Under My Skin
A. E. DOOLAND

Cover design and art by Yue Li
yue-li.tumblr.com

Edited by Nancy Phoebe Youssef

ISBN: 978-0-9941779-0-2

ACKNOWLEDGEMENTS

First and foremost to Anne Farmer, who not only encouraged me to go ahead and write this book in the first place, but also for her tireless support, critical analysis and opinions on each chapter and how it would land for the audience. This book would not only not be the same without her, but it wouldn't *be* without her!

Secondly to my poor partner Martina Vesela for her opinions, support and understanding.

Thirdly, thanks to Jieun, Seoyoon, Jude and Haley for their assistance, to Ken Dibbins for all his enthusiasm and help, and to the entire S.S. Endurance fandom.

This web series was crowd-funded, and the following fabulously generous people were major financial backers:

Anne Farmer
Miya
Aly M.
Ashleigh Wickens
Felicia F.
Naomi Leovao-Carpel
Brian Kane
Sten Sondre Johnson
Ken Dibbins
Stephanie Xie
Lake McGlone
Nikon Nevin

ONE

When I was choosing a career, I wish I had understood the difference between marketing and sales. If I had, I would probably be 'networking' right now—and by that I mean drunk under a table with prospective clients—and not sitting *at* a table on the 36th floor of an office building at 10pm on a Monday. I refreshed my email again, and surprise, surprise, nothing had come through. God, all those idiots needed to do was stagger over to a computer and type the letters 'O' and 'K' so I could finally go home. Apparently, that's too much to ask of our sales team, though. But, hey, would you like a Frost International-branded mouse pad?

The rest of my so-called marketing team had trickled out already—"You don't mind staying, do you, Min?"—and somehow I'd been conned into waiting for the final word from Sales on tomorrow's presentation. It was a stupid formality; we'd been working on the pitch for three weeks now, and it was solid. I learnt pretty quickly, though, that it was just easier to stroke the bulging egos of the sales team rather than piss them off.

"It's just you and me, Mike," I said, leaning back into my office chair and staring at the ceiling.

Mike didn't reply because Mike was a tacky souvenir turtle. One of my old friends from Melbourne had bought him for me when she went to Bali, as a joke. I'd never seen a worse paint-job on anything in my life—and that included my own paintings that I'd done when I was young and terrible. Mike was only barely recognisable as an actual turtle. I'd called him Michelangelo, but given the splotches of colour all over him perhaps Picasso would have been a more appropriate name. I reached out with a finger and wobbled Mike's head, and he spent a few seconds nodding at me.

If I was going to be stuck here all night I needed to start mainlining the caffeine before I passed out. I stood up stiffly from my desk. Over all of the partitions, I couldn't see a single head; I was the only sucker who was still at work at this hour. Well, aside from our co-CEO Diane Frost, of course. The light was still on in her office on the far side of the floor and I could see the top of a very tight bun behind the screen of her computer. I didn't think I'd seen her leave for dinner, either, but I *had* seen her saunter into the kitchen and make what looked like the world's strongest instant coffee a couple of hours ago. She hadn't said hello to a single person. 'Frost' was definitely the right surname.

There was practically no chance of her leaving her office again, so I figured I'd risk ducking over to the vending machine without my shoes on.

I grabbed my purse and walked over, the expensive new carpet soft under my stockings. Every second I could get away with not having those god-awful heels on was a relief, and there was something satisfying about giving a private 'fuck you' to the corporate dress code while I was chained to my desk subsisting on Red Bulls.

In case new employees had any sort of misconceptions about how much sleep they'd exchanged for their ridiculous salaries, on every single floor of the office was an energy drink vending machine. It was facing the lifts, too, just to remind you what you *should* be doing in case you even thought of leaving on time. Unfortunately, it only took coins and I was so deliriously bored that I'd forgotten that I only had a fifty. I sighed at it and then looked back towards the partitions. Well, I wasn't going to ask *Diane* for change, that was for sure.

While I was trying to decide if I was desperate enough to resort to instant coffee, the lifts dinged. I remembered that I had no shoes on at the exact moment that the doors slid open.

Fortunately, I recognised the black hair, brown eyes and ugly necktie on the man that walked out. I groaned. "Fuck, Henry! What are you doing up here?" I couldn't help quickly looking around to make sure no one had heard me swear. I wouldn't want them to think I actually had a personality.

"Being a good boyfriend and visiting you?" he said pleasantly, walking up to me with his hands full of his suit jacket and briefcase. He gave me a quick kiss. He was over six feet and one of those guys that actually needed to have their suits tailor-made because of it. Without my heels on, we were the same height. "By the way, you do know you're supposed to wear *shoes* in the office, right?" he used his I'm-an-important-manager voice for added drama as he looked critically down at my stockings.

"I'm probably not supposed to swear, either. Someone should tell HR," I said neutrally.

He didn't even flinch. "I can email you a link to the complaint forms, if you like."

"Great. Will they get processed faster because I'm dating the HR manager?"

He glanced up towards Diane's office and finally cracked a smile. "You," he said with his eyes twinkling, "are going to get me fired. I hope you make it worth my while."

He was giving me that look again. It made me uncomfortable. I was glad he had his stuff and was going back to his own place without me, because it meant I was off the hook tonight. He was great and everything, but on top of all the other stuff I had on my plate at the moment I just couldn't face having to put out. I wondered how many other women felt that way about sex with their boyfriends.

I laughed because it seemed like an appropriate reaction, and then changed the subject. "Since you're here, do you have any coins?" I gestured at the vending machine.

"Probably," he replied, as he held up his full arms and looked down at his pockets.

Of course he wanted me to dig around in them. Of course. I was actually *that* desperate for a Red Bull that I did, but I made sure he knew exactly what I thought of his methods when I looked at him.

He was grinning broadly at me. "Can't blame a guy for trying," he said as I found a handful of coins and straightened, looking down at them in my palm. There was plenty, and I was going to take all of it. He noticed. "I'm not sure I should leave that much change with you, though. Not until you admit you have a problem."

I rolled my eyes. "This is only my third," I told him, turning to the machine and feeding coins into it. "Did you decide if you're going back to Seoul at Easter?"

"Just booked my flights, actually. Are you coming this year?" I

3

glanced over my shoulder at him and my expression very effectively delivered my answer. He laughed. "I'll drop past your mother's and say hello for you, then."

Fabulous, I thought. In addition to nagging me to marry him, every time Henry visited South Korea, Mum called me and subjected me to a long lecture about what a bad child I was for never coming 'home'. This was ignoring the fact I'd been 'back' to South Korea three times in my life, and one of them I was too young to remember. It was her own damn fault I couldn't visit, because she was the one who'd convinced me to have a career in marketing in the first place. Not only that, but the last thing she'd done before she went back there five years ago was pressure me to apply for a top internship at international mining conglomerate Frost International. She was already gone by the time I'd landed it, so she never saw the ridiculous hours I had to work. Even though I explained over and over that Henry was a manager and I was just a marketing slave, she didn't seem to understand that I couldn't just take time off whenever I felt like it.

Secretly, though, I was pretty happy to have an excuse not to visit. She was my mother, but I'd rather jam a fork into my eyes than spend any time with her.

I opened the can and drank deeply from it. I swear that stuff was the elixir of life. "Okay, that's all I need from you," I said, in a deliberately flat voice. "You can go home now."

He chuckled, not fazed at all by me. "I did actually just come up to say goodbye to you," he said, but there was something about his smile which suggested that wasn't the only reason. "And also to let you know I told Omar to stop hitting on the sales interns and sign off on that diamond pitch you're working on."

Now *that* was something he was getting a hug for. He didn't abuse his position to help me very often. "Are you serious?" I asked him, and when it was clear he *was* serious I threw my arms around him and nearly spilt fluorescent yellow energy drink all over his white shirt. "Thank you, I might actually see my bed tonight!"

"Whoa!" he said, patting my back instead of whatever he'd rather have done to me. "If that's your third I'm pretty sure you won't be sleeping in it when you do get home."

I looked at the can as I pulled away from him, very skilfully ignoring another thinly veiled reference to what I knew he hoped we'd be doing tonight. "Nah, I'll be fine in a couple of hours," I said, and offered some to him.

He shook his head. "'Night, Min," he said. "Don't stay up too late."

I saluted him as he stepped into the lift, and then ran back to my desk. As if on cue, my inbox had an unread email waiting for me. A light practically shone down from the skies as I opened it and read the words, "...*looks fine, see you tomorrow.*" It didn't even have any typos. I was impressed.

"Yes!" I aggressively shouted, pumping the air with my fists.

My shout echoed around the empty office and I winced, slowly lowering my arms. That had been *much* louder than I'd been intending it to be; normally there were enough people around that I remembered to keep my mouth firmly shut.

In the office in the corner of the floor, Diane looked up from her computer screen towards me. It was yet another one of those horrifying moments I wished I was tiny and short and didn't tower over the partitions like some sort of female giant.

She looked straight at me and for a second I wondered if I should just start packing up my desk now. Then, she glanced up at the clock. When she made eye contact with me again her face relaxed into a smile. She nodded to acknowledge me, and then went back to her screen.

I just stared at her. My mouth was wide open.

Diane *fucking Frost* just smiled at me. International mega billionaire co-CEO Diane Frost just noticed and approved of the fact I was in the office at fucking 3am or whatever the fuck time it was now. *22:41*, my computer read as I shut it down.

"Sorry, Mike," I said to my ugly turtle as I reluctantly stepped back into my heels and collected my handbag from the bottom drawer, "you'll have to man the fort by yourself from here." I flicked his head so he nodded. *Diane Frost* had nodded, too. Jesus.

I was grinning like an idiot all the way over to the lift, but as the lift returned from ground I remembered I still had to survive the journey back down to street level. My smile faded.

The lift wasn't dangerous or anything. In fact, it was probably the most expensive lift in the southern hemisphere and I wouldn't be surprised if it had dual crash systems and airbags. The problem was that I worked on the 36th floor, and it took a full minute to get down. That minute was excruciatingly long: the lift was wall-to-wall mirrors and I was forced to stare at a thousand repeated reflections of myself for the whole trip. There wasn't anywhere else I could look.

My hair looked fucking terrible; no surprise, really, since it had been at least sixteen hours since I'd touched it with a curling iron. At least my makeup was still intact and I hadn't inadvertently smeared it across my face when I'd had my head in my hands earlier in the evening. The rest of me, though. I sighed at my reflection. I thought I'd chosen a dress that made my shoulders look narrower and gave me some semblance of cleavage, but from this angle I just looked as square as I usually did. I didn't really want to show cleavage at all, anyway—it just looked out of place to me and made me feel *really* weird—but at least if I had any I wouldn't look so angular. 'Swimmer's shoulders', Mum used to call them. How the hell did Henry get off on this, seriously? I looked down at the floor. I really didn't want to wreck my good mood by thinking about any of that right now.

Not even facing my reflection was enough to put a dampener on how great I felt to have had the co-CEO of Frost International acknowledge me, though. On top of that, it was a really pleasant temperature outside and it made my short walk down George Street feel shorter than usual, even in my stupid heels.

The bars opposite Circular Quay were already filling with the usual crowd of stoned backpackers and drunken tourists. The beautiful weather had made them spill out onto the footpaths and people were laughing and joking as I quickly walked past, hoping no one would give me any trouble.

On the way up the very steep road that led to my apartment, the clear evening gave me a great view of both the Harbour Bridge and Opera House. They were bathed in multi-coloured lights, and I stopped for a moment to try and capture that image in my head before I went inside. I liked the mix of colours, and it was about time I painted something to do with Sydney. Leaving Melbourne had made me nostalgic for all the places I used to hate while I was actually living there, and it was those cityscapes I tended to paint when I felt like going suburban. Mum would probably like it if I did some iconic Sydney sights instead; she might even print them out and put them up on the fridge for once. I think the last time I'd usurped the electricity bill on the front of it was when I was six.

Frost International owned several floors of one of the hotels bordering and overlooking The Rocks, and everyone who had been imported from other cities or countries usually ended up on one of them. Once people arrived, one of two things usually happened: they realised what an awful mistake they'd made and quickly broke their contracts and fled back home, or they cashed in their souls for *enormous* pay packets, signed permanent contracts and bought embarrassingly extravagant homes actually *in* The Rocks.

I hadn't done either. Well, apart from cash in my soul. Nearly four years later, I was still in number 2607 with uninterrupted views of the harbour. It was cleaned, and my laundry was done once a week; I could even order room service! It was just like living with Mum but without the constant nagging, and if I leant out the side of my balcony, I could actually see my office. So, why would I ever move?

The apartment was still pretty generic. I'd replaced all the linen with patterns and colours I liked, and I'd hung some of my own stuff on the wall, but it was still quite impersonal. In attempt to combat that, I'd put photos everywhere and proudly created a shrine for my extensive video game collection, but it hadn't worked. No matter what I did, the main room still looked like a display suite from *Better Homes & Gardens*. Eventually, I'd given up. What a first-world problem: 'Hi, I'm Min Lee and my free luxury apartment full of designer furniture feels barren and soulless.' Maybe I should start a support group.

As soon as I shut my door, I headed straight to the bathroom, leaving a trail of uncomfortable work clothes between the hallway and the ensuite. I didn't know how the hell women didn't go on homicidal rampages from wearing their stockings too much, and I thought indulgently about that as I wrenched them off my ankles and tossed them in the laundry basket. I looked fucking terrible; I was 25, and if I was expected to retire at 60, that was another 35 years of this crap. Still, maybe if I worked for Frost for a decade or two longer, I'd have enough money to retire early and go live in a cave somewhere where I didn't ever have to make myself look presentable to anyone.

Someone's bright idea was to put a mirror facing the door in the bathroom so you could watch yourself use it. I accidentally caught sight of myself before I stepped into the shower.

"I'm a fucking cliché," I said to my reflection, as I turned on the water. A woman who hates how she looks, now there's a plot twist. Cosmopolitan and those other mags were practically written for me.

I was getting pretty tired of whinging to myself about my body, so I didn't spend a second longer than I had to in the shower. I got out and put my pyjamas on: the oldest pair of tracky-dacks I owned, and a big t-shirt I'd stolen from Henry. The beauty of them was that they were so baggy that they completely hid my body and didn't give me the opportunity to notice and hate it. Trying to shut my brain up, I poured myself a glass of wine and went to the balcony to drink it.

I needed to get a fucking grip. I was 25, not a teenager. This 'I hate myself' crap wasn't cute anymore. I didn't have anything to complain about, either: I was already working for Fortune 500 Company in a permanent position being paid *way* more than other people my age, and I had a great boyfriend and a family who loved me. On top of that, my presentation slides tomorrow were a work of fucking art, *and* Diane fucking Frost had smiled at me. Everything was great. Seriously, what the hell was my problem? Whatever it was, I knew I needed to get over it.

There was a gentle, warm breeze outside. I was able to admire the lights even more from up here, and while I was waiting for the wine to take hold, I decided to have a shot at painting them.

I went inside to grab my laptop and tablet so I could set up shop on the deck. It was distractingly quiet out there, so I put some cartoons up on the screen of my laptop while I scribbled away.

Nothing was working, though. I couldn't get the angle right on the bridge, and my strokes were all over the place. After ten minutes there wasn't a single thing I liked about what I'd drawn, so I just erased the whole goddamn lot and sat back, seething.

I hadn't really been paying attention to the cartoon and now that I was looking at the screen, I realised all the characters were inexplicably opposite-sex versions of themselves. They were also singing for some reason. This show had always been a bit weird, but I think this episode was incontestable proof that all the writers were boiling mushrooms. I sat there frowning at it for another few minutes, but the random gender-bending was never explained. After some consideration I decided I actually preferred at least one of the characters that way.

I exhaled and looked down at my empty canvas. I didn't draw people that often anymore, so perhaps it would be good practice to draw that princess as a prince? More fun than lights on a bridge, that was for sure.

I'd been using my own reflection in the balcony door to get her head right and I was only three strokes in when I got caught on my body. The way I was sitting was the perfect reference; I was hunched and I couldn't see any sign of breasts at all. I'd also tied my hair back so it didn't get in the way. The screen from my tablet and the lights from the streets below lit me from underneath and were a very soft blue. I liked how it fell on me.

Well, I had been complaining about all that woman stuff, right? Fuck it. I sculled the rest of my wine in one mouthful and set to work.

Despite the fact I'd promised Henry *again* that I wouldn't stay up late, it was well past midnight when I finished the painting. I sat back and looked at it. There were some things I didn't like—like how I'd handled the pose and the lighting—but overall I'd captured the atmosphere really well. And then there was me. Because I knew I couldn't look at a picture of myself with any sort of objectivity, I flipped the canvas horizontally and hoped that would help.

It did, and my first impression was that I'd done a great job. I'd given myself a really funky haircut and dressed myself in a suit with a wide-collared shirt and a waistcoat. The tie I'd left kind of loose around my neck, and I'd copied one of Henry's *awful* paisley ones. It was hideous; I loved it. The rest of how I was sitting was basically the same. I grinned at it. There was something ultra-cool about wearing an expensive suit and then sitting with one leg scrunched underneath you and the other propped on a table. I'd put the tablet on my lap, too. I looked awesome, and all my angles looked really cool instead of really awkward. I sighed at it.

God, if only.

As soon as I'd thought that, I began to feel really uneasy about it. I looked down at the painting again, and my face stared back at me with a really intense expression, reclined exactly like I was. Seriously, what the hell was I doing? It was stupid. What a fucking stupid idea.

I closed Photoshop and went to turn off my tablet, but I hesitated as my mouse hovered over the shutdown button. Was it really as bad as all that? I opened the file again and had another look.

The execution was great, that much I had to admit. I had no idea what my weird problem with it was; it was a good painting. I should probably just upload it to Deviant Art before I started losing watchers who thought I'd abandoned my account.

I logged in and took a quick peek at my messages. I didn't get many these days—I was so busy with work I didn't get the opportunity to paint much anymore—but there were a few regulars I recognised. One of them was from a girl who was having some dramas with her friend and for some reason thought that because I could draw that I would also be full of wisdom. I resisted the urge to tell her I hadn't spoken to any of *my* friends outside of Facebook for *months* and basically gave her the text version of a pat on the back.

While I was uploading the painting, I got a bit stuck on the title and eventually settled on '*Lights Out*', and submitted it.

Leaning back in the chair, I stretched my arms over my head and yawned. It was probably about time I tried to get some sleep. I needed to be awake for that presentation tomorrow so I could soak in all the glorious adoration for my amazing, life-changing PowerPoint slides about why Frost was the best company in the world. There was only so much Red Bull could achieve.

I put my phone on silent and went to bed, but before I went to sleep I had to log in again to take another look at that painting. I wasn't sure what I was expecting, but it was still completely harmless. Normally there were things I liked and disliked about all my pieces, but why the hell did I love and hate this one so much?

I exhaled and put my phone back on my bedside table. Probably some weird body image thing, I decided, and then groaned and turned away from it, putting my head under the doona.

Min, for fuck's sake, it's just a painting. It's pixels on a screen. What sort of damage could it possibly cause?

TWO

It was a good thing I'd disabled vibrate on my mobile, because when my alarm went off in the morning, there were a 109 messages waiting for me on Deviant Art. I lay there, half dead, staring at the little white numerals on the corner of my screen and wondering if I had double vision or something. I'd never gotten that many messages for my stuff before. Maybe the painting had been featured on the homepage?

I tabbed through them, expecting the usual messages of 'OMG, wow!', or the extremely occasional detailed critique from someone who knew what they were talking about. That was *definitely* not the case this time. They were mostly from women, and mostly telling me how hot the 'me' in the painting was.

I kept scrolling down through them, the surprise waking me up a lot faster than usual. Sure, I'd selected 'self-portrait' as the category, but didn't they look up in the corner of my page and see that I was a girl...? Oh, right: I'd forgotten that a year or two ago I'd changed my profile so it hid my gender because I was sick of creeps hitting on me with lines like, 'looks like you're pretty good with your hands'. Yeah, *no*.

I put my phone down on my chest and lay flat on my back, staring at the ceiling fan rotating slowly above me. All those women were really into that guy in my 'self-portrait'. How ironic. I wasn't sure whether to laugh or cry, so I just laughed bleakly. I would have been great as a guy, too. Women *loved* tall men. And men hated tall women like me. Well, most men did.

I buried my head in my pillow and groaned loudly into it. *Okay, well*. I had a presentation today and I couldn't spend all morning thinking about that stupid painting and those poor women who had no idea they were lusting after a fictional character. I changed my mind several times over whether or not to display my gender again, and in the end I decided to just do it.

I was in a weird mood the whole time I was getting dressed, especially as I watched myself in the mirror, hopping around trying to get my stockings on. As nice as it was having people hot for what they thought I was, it was also kind of depressing. I couldn't let those women keep assuming I was some sort of stud when *this* was the reality.

I stopped awkwardly stumbling around for a moment and just stood and stared at my reflection. I was wearing a bra and undies that didn't match, and my stockings were cutting into my stomach. There was nothing in the world *less* sexy than this. It was a pretty far cry from that stylish guy reclined in an expensive suit on the balcony. Those poor women. It was just dishonest to let them keep complimenting me. Fuck, though, it felt good when they did.

While I was doing my makeup, I toyed with the idea of just taking down the painting. The trouble was, as much anxiety as it was causing me, I liked it. It was also good for my portfolio—it showed that I wasn't just good at landscapes and nothing else. Not that I should really care that much about my repertoire at the moment; there was no way I had time for private commissions and it wasn't like I needed the money. I decided I actually just really liked the painting. I liked it. And I didn't want to take it down.

After I finished my makeup, I wasted a minute or so frowning at my phone again before I slipped on my heels, collected my handbag and headed off to work. I was being ridiculous. Seriously. The sales team was running my team's pitch today and *that* was what I should be focused on.

Once I'd arrived at work, I didn't even get to sit down before one of my teammates came rushing over to me. "Hey, Mini!" he began, using the ironic nickname they had for me which I *hated*. "Did Sales give you a copy of the info pack? Because they're in a meeting somewhere and I don't think we transferred all the files onto the USBs. I want to check before I just go barging in on them."

I shook my head as I side-stepped around him and put my handbag into my bottom drawer. I never worked on those, which he should know by now since we'd been in the same department for *four years*. Anyway, apparently this file transfer issue was some enormous drama that required the whole team to freak out. I knew marketing was all about teamwork and I was supposed to actually care about stuff like this, but I was seriously too tired. I'd stayed back here while they were all home with their families or relaxing in front of the TV, so as far as I was concerned they could panic without me. Perhaps I was being a bit harsh. Most of them were pretty nice, I guess. Given the option, though, I'd design whole projects by myself. Even after several years, teamwork was still up there with group assignments, rocket lettuce and sunburn: things I'd rather avoid at all costs.

Whatever 'teamwork' they were doing on the other side of the partition was making Michelangelo's head nod. I watched it for a few moments. This was *way* too much energy for eight on a Tuesday morning on the amount of sleep I'd had. I needed a Red Bull.

Another marketing rep I'd worked with some time ago was already at the machine, stuffing coins into it as I walked up to her. Sarah, her name was, except everyone tended to call her by her surname, which was 'Presti', for inappropriate reasons. I didn't.

"Hey, Min! Long time, no see," she said, as I walked up to her. I smiled at her greeting. Her voice was husky; it was the kind of voice you ended up with after spending all night getting drunk at a bar and singing loudly along with the music. Even with makeup, she looked the part as well. The concealer was doing nothing for the bags under her eyes. She gave me about the same look I was giving her. "Guess you were here late, again?"

I sighed. "Til about 11," I said, watching her select a diet option from the panel. "How *are* you, anyway? I haven't seen you in ages."

She collected her drink, held it at me in a toast and then took a huge mouthful. "How's that for an answer?"

I laughed. I knew exactly how she felt. "I hear you. My team's running that Queensland pitch today."

"Oh, right," she said, leaning a shoulder on the machine. Her hair fell perfectly around her slender shoulders even though she wasn't paying any attention to it. How did other women just do that? "I heard about that. That's a major project, isn't it? You must be *so excited*." She said the last part with such exaggeration it was practically dripping with sarcasm.

I grinned. "Like it's my wedding day. I don't know how I'm containing myself." When she realised she was blocking my access to the machine, she shifted across a bit so I could get a drink for myself. I glanced up at her while I slotted coins in. "You look like you pulled a late one yourself. What's your excuse?"

She laughed. "My man just got back from Broome. He's doing fly-in, fly-out this year. It's, uh, great to have him back, if you catch my drift." She grinned smugly, and took a sip of her energy drink.

Well that explained the husky voice: it wasn't drunk singing, they'd just been keeping each other up. She seemed happy about it, too; I knew she was really into him. "How long has it been for you two now?"

"Three whole years." Her smile didn't slip at all.

"Wow," I said, opening my own can. I remembered when they'd met. "Three years? You do know I sell diamonds for a living, right? You're practically my target market."

She waggled her ring finger on the can. "You should study me," she said. "And write a report about my shopping behaviour."

"I'll make some illustrative graphs to explain you," I agreed. "Please specify your preferred colour scheme."

She laughed openly and patted me on the arm. I wasn't actually a big fan of being touched, but I quite liked her so I let it slide. She'd always made working long hours far less torturous. "Min, you crack me up," she said. "I hope we're on another project together soon. Anyway," she checked her watch, which had fashionably slipped to the inside of her wrist, "I should let you get on with it, your pitch is in like 45 minutes. Good luck!"

I smiled appreciatively; she was right about getting on with it. If I cared about career progression, I needed to at least feign interest despite my part being complete. Standing around, chatting at a vending machine wasn't likely to score me any points with the bosses.

"See you 'round," she said, and then with zero effort, sashayed gorgeously back to where her team were gathered. I wished it were harder to like her; some women just made everything look so easy.

The actual pitches were always completely anti-climactic, as far as I was concerned. My job was mainly managing the design and layout of the materials and presentation, and then someone far more bubbly and outgoing would deliver it to the clients. After that, we'd break for lunch and all the smooth-talking closers from Sales would casually mingle with the clients while they ate, engaging them in pleasant conversation until there were signatures on contracts. I found that part of the whole process sleazy and was glad I didn't have to be involved. Just in case there was a terrible PowerPoint crisis, though, I needed to be on hand to divert any potential catastrophic presentation failures. I was yet to figure out why IT couldn't do that, but I guessed it was more of this 'teamwork' thing I kept hearing about.

During lunch, we all stood at an acceptable distance from the conference room, waiting for the word on whether or not we'd been successful. Sometimes clients wanted to go away and have endless meetings before they'd make a decision, but occasionally we'd find out directly afterwards. We all loitered around just in case.

I had my phone with me because I'd missed a couple of calls from Mum before, and being a hopeless masochist, I'd opened the painting again to agonise over it. There were more comments on it, and the image was on the homepage of the category. I couldn't stop reading them, and the better I felt about the compliments, the more I felt like I was staging this huge lie to the women of the internet.

While my finger was hovering indecisively over the 'delete' button, all the boys started whooping and, remembering how close they were to the conference room, almost immediately muted themselves. Instead, they smacked each other's shoulders and made borderline offensive victory gestures. It was like being at the footy.

We must have signed the clients, but truthfully I wasn't really *that* surprised. It was a pretty hard market at the moment so as long as we were able to deliver, we'd most likely get the contracts.

Whoops, what was I saying? Of course it was *obviously* my amazing presentation that won them over.

When the clients had left and Sales started trickling out of the room with their chests puffed out, I saw Diane Frost shake hands with Omar, the Sales Manager, and then walk sharply over to us. I watched the boys all turn from drunken yobbos into executive marketing reps on six figure salaries in the space of two seconds.

She stopped in front of our team and stood there for a moment. Fuck, she was scary. "Congratulations on winning the pitch," she said cordially, but it was difficult to know if she meant that or if it was just her way of saying hello. Then, she held up one of the brochures from the info pack, like it was evidence in a murder trial. "Who did this?"

I immediately started to sweat; that was one of *my* brochures, and it stood out like a sore thumb in our greyscale office. I'd chosen a really bold colour scheme because the set of companies we were pitching to used similar themes in their own advertising and I wanted them to feel like they were holding their own material. Now that I looked at it, though, the colours were really fucking loud. Obviously *too* loud for Frost International. *Shit.*

I didn't say anything, not much to anyone's surprise. One of my teammates spoke for me. "That's Mini's work," he said, indicating me. "She does presentations and print."

"'Minnie'?" she asked, looking at me for clarification of my name. Recognition crossed her face.

I swallowed. No one was going to field this one for me. "Min. Min Lee."

She looked down at the loud brochure, and then thoughtfully back at me. "You again," she said obliquely. "'Min Lee'." Was she trying to commit my name to memory? When she spoke again, her smile was the epitome of 'professional'. "Good work, that contract is worth six million dollars." She nodded her head amiably towards the lifts. "Now get out of here and go celebrate."

She gave me one last look before heading back into her office.

We all just stood there. One of the boys exhaled. "I feel like I just watched a Kung-Fu movie," he said. "You guys will deck it out now, right? What the hell was that about?"

I shook my head, my heart still beating like crazy. She *seemed* to have congratulated us all for the pitch... And I was part of 'all', right? Still, I felt uneasy about that whole exchange and more than anything I wanted closure on it. It didn't look like I was going to get any, though, because Diane had shut her office door behind her and settled behind her computer again.

Our project manager, who had been working at Frost International for ten years, didn't look too bothered by what had just happened. "Nah, if Diane was pissed off at any of us, we'd know about it," he said. "That's just about as close as she gets to telling us we're awesome." He swung his arms around the shoulders over the two reps either side of him. "Come on, let's go have lunch and then get wasted on the company card."

We'd all gone back to our desks to collect our things when a familiar voice greeted me. "Min," it was Henry. I straightened to greet him and noticed his tie actually matched his suit today. That was a bit of a shock. Just to be safe, he stopped short of kissing me on the cheek; it probably would have been okay, but he didn't. He put a warm hand on my arm, instead. "I just read the email. Congratulations. Also would you answer your phone? Your mum's been trying to call you. She rang *me* to tell you that."

There goes any last remnants of a good mood, I thought, and groaned out loud. "Are you serious? Sorry," I said and took my phone out of my handbag. Sure enough, I had *another* missed call— as well as a whole series of new comments on the painting. I wasn't sure what was worse, strangers stressing me out or my *mother* doing it. "Give me a sec," I said to him, and put the phone against my ear.

It barely rang. "Min, why have you been avoiding me?" Despite the fact she spoke perfect English and my Korean was crap, she still refused to speak in English to me. "I've been ringing you all morning."

Even Henry heard that. He laughed as I said in English, "Because I'm at work."

"Henry's at work, too," she fired back, very pointedly in Korean. I gave him a look that warned him never to answer the phone to her again, and he threw his hands up in self-defence as she continued. "I've been worrying about your presentation all morning." I bet she'd even put it in her calendar. "How did it go? Did you all close that big contract?"

"About five minutes ago, actually." I decided not to tell her about my weird exchange with the Diane Frost, because it would only make her worry even more. "Now we're all going out to have a big lunch to celebrate, so I have to go soon."

"Don't eat too much," she said. "Henry will never marry you if you're tall *and* fat."

Henry snorted. "Don't believe anything she says," he whispered, making me feel really uneasy. He didn't notice my reaction because he was leaning into the phone and saying in perfect Korean, "Don't worry, she still looks like a supermodel." I sighed at him. "For now," he added, smirking at me. "She did just discover Krispy Kreme."

Both of them? Seriously. I couldn't roll my eyes enough and Mum was *still* having a go at me. "Nonsense, supermodels don't slouch like Min does."

Okay, I'd had it. That was enough talking about me. I looked directly at Henry as I asked Mum, "How's grandma?"

While that question stopped the torrent of judgments about me, it unfortunately got Mum started on a long story about their last hospital visit, and grandma's long list of conditions and medications. With my limited Korean, I could barely understand a single thing and so I just made affirmative noises intermittently to pretend I was following the story. I propped the phone between my cheek and shoulder so I could check that I'd taken my purse. All my co-workers were gathering in the annex to wait for a lift. Henry tapped his watch; I nodded. I wanted to get Mum off the phone, but she didn't have anyone else to talk to about taking care of grandma and to be honest, I didn't call her as often as I should.

When everyone was gone, Henry whispered something about needing to get back to work, kissed my cheek, and then disappeared as well.

It was twenty minutes before I managed to *finally* get off the phone with Mum, and as we were saying goodbye she dropped the whole angry mother thing and said, "Thank you for putting up with your terrible mother, Min. I know you don't like talking to me at all, but I want you to know that I love you anyway."

I nearly threw my phone on the floor and stomped on it. I *hated* it when she pulled that crap on me, *fucking hell*! Swallowing those words, I said as warmly as I could, "Don't be silly, thanks Mum."

I hung up and managed to not lob my mobile onto the closest wall—but I couldn't stop glaring at it and the notifications building up in the top corner of the screen. I didn't do anything about them, though. It was lunchtime.

My team had wandered down the road to a bar/restaurant on

the corner of George Street that fronted Circular Quay. There were nearly ten of my workmates there, and despite the fact they'd only been there for about twenty minutes, they were so loud it was like they were already completely wasted.

"Hey, look who's joined us!" one of them called as I stepped in the doorway. "Mini!"

There was nowhere for me to sit, and while I was scouting around for a chair I could use, one of the boys patted his thigh and said, "I got a seat for you!"

Someone else laughed at him and warned, "Frost International might not have a seat for *you* if the manager of HR finds out you're propositioning his girlfriend." They all laughed as I went and stole a chair from another table, dragging it over to slot between two of the others. I don't know what they thought Henry would do about it; we'd already decided between ourselves he wouldn't get involved in any disputes I had. It would make things too complicated for both of us.

That pretty much set the tone for the rest of lunch, though. There was some discussion about who was on which project team for the next pitch, but none of us knew what we were doing next so there wasn't much to speculate about. We tried anyway, but eventually that topic ran out of steam, and as they got progressively drunker, everything became progressively more awkward for me.

Every time the men would start talking about something other than work—women, money, sport—someone would remind him that there were *girls present*. Out of those, the only topic I could really do without was 'women'. I didn't mind them bitching about their girlfriends and wives, but I just didn't want to be involved in any sort of discussion about who was hot at work or who hooked up with who from operations.

Once we'd moved onto the topic of promotions, it was depressing how *little* they involved me. They all sat around the table together placing actual monetary bets on which one of them would end up being a project lead next... and no one put a cent on me. Or Sarah, for that matter. The hot favourites were a cocky guy who'd only been working with us for eight months, and the current project manager because he was mature—code for 'old'—and brought that whole fatherly thing with him to work.

As lunch progressed and everyone was boastfully handing around their phones with pictures of their wives and girlfriends, I just sat back and kept sipping at my wine. I had been admiring the far wall—someone had painted the stone so it resembled old wooden panels and had done a pretty good job—when I saw out of the corner of my eye a mobile being held at an angle that alarmed me.

I looked towards it just as it flashed. The guy behind it was the cocky new rep and he looked pretty proud of himself. "Hah, it's great!" he said, smirking and sending the photo to everyone.

Just to humour them I took my phone out and looked at it. I wished I hadn't. In the photo I was surrounded by drunk men, half of whom were shorter than me, and I was glaring towards the camera. It was a bit of an eye-opener because I had felt mostly invisible while they were ignoring me, and I'd had *no* idea I stood out so much amongst them until I saw that photo.

As each of my teammates got the message, they all started *laughing* like it was the funniest thing ever. Even though there was a level of sincere affection in them playing around with me, it kind of hurt.

"Is this Mini's happy face when she celebrates?" someone said. "Fuck, I'm sending this to Sales."

Yeah, send it to fucking everyone, I thought darkly. I don't think there's enough people laughing at me already, better make sure the whole company has it. The project manager, who had been setting a great 'fatherly' example by being the drunkest one of all, swung his arm out and whacked me on the shoulder like I was one of the boys. "You're fucking great, Mini," he slurred. "My wife would kill me if I did that. But no, you're totally cool about it."

Nope, right now you're lucky I'm not killing you, I thought while I smiled stiffly at him. Luckily, the reps quickly got over the photo and moved on to someone's 'smoking hot' bikini-clad wife.

I watched them, feeling more and more disconnected. No wonder those internet women liked *my* painting, if this was what their husbands and boyfriends were actually like. It wasn't that these guys were being cruel, either, at least not deliberately. They weren't *trying* to make me feel unwelcome. They were just having a good time and were completely oblivious to how out of place I felt.

Or that I was here at all. It just continued to get more depressing. Why the fuck *was* I here?

"I think I'll head off," I said suddenly, interrupting whoever was speaking. "Bye, guys." I didn't turn around to find out what their assessment of me leaving so early was, either. If they were going to be here all afternoon, I was just going to go home.

While I was waiting at the lights my phone buzzed. I took it out to look at it; it was from *Omar*. '*Nice photo, Mini,*" he'd texted. "*Definitely a character portrait, haha. They should put it on your ID tag.*"

Reading that just made me reach a point where I didn't even care what happened anymore. Whatever, I thought, closing the text. If that was what everyone thought of me, I didn't care.

There were still pending notifications from my painting as I went to put my phone away, so I paused before putting it back in my bag. I wanted to read them and feel good about myself for a fraction of a second, but it was all crap anyway and I couldn't be bothered dealing with it. The praise wasn't for *me*, that person in the painting wasn't *me*, was it? Actually, fuck it, I couldn't deal with any of it, full stop. Without really thinking it through, I uploaded that terrible photo that had just been taken as my ID on Deviant Art. There, I thought, turning off my mobile completely and putting it back in my handbag. Now those women can see who I actually am, be rightfully horrified, and then just leave me alone.

I felt strangely numb and detached the whole way home, and only started to feel like an actual human again after I'd had a shower and put my comfy clothes on. But then I had the choice of facing my computer, which probably still had Deviant Art open, or turning on my PlayStation. It didn't take a rocket scientist to figure out which option I chose.

Black Ops was already in my machine, so I flopped back on the couch and waited for a game to load. It was strange being home in the middle of a work day. I felt guilty, even though I'd been at the office past 10:30 last night, and even though I'd served a long enough sentence with my drunken co-workers.

I chewed through game after game until there was a knock at my door. It was like being woken in the middle of a trance. I sat up for a minute, feeling dazed. I looked over at the windows; it was dark outside already. What time was it? I turned my head back to the door, walked over to it, and peered through the peephole.

It was Henry, and he had champagne and takeaway.

I looked down my front at the faded t-shirt and baggy pants. Fuck, and I looked *like crap*. I didn't even have any makeup on. "Why didn't you give me a ten minute warning?!" I hissed through the door.

"I did," he said, not at all bothered by my reaction. "But I guess you're still avoiding your mother and you haven't checked your phone." I scrunched my face up. That's right, I'd forgotten I'd turned my phone off. My mother was the least of the things I was avoiding, but I didn't correct him. "It's okay, Min, I'll just wait out here for a few minutes. I don't mind."

I raced back into my bedroom and tore open my drawers, searching for the pair of pyjamas I always wore when Henry was over. They had an appropriately pretty, delicate pattern and were made of soft cotton and lace. They were comfortable enough, I guess, but I didn't really like them. I couldn't wear this t-shirt and trackies around Henry, though. I looked like such a dag in them, and I should really make the effort for him. Ugh, and I had to put all my makeup back on, too.

When I finally let him in, I looked presentable again.

He held the champagne at me as if I hadn't just made him wait for 15 minutes in a hallway. "Congratulations again," he said, as he leant and kissed me on the temple before walking past me into the kitchen. "How did you celebrate?"

"By killing hundreds of people," I told him. "Mostly with frag grenades, but I did experiment with a variety of assault rifles."

"How educational," he said, putting the takeaway down on my dining table. "Since you've bathed in blood, want to consume some flesh? It's pork." I came up behind him to peek over his broad shoulders as he opened the container for me. A delicious smelling steam poured out of it. "By the way, the champagne is a really good label."

I snorted. "Champagne is for wusses," I said. "I prefer the tears of my enemies."

He laughed. "I love you," he said, turned and leant against the table. "Now, are you going to tell me why you didn't return to work after team drinks? Not that it's an issue given the circumstances, but it's pretty unlike you." I had been grinning, but as soon as he said that, it fell away. I had no idea I was that transparent; normally people couldn't read me at all, not even Henry. He didn't miss my reaction this time, though. "Are you okay? Did your mother say something to you?" He pulled me close him and circled his arms around my waist.

I had an internal debate about whether or not to tell him about the painting, but I didn't. I just shook my head at him. "I'm just being emo again," I answered, as dismissively as I could. "Ignore me."

He didn't. He never did. Instead, he put my cheeks into his huge hands. "Min," he said sternly. "I haven't been with you for three years to not know when you're hiding something from me. It's okay, you can tell me, no matter what it is."

In the end he coaxed it out of me, including what had happened at lunch and the photo I'd uploaded. I reluctantly switched my phone on and handed it to him, pointing to the notifications in the top corner. He made a surprised noise and tapped at them with a fingertip.

I couldn't bear to look at what those disappointed women were probably saying about my terrible photo, so I turned away from the screen. "You can see my painting there, too," I told him, flopping back onto the couch and putting my ankles on the armrest and my forearms over my face. Through the gap in them, I could see he was concentrating as he tabbed through what he'd found on my profile. It was painful waiting for his assessment of everything. Really painful. "Don't read too much into the painting," I told him anxiously, "it was just something that I did while I was—"

"It's *good*, Min," he said, interrupting me. "Actually, it's a bit difficult to look at because of how good it is and how much it looks like you. I might have to question my sexuality." He glanced back over at me, grinning. "The photo is actually nothing like you said it was, and I don't know why you'd think I'd have a problem with a painting."

There wasn't much I could say to that. I had no idea what *my* weird problem with it was. Or why I liked it so much.

He came over and motioned for me to move my legs so he could sit under them. I lifted them up and put them back down across his lap. He was still scrolling—through what, though, I didn't want to know. "I think it's only natural you'd paint something like that," he said, pulling his psychobabble on me again. "For some completely unwarranted reason, you hate how you look. Of course you wish you were someone else."

I groaned. "You know what you can do with your psychology degree?" I asked him, good-naturedly.

He smirked. "I'm looking at the comments on your actual photo from those girls now," he told me, as if I hadn't been about to insult him. "Do you want to know what they say?"

"No."

He turned his head towards me, eyebrows up again. "Really? Because then you might start believing me when I tell you that *you're* the only one who thinks you're ugly." He held the mobile at me.

It made my heart race. "Henry, I really don't want to know."

Noting my expression, he nodded, then leant over me to place my phone on the coffee table. "Okay," he said. "But can I just say that there's a whole heap of women who'd step in for me if I bailed." He winced, thinking about it. "And I know this is really problematic on a number of levels, but that's actually a turn on."

"Imagining me with *other* people is a turn on?"

He shrugged. "I told you it was problematic. You want some champagne? Maybe that will make you feel better."

I made a face. "Nah, I haven't eaten anything." I was still thinking about what he'd said. "Did all those girls really say I looked good? Because on top of looking like the grumpiest person on the planet, that photo shows what an enormous giant I am."

He had such a warm smile. "Min," he said gently. "I like that about you. It's great to be able to actually feel I have my arms around another whole person, and I can't be the only one that feels that way."

I breathed out, watching my chest fall. I was hopeless. "It sucks that no matter how many times you tell me this stuff, I just can't believe it."

There was so much affection in his eyes as he nodded. "Okay," he said simply. "Then let me show you."

That was a really sweet, romantic thing to say, and I should have been completely touched and jumped lovingly into his arms, but instead, my heart sank. Of *course* this is where it was heading.

Even before he'd leant his torso down over me and put his lips against mine, I knew what was going to happen next. He had his eyes closed when he kissed me, too, which meant that he didn't notice when I jammed mine shut for a second. Fuck, and he was just so goddamn wonderful that I *couldn't* say I didn't really feel like it now, could I? Not when he'd been so nice. It had been a couple of weeks, too, so it was probably about time I let him do it again.

He slipped a hand under my pyjama top. I wasn't wearing a bra because I really didn't need to at home, and that meant he was able to take the little that was actually there into his hands. A sound escaped from the back of his throat as he slipped one crisply suited knee between my two bare ones.

I stared up at the light fixture above my head while he kissed down my neck. Come on, Min, it's going to be like fifteen minutes, tops. Quicker than doing the ironing. Quicker than doing my makeup, even. I should really have been counting my lucky stars that I'd landed an attractive, rich, wonderful boyfriend completely unlike the other idiots I worked with. He even *cooked*. Having sex with him was the very least I could do. Really, it wasn't his fault he'd picked a frigid girlfriend who had weird body image issues. I shouldn't turn those things *his* problem when they were obviously my own.

When he started unbuttoning my pyjamas, I realised I had just been stiffly lying there, and I only noticed because he leant away from me with a look of genuine concern on his face. "Min," he said, "you're not up for this, are you? Because it's fine if you're not, I'm happy to stop."

Looking down between us, I could already see how hard he was through his suit pants. Man, this just wasn't fair on him. I really should put in more effort. Rather than answer his question, I pulled him down into a firm kiss.

He leant heavily into me and I could feel his erection dig into my thigh. I slipped a hand between us to find a more comfortable position for it, and he exhaled forcefully when I touched it over the fabric.

"See?" he murmured in my ear as we continued, "you're gorgeous."

It would have been over much sooner than I'd anticipated, but Henry insisted on making sure I came first, so I had to put on a really convincing act about being into it. The whole thing took more effort than I had expected.

When we were done, he always insisted on kissing for a bit. We were both a bit sweaty and it was kind of gross, but I exhaled exaggeratedly for his benefit and pretended to enjoy it. "Thanks," I lied, feeling guilty even before I'd said it, "I needed that."

He'd put his head on my chest, and the beginnings of stubble scratched me as he smiled. "You're welcome," he said breathlessly. "Do you mind if I have the first shower?"

"Go for it. I had one before."

He pushed up, grabbed his clothes and then swaggered off into the bathroom. I just sat there for a minute after pulling my pyjamas back on. Well, at least that was done, now we'd go a couple of weeks without him asking for it again. I was due around then, too, so maybe even a bit longer.

My stomach grumbled, so I got up to explore what food Henry had bought us: boxes of noodles from that Hokkien place around the corner. I couldn't be bothered washing dishes—although to be honest, Henry would probably do them, but I didn't want that either—so I just grabbed a fork out of the drawer and took a whole box out onto the balcony.

In these frilly pyjamas and with all my makeup on, my reflection looked quite different than the one I'd painted the night before. I watched it as I ate a few mouthfuls of food. I didn't like how it looked, of course, but Henry obviously did. I just didn't understand that at all, and I wondered if he'd been lying about all those girls saying nice things about me. I wouldn't put it past him to be that nice...

Once that thought came into my mind, it was difficult to dislodge. Nothing was going to settle this except actually reading the comments, so I abandoned my dinner on the outdoor setting and went inside to get my phone. I didn't open the notifications straight away, though. I had to spend a few seconds psyching myself up in case he *had* been lying and they did say awful things.

When I finally opened it, it only took me one glance to realise that he'd actually been telling the truth.

I scrolled through the comments. They ranged from, '*Oooh you look so fierce! I love it!*', and '*I like this one too*' to '*OMG you're so tall!! I'm jealous!!*' and '*Yup, I'd still hit that, although it looks like it might hit me back*'. There wasn't a single nasty one. And, judging by the usernames, most of them were from women. That felt a little strange because I was so used to women being really judgmental of each other. It was also strange because many of them were clearly hitting on me, which must have been what Henry was referring to earlier. I took a second to try and imagine what being with a woman would be like. Women were usually a lot smaller than me, so being the tall one *and* being a woman didn't sit right. Also, the only women I could think of right then were Diane and Sarah, and both of them were just... no.

Alongside the comments there were a couple of private notes as well, so I opened my inbox and selected one. It was from one of my regulars. '*omg ur a girl??????*' I counted them, six question marks. '*wow okay this is a bit of a surprise!! ur still gorgeous tho! *^w^**' That particular one was from the girl who'd been having friend trouble yesterday.

Whoops, she messaged me quite regularly and had thought I was a guy the whole time? Even though she seemed pretty fine with it, I felt bad for her and typed a quick reply, '*Now that you know my secret, I'm going to have to kill you*'. I sent it before I realised that my sense of humour might actually not come across that well on the internet. Rather than risk having the police called on me, I quickly typed another one. '*Kidding. And thanks*'.

Taking my phone with me, I returned to my food. While I sat down and fished out all the baby prawns from the noodles, I reread the messages. It was pathetic how good it felt reading them, even though I couldn't figure out what they saw in me.

Henry came outside while I still had my phone out. "Plucked up the courage to read them?" he asked, kissing the top of my head as he sat down next to me with his own noodle box.

I nodded, swallowing my mouthful. "I've decided I'm going to leave you for this one," I said, and showed him the screen so he could read the comment.

He held my wrist to steady as he read aloud. "*'If you're married, leave him. I'm richer'.*" He laughed. "There's a wink, though. I think that means he's joking." He paused for a second, reading the username. "Wait, 'she'? Well that changes everything," he released my arm and opened his meal. "Invite her for dinner. I'll even cook."

I flicked a prawn at his cheek. It didn't hit him, but it did sail past his nose and fly off the balcony. He kept eating. "You'd better work on that aim if you want to beat my score in Free for All."

I couldn't scoff loudly enough. I *always* beat him. "You want to settle who beats who right now? I will camp your spawn points until you're begging for mercy."

"I like the sound of that," he said, and shovelled some more food into his mouth. "Come on, let's do it."

After the day I'd had, *that* was one 'do it' that I could really get into with him.

THREE

There was something beautiful about arriving fresh at work the following morning to an office full of groaning, baggy-eyed co-workers half of whom were cradling their head on their desks. The timing couldn't have been better, either, given that awful photo that they'd taken of me yesterday. I took far too much pleasure in making zero attempt to be considerate. Michelangelo nodded violently as I kicked my bottom drawer shut and sat down.

"Give me a break, Mini," a voice droned from the other side of the partition. It sounded suspiciously like it was being mumbled through a forearm. "I have the world's worst hangover."

And I'm playing the world's smallest violin. "Sorry," I said, aware of just how un-sorry I sounded. I may have even been grinning.

Working at a global company meant that most of my important emails arrived overnight, and I had to spend a few minutes combing through them for anything that needed my attention. It took more effort than usual today; some other poor sucker had drunk too much yesterday and passed out in a weird position on a bench. One of the reps had Photoshopped him into a series of settings, like footy matches, Lady Gaga concerts, Centrelink office stairs… the list went on. The pictures were being circulated with serious subject lines so when you opened them, you had no idea what you were about to see. My 'delete' key was certainly getting a workout.

There were actually some important emails in the mix, though. Frost was conducting explorations in a couple of countries in Africa, and my best guess about the next assignment we'd all be on was to canvas for investors to establish mines there. I sat back in my chair and read through some of the documents, ignoring all the email notifications popping up from my own team. I wasn't a big fan of marketing to investors—it was a really dry topic and I usually ended up using pretty much the same content and layout each time. On the other hand, it could mean scoring business trips to Botswana and New York. That would be cool.

I had been Googling the closest major airport to Botswana when hands loudly drumming the partition behind me made me jump. I swivelled towards the racket.

"Hey, Marketing!" our executive marketing manager Jason boomed over the top of me. He was possibly the only person aside from the two CEOs who wasn't known by a nickname, and that's because he was this imposing, extroverted man who everyone was a little afraid of. My usual interactions with him involved a combination of the following: him barking instructions at me on an airplane while, in the background, hostesses were telling him to turn his mobile off; getting emails at 4 am because he'd 'just had an idea about something' and as a result needed me to change 20 pages of documents right now; and having him suddenly appear behind me out of nowhere to drop documents on my desk and casually suggest I clear my calendar for the next two weeks. There was a rumour that he and the other co-CEO Sean Frost worked out together. Jason's biceps were so thick his shirt sleeves looked like they were about to tear open at the seams, so it was probably true.

I must have been looking at them while he was thumping away at the partitions, because I made eye contact with Sarah across the floor and she grinned at me. Two seconds later I got an email from her and the text read, *'Pretty sure you're not his type...'* I snorted and replied, *'what a coincidence, he's not mine, either ;).'* Sarah raised her eyebrows at me, and I quickly realised what I might have inadvertently implied in comparing myself to him. I didn't have a chance to correct myself, though, because Jason started his announcement.

"It's that time of the month again," Jason was calling. "And, no, I don't mean where I get neurotic and start crying hysterically. Although you guys will be doing that pretty soon, judging by the number of contracts we need. Nope," he leant theatrically on the partition. "Sales, management and of course, me, have picked teams for the next pitches and we'll be sending out an email in a sec with the details. Some of you might be on more than one team. Sorry about that. Not really, though. If you have questions, I'll be in my office." He gave us an exaggeratedly macho wave, and then disappeared.

I looked back over towards Sarah, but she had already been accosted by a couple of other reps. I watched them for a few seconds to figure out if they were just passing by, but from Sarah's expression it was actually business. To her it was, anyway. The two men were watching her white blouse a little too closely; it was both disgusting and fascinating. She noticed it, too, but didn't seem to care. She just tapped her pen on her glossy lips and read whatever document they'd handed her.

Someone groaned across from me. "You've got to be kidding me," he said aloud. "I'm on investment in Canada *again*."

I glanced over at him; he was leaning up to his computer screen with a frown on his face. Just as I realised that everyone else was doing the same thing, my computer chimed and a new email appeared—it was the one Jason had been talking about. Leaning up to the screen myself, I scrolled down the list of names for each project.

My name wasn't anywhere.

I must have missed it. I opened the search field and typed 'Lee', and it returned no results. I sat back for a second, my stomach dropping. Up until that point, I hadn't given much thought to my exchange with Diane Frost yesterday. Right now, though, that's all I could think about. Fuck, had my colour scheme in that brochure *really* been that bad? I'd heard of people who'd performed badly being transferred out of marketing into admin, but I'd never had anyone criticise my work before. Sure, management sometimes wanted me to change a few things, but it was never

30

serious. I couldn't lose my job, I just couldn't. I *was* my job. I took a deep breath to try and steady myself. Chill, Min, just chill. It was probably just an accident that they didn't assign you, I'm sure it's happened before. There are a lot of reps here, they probably just missed you. Despite trying to reassure myself that there was probably a normal explanation for why my name wasn't there, I had a *bad* feeling.

While I was busy stressing the fuck out, my chair spun around. It was Sarah's arm on the spine on it. "Can I borrow you for a second?" she asked with urgency, and then ushered me over away from the floor before halting in front of me. "Wow, Min," she said, glancing back towards everyone to make sure no one could hear us. "Who else knows?"

I gaped down at her, my heart still pounding from the email. Did she know something I didn't? "Who else knows what?"

She leant in a little. "You know, that thing with Jason…"

I had hardly spoken to Jason in at least three weeks, I was pretty certain that nothing had happened between us that would get me in trouble. Especially not something that Sarah would know about before I did. Just in case, though, I tried frantically to rehash my last few contacts with him to figure out if I'd done something wrong. "What thing? What did you hear?"

She just looked blankly at me for a second as if she had *no* idea what I was talking about. "Min, you sent me an email like five minutes ago."

Sent an email like… oh! *Oh.* That email where I might accidentally have implied I was gay by comparing myself with Jason. She thought I'd just come out to her? *That* was it? I was so relieved I laughed. It was a million times better than what I thought I was going to hear—that I'd transgressed and was going to be ejected from Marketing. "God!" I said. "*No.* No, no. I'm not… I'm sure I told you about Henry, didn't I? Wow, I thought you were going to tell me something else!"

"Well, yeah, I knew you two were together, but…" She didn't finish that sentence, shaking her head and laughing along with me. "Jeez, Min, I was like—am I the last person to know about this? You said it so casually. *Whoops.*" She took a deep breath. "Sorry for freaking you out. Anyway, which project did you get?"

I stopped laughing and winced, remembering what I'd been worrying about. "That's actually what I thought you were going to ask me about. My name isn't on the project list."

Sarah's brow furrowed. "Like, not at all?" I shook my head, and she blew a gust of air out through her lips. "Well, there are thirty of us. Maybe it's an accident."

"Maybe," I said, doubting it. "Which project did *you* get?"

She rolled her eyes. "Two, unfortunately. I'm doing web analytics and social media for private consumers again. I need to stop doing a good job with that." I remembered a year or two ago Sarah, who had previously been obsessed with Facebook, announced that marketing had put her off Facebook forever. I never saw her online anymore. "Also I'm on another project that doesn't have specs yet. It's called 'Pink', though, so it might just been one of Jason's really unfunny jokes."

I had opened my mouth to make a snide comment about that, but before I did we were interrupted. "Hey, Mini!" someone shouted across the floor. We both looked out towards the voice. A rep from my workstation was holding his phone with the handset pressed across his shoulder. "Phone!"

I looked back at Sarah. She gestured towards the rep, her elaborate bracelets jingling. "Maybe there's your answer?"

I swallowed. "It's been nice knowing you," I said darkly.

She laughed. "I bet it's just a mistake," she said, touching my arm amicably like she usually did with everyone. Because I had been distracted, though, I wasn't ready to try and feign being cool about it. She noticed my unease and quickly put it back down by her side, making me feel awkward. I could have *kicked* myself. She didn't mention it, and I didn't mention it, but I just felt like I'd failed a test.

I had to say something quickly so we could pretend it hadn't happened. "I *hope* it's a mistake."

Thankfully, she just let the whole thing slide. "I'm sure that's it. But, hey, if it's not and you are in trouble, me and some of the girls from Risk are going for drinks at Harbour View tonight," she offered. I knew the girls she was talking about; they were basically a catalogue of fully-clothed Victoria's Secret models who'd been friends since university, and Sarah fit right in with them. My face must have shown my hesitation, because she added, "I swear, Min, one of these days I'm going to get you to come with us. You can't work 24/7."

"Is that a double dare?" I asked as jokingly as I could, not really wanting to explain what it felt like tacking along with a group of people who knew each other really well. I'd rather let her assume it was purely because I was a workaholic. It had been four years since I moved to Sydney and somehow I *still* felt like the new exchange student.

We said our goodbyes and I went over to the rep, who was sighing heavily and impatiently fidgeting with the handset. "Took you long enough," he said, passing it to me over the partition and sitting back in front of his emails. I heard him mutter something about women and talking, but resisted the urge to make a dry comment about the extreme importance of catching up on the latest celebrity goss.

"Hello, Min speaking," I said, putting the phone against my ear. I glanced over towards Sarah's desk, but she'd sat down and was chatting with the rep sitting opposite her.

"Min Lee?" I didn't recognise the voice, but I made an affirmative noise anyway. "If you're free, Diane Frost would like to see you for a moment in her office."

That made me pay attention to the phone; my stomach dropped as soon as I heard her name. *Diane Frost* wanted to see me? Fuck, were my brochures really that bad?

I looked up at her office, but all I could see were the bun and perfectly coiffured hairline peeking over her monitor as she worked. She just looked busy, not angry, but that didn't stop me from being able to feel my pulse thumping in my neck. I looked around to see if anyone else was listening in; they weren't. "I'll be right there," I said, passing the handset back to the rep that it belonged to. Then I started to panic.

The voice ended up belonging to Diane's personal assistant. She must have been new because I hadn't seen her around, but she already looked like she was about to have a nervous breakdown. Her desk was *covered* in manila folders. She stopped what she was doing with them to smile professionally at me and indicate the door to Diane's office, which was open. "Go right ahead, she's waiting for you."

Behind the girl were floor-to-ceiling windows, showing a spectacular view of Sydney, all the way down to the road 36 stories below. I stared bleakly out of them as I walked past; jumping out of them was probably out of the question. Pity, because it was preferable to having to tell Mum that I'd lost my job.

I'd never actually been inside Diane's office before. It had the same big and airy feeling as my apartment, with the same lack of furniture. In this case, the only pieces of furniture were the bookshelves that lined a wall, and a mahogany desk with matching leather chairs in the centre. There was the same amazing skyline outside, but I couldn't pay any attention to it because Diane was seated in front of it and I was too distracted by what was about to happen.

She glanced up from the screen as I entered. "Min," she said, gesturing at the leather chairs facing her desk. "Take a seat, please."

Shit, she sounded *really* cold. I couldn't tell if she looked cold, though, because I didn't want to get caught staring. I just smiled and sat across from her, pretending to be unfazed about the CEO wanting to see me. The muscles in my legs were shaking. I don't think she could tell, though.

She was looking between the screen of her computer and a manila folder in front of her. With some horror I realised it was my personnel file; I recognised the terrible photo taken of me when I was twenty and a new intern. I stared at it. What was the *CEO* doing with my personnel file?

"How long have you been with us, Min?"

The fact she was asking that question made me really nervous, since I was sure my file had dates in it. "Nearly five years," I said. "I was in Melbourne for a year to begin with, and have been here for four."

She nodded. She wasn't even listening to my answer. "In marketing the whole time?" Again, she didn't look at me as I answered her. It was unnerving. "Mmm," she said, flipping through some papers. "There's a note here that you're not to deal with our HR manager," she observed. "The word on the street is that you're in a relationship with him."

Shit, is that what this was about?

It knocked the wind out of me; I hadn't even considered that might be an issue. "That's right," I said, trying to prevent my voice from wavering. I mostly succeeded. "I know it's against policy, but—" My brain went at a million miles an hour and I managed to not fumble with my words. "If it's a problem, I'm sure we can work out a solution."

She did the slightest of facial shrugs. "It's not a problem in itself," she said. "Unless it becomes a problem for business, that is. It certainly wouldn't be the first relationship at Frost." She sat back in her deep office chair, resting her elbows on the arms of it and lacing her fingers. She spent a few seconds watching me. "Min, I have a question for you and I want you to answer me honestly." There was only one correct response to that. I nodded. "Your career plan says that you're interested in management. Being a manager at Frost isn't a walk in the park, Min," she said, gesturing towards the floor. "You know the kind of commitment we expect from leaders here. My *cohort* has a family, but he doesn't spend much time with them." She couldn't have chosen a more unattractive word to refer to her brother, the co-CEO. "Are you prepared to make that sort of sacrifice? Of course, we have the statutory maternity leave arrangements for staff. However, it's very difficult for a company to replace managers for short periods of time without some interruption to business."

Right, don't get pregnant, got it. "Are you asking me if I'm prepared to make sacrifices for the sake of a promotion?" I couldn't imagine what sort of sacrifice they'd ask me to make; I basically did nothing else other than work, anyway. Having any sort of life was a distant memory. When she nodded, I answered automatically, "Of course I'm prepared." I felt as if I were regurgitating textbook lines fed to me by my career counsellor. "That's why I moved from Melbourne to Sydney. I'm prepared to do whatever I need to in order to progress my career."

Diane smiled slightly, and I think I saw a measure of approval in her face. "Good," she said, and as she pulled a stack of printed photos out from underneath my personnel file she added, "There are no management positions free at present. But I do like to have candidates in mind." She slid the photos across the desk and I took them, looking down at them curiously. They were macro shots of pink and champagne diamonds, in several variations and cuts.

While I was leafing through them, she asked, "Do you know what they are?"

These? They were a house. A *big* house, and early retirement. They were the most expensive and rarest diamonds in the world. "Argyle diamonds," I answered immediately. "From the Kimberley."

She let that sit for a moment, and then her smile broadened. "What I'm about to tell you is confidential: Frost has just purchased the rights to mine a pipe of diamonds like these in Western Australia," she said. "It's a small project but, potentially, an extremely valuable one, and of special interest to me. I'm looking to put together a group of people who can keep their mouths shut to work on it." I didn't miss her glancing out towards the floor. "That particular attribute is something that is surprisingly difficult to come by."

I knew what she meant. In any other circumstance I might have laughed at such a diplomatic way of calling the marketing department a rumour mill, but this didn't seem like the appropriate time. I put the pictures back on the table.

"Are you interested? It pitches in just a few weeks and I'm not exaggerating when I say there's a lot of work to do; I don't want many people on it."

Was she kidding? The less people, the better. "Yes," I said without hesitation.

"Great." She closed my personnel file and whatever she had been looking at on her screen. "I haven't picked the exact composition of the team yet. Jason or I will let you know."

Since the conversation was clearly over, I stood. Politely, she stood as well and gestured towards the door. "Thank you for coming so promptly," she said. She was the epitome of professionalism. She was terrifying, but I supposed this was as 'nice' as she got. That woman is a billionaire, I thought, and as I turned to leave, I glanced down at her sparkling watch. It was surreal to be standing a metre away from someone who could practically buy Australia.

As soon as I was out of earshot of her office, I exhaled audibly and put a hand on the wall to steady myself.

Wow.

Well, I guess being considered for a promotion and invited to work on a secret project was a *little* different from losing my job and my life as I knew it. Just, wow. I grinned. Those idiots on my old team would go *nuts* if I got a promotion. As completely ungrateful as it sounded given how much money I was being paid, it felt so good to finally have my years of dedication acknowledged with something other than an enormous paycheque. Even just hearing that she would consider me felt like a huge step. When I walked past the workstations of my hung-over team, I felt completely superior.

There were seven or eight new drunk guy photos in my inbox when I got back to my desk. I wondered if the rep making them knew that it was this kind of crap that was interfering with his career progression. I was tempted to tell him that in a reply, but as usual I held my tongue.

Before I read any more messages, I checked my phone. I really wanted to tell Henry about the conversation I'd just had with Diane, but I knew I couldn't. Diane had said the project was confidential and that she wanted someone who could keep quiet about it. I suppose that meant I needed to celebrate quietly on my own. I laughed to myself; now *there* was an evening unlike any other. A bottle of red and a hundred rounds of Free for All. I'd never done that before...

Sarah had BCCed me in an email to her friends in Risk about when they were meeting up. I clicked on it, remembering that weird touching thing and feeling stupid all over again. I needed a day or two to get over it, and the last thing I wanted to do tonight was be surrounded by gorgeous, perfectly relaxed women talking about Sex in the City or whatever its replacement was these days. I had a hard time imagining what people who didn't play video games did in their spare time, but I thought it was probably boring. Not wanting to ignore her, though, I replied with an excuse.

By the afternoon, I'd archived my material from the previous project, gathered Michelangelo and a sad-looking bamboo plant of dubious health, and was ready to sit with my new team, whoever they were. The office was basically empty, though, because everyone else was already in project meetings, probably arguing over who did what and establishing the pecking order. I literally had nothing to do, so I spun my chair around in slow circles and planned my evening. There were actually a couple of new games out that I'd been meaning to buy and play—maybe I could grab those on the way home.

It was 4:30 a lot sooner than I'd expected it to be, so I packed up early for once and went to brave the lift. It didn't fail to disappoint: I discovered my stockings were navy instead of black. I then spent the rest of the ride down wondering if Diane had noticed and judged me.

Outside it was still sunny and that made me worry even more about my black skirt and navy stockings combo. I knew I'd be home soon, though, and that meant I could just take everything off, burn it all in a ritual fire, and put something comfortable on. I was waiting at the traffic lights trying to decide which game I was going to play first when I heard a girl's voice say, "Look, that's definitely her." After some frantic whispering, another voice agreed, "Oh my God, you're right, it is! I can't do this. Okay, I can. I can."

I twisted a little to glance over my shoulder. There were two girls in Cloverfield Ladies' College uniforms hunched over a mobile and looking directly at me. I quickly looked forward again, and for some reason my heart was pounding. They both giggled, and that made it worse. It didn't matter that I was 25 and hadn't been in high school for seven years, those girls were the type of girls who used to make surfboard jokes about my body and call me 'telegraph pole' behind my back. I really didn't need this, especially not from school kids, not after I'd *finally* heard some good news. I quickly punched the pedestrian crossing button a few more times. Come on, lights...

"Min Lee? It's you, right?" One of the girls called out while the other one was hysterically giggling. When I heard my name, the blood practically drained from my face. How the *hell* did they know who I was? I stared in front of me, deciding to try and ignore them. Maybe they'd stop.

Some older woman had been standing beside me at the lights. She threw a glance behind us to see what the fuss was about and then peered up at me, too. I'd never wanted to just fade into invisibility any more than I did at that moment.

"Miss Lee!" the other girl called out again, leaning heavily on my surname like it was four or five syllables. Her voice sounded muffled as if she had a hand over her mouth.

"I'm going to fucking kill you, Courtney. Oh, my God. Okay. Min!"

The opposing lights were still green, and them calling out was starting to make *everyone* stare. There were even people on the other side of the road watching. I just wanted it all to be over, so I turned around. "Can I help you, girls?" I asked, trying to mimic Diane's impassionate tone. If they were going to make fun of me, they should just fucking get it over with so I could go home.

They both looked at me, then at each other, and giggled. One of them—the one who had been calling out to me first, I think—had very long, very straight brown hair but otherwise looked pretty average. Her friend looked like something straight off the cover of an Enid Blyton book, though. She was tiny with her blonde hair in big rolling curls and already had the kind of hourglass figure that men would probably fight to the death for. Just in case anyone hadn't noticed it, her plaid skirt was scandalously short and her shirt was a size too small. She pushed her friend in the head, straightened her school tie, and then marched up to me.

I looked down at her, aware that people all around us were practically reaching for popcorn.

"You really *aren't* a guy," she said, looking me up and down and making me feel self-conscious, and reminding me of my blue stockings again. She was so tiny she didn't even reach my collarbones. She noticed that, too. "And, whoa, you're, like, *tall*."

Shit, really? I'd been wondering why I found it so easy to reach everything. I didn't really want to get into a fight with them by being a smartass, though, so I just kept my mouth shut. It wasn't hard, because every moment, I kept waiting for them to drop the impressed act and just dissolve into giggles and make fun of me. I wondered what incredibly unintelligent insult *these* girls would come up with. *The Lee-ning Tower of Melbourne* used to be a favourite at my school.

Courtney was still looking between me and the screen of her mobile. "She *does* look like that painting. Like, really."

Well, there was only one letter difference between 'man' and 'Min'—something no one at my school had figured out despite the fact I'd been a hardcore tomboy back then. Perhaps these girls would, even if I was really careful to make sure no one could describe me as a tomboy anymore. I felt like my mismatched outfit was a dead giveaway about how much I hated wearing these clothes, though.

"It's me," the blonde said, as she gestured to herself. She wasn't teasing me and hadn't noticed my stockings, "*Hazumichan95*. By the way, if you're wondering, I really regret that username. Like, especially right now."

Comfortingly, I *did* recognise that username from Deviant Art. "Oh, you're the girl who had—" I was about to say 'friendship trouble', but then I realised that the person she was having issues with was probably that other girl who was with her. I didn't get a chance to figure out how to finish that sentence.

"I'm not Hazumi, though, *obviously*. I'm Bree." She gestured at her friend. "And that's Courtney. But don't worry; she doesn't use Deviant Art so you don't have to figure out who she is." The way she spoke, it seemed like she was trying to force out as many words as possible in the shortest period of time. Or like she'd had a little too much red cordial.

She—Bree?—grabbed my hand and shook it. "Min," I said automatically, before I realised how ridiculous that was because they both clearly knew who I was. At least *that* made sense now, because my username was '*MinLeee*'. The one with just two 'E's was already taken. What it didn't explain was how they'd sorted through the 4.5 million people in Sydney and ended up on this corner— outside Frost Headquarters. "How did you find me?"

Courtney laughed shortly. "Bree spent two and a half hours on Google," she said loudly, pretending to cough at the beginning and end of her comment.

Bree twisted around. "Oh, my God, *Courtney*, I'm going to tell my brother you have crabs if you don't shut up."

Did she just... I looked hurriedly around at all the people watching us. A couple of them were smothering their own laughter. I wondered if I looked as mortified as I felt.

Bree turned back to me. She still had my hand. I looked pointedly at it, but she didn't notice. "This is so awesome!" she announced, smiling brightly up at me while I struggled with the urge to just spin on my heels and run away. This particular girl seemed like the sort to give chase, and even with my long legs I didn't like my chances of outrunning her. I was wearing stilettos. "I love your art, you have *no* idea. It's *amazing*. It's so incredibly awesome to finally meet you!"

"Thanks," I said vaguely, wanting to follow up with, 'Listen, I'm really freaked out that you Googled me, you and your friend are too full-on, I feel extremely uncomfortable right now and wish everyone would stop looking at us, and your curls are perfectly symmetrical how do you even do that? I can *never* get mine that round...' But what I *actually* said was, "I have to go." Serendipitously, the pedestrian crossing went green.

I went to walk across it, but she didn't release my hand. "Come on," she said. "Courtney owes me ten bucks because *she* said I'd never be able to find you. I'll get you a coffee!"

It was approaching five in the evening. Not that it had ever stopped me from slamming caffeinated energy drinks before, but it at least sounded like an acceptable excuse. "Thanks, but it's a bit late for coffee," I said, and tried to pull away again before the lights went red.

Courtney was laughing away in the background. "She clearly thinks you're a scary stalker, Bree," she told her friend, as if I wasn't there. "Which you are, by the way. They should totally lock you up."

Bree snorted. "*Please,*" she said over her shoulder, still holding my hand between hers. "I'm not a scary stalker. It's not like I built some shrine to her that I sacrifice animals on and have a wall covered in photos that I *masturbate* to every night or something."

What on... I didn't think I'd actually heard right. Her sentence echoed in my head and it was only when several sets of people standing around us started to nervously laugh from the shock that I realised she *had* actually said it. I couldn't laugh, though; I felt sick. I really didn't want to be there. Somehow, I'd found something *more* humiliating than having people make fun of how I looked.

When I tried to tug my hand free this time, I managed to finally escape from her grasp. I'm not sure what I actually said—it was probably something apologetic about being in a rush—and I spun and ran out in front of traffic. Fortunately nothing hit me, and the flow of cars that followed prevented either of them from chasing after me. Once I'd turned the corner, I broke into a light jog and nearly rolled my ankles in the process. I couldn't get home fast enough, though some part of me was legitimately afraid they would follow me there.

Once I was upstairs and had the door shut behind me, I exhaled and leant against it. I listened for footsteps in the hallway, and then had a moment of clarity where I realised how *ridiculous* I was being. Min, they're *schoolgirls*. Like, little schoolgirls, and they're obviously completely harmless. You're not even *at* school anymore, you're a grown woman.

What was I afraid they would do if they had followed me, anyway? Embarrass me to death in the privacy of my own home? Oh, the *humanity*.

Fuck, though, I felt sixteen again. I took my phone out of my bag and was about to call Henry when I noticed it was only 5 pm. He'd still be in meetings, so I texted him instead. 'Really weird, a couple of schoolkids looked me up on Google because of my art and they just pounced on me as I left work...' Even as I was typing it, I felt stupid. This was *not* a big deal. I sent it anyway.

It must have been a pretty boring meeting, because Henry had replied even before I'd made it to the bathroom. "Hah, fans! Not surprising, your stuff is fantastic. Bet they were completely awestruck by the great Min Lee xoxo."

I read his text a couple of times, standing there in the doorway of my bedroom with the phone. I *was* being ridiculous. That Bree: she'd been messaging me for months and she had asked for advice on some pretty personal topics. It shouldn't be surprising she was being so familiar. She was really intense in real life, though. Fuck, she'd exhausted me after two minutes; give me the internet any day. It took me ages to get into the shower because I felt the need to go through every message she'd sent me. None of them were creepy; they were just ordinary, sociable messages. In some of them she was upset, in some she was happy... they painted a picture of an ordinary but extremely enthusiastic teenager. Not the scary monster I was acting like she was. Seriously, what the hell, Min?

After my shower, I investigated my almost empty pantry with a game controller in hand, still berating myself over those damn schoolgirls. I couldn't even comfort eat because all I had was a can of Homebrand spaghetti, a couple of packs of instant noodles and an ancient, half-finished jar of pickles from 2009. Vinegar preserved things for years, right? The date on the jar reminded me I needed to go grocery shopping at some point this year. I shouldn't always have room service.

What I did have lots of was red wine. I grabbed a bottle; it was the perfect method to start cultivating some serious amnesia. Wineglass and controller in hand, I settled down on the couch. Even though I'd forgotten to buy those games I was after, this was shaping up to be the evening I'd been expecting.

Time to try to relax, I thought, pouring myself a very generous glass of red. So I had a fan, so what? That was normal, right? My art was pretty good for the website, so it shouldn't really be *that* much of a surprise. And she'd probably Googled me because she'd only found out just yesterday that I was a woman; meeting an adult man as a schoolgirl was probably a big no-no. I took a big mouthful of wine. Fuck, I hoped that girl wouldn't try to accost me in the middle of the street again. Actually, I decided I should probably send her a message to let her know that I wouldn't be okay with it.

I opened Deviant Art, trying to figure out how I was going to phrase that sort of request without coming off sounding like a complete bitch, but she'd beaten me to it. There was already a message from *Hazumichan95*. I tapped it, a sinking feeling settling in my stomach. *"omg so amazing to meet u!!! sorry I was a bit star struck!!! :) :) :) :) wow I cant believe it u have been my art hero for like a whole year nearly. definitely worth the train trip into the city. btw that awesome pic of u on the balcony is my screensaver"*

I sighed. Well, fuck. I couldn't tell her to go away *now*, could I?

Since I had Deviant Art open, I checked the painting again. There were a few more comments, so I scrolled through them. Down near the bottom, I spotted another one from her. *"btw guys min lee is a totally amazing artist. she seriously looks exactly like this just check out her photo. how do people even make stuff like this omg i wish i was this talented at like anything!!"* There were a whole row of exclamation marks as though the key was jammed.

This was the girl that freaked you out, Min. I shook my head at myself; she wasn't a creepy stalker, or any sort of stalker. She was just being nice, and I was just a fucking hermit who needed to spend less time with a screen and more time with actual humans. I read her comment again. It *was* nice, but it was wrong. I didn't look exactly like that in real life. If I did, I wouldn't have to wear uncomfortable crap that I hated and I wouldn't feel so weird when I stood next to other women like Sarah. There was no point in getting upset about that, though, because I knew being miserable about it wouldn't change anything. It was just a painting.

I threw my phone on the other side of the couch and looked back at my half-empty wineglass. I was supposed to be celebrating that fantastic conversation I'd had with Diane Frost and instead I was stressing myself out over stupid crap again. Really, if I'd felt like having a painful evening, I would have joined Sarah and those beautiful friends of hers.

I topped up my glass and then switched on my PlayStation. Fuck all this crap, I just wanted to relax and celebrate. Why couldn't the world pause for just *one second* and let me be happy that after years of hard work, the *billionaire co-CEO* of my company told me she wanted to make me a manager?

I hoped mass murder and copious amounts of alcohol would shut my head up. It usually did the trick.

I hadn't realised I'd been drinking *that* much, but when I woke up at 3 am on the couch with no idea where I was, I had to concede that maybe the whole bottle might have been a bad idea—especially on an empty stomach. I drank as much water as I could then hauled myself off to bed.

As a result of my 'celebrating', I missed my alarm the next morning and gave myself twenty less minutes to do my hair and makeup. I had such a headache and was in such a rush when I opened my front door that I nearly tripped over something that had been placed in front of it. I stopped myself just in time.

It was a takeaway coffee cup with a little shortbread biscuit in the shape of a star on the plastic lid. Henry was known to do things like this, so I smiled and bent down to retrieve it. My boyfriend was the nicest man on the planet, I swear. After I'd picked it up, though, I noticed someone had scribbled in marker on the side of it. I held it up in front of my face to read.

"7 am isnt too late for coffee is it?? :) :)"

FOUR

"That doesn't look like a Red Bull," Henry remarked as he leant over my partition, his eyes on the full coffee cup in the centre of my otherwise empty desk. I was frowning at it, too. "Are you trying to quit again?"

Hah. I'd long since surrendered to the fact I would be drinking myself to death on those things. Instead of saying as much, though, I just bent forward in my chair, picked up the cup and held it at eye-level for him so he could read the text.

He squinted at it. "'*7 am isn't too late for...*'" His eyebrows lowered for a moment. "Am I missing something?"

I sighed and put the cup down on the desk in front of me, sitting back in my chair and staring at it again. "Those schoolgirls I told you about last night," I explained. "One of them left this on my doorstep this morning."

His frown disappeared. "Ah," he said, looking intently at me, "And let me guess, you're not going to drink it?"

"Doctor Freud, you've *cured* me," I said dryly. "Of course not! Who knows what could be in it?"

As usual, he didn't even flinch. "You're absolutely right. The milk might be *low fat*." He gestured at it. "They're schoolgirls, and by your account, big fans of yours. Do you actually think there's going to be anything other than coffee in there?" I pressed my lips together rather than concede that he was probably right. He wouldn't let it slide, though. "You didn't throw it out, either, so I'm guessing *you* don't actually think there's anything wrong with the coffee, either."

Of course I didn't throw it out. I had been going to, but in the lift on the way down, the creepy lopsided smiley faces on the cup and I had been staring at each other and I just couldn't do it. I'd paused by every rubbish bin between home and Frost International and not managed to toss it into any of them. When I'd made it to work, I'd even spent a couple of seconds staring into the bin under my own desk before just putting it beside my keyboard.

"Maybe I'm just keeping it as evidence to be tested in case I go missing," I said, half-heartedly. The thing that always got me was how quickly Henry cut through everything. He *was* right, they *were* just schoolgirls. What was I expecting? Arsenic? Rohypnol? There was almost no chance it was anything but coffee. I sighed. "It was just weird, that's all. If fans of yours ever went leaving coffee on your doorstep, you'd be freaked out, too."

"If they were that proactive? I'd hire them, actually," he said. "At the rate Diane goes through personal assistants, it would be good to have a standby waiting in the wings. And speaking of that," he waved a stack of manila folders he'd had tucked under his arm up in the air. "As much as I love your company, I actually came up here to give these to that poor girl."

They looked very similar to the piles and piles of folders that had been all over the assistant's desk yesterday. "What are they for?"

Henry sighed. "Diane and Sean are at it again," he said, making a frustrated gesture up towards the ceiling. It was common knowledge that the co-CEOs did not get along with each other, so that wasn't a surprise. They were also twins; sometimes it all felt like the premise of a B-grade movie. Between them they'd managed to draw battlelines along different departments so each of them was in charge of something they were better at than the other. There were turf wars all the time, though, and the HR department was always one of the contentious areas. Officially it was Sean's, and Sean was Henry's boss, but according to Henry that didn't stop Diane from meddling in it. Or with him.

I laughed once. "What happened this time? Did he forget her birthday or something?"

Henry shrugged his shoulders. "With them, who knows? I just do what I'm told." He pointed at my coffee. "Are you really not going to drink that?"

I glared at him.

His eyes twinkled as he reached over the partition and plucked the little star-shaped shortbread from the lid of the cup, popping it in his mouth. Then, pretending to look shocked, he grabbed at his throat with his free hand and made exaggerated choking noises.

Since I hadn't put my handbag away yet, I looked hurriedly around us to see if anyone else was watching and then thumped him with it. "Shut up! It's creepy, okay? She must have followed me home."

He stopped. "You're in the Whitepages," he pointed out. "It's how your mother got your landline." Well, *that* was true… "Anyway, let me solve your serious dilemma about what to do with the coffee." He lifted it off the table and drank deeply from it. Because it wasn't hot anymore, he was able to just pour the whole lot down his throat. When he was done he very politely returned the empty cup to my hand.

I placed it back next to my keyboard so those lopsided smileys could keep staring at me. "Well, I hope you have me listed as a beneficiary on your life insurance. I need a holiday."

He laughed, and then stopped being silly. "Sometimes people are actually just being nice, Min," he said with a smile, and then went to deliver the folders.

I swivelled in my chair so I could watch him leave.

He wasn't really a big coffee drinker, which meant he'd only done that to make a point. I couldn't figure out exactly what that point was, but whatever it was, a big component of it was trying to prove that he was right. I narrowed my eyes. The most frustrating thing was that he *was* usually right about people, and he was usually right about me, too. Usually. I hadn't figured out how he'd still not noticed how much I didn't like sex, though.

I spun back towards my empty desk. I *still* hadn't been assigned a team, and it was weird having nothing super urgent to do.

Being team-less actually continued for several days. I didn't hear any more about the top secret project Diane was planning and when I crossed paths with Jason in the kitchen, he didn't mention anything, either.

On the third day I'd been having grand visions of leaving work on time and finally getting to the game store before it closed, but as soon as word got around that I wasn't assigned a project yet, I suddenly became everyone's best buddy. Tragically, it wasn't because of my dazzling personality; if they could get someone to work on their layouts and colour schemes—namely, me—that was money they'd save in outsourcing design. The project leads didn't alter their timelines for me just because I was volunteering my services, either. They kept me back late with everyone else.

Leaving the building after dark *did* drastically reduce the likelihood I'd run into those girls, though. It was stupid for me to be worried about it; they were just kids, so they'd probably already be in bed by 9 pm, right? Still, just in case, I loitered around the doorway and peered down the street every night as I left the office. The security guards were just about ready to have me committed by the end of the week, but luckily, the girls still hadn't turned up outside.

That blonde one kept messaging me on Deviant Art instead. Each time I answered, I must have spent half an hour trying to make sure every word in my one or two sentence replies was clear. They had to say, 'I appreciate your attention, but I hope my disdain is enough to put you off trying to meet up with me again'.

By Monday I'd almost forgotten about the whole thing, so when I walked straight out of the building, looking down at the screen of my phone, I nearly collided with her. I stumbled at the last minute, nearly falling ungracefully onto the asphalt. I stood up straight again, staring down at those blonde curls and trying to steady myself. Who stands in the *middle* of the pavement right in front of the door of an office building?

This girl, apparently. She smiled brightly up at me. "Min!" she said, and then her smile faded. For a moment I thought she might actually apologise for nearly giving me a heart attack. That moment passed quickly. "Or should I, like, call you Miss Lee?"

Yes, I'm far more likely to be offended if you call me by my first name than, say, if you were to use the internet to stalk me to my house and work. "'Min' is fine."

As the shock faded and my senses returned, I remembered what had happened last time she had accosted me. Looking around us, I was grateful there were far less people on the street at this time of night than there had been last week. I checked my phone. "...It's *seven*."

The girl smiled. "I know," she said, and then changed the subject. "You can call me 'Bree'. No one can pronounce my surname anyway. Have you had dinner yet?"

I was still stuck on the part where she was waiting for me outside work *at 7 pm*. "Aren't your parents going to be wondering where you are?"

At the mention of her parents, she made a face and her nose crinkled.

"No," she said more firmly than I expected. "I said I'm at Courtney's and Courtney *owes* me, so she won't say anything."

I wasn't happy about a schoolkid lying to her parents about her whereabouts to lay in wait for me outside my work. Actually, it was as stalkerish as her putting coffee on my doorstep in the early hours of the morning. Bree didn't seem the least bit bothered by the fact she was lying to her parents, though. She didn't even have anything more to say about it.

"Anyway, I've been here for ages and I'm *really* hungry," she just said. "I was thinking we could go grab some dinner. There's this *great* restaurant in Darling Harbour, you'll love it."

Hang on a second, what? "Slow down," I told her, holding my hands up. "You're in the city at 7 pm by yourself, your parents don't know where you are, and you think it's a good idea to stay out even later? You need to go home right now."

She didn't look deterred at all. "I'm not by myself now," she pointed out. "Trains run until midnight, anyway, so I can just get one later. One of your earrings is falling out."

My eyebrows went up and automatically I reached up to my ears. She was right, so I fixed it.

As I was doing that, she slung her Cloverfield bag over her shoulder. "Come on," she said, as if I'd never told her to go home. "The restaurant is like ten minutes this way and believe me, the food is *awesome*."

I didn't budge. How the hell did she expect this to turn out? "Bree," I said, feeling weird about using her name, but wanting to get her attention. "What on earth are you doing, exactly?"

She turned back towards me with a blank expression. "Darling Harbour is this way and that's where—"

"Waiting here, I mean," I said, interrupting her. "The coffee, the messages, the lying to your parents. All of this—why are you doing it? What's the point?"

She looked at me earnestly. "I'm making friends with you," she said. "I decided last week. And it's not like I can just hang out with you at school, can I? So here I am now." She held her palms out to present herself.

I didn't even know which part of what she just said to be more alarmed by. "At *7 pm* on a school night." Then the rest of what she'd said hit me. "Wait a minute, you're just *making friends with me*? Just like that?"

She pointed a finger at me as if she was telling me off. "It's not *my* fault you work long hours. I've been waiting here since 4:30. You took so long to leave work even my iPod went flat. If you worked the hours of a normal person I'd be home by now."

The expression on my face said it all. "So the fact you're out late is *my* fault now?" I didn't even know what to say anymore. Was she *completely* insane? "And you've just *decided* that's how it's going to be? That we're going to be friends and that's that?"

She just nodded. *She just nodded?*

I didn't even know where to start. I'd only just met this girl and already I wanted to wrap my hands around her neck and shake some sense into her. She drove me *nuts*. Who the hell stalks someone to their house just to leave coffee for them? And Henry had just drank it, too, like it was nothing. If he'd have known what sort of nutcase she was, he'd probably have left it. No, wait. No; if he was here, he'd have said very calmly that some people are difficult, but that doesn't mean they are crazy. He wouldn't get angry; he'd just rebut what was said by focusing on key details.

But, fuck, I was no Henry. I tried anyway. "Bree," I said, trying to be calm and *not* strangle her. "I'm 25. I don't know how old *you* are, but—"

"18," she said, interrupting me. She paused for a second. "Okay, not really. But my birthday's in a couple of weeks, so..."

I had been about to explain that the age gap was too big for a friendship to ever work, but before I said anything I counted in my head and realised the age gap was seven years. Seven years, that was the same age gap between Henry and I, and we got along really well. Shit. I'd pinned her at maybe 14 or 15, and what I had been about to say was based on that. Now I didn't really know what I *could* say. If she was that close to being an adult, I also wondered if it was such a huge drama that she was out at 7 pm on a school night, too.

Sensing a moment of weakness, she went in for the kill. "Come on," she said, a big grin on her face and huge, puppy-dog eyes aimed right at me. "It's just dinner. What have you got to lose?"

I could feel myself wavering on that decision and I didn't like it.

Not at all. This *wasn't* going to happen. It couldn't, it was stupid. She was a *schoolkid*. "What makes you so sure you want to be friends with me?"

Leaning a hand on one of her hips, she smiled up at me like she already knew what was going to happen. "Uh, because you're *awesome*?"

Nice try. I wasn't 'awesome', that was for sure. I didn't like the smug edge on her smile, either. "I don't know why you'd think that or why you'd think it's going to work—"

"I don't *think* it's going to work," she told me as if she was delivering a universal truth, "I *know* it's going to work. My grandmother cured her cancer like that. It's all in the mind." She tapped her head and her curls bounced.

She was missing the point and I wasn't sure how I felt about being compared to a terminal illness. "But I'm not awesome, and I don't know who you think I am. A couple of weeks ago you thought I was a guy, so, no disrespect, but you don't know *anything* about me. I'm not just whatever you've decided I am."

She actually laughed at me; it was a really unexpected reaction and for just one second, I felt really humiliated. "Min, you are *so* uptight," she said, walking toward me. "Come on, let's just go have dinner!"

I put my hands up to stop her from coming any closer. I just... did this girl have *no* boundaries? This was absolutely and completely ridiculous and it was *not* going any further. But she wasn't even listening to me anymore. "Look, just stop." I said. "I don't want to see you, I don't want to have dinner with you. After work I just want to go home, put on something comfortable and relax. I'm going home."

"You can relax in this restaurant, it's really comfy," she said, *again* ignoring my dismissal.

Yeah, no. "Bree," I said firmly. "I'm going home." I even went as far as to attempt to keep walking up the road past her, but one of those little arms shot out and grabbed mine.

I looked down at my trapped wrist, and then up at those rosy cheeks. Bree beamed at me. "Trust me, you'd rather be in this restaurant with me."

That was the *last* place I would rather be and just as I opened my mouth to say as much, she released my wrist. Before I realised what she was doing and what was going on, she wrenched my handbag off my shoulder and ran a few paces away with it.

I couldn't say anything. I just gaped at her; did she *really* just do that?

She had a wide grin on her face. "Now you *have* to come," she said, holding up my handbag under her chin, and then glancing back down at it. "Wow, is this Coach? It's *really* nice."

"Bree!" I said, listening to the ragged edge in my voice. "What the fuck are you doing? This is *not* okay, give that back!"

She looked like she was really enjoying herself. "Come and get it!"

I still had my phone, and I held it up. "I swear to god I will call the police if you don't give it back."

"Or," she said mischievously, "You could just come and have dinner with me."

She waggled my handbag.

I literally dialled triple-0 and had the phone to my ear, rehearsing what I was going to say in my head when I realised how stupid it sounded. How stupid it made *me* sound. I put my phone down again. She was *tiny,* what the hell were they going to say if they *did* come? I sighed.

Bree lit up. "You're going to come? Really?" she asked, and the genuine excitement in her voice just gave me a stronger desire to beat her to death. It was *cute*, and that made it harder to focus on the part where she was a crazy fucking stalker-criminal.

"Give my bag back to me *right now*," I said. "And I might consider it."

Obediently, she trotted over and delivered my handbag. My original plan had been to get my bag back, lecture her on her *appalling* behaviour and then just storm off. But she was looking right up at me with those adoring eyes and, actually, I just felt *bad.* She wasn't 25, she was a teenager. She was just being young and stupid, and she just wanted to have dinner with her favourite artist at any cost. And what was her favourite artist doing? Being a grump.

Fuck.

"Okay," I said, regretting it even as I was saying it. "Just dinner, and just once. But you have to promise not to *ever* do *anything* like this again."

She stared at me for a second like she couldn't believe it, and then *jumped up and down*. "Oh my god, *really?*" she said, practically squealing. "*Really?* Yes, okay! I promise!" And just in case there was any way in which I *wasn't* extremely uncomfortable with everything that was happening, she reached across between us and took my hand to lead me. It was like being dragged along the footpath by the human version of a small fluffy terrier.

Bree talked the whole way. The *whole* way. By the time we were seated at the table on the balcony of an ugly modern restaurant that clearly took itself far too seriously, I think I knew everything about all of her classmates and could also draw some of their family trees. Slumped in my chair, I stared across the table at her as she babbled away. I had never met anyone who talked as much as she did; she filled every second of airspace. I actually wasn't sure I'd said as many words in my life as she'd said in half an hour.

I looked around us to see who was listening. One of the waiters smiled at me, but it was a very professional smile. I wondered what he was *really* thinking about what was going on. A chatty schoolgirl eating dinner with, well, whatever I looked like. I'd had a long day at work so however I looked, it was probably terrible. My hair was probably all over the place, and it probably looked even worse next to Bree's. There was no chance we'd be mistaken for relatives, either. Maybe they'd think I was her teacher?

"My cousin had her wedding reception here," Bree was saying, oblivious to my discomfort. "It was wild, there were like 200 people and we were so loud someone called the police on us and it wasn't even midnight. Are you vegetarian?"

I blinked. "Uh," I said. "No."

"Neither am I," she said, playing with the origami swan serviette. She put the serviette ring on its head like a crown while she kept talking. "I tried for, like, two weeks once but then this friend of mine had her birthday at Hard Rock and I was like, 'I could just starve or I could enjoy myself', you know? I only did it in the first place because there was this guy who was into me and he kept trying to make me eat at his family's restaurant and I wanted to make him feel bad so he'd never asked me again. So I was, like,

'Yeah, sorry, I can't eat any of those sweet little baby lambs you've hacked up and shoved on a skewer'."

While I was shifting awkwardly in my seat and listening to her, the smiling waiter walked up to our table and placed menus in front of us. I was glad I had something else to do other than just sit there and try to look relaxed when I really wasn't.

The first thing I noticed when I opened the gold-leafed menu was the price of the food.

I'm pretty sure I made some awful, strangled sound. It wasn't like I'd have trouble affording anything, but the presumptuousness of this girl was unbelievable. *Two hundred dollars for a steak?* Was the cow educated in a Swiss finishing school and ritually blessed before being hand-carried to the restaurant by 12 virgins dressed in white? What the *hell* could make a steak be worth that much money?

I was going to need some serious assistance to deal with all this. I held the wine list up at the waiter and pointed at one of them. "In a glass, please, but fill it to the lip." The waiter nodded and left us to select our meals.

Bree was giggling at me as I took a deep breath and braved the menu again. My opinion of the prices must have been obvious. "Now you know why I can't come here by myself!" she said, and then flipped the pages of her own menu. "So how much *do* you get paid, anyway? You work at Frost, so it must be *heaps*."

I looked up sharply at her. "Why?" I asked flatly. "Are you planning on robbing me? Because I hate to tell you, but you missed a golden opportunity to do that before."

She looked delighted I was finally speaking in full sentences. "Yeah, totally! I'm going to steal all your money. That would go really well. I'm like half your size, you could just, like, breathe on me and I'd blow off into the distance." She'd felt pretty strong when she was dragging me down the road. "You're *really* tall, by the way. That must be so cool. I always wondered what it was like to be tall."

Hah, 'cool'. Sure. I didn't really want to talk about what it was like being my height. "Have you thought about what university you're going to go to yet?"

She didn't look surprised by the fact I'd changed the subject at all. "Nah," she said, rolling with the topic change. "I don't even know if I'm going to go to uni. My cousin went to uni and now she doesn't have a job *and* she has an enormous debt." While she was talking, she'd stuck her knife into the prongs of her fork and was trying to balance them on the rim of her glass. "I guess it doesn't matter now, since she's pregnant. She'll probably just stay at home. Do you have any kids?"

She was giving me whiplash. "No."

"Do you want kids?"

Henry wanted kids. "Do *you*?"

Bree grinned. "Yeah," she said. "I'd have heaps just in case any of them turned out like my brother. Then I could just focus on the other ones. Would you be, like, really disappointed if I just ordered Fish and Chips? I just kind of want something extremely deep fried right now."

Yeah, I didn't know how I was going to cope with her ordering Fish and Chips because I'd pinned all my hopes on her ordering the Holy Steak. "Order whatever you like, I'm still going to be broke."

She laughed and stood up in her chair. Before I could stop her, she was *shouting* out to the waiter across all the softly talking patrons on the balcony. "Hey! We'd like to order!"

When she sat back down again, I think I'd shrunk as low in my chair as I could without actually sliding under the table. "You're supposed to wait your turn."

She shrugged, not at all worried. "Yeah, but they might take ages and I'm *really* hungry," she said. "What are you having?"

No idea, I thought, since you haven't given me the opportunity to decide. I'd probably just have a warm salad, anyway. I'd had a lot of bad food during the week, and as Mum said, I didn't want to be fat as well as tall.

After we'd ordered, I looked over the balcony and realised the sun was setting. Where we were seated had an unobstructed view of Darling Harbour, and with the sun disappearing behind the buildings, it was reflecting on the water. The scene was very beautiful, especially with all the neon lights and torches along the waterfront. It would make a good painting, actually, and this angle was just perfect.

While I was trying to figure out how I'd frame it, I heard a fake shutter click.

When I looked abruptly back at Bree, she had her mobile pointed at me. Tilting her head a little, she considered the picture. "That's the first time I've seen you smile," she said, glancing up at me over the screen and then raising her eyebrows when she saw my expression. "...*And* there it goes." She held her phone out at me so I could see the photo. "Look? It's nice."

If I was in it, it wasn't a nice photo. I did her the courtesy of looking at it anyway, but I just snorted. *That* was not a nice photo.

She made a face, snatching her phone back and examining it again. "Are you serious? It's great!" She tapped at the screen to zoom in. "Look! You have a dimple."

I did *not* have anything of the sort. *She* was the one with dimples. I looked again, anyway, and saw how high my collar was sitting and wished I'd worn something else. Or just gone home and taken everything off. As I was scrutinizing myself, her phone locked automatically again. That painting I'd done was her lockscreen.

A glass of red landed in front of me on the table and I thanked the waiter, glancing at Bree as she looked at her phone again and wincing. He gave me a secret smile back as he left. Bree was still looking at the photo, and I was worried if I just left it she might try to take more. "I don't really like being photographed."

"I'll fix that," she said immediately and with the same conviction she put behind everything she said. "Why, anyway? Do you have a thing about your nose or something?"

My hand shot up to the bridge of my nose. I'd never even thought about it. Was there something wrong with it? "My nose...?"

She looked surprised for a second and then laughed. "Oh, like, I don't mean there's anything wrong with your nose! It's just some people have weird issues with random body parts and don't want to be in photos, that's all!" She paused, watching me feel the shape of it. "Oh, my god, do you *really* have a thing about your nose? That's stupid. You're gorgeous."

Bree looked like the adult version of one of Bouguereau's cherubs, so I didn't think she'd understand what it was like to *not* resemble a classic masterpiece and therefore not want to be photographed. I certainly wasn't going to try and explain it to her, either. Anyway, it wasn't *parts* of me I had issues with, it was the whole thing. I took a sip of my wine as Bree took photos of her serviette swan with the serviette ring crown. Then again, was it actually the whole thing I hated? I'd really liked that painting I'd done of myself, and there weren't many parts of me I'd changed dramatically for that. Just two, in fact. I looked down at them in my blouse.

No sooner had I done that, my heart pounded. I put my wine glass back down on the table so I didn't spill it.

Dangerous fucking ground, Min, I told myself firmly as I closed my eyes for a moment. Just stop. You are who you are, learn to deal with it.

"Hey, can I have a sip of your wine?"

I opened my eyes again, still a bit dazed. "You're underage," I reminded her, "that's against the law."

She scoffed. "We jay-walked on the way here and that's against the law. It's too late, you're already a criminal. Just give me one little sip, okay?"

Before I could stop her, she'd reached over and wrapped her fingers around the stem of the glass. If I tried to struggle with it, red wine would probably spill all over the table and all over me. I couldn't do anything else, so I just let her take it.

She did *not* just have 'one little sip'. "This is gross," she said, wrinkling up her nose as she swallowed big gulps of it. "How can you even drink this?" Despite her assessment, she kept going and she'd drunk nearly half the glass before she gave it back to me. I stared at it while she said, "It's probably best you don't drink it all, anyway." She giggled. "I don't like my chances of being able to carry you home."

Home sounded *great* right about now. God, I was so damn tired all of a sudden. I just wanted to shut myself somewhere.

"Just you wait," she said, leaning across the table to pat my hand. "You're going to *love* the food! It's completely awesome. You're going to wish you could have dinner here every night." She stopped to think for a second. "You probably could afford that anyway, right? Oh, my god. If I could afford it I'd eat every meal at this place. Maybe I'd start a food blog."

I knew what I'd call it, too: *Adventures in Bankruptcy: Culinary Edition*. It was a great idea. I could go bankrupt *and* get fat, all in one. Then I could be tall, fat *and* broke. How attractive. Well, at least I'd be well-fed, I thought, as the waiter came bustling over and placed two very large plates in front of us.

Bree was actually right about the food. It *was* great. Although, given the fact the price rolled into three digits for each dish, I would have been pissed off if the food *hadn't* been life-changing. It was *so* great that it even succeeded in distracting me from my pathetic self-loathing for at least a few minutes. I'd have to remember to thank the 12 virgins dressed in white before I left.

I had thought maybe the food would shut Bree up, but she just kept talking through every mouthful. "So the school dance is in April," she was saying, "And *Courtney* wants to take my brother which is *so* fucked up I don't even know where to start. She was like, 'You can just take *my* brother', but her brother is this hideous monster who talks about girls like 'pussy' this and 'tits' that, and I'm like, 'why would you force me to spend time with that loser'?" Bree held her fork up towards the ceiling, examining a chip she'd speared with it, before putting it in her mouth. I supposed I should be happy she was at least using the knife and fork and not her fingers. "She just wants to feel like she's not an awful person, I guess. Whatever, though. Would you date your best friend's brother, even if you thought everything was fine in their family?"

"Uh…"

"Yeah, exactly," Bree said, interpreting that as my answer. "It is *so* not right. I don't know what I'm going to do about it. Maybe I just won't go. On top of everything, I *really* don't want to see them be all gross together. I hate it when people are like that. Do you have a boyfriend? Hang on, didn't you mention him in one of your messages? He works for Frost, too, right?" She didn't even stop for a breath so I could answer. "Wow, it must have been really hard finding someone as tall as you. Is he as tall as you?"

Even though I knew she wasn't trying to be mean, that comment stung me a little. I was already not feeling that great about myself. "Yeah," I said dismissively. "Do *you* have a boyfriend?"

She shook her head, peeling the batter off her fish and eating it first. "I go to an all-girls school," she told me. "St. Anthony's is our brother school because it's really close by, but all the boys there are total idiots and they only want one thing anyway, you know? They just stare straight at my boobs and, like, why would I *choose* to date that? So how long have you known your boyfriend? What's his name?"

"Does that matter?"

She gave me a stern look and waved her fork at me. "Friends know friends' boyfriends' names."

"It's Henry," I said, giving up.

"Henry," Bree repeated, testing the name out. "That sounds so totally proper. Is he Asian, too? Or Aussie?" *He's both*, I thought, but didn't say so because she'd probably miss the point, anyway. Trying to follow all of this was really draining me. "Must be weird to work with him. Weird and cool. Actually, it would kind of be cool to work in an office. I always wanted to work in an office."

I sighed at that, and she noticed. "Careful what you wish for."

She stopped eating for a second to watch me. "I thought you loved your job?"

Loved? *Hah*. "I've got a good job, that's true."

She actually spent a few seconds considering me when she *didn't* talk. "You're this amazing artist, so I don't really know why you do the whole Corporate Barbie thing, anyway," she said, going for another mouthful. "It *totally* doesn't suit you, and you shouldn't bother with it."

Wow, I... felt like I'd had a knife shoved into my chest. Had she really just said that?

It knocked the wind out of me and I sat there reeling for a moment. I *knew* it didn't suit me, did she think I needed some crazy, hyperactive teenager reminding me of that? I knew no matter how much I curled my hair or bought expensive makeup or wore Jimmy Choos, it didn't suit me. I still felt like an imposter. But I didn't have any choice, so what the fuck was I supposed to do? Go to work dressed in a sheet?

Just, no. No. I was exhausted. I'd had enough, I couldn't do this. I'd spent at least a couple of hours with this girl, I'd earned myself some space.

I just really wanted to go home and lock my fucking door and forget everything that had happened between 7 pm and now. I pushed back my chair and stood.

Bree's face fell. "Where are you going?" she asked, and I could hear the waver in her voice. "We haven't even had dessert yet!"

I shook my head, I didn't want to explain. She guessed anyway and looked stricken. "I didn't mean it like that, Min," she said, standing and trying to reach for me. I avoided her as I neatly collected my bag and walked up to the desk. While I was handing my credit card over, Bree abandoned her meal and came running up to me. "I meant that I just hate the whole Barbie thing in general and that you seem like the kind of person who would be above all that superficial image stuff!"

I had no idea if that was true or not and I didn't have the energy to think about it. The waitress looked between us, but didn't comment as she ran my card and let me sign the receipt.

Bree put both her arms around one of mine. "Please don't go, Min," she said. "I'll be quiet, I promise!"

Somehow I doubted it. "Where do you live?" I asked her calmly. She frowned at me. "How far away from here is your house?"

"Courtney lives near Parramatta," she said when she figured out what I meant. She sounded crestfallen. "I'm going back to hers tonight."

I took a 50 out of my wallet, opened her hand and gave it to her. She just stared at it. "That should be enough for a taxi," I told her, deliberately not looking at her so I didn't have to be subjected to those big puppy dog eyes. "I'm going home. Please don't try and stop me this time."

Of course she did, anyway. She followed me out of the restaurant, and as I was walking along the waterfront she grabbed my wrists and tried to put the 50 back in my hand. "Min, I don't want your money. I didn't mean it like that. Just come back in and have dessert." She didn't sound as enthusiastic as she had earlier in the evening, and I didn't think she was channelling her cancer-curing grandmother anymore. She just sounded really disappointed.

She probably *was* disappointed. But I just couldn't do this, I felt really weird and I just wanted to go home. "You managed to get your dinner," I said, probably sounding as tired as I felt. "Now can you just leave me alone?"

She didn't let it go. "Please," she said, sounding desperate. "Please don't go. I'm sorry. I know I say things without thinking, but whatever I say I never mean it like that. You're awesome. Please just come back inside. The dessert here is incredible, you'll enjoy it..."

I had to physically pry her fingers one by one from my arm in order to get her off me. This time, though, she let me. She didn't even steal my handbag again. When I was free, I gave her one last look. "Make sure you get a taxi," I told her. "Don't risk the train this late at night, okay?"

She just nodded mutely, her hands by her side for once. She didn't say anything else and I could hardly fucking bear to look at her because she just looked so upset. Over a goddamn meal, seriously? Who *was* this girl?

I turned away from her and continued towards the bridge, feeling my stomach sink. Now, on top of *everything*, I also felt like a terrible person. I just seriously didn't have the energy to deal with her right now. I just couldn't, no matter how upset she was. I felt like complete and utter crap, and my feet were killing me in these stupid shoes. What had I been thinking in the first place, anyway? I should just have gone straight home after work. Then I could have avoided hurting her feelings, avoided having *mine* hurt and felt like crap quietly in the privacy of my own apartment. Somewhere that didn't have people walking past me who all double-took when they noticed how tall I was. I wonder if *they* all thought I shouldn't bother, as well.

Before I stepped onto the footbridge, I looked back towards the restaurant. Bree was still standing there on the waterfront, watching me.

As if I wasn't feeling crap enough.

She'll be fine, I told myself, she can catch a taxi home. I kept walking.

FIVE

It took me a hundred metres and couple of odd looks from strangers to forge through my self-pity and come to a decision: I shouldn't have left her alone there.

I stopped on the other side of the footbridge, made a face and turned, walking back to the restaurant. She's just a schoolkid and it was, what, nine at night? I should at least wait for the taxi with her. Then, again, if her birthday *was* in two weeks and she *was* about to turn eighteen, was it really such a big deal?

I stopped in my tracks.

Okay, Min, think this through: going back in there with her means walking straight back into the situation you bailed out of, and you walked out for a reason. I scrunched up my face. Did I *really* have the energy to listen to more about Courtney, or Bree's pregnant cousin, or about that one time Bree found a huge chunk of frozen broccoli in her pasta? God, she was nice but just so damn *full on*. I winced as I remembered that photo she'd taken of me. No, I couldn't face any of that. Not right now, not with how crap I was feeling.

She'd be fine, I'd given her plenty of money for a taxi. If she could stalk me to my house before 7 am she could probably manage a taxi by herself.

I took a deep breath, turned, and went to continue walking back home.

I only made it two paces when I remembered how tiny she was. It wouldn't take a strong breeze to drag that girl into a car and drive off with her. Did I want to be responsible for something like that happening? Did I *really?*

I made a frustrated noise and then stopped *again*, turning sharply back towards the harbour and walking over to the railing so I could see across the water. Bree wasn't outside the restaurant anymore. Maybe I was worrying for nothing, maybe she was safely *in*side. Maybe I should call the restaurant and ask them to make sure she got into a taxi and *maybe I should get a goddamn grip*, Min, *she's nearly 18, not five.*

While I was standing in place and trying to figure out what it actually was that I wanted to do, an old couple who had been walking leisurely along the bridge made eye-contact with me. The woman had a pretty strange expression, and I realised how everything I'd just done had probably looked.

Great, now perfect strangers thought I was as crazy as the girl I was worrying about.

After they were gone, I looked down at my blouse and skirt, and beyond them, my heels. 'It totally doesn't suit you'; I could still hear how easily Bree had said it, as if it was no big deal to say that to someone. I would have been angry with her, but she clearly hadn't meant to hurt me. In fact, she'd looked mortified when she realised that she had. But just because she hadn't meant to be cruel didn't mean what she'd said wasn't true. Or... maybe I *was* being hypersensitive and she *had* meant it in an abstract sense?

That girl, I thought. Even just thinking about her was exhausting.

I pushed off the railing. I couldn't stand here all night feeling bad about myself and wondering whether or not Bree was safe. She was, everything was going to be fine, and I needed to just go home and avoid getting robbed or murdered myself.

By the time I got back to my apartment, my feet were aching so much I was just about ready to chop them off at the ankles. I decided a bath was the best remedy, but I was so distracted when I turned the taps on that I forgot about it and very nearly ended up with a bathroom-sized swimming pool.

It was actually embarrassing what I *had* been doing, and that was sitting at my laptop and checking my messages. She hadn't sent me one—and that *didn't* necessarily mean she'd been kidnapped, I reminded myself—but in the process of 'just checking' I accidentally got stuck reading some of the old ones. I was lucky I remembered the bath when I did.

I left my phone in the living room so I couldn't keep looking at it and stressing, shed my clothes, and climbed in to the water.

Since it was lovely and warm and I was exhausted in every way possible, I rested my head on the lip of the bathtub. With my chin on my collarbones, I stared down the tub at my body. I had a weird, philosophical moment where I reflected on how strange it was that people looked at this and thought it was me. There wasn't anything wrong with it, I supposed. If I saw it on someone else I wouldn't think bad things about them. It was just weird that it was *me.*

My body issues were exhausting, too, and apparently now I was also taking them out on other people. Was 'that totally doesn't suit you' *really* hurtful enough to be worth walking out of dinner over? Would Bree have walked out if I'd told her that her uniform didn't suit her? What about Sarah, would she have left dinner over it?

Regardless, I shouldn't have left. What I *should* have done–and what Henry would have said I should have done—was just say something like, 'I'm sorry you think that', or, 'Hah, I don't really like dressing up either', and just got on with dinner instead of storming out like *I* was the teenager. Bree hadn't been telling me I looked terrible in general, in fact she'd said the opposite a number of times. So then why did I take it that way?

It was just all so depressing. I was trying. I'd been trying *really* fucking hard with all this stuff since high school and I *still* hated it and it *still* gave me a massive headache. Winter couldn't come fast enough; I could just pile on all the layers and ignore my brain.

On that note, it was on the chilly side tonight so in the grand theme of hating my body and everything, after I'd got out and dried myself off I put on a big men's hoodie. Like all the comfortable clothes I owned, it used to be Henry's. He'd made the big mistake of leaving it at my house and the consequence was that it now worked for me.

I checked my phone on the way out to the balcony. I didn't have any messages, which, again, wasn't necessarily evidence Bree had been murdered in an alleyway. Rather than put my phone where I could see it and worry about it all night, I left it inside, set up my laptop on the balcony table and sat down to watch a few episodes of cartoons.

After another couple of wines, I ended up watching the last episode on my side in bed and was *finally* relaxed enough to be peacefully dozing off when my phone buzzed under my hand. I didn't even remember collecting it.

I opened my eyes and stared along the mattress at it. It was a Deviant Art note; that meant that Bree was okay. I exhaled and unlocked it. I could just get the reassurance everything was fine and then go to sleep.

"*i hate myself so much right now :(:(im so sorry min. i cant sleep. im really sorryyyy. i cant stop crying :(:("*

I sat up a little, read it again, and then groaned and flopped back heavily on the mattress. I'd been so worried about being an irresponsible adult and leaving a minor in a potentially dangerous situation that I'd forgotten how badly the dinner had ended.

And now she couldn't stop crying? Did she mean that literally, or was she just trying to say how sorry she was?

I held the phone in front of my face and squinted at the bright screen. I couldn't just leave this message for a day or two like I usually did, just in case she *was* actually upset.

"It's okay," I typed. "I'm glad you got home safely. Sleep well." I read that a couple of times, and then sent it.

I had been debating whether or not I wanted to get out of the hoodie and into my pyjamas when the handset vibrated again. I checked it.

"pls dont be like this :(:(ur really awesome. like really. i mean that its just sometiems when i say things they dont come out right.....it was just weird seeing ur this serious businesswoman cos online ur really funny and kind of smooth so i thought for like a year that u were a really cool guy with maybe some really cool job liek a real artist or something. i had this idea of how u looked from the messages and then u posted that painting and it was like exactly what i thought..."

My stomach knotted. That fucking painting. "I'm sorry I disappointed you, then," I typed, and immediately regretted it even as I was clicking 'send'.

I didn't have long to wait for a reply. "are u kidding me im the disappointment. i wanted to meet u for ages and then i screwed everything up :(:(u really are awesome though. And ur still pretty funny IRL. im sorry :(:("

I stared at those frowny faces for a good five minutes. If I hadn't been over the blood alcohol limit, I probably would have just said something nice and put my mobile on the bedside table and passed out. Unfortunately, I *was* over it, and all I could focus on was asking myself whether or not she'd been serious earlier. "Bree, are you actually crying?"

It felt like eternity before she replied, and it was only one word.

"yes :("

I closed my eyes for a moment.

Fuck. Could I *really* not have swallowed all my personal dramas for another half an hour and ended that whole dinner amicably? Okay, so she was seriously intense, and showing up at my home and my work and then forcing me to pay for that extortionately expensive dinner was *really* fucking not okay... but, come on, she was 17. Did she actually deserve to be crying at midnight on someone's spare bed?

I didn't know what to reply to that. On one hand I wanted to apologise to her for leaving, on the other, she shouldn't have dragged me there in the first place. I *was* sorry she was crying and I *did* feel responsible for it, despite the fact just about everything was her own damn fault.

Before I managed to figure out what I wanted to say, she sent me another note. *"btw im not trying to guilt trip u or anything. im just really sorry :(:(will u forgive me??"*

I exhaled. She'd done so many crazy things that I didn't actually know what she was asking me to forgive her for, but I suspected it was only for what happened at the very end of the dinner. Did it matter, though? Was I actually going to tell a 17 year old who really admired me that I didn't forgive her and that I wanted her to cry herself to sleep? Sure, I could double as Oscar the Grouch at times, but I was pretty sure there was actually a heart in there somewhere.

"Of course I forgive you," I typed, hoping I wouldn't regret it. *"Sleep well. I hope you feel better tomorrow."*

"thanks min goodnight and im sorry again xxxx"

I put my mobile on my bedside table and put a hand over my face. What a day, seriously. I couldn't even really think properly about it because my brain was just *so tired*. There was no way I was getting out of bed to put my pyjamas on, so I just turned over and went to sleep in Henry's big hoodie and my trackies. I didn't even bother to take my hair-tie out.

I wasn't exactly hung-over the next day, but I still felt a bit off and the blisters on my feet were aching as I swung them out of bed. I stretched, watching myself in the big sliding mirrors of my wardrobe which were facing my bed.

With my hair back and this huge hoodie on I looked really boyish, especially with the sleeves pushed up so the fabric bunched up around my shoulders. Because of the shoulders, the rest of me looked really narrow when I stood up, too, and I couldn't see my breasts. I was really glad Henry wasn't here to see me like this.

Just at the thought of work, I groaned. I *so* didn't feel like getting into my work clothes — especially putting my blistered feet into those heels again — and I briefly fantasised about just showing up at work dressed like this. I didn't even think people would recognise me if I did; they probably wouldn't let me into the building. Maybe then I could just quit Frost and get a 'really cool job' or whatever

Bree had said she'd pictured me with. Wow, when I imagined Mum's reaction to me quitting my job, though... Yeah, not an option.

I had been looking forward to getting to work and just sitting down at my desk all day, but unfortunately I got called into a team meeting for the Canada project and there weren't any seats left in the tiny little meeting room. It wasn't even my team, and I ended up being stuck standing up and hating the world while I listened to someone drone on about distribution contracts *forever.*

Not that I've ever made a particularly good damsel in distress, but when Henry stuck his head into the meeting and called me out I was pretty happy to be rescued.

I edged behind all the extra chairs and out of the room, shutting the door gently behind me. "Don't tell me," I said neutrally, "you were just so desperate to see my beautiful face you couldn't wait another second."

He smirked and motioned for me to follow him, looking excited. "Come with me."

Henry was rarely this cryptic, so he didn't need to steal my handbag to get me to follow him.

When he opened the door to the stairwell, he *still* didn't explain where we were going, he just grinned broadly as he made a 'ladies first' gesture and stood aside so I could walk past. He only ushered me down one flight, though, and that was to the level that HR was on.

I followed him all the way to the offices—a little stiffly because of my blisters—wondering what on *earth* we were doing.

He stopped short of his own office, and I couldn't figure out what the point of that particular place was at first. Then I followed where he was looking: it was at his assistant manager's out-tray. There was an A4-sized internal envelope marked *L36 MARKETING: LEE, MIN'.*

I picked it up and turned it over; there must have been a good fifteen or twenty pages in there. The envelope was closed and across the seal was stamped the words, '*STRICTLY CONFIDENTIAL'.* I didn't understand what the fuss was.

Henry was practically bursting, though. "I'm not supposed to have anything to do with this, so I didn't lead you here," he told me.

"Because of our relationship I'm not allowed to sign off on anything for you. But hardcopy, sealed envelopes stamped 'confidential' in HR's out tray only mean one thing," he said, smiling from ear to ear as he put his hands on my shoulders, "Min, that's an employment contract."

I just stared at him. It took a few seconds to sink in.

Remembering my conversation with Diane last week, I looked from the envelope to Henry. "Are you *serious*?" I said, my voice shooting off into the stratosphere, and then began to tear into it on the spot.

He put a hand over mine to stop me, glancing around us to see if anyone was watching. "It's marked 'confidential' for a reason," he said, and then kissed my forehead. "I understand why you can't talk about this stuff with me so I know why you didn't tell me. But I want to let you know that I'm really, really happy for you," he said and cupped my cheek with his hand for a moment. "Fuck, Min, this is great. Congratulations!"

I was at this terrible crossroads, because I didn't want to dismiss him when he was so excited for me, but at the same time *I really wanted to know what was in the envelope*. My dilemma must have been evident because he just laughed. "It's okay, it's okay," he said, and then kissed my forehead again. "I'll let you go. You go open that, sign it, and then we'll celebrate over lunch, okay?"

"Thanks, Henry," I said, giving him a quick hug when I was certain no one was watching.

He showed me out so I could rush upstairs back to my workstation and get stuck into that envelope. While I was checking around me to make sure no one was looking as I tore it open, it occurred to me that Henry had acted like I should already know what was inside. I didn't, really. Other than my brief chat with Diane last week about advancement opportunities, I didn't really know why I'd be getting a contract without someone explaining to me what was in it.

He still ended up being right, though, it *was* an employment contract. I couldn't scan it fast enough to figure out what was going on, and my eyes zeroed-in right on the words, '*Project Manager*'. I think my heart stopped.

I checked my name again. Yes, this was for me. Oh, my god. I read it further; it was actually only a four-week position, but it was substantially higher pay and, *fuck*, I'd get to call myself a Project Manager at Frost International! That would look fantastic on my resume, and I knew the experience would go towards a permanent management position.

I stopped reading and looked up, because I actually couldn't believe it. Things like this just didn't happen to me. I had one of those moments where I wondered if I was still asleep.

I sat back, taking a slow breath.

Wow, this was... this was *fantastic.* I looked down and beamed at it. Unexpected and *fantastic*. This was worth every goddamn second of overtime that I'd done in the last five years. Oh my god! *This* was why I wasn't assigned to any teams. I was going to be *running* one of them!

There wasn't much more information about the secret project Diane had mentioned to me in it, though, except the number of staff I'd have underneath me—only four, but it was a start, right?— and the name of the project, which was 'Pink'.

Wait a second, wasn't that the project Sarah had said she was listed for? I nearly cheered out loud. Fucking *yes*, I was working with her again? Yes! I couldn't sign on that dotted line fast enough.

There was a hand-scribbled note down the bottom of the last page that said, "*Please submit to Diane in person ASAP*".

You bet, I thought, and basically flew across the floor all the way to her office. She was on the phone, but she apologised to whoever she was talking to and hung up. Just that little detail made me feel *so* important. It quickly faded, though, because this was *Diane* I was handing these contracts to. I was suddenly unsure of whether or not I'd completed it correctly, and whether or not I would look incapable of managing a team if I hadn't.

"Close the door and take a seat," she instructed me, and I did what I was told, handing the contracts to her before I sat down. She flipped through them. "This all looks in order," she said, and then put them aside and looked back at me.

Even though I was really excited, I began to sweat as soon as she looked directly at me. It was stupid, I obviously wasn't in trouble. I also really, really wanted to thank her, but I didn't feel like I could say anything at that moment.

She didn't speak straight away, either. She considered me for a little while before finally breaking the silence. "Did you tell anyone?" I shook my head. "Not even your boyfriend? How close are you to him, anyway? You don't live together, do you?"

I smothered my surprise. That was a *strange* question, but I suppose since we were dating under the auspice of Frost overlooking their policy for us, it wasn't exactly inappropriate. It was still strange, though. "Henry guessed something was up because he saw the envelope in HR. But I didn't say anything. I am close to him, but we don't discuss everything. And no, we don't live together."

She nodded. "Good. Don't tell him anything about this. That's very important. He works for my brother."

I didn't contradict her because it was true, but it wasn't like Henry was Sean Frost's agent or anything. I didn't think they had *that* much to do with each other, and Henry was capable of keeping his mouth shut if he needed to. He was HR Manager for Christ's sake. He would know extremely confidential and interesting stuff about *everyone* and he'd never breathed a word of it to me. Anyway, if she was so worried I'd tell Henry, why had she picked me in the first place?

In response to her instructions, though, I just said, "I understand."

She nodded, opened her top drawer and took out a USB that was wrapped in a curled post-it. She held it up. "The brief is on here, and the password is on this," she indicated the post-it, "change it immediately. First thing you do. There's only four weeks, so you'll need to get started on the Marketing Requirements Document right now. All your team members are on here, too, and I've freed up 'Oslo' for your office." She held it out to me, but before she put it in my palm, she added, "I'm taking a *lot* of extra security measures for this project." I didn't miss the gravity in her voice. "A lot. The computers in 'Oslo' aren't even hooked up to the main network. Don't save *anything* to *anywhere* that isn't password protected and don't leave your laptops here overnight or anywhere your boyfriend can get at them if you're saving project files to them."

I accepted the USB. This all seemed completely over the top, but that observation wasn't exactly something I could say out loud to the co-CEO. My silence must have spoken volumes, though, because Diane was watching me. "My brother manages our IT," she said. "If it's on the network, he has access to it. I do *not* want him finding out details about the project. He thinks I've abandoned it and I want it to stay that way for at least four weeks. I had someone mention to him that all this extra security is because you're on a politically sensitive pitch, he believes it, and that's the way I want it to stay."

The more pressing question was why Diane was so desperate to make sure her brother, the co-CEO of their billion dollar corporation, didn't find out about one tiny little project. What could he really do if he did find out, anyway? Marketing was Diane's department.

It was all very weird, but I obviously couldn't say that. "I'll make sure everyone understands your instructions," I told her.

She smiled slightly. "Now *that* sounds like a manager talking," she said. "Jason chose you a compliant team. You shouldn't have any trouble telling any of them just once. If you have any questions, just ask Jason or myself, please, and for God's sake throw people off the scent if they start asking questions. I'm sure you're seeing a pattern here."

I nodded, thanked her, and let myself be ushered out of the office. It was actually really strange standing next to her because, like most women, I dwarfed her. Such a weird feeling, towering over Diane Frost of Frost International.

The office that Diane mentioned she'd had put together for us, 'Oslo', was one of the smaller offices on the corner of the building and close to hers. It faced out towards the Western Suburbs so it wasn't one of Sydney's best views, but it was still better than a felt-covered partition with postcards of places I wanted to go one day pinned on it. There were five workstations in there, four in the centre and one against the wall. I supposed that one was mine. I sat down at it and spun my chair sideways to face the huge windows.

All of Sydney looked like it was down there. I could see all the way to the horizon, and I was smiling again.

Looking out over it all with that USB clutched in my hand felt amazing. I felt like I was a king surveying my kingdom. Just, wow.

Five years and *finally* my career was going somewhere. Maybe I wasn't the 'really cool guy' Bree had thought I was for a year, but at least now I was working on having a really cool job.

A voice interrupted me. "*Here* you are!"

I swivelled my chair around as Sarah stepped inside the office and came rushing over to me. "Jason told me you'd be in here— what's this about you being Lead but it's all hush-hush? Is it true or was he just messing with me again?" She only had to take one look at my expression to know the answer. "Oh my god?" she said as a question. "Min, are you serious?" She looked ecstatically happy for me. "Wow, I suddenly have faith in humanity again — you've been working like a slave for years! So, what, you're my boss now?"

"Only for four weeks, and I only have four employees."

She laughed, grabbed an office chair from one of the work stations and pulled it over to where my empty desk was. "Best boss ever," she said. "They always start people off in small teams, though. Did you know the Head of Operations Australia used to be a marketing rep?"

I made a face. "Don't say that and get my hopes up," I told her. "I might screw the whole thing up and end up in admin."

Sarah gracefully crossed her legs and leant back in the chair. "Are you kidding me?" she asked. "When was the last time you screwed something up? Year seven?"

Last night, I thought.

"So what are we doing, anyway? Did Jason tell you?"

I put last night out of my head, and held up the USB. "Diane said it's all on here."

She sat upright in her chair and slapped her thighs. "Get out," she said. "*Diane* told you? To your face?" She leant back in the chair again. "Min, if you're not running the department in a year, something is seriously wrong."

"Stop it," I said, but I was smiling. I still couldn't get over it. "You want a see what's on this? I haven't looked yet."

We sat down, turned on one of the computers and went through the brief together; it was pretty straightforward. Frost was going to mine a pipe in the Kimberley, but in order to get finance for the project we needed to have already signed exclusive distribution contracts with strong projected end-consumer sales. Our job was to identify a good market to pitch this to, then to design the pitch and to provide a framework for Sales to deliver it. I sat back in my chair, exhaling at length. Diane wasn't kidding when she said there was a lot of work in this: this was a *huge* project for five people in four weeks.

"Shit," Sarah said as we both processed it. "I guess I won't be seeing too much of my boyfriend, then. When's the deadline?"

I checked. "April 29," I said, and then thought for a second. "Isn't that right after Easter?" Yet another fantastic reason I hadn't gone to Seoul with Henry. "That's more than four weeks, though. Do you think we'd be able to finish it before that long weekend?"

Sarah shrugged, and she was grinning. "Why are you asking me?" she said. "You're the boss! You tell *us* when it will be done by."

I mirrored her by leaning back in my chair and placed my fingers behind my head. "Wow, you're right." I laughed shortly. "This is just so awesome."

"So, how are you planning to celebrate?"

Hah. How did I usually celebrate? Red wine and a selection of semi-automatic rifles. "You don't want to know."

She laughed pleasantly. "You are such an enigma," she said, and then stood up. "Come on, let's go tell the tools we work with that they're all serfs and you're important now."

I made a face, and that stopped her. "Didn't Jason tell you? It's confidential," I said. "Diane was pretty specific about not saying anything to anybody about what we're doing. We're not even allowed to save to the network drives."

Sarah gave me the strangest look. "*Why?*"

I shrugged. "Something to do with Sean Frost."

She rolled her eyes. "Of course it is," she said. "So you can't even tell anyone that you're a project lead?" At my headshake she groaned. "Those two are going to end up killing each other," she said. "We'll have to celebrate quietly together then. Who are the other members?" She leant across me to the laptop, and her loose hair fell over one of my shoulders. Reading out the other team member's names, she made a face. "I don't really know those guys."

I didn't, either. "Guess we'll get to know them pretty well over the next four weeks," I said. "I'd better send them out an invite."

"And I'd better leave you to it," she said, "and move my 20 kilos of junk in here."

"Make me a coffee while you're at it," I said with a half-grin as she opened the door. "Lots of milk and sugar. Oh, and if you could pick up my dry-cleaning..."

At first she thought I was serious, and she might actually have made me that coffee until I mentioned the dry-cleaning. She burst out laughing. "You are *hilarious*," she said, as she closed the door. "I swear to god I'm going to get you out of the office one of these days. My friends will *love* you."

Somehow I sincerely doubted that, but I was glad *she* found me funny.

I finally met my employees, and aside from Sarah they were a quiet bunch who didn't seem to have any particular problems with the fact that I was their manager. One of them was fresh out of an internship and blushed fiercely whenever I spoke to him. Apparently he was one hell of an analyst, though, so I forgave him for how uncomfortable I felt speaking to him and watching his face go bright red. The other two were just your garden variety marketing reps, and one of them had been working for Frost for 15 years.

I ended up needing to cancel lunch with Henry so the five of us could figure out what on earth we were going to do with the brief. Eventually we put our heads together and assigned each other tasks. I drew up a project timeline, photocopied it and gave it to them.

By the end of the day I felt productive, like I actually might *not* screw everything up, and that, actually, despite my personal issues, life was pretty fucking great. Jason even said goodbye to me as I was leaving—he'd hardly acknowledged I existed before. God, could today get any better?

As it turned out it could, because EB Games was having a stocktake sale and was open later than usual. Not only did I get the two titles I wanted, but I got them for half-price and grabbed a third for free. The third one had co-op, too, so I figured when Henry got off work he could swing past and play a few rounds with me in celebration before he went home.

On my way up to my apartment in the lift I was so busy reading the jackets and wondering which one of them I should play first that I didn't notice what was outside the door of my apartment. In fact I'd almost made it there and was feeling around in my handbag for my keycard when movement on the floor caught my eye.

There was a *person* sitting cross-legged against my door, and the shock of that nearly gave me a heart attack. I took a step back and gasped embarrassingly loudly, putting a hand over my chest where I could feel my heart pounding.

No one would have given me prize for knowing immediately who it was going to be.

It was Bree, and she had a huge smile and an even bigger bouquet of flowers.

SIX

"You're here!" Bree said from where she was seated against my door, as if my showing up at my own apartment was a pleasant and unexpected surprise. "Hi!"

My heart was still going. "What the hell are you doing *at my home*?" I paused, remembering the coffee. "*Again!*"

She stood up a little awkwardly from the floor. "My legs went to sleep," she told me, because obviously that was the most appropriate answer. "You took ages. It's nearly 7:30."

I didn't even know where to start. Where could I, with this girl? I tried to think of what Henry would do. "Bree. You promised you wouldn't do this again if I went to dinner with you. *I had dinner with you*. What are you *doing* here?"

"Technically, I promised I wouldn't wait for you outside work," she casually pointed out. "And I didn't want to break my promise, especially after I kind of put my foot in it with the whole..." she gestured at my work clothes with her free hand. She still didn't look very impressed by them.

I just stared at her. Before I could even figure out what I should do or say, I lost my train of thought because she held up the huge bouquet. "Anyway, I had some money left from the taxi and since it's your money I figured I should spend it on you, you know? So I

bought you some flowers to thank you for forgiving me for being completely hopeless and to apologise to you for—"

"Bree, wait just one—" I said, but it wasn't any use, because she had already taken a step towards me and dumped the whole thing in my arms.

I had been about to tell her that it was absolutely unacceptable for her to show up at my house like this, but then I saw the flowers and double-took. I had been expecting lilies, or roses, or some other generic pretty flowers, but that wasn't what was wrapped up in the colourful tissue paper at all. Instead of a nice delicate arrangement, it was a native Australian bouquet and all the flowers were huge, twisted and really, really ugly. So ugly they were actually *monstrous.* I couldn't look away. Who in their *right fucking mind* buys flowers that look like they want to eat you in order to apologise to someone? Stupid question, I supposed: *this girl.*

While I was staring in horror at them, she kept talking. "They reminded me of you."

"*These* reminded you of me?" I said looking down at their furry leaves. They were fucking hideous. These were the sort of flowers you buy your much-hated mother-in-law to deliver a very clear message.

"Not because they're really hairy," she said. "I mean, you're Asian, so obviously not. But, you know, they were really different from all of the other flowers."

Wow, and there it was. My stomach knotted. Now I had a bunch of ugly flowers to remind me that I didn't fit in. And after my fantastic day at work, as well.

God, it was so awful, *they* were so awful, and yet the absurdity of the whole situation almost made me want to laugh. I was torn between feeling hurt by what she'd said, uncomfortable about her being here, *angry* that she'd shown up *again* and just, well, entertained by how *spectacularly* she was able to fuck up something as simple as giving someone flowers. I didn't even know what to think.

Bree looked alarmed at my reaction, and put her hands on my arms. "Oh, no!" she said. "No! I didn't mean it like that, obviously you are, like, surprisingly tall and then you wear heels for some reason on top of that, but I meant it more—"

God, she was still *going?* "Bree, really, I think you've said enough!"

"—special-different! I meant special-different, not anything else, no matter what it sounds like!" she finished. She looked actually upset, like she was about to launch into a really tragic story. "I just walked into the shop because I wanted to do something nice for you, and there were all these flowers and then these strange native ones here, and like, I thought to myself, 'I could buy her all of those ones that look the same or I could buy these' and then I picked them up and like, see?" She reached up and stroked the top of one of them gently with her fingertips. "It's really soft but I bet everyone just ignores them because they're not traditional. I bet they just sit there for days and days watching all the other pretty flowers get bought as they slowly wilt and die. Can you imagine what that would be like? It's so sad. I had to buy them for you, I couldn't just leave them there to rot."

I did not have the *slightest* idea how to respond to that. At all. Had this girl formed an emotional attachment to a *bunch of flowers*? I wasn't sure if that was tragic or terrifying, and I couldn't stand here gaping at her while I tried to figure that out. She was *still* affectionately stroking the monstrous furry flower.

"Bree, the flowers are a... nice gesture, but they don't make up for the fact you showed up at my home," I told her as calmly as I could.

And there were those big blue eyes again. "You don't like them?"

There wasn't enough air in my lungs for how much I wanted to sigh at that moment. "They're..." Ugly, hideous, probably evil, and *definitely* a waste of my money, "interesting. What I *don't* like is people just coming over uninvited. I don't even like it when people I know really well do that." She was still giving me those eyes, and for some reason I felt like I needed to keep justifying my feelings about her being here. "Look, Bree, I've had a really great day at work and I'd really like to relax and enjoy the rest of the evening."

She stopped touching the scary flower and nodded somewhat forlornly. "I just thought it would be a really nice surprise to bring you some flowers..."

Why did I feel guilty about that? She shouldn't even be here!

"Don't you see how this looks, though? You Google me and then show up at my house and work to give me things? If you want to meet people, you ask them and let them decide if they want to, as well."

She was still looking at me. "Yeah, but what would happen if I asked?"

I opened my mouth to tell her the honest truth, but then couldn't. The truth was that never in a million years would I have given anyone who asked on Deviant Art my home address or information about my work. And I wouldn't have agreed to meet them, either, no matter how long we'd been talking. Actually, that reminded me that I needed to change my username to something less obvious.

I couldn't think of a tactful way to answer her, either. I didn't want to be cruel. She was just trying to be nice.

She knew what I was going to say, anyway, and swallowed. "See? That's why I'm here."

In a creepy, intrusive way—she kind of had a point. There weren't many options for her because she'd idolised completely the wrong artist. God, I was being a grump again, wasn't I?

She gave the flower one more cursory pat like she was saying goodbye to a kitten. "Make sure you put them in water. They've been out of it for hours now and they're probably thirsty."

"I will," I said, with growing guilt about how dismissive of her I was being. She just looked so disappointed. Was I being unfair? Clearly she meant well, and she was right, if she'd just asked to meet me, I'd have said 'no'. Seriously, I'd known Sarah for... three years? Four years? And I'd never met up with her outside work, regardless of how often she tried to insist I did.

Ugh, was I being anti-social and unreasonable about all of this? She *did* just buy me flowers. Weird, creepy flowers, but she could easily have taken off with my money and spent it on something for herself. Henry had found that coffee thing charming, too, and he tended to be pretty level-headed. I doubted he would've been as angry as I was with her.

While I was second-guessing myself, Bree slung her schoolbag over her shoulder, looking like Christmas had been cancelled. "Well, I hope you like them anyway."

"Thanks, they're pretty." I was actually just being polite because obviously they were hideous and not pretty at all, but she didn't interpret it like that. She just looked up at me and *smiled.* It was the kind of expression a puppy might have as it realised someone had just decided to adopt it from the pound and it wasn't going to die cold and alone after all.

The hope on her face was completely disarming. "Min, I'm sorry I made you angry," she said, and she did actually sound sorry. "It's just that while I was buying them I was imagining how you'd react, and I wanted to be here to see your face when I gave them to you. I waited because I didn't want to miss it."

She'd waited here for three hours, in fact, and *this* was how I was reacting. Probably not what she'd hoped for, after all; my chest clenched.

While I was standing there feeling terrible, she winced. "Um, so," she began, "This is kind of embarrassing, but I've been here for three hours and it's another hour home. Would you mind if I used your toilet? The guys on the reception desk said I can't use the hotel ones unless I'm a guest, and I was worried if I left to look for some that I'd miss you."

I wasn't too keen on letting her in, but I was feeling bad already and, really, who would say no to that?

I exhaled, awkwardly trying to fish out my keycard with the games in one hand and the flowers clutched against me with the other. In the end Bree needed to take the bouquet back off me so I could open the door.

She dropped her bag *at* the door and I nearly fell over it as I was taking off my heels. I'd pushed it against the wall with an ankle, and when I looked up, Bree was already distracted on the way to the bathroom by one of my big paintings that I'd had printed and framed.

I liked that one, actually. Henry and I had gone up to Queensland a couple of years ago and had visited Green Island on the Great Barrier Reef. I'd only been in the water for about five minutes before I'd needed to go straight back to the hotel room and paint the reef. The colours and the light were so beautiful, it was like a different planet down there. The painting had turned out *really* well, and it was the first one I'd had framed when I moved up to Sydney. I put it on the wall that got the most sunlight so the colours were really bright.

"You don't have this one on Deviant Art," Bree said as she considered it.

It was the first time I really married up this crazy girl with the person online who I'd been discussing my art with. Multiple exclamation marks aside, we had talked *a lot* about it. I suddenly felt like a giant prick for completely dismissing her, even if she was *way* too full on.

I realised that her comment was also kind of a question. "I don't put everything on there. People steal things from it and I don't want this one stolen."

She leant right up close to it, really admiring the detail. That actually made me feel good; I'd put a serious amount of work into the picture and it was always nice to have others appreciate it. "It's incredible," she said eventually, standing back. "Like, this is better than most of the stuff in galleries. What do you do again?" She looked back at me. "At Frost?"

"Marketing." My heart fluttered as I remembered my promotion. "Well, project management, now."

Bree made a face, looking back at the painting. "I don't really know what that is," she said, and pointed at the painting. "But you should do this for a living."

I laughed cynically. If only; I'd lost that fight with myself *years* ago. "Wouldn't be much of a living. There's no money in art. I'd be on the street instead of in here." Now I sounded like my mother. "Painting is just a hobby. I enjoy it."

Bree turned a little to cast her eyes around the apartment. "This place *is* nice," she conceded. There was an unspoken 'but' as she looked back at the painting.

I suddenly realised who I was talking to. "Wait, weren't you on your way to my bathroom?"

She looked at me for a moment, a little disoriented, and then back at the flowers in her hand. "Oh, yeah," she said, and then made a face and put the flowers on the kitchen bench before disappearing through my bedroom.

I had to go past the painting to put the flowers in water, and I stopped to have another look at it, too. In the glass of the frame, I saw myself smiling at it. Yeah, I liked this one. The original file was so huge I'd even put individual scales on some of the fish, but this print wasn't quite big enough to see that level of detail. I would have needed to get a wall-to-floor for that, and I wasn't sure spending thousands on a quality printout was a wise investment. Looking at it all again made me feel like painting, though. Maybe I'd give the games a miss tonight and get the tablet out.

I'd put the evil flowers in a vase and was standing in the middle of the room trying to figure out where I could put them when Bree returned. "You have a lot of make-up," she told me, which meant she'd opened the cupboards in my bathroom. "It's weird. Not even my mum has that much."

I wanted to comment on how inappropriate it was to snoop in people's cupboards, but I had pads and stuff in there, too. I didn't want to embarrass her in case that's why she was looking.

Bree had already moved on from that thought, anyway, and was pointing to the kitchen bench. "You should put the flowers there," she said, reminding me I was holding the monstrous flowers. "The leaves kind of match the stainless steel."

She was right, and the flowers also would also be much closer to the stainless steel knives in the event that I'd need to defend myself against them. I was following her advice when she said behind me, "Oh! Should I have taken off my shoes?"

I set the flowers on the bench and was turning the vase to a good angle. "It's up to you," I told her, too distracted to realise what I was inadvertently saying. "It's just a habit. I'm not really fussed if people do or don't." There were slippers somewhere, too, but I think I'd kicked them under the hall-stand.

It was only when Bree went to take off her shoes by the door that I realised I'd just given her tacit permission to remain in my apartment. While I was trying to figure out how I'd managed to do something so absent-minded, she bounced back into the living area in her knee-high school socks and I just didn't have the heart to tell her to put her shoes back on again and leave. She didn't give me the opportunity to comment on it, either, because she was already at another one of my paintings.

It was of Federation Square in Melbourne, and I'd done it at night. It had started off as practice with lighting and had ended up turning into a completed print. "That's in Melbourne, yeah?" she asked, glancing back towards me to see me nod. "So you go to places and paint them? That's actually a really cool idea. Way better than buying souvenirs."

I thought so. "Well, yes. But I'm actually from Melbourne."

She gave me a cheeky grin, and I knew she was going to drag out the old rivalry between Sydneysiders and Melbournians. "That explains a lot."

"Whatever you're going to say, I've heard it before," I said, rolling my eyes as she moved on to the next one. This one was actually *not* a location shot; I'd had this dream where I was a character in a computer game and it was set in this beautiful phosphorescent forest teaming with tiny little glowing dragons. The print was darker than I'd have liked, but it still looked great.

Bree spent a few minutes looking at it, and then turned back to me. "You are actually my hero," she said. "I can't believe you did this all out of your head. It's like a superpower."

I tried to keep a perfectly straight face. "What are you talking about?" I asked her. "That's where I went the last time I took annual leave." She spun around to take another look as I kept talking, obviously thinking she must have seen it wrong. "I'm pretty happy with how the glowing ferns turned out, but I'm not sure I captured the essence of those baby dragons."

She turned to blink at me for a second, and then laughed. When she stopped laughing, she was gazing at me with what I could only describe as *total* adoration. I didn't know what to do with it, but it was really confronting. Fortunately, I didn't have to figure it out, because she toured the rest of my paintings and proceeded to give them a really gratifying level of appreciation. I was really proud of some of them, and I didn't think anyone had ever paid so much attention to them before.

I'd been standing near the small glass dining table where I'd left my tablet, and since I'd been thinking of painting anyway, I'd picked it up. Unfortunately, when Bree was done admiring my walls, the first thing she did was spot it in my hand.

She looked *really* excited. "Oh, my god, are you going to do something now?" she asked, already knowing the answer. She rushed over to me. "Can I watch? Please say I can watch! I've always wondered how you do it and you *never* stream, so it would be kind of interesting to watch how you go about it—"

"It's coming up to eight on a school night," I pointed out, interrupting her because I knew I wasn't going to be able to get a word in otherwise. "You really need to go home. Your parents are probably wondering where the hell their daughter is every night."

She made a face. "I told them I was at a friend's house," she said, and then looked hopefully up at me. "It's kind of true, isn't it?"

I closed my eyes for a second, remembering who I was dealing with again. She was relentless. "Bree, I don't know how to answer that," I told her, hoping honesty was the best call. "How would they feel if they knew you were at a 25 year old's house? It's probably inappropriate for you to hang around for much longer. I'm not sure what you want me to say."

She scoffed. "Well, it's not like you're up here getting me pregnant," she said. She didn't give me a chance to respond to that before moving right along again. "What I *want* you to say is that you'll be friends with me, so let's just be friends? You let me in, so obviously you don't *hate* me. There's no rule that says you can only be friends with people your own age, and if we're friends, it's not weird that I'm in here."

The way she put it, 'let's be friends', made it seem like she was suggesting I click a button on Facebook or change my status to 'friends with Bree'. I didn't actually know what she thought about the way actual friendships worked, but I doubted it generally started with a marriage-like friendship proposal. Then again, Bree's idea of things clearly differed a lot from most people's. *Those flowers,* I thought.

"Is there actually any way for me to say 'no' to that?"

From how much her brow was wavering, I think there actually might have been. "I guess so," she said, and then spoke with so much animation that her curls bounced. "But you can ask Courtney, I'm actually really nice. I always try and do nice things for people, and I'll try really hard not to accidentally insult you or do anything that you really, really don't want me to do. And if you're really tired from work and you want to relax I won't make you leave the house, we can just hang out up here. It could be awesome and I just really think you should try it first instead of just saying 'no' outright."

I listened to her deliver her pitch with total and complete conviction, heart on sleeve. God, I could really hurt her right now, I thought, watching her. I could say 'nope' and crush that little heart of hers. *Fuck*, I thought, I think I'm giving in to those curls. Shit.

"You should work in sales," I told her, and I was sure my resignation was audible. Before she could get *too* excited, though, I jabbed the air toward her with my stylus. "This is conditional on you *never* showing up or leaving anything anywhere again, okay?" She nodded mutely. "I'm serious about that. And I'm holding you to the 'I won't do things you don't want me to' clause, too."

"Whatever you want!" she said in the top register of her voice. "Oh, my god!" She looked like she was about to throw her arms around my middle. Before she managed to, I ducked into the bedroom to grab the laptop, came back with it and began setting up.

Bree shuffled one of the kitchen chairs around beside me and she still looked really excited. "This is so awesome, you have no idea," she said as I was trying to get comfortable. "I've wanted to do this for so long!"

I listened to her, trying to figure out how to position myself. It was a bit awkward, because normally I'd put a leg up and lean the tablet across my thigh. I was still wearing my work skirt, so that wasn't going to happen. I did bend my leg up experimentally, though, but the skirt was too tight and the fabric wasn't stretchy. Also, my stockings were slipping off the chair.

Bree noticed. "You need one like this," she said, smoothing the pleated skirt of her school uniform. It might have been passable when she was standing up, but as soon as she sat down it was *scandalously* short. I would never in a million years show that much skin. I did *not* need a skirt like that; even ten times that amount of fabric wouldn't be enough to make me comfortable. "Anyway, it doesn't matter, just put trackies on or something. It's not like you need to dress up so much to sit in your living room."

I thought about that for a second; I supposed my black tracksuit pants wouldn't look *so* out of place with my work blouse, and I *did* still have all my make-up on. I went into my bedroom, shut the door and put them on. Without the hoodie, they didn't look too boyish and the colour of them was such that they looked a bit like work-pants anyway. My white socks didn't match so well, but whatever. Fuck, this was way more comfortable. I did give my big hoodie a bit of a sad glance as I left the bedroom, though.

The trackies made everything so much easier, and I put the tablet across my knee and thought about what to draw. Bree was actually quiet for once, and I had been gazing forward trying to decide what do to when I noticed I was looking directly at those horrifying flowers. Bree sat straight up. "Yes!" she said. "It would be so poetic. I rescued them and then they went on to become famous!"

Hah, famous? "I don't have *that* many watchers online," I told her. "But okay."

I decided not to bother with a background—that would have taken ages and Bree did actually need to leave at some sort of reasonable hour—and just started drawing shapes. She obviously did actually know a thing or two about art, as well, because a couple of times while she was commenting on what I was doing, she used the correct terminology for the tools and asked me questions about my brushes.

"You know a lot. Do you draw?" I asked, working on giving one of the flowers a deep, open mouth with many layers of shark-teeth. I didn't remember seeing any pictures in her gallery on Deviant Art.

Bree laughed at what I was doing with the flower. "You want the truth?" I nodded as I kept painting. "You kind of taught me all that stuff."

I stopped for a second and looked at her. I did? I didn't remember those conversations at all, they must have happened ages ago. "Really?"

She relaxed back in the chair again. "Yeah. And no, I can't draw. I'll just hang around and be kind of in awe of you and a bit depressed." I shot her a strange look, she explained, "Well, it's like you have this totally amazing gift and you're not even using it."

I clicked through the palette. "It's not a gift," I said, "it's six years of locking myself up in a graphics lab every recess and lunchtime."

"Bit late for me, then, I guess," Bree said. "Plus at Cloverfield we only get half an hour for lunch and that's barely even enough to eat food. I think they just want to make sure we don't have time to cross the road to the boys' school. Are you this good at your job?"

There was that familiar whiplash again. "I think so," I said, and the corrected myself. "I mean, yes. I just got promoted."

Her face lit up again. "Oh, that's great! Is that what you were happy about earlier?"

I was actually surprised she'd been listening. She certainly hadn't *acted* like she was listening. I stopped for a second and looked at her again, and then went back to the tablet. I decided not to ask about it. "Yup."

"Well, if you're half as good at... project managing or whatever you call it as you are at art, I bet you're *awesome*."

There's something to be said for being heavily praised. I got it all the time online, but it's one thing to have disembodied text saying your art is amazing and another to have someone sitting next to you saying it. And Bree was just so damn genuine, I found it difficult to hang on to my reservations about having let her stay. This was actually okay. It wasn't exactly video games with Henry, but it wasn't ruining my evening. And she probably wouldn't be here for that long, anyway, because I was nearly done with the picture.

I couldn't remember the last time I'd done anything grotesque, but the flowers definitely belonged in that category by the time I was finished. I'd really only suggested the vase and painted these exaggerated, monstrous flowers full of teeth and tentacles pouring out of it like something from a horror movie. It was different from what I normally did, but I was happy with how all the textures turned out. I sat back from the tablet and examined it.

Bree loved it. "That's incredible. You did that in *half an hour*," she gushed, leaning over the picture. Then, she reached out and tentatively touched the tablet where the furry flower was.

I just stared at her for a second. What was she expecting? It was a *screen*.

She saw my expression and giggled. "Sorry, it just kind of looked really furry and I guess I just needed to remind myself that it's just a picture."

"You can touch the real thing if you want," I told her, and gestured at the actual flowers. "Just make sure you don't go anywhere near them without a sharp sword."

She laughed again. "It was actually really funny, because the florist asked me if I knew what to feed it, and I was like, 'um, you need to feed bouquets?' And I just had this weird image of, like, chopping up raw meat for it or something."

"Raw meat?" I snorted. "Please. *Those* flowers clearly hunger for the souls of unborn children."

Bree looked from my neutral expression to the flowers and burst out laughing. I hadn't thought it was *that* funny, but she kept laughing for a good several minutes, to the point at which she could barely breathe and her eyes were watering. She calmed down a little, and then saw the flowers and started all over again. I watched her at first because it was entertaining, but after her skirt rode a bit high I spent the rest of her giggle fit uploading the picture to Deviant Art. I didn't really think twice about the comment I put on the submission, but when Bree finally sobered up and bent forward to read it, she liked it.

"'*For Bree*'," she read aloud, and then from how she looked at me you'd have thought I'd done a hell of a lot more than dedicate a 30 minute speed-paint to her. "You don't know what this means," she said, basically articulating what I was thinking. Fortunately, she spelt it out for me. "Like, I've been a huge fan of yours for ages and now I'm here and you're painting for me and you're hilarious and just so *nice*."

She *was* actually going to make me blush if I let her go on, so I didn't. "Will you *finally* go home and leave me alone now?" I asked her, but I might have been smiling a little.

She grinned. "Yeah, okay," she said. "I kind of got what I came for earlier anyway."

"You mean I *didn't* need to do all this?" I gestured at the screen.

Instead of answering, she sat forward tensely for a couple of seconds, looking like she wanted to say something. Then, she lifted the tablet off my knee, flipped to Photoshop and scribbled down a phone number on one of the layers. When she finished it, though, she leant back, made a noise and then Control-Zed the last three digits and tried again.

I smirked. "That would have been a lot cooler if you knew your own phone number."

"Well, it's not like I call it all the time," she said, and then jumped up and rushed off to her schoolbag. "You should just give me yours!"

Yeah, no. My work number was the same as my home number, and she *definitely* wasn't getting it until I was sure I could trust her to not text me all day.

After she'd given me the right number, I shut the lid of my laptop. "Come on," I said, bustling her towards the door. "Let's get you home before your parents call the cops on me. Where do you live? If it's not too far, I'll come for the ride."

She looked alarmed. "No, that's okay, it's actually really far," she said. "I'll just take the train."

I looked pointedly towards the windows; it was getting dark outside. Bree was the last person in the world who should be allowed near strangers after dark. Especially in that skirt.

"I can go by myself," she said quickly, before I could speak. "I do it all the time, there's still always people around in stations until much later. I'll probably just go to Courtney's anyway."

I went to get my purse and take another 50 out. I didn't feel fantastic about giving away *more* of my money to her, but I also didn't relish the prospect of another night spent lying awake and wondering if she'd been kidnapped or murdered. "Okay, I won't come with you, but no trains," I said, making sure she took it.

When I'd put my skirt back on and Bree was on her way out the door, I cleared my throat and she stopped. I nodded towards the evil flowers. "You're just going to leave without saying goodbye to them?"

She giggled and bounced over to the vase, pretending to tickle one them under its chin. "Wow, I really love these things. Don't forget to feed them!" she told me, pretending to sound stern.

"Stockpiling human corpses as we speak."

She was still laughing when we'd made it down to the bottom of the building. Being a hotel in central Sydney, there were already taxis waiting to collect people. It was merely a matter of walking up to the one at the head of the rank.

She stopped in front of me. I'd just slipped on some ballet flats because my feet were still hurting from yesterday, but even without heels on I was just so much taller than her. The combination of me being very tall and her being very short made her seem almost child-like, but from this angle I could see pretty deep into her unbuttoned school-shirt. She definitely wasn't a child, that was for sure. I wished she'd do up that damn button, though. Being able to see inside made me uncomfortable and it was going to give people the wrong idea about her.

I didn't say anything about it because Bree already looked like she was about to explode with something. It made me even more uncomfortable. "What?"

"I'm one of those people who always hugs everyone," she said, sounding urgently worried about it.

I squinted at her. I was the opposite of one of those. "Please don't."

"I know I promised I wouldn't do anything you didn't like, but it's hard because you're really funny and I want to!"

"Then you'll have to be *really* strong," I told her, taking her shoulders, spinning her around and pushing her gently towards the taxi before she inevitably lost the fight with herself and pounced on me in front of everyone.

She let me usher her over to the taxi, hopping into it and winding down the window. I didn't miss the taxi driver's eyes dipping to that skirt and I made sure he saw me glaring at him.

"I had a great time!" she said out the window, oblivious to my exchange with the taxi driver. "And I'm sorry I just kind of showed up before," she reconsidered, looking torn, "but also kind of not really because it worked."

I just nodded and waved at her, watching the taxi drive up the street and then trudging back inside.

I had been wondering what I was going to do about dinner and waiting for the lift when a guy who was walking past the hotel ducked inside the lobby. I wasn't really paying much attention to him until I saw him disappear into the toilets beside reception. No one on the desk batted an eyelid, they just went about their business as he finished and went out the door again.

I missed the lift, because I was just gaping: Bree had said the reception staff *wouldn't* let her use the toilets, and that's why she'd asked to use mine, and *that's* why I'd let her in.

She wouldn't just say that. Would she...?

I couldn't leave it, I had to walk up and ask. "Excuse me," I said to one of them, "if people ask to use the toilets in the lobby here, do you let them?"

They all looked at each other. "Strictly speaking they're not public toilets," one of the staff answered me. "But we generally let people, anyway."

I sighed heavily; she hadn't told me the truth. *Bree,* I thought, scrunching up my face. It wasn't that not being allowed to use the toilets was a particularly serious lie, but I felt *so* stupid for not even picking up on it. I'd lived here for four years. Fucking hell, I was angry with her, but also really angry with myself because part of me was actually glad that I'd let her in.

I went back upstairs and spent a minute or two staring down at those monstrous flowers while I tried to figure out what I should do. Even without the lying, that girl had gone from stalking me to my apartment to somehow keeping me company *in* it. That had to be some sort of magic trick. Maybe she did have that creepy shrine in her bedroom after all. I groaned aloud and put my head in my hands. Goddamnit, what the hell was I going to do with her? How did this even happen?

I decided to consult Henry about it, and when I picked up my phone there was already a text from him. *"I could use some of those semi-automatics you keep recommending right about now. I know I generally advocate peaceful resolutions to conflict but I'm halfway up the clock tower right now with Sean Frost."*

You're halfway up a clock tower, I thought dryly. Speaking of clocks, I looked at the one on my wall. It was 8:15. Plenty of time for a few rounds of the new expansion. Maybe Henry could bring up some food and we could eat, shoot each other and just pretend everything was great and that no one was driving us crazy. I texted him back and then went to have a quick shower before he rocked up.

I was running the water and trying to decide if I could be bothered washing my hair or not when I caught sight of something on the glass as I opened the door to the shower cubicle.

The door was all fogged up, except for where someone had drawn a big lopsided smiley face on the surface with their finger and written '*made u look!!!!!*'.

SEVEN

Henry had ended up being *really* angry about something Sean had done. When I answered the door to him, I didn't even get to say hello before he'd walked past me with the takeaway and angrily hung up his jacket beside the door.

I had been about to rant about Bree, but when I saw his face, that plan went out the window. He was *way* more upset than I was.

Illustrating this point perfectly, Henry turned towards me and held up his hands. "I am working for an infantile fuck," he announced. "And I think I am going to kill him."

Right. I just stared at him; I hadn't seen him this angry in *ages*. He was normally calm and pleasant and it was kind of shock to see him so red in the face that his veins were standing out on his temples. I supposed it would be *really* inappropriate to make a comment about boss fights belonging in video games, so I just said, "Whoa. Want to tell me what happened?"

Before he did that, he marched on to my kitchen, took out two plates and began to divide the food between them with the most violent movements he could possibly have made without breaking anything. It was very telling that he *wasn't* shattering them; they were bone china and I'd broken a few myself just by using them. I actually found it kind of hilarious that even at his angriest, he was still careful not to accidentally break any of my plates.

"I watched him break the law today, Min," he said, throwing the container away. "Right in front of my fucking face, and knowing *I'm* the one who has to deal with the consequences of it. And you know what he said?" I mutely shook my head, and he pretended to speak in what I presumed was Sean's voice. "'Oh, you're a very capable man, Henry, I'm sure you'll be able to manage whatever happens'". It wasn't a very flattering imitation.

He walked sharply over to the table with our dinner and laid it out, and then went back to get cutlery. "Fork or chopsticks?" he asked me, trying to not sound as angry and holding both out for me to choose. I took the fork. He kept the chopsticks for himself, sitting down at the table. Before he started dinner, though, he gave the evil flowers he was facing a bit of a strange look.

"Don't ask," I recommended. That story could wait for later.

He gave me a strange look, too, but took my advice and just got stuck back into Sean and his dinner. "I can't fucking believe that man. I can't believe him." He took a mouthful, chewed, swallowed and then said, "No, actually, I *can* believe he'd do it. Fucker. Jesus, that man is a fucking asshole. He has *no* redeeming qualities whatsoever."

I sat down carefully opposite him. I didn't really know what to do because I didn't see him angry very often, so I tried to sound comforting. "Are you okay? What did he actually do?"

Henry shook his head stiffly. "Yeah, I will be okay, but I can't actually tell you what he did."

I made an 'oh' face, but I didn't push for details. He'd very respectfully not asked me for them about my project, after all. "Okay, then... Is there anything I can do to help?"

He shook his head and took another mouthful, swallowed again and then sat back, running his hand through his short hair and making it all stick up like he'd been electrocuted. "And now I'm so angry I can't even enjoy my Pad Thai." He looked up at me. "*And* I'm taking out all of my anger on my poor girlfriend who works at the same godforsaken hellhole as I do."

I squinted at him. "You are?"

He nodded stiffly. "When you express uncontrollable anger in front of others, it is stressful and potentially traumatic for them." He took a breath, making a 'calm down' motion with his hands. "So I will try and find a healthier way to express it. Min, I am very angry at Sean Frost for making me so upset that I came directly here to take it all out on you, and I am very angry at myself for transferring the blame when I should be perfectly able to control my own emotions."

"Those were some excellent 'I' statements," I told him. "But, seriously, it's okay, I'm not traumatised. I'm just a bit worried about you."

"Thank you," he said, still sounding frustrated. "And I'm glad I haven't caused you vicarious trauma. Fuck," he said, pushing plate away. "This is going to sound a bit weird, but do you have any tracksuit pants that might fit me? I think the solution to all of this adrenaline is to go for a quick run and all I have with me are my singlet and sneakers."

I only had the one pair that was unisex, and that was the pair *he'd* left here a couple of years ago that I wore all the time when there was no one around. He'd probably forgotten they were his by now, though. I almost had. "Yeah, I might," I said, and then went to get them. They did end up still fitting him, and so he put them and his sneakers on and went for a jog in the singlet he wore under his work shirt.

I chuckled to myself as I shut the door. At times I'd really wanted to strangle Jason, so I was completely with Henry about having an infuriating boss. I did feel a bit bad about my reaction to his anger, though; even though he was really upset, I still found him hilarious and entertaining. Poor guy. He was great, I hoped the run made him feel better. He worked too hard to put up with this crap.

On the way back to my Pad Thai, I spotted the scary flowers again and looked up at the clock. If Courtney lived near Parramatta, Bree should definitely be there by now. I took my phone out and went to send her a note, and then remembered that she'd lied to me.

I spent the next 15 minutes with my phone next to my dinner as I ate, trying to decide if I was angry enough not to check that she was okay. In the end my concern for her won out and I typed her a quick note to confirm she'd arrived at Courtney's in one piece.

It didn't take her long to reply. *"are u worried about me?? :) :) :)"*

I frowned at the screen. "Yes, and I'm not very happy about it," I told the phone, but I wasn't in the mood to actually reply.

Henry wasn't gone for much longer, but I'd nearly finished my food when he let himself back in. He looked calmer. "That's better," he said as he staggered into the living area. "I'm going to have a quick shower and then let's kill everything together."

"Sounds romantic," I called after him, and went to set up the console.

I didn't tell him much about Bree until we'd called it a night and were lying in bed, because he was finally enjoying himself and I didn't want to stress him out again. Furthermore, when I watched him put on the hoodie that was on my bed, I kept my mouth shut. It was difficult, though. I'd bonded with that stupid hoodie and I didn't like him wearing it.

Before we went to sleep Henry startled me by making a sudden noise. "Jesus Christ, Min, I'm the worst boyfriend ever," he said, remembering something. "You got *promoted* today and all I can do is talk about *my* problems. We should have been celebrating!"

I laughed shortly. "No, I'm way past that," I said, and then finally told him about Bree. At the end of the story, when I got to the point where I'd found out that she'd lied to me, he actually *laughed*. It sounded affectionate, but it was still a laugh.

I must have looked quite indignant because he laughed again. "I'm sorry, Min," he said, reaching over and rubbing my arm. "I am, really. I know honesty is a big thing for you after high school, but when you said she'd *lied to you* in that tone of voice I was expecting it to be about something serious and major."

"Does it really matter what it was about? She *lied* to me. That's not okay." He had a familiar expression on his face as he was listening to me which meant he was analysing what I was saying. That sort of stuff may have worked to calm *him* down but it wasn't how I dealt with my emotions. "And, Henry, if you pull that shrink act on me at this time of night I swear to god I'm going to murder you."

He sounded like he was smiling. "Min," he began, pulling it anyway. "Why do you think she lied to you?"

"I'm not playing this game," I told him, and he was very pointedly silent. "Henry, I know where you're going with this and I'm not going to rationalise it."

"Of course not. Then you wouldn't have an excuse to push her away and never talk to her again. Why do you think she lied to you?" he repeated, sounding gently insistent.

I *looked* at him. He raised his eyebrows at me and I rolled onto my back and groaned. "*Fine*," I said, rubbing my eyes. "She was trying to get into my house."

He didn't stop there. "And why do you think she was trying to get into your house?"

I turned my head back towards him and just glared. "Henry, I get it, she wanted to be friends with me."

He smirked, looking rather pleased with himself. "Wow, what a despicable human being, wanting to be friends with *you*. She clearly can't be trusted." The smirk faded a little and he did a facial shrug. "I don't know, Min. She just sounds like a normal teenager to me," he said, and then rethought it. "Well, maybe not *normal*, per se. But what is normal? You obviously enjoy her company, and that's all that really matters. What's the worst that could happen?"

"She's *17* and she keeps doing things that remind me of that. I'm pretty sure that matters."

He didn't look convinced. "Seven years," he said, reminding me of the age difference between him and me again. "Shall I go on?"

"No."

He chuckled. "Probably for the best. I'm a bit biased about this whole thing with—'Bree', wasn't it?"

Despite the fact I'd said I didn't want to go on discussing it, I couldn't help following up on that one. I looked across at him. "How can you possibly be biased about her? You haven't even met her."

His humour faded. "Well, you've been here for four years, Min. I'm just happy you're finally throwing down some roots." He snaked an arm across my middle, smiling. "Really happy, because I love *your* company, despite our colossal seven year difference, and I want you to stay in Sydney." He paused. "Although, obviously if I accidentally see you without make-up, I will dump you on the spot."

I thought back to how boyish I'd looked that morning in the hoodie he was now wearing, and winced.

He saw my expression and his smile dropped straight off his face. "Oh, Min, I'm sorry, I was just joking because I thought it would make you feel better," he said, sounding a bit panicked as he shuffled closer and wrapped his arms around me. "I didn't mean to say anything to upset you. *Shit*." He shook his head. "Sorry, that was *really* insensitive of me. I'm doing a great job tonight, aren't I? I'm so immersed in my own problems I'm not being very helpful about yours."

"It's okay, I'm fine," I said dismissively. "As in, I'm *actually* fine. Let's just get some sleep."

He did worry about it, but we eventually got to sleep anyway. Unfortunately, the following morning he had a couple of hours off because he'd been doing serious overtime even by Frost standards, so he left my apartment *in* the hoodie. I wasn't prepared for how upset that made me. That was *my* big, comfy hoodie, and I felt very not-fine about him taking off with it. Especially since my trackies were now all gross and sweaty, too.

I stood in front of my 'weird' amount of make-up—thanks, Bree—and got irrationally annoyed about the whole thing before I remembered that I was an adult and I could actually purchase my own clothes. By the time I made it into work, I'd decided I'd duck down to one of the places on George Street while I was getting lunch. Maybe I could even get some comfy clothes that I wasn't embarrassed to be seen in, too.

On my way into my new office I got accosted by the lead from the Canada project team.

"Mini," he said, in a voice I couldn't really ignore. I stopped walking and turned to face him as he asked, "Have you finished with the draft layout concept for the website?"

No, I hadn't, and I'd explained why to those guys yesterday. "I won't be able to volunteer for your project because I've been assigned my own team, now."

He put a hand on my shoulder which automatically got my back up. I looked at it, and then at him. "I know you've got other stuff to do, Mini, but we're really counting on you for this. We even reallocated the budget for design to something else and it's as good as spent. We can't afford to outsource now."

You had to be fucking kidding me. "Really, I'm not sure I'll be able to do it."

He squeezed my shoulder. "We're really going to be in big trouble if you can't finish what you started for us, Mini. It's going to put a lot of pressure on the rest of the team. And, really," he said, copying the way I'd said it to him, "it's not like you can't fit another design job in on top of whatever boring crap you're doing for the political pitch. Those never need to be flashy."

I'm a project lead, too, I wanted to say to him. I actually *can't* fit your dregs on top of my workload, and it's not a political pitch. Fuck confidentiality, seriously. Just fuck it, and fuck my complete lack of capacity to say 'no'. "Fine," I said, despite the fact it really wasn't. "Give me a couple of days, though."

He lifted his hand from my shoulder and patted my arm. "Good girl," he said, and then strode off somewhere on another mission.

I watched him go, and I'm pretty sure I looked disgusted. 'Good girl'. Was he serious?

That put me in a bad mood, and even Sarah noticed it. "Wrong side of the bed?" she asked with a grin as I walked into Oslo and put away my handbag. One of the other team members looked up and smiled at me. I managed to return it, but it was very difficult.

"Some of the people in this place..." I said to Sarah cryptically; I couldn't really discuss why I was so upset while there were other people around.

She spun her chair around to face me. "What I'm hearing is a *great* reason to get out of this place and vent to me somewhere else," she said. "Actually, Rob's going back to Broome next weekend and I was thinking that you and Henry should come on a double-date with us. I think you guys would really get along."

I shrugged. "I'm sure we would," I said politely, "but I just accepted another design job because I'm a doormat. I think I'm going to be Red Bull's best customer for the next couple of days."

She raised her eyebrows. "Why would you do that to yourself?" she asked me, but then said, "But you've got to eat, right? What do you say to Friday night? That way if you need to catch up with some work because of it, you can do it on the weekend."

I made a face. "Sarah, I'd love to, but I really can't. I'm just too busy."

"Me too," she said. "I'm on two teams as well, remember?" When I didn't say anything, she sat back in her chair and considered me for a few seconds. "I'm not going to be able to get you out, am I?"

I sighed. "It's nothing to do with you, I promise," I said, sitting down in my own chair and switching on the computer. "Please don't take it personally."

She made a noise. "Okay," she said, not sounding hurt or upset, which I was grateful for. She then swung her chair back towards her own computer and got back to work.

Not that I really should have expected *that* much in a single day, but I felt like the team wasn't making as much progress as I hoped they would when I'd been doing the timelines yesterday. They were all hard workers which was fantastic—not that they'd be employed by Frost if they weren't—but I felt like especially the younger guy was really missing the mark when it came to the depth of research required. I'd just have done everything myself, but I couldn't. Not even if I worked 24 hours a day.

I had actually planned to forgo my hoodie-buying expedition because of the extra work I'd taken on, but the oldest team member ended up chucking me out of the office at lunch time, saying I'd kill myself if I didn't take a break. I didn't argue with him because he was right, but I *did* spend the whole walk to the shopping centre worrying about being unfit for management. I was so busy stressing about not knowing my own limits that I nearly forgot to grab something to eat, too.

Well, apparently women the world over *did* cheer themselves up with shopping, so maybe I could give retail therapy a shot.

The store I'd been planning to get my own hoodie from was one of those surfie-type places that all of the beach-tanned blondes always bought all their bikinis and perfectly distressed denim from. I didn't look like I belonged there at all, and two separate sales clerks tried to offer me assistance because of that.

The women's hoodies were in all these pastel colours and some of them had strange embellishments like dead-end pockets or zips that lead nowhere. I wasn't a big fan of anything that wasn't very plain, but I took the last three 'XL's anyway and then went to go and try them on. On the way there, I spotted the men's hoodies hanging in their loose, completely plain glory over on the far wall.

That's more like it, I thought.

I looked furtively back toward the counter. Fortunately, the girl staffing it was busy doing something tedious and not looking in my direction. Feeling like I was about to commit some sort of felony, I crossed the floor and went to go have a look at what was on the men's side.

The colours were much bolder over there and the majority of the tops there had normal pockets and quite plain prints. I took a blue one from the rack. It was an 'XL' as well, and when I compared it to the women's XLs, they were like baby clothes.

I liked it, it looked *really* comfy and it was exactly what I was looking for. I held it for a moment. What was the big deal, anyway? There was nothing wrong with me buying this for myself. Women wore their boyfriends' clothes all the time, and men apparently found it cute. So I was buying it for myself instead of waiting for Henry to leave one at my apartment, so what? What was the difference?

I still felt really uncomfortable, though, and I couldn't put my finger on why that was.

"Hi, can I help you?" another one of the clerks asked, suddenly appearing beside me. I forced a smile but didn't say anything straight away. Because of that, she asked, "Oh, you don't speak English?"

I would have actually been tempted to go along with that if it would get rid of her, but I had a feeling she was one of those people who would try and help me anyway even if I pretended to not understand. "No, I do," I said. "Can I just walk straight into the change rooms or do I need one of those number-tag things?"

She indicated where the rooms were like an air hostess showing me the over-wing exits. "No, you can just go straight in. Also, we're having a promotion today. If you purchase one of the men's tops from this range or that wall over there, you get forty percent off men's jeans from the same line."

She proceeded to show me the jeans she was talking about and ask me about sizing, and while she was loading me up with them I just agreed they looked great and the deal was good value because I figured it would make her go away faster. It did, but by the time I went into the change room under the guise of trying on the women's hoodies, I had my arms full of men's jeans. I dumped them all in the corner of the cubicle.

The lighting the change rooms was actually pretty flattering, but I still had to face myself in a bra before I got the first of the hoodies on. It was one of the women's, and the sleeves were too short. That probably wasn't an enormous problem in itself because I always pushed them up my forearms anyway, but I felt like it was a sign. It also was a pastel purple and made me look as if I was trying too hard to be cutesy when I just wasn't. Well, so much for trying to buy something that I could actually wear in public, I thought. I scrapped that idea.

That hoodie had gone so badly that I didn't even bother with the other two pastel ones, I just went straight for the men's. It slipped over my head so much more easily than the purple one, the sleeves covered my arms and it hung at a really comfortable length down my middle.

It looked weird with a suit skirt, though.

In the reflection of the mirror, I could see the jeans I'd just dumped in a pile in the corner. I frowned at the glass. Min, you came here for a big comfy hoodie to wear at home. You'll leave with this one. What the hell are you going to do with those jeans? Hang around the house in them? You can save a 100 dollars and just do that in your trackies.

Then I remembered my trackies were currently soaked in Henry's sweat. I could use something comfy to wear while they were at the laundry.

So, wait, I was going to buy really expensive, really ultra-fashionable men's jeans because my 100 year old trackies were going to be gone for *two days* to be washed? And then what was I going to do with the jeans after that? Where was I going to wear them? I had never been a big fan of jeans.

On the other hand, the only reason I avoided wearing jeans in the past was because the skinny jeans I had at home were tight and uncomfortable. If I had big boot cut ones maybe I'd feel more like putting them on.

But, seriously, if I did really like them, *where* was I planning on actually wearing them other than at home? Those jeans *screamed* 'man'. There was nothing feminine about them at all. They belonged on a sepia-tone billboard under rippling abs and visible Calvins, not on me.

I bent down and picked up a pair of them. Fuck, they were so cool, though. I really wanted to put them on, regardless of who they were meant for. But what would it mean if I liked them?

I made a frustrated noise at myself. Who *cared* what it meant? Jesus, Min, get a fucking grip, the sky is not going to cave in if you put on a pair of men's jeans and like them. What the hell is wrong with you? This isn't high school anymore, no one's going to draw moustaches on photos of you and post them online just because you're wearing men's jeans.

I ended up just kind of holding them up and scowling. Great work, Min, I thought. How balanced of you. You're having a fucking personal crisis over a pair of jeans. A *pair of goddamn jeans*.

I was in there for ages, so long that the clerk came to check on me. "Is everything okay in there?" her cheerful voice called through the door. "How are the sizes?"

I looked at them in my hands. They were enormous. "I'm good, thanks," I called back, "I'll be out in a sec."

My final verdict was that I didn't have time to make this decision now. And since I wasn't sure when I'd be able to come back, I just decided to buy them and worry about everything later.

I wasn't sure what I had expected, but the girl at the counter didn't seem at all weirded out by the fact I was buying men's clothes. I supposed women did it all the time—probably not for the same reasons I was, though. I felt like she could read them all over my face as she greeted me and I was almost bracing myself for that smile to disappear. "Are these for yourself?" she asked, still smiling for now.

I *panicked*. "Why?"

That made her look a little surprised. "Because I can put them in a non-transparent recycled paper bag if you want to hide them from someone in particular."

I closed my eyes for a moment, feeling so, so stupid. "That sounds great." Then, completely unnecessarily, I added, "They're for my boyfriend."

The girl smiled while she was running my card. "I'm sure he'll love them."

Fuck, I was no better than Bree: 'they're for my boyfriend'. *Min,* really? You're going to *lie* to her? And Henry most certainly would *not* love them if he saw me in them, either. But whatever, I wouldn't wear them around him. Or anyone. They were for me.

Even in that paper carry-bag, I was actually too afraid to take them back to work. It was ridiculous, because if anyone saw the bag and what was inside it, they would assume I *had* bought them for Henry. Just as a means of avoiding that conversation, though, I walked all the way home and left the bag inside my door before I returned to work.

I was late back from lunch, but given the amount of overtime I did, the only comments people made were more of the 'long lunch date?' variety.

"Yeah, I'm cheating on Henry with clothes shops," I said dryly when Sarah asked. She laughed at it, though, which made me feel a bit better.

"I didn't think clothes shops were your type," she said afterwards, handing me a USB. "That's pink diamond sales in North America and Mainland China," she said. "Actually China's hedging out the US at the moment."

I accepted the USB from her. "Interesting," I said, and then asked, "and you didn't think clothes stores were my type?"

Sarah laughed again. "You don't seem like the kind of person to go shopping, that's all. I'm not having a go at your fashion sense. You dress *way* better than me, anyway. I'm lucky to brush my hair in the morning."

And yet you look amazing, I thought, a little bit enviously. I bet she never got stuck stressing for half an hour in a change room. Envy aside, though, she was right, I wasn't really a fan of shopping. Rather than think about why that was and spend too much time dwelling on what I'd just bought, I reviewed the figures that Sarah had dug up for me.

I didn't need our data-crunching ex-intern to tell me that the US was out, but I wasn't too sure sales in China were strong enough to justify positioning ourselves there, either. I gave the USB to the team members and asked them to see what they could mine out of it while I sat back and tried to think of what the hell we should do.

Okay, so it was only day two and I didn't think anyone other than me had really expected we'd be completing the marketing requirements document by now. Still, with only four weeks we *really* didn't have time to spend ages figuring out who we were even trying to sell these things to. There was just so much to do, and I had a sudden panic that the four weeks would be up and we would have achieved nothing, that I would be demoted, end up in admin and need to tell Mum what a terrible failure her daughter was.

Shit, and with everything that had gone on I hadn't even told Mum about the promotion in the first place. I was clearly losing the plot.

"Back in a second," I told my team, and then grabbed my phone to head outside.

Several of the levels in our building had their own alcove balconies, and ours was usually full of smoking marketing reps, especially around lunchtime. Today, though, there wasn't anyone out there when I pushed the door open and dialled Mum's number. As usual, she picked up almost instantly. "Min!"

Predictably, Mum was overjoyed for about five seconds and then started playing her usual game of running through a list of catastrophic what-ifs about if I blew the opportunity. I had been walking backwards and forwards and half-listening to her, while I privately what-iffed about those goddamn jeans, when the balcony door opened and Sean Frost came striding out.

I stopped walking. What was *he* doing here? He never came onto level 36 because it was Diane's stronghold. I didn't even think I'd been this close to him before.

He was supposedly an enormous heart-throb, but even from this distance I couldn't see it. What I could see was how fit he kept himself and how well dressed he was, but those things never really impressed me, anyway. He did seem much more easy-going than his sister; compared to her the only intimidating thing about him was his obvious self-confidence.

On that note, he smiled amicably at me when he saw me looking. The smile turned out a bit crooked because he had an unlit cigarette between his lips as he felt around in his pockets for a lighter. He didn't find one.

Because I was on the phone, when he walked up to me he just mouthed, "Lighter?" as he made a lighter motion with his hand. I shook my head. He nodded once, and then proceeded to search around the pot plants, seats and railings for an abandoned one.

I couldn't help being amused; this man was a co-CEO of a billion dollar mining company *on his hands and knees* in an Italian suit, retrieving a fallen lighter from underneath a bench.

He stood up and showed it to me as he triumphantly lit his cigarette. I smiled back, and I didn't even have to force it. Before I got too friendly, though, I caught myself: *this* was the guy that had broken the law and made Henry really upset last night. *This* was the fucking asshole fuck and all those other things Henry had called him.

I should have been really angry with Sean on Henry's behalf, but I was finding it really difficult. I mean, Sean definitely wasn't doing to me what he did to most of the female staff and maybe a few of the men, but he was very charismatic and very likeable one-on-one.

Definitely a far cry from the cool professional I'd seen give speeches at annual general meetings, and an even farther cry from the things Henry had called him last night.

"Min, Min? Are you listening to me?"

Shit, I'd completely forgotten about the phone against my ear. "Sorry, Mum, I'll call you back later," I said, and hung up.

Sean looked over towards me, and that's when he saw my expression. He cringed, clearly thinking it was about the fact he'd been scrounging around for a cigarette lighter and not to do with Henry's opinion of him. "I promise I don't normally crawl around on the concrete," he said. He had a pleasant voice. "It's just been a really hard day and I *really* needed a cigarette."

"I hear you," I said, surprising myself by actually speaking.

I meant that it had been a hard day, but Sean thought I was asking for a cigarette. He patted down his lapels and his pockets. "I'm sorry I can't offer you one, they're in my office," he said, and then considered me for a moment. "Min Lee, isn't it?" he asked.

I was too surprised he knew who I was to correct him about wanting a cigarette. When I didn't, he put the cigarette between his lips and dusted off his palms, walking over so he could shake my free hand. I was taller than him, but he didn't make me feel awkward about it. In fact, apart from the fact I knew Henry *hated* him for some reason, everything about him put me at ease. "I work with your boyfriend. There's a picture of you on his desk. Pleasure to finally meet you—I hear you're the rising star of Marketing at the moment."

I wasn't sure he was supposed to know about my position, but it was possible Henry mentioned something. "Henry does tend to exaggerate his praise of me."

Sean laughed. "I'm the same with my beautiful wife. So, how's your new team? Political project, is that correct?"

It seemed like a perfectly innocent question, but following Diane's advice I was careful to be appropriately dismissive. "You know how they go."

He was still smiling, and I could see where he got his reputation for public relations. "Fortunately, I'm pleased to say I don't," he said. "But according to my sister you get results, and since that's what she cares about, I'm guessing we'll have a politician or two in our pockets by June." He nodded politely, finishing his cigarette and butting it out in the bin. He gestured towards it. "Sorry again you had to witness the awful lengths I'll go to in order to feed my nicotine addiction. Now if you'll excuse me, unfortunately I have to run."

I smiled at him as he went back inside, but I didn't follow him straight away. Henry *hated* that guy? Really? I unlocked my phone with the intention of texting him, but then I saw I had a note on Deviant Art. I didn't have to check who it was from.

"*sooooooo,*" it said. "*did·u have a shower yet?? :) :)*"

I pictured the smiley face Bree had drawn on my shower screen and grinned for a fraction of a second before I remembered what else she'd done. *You lied to me, Bree*, I thought, but then I realised how many times *I'd* lied today and felt like a raging hypocrite. That didn't change the fact I was grumpy with her about it, though, so I decided to leave that message for now. I did end up texting Henry, but he didn't answer either so I figured he was already back at work and busy.

I'd better get to work, too, I thought, and then went back inside.

That evening I was the last one to leave as usual, but Sarah didn't leave very long before me. She gave me a bit of a measured look as she held the door open, but she didn't say anything other than goodbye.

"Bye," I said absently, trying to figure out why I hated the colours that Canada had chosen for their scheme so much.

I didn't get home until about 9 or 10. The recycled paper carry-bag was still inside my door, so I took it with me into the bedroom and only faced it again after I'd had a shower.

Since my trackies were off with the laundry, I was sort of forced to put on my new comfy clothes. I wasn't too unhappy about that. Despite my inner conflict, part of me was looking forward to wearing them.

The jeans *were* seriously fucking cool, and when I pulled them on they were *really* comfortable. Not baggy, exactly, but nice and loose. I'd bought one size bigger than I probably needed so they sat low on my hips; if I was going out in them I'd need to wear a belt. I stopped for a moment: yeah, right, 'going out in them'. Just, no. As if people didn't stare at me enough already because of how tall I was, I didn't need to add 'wearing men's clothes' to that. I put a soft t-shirt on under the hoodie, and then shot myself a passing glance in the mirror while I was throwing away the bag.

It was just supposed to be a quick look, just to check nothing was on back-to-front and no tags were still attached. It didn't end up being quick, though, because my reflection was just so different from what I had expected to see.

I wasn't wearing any make-up and I had my hair tied back because I'd just been in the shower. Between my hair seeming short and the fact I was wearing men's clothes... fuck, what was I *doing*? They were only supposed to be comfortable, *that* was why I'd bought them. It wasn't even about how I looked at all.

But that didn't change the fact that I looked good like this, really good. And better than that, I looked *right*.

My heart started racing again, and I forced myself to look away from the mirror. *No*, I thought. *I'm not doing this, not now*. I had way too fucking much going on in my life to want to add more stupid, whimsical complications to it. Work was already making me feel like I was on the brink of losing it, I didn't need something else to worry about. I just needed to dag around my home and enjoy my new comfy clothes like anyone would. That's enough, Min, please just leave it there and stop thinking about it.

I followed my own advice, poured myself an enormous mug of wine and went to quickly eat some dinner. In doing so, I was sitting opposite those evil flowers and they reminded me that it had been a while since I'd replied to anything Bree had sent me.

When I went to get my phone so I could, there was already a message waiting for me. It wasn't from Bree, though, it was a text message from Henry. *"Hey, Min, one of your co-workers—Sarah, she said her name was—invited us out for dinner on Friday night with her and her boyfriend. Obviously, I said yes."*

I stopped chewing mid-mouthful.

You've got to be kidding me, I thought, she went behind my back and just asked Henry?

God, she was as bad as Bree. I reconsidered that and made a face: okay, no she wasn't, no one was as bad as Bree. She *was* sneaky, though. I still had no idea what to do about Bree, but I knew one employee who was about to find herself with *a lot* of very boring paperwork for the next four weeks as penance for ganging up on me with my boyfriend.

EIGHT

I got to work early the following morning so that when Sarah arrived, it was to a desk *covered* in analytics printouts. She stopped in front of them, looked from them to me, and then walked over to my desk and placed a can of Red Bull between my keyboard and my monitor. "Still glad I did it," she said as she went and sat at her own desk. She sounded like she was grinning.

"You say that now," I said neutrally as I pretended to be very busy, "until I tell you that I 'accidentally' deleted the spreadsheet for those and I need you to re-enter all the data."

Even after all those years she'd been working with me, she still hadn't learnt. "Oh my god, Min, are you serious?" She turned back to all of the printouts on her desk with this look of total horror on her face. "I can't believe you'd seriously do that to me because I *asked you to eat food with me and...*" She never finished that sentence because apparently I was doing far too good a job at looking completely innocent. "You're *messing* with me!" she accused. "And after I bought you a Red Bull, too!"

I shot her a half-smile before I looked back at my screen. "Of course I'm not. I'd never do such a thing. Now get to work," I said, nodding my head sideways at her printouts. A crumpled-up ball of one of them flew past my face and I gave her an unimpressed look. "Good thing it's only contracts you pitch."

I saw one of our teammates who was sitting beside Sarah roll his eyes. I left it, though, because Sarah had started laughing and that made *me* chuckle.

Since my cover was blown, there was nothing standing between me and the Red Bull. I plucked it from between my keyboard and monitor and I toasted it in the air towards Sarah. "Cheers," I said, opening it to a very satisfying hiss. "A-plus job at sucking up to the boss. Now I need you to tell me what rich 25 to 34 year olds on Facebook are saying about pink diamonds."

"Yeah, okay, okay," Sarah said, pushing aside all of the paper to get to her keyboard, still smiling ear to ear. "Hah, Rob is going to *love* you. Is it Friday yet?"

I wasn't looking forward to Friday as much as Sarah was, and so when Friday *did* roll around, I was too worried we hadn't completed the framework documents to think about much else. Actually, we'd barely even started them. It was only a week into the project and already we were way behind the timelines. I was so worried about it I sought out Jason to have a quick word with him. It was never a pleasant experience; I had to be pretty desperate to bother talking to him.

He listened to my concerns while he tried to pick something out of his perfectly white teeth with a fingernail. "Well, ordinarily I'd give it a few weeks," he said, giving up on his teeth. "But because you've only got a few weeks for the full project I'd suggest getting your arse into gear. There's probably still enough time." He pointed his finger at me. "But what's this I hear about you doing Canada's design?"

I made a face. "I promised them I'd do it before I got committed to Pink. I've finished it now, though."

He didn't look impressed, and that made my heart sink. "I know hard work is kind of an Asian MO, but maybe you'd have finished the docs by now if you focused on the project we actually assigned you to."

After I'd been told that, I felt like the most appropriate course of action was to book a ticket back to Melbourne and apply for a job at McDonalds; something I might actually be capable of doing properly. I didn't, though, and I didn't even go hide out on the balcony, either. I went back to my desk at Oslo and tried to focus very hard on reviewing the data I'd been given and not think bad thoughts about my lack of skills in project management.

I had been so preoccupied I jumped when Sarah tapped me on the shoulder with a smile on her face. "Your phone," she said, and pointed towards my drawer. "It's been going crazy in there for like the last 15 minutes."

I stared blankly at her for a second, and then looked at my drawer. Just as she'd said, it buzzed. I'd better turn vibrate off. "Sorry, I hope it hasn't been distracting you."

She snorted. "*Please* distract me," she said, going back to her desk. "I'm watching a terrible Russian TV show that has so much product placement I feel like it's one big infomercial." She imitated a Hollywood-style Russian accent, and actually didn't do too bad a job at it. "'Please, let me present you with enormous pink diamond. Let me to show you where you are buying such this diamond. Let us reflect on this most wonderful store full of diamonds. Look here at store'."

That made *me* laugh for once, and when one of our teammates cleared his throat I realised we were probably bothering him. I felt a bit guilty about that, because I'd asked him to finish something today that realistically should have taken two or three days, and here I was, dicking around and annoying everyone. I scrunched up my face; a job at McDonalds was looking pretty appropriate at this point.

I'd gone to open my drawer and take my mobile out to turn the vibrate function off when I noticed it was a series of notifications from Deviant Art. I paused for a moment. It had been a couple of days since I'd replied to Bree. I still wasn't happy about her lying to me, but the more I thought about it, the more I recognised Henry kind of had a point. It wasn't malicious, and seriously, I wouldn't have let her in if she hadn't lied in the first place. I sighed. I shouldn't defer replying to some fictional point in the future where I wasn't overworked.

I had literally only just opened up my notes and was tapping out a quick reply when Jason powered through the door with a big fat book in his hand. He stopped when he saw me on my phone, looking directly at it and then laughing.

"I just came in here because I thought you might be more comfortable using some of the timeline templates in this," he said, holding up the thick book. The title was '*Essentials of Effective Time Management in Marketing*'. "But maybe you should just read the whole thing." He dropped it on my desk in front of me, gave me a pointed look, and then left.

Sarah and I glanced at each other, and she rolled her eyes and shook her head about him. It felt like something the naughty students sitting up the back of the room would do to each other if the teacher had told them off.

My other teammates had been surreptitiously watching and of

course they didn't say anything, but they didn't need to. I knew what they were thinking and I just felt *stupid*. And it wasn't as if I could run after Jason and tell him that he just had bad timing and I'd been working really, really solidly.

God, was I kidding myself, though? Was I *really* working as effectively as I could?

I had spent nearly half an hour earlier in the week printing out all that analytics stuff to arrange artfully on Sarah's desk. That was definitely time that could have been better spent. And Jason was right about accepting Canada's design project. Goddamnit, why hadn't I put my foot down with the arsehole lead from that team? Did I *really* need his approval? And what the fuck was that 'good girl' crap he'd said to me, anyway? I had a brief fantasy where I was a guy and instead of accepting his stupid fucking design project, I just punched him as soon as he opened his mouth and kept walking.

I chuckled to myself about that and then realised what I was laughing at and immediately stopped. Why the hell would I imagine being a guy? I tried to correct myself by imagining it again just with how I looked right now, and the fantasy didn't have any of the same oomph or satisfaction about it.

I felt really uncomfortable about that, and I didn't want to think about what it meant. Fuck, I really didn't have time for this crap. We were so behind, and my team had all probably given up on me and decided I was terrible at my job. I didn't need to have any more time-consuming personal crises.

I didn't take a lunch break. I did, however, exceed the recommended maximum number of cans of Red Bull and eat a decrepit muesli bar I found at the very bottom of my handbag.

In the evening, Sarah had to go pick Rob up because he lived somewhere out in suburbia, so she said goodbye a little bit after seven, and reminded me the booking was for eight. My other three teammates all disconnected their laptops from everything and went home with them shortly after that, presumably to continue working there.

I hoped that I'd regained at least some credibility by being the last one to leave. I actually had most of the data by now, and we'd had a meeting to discuss the strongest leads, and it was really looking like it was going to be Russia. I hadn't done any sort of business with Russia before, and neither had the rest of the team. It would probably be wise to spend some of the budget on getting a consultant to train us and the sales team on cultural appropriateness. There was also the off-chance that we'd need to go and deliver the pitch *in* Russia given the tight timeframes for getting people out here. That was kind of cool, at least. Moscow was supposed to be beautiful.

I caught myself. Wait a second, Min. That was *if* we had stuff done on time and *if* I didn't fuck the hell up. And, fuck, I *really* needed to write the marketing statement tonight. I'd told the team I'd email it to them tomorrow and I hadn't even started it. I opened a blank file. Shit, shit. I was running out of time.

"Min," that was Henry's voice, "there's this thing called a mobile phone. I think you might even have one."

I looked up, kind of startled. Henry had his head poked in through the doorway. I briefly wondered what he was doing here instead of just texting me, but then I remembered I'd turned off vibrate on my phone because of Bree's messages. And now Henry was here, and *shit Henry was here.* I hissed and hurriedly shut the screen of the laptop. "Henry, you're not supposed to be in Oslo!" I gestured out behind him. "Diane's office is just around the corner!" The last fucking thing I needed was to have one of the CEOs unhappy with me, too.

He had his briefcase with him, I could see the corner of it halfway down the door. "I wouldn't be except you haven't answered three texts and the phones aren't connected to this office. We really need to leave now or we'll be late. It's 7:50."

I looked back at my screen. I really, really, needed to write that statement. It wouldn't take more than about half an hour. An hour, at the most. "In a second," I said. "Sarah knows the pressure we're under, she'll understand if I'm late. You just go on without me."

"...and yet she's probably already at the restaurant, waiting for us. Come on." He pushed the door all the way open and stood in the doorway. "You can do the rest over the weekend."

"Henry," I said. I could hear the note of desperation in my voice and I hated it. "I will literally be done in about half an hour. You just order me something and I'll be there on time to eat it." He didn't budge. Since there was no one else within earshot, I added, "My team's already basically given up on me and Jason thinks I'm hopeless. I *have* to get this done!"

He walked into the room towards me. "Min, by all reports you're great at your job, so I'm sure you're just overreacting." He stopped behind my chair. "Are you actually going to make me drag you there? Because I will try." Despite saying that, though, he didn't. He just stood behind me and looked down at me. He always looked quite imposing in a full suit with his jacket on. "Min. Let's go."

My heart was racing. "Henry, you don't understand, I really just need to get this finished, so if you could just give me—"

"Can we help you, Henry?" said a cool voice from the doorway.

We both turned looked over towards it and to my horror, Diane Frost was standing there. She wasn't looking at me, she was looking at Henry, but it didn't matter. I knew who was going to cop it. "I hope Min explained to you this is a closed office." When she looked down at me, I felt sick.

"She did, and very clearly, but I'm just trying to drag her out of here for food," Henry explained, trying to soften her. Fuck, he was good with people; he sounded *so* lovely. "Taking appropriate breaks is an OH&S issue, after all."

She smiled, but it didn't reach her eyes. "I'm sure she appreciates the gesture," Diane said. "But you still shouldn't be in here. Political pitches are strictly confidential."

"You're right, and I shouldn't need to have that explained to me, I apologise," he said easily. He seemed so relaxed, but I could hardly move. I was frozen in place as Henry bent down beside me and opened my drawer. I didn't actually know what he was doing until I saw him walk out of the room, nodding respectfully at Diane as he passed her. Once he was out in the corridor he held up what was in his hand.

My handbag.

My jaw dropped. I'd told him about what Bree had done, but never in a million years would I have thought he'd take *tips* from her. He went off towards the lifts with it while I sat there feeling ill.

Diane directed me a very hard stare. "Don't let him in here," she said once he was gone. "I don't care what his excuses are. Did I not make that clear enough for you?"

Apparently not. I felt *so* stupid. "Of course you did, it won't happen again."

She kept glaring through me. "Jason tells me there are some holdups with the documents?"

I felt like I'd been kicked in the stomach. God, could it get any worse? Of *course* Jason had told her. I bet he'd told her how I'd been wasting time on my phone, too. "It's nothing that hard work can't fix," I said, probably sounding much more confident than I felt.

She nodded once. "Good," she said. "You won't make me regret choosing you to lead this project, will you?"

From the way she said that, I think she already was. And she *should* regret it, too. If I needed Diane Frost to come in here to tell me how to do my job, I was majorly underperforming.

I watched her leave, feeling sick, so fucking sick. I'd been so excited about this opportunity. I had been looking so forward to impressing her and exceeding her expectations and now... Well, now everything was turning to shit and I *still* hadn't finished the fucking framework docs we needed. She should have chosen a more experienced project lead even if they were all loud, egotistical fucks. I wasn't up to this, but I couldn't pull out of it now without destroying my career. I just had to do it and not fuck up any more than I had. Somehow. Fuck, I needed sleep, but I had this stupid dinner.

I really needed to touch up my makeup before I met Sarah's boyfriend, and, *shit,* all my makeup was in my handbag and Henry had taken off with it. I didn't know how far he'd go with it, but if he was making a point he might actually take it all the way to the restaurant.

I hurriedly shut down my laptop and pulled out the USB. I gave my desk a cursory glance to make sure I had definitely shredded everything that showed anything about the project, and then left the room. I could come back tomorrow and grab the computer if I needed it.

After I'd shut Oslo, I jogged all the way to the lifts, but Henry hadn't even pressed the button. He was just waiting there. "I actually am very sorry about that," he said as he passed me my handbag. "I hope I didn't get you into too much trouble."

I couldn't think straight, the adrenaline was making everything feel a bit surreal. The bottom line was that I was fucking up, though. Henry couldn't be blamed for that. "No more trouble than I already got myself in," I said dismissively. "Fuck, I need alcohol. Lots of alcohol. And then I need to pass out and wake up at in the middle of the night and keep working."

Henry nodded once. "Sounds balanced," he said mildly, and then offered me his hand. "It'll all be alright, Min." I looked at it. I felt kind of sweaty and restless, so I shook my head. He nodded again and put it back in his pocket.

When we entered the lift, I stood facing the mirrors to fix my lipstick and my eyeliner and try to do something about my hair. I looked fucking terrible, as usual. Definitely not in form to punch Canada's project lead.

"How do I look?" I asked Henry, anyway.

He had been watching me with concern and it was a little claustrophobic. "Gorgeous, of course," he said. "But like someone who could use a holiday. How many annual leave days do you have? I was thinking we could go across to New Zealand for a week or two. There are some great landscapes there..."

I knew he was just being nice but I actually felt a little patronised, like he was suggesting I wasn't able to cope with my job and that I needed *him* to help me find ways to relax. "It doesn't matter, I can't use them until after this pitch anyway," I said, and then winced as I remembered Diane's expression. "*Fuck*, how the fuck am I screwing this up so badly?"

He put a hand gently on my back. "Min," he said. "You are fantastic at your job and *the CEO* would not have hand-picked you for a key project if you weren't. You'll work things out, and that mix-up back there was clearly all my fault, anyway. Let's leave work at work and relax for once. Sarah seems very nice."

He was right, she *was* nice, but that didn't really help me feel better about how I was doing at my job. Once we were out in the fresh air and walking towards the restaurant, though, I did feel a little better. Henry was right, and I had the whole weekend to work solidly on that stupid document. Additionally, Sarah had been really looking forward to this dinner so the least I could do was try and forget work and enjoy it. She was fun, I decided. It would be okay.

The restaurant was just off Darling Harbour and the outdoor dining area had palm trees lit underneath by real torches. All the furniture was heavy, rustic wood, too. It was very atmospheric.

"Hey, guys!" I recognised Sarah's voice and looked over the sea of tables for her. She was already up and walking briskly over to us. A big, burly man was following her.

He couldn't have looked any more like a tradie if he tried; he had the shaggy hair, the only-just-barely-dressed-enough-for-dinner look, and a walk that said, 'I do manual labour for a living and check out my real muscles, eh?' He had a bit of a pot-belly, too, but because he was already so stocky it didn't look out of place. His broad smile I recognised from the photos on Sarah's desk.

Sarah had changed for dinner and she was wearing jeans, boots and a big loose t-shirt that fell perfectly everywhere. Beside him she looked incredibly slender and stylish. "Min!" she said, touching my arm like she usually did and standing aside for her boyfriend as he caught up to her. "This is Rob, Rob, Min Lee, my boss, now!" I flinched as she said that, but took Rob's hand when he offered it to me to shake. He was taller than me and his hands were as big as dinner plates. I managed to smile at him, despite how shit I was feeling.

Henry leant forward as well and shook Rob's hand with an incredibly practised, smooth movement. "Henry Lee," he said.

Rob's eyebrows went up. "Oh, 'Lee' as well? Are you two married already? How long?"

"Since birth," I said, and was about to explain that it was just a really common name, but Rob clearly took what I'd said literally.

He just kind of squinted at me. "One of those arranged marriages?" Sarah was already trying really hard to smother her amusement beside him. I watched her, thinking that if I'd been in a better mood, I might have played along to see how far I could have taken that 'arranged marriage' thing.

Henry ruined it, though. "No, no. 'Lee' is just like the South Korean version of 'Smith', there's a lot of us."

"Oh, right," Rob said, and then laughed openly. "Sorry, I'm a bit of a dick when it comes to all this cultural stuff. I grew up in far north Queensland. But don't worry, I didn't vote for One Nation," he added as we started to move back to the table. "So what do you do,

Henry? You remind me of the guy who hires and fires at the mines."

That made Henry laugh. "That's my job in a nutshell," he said. "I'm guessing you don't work in an office?"

Rob held the chair out for Sarah; it was actually very, very cute. She looked delighted, accepting it as he sat down beside her. "Is it that obvious?" He grinned at Henry. "I'm a fitter and turner. I work at Frost Energy up in Broome, FIFO at the moment but we'll see." He put his arm around Sarah.

Henry deliberately copied Rob's chivalrous chair-move with me, giving me a little smirk. I accepted it and sat down, but I felt a bit weird. Henry and I didn't have the sort of relationship where that happened very often and to be honest, I kind of didn't like it. I wondered how much of that was to do with me being stressed and irritable, though.

Sarah caught my discomfort and I shrugged at her. She didn't say anything about it, though, she just leant into Rob's arm. "Rob has got this amazing place up in Broome," she gushed to us. "It's just out of town and it's practically on the beach. I spent all my three and a half months of annual leave up there. It's like a different world, I love it."

My smile fell. Broome? Sarah's long-term boyfriend actually owned a house in Broome and wasn't just up there for work? I panicked for a split second before I remembered that there were no offices out there. I doubted Sarah would be at home in a mining town, so Frost International probably wasn't going to lose her just yet.

While I was stressing about that, Henry was already looking at the wine list and had flipped over to the reds. He didn't drink red. "I hear Broome has some beautiful natural scenery," he said, leading the conversation. I knew what he was alluding to and really wished he would stop trying to look after me, even if he was just trying to be a good boyfriend.

However, in doing so he'd apparently asked the right question because he set Rob off. "It's fucking beautiful, you should see it." His very broad accent was quite entertaining to listen to. "Like, I grew up in a real leafy area, you know? And out west is completely different. You're there and you're like, 'Yeah, I'm definitely in Australia'. The colours, man." He laughed. "Not that I get to see

116

them during the day much, because I'm down the mines from sunrise to sunset."

Hah, *that* I could relate to. "I hear you," I said. "I basically haven't seen daylight since 2007."

Sarah had the wine list out, too. "Min works a bit too hard," she explained to Rob, who had been looking confused and like he was about to ask me if I worked in mines, too. Not the sharpest tool in the shed, apparently, but his big open smile made up for it. I decided I quite liked him, despite the fact I wasn't really in the mood to like anyone.

Henry nodded, smiling briefly at me, "Yes, Min's work ethic is a little intimidating. Though it's why she got flown up here from Melbourne so I can't complain too much about it! How did you two meet, anyway? At work as well?" He was looking back at the lovebirds.

They both laughed and looked a little sheepish. "You go first," Sarah suggested, making an 'after you' gesture with her perfectly manicured hand.

I could feel Henry looking at me as he opened his mouth to speak, and I couldn't resist the urge to mess with him. I spoke instead. "I was an impressionable young intern fresh out of university," I said to them, knowing Henry *hated* the way I told this story. "I didn't know anyone in Sydney when they flew me up here, but, boy, did the guy in HR really take care of me."

Henry laughed nervously. "It didn't happen quite like that, I'd never use my position to take advantage of anyone," he said. "Plus, I wasn't a manager then, and we were friends *well* before anything happened, anyway."

It was just too much fun working him up. "But I *was* up here all by myself... I mean, what would have happened if he'd decided for some reason not to help me? I couldn't risk it. I had to do whatever he said."

Henry gave me a measured stare, and I waggled my eyebrows at him. "Excuse me," he said neutrally to our dinner guests as he turned bright red, and then pretended to strangle me.

They both laughed, and that made me feel better. Sarah flagged a waiter from across the patio. "Just as I suspected, it beats our story. I saw Rob at my local and we only made it as far as his car."

"Yeah, now she's stuck with me," he said, sounding chuffed. He hugged her up against his side so he could kiss the crown of her head. He was so strong that her thick chair actually tipped sideways as he did it. It was like watching a Rottweiler trying to cuddle a kitten. He left his arm around her as we all kept chatting.

After we'd ordered our wine and food and gotten stuck into the complimentary bread, we spoke about our respective hobbies. Rob was a bit of a sports nut—no surprises there—but since neither Henry nor I were at all interested in sport we had to look for something else to discuss.

Sarah sat up in her chair. "Oh! That's right!" She fished around in her pockets for her phone. "Min's like this *mad* artist. What's that website where you put your stuff again?"

I had finally managed to start relaxing, but as soon as she mentioned my artwork, that all faded. The painting of me as a guy was still the first thing in my gallery. I suddenly had *awful* visions about what they would both say if they saw it.

Before I could stop him, Henry told her, "Deviant Art dot com." He smiled at me, obviously not realising that I wasn't just panicking because I was shy about my art. "It's 'Min Lee' with an extra 'e' at the end. She has some *amazing* landscapes on there."

Rob was leaning over to look at Sarah's phone. "You sound pretty proud of her," he commented to Henry.

Henry beamed at me. "You bet."

Just you wait until you hear what they have to say about that painting, Henry, I thought, wondering about the possibility of just running off with Sarah's phone before my profile loaded. I obviously couldn't do anything so melodramatic, so I just sat there bracing myself for their reactions.

"Oh, wow," Sarah remarked as she watched something load on her screen. "I haven't seen this one before, it's great. When did you have short hair? It really suits you." My heart almost stopped; she was looking at the painting. I kept waiting for her to say something about the fact my chest was flat in it, but instead of commenting on anything to do with that, she just looked up at me. Her eyes went straight to my hair, I think trying to judge whether or not it could have grown that much in the months that I hadn't been working with her.

I didn't know how to answer her question, though. How do you say, 'I haven't had short hair since I was fourteen, but I just felt like painting myself as a guy'? I couldn't speak at all; I felt strangely disconnected from everything.

For all that Henry had been subtly annoying me with his over-attentiveness, he did actually rescue me there. "It's been a few years since her hair was that short," he said vaguely, and then shot me a bit of a quizzical glance about why I hadn't answered that one myself.

Sarah looked between us, and then back at the phone. Rob took it from her so he could get a better look. "Fuck, you painted that?" I nodded mechanically. "Jesus. I can't even draw a map of how to get from the airport to my house and it's three roads. That's fucking impressive. What else is there in here?" He started tapping at the screen, presumably flicking through my gallery.

And that was it. There was no shock, no disgust. No anything, really. Rob didn't seem like the sort of person who could diplomatically gloss over a bad reaction to something. So, they thought that painting *was* a genuine self-portrait, and the fact I was clearly cross-dressing in it didn't even warrant a mention. The only thing they'd been judging was the quality of my art. I should have been relieved, but I wasn't. Deep in my gut I felt like there wasn't a more dangerous reaction they could have had than being fine with me in that painting.

It meant I could do it. I could actually do it, I could *be* that cool. I remembered those clothes I'd bought yesterday and how I looked in them. I could do it, I thought, all I'd need to do is cut my hair and deal with my breasts somehow and then *holy mother of fucking god, Min, what the fuck are you thinking*?

Had I forgotten I had a boyfriend? A job? Family? How did I really think that would *actually* go? And it wasn't like I just wanted to cross-dress, either; how the hell did I think I was going to 'deal with' my breasts? Magically make them disappear? God this was so fucked up. And where did it stop? If I somehow 'dealt with' my breasts, *then* what? I remembered fantasising about being a guy punching Canada's lead, and I felt so, so sick. No, *please* no. Please don't let *this* be it.

"Oh, hah!" Rob said really loudly, mercifully distracting me. He

119

looked around as he startled people on nearby tables. "Sorry," he said more quietly. "I'm used to yelling at people in mine shafts. Anyway, you play *World of Warcraft*? I haven't played that in ages."

I guessed he'd found a painting I'd done of one of the locations in the game. "I used to," I said, trying very, very hard to focus on that instead of how shaky I was suddenly feeling. "I don't have the time now. Mainly I just play first person shooters."

"Xbox or PS?" he immediately asked, leaning forward and giving the phone back to Sarah. Sarah rolled her eyes and leant back, a long-suffering smile on her face. She kept tabbing through my paintings while Rob waited for my answer. "I hope you say Xbox, because *Halo* is unreal."

I kind of wanted to hear what Sarah had to say about my art, but I didn't want to be rude. "PlayStation, actually," I said a little apologetically. "Although I do have an Xbox that I never use. And I think I actually have one of the Halos, too."

"Is it *Reach?*" he asked. "Fuck that was good. I never stop replaying that. I tried to get Sarah into it, but no dice." He hugged her.

"Not a game person," she said, looking up from her phone. "Sorry, guys! Although it's pretty hilarious watching him flip out when he gets killed."

Rob looked indignant. "Which is hardly ever," he said, puffing out his thick chest. "I'm a pro."

Henry had been watching me with a smug grin. "That sounds like a certain someone I know."

I scoffed, feigning being absolutely fine. "You're just jealous you can't beat me."

For all Rob looked like a bit of a simple creature, he had some great things to say about various game series. It was particularly amusing to sit and listen to him rant about what he didn't like about *Grand Theft Auto* and why the franchise was 'losing its way'. I wasn't a big fan of the series myself—I hadn't even finished the last one—but what he was saying made me want to play it again to see if he was right. That, and listening to him meant I didn't have to think about myself.

He didn't stop when our food arrived, either. In fact, he quickly forgot about his dinner. Henry had asked him some questions about the Arkham series and he needed to passionately list all the ways in which it had ruined one of the characters.

I wasn't really that big a fan of that universe, so I'd been picking the bits of food I liked out of my pasta and half-listening as I tried not to let my mind wander. Sarah had been eyeing off Rob's food, but every time she'd tried to ask him for some, he hadn't noticed because of how loudly he was speaking. The last time she tried, I made eye-contact with her and we both laughed silently.

I lifted my fork and made a very subtle gesture with it towards Rob's plate, mouthing, 'Go on'. I looked up at him deep in conversation with Henry.

She smirked, and reached carefully under his arm to steal a prawn. He didn't notice, and I pretended to applaud her. While the boys were talking, Sarah slowly escalated her food stealing until she just took his plate and said casually, "Mind if I take this for a sec?"

He sat back automatically to let her, still talking to Henry, but halfway through her putting it in front of herself, he double-took. "Hey!" he yelled, again startling the other patrons around us. "I've got a figure to maintain." He patted his pot-belly with a grin. The two of them proceeded to play tug-o'-war with the plate. He let her win, but she gave it back to him, anyway. I laughed right the way along with them until they leant in and started kissing. Then I stopped.

Henry and I just kind of sat there awkwardly, not looking at each other. Under normal circumstances I might jokingly have given Henry a really exaggerated kiss, but I just couldn't face doing that right now. I kept thinking about the whole cross-dressing thing, and worrying about what would happen if Henry found out. I sighed, took my wine, and poured it down my throat.

Rob caught the movement out of the corner of his eye and stopped kissing Sarah. "Whoa, did you just drink all of that in one go?" I looked from him to the empty glass, and swallowed. He was clearly impressed. "Respect," he said with conviction. "I dated a girl up on the mines who was the same. She could do a pint in under four seconds and she drank us all under the table, she was basically a bloke in a skirt. I always thought I'd end up with a tomboy like you guys, you know, with the video games and stuff." While the colour was draining from my face, he looked affectionately at Sarah, and ruffled her beautiful hair. "Somehow I fell for Miss Girly, here, instead. What are the odds?" She gazed up at him adoringly.

They kissed briefly again, while I just sat there with my mouth open. 'Basically a bloke in a skirt'? He hadn't meant it as an insult; in fact, it sounded like he meant it as a compliment. It didn't feel like one, though. I looked down at my own skirt, feeling all that adrenaline that I'd managed to quell before starting to surge back.

The worst part was that he was *right.* Everything just fit into place in my head like a completed jigsaw puzzle. I got it, and it made me feel *sick.*

At what point was I going to actually address how looking like *this* made me feel?

My heart started going again, and I panicked. No. *No.* Not at this point, I thought, not with work. Fuck! Not at this point. I took a few deep breaths while I stared down at my half-eaten dinner and tried to conceal my anxiety. Not now, I couldn't have a personal crisis right now. I had too much going on, I could worry about whatever issues I was having in a few weeks when the project was complete. I just didn't like my chances of being able to cope with this *and* the shit that was going on at Frost. I tried to calmly tell myself that I was probably jumping to conclusions and maybe when work wasn't so crazy it would all make sense. I could deal with all of this much later after I'd had time to think and reflect and *god fucking damnit why wouldn't my heart just chill the fuck out?*

I needed to not be around anyone. "Excuse me for a second," I said as evenly as I could, standing up.

They stopped kissing, and Sarah wiped her mouth. "Sorry, that was pretty inappropriate, wasn't it? I think I've had too much wine." She laughed.

I smiled tensely, stepping away from my chair and heading straight for the restroom.

It was empty, thank god. I went and shut myself in the far cubicle and leant on the door. My heart was pounding in full force, so much so that I could even feel it in my neck.

I can't do this, I thought, over and over. *I can't. I can't do this.* Every possible scenario started to crystallise in my head: Henry and I breaking up over it and me having to go to work every day and see him, me having to leave Frost because of it... or even me just needing to leave Frost anyway because if they didn't respect me now, would they respect me if they found out what I wanted to do to myself? I'd be the laughing stock of the work place, just like high school. They were probably all either laughing or grumbling to each other about me already. What would they say if I just rocked up in a suit? What was I fucking thinking about dressing up like a guy anyway? How the fuck was that going to solve anything? It didn't change reality. It didn't change *the fact I was in this stupid female body*. It didn't change anything, it just fucked *everything* up a hundred times worse than it already was. Why did I want to do that?

And why couldn't I just forget all this, accept that it wasn't possible and just be happy with myself? Why*?*

I leant against the wall and closed my eyes, trying to slow my breathing. Now was *really* the worst possible time ever for me to be flipping out, just when I needed to be able to focus on working really hard. Could it all just fucking go away? Could everything?

The restroom door opened and I stepped against the back wall so no one would guess what I was doing in here.

"Min?" *Henry?*

"This is actually the women's toilets," I pointed out, noting the irony.

He ignored me. "Min, are you okay? You've been in here for a while." I could see his work shoes underneath the door of my cubicle.

I sighed at length; my breath wavered. "I just want to be alone for a few minutes."

The door rattled as he leant on the other side of it. "You've had a few minutes. What's up? Work?" God, he was being so lovely and all I could do was being irritated by it and wish he'd go away.

You want to know what's up? I thought. I closed my eyes and imagined actually being able to say it to him: 'there's something *wrong* with me. Henry, there's something wrong with me. Please, please, make it stop.' Fuck, now I was crying. Could I get any more pathetic?

"Min," he gently prompted me.

I didn't tell him. "I just want to go home," was what I actually said. The depth of resignation in my voice surprised even me.

Henry didn't say anything for a few seconds. In the end, he didn't argue with me. "Okay," he said. "I'll tell them you're not feeling well."

I didn't want to sound like I was crying, but I think I did, anyway. "And... Is there a back way out of this place?"

When he spoke there was so much compassion in his voice that it hurt to hear him speak. "Oh, Min," he said through the door. "I'll sort it out."

There *was* a back way out of the restaurant, and it was through the kitchen. It meant I needed to be herded past a series of chefs, sous-chefs and kitchen hands who all stared at me like I had three heads.

Henry didn't tell me what Sarah and Rob had said about me leaving early, but it didn't matter. I was convinced they both thought I was crazy. This was the *second* dinner I'd walked out of halfway through because of my stupid issues. I couldn't even get a fucking dinner right.

Henry offered to hail us a taxi, but I shook my head. We walked.

Despite having failed to comfort me so far, he still insisted on trying. "Everything just seems worse at the moment because of how much pressure you're under at work," he told me as soon as we were walking alone. "I know you've got a big project running, but I really think for your own sanity you need a week off. Everything will be okay, Min. You just really, really need a holiday."

From myself, I thought. "I can't," I said. "If I blow this it's over for my career."

We'd walked nearly the whole way home before he spoke again. "I know work is one of the main issues here, but are we going to talk about why you left dinner? The timing was pretty specific."

I swallowed. That was the *last* thing that I wanted to do. Not with Henry. "No." When he went to speak anyway, I stopped walking for a moment to accentuate my point. "Please," I said, interrupting him. "I don't want to discuss it."

This time, he pushed me to talk. "Because I know you have some serious self-esteem issues which are linked to how you look, and I know that Rob said you were a—"

"—Henry!" I said, throwing my hands up to stop him from speaking. There was a really raw edge to my voice, and I was too tired to disguise it. "Can you stop being so fucking understanding for like two seconds? You have to be fucking sick of my bullshit by now, you really want to hear more detail about it?"

He watched me, not reacting to what I was saying.

I didn't want to cry again. "Yes, I have some fucking 'serious self-esteem issues that are linked to how I look', and if you knew the half of them you'd run a fucking mile. Do you really want me to go into all of that? *Really?*"

His eyes swept my body and then ended up locked on mine. He took a step towards me. "I want to do whatever makes you feel better, and you're obviously desperate to tell someone," he said, and went to reach towards my face. I shook my head, and he let his hand drop. "And not that I've ever particularly cared what my girlfriends looked like, but I'll say it as many times as you need to hear it: Min, I've always genuinely loved how you look."

I could barely speak, and I lost my fight against tears. "Henry, I just *hate* it."

He held his arms out to present himself, looking down at his shoes for a second and then back at me with a gentle smile. "And look, I'm still here with you, regardless of how much you hate yourself. Or why."

Just that image of him standing there on the side of the road with a gentle, accepting smile. Loving me despite everything. God, it *hurt.*

"I don't understand," I said, and meant it, about everything. About Henry loving *this*, about the fact I was doing so badly at work suddenly, and most of all, how wrong I felt about how I looked now. "I just don't understand anything, and I don't know how to explain it."

"Do you want to try?" he asked me very carefully. I shook my head. "Don't forget I'm a psychologist."

I shook my head again. He respected that, and we just walked home together. He did pause in the door of my apartment as he gave me my handbag, though. "I know you *want* to be alone right now," he said, "but I'm not sure I should leave you alone. You're not in a good place."

I rolled my eyes. "Henry, I'm not going to kill myself."

He looked a little alarmed. "Well, that's good," he said, I think satisfied that I wasn't, "but I meant in general. No one should have to feel like you're feeling and also be alone."

And yet that was exactly how I wanted to be. "I'll be okay," I said. "I'm just going to go to sleep, anyway. I'm exhausted." It didn't look like I'd managed to persuade him, so I added, "Literally, I've had a really long week at work and I'm going to have a shower and then go to bed. I'll feel much better after I've slept. There's no point in you staying."

"There would be a point," he said, but he stepped out of the doorway anyway. "I'm not going to force you, though. I know you like your space. I hope you won't be too upset if I decide to check on you over the weekend, though."

I shook my head. "Goodnight, Henry."

He put a warm hand behind my neck and kissed my forehead. "I'm here for you," he said simply. "Whatever's going on."

I didn't actually end up having a proper shower. I was too exhausted, I just kind of ran the water over myself and then at some point realised I should probably get out.

I had to face myself naked in the bathroom mirror when I was done, and it was *still* so weird. My hair was plastered against my neck and shoulders. I had a vision of myself just going 'fuck everything' and taking scissors to it. They were right there on my bathroom vanity, beside some makeup that I'd left out. I looked down at them for a second. They were new, they'd be really sharp. It would be so easy, I thought, but, *fuck*, who was I kidding? I couldn't do that, I had my job to worry about. In one movement I just swept everything off the vanity and listened to it clatter across the tiles. Whatever, I thought, and went to put on my pyjamas.

The track-pants hadn't come back from the wash, yet, so I just put on the jeans with Henry's big old t-shirt and shut the wardrobe to a reflection of myself in the door. I looked like an 18 year old guy.

"Are you happy now?" I asked the mirror. "Is *this* what you want?"

I watched myself for a few moments, completely not understanding why *this* was how I felt comfortable. In the end I was the same person, so why was how I looked so critically important to me? I exhaled and shook my head. I had no idea how I was going to sleep. Wine might help.

I was so busy glaring down my front that when I went into the kitchen, I'd forgotten about the flowers Bree had gotten me. I looked up just as I passed the kitchen bench and found myself staring straight into the gaping maw of one of the bigger ones.

There was already so much adrenaline in me that it gave me the fucking fright of my life. For about a second I literally thought there was an alien creature jumping at me from the bench.

I'd backed against the oven with my heart going again when I realised that it was actually just a flower. The rest of them were sinisterly lit by the glow coming from the city outside, and because they'd started to die, all their colour had faded and they looked slightly skeletal. Who the fuck *buys* these?

"Fucking Bree!" I said aloud, putting a hand on my chest. Those fucking flowers. Even as I said it I could hear her saying soulfully, 'But it's not their fault!'

God, it was so ridiculous. I ended up drinking a few mouthfuls of red wine out of the bottle while I stared at them and tried to calm myself down. They were hideous, and I kept discovering new hideous things about them as they withered. I remembered Bree had said they'd reminded her of me, and I was feeling pretty fucking hideous right now, so it seemed apt. Shit, and I hadn't replied to her before, either. I should do that quickly unless I wanted to add *another* person to the list of 'casualties of Min's issues'.

I put the wine back in the cupboard and then grabbed my phone from my handbag and went and lay on the bed.

Sarah had texted me, '*Hey Min, hope you're feeling okay. Rob's a bit sick, too! Must have been something in the food. Had a great time anyway, great to finally get you out of the office! See you on Monday!*'

I exhaled at length; at least she didn't think I was crazy. On one hand I was glad I could keep her quarantined from my personal crap, on the other hand I hated lying to her. I closed the message and opened Deviant Art, going straight to my notes.

Bree's latest message just read, "*im sorry if i said something wrong again i didnt mean it :(:(:(pls dont ignore me :(:(:(*"

I took another deep breath. Fuck, I couldn't do *anything* right; now Bree thought I was angry with her, too. To be fair, I *had* been, but it all seemed extremely hypocritical now. I sighed and ran my

127

hand over my face. I wasn't sure I had enough energy to comfort her, to be honest. I was too fucking tired to deal with my own crap, let alone anyone else's. But, in all honesty, I couldn't leave her feeling like that, could I?

I hit reply and thought for a second. *"Sorry, Bree, I'm not deliberately ignoring you! Things are just crazy for me at work at the moment. We'll talk soon."* I read it a couple of times to make sure it seemed chirpy enough, and then sent it.

It took her literally two seconds to reply, *"before we met u used to reply really quickly :(:(:(so like u can say its about work all u want but yeah.........:("*

I had really only been planning to tick the 'replied to Bree' box so I didn't feel like shit about it. I didn't want to start a conversation with her, but the thought of her being heartbroken and thinking I didn't like her was awful. God, she needed to just not open herself up like that to people, she was going to get hurt.

Since I didn't want to be the one to actually hurt her, what should I say to make her stop feeling like everything was her fault? I could make something up, but I'd been grumpy at her for lying to me so that wasn't a great option. On the other hand, I really didn't want to confide in her. I'd have to be vague.

"I've been having a hard time recently over some personal stuff I don't want to discuss. It's not you at all." As soon as I sent it, I regretted it. Why would I share that with a *17 year old?*

She took a bit longer to reply this time, saying, *"hang on a sec im gonna make something for u,"* and leaving me in limbo.

I didn't know how long she wanted me to wait, all I really wanted was to go to sleep and just pretend today had never happened. Unfortunately, she was quite unpredictable and the thin slither of me that didn't just want to go to bed forever was curious about what she was up to.

It took her about five or ten minutes to get back to me, and when she replied, it was with a link and several wink emoticons.

I tapped it, and my media player opened. That made me raise my eyebrows, but not half as far as they went up when I heard her voice blaring out of the speakers of my phone.

"Hey, Min!" she said. "I'm sorry you're feeling like crap, but I bet I know something that will cheer you up!" She giggled. "I don't know how good your Korean is because you sound like a total Aussie, but on the off-chance that you actually speak it, I spent all evening learning something for you. I hope I don't screw it up too much!"

Then, she began to sing.

She was *terrible.* All her high notes were just a little bit flat, and her timing was way off. Despite her abysmal musicianship I could still understand her: she was singing Kpop. A Girls' Generation song, I think, but Kpop always sounded completely generic to me so I couldn't be sure. I had no idea if she knew how bad she was, but she was so darn enthusiastic about it that it was hard to criticise her.

Towards the end of the song, the second-hand embarrassment factor was just so high I ended up with my pillow over my head, laughing from the pain.

She finished off by saying, "Hope I didn't do too badly and I hope you liked it!"

When my phone fell silent, I took the pillow off my head. She hoped she hadn't done too badly? She could *not* have done worse. That was almost a YouTube infamy level of terrible.

I didn't really know how to tell her she was potentially one of the world's worst singers, so I decided not to comment on the song at all. I just typed, "*You're silly ;)*".

"*I know ;) ;) ;)*" was her reply.

I decided to leave the conversation there and get some sleep, and when I leant up to put my phone on the bedside table, I caught sight of myself in the mirror and everything that had happened just hit me again. I flopped back against my mattress and pulled the doona up under my chin. *Whatever*, I thought, *the wine will kick in soon.*

NINE

Because I hadn't gone to bed before ten since I was about eight years old, I did end up wide awake at 3 am after all. And because I was awake in the dead of the night and there was nothing else to do, I discovered I had two choices. I could either lie in bed and rehash yesterday over and over again until I felt like just cleaning up all the wine in my cupboard, or I could get up and work solidly on the framework docs and give myself a fighting chance at getting ahead. God, though, it was early and my eyes hurt as I got up and turned on my laptop. Fortunately, I was too tired to focus on anything except who was buying pink diamonds, so when the sun came up my first thought was, 'Wait a minute, aren't the days getting *shorter?*' It was 7:30 and I was nearly done with the statement.

I was also kind of hungry, but rather than interrupting my work I opted just to push through it and by 10 I had the statement and the target consumers defined. After some deliberation I decided I didn't have time to stress about whether or not Russia was the right direction; leadership was apparently about having to make risky decisions so I just needed to call it. After I'd set up the stupid encryption software on my laptop, I emailed the docs through to everyone's private emails and CCed Jason.

I had sat down on my bed with the full intention of ordering room service to shut my stomach up, except somehow I fell asleep and woke up after midday. I sat upright, feeling fucking *awful* like I always did after daytime naps, and had the misfortune of catching sight of myself in the mirror. I looked like that chick out of *The Ring* if she'd been cast as a guy instead. I put my hair up so I didn't look like I was ready to haunt anyone.

Swinging my legs over the edge of the mattress, I just sat there for a few seconds, slowly remembering everything that had happened yesterday. It felt really far away, like I'd dreamt it all. I hadn't *really* run out on dinner with Sarah and Rob, had I? And that conversation with Henry? All the adrenaline was gone and, even looking at myself in these clothes, I felt numb, as though I wasn't awake enough to hate myself yet.

I looked *so* much like I used to in high school before I started wearing makeup. Without any of it on I seemed younger; I could easily have told people I was 20, or even maybe 18 and gotten away with it. I'd definitely get carded if I tried to buy alcohol looking like this. I swallowed. Younger, and, well, guy-er.

'Bloke in a skirt', Rob had said, and I'd felt that assessment like a tonne of bricks. I knew why, and for a second, I was scared to even *think* about the question. I forced myself to.

Did I actually *want* to be a guy? Like really, not just, 'Yeah, it would be easier'?

In finally just asking myself, I had kind of expected to get a really definite answer. I didn't have one, and I couldn't separate those questions from *oh god what happens if I really do and Henry and Mum find out.* My brain felt like scrambled eggs and as soon as I'd asked myself one question another twenty were waiting to be answered. I settled on, 'I *think* so', and then felt like an idiot for not knowing for sure. The best I could manage was that I liked how I looked in these clothes, I liked how I *felt* in these clothes, and it was a welcome change from hating myself and my reflection.

I stood up stiffly and got a better look at myself in them. Wow, I could seriously pull off the guy look, especially when I tried to. I experimented with different postures and expressions and, feeling a bit disconnected and scientific, analysed the results. I looked quite feminine when I smiled with my teeth—not that I did that very often. Also, the fabric from the t-shirt was brushing on my nipples and when they were hard it was a dead giveaway I was female, too. Men didn't have nipples like this. I thought about that for a second. I actually used to wear a really tight crop-top to the gym downstairs to stop them from standing out so much. I probably still had it somewhere...

I actually did, and I found it when I burrowed all the way down the back of my underwear drawer. I put it on and put the t-shirt back on over it and my nipples were gone, and actually I looked a lot flatter, too. That felt better, I preferred there being absolutely no sign there was anything on my chest at all.

I wasn't sure what to do now, though. What *did* people do when they felt like this?

I went to go get myself a drink of water and fantasised about living alone on a desert island and wearing whatever the fuck I wanted forever and not having to worry about it. I drank half the glass and gave the rest to the evil flowers. Well, I guessed there was no harm in just wearing this stuff around the house, as long as Henry wasn't around. I kind of had been for years, anyway, I'd just never really understood what the appeal was until yesterday.

Ugh, *yesterday*. Just thinking the word was *exhausting*. It did remind me that my team would probably have replied to my email by now, though. I went and sat at my laptop and read through them; my colleagues were all giving me indications of when their components would be done and none of it was before Sunday. Jason had even sent me a one-liner: "*I guess my book came in handy after all.*"

"You fucking prick," I said at the screen, conflicted as to whether I should be flattered by the fact he was saying I had good time management, or pissed off by what a snide bastard he was. At least he might give Diane good feedback about me for once; maybe I wouldn't get demoted to admin after all.

While I was updating the timelines and really struggling to ignore my loud stomach, my phone went off next to me. I checked the screen: Henry. I hesitated before I answered, momentarily panicking about my clothes. Then I laughed at myself. *Min, you idiot*, I thought as I answered it. He can't *see* you, it's a *telephone* call.

I put it to my ear. "Told you I wouldn't kill myself."

He made pained noise. "I'd prefer if you wouldn't joke about that," he said, in his serious voice. "Are you alright, Min? You were in a pretty bad way last night. I hope you slept more than I did."

I sighed internally; it looked like he wanted to *talk* again. Leaning back in my chair, I went to run my hand through my hair. It was something I used to do when I was fourteen, and it didn't work because I had long hair now and it was tied back. My fingers got stuck near my hair-tie and I disentangled them from my hair as I answered. "I slept okay, considering."

He didn't say anything straight away, and there was an unspoken question that kind of hung in the air: he wanted to know what had been upsetting me. My immediate fear was that he'd figured it out and just wanted me to say it for confirmation. He had to have *some* idea, because I'd told him about high school and he *did* know what Rob had said that had upset me. What if he had guessed? Would he know what to do? Actually, that was a stupid question. He would know exactly what to do, he always did. But this wasn't just some client of his, this was his girlfriend. I could just imagine him politely trying to pretend he wasn't upset about the fact his girlfriend had some strange desire not to be a girl anymore.

When he eventually spoke, he didn't ask me what was wrong, he just sounded relieved. "Okay, well, you do *sound* a lot better. Fuck. You have no idea how many times I wanted to just get in the car and show up at your place just to make sure you were alright."

It was completely left field, but at the mention of 'showing up' I smiled at the memory of Bree waiting for me with those *awful* flowers. "Don't forget to figure out what you're going to lie about to get in."

"Min." He didn't sound pleased, which was actually a bit of a surprise. He usually would jump right into joking around with me. I felt a bit guilty.

"I'm sorry," I said quickly. "That was kind of inappropriate. It's okay. I'm okay. I only brought her up because she sent me something *terrible* before I went to sleep last night."

There was a pause. "Terrible how? Is she crossing lines again?"

"No, actually," I said, leaning back towards my laptop and opening Deviant Art. I copied the address and emailed it to him. "Click that," I said. "She made it to cheer me up."

I could her him thumping away at the screen of his mobile. "Shit, it says I can't while I'm on call," he told me. "I'll do it in a sec."

"Okay," I said, still feeling guilty about joking around when he'd obviously been really worried about me. I would have been so lost without him last night, he'd been wonderful. I didn't tell him how much I appreciated him often enough. I really should. "Look, Henry..." I began, feeling uncomfortable, "thank you for being there yesterday. I'm sorry I ruined our evening out by having a mini-meltdown."

He chuckled. It was a quiet, gentle sound. "It's my turn to sound inappropriate," he said. "But I can't hear the word 'mini' now without feeling pangs of hatred for everyone who calls you that." I smiled at that. He sobered. "But, Min, regarding last night... I need to ask you something important. I went home and kept thinking about how you'd brought up killing yourself right out of the blue and just *worried* that the idea was already in your head. You've never mentioned it or joked about it before and it scared me. You'd talk to me about it if you had those thoughts, right?"

At least I could be completely honest. "This time you *are* over-analysing me," I reassured him. "I don't have those thoughts. I just thought it was what you meant about not leaving me alone."

"Okay," he said, and then laughed a little nervously. "Just don't you do it and leave *me* alone, okay?"

Don't you leave *me* alone, either, I thought, looking down at the knees of my men's jeans. God. Please don't figure out what's going on for me and just leave. "I won't, Henry," was all I said.

Fortunately he changed the subject. "Okay. Speaking of alone, I hope you don't lock yourself up and work *all* weekend."

I glanced at my laptop. "I can't anyway," I said. "Because unfortunately I've delegated stuff to my team and I have to wait until they send me their components before I can keep going."

"Good," he said. "Sean's wife's huge baby shower is tonight, which I totally forgot about until Outlook reminded me this morning, and unfortunately I think I'm obliged to go. Would you like to come? It's casual dress, apparently, so that's something."

I looked down at my t-shirt and jeans. How casual? Casual enough for me to rock up in this? Hah. "Yeah, I think I'll give it a miss," I said. "Have fun, though."

He snorted. "Yes, 'fun', that's definitely one word I associate with Sean Frost. At least his wife is quite nice. Well, you make sure you have fun, too, okay? Call your Melbourne friends or your Mum or see Bree or something. Playing multiplayer for twelve hours straight doesn't count as social interaction, especially when you mute everyone."

"Please, I don't play for twelve hours straight," I scoffed. "I stop for food. Actually, speaking of which, I'm *really* hungry now."

He laughed. "I'll let you get to that," he said. "And I'll listen to this 'terrible' thing Bree sent you. Bye, Min. I'm glad you're okay."

I didn't feel very okay, but I did grin at the thought of him listening to Bree's sound file. "Thanks again, bye."

After he'd hung up, I decided to have another listen to Bree's agonising singing so I could imagine what Henry was thinking as he was, too. I clicked the link on my laptop and played it again; god, it was even *worse* through proper speakers. It was all I could do to not just put my hands over my ears and try and sing over her so I couldn't hear it. Despite the fact it was making me laugh, I had to stop halfway through. The bridge of the song had some really high notes that Bree was just spectacularly missing and the pain was too great.

After a minute or two, Henry texted me, *"Oh, dear."* I laughed. 'Oh, dear,' was about right. He followed it up with, *"Oh, and thank her for the handbag tip on getting you to restaurants when you next see her. Much appreciated."*

I groaned. "I don't think so," I said at my phone as I closed media player on my laptop and opened my browser. "I don't want to give her any ideas."

I decided to forgo room service in favour of an enormous cheesy pizza and a garlic bread from up the road, and before I'd ordered, I opened a new Google tab.

I stopped for a second. I wanted to search about the whole man-thing, but I didn't even know the terminology. Was it 'transsexual'? Wow, okay, no, I was *not* searching for that. Fuck, I couldn't even imagine saying that word to Mum, she didn't even like it when I didn't match my lipstick with my blouse properly. Whatever, it didn't matter what it was called because it didn't change anything. I was only going to be like this at home, anyway. Fuck. Time to drown my sorrows in grease.

After I'd ordered it, I had to wait forty-five minutes for them to bring it up. That wasn't really long enough to get any serious gaming in, and I didn't really feel like painting.

I stared at my laptop. I could just do that search.

Since I *really* couldn't bring myself to type 'transsexual', I just typed, *'I think I want to be a guy'*, and hit enter. There were a lot of results from forums and blogs, and I clicked quickly through them. People asking themselves the same question... but they all seemed to be young teenagers. Even people *answering* their questions were teenagers. They were using the term 'transgender' or 'trans' which was happily less clinical, but when they started to discuss 'transitioning' and 'coming out' I could feel my pulse start to race again. Coming out? Fuck that, seriously. *Never.* When I read the terms 'medical diagnosis' and 'surgery' and then saw some pictures of it, that was the final straw—no. Just no. No doctors, no one was examining me or injecting me with anything and *no one* was cutting into me. I'd rather live in limbo forever than that. I closed the tab and sat back in my chair, taking a few deep breaths.

I was 25, not 13 like these kids. They all talked about 'just always knowing they were men'. If that was the case, wouldn't I have known by now if I was like them? I looked down at my jeans. Apparently not, because here I was wearing men's clothes and searching the internet about wanting to be one. I had a sudden thought about how Mum would react if I told her and my throat tightened. She'd ship me off to every therapist in the fucking country, and, regardless of how often Henry sang praises to counselling and psychology, just *no*. I was done with counselling. Henry... fuck. *Fuck*. What would have happened last night if I hadn't had him? God, and *work*. I would be infamous at work, I'd never live it down. It would be worse than high school. No, there wasn't going to be any 'coming out'. I was going to wear my fucking uncomfortable, fucking godawful work clothes at work and I could deal with whatever this man-thing was in the privacy of my own home.

I could feel my pulse in my *hands,* my heart was beating so hard. I was getting so sick of that feeling. Was I going to get like this every time I thought about it? I was going to need a hell of a lot more wine in my cupboard if that was the case. God, it was too hot inside.

I stood up and went out onto the balcony. It actually wasn't any cooler out there because the sun was directly on it, so I came back inside and just stood restlessly in the centre of my living room. I'd lose all of this if work found out, I thought, looking at my home. I couldn't stay living here if I left Frost. Thinking about that made me worry about my timelines again, and *again* I checked to see if anyone had sent me their components but my inbox was empty. I sat and refreshed my mail constantly for about five minutes before I realised that wasn't going to make work magically appear there.

I was stuck until people emailed me their components; stuck stressing about work, Henry, Mum and whatever the hell was going on in my head.

When my eyes fell on those withered, evil flowers, I remembered what Henry had said and had a bit of an odd thought: I could invite Bree over. She was completely crazy and would definitely give me something else to think about, and I'd also be able to boast to Henry that I'd had human-to-human interaction. I hoped the shock wouldn't cause him to drop dead on the spot. Plus, the idea of someone getting *really* excited about seeing me was actually kind of flattering. And, honestly? I'd enjoyed myself last time. She didn't need to stay that long, either.

I'd picked up my phone to message her, but before I sent one I had second thoughts. Goddamnit, I'd need to change back into *those* other clothes. Could I be bothered? Maybe I should just watch a couple of TV shows I'd downloaded, instead. I probably shouldn't be around people now; look at what I'd done last night with Sarah and Rob.

I went and flopped down on my couch with my phone, and just as I'd done so, it vibrated in my hand. There was a notification in the corner of the screen for Deviant Art. Really?

I selected it. It was from Bree. I'd started to think, 'Great minds think alike', and then laughed to myself about using the term 'great mind' to describe Bree. She probably wasn't stupid, but 'ditzy' was understatement of the century. I opened it.

"uh so dont kill me but im in the city and i kinda thought i could come up and say hello??"

I frowned at the screen; she was asking? That was progress. Well, maybe she could come over for a bit after all; those pizzas were really big. *"Okay. How far away are you?"*

"ummmmm..........."

There was a knock on my door.

I sat straight up on the couch, my jaw open. Looking up at the clock, I realised it couldn't be the pizza guy yet, it hadn't even been half an hour. In case I was wrong, though, I jumped up and rushed over to the door, looking through the peephole, and there was a blue eye staring back at me on the other side of it.

I smothered a startled noise and stood away from the door, putting a steadying hand on my chest. I was about to have a go at her for breaking her promise and just showing up, but she beat me to it.

"I'm sorry..." she said meekly through my door. "I promise if you'd have said no I would have just snuck away!"

I groaned and ran a hand over my face. Min, you'd actually been about to invite her, I had to remind myself, 'crazy' is what you *wanted,* remember? I very nearly opened the door before I realised what I was wearing. I needed to change first. "You're going to have to wait out there for a sec."

"Why?"

I sighed at her through the door. "Because I need to hide the body and clean up all these bloodstains," I said flatly, and then rushed off to change while she stood giggling in the passageway.

I rushed into my bedroom, pulled off the t-shirt and jeans and just stuffed them into a shelf in the wardrobe. Pulling on a blouse and my skinny jeans, I was just zipping up the fly as I closed the wardrobe door when I saw myself. My legs looked so weird in these stupid tight jeans. I stopped doing them up halfway, groaned, and then opened the door again to look for something else. I eventually gave up and settled on a cotton skirt because I couldn't leave her out there forever.

I put on as much makeup as I could in a few minutes, and by the time I opened the door, Bree was standing there having a deep and meaningful with the pizza delivery guy, holding the pizza box in her arms.

She looked me up and down with a bit of a strange expression, but then gestured at the delivery guy. "This is Sandeep," she said. "He's a qualified dentist but Australia doesn't recognise his qualifications so he's delivering pizzas for a living."

Sandeep gave me a bit of a pained look. I felt for him as I reached over and took a couple of notes out of my purse which was hanging by the door. "Don't worry about the change," I told him. I figured he'd earned it for keeping Bree entertained. He nodded and then looked at me with pity as he left.

Bree was still busy frowning at me. "Did you seriously go and spend 15 minutes getting dressed and putting on makeup to *eat pizza* with me?" I didn't know what to say to that. "Because, like, I'm flattered, but that's really weird?"

I looked down at her. She really couldn't lecture *me* on clothing. Being Saturday, she wasn't in her uniform, and she'd switched her pleated skirt for what I *assume* should be described as shorts, but I wasn't sure there was really enough material to call them that. And not to say she was chubby — because she wasn't, really, just short — but she wasn't very slender like I was and her thighs had volume to them. That, in combination with her thin scoop-neck t-shirt, looked almost pornographic. How the *fuck* did her parents let her leave home like that? I felt uncomfortable just looking at her.

She noticed my line of sight. "Bit different than a Cloverfield uniform, yeah?" She was grinning. "How do I look?" She did a little turn.

Like you're ready to lap-dance someone. "Older. But not old enough to wear that."

She laughed. "I *still* can't believe you made me wait out here while you put on *makeup.* That's so hilarious." Something occurred to her and she stopped giggling. "Not that you look bad or anything! Although that is kind of *heaps* of makeup. Can you smell that?" She looked down at the pizza box in her hands. "Oh my god, I can't believe you invited me over for pizza! Let's eat. I'm starving."

She ducked under my arm on the doorframe, kicked off her thongs and then went straight into my kitchen. Chuckling to myself, I followed her in there to find her already banging around in my crockery cupboards. She had one of them open and was apparently planning on splitting our pizza between two plates, but instead of taking them she just kind of looked back at me.

"I can't reach," she said, perched on her tiptoes by an open door. "Who puts the big plates *all the way back there*?"

I gave her a smirk and then reached easily over her head, took two plates, and handed them to her.

"Show off," she said, grinning, and then went to split the pizza. I leant back against the counter and watched her trying to separate the slices. She was making a mess of it. "How many pieces you want? Because we can both try to do four each but these pieces are seriously *huge* and if I eat four of them I'm going to be really sick."

I observed her take four slices, anyway. "Should I go and get the bucket?"

She handed me my plate which was laden with garlic bread and pizza, looking determined. "It smells really good. I have to try, I promise I'll stop before I need a bucket. Let's go and eat on the balcony!" She stopped on the way past to pet the evil flowers and then continued outside. I followed her, giving the flowers a bit of a measured stare as I went past.

She'd only taken a few bites of her pizza before she'd discovered the view. "Wow, I can't believe you *live* here!" she said, and then took her phone out of her 'shorts' and took a panorama of the city. "Look, you can see the Harbour Bridge." She pointed at it. I pretended to be surprised and extremely impressed, and she narrowed her eyes at me. "Well, it's exciting to me, okay? I can see a brick wall through *my* bedroom window."

She turned back towards the view and leant her stomach over the balcony. "Whoa, it's *really* far down to the ground," she said. "It makes me dizzy." My grin faded a little; I didn't like her leaning over the edge like that. I put my pizza slice back on my plate as she peered downwards. "Can you imagine falling off the edge? Like what it would be like sailing through the air and knowing you're about to die?"

"Why don't you lean a little *further* over? Then you won't have to just imagine what it feels like." I thought I sounded pretty casual, but Bree looked back at me as if I'd asked her to get down.

"You worried I'm going to fall?" she asked, looking amused. "What am I, like, six?"

"What you are is leaning over the edge of a 26th floor balcony."

She watched me thoughtfully for just a fraction of a second, and then her foot slipped from under her and she lurched towards the railing.

Fuck, my heart stopped. I leapt out of my chair with the intention of trying to grab one of her limbs... and then realised that although the movement had been very sudden, it wasn't something that was likely to propel her over the edge.

Bree stood up straight again and turned so her back was against the rail, giving me a very cheeky grin.

I opened my mouth and then closed it again. She didn't. "You did that on purpose."

Her eyes twinkled. "Did I scare you?"

I looked down at me and then back at my chair. "No, I just suddenly needed to stand up," I said flatly, and then sat back down in it and took a deep breath. *Fuck*.

She looked both delighted and pleased with herself, and then came back to the table and sat in front of her pizza. "So, like, not that I'm complaining at all because it's awesome, but what made you invite me around? Just bored?" She carefully took a big bite.

I swallowed mine. I knew why I wanted her here, but I wasn't going to tell her why. She didn't need to know. "It's all part of my plot to kill you."

She laughed and said through her mouthful, "Nice try, but I saw you about to rush over and stop me from falling."

"Of course," I said. "Your body needs to stay in my apartment so I can feed it to the flowers."

The next sound she made was alarmingly like choking, but then I realised she was laughing. When she saw me panic again, she just laughed even harder and eventually she needed to put her pizza slice down while she got a hold of herself. "Oh my god," she said when she did. "You're so awesome. I have no idea how you say all those things with such a completely straight face, it's great. Those poor flowers, though," she leant back in her chair and looked at them through the open door. "I still feel so sorry for them. It makes me so happy that they found a good home."

"So what brings *you* into the city?" I asked her since she'd stopped laughing at me. "Did you have something to do, or is it just really comfortable sitting against my door?"

She made a face. "It's actually kind of a long story."

I looked pointedly at my plate. I still had three slices and some garlic bread to go. "Well, I have rations. I can go the distance."

Her nose was still scrunched up. "Nah. I just had a really shit day and the end of the story was that I wanted to see you."

Well, I wasn't going to push her to tell me, because I sure as hell wasn't going to tell her why *she* was here. Instead, I held my arms out and looked down at myself. "And now that you can look upon me, is it everything you'd hoped for?"

She giggled again. "Oh my god, you crack me up! I still can't really believe you let me come over. Like, I know you said you'd be friends with me and stuff but you're so, like, I don't know, '*how dare you talk to me*', that I thought maybe you'd just said it to be nice." She took another bite of pizza, looking very content. "You know when you imagine something really great and then it actually happens? Yeah."

I snorted. "All I did was open the door and give you pizza," I said. "If that's what you were imagining, you're really easy to please."

Something passed over her face for a second. "Yeah, I am." She actually waited until she'd swallowed before changing the subject. "Anyway, it's my birthday tomorrow."

Her birthday tomorr— oh, that's right. When I'd first met her she *had* mentioned it was soon. "Happy Birthday for tomorrow," I said automatically. "If you'd told me earlier I would have put candles on the pizza. You going to do anything special?"

She laughed bleakly, and in the process slopped cheese topping all over her t-shirt. Instead of looking distressed about it, though, she just peered down her front and casually scratched at it. "Some of my family is coming over," she said, and then put the cheese she'd picked off her top in her mouth. She saw my expression. "What? I'm not wasting good cheese, and it's not like this tee is *gross* or anything."

I opted not to say anything about the cheese. "You're not going to have a big party for your 18th?"

She shook her head. "My parents don't like me having friends over."

Something about the way she said that didn't invite further questions, so I left it. I found it kind of weird that she apparently had strict parents when she went running around Sydney in little more than her underwear.

Illustrating that point exactly, while I was watching her, she looked down her front and pulled her t-shirt out so she could inspect it for any remaining cheese. In the process of doing so, she showed me her stomach and the bottom of her bra, and the rest of Sydney far too much cleavage.

Jesus, did that girl have no concept of how she looked? "I can see what you're spending today doing," I said neutrally. "Celebrating your last day of childhood dressed in clothes you should have retired when you were five."

She smirked. "I'm so not a child," she said, glancing down at her breasts and grinning as she examined the grease stain from the cheese across the front of them. "And *these* are adult clothes."

"You can say that again." I watched her try and blot the stain with some serviettes. "Bree, are you sure that's the impression you want to give people?"

Bree gave up on her grease stain. "I don't care what impression people get," she said easily. "You only live once, and I really like this top, it's really cute and soft and it lets the air in."

When she went to take another bite of pizza, I sighed. "You're going to ruin your 'cute' top if you don't get that grease stain out now," I said, standing. "Cheese stains are terrible. Come on, I'll lend you a top and we can soak that one."

She put her pizza down. "You just want to dress me like a nun," she accused me, but she followed me inside anyway.

I had only walked into the bedroom to find her a new top, but when I turned to ask her if she'd mind sleeveless, she'd already whipped her top off and was holding it scrunched in one hand.

Her bra was too small, too, and her big breasts were spilling out of it. "Jesus, Bree!" I said, turning my head sharply away from her. "You could have at least waited until you had something to put on instead!"

She sounded indignant. "It's not like it's nothing you haven't seen before, you're a girl too!" she said, but as she said that, something occurred to her. In the reflection of the wardrobe, I could see her giving me a *really* weird look. I chose to ignore it.

I was busy sorting through my tops for something small enough to fit her and yet something she couldn't accidentally ruin when she spotted something in one of my shelves and finally stopped staring at me. "Cool!" she announced and went for it.

Before I could stop her, she'd pulled out my men's jeans and was holding them out to admire them. She was so short that the hips of my jeans came up under that pornographic bra of hers. The colour drained out of my face. Even if those jeans had had a big Mars symbol painted across them, they couldn't have more obviously been from the men's department.

She didn't seem to care about that. "Wow, these are *way* cool. This is more like the stuff I kind of imagined you'd wear. They're yours, right?" She looked up at me for confirmation.

On the tip of my lips I was about to say, 'No, they're my boyfriend's', but then I remembered how angry I'd been at her for lying to me. I considered doing it anyway, but I found myself at an impasse. I didn't say anything, I just felt sick.

"Put them on!" she said, and I could hear the excitement in her voice. "They are *so* much cooler than that skirt. I don't know why you dressed up for me, anyway. It's stupid. I don't want you to feel like you have to be super formal around me or anything. You can be comfortable, I don't mind!"

She walked up to me to give me the jeans. I didn't take them from her. "Actually, I'm pretty comfortable now," I managed to say. I wasn't sure how convincing I was, though.

She wasn't fazed. "Okay, well, do it for me? I want to see how they look. My brother would be *so* totally jealous, they're such an awesome brand."

For just a second I was tempted; what she'd said earlier, the 'you only live once, and I really like this top' was fresh in my mind. But then I thought about what I'd Googled, and remembered all the surgery and doctors and psychologists and I... couldn't. I just couldn't. I didn't want *anyone* to think I was like that, even if maybe I was. I felt like if I put them on it would be like opening a floodgate and just by looking at me she would know. But I couldn't say anything, I just kind of stood there like a fucking idiot with this topless 17 year old pushing men's jeans into my stomach.

After a few moments, she gave up and stood back. She was directing me that really strange stare again, and I didn't know what to make of it. She probably thought I was a fucking head case, and she was right. Fuck. Why did I think it was a good idea for me to be around people, again? I needed to go be a hermit in a cave somewhere.

"Min," she said carefully. Her eyes were dipping between mine and my chest. "I want to say something but I'm scared I'll say the wrong thing and you'll be really upset again."

I felt numb. "Just say it."

Her brow was actually shaking. "Are you, like, actually a guy? Like, is that your secret?"

I didn't think I'd heard her right. "What?"

She looked uncomfortable. "You know, like, are you just pretending to be a girl?"

I just stared at her for a second. I didn't know if she'd guessed or not, but I panicked anyway. "What makes you think that?"

She looked upset as she counted off reasons on her fingers. "Like, okay, on Monday I *swear* you had boobs. Like not big ones or anything, but definitely boobs, and today..." She looked at my chest; I was still wearing that crop top and it flattened them out. "So maybe you were wearing those chicken-fillet-type things flat girls wear. And you won't hug me, and it's like, what are you afraid of me feeling? And then you needed to go and spend like twenty minutes

144

putting on a drag-queen-level makeup before you'd let me in and then I find these boys' jeans in your cupboard, and you're totally uncomfortable with me showing any skin and you won't change in front of me..." She ran out of fingers. "And you're *really* tall for girl, and you look so ultra-super girly like those pretty Thai ladyboys who are, like, *way* more beautiful than female women are..." She looked distressed for a second. "Was that a really awful word to use? 'Ladyboy'? I never know the right way to say anything. Just pretend I said all of that but I used the right words, okay?"

I didn't even know where to start. She thought I was physically a boy? Fuck, that would have made life a hell of a lot fucking easier. Female woman? 'Drag queen' makeup? God, it all hurt so much that it got to the point where it didn't.

She took a step back, like she was afraid I was about to yell at her or hit her. "Because it's okay if you are secretly a guy. I'm not, like, hardcore religious or anything, I don't mind, I won't tell anyone!"

It was just so fucking ironic that the only thing I could do was laugh, and that made her look even more scared. Fuck, all I could do was laugh!

"You're scaring me," she said, looking tiny. She was still just wearing that bra and those shorts.

I tried to stop laughing. "I'm sorry," I said, sitting back down on the bed so at least I didn't tower over her. "No, I'm not 'actually' a guy." After I'd said that I decided it didn't ring true to me, so I tried to think of a different way to describe it. "I mean, yeah, my body's the same as yours." She didn't look like she believed me, though, because her eyes kept going back to my chest. "I'm not showing you, Bree," I told her firmly.

"If it's not true, then why are you being so weird?"

I closed my eyes. "I can't even begin to tell you. Fuck," I said, shaking my head. It eventually ended up in my hands.

I felt the bed give as she sat down beside me, and I could see us in the reflection of my wardrobe door. The only other person who'd been on this bed was Henry, and compared to him she was so little. Compared to *me* she was little. She didn't give me much time to think about that at all, though, because she had already come up with another theory. "Well, did you, like, *used* to be a guy?"

I threw my hands up. "Oh my god," I said, and then I started laughing again. "No. Bree..." What do you even *say* to that? The truth actually seemed far less dramatic than everything she was coming up with. Even still, I couldn't say it straight away. I was surprised I could even say it at all, since I hadn't managed to say it to Henry. Henry didn't often look so close to tears as Bree did now, though. She was hanging on my every word.

"It's just that I think I'm supposed to be a guy," I told her. I sounded far more definitive than I felt, though, so I added, "Maybe. I don't know. It's difficult to think about."

There was a long silence. I didn't look at her, and I didn't look at the reflection in the wardrobe. I didn't even know what was going to happen until I felt a pair of arms around my shoulders. "Oh."

"'Oh'?" I asked her, looking across at her. She had her head on my shoulder and all I could see was a mop of blonde curls that smelt like vanilla shampoo.

She looked up. "Well, I wanted to say something nice because I can see you're really worried about it, but I couldn't because I don't see what the big deal is," she said. "If you want to be a guy, just go for it?"

If only it were that simple. "But how do I 'just go for it'? My life's already set up. I can't just, I don't know, get some injections and then tell everyone I'm a guy and expect nothing except my voice to change." And I wasn't even sure I *wanted* injections, anyway, because then I'd get hairy and I didn't like the idea of that at all. Fuck, maybe that meant I *didn't* want to be a guy? Or was I just scared of making changes that would mean I wouldn't be able to put on a skirt and keep pretending to everyone that everything was fine? There were just too many questions to even start to answer them all. Where did you start with this stuff?

Bree's eyes widened as she thought of something. "Are you going to get a dick?"

Those surgery photos, *oh my god*. My heart sped. "I actually don't want to think about that now." Or at all, ever. Instead of dwelling on the pictures I'd seen, I looked across at her next to me. She still had an arm around my shoulder, and she was deep in thought. "How are you okay with this?" I asked her. "It's so fucked up."

She looked surprised. "Uh?" she said. "It's actually kind of interesting, and I told you, I'm not some psycho religious nut or something. If you want to be a guy, then *que sera sera*? And anyway," she gestured at the women's clothes I was wearing. "You looked better in the painting than in these. Not that you're not a cute girl or anything," she hurriedly added. "You're totally cute. But, yeah. So are you going to put them on?" She placed the jeans in my lap.

This time I accepted them and sighed.

"And take off all that makeup, too," she instructed me as she sat back. "It's weird. I don't like it."

Bree. "Okay," I said, and stood with the jeans. I grabbed the big faded t-shirt from the wardrobe and then pointed at it. "Just look in there and see if you can find something that will fit you. Nothing that looks too expensive, please."

I went into the bathroom and slid the door shut. My reflection stared at me from the mirror.

Well. That wasn't at all what I imagined would happen when I thought about telling someone; there wasn't even any hint of disgust or judgement in her. It was actually a bit of an anti-climax. I wasn't stupid enough to think that everyone would be like she was—the world would be a pretty scary place if everyone was like Bree—but it was at least a little bit comforting. I changed into the jeans and t-shirt.

Once I was dressed, I filled the hand basin with water, tied my hair back, and just washed all my makeup off. Then, drying my face and neck, I looked up at the mirror again. I wondered what her reaction to this would be. I looked *very* different.

When I went back out into my bedroom, Bree had found my new comfy hoodie and put it on. Hilariously, on her it came down to her knees and the sleeves dangled almost as far. She was lying on my bed in it waiting for me, but she sat up as soon as I walked in. Her face lit up. "Yeah!" she said, leaping up and bouncing over to me, long sleeves flopping everywhere.

I felt a bit self-conscious. "Yeah?"

"Yeah," she said with conviction, and inspected me from all sides while I just stood there. "Wow, you really look like a guy, especially with your hair back. That's fucking crazy, because like five minutes

147

ago you were the girliest girl in Australia. Anyway, this is *way* better. I prefer you like this."

Me too, I thought, and then stressed about Mum, Henry and work.

"So, like, you want to go for a test drive? We could go shopping or something."

Fuck, no. "Not going to happen," I said firmly. "I'm not leaving my home in these."

She looked a bit disappointed. "Okay," she said, and then shrugged. "I kind of want to finish my pizza anyway."

After I'd put talcum powder on her stained t-shirt to soak out the grease, she lead me back out onto the balcony. We sat there and ate and chatted—about what I have *no* idea because I was running on autopilot—until I'd made my way through two slices and was attempting the third. Bree had barely managed two. "You might need to get that bucket after all," she joked as she held up the third slice and looked apprehensively at it.

"You could just not eat it," I pointed out.

She looked at me like I was crazy for suggesting such a thing. "I'm going to do it," she said stoically. "I am."

"Good luck, then," I said and then laughed openly at her expression.

She didn't end up taking a bite because she put her pizza down to stare at me. "You look really great when you're not so uptight," she said, and then out came her phone.

However relaxed I had looked, I stopped looking that way immediately. I threw up my hands in front of my face and looked away from her. "No, Bree," I told her as she pointed it at me. "No photos, not of this. Please."

"But I want to show you how good you look now," she said, sounding a little disappointed. "I think you'd really like it."

I probably would, but I really didn't want anyone having any sort of photographic evidence of this. A painting was one thing, actual photos were another, and Bree seemed like the sort of person who'd make bad choices about who she'd showed them to and where she'd upload them. I couldn't risk anyone finding out. "Bree, *no.*"

"I won't, I won't," she said a little forlornly. "I'm sorry."

When I saw her expression, I winced; you'd think I'd just run over her new baby kitten. Listening to her sing had nothing on how painful it was to look at her when she was upset. I could hardly bear it. I leant across the table and did a 'gimme' motion towards her phone. Perhaps I could do something else for her, instead.

Looking surprised, she passed it over to me and I fiddled with it. She watched me. "What are you doing?"

I pressed a button, and then looked up at her and waited.

In the living room, my mobile rang. "Happy Birthday," I said easily, cancelling the call and handing her phone back to her with a smug grin.

Her disappointment transformed into delight in the space of half a second. She stood up to accept the phone from me. "Did you just *put your number in my phone*?" she asked, in the same tone as she might ask if daddy just bought her a sports car or her team just won the Grand Final.

"Don't text me constantly," I told her sternly, but there may have been a smile on the corner of my lips. "That's my work phone, too."

She wasn't at the stage where she could listen to instructions yet. "Did you just put your number in my phone?" she asked me again, and then came to dance around me, shrieking. "Oh my god!" I couldn't not laugh as she literally bounced around my chair. She stopped as suddenly as she started, though, and then looked extremely serious. "I have to hug you now," she told me gravely.

"You hugged me before," I pointed out. "That's your quota for today."

She swatted my face with an empty sleeve. "I can't tell whether you're joking!" she accused me. "It's stressing me out. Just stand up so I can hug you!"

I rolled my eyes and stood, exaggerating my reluctance. I actually didn't mind; she'd touched me so much already I think I'd begun to develop an immunity to it. As soon as I was up she flung her arms around my middle and squished the air out of me. I coughed. "You're really thin," she said into my ribs, her voice muffled by my t-shirt. "Like, really."

She couldn't talk, she was so short I couldn't even hug her properly; my arms rested on her shoulders. "That's a pretty bold statement for someone who's not even a whole person to make."

"Shut up," she said into my ribs. "It's not my fault. My mum is like four foot ten or something. Besides, I only seem ultra-short because you're *huge*." She looked up, panicking. "I didn't mean it like that!"

I expected it to hurt, but it didn't. I just pushed her head back into my stomach to shut her up, anyway. "If you're not careful I *will* feed you to the evil flowers."

As she giggled into my t-shirt, I was struck for a moment by how normal this all was. We were just joking around like we had been before, and the fact that I now looked like a guy and was wearing guy's clothes didn't matter. It didn't even matter that I had no idea what I wanted to do with what was under my clothes, either. The sky hadn't fallen in, the world hadn't stopped turning. Though Bree was hardly Henry, or Mum, or anyone at work, it was still reassuring. I was suddenly really glad she'd lied to me.

"You're breathing funny," Bree told me, and I looked down at her.

Probably, I thought, *I'm high on pizza and garlic bread*. I didn't joke this time, though, I just tried to decide if I really wanted to explain to her why I was feeling so good. I might as well. I'd come this far, right?

"You're the first person I've told about me. And instead of being fucking horrified, you're hugging me."

She hadn't been expecting me to be serious, and the look she gave me... Wow. "Can today be my birthday instead?" she asked in this tiny little voice. "There's no way tomorrow can beat this."

I ruffled her curls and peeled her off me. "Come on, let's eat ourselves into a stupor and watch bad TV," I suggested. "If you're *really* nice to me I might draw you an actual birthday present."

"Oh my god, are you serious?" she asked, galloping after me as I took the rest of our pizza inside so I could set up my laptop. "Are you fucking serious? Just tell me what I need to do!"

I set myself up on the floor with the laptop and tablet and while I was scribbling away on it, Bree leant over the edge of the couch and dropped crumbs all over me and into my hair. I'd drawn a rectangular shape and was choosing colours and levels when she realised what I was painting.

"You're going to draw an *actual* present?" she said, giggling. "Like a wrapped present?"

I picked a few colours for the ribbon. "Yup," I said. "What colour would you like for the wrapping paper?"

She brushed some of the crumbs off the top of my head. "Sorry," she said sheepishly, and then answered my question. "I don't care about the wrapping paper, I want to know what's inside it!"

I held up the tablet so she could see it better. "What do *you* think's inside it?"

She gave me a look. "You're the artist, you tell me!"

I shook my head. "Don't you know anything about art? It's all about the viewer's interpretation," I joked, and then chuckled as she flopped me with a sleeve again.

"Fine," she said, rolling onto her back on the couch so her head hung upside-down next to mine. She watched me down over her forehead. "I think you bought me some new clothes."

I laughed at her, and we went backwards and forwards guessing what might be inside until I'd finished the painting. The suggestions got slowly more and more absurd until Bree was insisting that I was buying her a carpet python. "That'll go with the evil flowers," I told her. "All I need now is a hairless cat and my collection of evil familiars is complete."

I pulled the laptop onto my actual lap to upload the painting to Deviant Art, when I noticed an unread email icon down the bottom of my screen. It was from one of my team members, and it had an attachment.

My heart sank. I had work to do.

For about ten seconds, I considered not mentioning it and not doing anything about it. I was enjoying myself and didn't actually want to start working again just yet... but then I remembered yesterday. Yesterday I'd been practically having a breakdown about my workload and how behind we'd been, I didn't have the luxury of leaving the docs an hour or two so I could be silly with Bree.

"I thought you were uploading the painting?" Bree asked me, sitting up.

I took a deep breath and then released it. "I just got an email from someone at the office," I told her, feeling myself deflate. "I'm going to need to do some work now."

"Oh..." That girl could put so much emotion in a single syllable. She sounded *so* disappointed. "I'm going to have to go, aren't I?"

I nodded slowly. "I'm sorry, Bree. Work is insane at the moment." I pushed myself up off the ground and put my laptop on the table. "Thanks for coming, though."

"Thanks for having me," she said automatically. "And thanks for the pizza and the carpet python in a box."

I grinned, ducking into the bathroom to see if her t-shirt was doing okay. "If you'd given me more warning I could have bought you a real present," I called back to her. The talcum powder hadn't soaked up all the oil yet, and her top probably should be washed properly. I could get room service to do that.

That made her perk up. "Really? You'd buy me something?" she asked me as I went back into the living room.

"Sure," I said, looking out towards the balcony. "I'll give your t-shirt back to you next time I see you, it's not done yet. It's still light, are you okay to catch the train home? I can always drive you if you're not."

She stood up, still in my hoodie. "Yeah, I probably won't go home straight away," she said, and then pulled the hoodie off to give it back to me. She wasn't wearing anything except the bra underneath, and it was still a shock seeing that much of her. I didn't say anything about it this time, though, I just went and grabbed her the first cotton top I found in my drawer. I handed it to her and she pulled it on, being uncharacteristically quiet. It was so big on her it covered more of her thighs than her 'shorts' did.

"Happy Birthday for tomorrow," I said to her at the door as she put her thongs on. "We can have a drink next time I see you, right?"

"Hah," she said flatly, and the stood in front of me. "At least you have to see me again. You promised to buy me a present *and* you have my t-shirt. You have to give it back."

I shot her a half-grin. "Yes, that's definitely the only reason I'd want to see you again, Bree."

She actually blushed. "Okay," she said, giving me a quick hug. "Don't actually buy me a carpet python, though."

I laughed. "Got it. It would probably just eat you anyway," I said as I showed her out and we said our goodbyes.

Once she was gone, I sat down in front of my laptop and just stared at the email. I *really* didn't feel like working, but I also didn't feel like having any more meltdowns over being behind in the project, either. Not with everything else I had going on with me.

I downloaded the component and read it through. It was from that young guy in the team, and the quality of it was *terrible*. I put my head in my hands for a moment. It was going to be a *long* night.

TEN

After a full weekend of dressing exactly how I felt comfortable, I wasn't prepared for how difficult it was to face my work clothes on Monday morning. I hadn't even thought about it because I'd been putting them on for five years, but now here I was, standing with my wardrobe open, taking ten minutes to talk myself into putting on a proper bra. I'd never liked bras, but I guess I'd always just figured they were an unavoidable part of being female. Now, it was like a switch had been flipped. I was looking at this lacy black bra in my hands asking myself, 'why the hell would I wear *this?*'

When I'd finally managed to get it on and put a blouse over it, looking at the shape of my breasts in the mirror felt really strange and uncomfortable. I felt exposed. I felt like people could see something I didn't want them to and I had to spend a good minute or two convincing myself not to take everything off so I could just put the crop-top on underneath. All my summer work blouses were floaty and thin anyway so even *with* the tight crop-top you'd be able to see I had breasts.

The skirts were a different matter. I did actually own a pair of work pants, but they were tailored to give me the illusion of curvy hips. Mum had had them made for me and I'd only kept them because I was terrified one day she'd demand to see me in them. I'd never liked them, but I put them on anyway and then inspected myself. Not surprisingly, they gave me curvy hips. I made a face at my reflection; I preferred the way my hoodie narrowed me out. Still, I couldn't manage stockings today, so pants it was.

Then I did my makeup, slipped on a pair of heels and rushed out the door.

I made slower progress than usual to work because I'd run out of bandaids and without stockings I kept reopening my blisters. Furthermore, all the reflective surfaces I normally needed to brave on the way to work seemed to have multiplied over the weekend. Looking at myself from every angle like this was depressing, I hated it. Whatever I ended up privately deciding I was, it definitely wouldn't be *this*.

It was early when I got to the office and none of my team were in yet. I could see the light on in Jason's office so I thought I'd stick my head in there.

"Sorry to bother you," I said, knocking on his open door as I entered. "Did you get a chance to have a look at the Pink docs?"

Jason turned his attention from the screen to me, and gave me a very obvious once-over. If I thought I was going to be able to forget about my body today, boy, was I wrong.

"Mini in *pants,*" he said, ignoring my question. "I didn't even know you owned pants, I don't think I've seen you in anything except a skirt in five years. Must be hard to find pants long enough with those legs, hey?" He laughed at himself.

There probably wasn't anything else this man could possibly do that could make me dislike him more than I already did. "I felt like a change," I said pleasantly, instead of telling him he was a fucking prick and suggesting alternate places he could shove his observations. "So, did you get a chance to read the framework and what we've done with the requirements so far?"

His laugh tapered off and he nodded. "I did, it's not too bad," he leant back in his chair, considering me. "I like your reasoning, Russia looks like a good direction and there's definitely a market for ridiculously expensive jewellery over there. The upper class is just drenched in oil and mineral money. Did you know the minerals department have trade partners in Vladivostok and Moscow?" I shook my head. "Speak to Frost Energy about getting some leads for buy-ins there. I'll forward you an email from the guy you need to meet with. He'll probably know people who know people. Be discreet when you set up meetings, though; don't put any details in writing." At my nod, he remembered something and added, "And for fuck's sake do something about that kid in your team." He sounded annoyed. "What's his name? Ali? Mohammad?"

He had to be fucking kidding me. "It's '*John*'," I said, discovering there *were* actually things Jason could do to make me dislike him more.

"Yeah, whatever," he said dismissively. "Anyway, he sent that last component unencrypted and that's just not good enough."

I winced. I hadn't noticed, but it didn't surprise me. It was frustrating that Jason had been the one to pick up on that, though, because I'd rather have been on top of that issue myself. "Will do."

As I was leaving, he stopped me. "Oh, and Mini?" I turned back toward him. I couldn't tell if he was going to say something serious or not. "You did a great job of turning the project around on the weekend. But let's make sure we stay on track, yeah?"

I kept expecting him to finish off with a snide jab at me, but he didn't. He just went back to whatever he'd been doing before I'd called in on him. That actually just made me angrier, because the fact that he'd complimented me made me felt really proud. I shouldn't enjoy getting the approval of pricks like Jason, but apparently I did. Bastard.

I'd gone back into Oslo and sat at my desk, conflicted as to whether I wanted to be angry at Jason or relieved that the project was on track again. In the end, my relief won out.

My meltdown last week apparently hadn't ruined everything for us after all. We were making good time if Jason thought we were up to the point of scoping contacts; contacts were just one step away from setting up pitches, and that meant we might actually have signatures right after Easter. There was a good chance I could avoid fucking this up if I could just keep my head together and make good use of my time.

There were no clocks in Oslo—on purpose, I think, so we couldn't gaze at them and lament all the hours of our lives we were losing—so I took my phone out of my handbag to check what time it was. If it was before 8:30 I could probably go downstairs and buy Henry some sort of pastry to thank him for being wonderful. As I glanced at the time I noticed I'd gotten a text message.

Bree, I thought, feeling even better. I opened it. *"so ive picked like the top 3 places id go if i had to run away....have u been to new zealand canada or sweden???"*

I grinned. I had actually been to Canada a number of times on business, but I'd never been able to see any of it because I'd spent the whole time working. I didn't think that was her point, though. *"I take it your birthday went well, then?"*

"i saved u some cake. can i bring it over before it goes gross??? :) :) :)"

I sat back in my chair. I *really* needed to focus on my work, but since it had been her 18th and she was hinting at it not having been so great... well, I supposed I could make an exception, maybe just an hour or so. She'd been over on the weekend and I'd still managed to get everything done, after all. *"Okay, but I won't be home until after six, and an hour at the max because I'll still have a lot of work."*

"did u buy me that present yet??? :) :) :)"

I groaned. Did she think I just sat around looking for stuff to do? *"I haven't had time to, and if you want to come over tonight I won't have had time to, either."*

"Must be a pretty interesting conversation," a woman's voice said from behind me. She sounded like she was smiling. "'Morning, Min."

The suddenness of it got my adrenaline pumping; I hadn't noticed anyone come in. It was just Sarah. "Jesus, you scared the hell out of me!" For a moment I was relieved, and then I remembered I'd run out on her and Rob on Friday.

She slung her handbag off her shoulder into her drawer, looking kind of smug. "Why, what were you afraid I'd see you doing?" she said, grinning at me. "Something naughty? You look guilty enough."

I blushed, which was stupid, because I *wasn't* doing anything naughty. "Yeah, nothing naughtier than making birthday plans with friends," I said. "God, and you interrupted us just as she was about to describe her cake to me!"

Sarah had a big smile on her face as she rummaged around in her bag for her purse. "Hah! I'm guessing you're feeling better, then? You didn't look great when you got up from the table on Friday."

That. The memory of it didn't make me feel that great, either. I hoped I looked as apologetic as I felt. "Yeah, I'm sorry I disappeared on everyone like that," I said. "I was feeling pretty crap."

She shrugged. "Rob wasn't great either, actually. If anyone's sorry it should be me for choosing a place that made everyone sick!" I felt bad about letting her believe that, but there weren't many other options. "You can choose somewhere next time," she said, finding her purse and then standing up. "And by the way, Rob *loves* you. He was bothering me all weekend before he flew out to invite you over for games and I had to explain to him that some of us have work to do."

I laughed at that. "We can do that next time he's in town, I guess. He's great."

She immediately dissolved into a mushy smile. "Isn't he just? I don't think I've ever met a nicer man. I get that he's not Einstein, but it doesn't matter. He's everything else." She remembered something and cringed. "Also, by the way, sorry for basically making out in front of you. I keep forgetting how bad I am on alcohol."

I was still snickering at the Einstein comment. "It's okay. I can't be certain, but I'm pretty sure it was just the food that made me sick."

"I did wonder," she said, grinning again. "But I didn't think we were *that* disgusting! He wasn't groping me or anything."

At the mention of groping my eyes darted downward on her. I wished they hadn't, because *her* curves were all deliberately on display and looking at them made me self-conscious. She was clearly so comfortable with who she was and that was in stark fucking contrast to how I felt. Fuck, she was so lucky. She probably didn't even know how lucky she was. I liked her, though, so I couldn't really resent her for it.

Unfortunately, she caught me looking and craned her neck downward. "Don't tell me I've put this top on inside out again."

I think I might have gone a bit red. "No, I was just looking at what you're wearing."

Her eyes went straight to *my* body, and she seemed to think she understood. "Oh, because you're wearing pants for once? Yeah," she looked down at her own pants. "I can't be bothered with stockings most of the time. I like how sexy they make me feel but I always seem to catch them on stuff and rip them."

Sexy was something I'd *never* felt in stockings, not a single day in the five years I'd been wearing them. I'd never felt even slightly sexy in these clothes. The thought of needing to wear them every day until I retired was exhausting. 35 more years of feeling unsexy and weird. The eternity of that number was *so* depressing.

She had her hands on her hips and was watching me a little too closely. When I realised, it made me nervous. "Min, is something up? I didn't really want to say anything, but you've been kind of off-colour since I came in."

I had no intention of telling her; she was the only person I actually liked at Frost aside from Henry. Oh, and speaking of him, I'd actually been on my way downstairs before I'd gotten Bree's message and Sarah had rocked up.

"Just stressed out, I think," I said dismissively, and reached into my bottom drawer to grab my purse. "I'm just going downstairs to buy something sweet for Henry. You want a coffee?"

She didn't press me for an answer, which I appreciated. "Okay," she said, still giving me a bit of a sceptical look. "I was just going to get an energy drink, but I'll come for the walk."

I ended up buying Henry a custard Danish, and when I went to visit him in HR, Sean Frost was sitting on the edge of Henry's desk playing with a gun-shaped stress ball I'd bought Henry a couple of years ago. Henry was trying his best to look calm and professional, but I didn't miss the pinch at the corners of his mouth. When he spotted me in the office, he looked markedly relieved. "Min!"

Sean looked up at me, too, and flashed me a friendly smile. I nodded politely at him. "I hope I haven't interrupted anything. The door was open."

Sean shook his head. "No, you're fine. I'm about to head off anyway."

Henry seemed just about ready to push Sean out of the door himself. "Pants," he commented as I walked around the table to him, leaning back in his chair for a moment to inspect them. "You look lovely, they really suit you. Change is as good as a holiday, right?"

Those compliments made me uneasy. I didn't feel like they suited me, I didn't *want* to look 'lovely', and if he only knew the type of changes I wanted to make... He was just being nice, though. Like he always was. Sarah wasn't the only one with a great boyfriend. On that note, I handed him the paper bag with the Danish in it. "I bought you some breakfast," I said. "I know it's not low-fat muesli, but it's better than nothing, right?"

He chuckled. "Thank you," he said, accepting it and peeking inside. "Ooh! Now that's definitely more interesting than muesli. Thanks for thinking of me, Min." He smiled up at me and patted my hand. That smile... fuck, he was wonderful. He was *so* wonderful. I could *never* tell him about me, never, because watching that smile be replaced by something else entirely would just *kill* me.

I let my hand linger on his, wanting to tell him just how great he was, but Sean was still sitting across from us and it would probably be inappropriate. I just smiled back at Henry for a moment instead, and then nodded politely at Sean again when I went to leave.

Just as I was going, Sean said, "Actually, I need to duck upstairs for a couple of minutes," and hopped off the desk. He threw the stressball at Henry, who caught it automatically and then set it carefully back down where it belonged on his desk. Sean was already walking towards me. "Want some company?"

I didn't mind—and he was the *co-CEO of Frost International, for Christ's sake*—but over behind Sean I could see Henry looking like he was going to leap across the room and throttle him. I smiled tightly at Sean anyway and let him lead me out, throwing an apologetic glance over my shoulder at Henry.

Sean moved briskly as we went towards the lifts, but because my legs were longer it wasn't a problem for me to match his pace. "So how's that project coming along?" he asked me, just to make conversation. "I hope my sister isn't riding you too hard."

"We're on track," I said, feeling relieved about being able to say that. "So the hard work is worth it."

He looked sideways at me as he pressed the button. The doors from the lift I'd used a couple of minutes ago opened. "I suddenly understand why she put you on the team," he said, I think commenting on my work ethic. "When do you pitch?"

I shook my head as we stepped inside. "No dates yet."

He raised his eyebrows. "Even with the state election coming up in a couple of weeks? That's strange."

I wasn't sure what he wanted me to say, he *knew* the project was confidential. "Well, you know what it's like setting up meetings with people in cabinet."

He tilted his head. "You're probably right. I mainly get other people to set that sort of thing up, so I'm not likely to know what I'm talking about." I must have been looking a little too hard at my reflection, because the next thing he said was, "New pants?"

That surprised me. Had I been *that* obvious? "Not new, exactly. I just haven't worn them before."

He nodded. "And you don't like them?" I pressed my lips together and he laughed. "I hear you. Try being a CEO and having to spend 24/7 in a suit," he said. "And my wife gets so upset when I crease them, too. I can't have any fun. I can't imagine how uncomfortable it must be to have to do all of that but also in *heels*."

Jesus, he was *so right,* so right that I just had to laugh. When I stopped, he was smiling at me in the mirrors. It wasn't flirtatious, I don't think. My best guess was that he could see how nervous I was in his presence and he was trying to make me relax. It was working. Why the fuck did Henry hate him so much? And Diane, too? He was *nice.*

As the doors slid open on 36, they opened to two people, Jason and Sarah.

They had been discussing something in front of the vending machine, but stopped when they saw us. Sarah looked pleased to see me, but Jason's eyes couldn't have been narrower. He abandoned whatever conversation he'd been having with Sarah to walk over to us as we got out of the lift. "What are you doing with this tool, Min?" he asked, grinning at Sean. "Didn't Diane tell you he's bad news?"

Sean didn't look offended in the slightest. "Not doing a great job of selling me to your employees, Jase," he fired right back. "What is it you do again?"

"Shitloads of paperwork, mate," Jason said, freely swearing in front of the CEO. "Paperwork forever. Want a smoke before the meeting?"

Sean patted his chest and hip pockets. They were empty. "I hope you've got some."

As they left, Sean turned around and nodded a goodbye to me. It felt really good to be acknowledged, especially by someone who wasn't a total prick like Jason.

They swaggered off together like old high school buddies. I might actually have thought that's what explained their familiarity with each other except I was pretty sure Jason was quite a lot younger than Sean.

I walked up to Sarah, and she handed me one of the Red Bulls she'd been holding. "What was *that* about?" she asked me, and I shook my head as we followed them away from the lifts.

Out across the floor on the way back to Oslo, we could see them walk out onto the alcove balcony. They were deep in conversation, laughing and joking around with each other as they lit their cigarettes. At one point Sean flexed—he actually was kind of built— and Jason made some comment we couldn't hear through the glass. With their muscular, broad shoulders and flat abs, they were both in pretty great shape and the very epitome of 'men'.

That's what I wanted to be? *That?* I frowned at them. I did recall reading on the forums that a lot of trans men wanted to bulk up, but I was ambivalent. Did that mean I really didn't want to be one? Because I didn't want to be hairy and I didn't care about muscles? Then again, Henry wasn't muscular or particularly hairy, there was nothing unmanly about him. I briefly asked myself if maybe I just wanted to wear men's clothes and that was all, but as much as I *really* wished with all my heart for that to be the case, I knew it wasn't. Women didn't normally want to make their breasts disappear. Just wearing a suit wouldn't be enough for me.

"What do you think's going on with those two?" Sarah asked me thoughtfully, distracting me from my identity crisis. We'd stopped to lean on the wall outside Oslo, which was still empty. It was nearly nine, so I didn't know where the hell my team was. I'd need to speak to them about that.

I didn't really understand Sarah's question, though. Was she asking about how Sean and Jason knew each other? "What do you mean?"

She snorted. "Well, if you believe the rumours about what they do together..." she said, making a circular motion towards them with her drink and grinning.

I made a face and shook my head. "Nah, Sean's married," I said, thinking of that smile he'd had on his face when he'd talked about his 'beautiful' wife.

Sarah just turned her head to stare at me, and then laughed like she did when I'd said something really funny. "Okay," she said as she recovered. "Wow, you're serious. Okay. You want to know something?" I narrowed my eyes at her as she kept going. "I actually kind of thought when I caught you texting this morning that you might be cheating on Henry, and that the Danish was maybe a guilt-apology thing even though he didn't know."

It took me a second to really process what she'd said to even gape at her. "*What*? No!"

She laughed tensely. "I know, I know. It's just kind of obvious something is up with you so I thought maybe that's what it was. But your whole, 'no, Sean couldn't *possibly* be sleeping with Jason, he's *married*' blew that theory out of the water." She paused, looking mildly disgusted with herself. "I did not just use 'blew' in the same sentence as that other stuff."

I was still so spun out by her suggestion I'd cheat on Henry, I couldn't even think about Sean and Jason. "Henry and I are fine," I said, and it was true as long as he never found out about the me-wanting-to-be-a-man thing. And cheating on Henry with *Bree*? What a suggestion. "The friend I was texting is a *girl*," I told her, as if that would obviously put Sarah's insane theory to rest.

I wasn't sure it did, though. She just laughed at me, clapped me on the back and clinked her Red Bull against mine. "Okay, Min," she said, and then started to walk into Oslo, saying over her shoulder. "But I'd be willing to put a grand on those two guys sleeping together. More, even."

I looked back at them on the balcony. Jason leant forward to give Sean a light, and perhaps it *might* have been a little close. Then again, all I knew for sure was that Jason was gay and Sean was married. And even if Jason was into Sean, it didn't necessarily mean they were sleeping together. I had been getting comfortable with my own assessment, and then I saw Sean make a couple of smoke rings. Jason blew a big puff of smoke through one of them and they both smirked at each other. That was... kind of sexual.

Fuck, I think Sarah's right, I thought. I worried about that as I followed her into Oslo.

"See?" she asked me knowingly when I closed the door behind me.

I nodded at her, scrunching up my face. "I'm not cheating on

Henry, though," I said. "You're wrong about that. I'd never do that to him. The person I was texting *is* actually just a friend."

She nodded. "I got that far by myself." She then spent a couple of seconds watching me, obviously wanting to say something else.

I didn't let her. I was uncomfortable enough about the conversation as it was. "So, speaking of Jason, I had a word with him about the framework this morning," I said, sitting down at my desk and feeling around in my handbag for the USB. "He thinks Russia was a good choice and is forwarding me some potential leads..."

I watched her roll her eyes at me, but she let me change the subject.

My team trickled in between nine and nine-thirty, and while I was aware they'd been working all weekend, I couldn't have them think that was a good reason to slack off during the week. Ian, the older guy, actually showed up a full half an hour late and really should have known better. I called a brief meeting under the pretence of going over the framework, and then said at the end, "And, guys, I understand that you've been working all weekend, but this project is only running for a few more weeks. I'm sure I can negotiate some time off for you after contracts are signed, but I really need your full commitment until then so we can make this project successful." I wasn't sure they'd really got my point, so I added, "That means showing at up on time at nine o'clock. Or earlier, if possible."

I could see them collectively nodding, but their eyes were a little glazed and that made me feel like a school teacher. It was *awful* telling grown men what to do and I wished they wouldn't make me. And, while they were all clearly taking me seriously, I really felt very female right then in comparison to them and that made me self-conscious. I wondered what they *really* thought of a chick telling them off, and whether Jason or Sean got different responses from people than I did. And then I wondered if I was being paranoid.

"I took my wife to the doctor this morning." Ian was more explaining himself than giving me attitude, but I was annoyed anyway because he hadn't even bothered to call in about it. "She wasn't feeling well and I was busy with the requirements framework all weekend."

"Yeah, my partner's really sick at the moment, too, there's something going around," Sarah said easily, knowing full well everyone had seen that she was here on time.

I exhaled, shooting Sarah an appreciative look. She gave me a little smile.

"Also," I said, remembering Jason's comment to me and not wanting to single anyone out, "please make sure you *always* send any info to do with the pitch using the encryption software. That's very important."

"I just wish we knew *why*," Ian commented as I closed the meeting. "Frost International sells diamonds. *This* is a diamond pitch. I don't get it." I tended to agree with him, but I didn't think it would be appropriate for me to say anything more.

After they were sitting at computers working again, Sarah came up to me and put a hand on my arm. "Good job," she whispered. "That went okay."

I sighed audibly. "You want to be lead? I'm done."

She laughed and rubbed my arm. "No, thanks," she said quickly, and then got straight to business. "Can I borrow your USB for a second? I just want to grab that spreadsheet."

I was so glad she was on my team, she was a great support. The whole project would have been hell without her, and she kept doing little things like bringing me lunch and offering to run stuff past Jason for me. I hardly needed to get up out of my desk for the entire day, which allowed me to really get some serious work done.

I still had a lot more to do in the evening, but at about quarter to six I figured I'd better leave so I wouldn't be late for Bree. Deciding I could just work from home later, I packed up and went to grab some bandaids out of the first-aid kit near the lift for my poor feet.

I pulled the box down off the wall and flipped it open on the floor, searching around in it. I'd found them and was grabbing a handful when I caught sight of some packaging with diagrams on it in one of the bigger compartments. I never would normally have paid any attention to it, but the diagram was of how to treat a chest wound and it had a picture of a guy's chest and elastic bandages all around it.

I stopped what I was doing and picked up the package. It had three elastic bandages and some other stuff in it and I just kept looking at those diagrams on the front. '*Wrap tightly and press down for adequate compression*', it read. I could use adequate chest compression, I thought, and there's no way anyone working at Frost is ever going to end up with a gaping chest wound.

I looked up. No one was watching so I took it out, closed the kit, and mounted it back on the wall. I tucked the package in my bag, not really understanding why I was feeling so goddamn guilty about it. We were *allowed* to take items out of the first aid kit, OH&S was very clear about that during orientation. We were just supposed to fill out a whole lot of paperwork when we did. The thing was, there was no way I was ever going to leave any evidence that I'd taken *chest* compression bandages. How did you explain that? 'Oh, I just had a small chest wound on the way home and needed to use these?'

While I was waiting for the lift, I opened my bag a little and examined the bandages, squeezing them through the packaging. They felt really firm. I wondered if I'd be able to breathe with them wrapped around me.

"You're off, too?" Sarah's voice startled me again. I hurriedly closed my handbag, drawing a sharp breath. From her expression I didn't think she'd seen what I was looking at, but her timing was a bit suspect. It seemed like she was following me out but, then again, spending too much time with Bree was probably just making me overly suspicious. She came and stood beside me at the lifts. "This is early for you."

I nodded. "Seeing that friend," I said as we caught one downstairs together.

She didn't say anything for half the lift ride, and when she spoke, it was after visibly gathering the courage to. "Look, Min, I didn't mean to be too nosy this morning," she said as I touched up my lipstick in the mirrors. "I shouldn't feel entitled to know anything about your private life. I'm sorry about that."

I put my lipstick away, thinking carefully about how to answer her. Sarah had never shown any sign of being judgemental, and aside from Henry and Bree she was the closest thing I had to a good friend in Sydney. It was just that I couldn't bring this thing I had about myself to work. I didn't want to lose her support on the team because it would be hell without her. It was bad enough that she'd nearly seen me with those fucking bandages.

"It's okay," I said, anyway. I think I *wanted* to tell her, but then when I imagined the words actually coming out of my mouth I knew I'd choke on them. I couldn't pretend it was nothing, though. I wanted to stay friends with her. "You *were* right about what you said," I told her. "There is something 'up with me'. It's just personal and I just really can't talk about it. I'm sorry."

She nodded slowly, and I could see her brain ticking over. "Okay," she said as we stepped out of the lift and walked through the lobby. "You don't have to tell me. Maybe we can both go and get drunk together instead."

Unexpectedly, that made me laugh. "That actually sounds fantastic," I told her, meaning it. "I've always found there's nothing more therapeutic than drinking myself into a coma."

She grinned. "You'll love it: I'm a cheap drunk, too," she said. "Rob always tells me how much money he's saving by dating me instead of his last girlfriend."

"Oh, I'm taking *you* out, am I?" I asked her as we walked through the revolving door. "Doesn't the inviter normally pay?"

She grinned. "Yes, but you're my boss now," she pointed out. "That's generally how it goes."

I was about to joke about that, but as we walked out onto the street, I heard a familiar voice shout, "Min!"

Bree.

Despite having *promised* me she wouldn't, she was waiting for me outside work again. She came rushing toward me in her school uniform. Unfortunately, she got halfway to us and realised she'd left her schoolbag on the corner. She stopped, made a face, and then ran back to get it.

I was torn between being pleased to see her and angry at her for breaking her promise again. And, fuck, Sarah was with me!

Rather than disapproving of Bree, Sarah could *not* have looked more amused. "That's who you were texting, isn't it?" I nodded.

The look she gave me made me cringe. "She's actually very nice."

Sarah looked back at Bree dragging her full schoolbag toward us and snorted. "Yeah, I bet she's a lot of things."

Bree caught up to me and looked like she wanted to hug me

around the middle. She didn't, though. "I'm not sure if I can hug you in those clothes," she explained, gesturing distastefully at them. "I'd probably ruin them. Although that wouldn't be such a bad thing. You look *weird*."

I took a sharp breath. Sarah was standing right next to me, and that was far more than I ever wanted her to hear. I looked at Sarah a little panicked, but I don't think it was until she'd seen my expression that she thought twice about what Bree was saying. After she'd seen it she began listening very closely.

I wanted to yell at Bree for being so indiscreet, but that would have been even more obvious. So rather than replying to her, I indicated Sarah with a wave of my hand. "Bree, this is Sarah, a friend from work. Sarah, this is Bree..." *a friend from hell*, I thought, and winced as I remembered her 'you look weird' line and Sarah's expression.

Bree looked up at Sarah. "Hi," she said, offering her hand to shake. "You're Min's friend, too? You're really pretty. I like your hair."

Sarah looked from Bree to me and then burst out laughing. "Thank you!" she said, shaking Bree's hand. "Cloverfield Ladies' College, right? I hear that's a great school, I have a couple of friends who went there." She paused, looking sideways at me with that same amusement. "A really, really long time ago." I half glared at her. "Anyway, I'd better head off. I'll leave you two to it. See you tomorrow, Min." She shot me another puzzled glance, and then turned and walked towards the train station, still chuckling to herself.

We watched her go. *Shit*, I thought, *I hope she didn't figure anything out*. God fucking damnit. "Jesus, Bree," I said to her when Sarah was out of earshot, watching who was walking past us to make sure no one else was listening, either. "I swear to god if you say *anything* about what you know about me in front of anyone again, I will fucking kill you. This stuff is *really* private. And you showed up here after saying you wouldn't, again."

She pouted. "I didn't say anything about you wanting to be a guy," she said, at least making the effort to speak quietly. "And you *do* look weird."

"Don't you think I fucking know that?" I said to her. "But just don't, okay?"

Bree did at least finally start to look a bit remorseful. "Okay, I get it. I'm sorry I showed up here again," she said. "I just thought we could go shopping together so you didn't feel, like, pressured to do it later when you had work to do. And then I just wanted to hug you, and then I realised I couldn't. It just all came out." She was giving me those big soulful eyes again.

I sighed at her. "You're unbelievable."

"I know," she said. "But I don't think your friend knows. She just thinks *I'm* weird, and I don't mind what she thinks about me." She paused. "Also she has really nice hair kind of like Courtney's. I always wanted hair like that."

"I like your hair the way it is," I told her, pulling one of her curls and releasing it. "But if you show up here again and ever fucking talk about what I told you in front of anyone, I swear to god, Bree..."

"Okay, okay," she said, looking chastised. "I'm hopeless, I get it. Can we just go and eat the cake now? It's really heavy."

The cake actually turned out to be almost the *whole* cake, with only a couple of slices cut out already. She'd been carrying the whole cake inside a Tupperware cake container in her schoolbag. It was clearly homemade, and someone had actually put a lot of effort into delicately icing and decorating it. There were even little marzipan flowers all over the top of it.

"Are you sure your mum is okay with you taking this?" I asked, gently touching one of the pretty little flowers.

"It's my birthday cake. I'll eat it with whoever I want," she said with surprising conviction, but didn't elaborate. We dropped it off at my place so I could put it in the fridge, sitting down at the table and sharing a slice before we went out again. It was actually a really great cake, but I wasn't sure how much I could really say about it because Bree was shovelling at it like she *hated* it.

She'd perked up again by the time we left the house, though. "You're not going to put on your other clothes?" she asked as I slipped my heels back on. I gave her a look and she scrunched up her nose. "Now that I know what you *really* look like, I'm never going to get used to you wearing all of this other stuff."

I ruffled her hair as I passed her. Just very occasionally, she did actually say the right thing. "You and me both," I said as I grabbed my handbag.

We went to a shopping centre off George Street. Bree was one of those people who always wanted to walk arm-in-arm, and that, coupled with the fact my blisters were killing me and I hadn't put the bandaids on them, made the walk there rather uncomfortable.

"You shouldn't have worn heels," Bree told me when I mentioned it. "I never wear heels."

"Maybe when you're a big girl mummy will buy you some," I said, and she shoved me. I laughed. "It's not the heels that are the problem, I'm used to them. In the last few weeks I've just been walking a lot further than I usually do."

As we passed a skate store, Bree stopped suddenly by the window. She had my arm, too, so I nearly fell over. "Look," she said as I glanced around to see if anyone had noticed me being so ungraceful. "*Those* look more comfortable than heels."

She was pointing at a pair of men's high-top sneakers. The tongue hanging out of them was so puffy it looked like it might need a shot of antibiotics to get the swelling down. "Yes, I'm sure they'd go particularly well with these *tailored suit pants*," I said dryly, but Bree had already released my arm and rushed inside.

To my horror, I heard her call out, "Hi!" to the clerk as he looked up at her. "Do you have those men's ones," she pointed at the high-tops, "in her size?" she pointed at me like what she was asking was perfectly normal. I couldn't believe it. *Way to fucking out me, Bree*, I thought, feeling all the colour drain from my face. If I wasn't so fucking embarrassed I may actually have killed her on the spot.

Fortunately, the clerk clearly wasn't making assumptions about me at all. In fact, the expression he gave me was much the same one Sarah had. He was assuming *Bree* was the head case. "Do you know what her size is?" he asked Bree as I walked up to them. "I'll have a look."

"Eleven in women's," I told him, and he nodded and went out the back of the store. I looked down at Bree, who was trying her best to give me a really sweet smile. "Bree. Are you actually trying to get me to brutally murder you? Because it's working."

She bounced up and down in front of me and grabbed a handful of the fabric at the front of my blouse. "I'm sorry," she said. "I'm sorry! They're just really cool and they'd look great on you! Anyway, no one's going to know everything just because you're buying men's sneakers. They'll just think you have really big feet and can't find your size in women's."

I ended up walking out of that store with a pair of men's sneakers and a very sheepish little schoolgirl who was about ten times more excited about them than I was. When she pulled me into another men's clothes shop, I stopped her. "Aren't we supposed to be buying *you* a birthday present?"

She shrugged. "I'm having fun!" she said, and then loaded me up with more button-up shirts than I'd ever seen in my life and pushed me into a change room. I would have been embarrassed about that, too, except the clerks were all giving me secret smiles like they thought I was just patiently putting up with a crazy teenager. Bree saw and didn't seem to care. "Tell me when I can come in!" she called over the change room door as she pushed it closed.

I stared at myself in the mirror of the door. Well, well, well, I thought at my reflection, we meet again. I tried to ignore it while I tried on the clothes.

I did actually quite like the style of the shirts. That was, until I'd put them on. Bree had insisted I try a medium size instead of the XLs I usually preferred, and they buttoned up perfectly all the way to my chest where they pulled tight across my breasts. Despite the fact my breasts were quite small, they still managed to very effectively ruin the way the shirt looked. I looked ridiculous, and I just had this *wave* of self-hatred, like who the fuck was I kidding trying to look like a guy? I was a fucking *girl.*

"Can I see?" Bree called when she heard me stop making changing noises.

"No," I said, and went to take the top off.

"Why not?" she asked through the door. "Is the medium too small?"

She ended up convincing me to let her in, and I showed her, expecting her to immediately see my dilemma. She shrugged. "If you, like, hunch they'll probably just look like pecs?"

The top was short-sleeved and I held out my arms. "With these scrawny things?" I asked, and then groaned. They didn't look at all like Jason or Sean's arms at all. "I'm too skinny for people to think I have pecs."

"You know you can get surgery to remove your boobs, right?" Bree asked, looking at my breasts in the reflection. I wondered how she knew about that. "Maybe you could get that, and then use those chicken-fillet-like things you can put in your bra to pretend you have them at work."

I laughed once. "Yeah, Henry wouldn't notice at all." I reached for the door to let her out. "Okay, I'm taking the shirt off."

She didn't go anywhere. "You've seen me in a bra," she reminded me.

I took her by the shoulders, turned her around, and pushed her out the door. "You actually like how yours look, though."

She giggled. "Well, they're DDs," she said as I closed the door and locked it. "What's not to like? They're great."

I could only see her feet under the change room door, and right then she jumped experimentally up and down. I laughed to myself while I took the shirt off, knowing what she was looking at. I hoped her bra was more supportive than the one she was wearing on the weekend, because I could just imagine how she'd have looked if she'd jumped up and down in that *and wow I really shouldn't have been imagining that.* Bree did have a great body and she clearly enjoyed showing most of it to people, but there was just this sweet sort of naivety about her which stopped her looking like she was inviting people to touch it. I wondered if anyone *had* touched it, and then mentally hand-smacked myself. That was none of my business.

I'd gone to put that shirt neatly on the floor to try a bigger one, when I noticed my handbag in the corner and I had a thought. Those compression bandages. I wondered if they'd make the shirt fit. I took the package out of my bag and looked at it again. Well, there was no harm in trying, right?

I slipped off my bra and undid the wrapping.

"What's that noise?" Bree asked through the door.

"I'm hungry," I said flatly. "I felt like a packet of chips." She giggled.

The bandages were actually really good; they were made out of some strange fabric that stuck to itself so I only needed to press them down and they were secure. I had to try a couple of times, though, because the first time I did it I wrapped my chest too tightly and it *hurt.*

When I was done, I looked at myself in the mirror. I wasn't sure how I felt about myself from the front because of my hips, but from the side, I was completely flat. Completely. There was no sign at all that I had breasts. Just to check I wasn't imagining things, I put on the shirt that hadn't quite fit before.

It worked, they were completely gone. *That* made me smile, so I opened the door to Bree and let her squeeze in. "What do you think?" I said, and presented myself.

Her eyebrows went up. "Wow," she said, and reached out to touch my newly flat chest, curious about it. Fortunately, she realised at the last minute that it probably wasn't appropriate and didn't actually put her hand there. "How did you do that?"

I bent down and handed her the empty bandage wrapper. She took it from me, but didn't really understand until she saw the diagram. "Oh, that's a good idea," she said. "And probably a whole lot easier than just getting a surgeon to hack them off."

I winced at her choice of wording. "What do you think of the shirt?" I asked. "Should I get it?"

She looked back up at me. Even though I had my breasts taped flat, it was actually really uncomfortable having Bree so openly staring at my chest. I'd have to get over that if I was going to pass as a guy, though, because guys didn't care about their chests. I caught myself thinking that and made a face. Pass as a guy to *who*, Min? Who else are you planning on showing this to?

"Yeah, get the shirt," Bree said as an afterthought. She was looking down at her own breasts and tried to push them against her ribcage with her hands. The result was just a hell of a lot more cleavage around her collarbones. "I could never get mine that flat," she said, releasing them again, which I was grateful for. Watching her so freely holding them in front of me was a bit awkward. "You're lucky you don't want to be a guy and have *huge* boobs. That would suck. You'd *have* to get them cut off."

"Small mercies, I guess," I said, and then kicked her out so I could change back again.

When I'd put my work clothes back on and opened the door, Bree was all the way up against the mirror at the far end of the fitting room, pulling at her hair. "How do you think I'd look with straight hair like Courtney and Sarah?" she asked me.

"Just as terrifying as you look now," I said. "But straighter."

She snorted. "*Straighter?*" She started to giggle.

That hadn't come out the way I'd intended it to. I pushed gently as I passed her. "You know what I mean."

She did, but she found it hilarious anyway, and spent the whole time I was putting the clothes back trailing after me and giggling incessantly. She continued into *another* clothes shop, and came rushing over to me with a women's t-shirt which she held up across her front. It read, '*Looking 4 Prince Charming'.* She was laughing too much to say whatever she'd wanted to say about it.

I rolled my eyes at her. "Yeah, yeah, I get it, very funny."

The last set of shops in the centre were several jewellery stores and a supermarket. We passed by the window of one of them and there were a whole lot of engagement rings.

"Hey," Bree said, on her tiptoes peering at the rings. "Doesn't your company sell diamonds? Are there any Frost diamonds here?"

I leant back to read the shop signage. "Nope."

She rolled her eyes at me. "You didn't even *look* at them," she accused.

I came up to the display window beside her. "I don't need to. Frost does prestige diamonds, and this isn't a prestige store."

She groaned. "Well, sor-ry," she said, clearly still playing with me, but there was an element of something else in her voice. "Not all of us live in super awesome expensive apartments and can just buy awesome *prestige* diamonds whenever we feel like it." She walked into the store. "Some of us regular people like regular things."

I walked in after her while she looked around at all the stuff on display. "Actually, Frost diamonds are probably a bit out of *my* price range, too," I corrected her. "The cheapest ones retail for about $20,000, but our most popular selection is in the $100-to-$150,000 price range."

Not only did Bree gape at me, but the clerk behind the counter who'd overheard us did, too.

"That's enough for a house," Bree said, sounding actually kind of distressed about it. "Like, a small house, but a house. You can't live in a diamond."

The clerk's expression was quite funny as well. "Well," she told us in her professional voice. "We have a lovely selection of jewellery in the 100-to-150 *dollar* range." Both Bree and I laughed.

Bree turned her nose up at me. "Okay, you can show *me* that stuff," she said to the clerk, and then they chatted about some of the items on display while I stood back and watched, holding my shopping bags.

It was odd talking about the price of Frost merchandise like it was worth actual money, I thought, reflecting on how we normally talked about contracts and units and profit. Discussing it with Bree reminded me that, actually, Frost was raking in *enormous* amounts of money just from the comparatively small diamond division. Money 'regular' people didn't usually have, and money Bree definitely didn't have.

I watched her talk animatedly with the clerk as she leant over the counter. The clerk was even older than me and *she* was enjoying chatting with Bree, too. Henry was right, the age difference wasn't actually a problem, but Bree did have a point about money. She wasn't old enough to have a job that paid anything like mine did. And I didn't just have a 'regular' job, I worked for Frost International. And what was the fucking point of working for someone like Frost and having all this money if all I did was either buy cosmetics or send it back to Mum?

I looked at Bree cooing over a gold bracelet with the clerk. Well, it *was* her 18th birthday yesterday, wasn't it?

I made a gesture to get the clerks attention, and then indicated the bracelet. The clerk smiled ear to ear like she was absolutely delighted and nodded at me.

When the clerk started to take the bracelet away from Bree, Bree stood up straight and looked really confused. "Why are you—?" The clerk glanced at me and Bree turned back towards me. I was just smiling, and Bree's jaw dropped. "Are you...?" I nodded. She just stared at me for a second. "But it's *real gold,*" she said. I pretended to be very impressed and she pointed her finger at me. "Stop that," she ordered. "This is serious. You're buying *real gold* for me?"

"Would you prefer *fake* gold?"

The clerk snickered as she finished polishing the bracelet.

"Would you like it gift-wrapped?" she asked us.

I looked at Bree. She just looked stunned. "I don't know," she said.

The clerk seemed to be finding Bree's whole surprise very sweet. "Would you like to wear it now, instead?"

Bree looked back at her and just stared for a second. "Okay," she said, and presented her wrist.

The clerk helped her put it on, and then I handed my card over while Bree just stared mutely at her new bracelet.

When we were done and had made it out of the store, Bree kind of just stopped beside the wall. "Did that just happen?" she asked me with no trace of humour in her voice.

I smiled and ruffled her curls. "Happy Birthday."

She was still looking at her wrist. "When I told you to buy me something, I just thought you'd just get me something cheap and silly," she said, and there was something about her voice. "I never thought you'd *actually* buy something really awesome for me."

When she looked up at me, I realised why she sounded so strange. Her eyes were *swimming* in tears.

Fuck, had I done something wrong? "Bree...?"

Without waiting another second, she threw her arms around my middle. There were people everywhere and I felt a bit uncomfortable about it, but given the circumstances I couldn't push her away. I put a hand on the back of her head, not really sure what to do. That certainly hadn't been the reaction I was expecting, and I worried about it.

"Are you okay?" I asked her quietly after a minute or two. She was still hugging me just as tightly. "I didn't mean to upset you."

She took a deep breath and exhaled, warming my stomach. "I'm sorry about crying, it's really dumb," she began. "It's just, like... I thought you might really like a coffee before work so I got up *really* early so I could get into the city on time to get you one. And then I thought you might like some flowers because I upset you that night and I wanted to say sorry, and flowers are a nice way to say that, right? And I thought maybe you'd like to have some of my birthday cake because it's really pretty, so I had to wait until Mum went to take the rubbish out so I could sneak it into my bag and show you." She took a short breath. "It's just that, you know, I always try to do all these nice things for people..." She looked up at me with those big eyes of hers. "I *always* try and do nice things for people. But you did something nice *back*."

I stroked her hair. So that's what it was about. "Happy Birthday," I said again, quietly.

After a minute or so she released me, standing back and gently touching the bracelet. "I'm going to help you," she announced eventually, after spending some time deep in thought. When it was clear I didn't know what she meant, she looked around us to make sure no one could hear, and then elaborated. "Like, you want to be a guy? Well, I'll help."

I winced. I still wasn't comfortable hearing her say that, and especially not suddenly with no warning. "I'm not actually sure what I want, and you help already," I said. "You don't need to *do* anything. Just be your crazy self."

She didn't look convinced. "But I'm sure I can do more than that," she said. "There must be something else."

I laughed bleakly as we started walking again. "If you could spontaneously develop some magical powers, that would be great."

It was getting to that time of night: the lights around us in some of the stores were beginning to switch off, and here and there roller-doors were being shut.

"I guess you have to go do work," Bree said in that desolate tone of hers she reserved for when she needed to leave. "And I have to go home."

"You're not going to Courtney's tonight?"

She shook her head as we walked out of the entrance. "My brother's there. It's too weird." She didn't say anything else. It was dark outside already, and there was a bit of a chill in the air as we headed back home.

When we got upstairs, Bree looked hesitantly at her schoolbag by the door, and then up at me. "Can I just stay for a bit longer? I'll be *really* quiet. I have homework to do, anyway."

I had been ready to refuse, but there was a note of something in her voice. It made me wonder. "Bree, do your parents know where you are?"

She shrugged. "I'll seriously be really quiet."

I watched her for a second. There was obviously a reason she didn't want to answer, and I didn't want to push her, so I left it. She was 18 now anyway, and all the evidence pointed to her having had a *crap* birthday. She enjoyed herself when she was here. "Okay," I said. "But literally, you will need to be dead quiet. I'll need to be able to concentrate."

She brightened. "Really? I can stay?"

I took the bags into my bedroom and went in there to change. "Really. I'm using the table, though. Or I will after I have a quick shower."

I had my shower and threw on the hoodie and the jeans, and by the time I came out of the bathroom, the doona was missing from my bed. I followed the trail of discarded bedding and found it draped over the spine of my couch and hanging over the front of it. I lifted the end of the make-shift doona-tent near the arm. Bree was lying on her stomach inside it reading something on her phone.

She looked up at me when I peeked in.

"Okay..." I said slowly.

"If I can't see you I'll be less tempted to talk to you," she said very matter-of-factly, and then went back to reading whatever she had been. "Also, it's really warm in here."

I had to laugh. "If you suffocate, I'm feeding you to the flowers," I told her, and then set myself up at the table to do some research on the leads Jason had sent me.

Most of them were just contacts in large mining or construction companies in Russia. I couldn't find any connections to more consumer-oriented products at all. Leads were leads, though, so I wrote somewhat cryptic emails to a few of them and then stopped short of actually sending them. If I was going to send communication that had anything to do with Pink externally, I'd probably have to clear it with Jason first, and, fuck, that young guy John had sent me a link to a webpage about Argyle Diamonds unencrypted *again*. I put my face in my hands; I wasn't sure how much clearer I could have made the message about the importance of information security. Well, I couldn't do anything now, but I'd need to jump right on it tomorrow. *Fuck.* Why couldn't people follow simple instructions? I saved the emails onto the USB, shut my laptop and then leant back in my chair and stretched. That was probably enough for today; it was bedtime.

That reminded me that Bree was still here. I flopped my arms back down and looked over at the couch; she'd been *dead* quiet. I decided I should probably thank her for that because it was a bit of a feat of self-discipline for her, so I wandered over and lifted the edge of the doona.

I had opened my mouth to say something, but I stopped when I saw that she'd face-planted on her phone. It was half-buried between her cheek and the cushion and she was fast asleep. I laughed soundlessly; that explained why she'd been so quiet. I should have known 'self-discipline' and 'Bree' weren't two words that belonged in the same sentence.

Carefully excavating her phone, I rolled the doona back to her shoulders so she didn't actually suffocate, and then I stood back up.

Well, I couldn't kick her out now, could I? I looked at the clock 11:30. It was probably better if she did stay over rather than going home at this hour. I wondered about her family, though. How the fuck did they not worry about where she was all the time? Unless she was lying to them, that is. Still, my mum would *never* have let me out so much in my last year of school, regardless of what I'd told her. I knew Aussie parents were a little less hardcore, but I didn't think they were *this* lax about where their teenage daughters were.

Kind of hating myself for it, I unlocked her phone to just check she hadn't received a hundred phone calls from scared family wondering where their daughter was. She hadn't, there wasn't a single one. And in fact, the last thing she'd been reading *wasn't* actually even homework, it was a blog that called itself *The Queer (A)Gender.* I sighed at that, and then put the phone down on the coffee table and just looked down at her.

What's the deal with you, Bree? I thought, bending down so I could tuck her in a little better. That delicate little bracelet was still on her tiny wrist, and it reminded me how small she was, which made me worry even more. I hadn't seen bruises or anything on her torso when she'd had her top off, and I didn't *think* it would be something like that, but I still worried. I worried about what was going on for her. Fuck, it was just so easy to worry about this girl.

Still, I had several more pressing issues also competing for brain-space, like not being sure if I definitely wanted to be a guy or not and the fact that when I gave my team instructions it all seemed to go in one ear and out the other. I sighed, turning off the living room light and heading into my bedroom. All of this could wait until tomorrow.

ELEVEN

I woke up to the sound of someone opening and closing the cupboards in my kitchen. Yawning, I felt around my bedside table for my phone and held it in front of my face, half-blinding myself. *6:02 am.* Bree was very awake for this time of the morning. Weren't teenagers supposed to be impossible to wake up before midday?

Just as I was trying to decide if it was too early to get out of bed, my bedroom door swung open and a silhouette with very fluffy hair appeared. "You have *no* food," she announced, not telling me anything I didn't know. "I had this really nice idea where I was going to make you breakfast and have it ready for you when you woke up but the only thing you have in your pantry is this one single pickle and the most plastic-looking two minute noodles in the world. The cake is the only thing in your fridge. You don't even have *milk* anywhere, just, like, four hundred thousand bottles of red wine."

"Good morning, Bree," I said pointedly in my croaky morning voice. "How did you sleep?"

"Okay," she said, still lecturing me, "and you *sound* like a guy, now, too. I've discovered the reason you look like some skinny teenage guy when you don't try to do the feminine thing is because you hardly ever eat. If you didn't have your hair, like, down around your face like that then no one would think you weren't a dude." She paused, touching her own messy hair. "Also, can I have a shower? I look like a pom-pom."

It was too early to deal with her, so I washed my face quickly and then got dressed while she was having a shower. Since I couldn't wear my tailored pants two days in a row, I ended up needing to brave a skirt with stockings. 34 years, 364 days to retirement, I thought, sighing heavily. I toyed with the idea of

179

pulling my hair back—especially after what Bree had said—but 'guy' really wasn't the impression I was trying to give people at work.

When Bree *finally* emerged from the bathroom, she'd done a pretty good job of fixing her hair and smoothing her uniform and it wasn't at all obvious she'd crashed on someone's couch overnight. "Can I just leave my undies in your washing?" she asked. "It's a bit weird to carry them around."

Was she serious? Her skirt barely made it halfway down her thighs. "Bree, you can't go out like that without any!"

She looked at me for a second and then laughed. "I have spares," she said. "But oh my god!"

She continued to laugh about that while she was watching me do my makeup, and then all the way downstairs. I had automatically started walking to work when I realised I couldn't send Bree to school without having fed her. It was really too late to sit down anywhere, though.

"Would a muffin and a coffee be okay for breakfast?" I asked her, as we passed a café.

"Sure!" she said, and ended up talking the barista into making her a ham-and-cheese toastie, instead. She ate it with an expression of total contentment as I walked her to Circular Quay to catch her train. We'd just missed one, so we sat and watched the ferries dump hordes of business people in suits onto the quay.

"You should wear a suit to work," Bree said, offering a wedge of her sandwich to me. "That would be so awesome."

Yeah, in my dreams. "Hah," I said as I had a small bite and gave it back to her. "World peace would be awesome, too." I half-heard an announcement over the speaker system. "Hey, isn't that your train?"

She nodded, dusting her hands as she stood up. "Thanks."

Her hair was a bit damp, and if I ruffled it I'd probably make it frizzy for the rest of the day, so I didn't. "You're welcome," I said. "Come on, you've only got a couple of minutes, you'd better go."

I walked her up to the barriers and she just stood there, glancing up at me and looking uneasy.

"You've got to go to school," I told her. When she didn't say anything to that, something occurred to me as I watched people hold their Opal cards next to the readers. "You *do* have enough money on your card, right?"

She didn't say anything, so the answer was obviously no. And she wasn't going to tell me, I thought, looking around us at all the ticket inspectors making sure everyone was tapping on. How the hell was she planning on getting to school?

I leafed through my purse for *my* Opal card which I hardly ever used, took her hand, and placed it in her palm. "Here. It's full-fare, but I don't think anyone will notice." As I was closing my purse, I caught sight of the blue-green of a couple of ten dollar notes, as well. "Do you have lunch?" Again, no answer. I made a short noise and put one of the tens in her palm with the card.

She was being uncharacteristically quiet again, and I led her aside from the barriers so we wouldn't get in anyone's way. "Bree, is everything okay?"

She nodded, looking down at the note and the card in her palm.

What was going on for her? It *couldn't* be that her parents had no money, because Cloverfield was a pretty expensive school and Bree, while being very sweet, did *not* seem like the type of person who'd be there on a scholarship. I wanted to ask her, and I suppose I probably would have been entitled to because I *was* spending heaps of money on her, but I also kind of wanted her to want to tell me on her own terms.

"It's not fair," she said quietly.

I frowned a little. "What isn't?" Putting a hand underneath hers, I closed her fingers around the card and the ten. "If you're worried about the money, don't be. It's not a problem."

"Yet," she said. "It will be."

It was on the tip of my tongue: 'what's going on, Bree?' I couldn't say it, though. What if it was something *awful* and really private I was forcing her to tell me in public? I just put a gentle hand on her back and lead her up to the barricade. She tapped my card and went through.

I raised my hand a bit hesitantly and waved at her, and she smiled for a second and waved back. There was something haunted about her, though. It seemed forced, but she'd turned and gone to climbing stairs before I was sure. I watched until she'd reached the platform, trying to imagine what the problem could possibly be.

When people started to give me frustrated looks and push past me, I realised I couldn't just stand there against the barriers because I was half-blocking them. I stepped aside, looking one last time up the stairs just to make absolutely certain Bree wasn't coming back down them before I headed off to work.

Something is seriously up with that girl, I thought, focusing on the pavement in front of me to avoid catching sight of my reflection in shop windows as I passed them.

The beautiful cake was evidence Bree hadn't been kicked out of home and that her parents still obviously loved her. She didn't have bruises or anything on her and she didn't seem to have any hang-ups about her body at all so it couldn't be... anything more serious than that, could it? I didn't feel like that made sense, but maybe I should ask Henry about it. Yes, I thought as I walked into the lobby of Frost and pressed the lift button, I'd have to ask Henry what he thought. He always knew this stuff.

I was the first one in the office, *again.* Sitting down at my laptop, I fished around in my handbag for the USB and then flipped it between my fingers while I was waiting for my system to boot up. Bree had dragged me to that expensive restaurant and made me pay, and she hadn't seemed to have any issues with that. I supposed she had been getting progressively more uncomfortable with the money I was spending *since* then, but I thought I had been making it perfectly clear it was fine? Actually, to be perfectly honest, part of me kind of enjoyed it. Spending money was a complete non-event to me, and I'd never had anyone to spend money on before. I liked that something so simple meant so much to her. It felt like I was cheating at friendship, somehow. Seeing that gratitude on her face when I'd bought her the bracelet was a great feeling.

Why wasn't it fair, then? Goddamnit, what was going *on* with her?

This was driving me nuts. Was I overreacting? I had to text her. I took my phone out of my bag and spent at least five minutes trying to figure out what to say, in the end settling on, *"Are you going to be okay? I'm worried."*

She took longer to reply than usual. *"thats because ur a stressball lol btw i hardly have any credit left"*

I groaned. "Avoid the fucking question, why don't you, Bree!" I said at the phone, and then put it away. She clearly didn't want to talk about it, and while I was *dying* to know, it wasn't my place. Unfortunately, the fact she hadn't answered whether she was going to be okay or not seemed very important and I ended up staring at Michelangelo underneath my monitor rather than the timeline actually on it.

Predictably, Sarah was next through the door. She stopped in the doorway and looked at me. We watched each other for a few seconds, and then she burst out laughing and went and put her bag in her drawer.

Bree, I thought, remembering when I'd said goodbye to Sarah yesterday. "Sorry about last night," I said mildly. "Bree is..." I searched for a good adjective, but I didn't find one. "Well, you saw what she's like."

Sarah was still laughing away. "I actually have a confession," she told me, turning her laptop on and spending ten seconds trying to get her USB into one of the slots. She printed something out and then walked over and dumped it on my keyboard. "I'm a bad person."

I picked it up; it was a marketing analytics report from social media. Facebook, this time. Only instead of analysing a demographic, it was just analysing a single person. "'Briana Dejanovic'," I read, pretty sure I was pronouncing it wrong. Was this... I looked up at Sarah. *"Bree?"*

Sarah looked *very* guilty. "I shouldn't have, I know. Her profile's public, though, and I have all those really powerful search and analytic tools..."

I probably would have been a *whole* lot angrier if I wasn't really, really interested in what was on the report. It might help me figure out what was up with Bree and if everything was okay.

I pretended to glare at her. "Using your powers for evil?" She nodded meekly, and that made me laugh. "How the hell did you find her, though? I wouldn't have told you her surname, because I didn't even know it."

Sarah looked like she couldn't believe that. "She was all over you and you don't even know her surname?" At my expression she held up her hands, bracelets jingling. "I didn't mean anything by that, by the way. You two just seem too close for you to not know those kind of details."

There were a lot of details I didn't know about Bree, but I still enjoyed her company. I shrugged at Sarah. "I met her online and it didn't seem important. So how did you find her profile?"

Sarah leant over and flipped to a print-out of her 'about' page. It was pretty bare, but *did* have her school listed. "It was actually a no-brainer, I didn't even have to filter by themes until I got her. I just tabbed through photos of kids in her school and stopped when I saw curls." She stood up, taking a couple of pages with her. Then, clearing her throat dramatically, she spoke in the same voice she'd use to deliver a series of analytics in a project meeting.

"Briana Dejanovic, 411 friends, 86% of them further than 25km from her hometown and current location which are both listed as Sydney. Her follows are unremarkable, really, nothing we wouldn't expect from the demographic. Her friends-of-friends is in the tens of thousands so she has excellent reach with her posts, and there are some," Sarah glanced up at me, "very interesting topics on her recently liked list. Overall an interesting analytical exercise but unfortunately through examining her status updates, clicks and click-throughs, the likelihood of her being interested in purchasing a pink diamond or any other Frost merchandise is very low."

I was too worried about this 'recently liked' list and what I'd seen on Bree's phone last night to laugh very hard at Sarah's consumer analysis of Bree. Fuck, I hoped Bree hadn't liked any of those gender-related blogs she'd been reading, because together with the things Bree had said last night, I wouldn't have put it past Sarah to guess. I didn't want to rouse her suspicion, though, so I just asked innocently, "'recently liked'?"

Sarah showed me the list. There were a couple of pop stars, *Girls' Generation* again, and, unfortunately, some sort of queer blog with a big rainbow flag as its display picture. It was buried in amongst her other likes, though, so I just pretended not to notice it. "She likes Korean pop music?" I asked dryly. "That *is* concerning."

Sarah looked *wholly* unconvinced, but didn't say anything. "Move over," she said, glancing nervously over at the door. "I have to show you this girl's Facebook page."

She reached across me and opened up Facebook in my browser, logging in as one of Frost's analytics usernames and then going to Bree's page.

Bree's display picture was a pretty unremarkable selfie, but as soon as Sarah clicked on the 'Photos of Briana' header, fuck, *I* had to look over *myself* to check the door was shut. Bree had probably... dozens of photos of herself there, and while none of them were actively pornographic or showing anything beyond a lot of thigh or a lot of cleavage, the positions she was in and the *expressions* she had on her face... *Jesus.*

Sarah and I scrolled through them with our jaws open.

"Yup," Sarah told me as we reached the end, her eyes as wide as saucers, "it's still just as shocking the second time around."

The last one was Bree with the two top buttons of her school uniform undone so you could see deep into her cleavage. She'd angled the camera accordingly and was pretending to bite her lip, like she was inviting the person behind the camera to reach out and touch her. Fortunately it was a selfie so there was no one behind the camera, but it was so sexual that I found it incredibly fucking uncomfortable to look at and had to close the page.

"Oh, my god," I breathed, putting my face in my hands for a second. Even with my eyes closed I could see the echo of that cleavage on my retinas. "Why would *anyone* put photos like that on the internet? Is she *trying* to get stalked?" That seemed a pretty ironic question to be asking about *Bree, S*talker Extraordinaire.

Sarah shrugged, leaning back in her chair, clearly finding my reaction very entertaining. "Well, I suppose she *has* got a great rack so she probably just wants to boast about it." When I *looked* at her, she shrugged. "What? Objectively speaking, she has. I can say that, can't I?"

I groaned and put my face back in my hands again. "Oh my god..."

"Also, and I'm not drawing any conclusions, really," Sarah said, giving me adequate time to prepare for *more* Bree, "but *this*," she flipped through the pages and showed me a status update. "I found it on her friends-of-friends."

I read through it. Someone had replied to a status last night with 'GAY', and then Bree had *gone to town* on him about how offensive that was, complete with all caps and zero punctuation. My first thought was she'd probably just been reading a whole lot of those queer blogs I'd found on her phone and was just playing white knight, but then I remembered that whole 'straighter' thing in the shopping centre yesterday. Could she be...?

I didn't even finish that thought because I was already panicking that maybe she was into me. *Then* I started telling myself off, because it was stupidly narcissistic to think that just because a girl was gay and I was also currently masquerading as a typical girl that she'd be into me. Especially because I kind of *wasn't* a proper girl, and especially given that Bree's assessment when I was dressed like a girl was: 'weird'. Bree probably didn't even really think of me as a peer, so that would mean we were safe, wouldn't it? Although, going over everything that had happened in the last few weeks didn't provide me with much comfort. Especially with what Sarah was implying.

Sarah patted me on the back, a mischievous glint in her eye. "Happy reading," she said. "I'm going to get us some caffeine."

While she was doing that, I flipped through some of the other pages looking to see if I could find actual confirmation that Bree was gay. In the process I found out a series of things I'd never ask Bree directly: her parents were still married and appeared to still live together because there were a number of recent photos of them together in the same house. Her brother's name was Andrej and he and Courtney had posted about the same number of suggestive photos Bree had except with each other. That was almost as bad. There was one photo where they almost looked like they were fucking and I got to the stage where I was actually asking existential questions to the universe about why *anyone would ever voluntarily show that to people*. There were no photos of Bree in any sort of suggestive fashion with other girls, but there weren't any with any boys, either. And in all the photos of her and her family, everyone was smiling. Even Bree. Despite all of that, there was nothing else gay or queer or whatever on her Facebook.

I was probably making a big deal out of nothing. She was probably just being a nice person and standing up for the community.

I paused. 'The community', I thought, remembering *my* body issues. I was potentially secretly *in* that community, wasn't I? 'LBG'...'LBT'... Whatever it was. I couldn't remember the acronym, but I was certain there was a 'T' for 'trans' in there, somewhere. So maybe Bree was just standing up for me in the event that I *did* turn out to be? But then, Bree had specifically been defending the term 'gay', and I wasn't gay. Although... if I *was* supposed to be a guy, and I was with Henry, did that mean I *was* secretly gay?

I sat back and just stared out the window towards the Western Suburbs, completely spun out. I felt like I'd just been told I was adopted or something, and everything I'd thought I knew about myself was bullshit. *Fuck*, this was a headache, what the hell did anything mean anymore? I didn't even know where to *start* on this one. Bree's suggestion of running away to Canada was sounding *great* right now.

I think I may have torn out half my hair by the time Sarah came back with my Red Bull. She laughed at my expression as I accepted it from her and opened it.

"I think I hate you a little bit," I told her as I took a sip. She had *no* idea about the can of worms she'd just opened. "Did you do this to *my* Facebook, too?"

She grinned. "There's nothing interesting on yours."

I sighed heavily and took one last cursory look at Bree's profile before I closed the page. I had the print-outs, I could pour over them later for evidence about what was going on with her. "I'm beginning to understand why you hate social media."

"Facebook's evil, I told you," she said, which was very interesting to hear out of the mouth of a social media marketing specialist. "I'd delete my account but then I'd never get invited out. Speaking of which," she said, "the girls are all going for drinks at that pub in The Rocks on Friday. Should I send you and your exhibitionist friend an invite?"

"Probably not worth it," I said, closing the browser. "I'm going to go home and delete my account tonight."

I'd swivelled back to face my monitor and I could feel her staring at the side of my head. When I glanced at her, she asked, "Okay, so you didn't know her surname, which kind of means you don't really know her that well, but *she* gets to take you out just like that? She doesn't even have to sic Henry on you?" She was smiling, but I could tell she wasn't just teasing me. I started to worry I was hurting her feelings, but then she added. "Like, is it a great rack you look for in a friend? Because, *hello.*"

She stuck her chest out, and I nearly spat Red Bull all over my monitor. While I was reaching for a tissue and my eyes were watering, she added, "Not that I want to nag you. I'm just wondering."

I winced, blotting my nose. "I know how it looks, but it's not personal." When she kept listening, I sighed. "Sarah, seriously, though, you keep trying to get me out of here. Why? What makes you so sure that I'm the type of fun you expect me to be?"

She shrugged. "I don't know," she said. "Looking at you, you're this serious workaholic. But I know you play video games, prank your poor unsuspecting co-workers, you have this killer sense of humour and hang out with wild schoolgirls." She crossed her arms as she considered me. "All is not what it seems. So I compiled the evidence, analysed it, and all signs point to you being stacks of fun."

All isn't *what it seems, Sarah,* I thought, but I disagreed that it meant I was 'stacks of fun'. I probably *would* enjoy myself, though. Particularly if alcohol was involved. "Well, then, prepare for the incredible excitement of watching me sit and silently drink wine," I told her. "I'll definitely go drinking with you on the day we close this. Mainly to shut you up, though." I winked at her.

Sarah nodded once and looked victorious. "*Good,*" she said. "Just out of curiosity, though, how *did* that girl do it so easily?"

I exhaled audibly. That was a good question. "She'd have physically carried me out of here if she was strong enough, and I'm not exaggerating. 'No' wasn't an answer she was going to accept."

Sarah nodded slowly. "I can't wait to get you *really* drunk," she said cryptically, and then turned back to her spreadsheet, ending the conversation by doing some actual work. I followed her example.

As soon as the rest of my team got in, I needed to have a quiet word with John about him sending unencrypted emails. The discomfort of telling someone off, especially while the humiliation showed on his bright red face, was enough to distract me from Bree and the vortex of chaos surrounding her. Furthermore, Jason stuck his head in before lunch and told me that Diane wanted to speak briefly with me and him tomorrow morning before work.

While I was screaming internally and absolutely certain it was to do with that unencrypted email, Sarah gave me a look that basically said, 'You're our next CEO, right?'. I scoffed at her.

Jason had also approved my emails to the contacts he'd recommended, and so I spent an hour or two making sure I was completely happy with the vague wording and sent them off. Vladivostok got back to me quickly and teed up a teleconference for later in the week, but I'd have to wait overnight for Moscow.

It was productive day, but Sarah had been in and out of consumer profiling meetings for her other team which meant I had no one to bring me lunch and I hadn't eaten all day.

I was *starving* by dinner, to the point that I was considering drinking milk and/or eating sugar directly out of the kitchenette. When I was finally done with the requirements doc and Henry sent me an SMS, I was about ready to start going on the half-dead plant on my table.

"*Want company tonight?*" he'd texted. "*I thought maybe we could go out for dinner, somewhere quiet and low key. What do you say?*"

I was waiting for my laptop to shut down as I texted him back. It would actually be a great opportunity to pick his brains about Bree, and I was so hungry I would have said yes to just about any suggestion as long as it involved food. "*I am DYING of hunger. I will literally eat ANYTHING as long as you can give it to me quickly.*"

Of course, I shouldn't have left an opening for him. "*I'm assuming that doesn't mean what I hope it does...?*"

I groaned. I caught myself thinking '*Men!*', but then had a sudden thought about how *I* felt about myself. Was I differentiating myself from them after all? It was such a strange, disorienting feeling. I just seriously had *no* idea what I was supposed to be. I was much too hungry to think further on it now, though. "*Nope, it doesn't mean you can give* that *to me,*" I texted back. "*Not unless you can serve it sliced in a baguette with mayonnaise and chips on the side, that is.*"

"*...Ouch. I'll be downstairs in five.*"

I stuffed all of Bree's Facebook analytics into my handbag, and headed downstairs to meet him.

Henry had picked a boutique Japanese restaurant in The Rocks; it was a tiny little place I had no idea about despite living about three streets away. There were only a couple of people seated when we walked in, and so the waitress was able to show us to a table straight away. She put the menus in front of us as we sat down. "Drinks?"

"A glass each of house white and red," Henry said, and then added, "If you want to hang around for a couple of seconds, I'm pretty sure my girlfriend wants to order straight away." He grinned at me.

I literally picked the first thing on the menu, and as soon as the waitress was gone I started to undo my handbag. "Not that you're not wonderful anyway, but I actually have an ulterior motive for going to dinner with you," I said, heaping together all the Facebook analytics print-outs.

"I should have known being wonderful wasn't enough for you," he told me with a completely straight face.

"Yeah, you should have. Some shrink you are," I said and then showed him all the Facebook analytics, explaining everything I was worried about with Bree. The waitress came back with our wine halfway through it and gave me a *really* strange look about all the paper I'd spread everywhere.

When I was finished, Henry sat back with the wine in one hand—there was nowhere on the table to put it—and squinted at me. "So what are you actually asking me?" he said, "Because I'm getting a lot more about you than I am about Bree just at this moment."

I wasn't interested in hearing about how crazy he thought I was. "I really don't know what to think," I said. "But I'm kind of worried something terrible is happening. You don't think anything... really bad is happening to her?" When he waited for me to elaborate, I added, "You know, do you think anyone's abusing her?"

Henry's eyebrows went *right* up, and he took a big mouthful of wine. "Wow," he said, and then had another one. "Wow, that's a heavy topic for a light dinner." He spent a few seconds thinking over his answer. "To be honest, Min, unless you're going to show me photos of bruises, I'm not going to be able to tell you anything without speaking with her one-on-one in a therapeutic setting." I leant back in my chair and made a face. He winced. "I'm sorry, I know that's not the answer you're looking for."

It really wasn't. "You don't have any idea at all? Not even a, 'Well, that's unlikely'?"

He shook his head. "If I knew the answer I'd just tell you."

I frowned back down at the print-outs, and then gathered them all up and shoved them back into my handbag. While I was doing that, he commented, "But *you've* gone to a lot of effort to not just ask her what's happening in her life. Why is that? What are *you* afraid of?"

Wow, he always cut *straight* through things. I put my bag under the table, thinking. "What I'm going to do if she says yes," I said, and then made a face. "And that I'm going to feel like absolute shit for spending two weeks trying to avoid her."

He chuckled. "I'm not going to remind you what my initial advice about Bree was."

"Good. Because then I'd have to punch you."

The chuckle turned into an outright laugh for a second or two. "Anyway, you shouldn't feel that bad if it does turn out to be something serious, because since those initial meetings you've been a good friend to her."

"That's true," I said, remembering the last few days. "And I've spent a tonne of money on her, too, I don't think I've got anything to feel bad about."

That caught his attention, but he was careful to be mild about it. "Just out of curiosity, how much *have* you spent on her?"

I immediately felt self-conscious. It didn't look that great, did it, buying a gold bracelet for someone I'd met three weeks ago? I glossed over that part. "Oh, you know. Money for food, taxis to get back to her friend's..."

He nodded, accepting that. I felt awful about not telling him about the bracelet, but I didn't want him to think Bree was just using me for my money. She wasn't like that.

He put his wine glass on the table. "Well, it just sounds like you're being a good friend," he said, "whatever's going on for her. And judging by what happened over the weekend, she's being a good friend to you, too."

I really wanted to keep discussing Bree to try and figure everything out, but shortly after that, the waitress brought our dinner. I stopped talking to inhale mine in under three minutes, but Henry dawdled over his as usual, chatting about his sister who was pregnant *again*. She was younger than him and already had three children.

"I guess I'm lucky she went and married a Chinese guy," Henry said. "Or I'd probably lose my place as star child of the family." He remembered something and laughed. "You should have seen Mum's face when Alice was first pregnant. She didn't know whether to be overjoyed she was going to be a grandma, or horrified that the child was going to be half-Chinese."

I rolled my eyes. "You think your mum's traditional? When I first moved to Sydney, on every single phone call, Mum would always say, 'Don't date white men, and don't date Chinese men, and make sure he's Christian. Not Anglican, though'." I paused, looking around us. "Actually, she'd probably be horrified we're eating in a Japanese restaurant, too."

Henry nodded once. "Note to self: next time I visit your mother, pretend I've converted to Christianity and don't mention how much I like sushi. Got it."

I was laughing with him, but in the back of my mind I was still acutely aware of what I was saying. My mum *was* traditional. If she knew what I was thinking about my body these days and how I wished I could change myself... *fuck*. At least she was thousands of kilometres away and had to look after grandma so she couldn't suddenly show up at my home and accidentally catch me trying to look like I wanted to.

It was dark when we'd finished our dinner and went to leave the restaurant. "Mind if I stay over?" Henry asked me. "I'm probably over the limit to drive back to the bay tonight."

I pressed my lips together. "I need to do some more work on the project," I said, remembering Diane's insistence Henry not be exposed to it. "Which means I'm probably going to need to lock you in the bedroom or something."

He grinned sideways at me. "That'd be okay..."

I narrowed my eyes at him. "Alone."

He tilted his head. "Knew there was a catch. That's fine. I need to finish the book I'm reading, anyway."

We walked back to my building through a road in The Rocks, and it bordered a park lined with palm trees. The street lights were a gentle orange, and they cast a sort of tropical light on the gardens of the townhouses on the other side of the road. We could have been walking up a street in any nice part of Sydney, except here every single car parked along the road was gold-plate prestige. Behind us, the Sydney Harbour Bridge loomed over the houses.

Henry had his hands in his pockets as we walked, smiling at the streetscape. "This is a nice area, isn't it? Very cosmopolitan, but there's something quiet and suburban about it, too."

My favourite thing about it was its complete lack of reflective surfaces, but I didn't say as much.

When we got back to my building and stepped into the lift, Henry's hand was idly stroking my lower back. He didn't usually inadvertently touch me like that, and he was generally pretty upfront about just asking for it if he wanted sex. I wondered about that hand.

I didn't wonder very long about it, though, because when the doors slid open on my floor and Henry stepped out of the lift, he

193

stopped suddenly and I nearly walked straight into him. Over his shoulder, I could see a familiar shape seated against my door. She didn't see us straight away, though, because she had her eyes closed and headphones in her ears.

"That's Bree, isn't it?" Henry asked in a really philosophical tone.

I groaned audibly as I walked out of the lift behind him. "That's her."

I wanted to be annoyed at her for *again* showing up whenever she felt like it, but I was too relieved that she wasn't at home with whatever was going on there. Especially after all the possibilities I'd been discussing with Henry.

She opened her eyes and looked up at us. I had expected her face to light up like it always did when she saw me, but she didn't. Instead, her eyes were swimming and she looked *really* upset. My stomach dropped. What had happened?

"Wow, okay," Henry said quickly. "I think that might be my cue to leave." He kissed my cheek.

"Fuck," I said, closing my eyes for a second. "Fuck. I'm sorry, Henry."

He nodded. "It's okay. I'll take a taxi home, we can talk tomorrow." He then glanced back at Bree and said quietly to me as he stepped back into the lift, "Good luck."

Bree hauled herself off the floor, but she didn't come running up to me like she usually did. Instead, she waited for *me* to walk up to *her.* When I got to her, she just swallowed and looked up at me. "I'm sorry," she said in a tiny little voice. "I ruined your evening with Henry."

I sighed; *Bree.* "Not really," I said. "I was just going to come home and do work. Come on. Come in and tell me what happened."

I let us both in, and literally as soon as I'd closed the door, she had her arms around me. I braced myself against the wall so I didn't fall over. I was still wearing my heels, and I tried to awkwardly kick them off.

"I'm sorry," she said again into my blouse. "I'm sorry..."

I put a hand behind her head. It was *so, so* strange to think that this was the same girl posting all those awfully sexual photos of

194

herself on the internet. Fuck. What could turn that giggling, energetic, frighteningly extroverted girl into *this*? It *must* be something awful. God, I felt sick about that. I felt sick. I was scared about what she was going to tell me.

"Bree, what happened?" She shook her head. I wasn't sure if that meant 'no' as in I'm not telling you, or 'no' as in nothing. "Seriously, you look really upset."

She pulled away from me for a moment. She was a mess. "Can I have a tissue?"

"Yeah," I said, and led her into the bedroom, grabbing one from the bedside table and handing it to her.

She sat down on my mattress, blowing her nose and then staring at the scrunched tissue in her palm. She looked absolutely miserable. It actually hurt to look at her like this. "Can I do anything to help?" I asked. "Anything?"

"You should change," she said, as if I'd never asked her anything.

I did feel uncomfortable like this, but honestly, it could wait. Everything could wait. I sat there silently beside her for a little while, hoping she would spontaneously tell me. She didn't. Maybe Henry was right when he'd said, 'You're doing a lot to avoid asking her'. Maybe I should just do it. Not knowing and having to imagine all the awful things that might be happening to her would be *far* more fucking agonising than whatever she could say. It took me a minute or so to work myself up to it.

I took a breath. "Is someone hurting you?" I wasn't even sure how to ask it. "Or, is someone, like..."

"No," she said almost angrily, jamming her eyes shut and spilling fresh tears down her cheeks. "No, no one's beating me up," she said. "Or doing anything like that. But it would be *fucking easier* if someone was, because as soon as I say 'no, I'm not being abused' people are like, 'oh, well, it can't be that bad, then' and they treat me like I'm overreacting."

It would be *easier* if she were being abused? Did she *really* mean that? "Overreacting to what?"

She closed up again, and shook her head. "You can't do anything about it anyway, no one can. I'm just *stupid.* I should just be happy I'm not living in some terrorist war-zone or something."

"Bree," I said. "I've been worrying about you all day. Seriously, all day. I was sitting at my desk this morning trying to figure out what the hell is going on with you. I know it's your business and you don't have to tell me, but it's driving me *fucking nuts* not knowing," I said. "Especially when you show up here, like, distraught and then expect me to be content just watching you cry and not being able to help."

She took a deep breath, gently scrunching the tissue in her hands. *You're going to tell me finally,* I thought.

I was wrong. "I'm sorry," she repeated *again*, and then came more tears. "I shouldn't have come here, I just," she took a ragged breath, "I just—you always make me feel better. But now *you* feel *worse*." She leant into my hand. "Did you really worry about me all day?" she asked. I nodded at her and her face crumpled up. "I told myself, 'when you meet her, be really nice, because she has this really hardcore job and she works like a million hours...'" She swallowed. "And now I'm just making it worse."

"Bree..."

There was something in her eyes as she looked up at me. "Okay," she forced out of her mouth, but her jaw was so tight she could hardly move it. "Okay, but it's a long story, so you should have your shower and get changed first."

"And then you'll tell me?"

She could barely speak, so she just nodded.

I touched her cheek and sighed. "Okay," I said, releasing a long, measured breath. "Okay. Go grab yourself a slice of cake or something while you're waiting. Carbs are supposed to cheer people up. I'll be really quick."

I was as fast as I could be in the shower; I didn't need to wash my hair tonight anyway, so I just got rid of all of my makeup. At least I couldn't focus too much on how jarring it was to see myself topless, because I was too worried about what Bree was going to say. What if it *was* something really, really awful that was happening to her, even though she said it wasn't? She'd lied to me before, maybe she was lying to me now. Fuck, I hoped it wasn't that, I did. But what if it was?

I threw on the hoodie and jeans, and then walked out into the living room, expecting to see Bree on the couch, maybe eating her cake.

She wasn't there, though.

"Bree?" I called, checking the kitchen, the balcony—I even ducked back into my bedroom and made sure she wasn't curled up in the doona somewhere.

Walking back into the living room, I realised how silent it was. It was at that point that I saw she'd left my Opal card and some small change on the kitchen bench.

She'd left. Fuck, she'd *left*. And she had no money, no means of getting home and it was fucking dark outside. I took a breath. *Shit.* Shit! Why the *hell* would she do this?

I rushed over to my handbag and picked up my phone, hurriedly fumbling around with it and calling her number. She rejected the call, and when I tried again she rejected that one, too. Fuck! Now, on top of what was going on at home, she was wandering around the laneways in Sydney at night in that tiny skirt with no way of getting anywhere safe.

I leant against the kitchen counter for a second. I'd only been five, maybe ten minutes in the shower. She can't have gotten *that* far, and she was probably going towards the train station. I'd stepped into my old sneakers and rushed out the door before I'd even thought about it, and only realised when I saw myself in the mirrors in the lift that I was still dressed like a guy.

I stared at my reflection. I wasn't just *dressed* like a guy, I was dressed up *as* a guy. I didn't have time to go back home and change, though. If she was close by the hotel I could still catch her.

I put the hood over my head and belted through the lobby as fast as I could, hoping none of the staff would recognise me.

It was dark outside, and the laneways that lead towards the station weren't actually that well-lit. I half-walked, half-jogged along them, looking for her. Aside from the odd person walking back home from work and one very concerning group of suspicious-looking teenagers, there was hardly anyone out. It was the perfect environment for someone to pull over in their car next to a sweet little blonde girl and pretend to offer her a ride home.

While I was imagining all manner of fucked-up scenarios, I recognised her silhouette down the end of one of the lanes. God, the *relief*. She was in one piece and thank *god* she hadn't done something stupid like trying to hitch-hike home. "Bree!"

She stopped walking and turned back towards me as I jogged up to her. I hugged her briefly, and then stood back, holding her shoulders. "Bree, what the fuck? Just–*what the fuck*?" I hugged her again, and she let me, just standing passively in place. "Why did you *do* that? Are you *trying* to get yourself mugged or killed?"

She shook her head slowly. It was like all the energy I usually expected of her had been sucked out and she was just this shell of herself. "I didn't want to make everything worse for you and just be another thing you have to stress about," she said. "So I left."

"...thereby causing me to fucking stress about you!" I pointed out. "It's too late to just disappear, Bree, I'm already stressing. If you wanted me not to, you never should have dragged me to dinner in the first place." I stood up, and went to run my hand through my hair, *again* forgetting it was long. Thank *god* she was okay, but how the fuck was I *this* tied up in what was going on for her? I may have been casually messaging her on Deviant Art for ages, but I'd only met her three weeks ago, and *seriously*, I'd only really been close to her this week. *One week!*

"Why?" I kind of asked the universe.

She thought I was talking to her. "I'm sorry."

I took her by the shoulders for second. "You drive me fucking crazy," I said. "You *are* fucking crazy. But, please, *please,* don't ever do anything like this again. You'll kill me."

I released her and stood back, taking a deep breath. I didn't know what else to say, either about her running out like that or whatever was going on at her home. If she wasn't going to tell me, she wasn't going to tell me. And it was driving me *fucking crazy with worry* but I guessed I'd just have to deal with it.

"Come on," I said, giving up. I took her arm the same way she'd taken mine dozens of times when we'd been walking around Sydney. "Come back to my place. You can't go anywhere at this time of night. Maybe you can call Courtney or something and talk to her instead, if you don't want to tell me."

She sucked air through her teeth. "Yeah, right. She's fucking in love with him," she said quietly.

I stopped in my tracks and looked down at her, my jaw open. Her brother?

Bree didn't look up at me. I didn't want to push her, and it took her some time to be able to say anything else. "It's really complicated," she said. "Like, really. When I start thinking about how I would explain it to you, everything's just so fucking unfair I can't even breathe. It's just so fucked up. I don't want to tell you because it sounds like it's nothing, but it's not. It's *really* not. I don't even want to think about it."

I wished I had Henry's ability to cut through everything and just ask the right questions, but I didn't. I just wanted to know she was safe. "Is he... doing anything to you?"

She deflated. "Not in the ways people actually care about."

I watched her for a moment, and then exhaled. I just couldn't imagine what sort of person could want to hurt Bree—other than nameless, faceless kidnappers, that is. But her *own brother*? Henry was so fiercely protective of his sister. I wondered what sort of person wasn't. Who would hurt someone like Bree?

At least now I had some idea why talking about it was difficult for her. "Come on," I said, starting to walk. "You're 18 now. Let me show you why 'four hundred thousand bottles of red wine' in the cupboard is better than having milk in the fridge."

She took my arm, and I think she might even have smiled a little when I quoted her. I flashed her a lopsided one of my own, and led her home.

TWELVE

Fuck, my *head*. I wasn't even properly awake yet and it was *killing* me. With my eyes still closed, I put a palm against one of my cheeks. My face felt hot, and that was in direct comparison to the fact the rest of me was shiver-cold.

Where was my doona?

I felt around the mattress for it, expecting that I'd probably kicked it off at some point. But when my hand landed on something solid, warm and *breathing* I had one of those panicked moments where I *really worried* about what I'd done while I was drunk. Had Henry come over last night after all? I didn't think I'd—

—shit, *Bree.*

Despite my splitting headache, I sat bolt upright in bed, twisting towards the something. It *was* her; her curls were spilt out all over the second pillow and she had both the doona and the extra blanket coiled around her. I could only see below the knee on one of her legs, but it looked bare. I gaped at her, feeling the panic set in.

Fuck, had we—? I stared open-mouthed at her as she stirred, yawning. Fuck. *Fuck!* Had I gotten so completely wasted that I'd slept *with a girl*?

Even as I was asking myself that, though, I had a patchy memory of pretending to smother her with the doona as I'd tucked her in on the couch. Yeah, I was pretty sure she'd fallen asleep on the couch and I'd staggered in here and passed out by myself. God, that was a relief.

I lay carefully back down again, staring up at the ceiling and laughing at myself. As bits and pieces of the night started to slowly come back to me, it became very clear nothing like that had happened. Before we'd gone to bed separately, Bree had made me watch three or four episodes of *oh my god the best TV show on earth*—which, by the way, was *far* from actually being the best TV show on earth—and we'd been sitting across the couch from each other.

That didn't answer the question about what she was doing in my bed, though.

Her eyes fluttered open. "Good morning," she said sleepily.

I narrowed my eyes at her. "You're not where I left you," I observed.

She scrunched up her nose. "The couch was hurting my neck," she said. "And then I came in here, and you had this *whole ginormous* bed and you were only using, like, the very edge of it."

"So, naturally, that was a sign you needed to hop in."

"I was very careful when I climbed over you," she told me. "And then even though I was really cold I slept all the way over here so I

200

didn't wake you up." She adjusted the doona while she was speaking, and I could see the blue of my hoodie above it, which further explained why I was so cold. I must have given it to her at some point, because I was just in a t-shirt and jeans.

I looked back across the pillow at her in my bed, wearing my clothes. I didn't know why I was so surprised, though. Of *course* she was randomly in my bed: this was Bree we were talking about. Personal space was completely optional to her. I started to laugh but I just ended up in a long, pained groan with my hands over my face.

"Fuck, Bree..." I said, rubbing my sore eyes. At least she was happy again, though, and that was what counted. Remembering those red, puffy eyes and that tragic little voice... "Well, better in here than on the streets of Sydney, I guess."

She snorted. "And way more fun. And don't try and pretend you didn't have fun last night, because, look..."

She half-sat up and felt around inside the doona, rescuing her phone. After a few seconds of waiting for something to open on it, she held the screen towards me. I could hear the tinny buzzing of bad speakers and someone laughing quietly. When I squinted at the screen, it was *me*. A video of me. I'd obviously tripped and fallen on the rug because I was on all fours, *laughing* forever about it instead of actually getting up. Bree was giggling so hysterically from behind the camera you could hear her struggling to breathe.

At least my face wasn't really in the video. I would have deleted it anyway, but before I could touch the trash can icon on the screen, Bree snatched it out of my reach.

"You'd better delete that," I told her.

She gave me a pixie grin. "No way," she said, and then played it again to herself.

I gave up, rolling onto my back and yawning, half-watching her beside me.

There were obviously some missing parts of last night; I didn't remember her taking that video at all. I strained to remember what we'd done before we'd watched that TV show; I think I'd spent about twenty minutes or so trying to do some work. Bree had come up behind me and had proceeded to tell me that it was stupid to call pink diamonds pink when they weren't. I'd Google-imaged some 1P-category pink diamonds to prove they *were* pink, but then we'd ended up having a brief argument over whether her school tie was pink or coral. It was obviously coral and the fact she vehemently declared it wasn't *drove me crazy to the point of wanting to strangle her*, because who was the schoolgirl and who did professional design work for the marketing department of a Fortune 500 company here? Obviously I knew what I was doing which was probably partially why Jason and Diane had chosen me for... Wait, didn't Jason say something about...

I sat upright again. *Shit!* I had that meeting before work this morning with Diane and Jason!

"Oh my God!" I checked the clock on my phone and then clambered off the mattress, head pounding. "I have a meeting this morning I forgot about!"

I staggered into the bathroom to wash my face, wrestling some hardcore nausea. This was one serious hangover; I felt like I really needed the whole day to sleep it off. However, taking sick days at Frost was code for 'never promote me', and, on top of that, I really couldn't waste a single day on this project. I didn't have the time. Speaking of time, *fuck*, I was going to be late for this meeting!

Bree was only just getting out of bed when I rushed back in there. As soon as she stepped out of the doona, all I saw beneath the hoodie was skin. I stopped. Was she *serious?* "Bree, are you *not wearing pants?*" I asked her with the wardrobe open almost as far as my jaw was. "Were you in bed beside me and *not wearing pants?*"

She shrugged. "I'm wearing undies," she said, like that made it perfectly fine. "And your jumper is kind of long anyway."

I put my palm to my forehead and *groaned* as she shut the bathroom door behind her.

Despite the fact I was in a huge hurry, I still struggled to get my dress on. I kept telling myself it was ridiculous of me to be this hung up on *fabric,* and it was the same fabric that people made men's suits out of. No matter how much I deconstructed it, though, it didn't make it any easier. And actually, the only thing that ended up getting me into it was hearing Bree turn off the water in the shower and worrying that she'd see my breasts in this godawful lacy bra if I didn't put the damn thing on.

I rushed putting on my makeup and I rushed my hair and in the end I had us out of the door at a reasonable hour. I didn't have time to take her to the train station, though, so I parted ways with her under the George Street overpass, pushing my Opal card and a few small notes into her hand.

She was laughing as she stuffed them into the front pocket of her bag. "Min, you look *so* hung-over," she said. "I bet you have a terrible headache."

I wondered if the heavy sunglasses I was wearing gave it away. "Not at all," I said flatly. "I feel fantastic."

"Oh, yeah?" She grabbed my hand and pulled me downwards, trying to say really loudly next to my ear, "Then I guess you won't mind *if I do this*!"

She was lucky I'd taken some serious painkillers, because even on them I felt like blood was going to start pouring out of my ear after she'd shouted in it. I shook her off. "I hate you."

She looked delighted, still giggling. "No you don't, you're *smiling*."

I tried to do something about my smile. "I do. I actually hate you. It's why I watched that terrible TV show with you for hours last night and why I bought you that bracelet." My smile had crept back by the time I'd finished that sentence, but Bree's had dropped right off her face as soon as I'd said 'bracelet'.

I glanced down at her wrist; it was bare. "You're not wearing it," I noted. Maybe she *didn't* like it?

Bree made a face. "I can't wear jewellery with my school uniform," she said, glossing over the fact her uniform skirt was so short it could cameo in a B-grade porno. "So I left it at home."

Well, that made sense: she wasn't wearing any other jewellery, either. My old high school had been just as strict and randomly hypocritical. And, speaking of school, I checked my phone—*shit*. I had ten minutes to be in the office and she was going to miss her train.

"Okay." I looked her up and down. "Well, as much as I'd love to have my ears shouted in all day, I have to run. Are you staying over tonight, too?" My weather app said it was going to be a really nice night, so I figured that maybe we could watch more of that terrible show of hers out on the balcony over some dinner.

She looked down at her feet and shook her head. "Nah, Mum doesn't work nights on Wednesday, Thursday or Friday."

"Oh," I said. No dinner and TV on the balcony, then. "Well maybe Saturday?" She nodded, still looking at the ground. I didn't want to make her sad again, but... I couldn't help but ask. "Are you going to be okay until then?"

She shrugged. "Yeah, I guess."

I winced. I wanted more assurance than that, but I also *really, really* needed to not be any later for this meeting than I already was. "I hope that's true, Bree," I said, and then cupped her cheek for a second. "Okay, I *really* have to go."

She nodded, and then smiled a half-hearted goodbye at me, turning and walking towards the pedestrian crossing. I waited until she waved at me from the other side of the road before I spun and rushed uphill towards Frost, trying as hard as possible not to think about how much my head hurt or how sick I felt.

It was 8:30 when I got into the office, and Jason was waiting for me by the door of Oslo with his arms crossed. He did *not* look pleased.

"I'm sorry, I'm sorry!" I said, jogging past him into the office and dropping my bag into my bottom drawer. "I'm not feeling that great, but I'm ready."

"The one day that you're not here before six..." he said, shaking his head at me. "Well, at least you *look* sick. Maybe we won't both get caned."

I wasn't sure what hurt more: my head or being told off by my boss, but the strong painkillers I'd taken weren't touching either of those things. I was starting to worry that I was going to get in trouble again, but Diane's assistant was only just handing her a jumbo latte as we went into her office, and her computer hadn't even finished booting up.

"Thanks," Diane told her assistant, and then sat down and gestured hospitably towards the chairs opposite her desk. "Good morning, take a seat."

Jason sat down easily, and I slowly lowered myself into the chair beside him, my head throbbing so much from running that my vision was pulsing in sync with it. And my stomach... I had a horrible image of myself just throwing up all over Diane's desk. Oh, god, there wasn't anything *worse* I could do. Why did I drink so much last night when it was *Bree* who really needed the distraction? *Why? Why did I do this to myself?*

"Min." I looked up at Diane as she spoke to me. It must have been apparent how bad I felt, because she frowned. "Are you not feeling too well?"

"I'm fine," I lied, palms sweating. "Probably just a virus. I'll get over it."

She watched me for a moment. "Hmm," she said, giving me the smallest possible smile. "Good thing you're all the way over there, then. Anyway, if you could provide with me an update on the project, that would be fantastic. Jason's given me some details, but he *is* in charge of 14 other teams, so I'd rather hear it from you."

Thinking straight enough to relay our progress was actually a bit of a challenge, but I thought I sounded coherent and professional enough just to pass as someone who was a bit sick. I went over the project so far, explaining the decisions we'd made at each point and what was still left to be done.

She nodded slowly as she listened to me, occasionally asking me questions. Eventually, she said, "Well, that all sounds on track. Russia is an excellent choice, and if you're selling to Vladivostok, it's quite likely we'll get some demand out of Beijing, too."

I hadn't even thought about future expansions, but I obviously wasn't going to tell Diane that. I pretended it had been part of the decision all along. "Strategically, it's a good place to position ourselves."

Diane looked satisfied by that. "A solid plan," she said. "How's information security?"

"Terrible," Jason butted in, abandoning his professional vocabulary again. "Mini has that Arab kid in her team, and he doesn't understand the meaning of 'encryption'."

I flinched as he said that, and I think Diane noticed. She didn't say as much though, focusing on the rest of his complaint as she directed me with a frown. "Why aren't you dealing with this?"

"I spoke to John yesterday and I haven't received any unencrypted emails since," I assured her, sounding far more confident than I felt. "But yes, he needed to be told several times."

She didn't look pleased. "Watch him," she said. "There will be trouble if my brother finds out where we're planning on setting up in Western Australia."

"Understood," I told her.

"And," she said, remembering something and pointing at me. "I saw you two together last week. Why was that?"

My eyebrows went up. "I've bumped into him a few times," I said. "We talked a bit, but it was purely small talk."

Jason scoffed. "It's never small talk with that man," he said coarsely. "Excuse my language, Diane. But Mini, he's a fucking asshole."

Diane didn't look shocked or angry, and she didn't ask him to watch his language, either.

It was the strangest fucking conversation. I was listening to the guy who was joking around with Sean at every possible opportunity—and maybe doing more than that with him—calling him a 'fucking asshole'. Suspect choice of wording aside, it didn't really seem like the way you'd expect someone to describe a person they got along that well with. And, Diane? Diane was Sean's *sister,* the very essence of decorum, and *still* she was happy for her employees to call him derogatory names. I was beginning to think that maybe Henry and Alice were the only balanced siblings on the planet. What the hell was going on in people's families? I just couldn't imagine how siblings could end up so much at odds. Like, Mum and I didn't get along at all and sometimes it felt like ten thousand kilometres wasn't enough, but she was still my mother.

It was all incredibly screwed up, and I wondered if Sean knew the way they were talking about him. Hell, I wondered if *Diane* knew how close Sean and Jason appeared to be and that they might even be involved with each other.

"I'll be careful with what I say to Sean," I promised them, and apparently that marked the end of the meeting.

Family feud aside I thought it went quite well, and while I was congratulating myself for not throwing up on Diane's table as we left, Diane stopped me as soon as Jason was gone.

"Min," she said, briefly closing the door beside us. "Mind if we have a word?"

That wasn't actually a question, so of course I nodded.

She was watching me with a very measured gaze. It unsettled me even though she was so much shorter. "How do you like working in marketing, Min?"

"I love my job," I said with practised ease.

She nodded, and then appeared to very carefully choose her words. "Marketing is a bit of an anomaly in most large companies," she began, somewhat cryptically. "The skillset required to excel in it generally differs from that of other departments. Take Aaron, for example," she said, referring to one of the older 'fatherly' leads I'd previously had. I'd hated working with him; he'd spoken down to me and treated me like a secretary. "He's a fantastic networker. We'd lose a huge web of contacts if he were to leave us. And Gerard, he's another fantastic member of our team." I didn't like working with that man, either. He had the tendency to freely laugh at other people's expense.

She reeled off a whole list of names, and I began to see a pattern; all the people she was naming and complimenting were *fucks*. Actual fucks, there wasn't a name on the list that I'd want to be put in a team with. "And, of course, Jason is the best closer this department's ever had. He's a real asset to Frost International."

She paused, letting that sink in. "When I'm hiring for this department, I'm often presented with the difficult choice of hiring the type of employee I might choose for another area of the business, and someone who's going to shake hands and seal the deal, so to speak. This can make marketing teams operate a little less smoothly at times. However, what matters is that we get signatures on those dotted lines. If we can't sell our products, we don't *have* a business."

I nodded, not following her completely.

"So," she said. "Occasionally I'm required to overlook certain behaviours I see in order to ensure that I still get those signatures and we still have a very healthy, very profitable business. Working closely with very strong marketers like Jason, I imagine you've discovered you have to do the same. I trust this hasn't been a problem for you?"

I finally understood what she meant, and it left a *really* bad taste in my mouth. It must have been triggered by that 'Arab' comment she'd seen me react to earlier.

She was asking me a trick question, though. Of course Jason's complete lack of regard for people was a problem—he was a manager for Christ's Sake—but I knew actually saying as much would give my career the kiss of death. So I looked right back at her and forced a calm smile. "I have no trouble working with Jason," I said through my teeth. "I've been working in marketing for five years, after all."

She smiled faintly and nodded. "That is a very good point," she said, visibly relaxing. "And good to hear, too: you're doing some great work on this project. It would be a shame if you decided to transfer out for something minor. Anyway," she opened the door again and stood aside politely so I had room to step through it, "thanks for your work. I look forward to attending functions in Russia and seeing women wearing our merchandise."

She showed me out and I stood by the door for a second.

Under all the compliments and explanations of how marketing departments functioned, there was something sinister in there. I didn't think she was *threatening* me exactly, but I didn't like it. It was one thing to just kind of know I needed to put up with Jason, and quite another to be told my career in marketing was over if I didn't.

That, on top of the Sean-Diane stuff, the Sean-Jason stuff and the fact happy families seemed to be a fictional construct in Australia was just making my terrible headache even worse. *Ugh.* I sighed, and started to walk around the corner to Oslo. I'd need to ask Henry what he thought about all of that.

I walked back in the office to find Sarah already seated at her desk.

"You *are* here," she said, and had started to say something else, but she cut it short and laughed. "Whoa, *someone* didn't get any sleep last night. Did Henry stay over?"

"Nope," I told her. "I was out fighting evil."

I did *not* want to tell her that it was Bree who had stayed and that it was because of Bree that I looked like this, because knowing her, she'd take it the wrong way. It was difficult to take it the right way, actually, especially given that we'd ended up in bed together. I didn't want to have to explain to her that Bree needed to be held to different behavioural standards than normal people.

She laughed. "Looks like evil won," she said, and handed me a Red Bull. "I have Panadol if you want some, too."

I shook my head, and then winced as the movement made it throb. "Diane says our project is going well and she congratulates us," I told her instead, changing the subject.

Recognition passed across her face. "Oh, that's right, *that's* where you were," she said. "And hey, go us! You should buy us lunch to celebrate."

She was probably right. "I should, shouldn't I? Maybe I'll go down at lunch and buy Chinese from the place around the corner for us all or something." Just talking about food made me feel ill, I didn't relish the idea of having to deal with the smell of it.

"Looking forward to it," she said, and then she watched me intently for a few seconds. "So," she began in a playful voice. "I noticed you *didn't* delete your Facebook last night as promised, so I sent you and your friend an invite for Friday."

She did *what?* I leant back in my chair and sighed at her. "You're lucky I'm way too sick to bother doing all the paperwork required to fire you."

"There's more..." she said, and then turned her laptop toward me. She had Facebook chat up, so I leant towards the screen.

Sarah had hit up Bree on Facebook last night about the invite, and when she'd told Bree where the venue was, Bree had replied, *"wow thats really close to here"*.

Sarah looked smug. "Close to 'here', Min," she said. "Not 'close to Min's'." She closed Facebook while I was glaring at her. Why had she asked about Henry if she knew who was with me last night? "Anyway, I was actually thinking that stunt I pulled with Henry in getting you out of the office might also work with Bree. But she was pretty hesitant and wouldn't accept the invite on your behalf."

That made me smile a little. If Bree was angling herself towards more quasi-expensive jewellery, it was working. "Good," I said. "At least I know who's on my side and who isn't." I gave her a sideways look. "Anyway, I think I actually agreed to come drinking with you when the project is done. You don't even need to pull any stunts. And you don't need to go using Facebook to check up on the location of my friends or invite me to stuff, either."

She shrugged as we both reluctantly got ready to start working.

"Maybe not, but it's more fun this way." She grinned at me and then turned back to her screen.

I swung my chair back towards my own. I had trouble focusing on work because of how crap I felt, though. I might have ducked into the bathrooms to put a wet towel on the back of my neck for a bit, but there were giant mirrors facing the basins in there. I was pretty sure seeing myself in a dress and plastered in makeup had zero chance of making me feel any better, so I ended up deciding just to push through how sick I felt.

Moscow had gotten back to me to set up a video conference at 4pm which meant that I needed to hurriedly book meeting rooms and equipment and find an interpreter. Jason insisted that the stream shouldn't run on the main network, and it turned out to be a nightmare trying to get wireless coverage from Oslo reaching down to the meeting rooms.

Because of all that hassle, I didn't get to see Henry. About half an hour before the video conference started and while I was sitting in the meeting room with Jason and worrying myself half-to-death that I wasn't ready to set up a pitch, Henry texted me.

"The suspense is killing me," it read. *"Is Bree okay? Are you okay?"*

I looked up; Jason was busy on his tablet and wasn't paying any attention to me, so I texted back, *"Yeah, it's something with her brother, she didn't say what but at least it's not physical."* I wasn't sure what else to tell him and whether or not I should say she'd run out, but I knew what else I *wouldn't* be telling him: 'Bree and I got drunk together, she slept over and we ended up in the same bed. Also she wasn't wearing pants when I woke up.' Oh, and the part where I was dressed up as a guy the whole time, too. I shouldn't forget to mention that.

I squeezed my eyes shut and groaned. I'd better just change the subject. *"Actually I have some work-related and Bree-related stuff I need to discuss with you. I'll probably need to sleep tonight but do you want to come over tomorrow?"*

"No can do," he sent back, *"tomorrow I have to fly down to Melbourne and help interview graduates again. Frost had so many applications this year that they almost need to hire more HR staff to chew through them all. Sunday is looking good. Want to catch up*

then? Maybe we could do something a bit more romantic than usual and go and see a movie. I'm thinking Horror. Nothing more romantic than Horror."

I chuckled, and then smothered it when I remembered who was in the room with me. "*Sounds great. Come over after lunch.*" After I'd sent that, I put my phone away and got straight back to stressing that I would fuck up this meeting.

I had expected Jason to run the teleconference, but when I'd asked him what he'd planned to say, he said he hadn't planned to say anything because it was *my* meeting. "It's just a first contact meeting," he'd said, checking NRL scores on his tablet. "Aside from actually insulting them, there's probably not that much you can stuff up."

"But you're here," I'd observed.

He grinned. "In case you stuff up anyway."

I didn't stuff it up, though, the interpreter arrived on time and Moscow called in a few minutes later. The three people I ended up talking to on screen were a guy who was obviously the boss—he introduced himself to me as the contact I'd emailed—a female personal assistant who looked about Bree's age and another guy who didn't say much.

I explained in as little detail as possible about the products we were planning on selling and timeframes around the construction and operation of the mine. All three of them listened carefully until I was finished. Then, my contact and the other guy with him had a brief quiet discussion, too quiet for the interpreter to get much of it. When they were done, I asked, "So, can you think of any companies or people I should approach who might be interested? And if so, are you able to introduce us?"

The quiet guy finally spoke. "You know of Sasha Burov?" he asked me in excellent English.

"Of course I know about him," I said immediately. His name had come up repeatedly during scoping, it would be remiss of me to *not* know who he was. "He's one of the top diamond brokers in Eastern Russia. He buys for those intricate Korzhakov collections and that Russian-Italian designer," I thought for a second. "'Poletti-Pisani', I think it is? There are a whole host of even Western celebrities that commission jewellery from those collections."

The quiet man looked *very* impressed. He nodded once. "I am him," he said simply. "You can speak with my assistant here. Make me the appointment, book tickets. Frost International will put me in a nice hotel, I think, give me a good view of Sydney while I am there." He smiled, showing two rows of perfect teeth. "I look forward to meeting you. Perhaps we can do some business." He shook hands with my contact and then stood up out of frame and walked off.

Jason had looked up with surprise in the middle of that whole exchange, and then across at me. I must have had much the same expression. Had I just accidentally booked a sales pitch on my *first contact*?

I hurriedly checked dates with the young assistant, penned in Mr. Burov for after Easter and then ended the call and dismissed the interpreter.

For a minute or two Jason and I just sat back in our chairs. Had that just happened? Had I really just *booked a sales pitch on my first contact*?

"How the *fuck* did *you* do that?" Jason asked, lapsing back into his habit of swearing. I shook my head. He blew a stream of air through his lips. "I need a cigarette." He stood up. "Fuck. Good work, Mini. Very nicely done," he said, but his congratulations seemed more of an afterthought to his surprise.

I followed him upstairs, and went back with him to his office to lock up the tablet. His office wasn't empty, though: Sean Frost was seated in his chair, playing with a set of perpetual motion balls Jason had on his desk. Sean had obviously been waiting for Jason.

"Don't you do any actual work?" Jason asked him as he took my tablet from me and locked it with his in the filing cabinet.

"Jason, Min," Sean greeted us cordially, standing up. "If I'm not mistaken, supporting and socialising with my employees *is* part of my role?" He grinned. "Cigarette?"

"You fucking bet," Jason said, grabbing a packet of them out of his jacket. "Ms. Genius right here just scored us a pitch."

Sean looked over at me and smiled. It was really warm and genuine. "I'm not surprised," he said. "I hear good things about her. Congratulations, Min."

I was still completely spun out about what had just happened, but wow that felt good. The *other* co-CEO congratulating me, too? I could hardly believe it. I could actually hardly believe the whole last hour. I beamed at him.

Jason didn't look quite as sold on me. "Yeah, you hear good things from her boyfriend, right?" He laughed. "If he wants to get any ever again he's kind of obliged to say she's fantastic." Instead of inviting him to shove it, I laughed appropriately like Diane would have wanted me to as they walked out together.

They kept joking all the way to the balcony, and I watched them for just a second, wondering if Sean knew the things Jason said about him behind his back. Jason lit Sean's cigarette again, and Sean leant into the lighter. I watched as Jason grinned broadly at him; there was something predatory about it. If they weren't sleeping together, Jason was certainly acting like he wanted them to be. Why, though? Was he just trying to cover all his bases by cosying up to both CEOs? He worked pretty closely with Diane, and I remembered Diane saying he was the only other person she'd trusted with regard to the project.

I made a face. Whatever, I wasn't going to learn much by standing here and staring at them. I also really couldn't be bothered with the sort of teasing I'd get if anyone else in the department caught me staring at two attractive men.

I had better things to be thinking about, anyway. Like *the fact I'd booked a sales pitch on my first contact.* I might actually have skipped back into Oslo, if not for these goddamn heels.

Since my team were all probably going to work through the evening and I was *fucking ecstatic* that I'd somehow managed to fluke a sales pitch, I shouted them to dinner, too, in order to congratulate them. Hell, I'd shout them to as many meals as they wanted as long as we kept pushing along at the pace we were tracking at. I hadn't even spoken to Vladivostok yet.

While we were preparing for that meeting the following day I bought food for everyone again, and later I found Sarah with her head in her hands over a half-finished rice and black bean stir-fry. "This project is going to *really* put me off Chinese takeaway," she said, and then tried to soldier through the rest of it as she copied and pasted some stats to me.

Unfortunately, when I did have my meeting with Vladivostok on

Thursday, it didn't go quite as spectacularly. I did get a few names and a few numbers to follow up on, however, and my team spent all the rest of that day doing research on those people. Meanwhile, I went and read up as much as I could on this Sasha Burov to try and decide what sort of material we should develop for him. I thought over what he'd said: 'Give me a good view of Sydney'. Maybe he didn't get down to Australia very often? That might be something I could use in the marketing materials.

I went home on Thursday night and watched about four hours of Tourism Australia commercials and some related documentaries. Bree even sent me a few links on Deviant Art to the ads her extended family in Europe really liked when I told her what I was doing. And, as soon as I was sure Moscow was open on Friday, I called in to speak to Sasha Burov's assistant in order to ask about the last time he'd been down here. She had to double-check, but she actually thought it might have been more than a decade.

That settled it, I thought, lacing my fingers behind my head and spinning around in my office chair. I was going to exploit my country's natural beauty to get his name on that dotted line.

I spent most of Friday evening tabbing through thousands and thousands of images of Australian landscapes. I wasn't sure exactly what I wanted to use or how I wanted to use it, but usually in this sort of circumstance I would just come across something and get an idea. There didn't seem to be any reason to work late in the office if I was just looking at photo collections, though, so I went home and spent hours using up my bandwidth on high res landscapes, dressed comfortably in clothes that didn't make me feel like everything sucked.

Around midnight, my stomach started to grumble. It was annoying, because I only had a few hundred photos left on this particular site and I didn't want to leave it half-finished before bed. I tried to keep working anyway, but I kept being distracted by how hungry I was so I decided I'd just duck down to the late night pizza place on Cumberland. It would take me ten minutes and then I could probably keep going for another hour or two.

I went into my bedroom and opened my wardrobe, automatically going to get the same dress I'd worn all day so I could change into it before I left.

When I picked it up, I had that familiar wave of resentment. I didn't *want* to put it on again. I'd have to put on stockings and a bra, and makeup... It was almost enough to drive me back to the fridge to just eat Bree's crusty old birthday cake that was still in there. I really felt like pizza, though, and why the hell should I have to forgo it just because I couldn't face putting on any of my girly clothes again? I'd done my time in them this week.

Stop being ridiculous and put the damn thing on, I told myself as I looked down at the innocent fabric in my hands. It's not rocket science, Min. Just take off your comfy clothes, put one leg into it, followed by the other and zip it up. That's all you have to do.

I couldn't, though. I couldn't do it. I just couldn't spend one more second today dressed like something I wasn't.

I left the dress in the wardrobe and closed the door to the reflection of me in my jeans and hoodie. It was a relief, especially since I'd decided to try the bandages on again this evening. I probably didn't really need to wear them with anything except those tight button-up shirts, but I'd put them on earlier anyway, just to see what they looked like. They were actually quite uncomfortable; maybe I was wearing them wrong. Still, they weren't as uncomfortable as heels had been when I'd first started to wear *those,* and they *did* make my chest look completely flat. I turned sideways for a moment and held my hoodie against my stomach, admiring the smooth plane between my collarbones and my hips.

Fuck it, I thought, I'll just wear this down to the shop. It had been a complete non-event yesterday when I had been running around after Bree in this, and it was the middle of the night now. No one was going to see.

I did put my hood up as I went through the lobby, though, because I was still a bit worried the staff or other new employees staying at the hotel would recognise me. And while I was sure the staff saw some pretty dodgy stuff come in and out of the hotel, I didn't want to be anyone's 'Hey, you'll never guess what I saw at work today' story.

It was beginning to get a bit chilly outside; the breeze was pleasant, though, even this late at night. If it was nice weather again tomorrow, maybe Bree and I could sit out on the balcony after all.

I'd made a pact with Bree over text message that for every episode of her TV show we watched, she'd have to watch one of my cartoons. She'd pinkie-sworn, so it was settled. We could relax with the balcony door open, eat junk food and watch stuff. Sounded like a great Saturday, to be honest. Just like the last one I'd had with her.

Walking around in the dark like this reminded me of when she'd run out, though. I hoped again that nothing had happened to her while she'd been home the last couple of days. Maybe I should buy her something to cheer her up just in case? Not jewellery, though, something she didn't have to take off or put away.

I was so busy trying to decide what an appropriate Cheer-Up-Bree present was, that I didn't notice someone staring at me from the other side of the street. When I did notice, I didn't want to stop and turn my head around towards them because I was worried I'd get drawn into a conversation. I still wasn't convinced I *sounded* like a guy, and I really didn't want to find out how people would react to the discrepancy. I had enough fucking trouble dealing with it myself.

I'd hoped she'd give up if I just kept walking, but she didn't. She followed me all the way up the street, jogging as I walked faster. I could see her silhouette out of the very corner of my eye, and I could hear her heels clopping on the pavement.

It was completely irrational because I was much bigger than she was, but I was actually scared what would happen if she caught up to me.

Ahead of us, there was a pub on the corner and people were sitting along the walls of it, drinking and laughing. I exhaled. Maybe I was wrong; maybe she was just rushing to meet someone in there.

My relief didn't last very long though, because she crossed the street to get to me and reached up to pull my hood back, laughing. But as I faced her, for some reason absolutely certain I was about to cop a torrent of abuse like in high school, a familiar voice caught me *really* off-guard by saying, "Min! I knew it! It *is* you!"

I recognised that voice well before there was enough light for me to see who it was. You'd hope I would; I spent enough time at work. My stomach bottomed out as the silhouette stepped into the light. I saw her big grin before the rest of her features, and that her long hair was braided for once instead of loose around her shoulders. She was wearing significantly less than she did at work; no wonder I hadn't recognised her.

Now, I did. While I was frozen solid to the pavement, she grabbed my forearms—as touchy-feely as she always was—and looked delighted. "Fuck, you actually came, I can't believe it! This is *insane!*"

"Sarah?" I rasped, because it was all I could manage.

Shit.

THIRTEEN

"You look so different!" Sarah said as she held me at arm's length, looking me up and down. It was too late to stop her. It was too late to do anything about what she'd seen, so I just stood there, panicking. "Sorry for chasing you up the road, but I didn't want to yell out at some random person if it wasn't you. *Wow,* though. Bit of a difference from you in corporate getup..."

There was an implicit question in that and instead of answering it, I wanted to just turn around and run home. It was too late for that, too, wasn't it? She'd seen me in these clothes, and it was probably really obvious what look I was going for. Fuck. *Fuck,* I hoped she wouldn't tell anyone at work. Why did she have to find out *now*? Like *this*?

"I'm in the middle of doing some graphics for Pink and I just ducked out to grab some dinner," I stammered, conveniently neglecting to explain why I looked like *this* specifically, "and there's a little pizza place up further..."

She groaned. "You were going to buy pizza?" When I nodded, she shook her head at herself, looking a bit disappointed. "Hah, I should have known it was too good to be true. You *aren't* here to hang out with me," she said. "Well, you're going to anyway. By some fantastic coincidence, this place has table service open until one. You can just keep me company until the girls arrive later." She gestured for me to follow her.

I stayed put. When she raised her eyebrows at me, I held my arms out to indicate what I was wearing. "Sarah, I can't go in like this."

She didn't sound too concerned. "Uh, it's a pub? Pubs don't have dress codes. As long as you're wearing actual clothes, no one's going to throw you out."

I opened my mouth and took a breath, but I ended up just releasing it. I didn't want anyone from work to see me like this. I didn't want *any possible way* anyone in marketing or, most importantly, any possible way *Henry* could find out about this. Sarah... well, Sarah, herself, she was maybe okay. She hadn't told anyone about Bree, after all. But she was still *from* work, and I worried about mixing her in with this stuff.

When I didn't say anything, her frown deepened. She was onto me. "The dress code isn't what you meant, is it?" I shook my head. She pressed her bright red lips together for a second, looking intently at me. It seemed like she was having trouble figuring out what *she* wanted to say, too. Finally she took a tentative step towards me. "Can I just do something for a second? It won't hurt."

I didn't know what to expect, but I didn't think she'd do anything inappropriate. She wasn't Bree. "Okay..." I said hesitantly.

She glanced over her shoulder toward the pub to make sure no one was watching us, and then stepped in closer to me. Taking the hem of my hoodie, she pulled it gently downward. The fabric pulled flat against my body and it was very, very clear I'd done something to my breasts. There was no point in pushing her away now, she'd seen what was going on. I braced myself to be *really* ashamed by it; I was usually hugely uncomfortable with anything to do with them. It didn't happen this time, though. I mean, I was worried about what she was going to think, but I didn't feel self-conscious about my lack of chest. With the thick material the hoodie was made out of, the bandages weren't visible, either. It looked like there had been nothing there to begin with.

Her eyes widened and she released my jumper. "Wow," she said as she stood back with her jaw open for a second. She closed it quickly, though. "Wow. Okay."

She didn't ask, but I knew what her question was. "It's complicated."

Her eyes were still wide open. "Yeah, apparently," she said, considering what she'd just seen.

I looked down at the ground and nodded. Fuck. Well, she knew now. At least now she'd understand why I wasn't going to come inside with her. "Yeah, so," I said, "I'm going to go and get that pizza I was after."

She snapped out of her surprise and stepped in front of me when I went to leave. "No you're fucking not," she said. It was jarring to hear her swear; she didn't do it that often. "You're not getting away *this* time, not now." I opened my mouth to contradict her, and she interrupted me. "I don't care what you're going to say, your argument is void. It's pitch black in there and I promise you *no one* will recognise you, seriously. I almost didn't, and I wouldn't have if you'd never shown me that painting you did of yourself."

"Sarah, I—"

"Nope," she said shortly, leaning on one hip and crossing her bare arms. "I have bought you lunch almost every day, and every day for the past two weeks I've been doing all that menial crap for you. Now, I may not be as young and cute and blonde as that little friend you've got on the side, but if *she* can refuse to take no for an answer from you, I *certainly* deserve to do the same." I just stood there gaping at her as she added, "You said she'd carry you out of work if she wasn't so small? Well, I'm bigger, and I swear to god I'll carry you in there myself if you try to keep making excuses. It's *dark* in there, Min, and you cannot just leave me hanging now after the whole 'it's complicated' thing."

There... wasn't much I could say to that. She was clearly *not* going to let me get away, and she was right, anyway. She *had* been doing a lot of stuff for me, and I *had* run out on her last time we'd eaten. Fuck. *Fuck!* Now I felt bad, too. She'd been really great the last few weeks.

I looked past her at the pub. There was a gauntlet of people along the walls to get into it, though. "Are you sure no one will recognise me?"

She snorted. "Uh, *yeah*. You look like a—" she winced, "well..."

I looked back down at her. "A guy? You can say it, it's okay."

She sighed with relief. "Yeah, even with the whole," she indicated my chest with a wave of her hand, "I wasn't sure if you'd be insulted if I said that. But seriously, Min, it's kind of creepy how my boss now looks like an 18 year old boy." Her eyes were wide again. "Like, *really* creepy. Although you and that schoolgirl kind of makes more sense, now."

I was *not* following that topic anywhere. "My ponytail doesn't give me away?"

She considered it for a moment. "It actually just looks like a really bad fashion decision," she said, leaning around me to get another look at it. "Like you're some kid who's trying really hard to be cool and mature."

"Great," I said flatly. "Because I was worried people weren't going to be able to judge me, after all."

That made her laugh. "I think you've just about run out of excuses. Let's eat, I'm basically dying of a combination of starvation and curiosity." she said, and then took a few steps towards the pub. I didn't move. "What now?" she asked.

"Didn't you offer to carry me in, before?" I said in a complete deadpan. "Because I'm not going to walk if I don't really have to."

She groaned, waiting for me as I caught up to her anyway and we continued to the pub. "I think I've done enough for you this week," she said, looking sideways up at me. "Go on. Get in there and let's get dinner."

No one paid any attention to us as we past them. Sarah got a couple of second glances because she looked good, but otherwise we could have been any two people off the street walking into the pub.

When we'd stepped inside, I quickly realised Sarah wasn't kidding about the place being dark. It was nightclub dark, but there weren't any laser lights to break it up. Several groups of people were sitting in little booths that lined the walls, laughing, chatting and drinking, but whether or not they were Frost employees, I had no idea. That was because, unless we got right up close to people, there wasn't enough light to see the details of their faces at all.

Sarah led me over to a corner booth that had a 'Reserved' placard on it. She brushed it aside, explaining, "The guy who owns this place always does that for us. We've been coming here for like seven years."

No sooner had she said that and we'd sat down, a greasy middle-aged guy leant over the bar. "Sarah!" he called halfway across the floor, instead of actually coming over to our table. There was no music yet, but because there were so many people inside it was still difficult to hear him. "You want food?"

It was an interesting way of taking our order, that was for sure. "Some table service…" I said to Sarah with a smirk, and she kicked me underneath it.

"Potato wedges!" she yelled back. "A huge bowl with lots of sour cream and at least something resembling a salad." She looked at me, and I shrugged. I was almost too nervous to feel like food anymore. Turning back to the guy, she shouted, "Times two. And a bottle of something bubbly."

He gave us the thumbs up, and then disappeared behind the bar into what I presume was a kitchen, throwing a passing glance at a television mounted in the corner of the room. There was some sort of sports game playing on it.

"Min," Sarah said to get my attention. I looked back at her, and she was leaning forward across the table, watching me intently. When I didn't say anything, she prompted. "Come on, I'm dying here. This is the part where you tell me what's going on with you. Is this the 'personal thing' you were talking about the other day?"

"It *used* to be a personal thing," I said, and then glanced around us. *And I'd kind of like to keep it that way*, I thought. "What time did you say your friends were coming again?"

"Not for ages," she said dismissively. "Their time management skills leave a lot to be desired. So, this… thing, are you…" She stopped and made a face. "Sorry if I screw up, I don't know any of the words for this stuff. So, the point is to look like a guy, right?" I nodded, and she leant back in the booth, staring at me. "Is this just like some secret hobby, or…?"

If only. "Hah. I wish it was that simple." She had her eyes fixed on me with an intensity which said 'elaborate', so I did. "I mean, it's secret in that I don't want anyone to know. I wish it didn't have to be, but it does."

"*What* needs to be though? What is 'this' and 'it'? I won't tell anyone."

Before I even considered explaining I spent a few seconds checking around us again to make absolutely certain no one could hear. It took me several more to gather enough strength to actually say exactly what was going on for me in so many words. "I don't feel comfortable as a girl."

I don't know if Sarah had expected me to be so succinct, or if she just hadn't expected *that* to be the issue or what, but she looked *really* stunned. She sat back in the booth, staring at me. She didn't say anything straight away, either. "This is such a trip out," she said eventually. "You're *so* incredibly girly at work, even more girly than I am. You're always immaculately dressed, with pearls and earrings and stockings and even though you're six-foot-a-thousand, you still always wear really nice heels..."

I sighed deeply, and shrugged. "It takes me 20 minutes to get into my dress every morning. I hate it."

She spent a few seconds letting that settle. "Fuck," she said, swearing again. "So, you think you'd be better off as a guy, then?

I shrugged. "I don't know. I don't really know *what's* going on, to be honest. I just know what feels right and what doesn't." I paused. "You're only the second person who knows."

She still looked spun out. "Henry?" I shook my head. "*Bree?*" When I nodded, she needed to think about what that meant, too. "Fuck, Min... I mean, I kind of wondered about that painting, but I had *no* idea it would be something like this."

"That's kind of the way I'd prefer it, to be honest," I said. "I don't want this to get around at Frost."

She made a noise. "Yeah, you really don't," she said, and then looked more troubled the more she thought about it. "Wow, yeah, you *really* don't. Can you imagine what—Ah, here we go..." She was looking across at the bar and getting distracted by approaching food.

The greasy man walked out from behind it with a tray in one hand and a bottle of wine in the other. He plonked it all down on the table in front of us. "*Bon Appetit,*" he said in a really broad Australian accent, and then instead of pouring the wine or laying the food out nicely in front of us, he swaggered back behind the bar, sat on a barstool and stared upwards at the game on TV.

"Classy place," I commented as I tried to force myself to eat a potato wedge.

Sarah went straight for the wine, filling my glass to the brim and then pouring one for herself. "Eh, he always lets me eat for free because I drunkenly kissed him on his birthday like five years ago. Actual guests get reasonable service, but me and my friends are just part of the furniture so he's stopped bothering."

"So much for buying you dinner," I said with a tense smile as I accepted my wine glass from her. "I'll just have to pick up the bar tab, instead."

She pointed a potato wedge at me. "You'll be sorry you said that."

"Didn't you say you were a lightweight? I think I'm getting a great deal, here. Free food and all I need to do is get you trashed on a couple of glasses of sparkling."

She indulgently poured her sour cream *all* over her wedges. "A couple? I'll be on the floor after one."

"Even better. I'll help you out of here looking like I scored the hottest girl in the place." She stared at me for a second, and I faltered, remember what we'd been talking about. "Uh, I didn't mean—"

She broke into a laugh. "It's okay. I was just messing with you. But since I'm playing a long game of truth with you: I believe we were up to 'Bree'."

"We were?" I cringed a little. "What about her?"

"Come on, she's basically a cut and paste job from one of those 'Bid-on-my-virginity-dot-com' sites, school uniform and all. She's got the puppies out *all* over her Facebook page, and she was about ready to jump you in the street when I met her. Tell me with a completely straight face that you've *never* slept with her."

I opened my mouth to say exactly that, and then remembered waking up next to her earlier in the week. Technically, that was sleeping right?

I paused for too long apparently. "I *knew* it!" Sarah announced, holding her hands up in the air. "I totally knew it! Oh my god, Min, you are unbelievable!"

I put my face in my hands for a second. "It's not what you think, and she is *not* like that," I said. "She does show skin, sure, but she's just so sweet, she's *not* like that!" I realised how all of that sounded, and so just to make it perfectly clear to Sarah, I looked up at her from my hands and said, "I've slept *beside* her. Not with her. *Because she's a 'she' and we're just friends and I have a boyfriend.*"

Sarah stopped cheering, but she still looked pretty smug. She gestured at my torso. "Yeah, but you look like a 'he' and you *feel* like you might be a 'he' so I'm actually not sure what's more gay: you sleeping with Bree or you sleeping with Henry."

"Sarah, I'm straight," I said, pretending to cry into my hands.

"Again," she said, making a 'tada' motion at me and how I looked. "You being in the situation that you are, what does that even mean?" She reached across the table and gave me a solid pat on the shoulder. "Sorry to give you the third degree but your mysterious behaviour over the past few weeks has been driving me absolutely crazy. Here, drink your wine." She pushed the glass towards me again. "It's going to be okay, I promise."

I obediently drank deeply from it. "Put that in a contract so I can sue you if you don't deliver," I told her, giving up.

She sat back against the padded spine of the booth, eating another few wedges and washing them down with more wine as she watched me thoughtfully.

After she'd finished them, she said, "You know, when I thought you might be fun to drink with, I just had this sort of vague idea that you might have a wild streak. Understatement of the year: at the rate we're going you might as well tell me you're a dominatrix or a wizard or a spy or something. I suddenly feel like I don't know the first thing about you."

I laughed darkly. "Yeah, well, join the club."

"Count me in," she said, and then shrugged, holding her glass up in the air as if she was making a toast at a wedding. "Whatever, Min, I couldn't care less what you end up as. Working at Frost is hell on earth most of the time, especially with the bastards in marketing. But these past two weeks haven't been like that at all. It's been great. Working with you is stacks of fun. I don't even care what project I'm on: I wouldn't want to work with anyone else but you."

My chest clenched; it felt *so* good to hear that. Just so good, and I think I might have teared up a little if the wine hadn't been starting to get to me. Sarah was great about this stuff, why hadn't I just told her in the first place? "Thank you," I said, meaning it. "And I *do* have something to tell you."

She put her glass down, all serious again. "You do?"

I nodded, looking with exaggerated drama at my wedges, and then up at her. "Sarah, I'm a wizard."

She threw a wedge at me, and, predictably, she missed. "You're a dag," she said as we kept eating, "that's what you are."

I was comfortable around her; too comfortable, in fact. The bottle that her owner friend had got us was sparkling wine, and while I was perfectly able to hold normal wine, sparkling just went straight to my head. I'd finished my third big glass of it when Sarah whistled at the owner and got us another one.

"We've got to stop," I said as she filled my wine glass to the brim for the *fourth* time with the second bottle. "I'm never going to get any work done. I need to get home at some point and get through the last couple of hundred images." I wasn't slurring yet, but I wasn't too far away from it.

Sarah took a big swig from the bottle and then poured her own glass full. "Yeah, sounds *fascinating,*" she said sarcastically. "Or you could stay here with me and get completely wasted. They clear the floor and play bad music after one. I'm a terrible dancer, it will be really entertaining."

I laughed once, and had been about to inform her that I was also a top contender for the World's Worst Dancer title, when someone said something behind me. It took me a few seconds to realise it was to us, and by that time there were two gorgeous women looming over the booth. As if that wasn't intimidating enough just in itself, it reminded me of high school when some of the girls would surround me after class. If I hadn't been so very drunk at that moment, I think I might have actually tried to get away.

"Hey, Sarah, don't you already have a boyfriend?" one of them asked her light-heartedly, and then gave her a bit of a clumsy shove. We weren't the only ones who were drunk, apparently. I couldn't tell if the girl was being nasty or not—did she *actually* think I was a guy, or was she having a go at me?

Sarah looked at me with alarm, and then glanced at the screen of her phone. "*Crap!*" she said. "What time is it? I completely forgot you guys were coming!" She held a hand out towards me. "It's okay, though, they're totally cool..."

These were her work friends? I inhaled sharply and looked back up at them; the two of them *did* share Sarah's grade of good looks, dress sense and the I-kind-of-know-I'm-hot self-confidence, but I didn't recognise either girl. Maybe they were other friends of hers?

At Sarah's and my panicked expression, they both laughed openly. "Busted!" the shorter one declared and then held her hand out to me to shake as she spoke to Sarah. "Are you going to introduce us to your toyboy? He's cute."

'Toyboy'? *'He'?*

Instead of taking the girl's hand, I looked back at Sarah.

"I'm really sorry, but seriously, it's okay," she promised me. "They won't care."

"Won't care about what?" the taller one asked Sarah as I looked back at the hand in front of me. "What's going on?"

There wasn't anything else I could do, really, so I shook the hand being held at me for a second. "Min," I somehow managed. I hoped she couldn't feel how sweaty my palm was.

The girl attached to the hand looked stunned for a second and then squinted at me. "*Min?* As in, 'Sarah's Boss Min'? 'Min Lee' Min? No *way!*" Wait, she *was* from Frost? I looked harder at her again, but in the low light I couldn't tell if I recognised her or not.

"That's her..." Sarah confirmed, sounding pained. At 'her', both heads turned back towards me with surprise. That was very telling. They *had* thought I was a guy, after all, and wow, it was actually a relief. They were probably just being flirty before rather than trying to insult me.

Sarah presented me with a gesture. "Everyone, this is Min. Min, this is Liz," she pointed at the tall blonde, "and Gemma," she said, pointing at the shorter brunette.

The girl who had gone to shake my hand had been Gemma. "You're a *chick*?" Her eyes kept flicking between my flat chest and my face. She sounded genuinely surprised. "Are you *sure*? Because, like, wow."

That is a very good question, I thought, but I just forced a smile. I still wasn't sure about them.

Liz shoved her. "Don't be fucking rude, Gem," she said. "And can you sit down? These heels are killing me."

I shuffled along the seat to the back of the small circular booth so that they could both fit next to me.

Liz was already talking as they sat down. "Sorry we're late, by the way," she said to Sarah. "My husband did his knee in last weekend's game and the way he's carrying on about it you'd think that he'd lost the whole leg. Gemma was over at eleven and he was all like, 'But who's going to change the heat pack?' and 'what happens when the boys come around and I can't get to the door?', and I'm like, 'Geez, Chris, I'm not your slave, tell them to come around the back or something...'. We were seriously waiting for him to stop crying like a toddler and we didn't get out the door until half-past 12..."

Sarah was starting to relax, even if I wasn't. "That's okay, Min's been keeping me company," she said. "And I guess Chris isn't coming then?"

Liz shook her head. "Not tonight. None of the boys are, they're all going back to my place." She gave us all a very pointed look. "And by the way, if anyone asks, we actually just went and had a quiet late night dinner somewhere for someone's birthday. Chris would kill me if he knew I was just going out on the town without him. He's such a sook."

Sarah laughed. "Got it," she said. "And by the way, if anyone at work asks, you never met Min, either."

Both the other girls looked at me, and a very loud 'why' hung in the air. No one answered it, though.

Gemma shrugged, and Liz said, "Uh, okay?"

"It's a pleasure not meeting you," I said with a slight grin, before I'd given it any thought. Internally, I *winced.* Really, Min? I asked myself, you want to be an idiot around Sarah's work friends?

The two girls didn't seem to think I was an idiot, though. They laughed a little and the hesitant, polite smiles they'd been giving me relaxed into regular ones. Apparently that stupid comment was enough to make me fair game to talk to, as well.

Gemma flipped her hair over her shoulder—a little self-consciously, I thought— which made *me* self-conscious again, too. "So how long have you been working at Frost?" she asked.

"About five years," I said. "Which is coincidentally also how long I've been addicted to energy drinks and takeaway food."

They laughed. "I hear you," Gemma said. "There's a 24 hour Subway two doors from my house and I think they *actually* stay open after midnight *because* of me." She considered me for a moment, "Marketing, yeah?" I nodded, and then she forehead-slapped and laughed a bit nervously. "Sorry, that's a stupid question, fuck, I'm drunk. Of *course* Marketing if you're Sarah's boss... anyway, I don't think I've seen you around?"

Sarah and I glanced at each other. "She looks a bit different at work," Sarah said carefully.

Liz laughed and leant out from behind Gemma to say to me, "We all do. As if I could wear this into a Risk meeting with Diane Frost." She held her arms out so I could see how tiny her dress was. Actually, Gemma's was pretty small as well, and all three of them had their hair back off their faces. Sarah looked really different with hers back, maybe that's why I didn't recognise them?

Gemma adjusted her dress a little. I noticed how nicely it fell across her hips. "Now, on the other hand, if the meeting was with *Sean* Frost..."

"—Then you'd probably need to be dressed more like me to get his attention," I said before I thought it through, adding for extra embarrassment, "I realise I need to work a lot on my guns, though."

They all stared at me for a second and then burst out laughing. "Oh my God, though," Liz said, leaning forward on the table again. "You're so right. What's going on with him and that manager from Marketing? They're always together. Do you think they're..."

Sarah looked smug. "I was telling Min the other day that I'd put big money on that."

Liz took the wine bottle from the table beside Sarah and drank from it. "Well, I'm sure Chris would go in on that. Since he stopped being allowed to bet on games he'll bet on just about anything else."

I must have looked a bit confused, because Gemma leant towards me and explained, "Liz's husband plays for the Waratahs, and you're not allowed to bet on the league if you're playing in it."

Sarah managed to get the bottle back off Liz and poured herself another wine. "Also, he's really hot," she said, "and Liz totally doesn't appreciate him."

Liz made a face. "Because he's a jealous fuck, that's why. He's lucky he's so cute."

Gemma gave them both a dirty look. "Shut up, both of you. You know who I share my bed with?" she asked, waiting for a second, and then answered pointedly, "*My cat*."

I shrugged and said 'quietly' to Gemma, "To be fair your cat is probably less hairy than Rob." I made sure it was loud enough for Sarah to hear.

Sarah did hear it and threw a scrunched up serviette at me. "Quiet, you!" she told me, but looked all rosy-cheeked at the mention of Rob.

I ducked behind Gemma to avoid the serviette, laughing. When I sat up again, Gemma was giving me this measured look. There was curiosity in it. "Are you married?" she asked, and it seemed just a little bit out of place. "Kids?"

"Neither," I said, because Henry and I weren't married and I didn't really want to bring him into any of this. Across from me, Sarah raised her eyebrows when I didn't elaborate. Gemma looked like she wanted to say something else, but talked herself out of it.

Because I felt like the two girls were okay with me, and because I was *fucking drunk* and Gemma called me 'cute' before she'd realised I was female, I looked down at her and said with a low voice and a charming grin, "Was that the answer you were hoping for?"

No sooner had the words left my lips, I could have buried my head in my hands. *Min*, I scolded myself, *what are you doing*? I was about to actually apologise for being fucking inappropriate, but before I'd done that, Gemma had put her own hands to her cheeks. Even in this low light, I could see she was blushing fiercely.

Sarah looked between us, a smile growing on her face. "I think this calls for more alcohol," she said, and tried to wave over the owner. He was busy watching the game, though, and didn't see us.

Liz put her hand on Gemma's back. "Not for Gem, though, I think she's had enough," she said, looking very, very amused by what had just happened.

'Gem' managed to compose herself. "No, actually, alcohol sounds pretty good right now," she said, a little too embarrassed to make eye-contact with me again. "*Lots* of alcohol."

Sarah wasn't having any luck with the owner and I couldn't decide if I was horrified by what I'd done or not, so I half-stood, hampered by the table. "I'll go over and get it," I said, and then looked at Gemma and Liz who were blocking my way out of the booth. They shuffled along the seat, getting out so I could as well.

I don't think either of them had realised how tall I was until I stood up beside them. Gemma looked up at my body with the same surprise that Bree had had when I'd first met her. Unlike Bree, though, she didn't say anything. She actually didn't need to, because I could tell from her reaction that 'tall' was something that worked for her. Before I could talk myself out of it, I winked at her and sent her into another deep blush.

Liz laughed at Gemma's red cheeks, clapping her on the shoulders and steering her to sit back in the booth again.

I watched them for a second as Gemma pulled herself back together and Liz and Sarah started chatting again. I did that to her, I thought as I watched Gemma, remembering her playfully describing me as 'cute'. It was really difficult for me to accept it when I thought about it. Not only were the two girls completely okay with how I looked and dressed, they were *so* okay about it that they were letting me tease them based on their reaction to it.

Sarah had said they would be fine, but I still couldn't believe it. I'd been *so* sure no one would ever talk to me again if they found out, but there were three people here who didn't even care. It was surreal, and I felt... wow, *really* drunk. And I was just standing there staring at the three of them with my jaw open like a total idiot. Hadn't I been about to do something?

Trying not to look as drunk as I felt, I went to go and grab that other bottle I'd been after from the owner.

"Are you over 18?" he asked me a little suspiciously, but he was smiling. He'd seen me with Sarah, so I didn't think he'd *really* cause me any trouble. "How old are you?"

"12," I said flatly, looking down towards him because I was taller. "And a half."

He chuckled. "Yeah, okay, I get it," he said, easing the cork out of another bottle of sparkling and passing it over the counter.

I accepted the bottle from him, glad he hadn't made me show my ID because then I'd have a *lot* of explaining to do. I pointed at the glasses hanging in the racks above his head. "Can I take two of these?"

He'd already turned back towards his rugby game, and waved his hand dismissively at me. "Yeah, yeah."

I grabbed a couple and then headed back to the table, pretty impressed with the beautifully straight line I was walking in.

I *felt* drunk, but at least I didn't look it.

Back at the table, I practically got a hero's welcome. "Yes!" Liz announced, letting me pour her a glass. Gemma, I teased a little. She asked me to stop when I got to what was probably one standard drink, but I pretended not to hear her and kept pouring.

She nearly snatched her glass out from underneath the bottle. "That's enough! That's enough!" she begged me, giggling.

I pretended to be very innocent. "I thought you said you needed *lots* of alcohol?" I asked her, and then flashed her a grin. "I'm just getting you drunk like you wanted."

She stared at me for a second, and then looked away while the other two girls laughed.

Sarah stood up so I could get in behind her, giving me a secret little smirk as I slipped past. I didn't really think about why I hadn't just sat in front of her instead, until I realised that she'd done it on purpose to make sure that I sat next to Gemma. I mock-glared at her while I gave her wine a top-up. She took the glass and drank from it, looking pretty pleased with herself.

Liz filled me in on what I'd missed. "Gemma has a conspiracy theory about Sean Frost," she told me, with exaggerated seriousness.

Gemma smacked her good-naturedly. "It's not a *conspiracy* theory," she said, turning back towards me. "It's just a theory, and, actually, I think it has merit."

Since we were all apparently humouring her theory, I nodded with the same sense of exaggerated seriousness and pretended to give her my rapt attention. I didn't have to pretend, really, but she still smacked my arm, too. "I mean it!" she said, laughing. "You know his wife is Belinda O'Dougherty, right?" I nodded. "Okay, think about it. She's a supermodel, but—"

Sarah, who had checked her phone in the middle of Gemma's explanation, said abruptly, "Oh my god *what*?" She was looking at her phone.

Gemma and Liz both turned back at her, surprised, Sean Frost and his wife were quickly forgotten. Sarah held her phone at them and they stood a bit off the seat so they could lean towards the screen. I could see it from where I was, and it was a blurry photo of two people I didn't know pashing.

"Oh my fucking god," Liz said as they both sat down again. "I *knew* he was into her. I *knew* it. I told you they'd end up together."

When Gemma sat down again, she was a lot closer to me than she had been before, a lot closer. So close, in fact, that her leg was pressed against mine from knee to hip. In that short dress, her skin was warm against my jeans. I normally *hated* people sitting close to me. Henry frequently joked about the size of my 'personal space bubble'; once, he'd even stood on the other side of the room and pretended to knock on it. I didn't hate this touching right now, though. Not at all.

I half-listened to the three of them all gossip about this new couple while I was watching Gemma. Was she doing it on purpose, I wondered? Or was she just quite drunk and not coordinated enough to care what part of the seat she was on?

"Sorry, Min," Sarah said, startling me a little. I looked up at her and away from Gemma. "Whether or not two people you've never met are going to hook up and get married is probably the last thing you care about."

I made sure I kept a completely straight face. "Actually, I care very deeply about it." They all gave me weird looks. I waited for a couple of seconds, and then explained, "Well, what do I actually market for a living?" I grinned as they all groaned and rolled their eyes at me. I pointed a finger at them. "Who's hooking up and getting married is critically important to me. Someone's got to buy stupidly expensive diamonds."

Sarah locked her phone and put it back in her handbag. "Yeah, that's what we were doing," she said, "we weren't gossiping, we were doing demographics research. I'm totally using that."

Liz took a sip of her wine. "Research yourself," she told Sarah, "You're next."

I looked down at Gemma beside me. "What about you?" I asked her, and I think her cheeks went a little pink again.

"What about me?" she asked.

"How does your cat feel about diamonds?"

She laughed, giving me this somewhat embarrassed smile as she glanced up at me. We held eye-contact for a little too long, and then both panicked and looked away. I would have probably been a lot more freaked out if I hadn't been drunk, but even with all that wine in me I was still scared to look back at her. What was I *doing?*

While I was trying to figure that out and pretend I was focusing on what Sarah was saying to Liz, Gemma put her hand on the inside of my knee. It was an innocent enough gesture, but, *wow*, I felt it. So much so that I couldn't breathe for a second, and it was exactly at a time that I wanted to. A lot.

She left her hand there, too, and I was acutely aware of all the tiny movements her thumb was making as it moved in slow circles on my jeans. With a sense of dread that would have been *much* more pronounced if I'd been sober, I realised what all of this meant, and it wasn't just that I was having fun teasing her.

Fuck, I thought, *fuck*. I'm *attracted* to her. She's a girl, and I'm attracted to her. As if that wasn't a dangerous enough thought on its own, the absolute worst part of it was that my next one was, 'so this is what it feels like'.

"Weren't you in the middle of telling us your thing about Sean?" Liz asked Gemma.

"Huh? Oh!" she said, sounding a bit distracted herself. She hardly looked at me as she spoke this time, but her hand was still on my thigh. "Okay, so." She tried to compose herself—should I have been that delighted that she *wasn't* composed?—and then asked, "...wait, where was I?"

"Belinda O'Dougherty," I prompted, a bit breathless.

"Oh, yeah," she said. "Anyway, she's this huge supermodel and she wasn't famous before she and Sean hooked up, right? And now she's *super* famous and in everything with her baby and her big, pregnant belly..." Gemma paused. "I think it's a Katie Holmes-Tom Cruise-type of deal. I reckon Sean's not even in love with her at all, I think she's just this really respectable wife for a billionaire mining magnate and in return he helped her with her career."

We all sat back to consider that, and I found it such an interesting theory that I totally forgot Gemma had her hand on my thigh.

It was possible she was actually right, I supposed, but Sean had looked genuinely enchanted when he'd brought up his 'beautiful' wife with me. I hadn't prompted him, either. And Henry had never mentioned thinking their marriage was a fraud. It seemed like the sort of thing Henry would pick up on, especially given how much he hated Sean.

"Think about it," Gemma continued. "He's always with that beefcake marketing director and *everyone* knows they're totally giving it to each other, and he couldn't just go and be this big gay mining billionaire. That's bad for business, even now, so he made some arrangement with Belinda. I mean, have you ever even seen them together?"

"Henry has," I said automatically, without thinking. "He went to their baby shower last weekend. He says she's really nice."

Gemma's brow lowered for a second. "Who's Henry?"

My stomach dropped; *whoops*. I shrunk a bit in the seat. "My boyfriend..."

The expression on her face... "*Boy*friend?" she looked over at Sarah for confirmation I wasn't messing with her.

"Yup," Sarah said, and then gave me a weird look, like 'why would you say anything?'

Gemma took her hand off my thigh and sat back, quiet for a few moments. Her disappointment was actually palpable. I felt *stupid*, like I should apologise for not telling her sooner.

"You're *straight*?" Liz asked me, like she'd just found out everything she'd ever believed was a lie. "Okay, I'm sorry for just being out there like this but, seriously: *what?*"

I remembered Gemma's hand on my thigh. Apparently not, I thought, and then panicked. "It's fine," I said, and then it all just suddenly caught up with me and even the several litres of alcohol wasn't a match for my adrenaline. "I think I'm going to go get some fresh air for a second," I said, fanning myself momentarily with the drinks menu. "I've had a bit much. Sorry."

A fucking oracle as always, Sarah grabbed my wrist as I climbed awkwardly over her to get out of the booth. "Don't leave yet," she told me sternly. I nodded, and then made a beeline for the hallway.

The beer garden was closed, but there was a quaint little brick courtyard filled up with cleaning equipment and other stuff that was unlocked. I slipped out into it, staggering and knocking over a pile of crates in the process. Rather than just picking them up, I sat on them.

Fuck.

I wanted to just ignore the fact I'd been really attracted to Gemma. I spent a few seconds chalking it up to too much alcohol and how much I'd enjoyed making her blush, but that hadn't had anything to do with what I'd felt. And I didn't just like it on an emotional level the way I generally did with Henry, either. This was different. I'd *felt* it. Under my hand, in my stomach, and—I winced—well, everywhere you would ordinarily expect to feel something like that.

At least I wasn't having a full on panic attack over it; I'd had too much alcohol for that. Even with all this dumped on me, I felt far too relaxed. Kind of good, actually, I really liked when I'd drunk enough to reach that point that I could close my eyes and just kind of drift away on my thoughts... I'd have to make sure I drank bucket loads of water before I went to bed, though, or I wouldn't feel like getting out of it. Then Bree would be stuck with me tomorrow while I slept in and felt sorry for myself. Although, maybe if I was lucky, she'd just get into bed with me...

I opened my eyes wide again.

"Hey..." a voice said from the doorway and I had to try and conceal how startled I was.

I looked over, and Gemma was leaning on the door frame. Because there was light coming from the kitchen window, I could see her much better out here than I could inside. I'd actually pegged her colouring a bit wrong; I'd thought she was a dark brunette, but now I could see auburn highlights in her hair and a dusting of freckles across her face. It was gorgeous. *She* was gorgeous. I felt nervous again.

"Hi," I said, and then looked around me at all the fallen crates. "Just in case you were wondering, they were already like this, I swear."

She chuckled. "Sarah said you had a habit of taking off, so I thought I'd just come looking for you and try to convince you not to."

I laughed once. "Good luck," I said, and then patted the crate beside me. I pointed up at the gap of sky a couple of levels above the courtyard. It was completely overcast. "Want to stargaze with me?"

She came over and sat next to me, wobbling a little on her heels.

She was at least as drunk as I was. Maybe because of that, she didn't say anything straight away, and I was too fucking nervous about her sitting that close to me to think properly myself.

She did speak eventually. "I'm sorry," she said. "I didn't mean to, you know..." she gestured vaguely at my knee. "Don't leave because I can't keep my hands to myself."

I shook my head tightly. "I should have told you earlier."

She laughed nervously, shifting on the crate. Her nervousness was actually really gorgeous, too, and I would have been much more affected by that if I wasn't terrified about the fact that we were both out here alone. I was actually shaking a little, but I managed not to make it obvious.

"It's just...well, it's a bit of a surprise for me, I don't normally go for girls, but it's like you're—"

"—it's fine," I interrupted her, completely fucking agreeing with her. I didn't want to talk about it, though. It was the last thing I wanted to talk about. I'd barely come to terms with the other stuff that was going on for me, and now *this*. In case she was going to try again, I repeated, "It's fine."

"Is it?" she asked, and there was something more about that question. I was terrified of looking at her—almost to the point of feeling a bit ill—but I did anyway. Once I did, it was too late to look away.

She was watching me so attentively, her eyes dipping between my face and my body. I don't know what she found so interesting about it, and while I was trying to figure that out, she looped a hand around the back of my neck under my ponytail and pulled me down to kiss her. I froze.

Her lips were so soft, much softer than the ones I was used to. I was so completely shocked that I just kissed back out of reflex, but when the blades of our tongues touched she made this noise at the back of her throat... *Fuck.* I felt it somewhere deep inside me. *That* wasn't alcohol.

For just a second I started to wrap my arms around her, but instead of Henry's big, strong body, she was this smaller, softer version. Alarm bells were going off everywhere in my head, but I could hardly pay attention to them because of how wasted I was. What I *could* pay attention to was how she felt against me, right up against me, pressing up into me and kissing me and touching my neck and god, that dress was so short and her thighs looked so *good* and okay, no, I needed to stop, *fuck, I needed to stop, this needed to stop*!

I pulled back far more forcefully than I'd intended. I was breathing heavily, and I had no idea if it was from panic or the fact I'd been about to get *really* into that. "I can't, I can't do this," I said, and it sounded like a plea.

"I'm sorry," she repeated, looking horrified at herself. "Shit, Min, I'm *wasted*, I'm really sorry!"

I stood up, because I couldn't be trusted to sit next to her for a second longer. "It's not your fault," I said, losing the fight against how much I was shaking. I went to change how I was standing to hide it, and instead of succeeding I nearly fell backwards over another set of crates.

She tried to help me stand up, but I couldn't let her touch me anymore. "This isn't your fault," I told her, taking a step away from her. "I actually *am* going to 'run off' again. But it's not your fault, okay? You're gorgeous. I can't stay here tonight or I'm going to do something I'll regret."

She was still looking really angry with herself. "Okay," she said, nodding. "I get it."

I mirrored her nod, still breathing heavily, and then went straight for the exit. I could just text Sarah later; from what she'd told Gemma it sounded like she knew I was going to leave, anyway.

I walked briskly out onto the street, thinking I was probably right just to try and make my way home unassisted. Actually, though, I wasn't really that sure how I made it home. I managed somehow, and I didn't get robbed, or murdered or hit by a car despite the fact I was all over the place. It took me five or six swipes with my keycard to get the door to open, and when I went to go put on something cooler than a hoodie, I saw I had Gemma's lipstick smeared all around my mouth. I'd walked out of the pub and home like *this*?

I propped myself upright against the wardrobe, staring at my reflection. Now that I was home and everything was normal again, I could hardly believe what had happened. If it wasn't for the lipstick, I may have thought I was so drunk that I'd been hallucinating.

Once I'd washed my face, I sat back down in front of my laptop, in my drunken haze determined that the solution to feeling like everything was completely out of control was to finish reviewing the graphics. At the very least it would mean that I wouldn't have to do it when Bree was over tomorrow and I could just relax and have fun with her.

I couldn't concentrate on photos of landscapes, though, I could only think two thoughts: how amazing it had felt to be *really* attracted to someone, and how *fucked up* it was that I was feeling that way about a girl.

I was stuck on the see-saw of those two thoughts for god knows how long, until I caught sight of a photo that actually mattered on the other side of the room: me and Henry in Queensland together.

Henry. I squeezed my eyes closed for a moment.

Yeah, 'conscious' wasn't going to work for me right now, I decided, standing up and weaving haphazardly across my apartment towards my bed. With any luck I'd just pass out and wake up remembering absolutely nothing that had just happened.

FOURTEEN

For a few beautiful seconds after I woke up, it felt like any other weekend. The sun was peeking through the blinds and hinting at a great day to do work on the balcony, it was kind of a pleasant temperature, and if I checked what time it was, maybe I could... not move my head at all because *wow* it *hurt*.

I rolled onto my back very, very carefully, and bits and pieces of last night started coming back to me. I'd been drinking, obviously, and since I had lots of different memories of Sarah refilling my glass, I could hazard a guess that it was a *lot*. I clearly remembered coming out to her and it being a huge relief, and then after that things started to get a bit hazy. One memory shone through the rest: Gemma. Not really her herself, but how much fun I'd had flirting with her, how terrified and exhilarated I'd felt when she'd touched me and then how we'd ended up pashing in a courtyard.

I'd never been turned on like that. At the time it was wonderful, but In the light of day, all I could do was lie in bed and be *absolutely horrified* that I'd let it get that far.

Min, I thought. How *could you*? Henry would *never* go behind your back with someone else. He's done absolutely nothing except be there for you through *everything*. How are you going to tell him that you cheated on him?

I couldn't figure out what I'd say. I felt sick, angry at myself and almost numb to what I'd done. What was I going to do? I didn't know, and my head was *killing* me, but I had to do something about it.

I sat up very slowly in bed. I could see myself in my wardrobe mirror—I didn't get any prizes for guessing how I looked—as I very carefully stood and walked into the bathroom. I was nearly out of my strongest painkillers. I popped the last two out of the phial and then cupped water in my hands from the tap to swallow them. Since I was in there, and because I felt kind of gross from having been so drunk last night, I decided to have a quick shower, too.

At least, I'd planned on it being quick, but the water was warm and I was feeling so fucking awful that I just leant my head against the tiles and let it run over me as I stressed about last night. Being physically relaxed did actually make everything seem a bit clearer, too; I was beginning to understand why Henry kept shoving his whole 'the mind and the body are one' mantra down my throat.

What would he *really* think about what had happened, though? Level-headed Henry? With my own very un-level head against the warm tiles, I tried to copy the way he worked through everything.

Okay, Min, so, you were turned on by a woman and she kissed you. Does that *actually* mean your relationship with Henry is doomed? With some relief, I sighed. No, I thought easily, of course not. There were even pop songs about it, and for there to be pop songs about it, it must have meant that it was actually a really common occurrence. I did need to ask myself why it hadn't happened before, though, because I'd been around attractive women in the past and had no desire to do anything with them. Then again, I'd never been able to *relax* around women, so maybe *that* was the key: bucket loads of wine.

While I was on that point, I had a really heartening thought. What if just being relaxed enough to go for it was the key to me being turned on in general? Maybe I *was* still mostly straight after all, just too stressed out to ever enjoy myself. Henry was coming over tomorrow, which would be a great time to see if alcohol made the difference. God, it would be wonderful if I could just figure out how to enjoy sex with him, then I wouldn't have to dread it rolling around every two or three weeks.

The painkillers were already starting to kick in by the time I got out and got dressed, which was a mixed blessing. It was nice to not be in serious discomfort, but I just kept thinking about that kiss and needed to keep repeating to myself that everything was fine and that I didn't need to worry about it. I had been sitting on the edge of my bed wondering how the hell I was going to get through today without going nuts, when I remembered it was Saturday.

I sat up straight. That meant Bree was coming over today, I thought, and felt better. What time was it? I leant stiffly over to my bedside table to grab my phone. *10:02AM*, it read, which was a bit of a letdown because Bree was due around midday. I turned it over a few times in my hands as I thought about it. I didn't feel like waiting a couple of hours for her. I mean, I had work to do but I just couldn't face any of it, and I didn't want to be stuck here, hung-over, and on the verge of a completely unnecessary meltdown over something that wasn't a big deal and didn't mean anything.

What's the harm, really? I unlocked my phone and typed Bree a message. *"Hey, feel like coming over a bit earlier?"*

She didn't take very long to reply. *"funny u say that.................."*

I looked up from my phone, suspicious. I had a feeling I was beginning to get how Bree was.

To check my theory, I stood up carefully and walked down the hallway, stopping in front of my door. When I opened it, I actually wasn't surprised when a small teenager who'd been sitting against it and listening to her old iPod fell backwards inside. She looked sheepishly up at me from the floor with her curls fanned around her. "Hi..."

She was silly, and terrible, and I was *so* pleased to see her. Despite the fact my whole body ached, I helped her up. "You don't have to sit out there all morning and wait," I told her. "If you hold your hand like this," I made a fist, "and you bang it a few times against a surface like a door..."

She let me pull her up and then brushed the creases out of her skirt. "You can't really say that when you keep going off at me for showing up here," she pointed out as she straightened. "You said you hate it when people do that, so I was being good and waiting."

"Yes, but when did you ever listen to anything I asked you to do?"

"Hey, I listen to you!" she protested, and then went to give me a big hug just like she'd done several times before. This time, though, I bristled a bit when she touched me. She must have felt me go stiff as a board, because she let go and looked up at me with a frown. "What's wrong?"

That was a good question. I felt really strange this morning. "I'm probably still a bit out of it from last night," I decided aloud. "I had a really big one."

She squinted up at me. "Yeah, I can tell," she said. "You look even worse than you did on Tuesday morning. Why do you keep *doing* that?"

I laughed bleakly. "Because everything continues to be stressful." I opted to not tell her any more about last night. It wasn't important, anyway. "And how are you? Is everything okay?"

She echoed my bleak laugh. It was such a strange thing to hear from her. "Pretty much the same as you," she said, bracing herself against the wall as she slipped off her thongs. "Everything sucks, and it keeps on sucking, and it doesn't fucking stop. I can't get drunk at home like you can, though."

"So what do you do?"

She shrugged. "Nothing."

I sighed. We were such a pair of sad-sacks today. "I think you had a great idea earlier in the week," I told her, shooting her a grin as we walked into the living room. "Fuck everything, let's just run away together."

That made her laugh properly. In the middle of it, however, she suddenly stopped laughing and stood in place. After a few moments of consideration, she looked thoughtfully up at me. "Okay, I know you're joking about running away, but why don't we just do it?"

Hah. "Because there's this thing called work that I—"

"No, silly," she said, interrupting me. "I don't mean, like, fly off to Canada forever or anything like that. I don't even have a passport. I mean just... I don't know, just go somewhere for a day. Somewhere like miles away where there's no one and we can just pretend everything is great?"

While I was wishing such a mystical place actually existed so I could buy real estate there, she'd already taken off on that idea at a million miles an hour. "Yeah, like maybe in the mountains or something? There are some really nice parks there." The more she thought about that, the more excited she sounded. It was fun to watch her transform from miserable into enthusiastic in such a short space of time. "Actually, that's a really great idea! You can just look like whatever you want, because it's not like you can wear heels in a national park, can you? And maybe we can go to this place that I used to love when I was kid. Anyway, come on! Let's do it! You have a car, right?"

"Well, yes..." ...but I could count the number of times I'd driven it on two hands. I kept needing to replace the battery in it because I hardly ever turned it on.

"Then...?" she said, leaving the sentence in the air and squirming around in front of me.

Honestly? She could have suggested anything right then; there was no way I was ever going to say no. I had this really weird sort of disconnected feeling about everything, and I was too tired and hung-over to argue with Hurricane Bree. And, anyway, this was *Bree* we were talking about. If she had her heart set on it, she was going to find some way to get me to do it. This time, though, I actually quite liked her idea. Road trips could be fun. I hadn't done something like this in *ages* and 'completely different' sounded like the shake-up I needed to stop those thoughts about last night creeping in.

I chuckled and shook my head at her. "Fine."

"Yes!" she shrieked, reminding me that my painkillers weren't completely working just yet. She bounded off into my living room. "I'm going to pack your laptop and your tablet!" she told me, poking her head over the kitchen bench. "You're going to want to paint this. *Trust* me!" She then went zooming off around my house to look for my laptop bag.

I wandered over to the wall and leant against it, still feeling kind of sluggish and tired while she was buzzing all around me. She emerged from my bedroom with my laptop bag, and, by the looks of things, she'd also been digging around in my wardrobe. She'd found the button-up shirt we'd bought together as well as an old baseball cap I used to wear aeons ago when I actually had the energy to go jogging.

"Here," she said, coming up to me and handing me the shirt. "Put this on. Also I found this so you can hide your hair." She gave me the baseball cap and double-took, putting her hands on her hips. "Whoa, you seriously look terrible. How much *did* you drink?"

"No comment," I said dismissively. "Why do I have to wear the shirt with the buttons? What's wrong with this?" I gestured down to my old t-shirt. "If no one's going to be there, does it even matter?"

"*I'm* going to be there," she said primly. "And I *like* you in the shirt with buttons." I couldn't really argue with that.

Once I'd changed and she was happy with how I looked, she only let me grab my handbag before I was bustled out the door. Sniggering at me as we stepped into the lift, she pointed at it. "That kind of ruins the whole tough guy image."

"Good," I said, slinging it over my shoulder. "I'm not a tough guy, I'm a nice guy who's obviously carrying his—"'—girlfriend's handbag', I'd been about to say. I managed to not finish that sentence just in time. I just kind of stood there staring at my reflection, horrified by what had been about to come out of my mouth.

Bree raised her eyebrows, suggesting, "...his 'girly Coach handbag'?" as a closer for my sentence. She thought about that and shrugged, watching the numbers scroll down on the lift. "Well, I guess technically if you end up a guy you'll end up as a *gay* guy. So maybe it's not so weird after all."

That reminded me of Henry, and by extension Gemma, and then everything that I had been thinking about this morning. Fuck, I needed to just not be so worried about all of that because it didn't mean anything and it wasn't important. Besides, weren't Bree and I running away for the sole purpose of taking a day off from everything stressful? I could worry about this tomorrow when Henry was actually here.

I was still stuck trying not to think those thoughts when Bree and

I exited the lift and I was rummaging around in the bottom of my handbag for my keys.

"Is it a nice car?" she asked me, holding onto one of my arms and making it more difficult for me to search for the keys to it. "Like, an expensive one? Or just like a regular old bomb?"

I narrowed my eyes a little, finally locating my keys and pointing them at my car.

It chirped and the blinkers flashed. Bree turned towards it with a big smile, but as she looked back at me, it had disappeared completely. "Min. It's a *Lexus*."

"Congratulations," I told her neutrally. "You read at the first grade level."

She ignored me, shaking my arm. "You drive a *Lexus*? Are you fucking *serious?*"

I shrugged as we walked up to it together. "My mum chose this car and I shouldn't have let her because I don't even *need* a car. So it just kind of sits down here while the repayments get debited from my account every month. I haven't even turned it on for a few weeks."

She looked at me like I was absolutely crazy, and then quickly disappeared into the passenger seat. After I'd climbed in and started the engine—it took a while to turn over, and I was worried I'd let *another* battery run flat—she discovered the stereo and was treating the entire hotel to some cheesy pop music as we pulled out of the car park.

As happy as I was to have my thoughts drowned out, the bass was killing my head, so I reached over to turn down the volume. I happened to glance at her as I did it; she was *dancing* to it in her seatbelt with a big open smile. When she saw me looking she did a little flourish and then kept going. "This sound system is fucking *amazing!*" she shouted to me.

Well, at least she's having fun, I thought as I took my hand off the volume dial and put it back on the steering wheel. It was *her* day off, too, and my head would be okay.

She continued to dance to that garbage as I merged onto the highway.

Even though I'd sworn I'd never do it again about a hundred times, we had McDonalds for breakfast. As we pulled up to the

Drive-Thru, Bree kept changing her mind so often about what she wanted that I ended up just ordering her porridge as penance.

"I *hate* porridge!" she told me and then leant across my lap when we got to the window and begged the clerk to exchange it for something that contained actual flavour. Because she was upside down, in the process of watching her beg for 'real' food, I'm pretty sure the poor guy got to see a lot more cleavage than he'd expected to see at 10:30 in the morning. I certainly did.

Probably as a direct result of it, though, she ended up scoring some free pancakes and as she was laying them triumphantly across her half-naked thighs, I shook my head. "I worry about you," I told her.

"I know," she said, lifting up her pancake box to show me her pleated denim skirt. "That's why I wore my longest skirt today." I couldn't tell if she was joking or not because she looked completely serious, but that skirt did not look a single inch longer than any of her others.

After she was done with the pancakes, she spent fifteen or twenty minutes silently typing away on her phone. I figured she was chatting to someone so I just relaxed back in my seat, watching the road and trying not to fall asleep. Bree couldn't remember exactly where the park she wanted was or even what it was called, but she gave me some vague directions anyway and we'd ended up on this road winding up a mountain.

Without Bree's incessant chatter to distract me, though, my mind had drifted back to Gemma and Henry. It was so goddamn frustrating that I kept thinking about it when I was trying to relax and enjoy myself, especially when I didn't even need to worry about it because it didn't have to mean anything. I had been lecturing myself on that when the road came to an abrupt end.

I slowed down, and that made Bree look up from her phone. "Are we here?" she asked hopefully.

I looked around us. We were in the middle of nowhere. "I don't know, I've never been 'here'. *Are* we?"

We got out of the car to check. There was a National Parks and Wildlife sign with an arrow pointing down a track, but Bree didn't look very heartened by it. She walked up to me with a very sheepish expression. "Um, Min," she said thoughtfully. "I think we're lost."

I sighed at her. "Well, where do we go now?"

"I don't know..." she said, looking back down the road we'd come from. "We should probably just keep looking?"

We belted ourselves into the car again, and as I drove off she took her phone out and continued to tap away at it.

"Pretty intense conversation you're having there," I commented eventually when I was trying to decide whether I should turn left or right at a T-junction without her help. Leaning towards the windscreen, I tried to figure out which way looked prettier.

"I'd be kind of tragic if I tried to have an intense conversation with Google," she told me, giggling. "I'm trying to find this place that I want to take you, so I Googled, like, 'beautiful national parks with streams near Sydney', and then I seriously went through *all* of Parks and Wildlife's recommended rivers, and then I got desperate and opened Google maps," she said. "And I'm dragging the little orange man around hoping I find, like, *anything* pretty, but the data reception out here is crap and it takes about five minutes for anything to load."

Since I was stopped, I turned to look at her and she showed me her phone. She wasn't kidding. She was actually skipping through Street View, block by block, looking for nice parks.

I had to laugh at us both. "I think we're the type of people who get lost in the bush and need to be rescued," I told her. "Are you sure you want to go hiking about in the wilderness looking for this childhood creek of yours? It might be the last thing we ever do."

She shrugged. "I just thought it would be really great to take you somewhere nice so you had something pretty to look at while you painted."

I've had you for a few weeks now, I thought, glancing across at Bree in the passenger seat. "That's a nice idea, but when I paint I mainly look at my tablet," I pointed out. "I don't tend to notice anything else. You'd be better off giving me something pretty to listen to, instead."

"Well, I think there were birds there, but whatever," she said, leaning back in her seat and stretching out her legs. "What do we do now that we're all the way out here?"

I think it starts with figuring out which way to turn at this stupid intersection, I thought. The main problem was I didn't care which way we went. It didn't matter, did it? The point had always been to spend the day with her, which I was, and I *really* didn't want to go home yet.

I opened my coin tray and put a twenty-cent piece in her palm. She looked quizzically at it, and then up at me. I winked at her. "Heads we go left, tails we go right," I said. "Let's get *lost*."

Bree's eyes lit up as she looked at me. "I wish I had a passport right now," she said cryptically, and then flipped. Heads it was.

We kept flipping and turning for a good hour or two; I disabled the GPS in the Lexus and neither of us were allowed to use our phones. I *did* get a bit concerned when I saw a sign telling me how far away Canberra was, but we did have all day, so it didn't really matter.

At lunch time, we pulled up in this tiny little town so I could fill up, and Bree had already gone into the little servo to see what food they had. I followed her inside when I was done with the petrol.

The store itself was a bit of everything; I supposed when it was in a tiny town like this it needed to be. It also doubled as a Post Office and Bree was holding up a postcard. "Perthville," she read. "Original. I'm going to start a town and call it Sydneyville."

"There's already one of those in Victoria," I told her, walking past her towards the food.

She came running after me. "Really?" she asked.

I winked at her again. "Nope." She muttered something and gave me a shove. I ignored her. "What are you going to eat?"

She spent ages fussing over the sausage rolls and pies, but finally made a decision when I was already halfway through my Red Bull. The owner had been chuckling to himself at the register when she tapped the glass. "Can I have the mushroom one?" she asked him, pointing to a homemade pie. "With the gravy in it?"

"You can," he said, and then nodded over at me. "What's your boyfriend having?"

I nearly choked on my Red Bull. *He's having a coronary, that's what he's having*, I thought, coughing and trying to get the burn of it out of the back of my throat. Bree, far from looking shocked or upset, just looked *very* entertained.

When she turned back to the owner, I think the colour drained from my face. Don't you out me, Bree, I mentally willed her. Luckily, she was having far too much fun to do anything of the sort. "He should probably have a salad," she said, paying me back for the porridge incident while I was coughing unable to defend myself. "He was just telling me how he doesn't eat enough greens. No dressing, though. Just the plain old veggies."

I glared at her, still trying not to cough. The only thing I was actually capable of doing was handing my card over to pay, but just as I was doing that, I spotted the words 'Miss Min Lee' and panicked, snatching it back. I didn't want to risk any trouble; I already probably looked like I was too young to be driving a Lexus and like I shouldn't be taking two fifties out of a very feminine ladies' purse. I didn't need to add a card with 'Miss' on the front of it to that equation.

Bree caught me hurriedly shoving the card back into my purse, and the smile fell right off her face.

"Actually, I'll just pay cash," I rasped, giving him both the fifties and giving Bree a bit of an inquiring look.

The owner looked a bit confused about all of it, but smiled at me just the same. "Have a nice trip, you two," he said amicably, and then waved to us as we left.

I stuffed the receipt in my pocket as we got back into my car. *That was close*, I thought. I was going to need to sign up for a bank that didn't put titles on cards.

As I started the engine, I realised Bree was watching me with a really strange expression. "Why did you do that?" she asked, as if she'd caught me holding up a bank or something. "Why couldn't you pay with your card?"

I nodded towards my handbag as I pulled out of the servo. "Look at it," I told her. She watched me suspiciously for a moment, and then took out my purse and leafed through the cards until she found it.

It took her a second to understand, and her relief was palpable. "Oh," she said, a smile growing on her face. "'Miss'." She laughed longer than she should have for that, and then relaxed back into the seat.

I took my eyes off the road for a second to glance across at her. She didn't explain herself, though, she just smiled contentedly as she picked at her mushroom pie and snooped through the rest of my purse. It was at that moment while I was trying to figure out what was up with her that my eyes dipped to her wrist. She *still* wasn't wearing her bracelet.

This is all going to be something to do with your brother, isn't it? I thought, *dying* to ask her what was going on and what she'd done with it. Did she not want him to see it? I didn't say anything about the bracelet or the credit card, though, because she was happy and I didn't want to make her cry. She'd tell me when she was ready to, and in the meantime I would just have to find a way to be content with not knowing. Like I wasn't already perfecting that skill in my personal life, anyway...

She was still watching me. "That shopkeeper person called you my *boy*friend," she said, reminding me of how uncomfortable that had been. "Should I do that, too?" I glanced across at her, and my eyes must have been pretty fucking wide because she burst out laughing and clapped her hands over her mouth. "Oh, no, no!" she said through them. "Oh my god, that came out wrong! I meant, like, should I call you 'he' and all that?"

I was still recovering from the 'boyfriend' comment. "If you want," I said, trying to focus on the road.

Her giggle fit made her turn *bright* red. Even her neck and cleavage were red, and even though she was fanning herself with her hands, it wasn't helping. "Do you mean that like a really polite way of saying yes, please call me 'he', or do you actually mean *if you want* if you want?" she asked me. "Because isn't it supposed to be about what *you* want?"

What I *really* didn't want was to be asking myself that question right now, so I tried not to think about it. "When I figure out what that actually is, I'll let you know," I told her. "I don't mind which pronouns *you* use, just don't do anything that makes people look twice at me."

While we were looking for somewhere to pull over so I could eat, Bree spent some time thinking about my answer. "I'm going to use 'she'," she decided. "I think. I mean, like, because half the time I see you in dresses and I can totally see myself just accidentally making a mistake in a shop or something." She paused, making a face. "But then I could accidentally call you 'she' when you're dressed in your normal stuff, too, so like... okay, this is *really* hard."

I had to laugh at her. "Yeah. Now just imagine being in here," I said, gesturing to myself. As I was saying that, I spotted a picnic table in a park on the side of the road. "Here we go," I said as I pulled the car over beside it.

I almost wished I'd given it a miss, though, because my garden salad definitely didn't deserve its own rest stop. In fact, it was *disgusting*, and as I tried to choke back the world's driest carrot, Bree was busy giggling herself half to death as she watched me struggle with it.

"I hate you a little bit right now," I told her, holding a paper-dry piece of lettuce up to the light so I could inspect it and make sure it actually *wasn't* paper.

She looked very pleased with herself. "That's Karma for you," she said sweetly. "My porridge is still in the car somewhere if you'd rather eat that instead." Her eyes twinkled. "Some guy who was *actually* nice gave me pancakes so I wasn't brutally forced to eat something I hate."

"I saw what you had to do to get those pancakes," I said, waving my fork at her. "And I'd rather have the salad."

She looked down admiringly at her breasts, confirming they'd been part of her plan all along. "Your choice," she said smugly. "If you'd been more patient at breakfast maybe you wouldn't be in this situation now. Or," she said, shaking them a little, "maybe you could have used *mine* to get free stuff!"

I felt uncomfortable and had to glance around us to make sure no one else had seen that.

Bree's smile faded. "You're being *really* weird and uptight today," she told me. "I mean, not as bad as you were when I first met you, but yeah." She leant her elbows forward on the table. "It's a pity we couldn't find that place I used to like when I was little. It's really quiet there. You'd probably be *way* more relaxed, and you always chill out when you paint. Plus I was kind of looking forward to watching you do it..."

I finished my salad as I wondered exactly how good her memory of this creek was. Let's find out, I thought. "Well, why don't I give it a shot anyway?" I asked her, standing up a little stiffly and going to grab my laptop and tablet out of the car.

"Are you serious?" she asked me as I took the laptop from under the passenger seat and came back to the table. "You're going to paint it *here*?"

I shrugged, unzipping the bag. "If you can give me a good description of it, yes," I told her, and then patted the bench beside me with a very distant, vague memory of making a similar motion to Gemma last night. I pushed that thought aside as I pulled my laptop out and opened it.

She came around to sit beside me and waited for Windows to resume while I was getting the tablet out. I'd left the browser open at the photo bank site I was using for work, and since I didn't really need the main screen while I was using the tablet, I let Bree look through the photos a bit while I set up a canvas.

"These are really amazing pictures," she said as she scrolled through them. "The colours are fucking awesome."

I scribbled a bit with the stylus to make sure my settings were intact. "Eh, they're okay. None of them are what I'm looking for, which is an *amazing* photo of Australia that says, 'sign a multi-million dollar distribution contract for pink diamonds!'"

"For that Russian guy you said about?" I nodded at her, and she tilted her head at the photos, considering them. "They're still great, though."

I was actually very over those photos after *hours* of looking at them, so I turned my attention to the tablet. "Now," I said, gesturing at the blank canvas. "Describe your creek."

Bree didn't do that bad a job of helping me paint it, actually. Her idea of composition wasn't terrible and she was able to give me detail that built a good atmosphere—water mist over the creek, dappled sunlight through the trees and crunchy autumn leaves all over the ground. However, it wasn't so much that she was good at describing pictures that helped me, it was how goddamn bossy she was about making sure I was getting everything exactly right. Boy, did she let me know if something wasn't turning out the way she remembered it.

The final piece didn't fill up the whole canvas, just an oval in the centre of it. I was pretty certain my battery was going to die before I'd have time to fill in a whole background, so I left it at that.

When I'd finished, Bree still acted like it was the most beautiful thing she'd ever seen. "That's exactly right," she said with a whimsical sigh. "Like, exactly. I kind of want to show Mum and Dad to see if they recognise it, but at the same time I don't. It's so creepy, I can see it in my head and it looks like this. "

"That's from your head, remember," I said to her, but was still secretly very proud that I'd done her childhood memory justice.

She took the tablet from me and was holding it up against the laptop screen while I stretched my wrists out.

I didn't realise what she was doing until she said, "Oh, right, I can see why you don't like the photos." I looked down at her for an explanation. "Well, when you compare this," she indicated the tablet, "with this," she pointed at my laptop, "the photos are really flat and really boring. Your picture makes the place look, well, kind of magical," she said, smiling down at the tablet again. "Fuck those stupid photos, *you* should do all the landscapes for your project thing."

I had opened my mouth to immediately contradict her, but didn't go through with it. Actually, that wasn't such a bad idea. In fact, it was unexpectedly a really *good* idea and it had very unexpectedly come out of *Bree*.

"You're welcome," Bree said smugly, tossing her curls.

I rolled my eyes at her. "If I close this contract using that suggestion, I will take you out for a few drinks," I promised, and then gave her a bit of a surprised look again. She'd come up with that?

My laptop hardly had any charge left, and since it was going to take us three or four hours to get home, we packed up, piled into the car, and headed back to Sydney.

Bree had been treating me to some very frightening renditions of Mariah Carey songs as we drove, but quietened as soon as Sydney loomed on the horizon in front of us. I didn't want to go home, and there was something nagging at me that I didn't want to have space to worry about, as well.

As we gave way at the turn off to the final tollway that lead into the city, Bree abandoned her silence to flip the twenty-cent piece again. "It says go that way!" she said, pointing back towards the mountains.

I worried about that. "Do you want to stay over?" I asked, hoping she'd say yes. "It's fine if you do."

She sighed and shook her head. "No," she sounded miserable. "I mean, I totally want to, but I can't tonight."

Why not, Bree? I asked myself as I looked across at her and nearly side-swiped a road train. I swore and corrected my steering. "Okay," I said, both hands on the wheel and my eyes on the road. "Want me to drop you home, then?"

She nominated a train station, and then hugged me awkwardly through the driver's side window as I left her. "I had a great time today..." she told me, but left the sentence hanging and then looked like she wanted to say something else. She never said it, though, she just turned and walked towards the platform. I leant forward to look up at her before I drove off; there were just a selection of regular people waiting for a train. She'd probably be safe, even in that 'long' skirt.

When I got home, I usually had makeup to wash off and clothes to squish out of and generally had a shower. Not needing to do that was *really* disorienting, it wrecked my whole routine. I decided to strip and have a shower anyway.

I felt better than I had this morning in it, especially about the Gemma thing. It was fine, I decided. It was just something a woman had done to me when I was drunk, Henry probably wouldn't even care about it. In fact, he'd probably be able to give me some advice for how to stop constantly thinking about it all the time.

After I'd thrown on my hoodie and the old trackies, I decided to start looking at Bree's suggestion for the project. I'd plugged in my laptop and had been going through some of my old landscapes to decide if I had the skill to pull something like this off when my phone buzzed in my pocket. I took it out to check it.

It was Sarah, and that reminded me that I'd run out on her last night. Again. I braced myself as I opened it in case she was going to yell at me. Her text wasn't angry at all, though. "*How's the head, Toyboy? ;)*"

It would be better if I had better painkillers, I thought, as I read her message again. There was something comforting about the fact she was so okay about my guy-thing that she could joke about it.

Even though she wasn't angry, I decided to apologise anyway. "*I suppose I can't really say it was the food this time, can I? I should have at least said goodbye. I'm sorry.*"

"Are you kidding? Watching my female boss completely dismantle my female friend was the highlight of my week." There was a pause, and then another message came through. I'd been fine with the 'Toyboy' comment, but as she kept going, I was already beginning to feel a very familiar discomfort, and my heart was beginning to race. "Just fyi Gem is totally questioning her sexuality over you. Should I tell her that you might decide there's a guy in there after all?"

I couldn't type fast enough. "No, just leave it, it was absolutely nothing anyway," I said. "Just a drunken pash in a pub with a girl. It probably happens all the time. And I doubt I'll run into her again so it doesn't matter."

"1. You work in the same building. 2. You're both friends with me. 3. I've actually never pashed another chick in a pub, and to my knowledge Gemma hasn't either. 4. My hand slipped and I accidentally gave her your phone number. In my defence, you weren't there to stop me."

It was the last part that made me start to panic. This was getting out of hand. I felt sick. *Really* sick. "It was nothing, Sarah," I texted back, but my hands were shaking a bit. "Really, it was just one of those drunken things. It didn't mean anything. I have a boyfriend."

I had to wait a second for her response, and when I got it, it floored me. "OMG, who you are SO not into. If you don't mind me saying, that whole thing with him is so obviously a 'should'. He's nice and all that, but why would you settle for someone that you're not into when you can set the whole room on fire with a chick like you did with Gem?"

My jaw dropped.

I couldn't even look at that message a second longer. I put the phone down and felt my pulse race. Even without it in front of me, though, I remembered every word and I felt every single one of them like punch in the stomach. I couldn't argue with her, because she was *right*.

Oh, no, I thought as my chest tightened and I got light-headed. No. No, no. Not this again. *Please*, not this again.

My throat was starting to feel like it was closing over and as if that wasn't a big enough problem on its own, I couldn't *breathe* because of these stupid fucking bandages and everything was just *so fucking fucked* and *what on earth* had fucking possessed me to think anything could ever be fine and okay after I'd cheated on my boyfriend with a *woman?* Sure, I'd pushed Gemma away, but I'd wrapped my arms around her first. I couldn't fucking put this all on her.

I sprung out of my chair and wrenched my hoodie off, pulling at the bandages with quivering fingers, searching all around them for the claw. When I finally found it and tore them off me, the relief lasted for about two seconds until I realised that the burning in my chest was still there. I paced, trying to get rid of it, my hand on my ribs.

Stop it, Min, I told myself as my apartment began to feel extremely fucking small all of a sudden. There wasn't any air in here, either, but I kept trying to breathe anyway as my heart thumped against my palm. *It's going to be fine, Min.* It's fine, you've been with him for *years* and not really been into him and it's been perfectly fine. Nothing needs to change just because you know *why* you're not into him and, actually, won't it be easier now? Now that you know what the problem actually is?

It didn't feel fine. It didn't feel fine *at all*. And if he saw me dressed like this and heard people call me Bree's *boy*friend...

I was breathing and breathing and *still* no matter how much I tried I felt like I couldn't inhale deeply enough to get all the oxygen I needed. As my vision started to grey, in the back of my mind I could hear Henry's voice saying *so* calmly, 'It's okay, Min. It's okay. It's just adrenaline, it will be gone soon,' and while that was normally a comforting thought... now?

Now I was going to have to tell him. He deserved to know. But, *fuck*, what was I going to do? I didn't want to lose him. He was just so much fun and so wise and loving and Mum would *fucking kill* me. How would I even show my face at work if we broke up? And if I couldn't show my face at work, how could I stay there, or even here? My home belonged to Frost. I didn't want to lose it or him or anything and I didn't *want* to break up with him. I just wanted everything to be okay.

I had been circling the inside of my apartment and trying to talk myself down when my phone buzzed on the table. As I looked at it, my heart started pounding again. I was worried it was going to be

Sarah with some more home truths so I almost didn't check it. I was glad I did, though, because it was Bree this time.

"*why were u so distant with me today.....?? :(:(i mean u were nice and we had fun i guess but it just felt like..... i dont know.... u dont even want to hug me anymore :(:("*

My chest clenched. *Bree.*

On the one hand I wanted to invite her over right now because I couldn't face thinking about all this stuff, but on the other, I doubted I was in a fit state to entertain. It was a bit of a moot point anyway because she'd told me she had to stay home tonight. I couldn't not reply to that message, though, because Bree wasn't like Sarah. She'd be upset if I didn't.

"*I'm just going through some stuff right now,"* I typed, after thinking it through. *"It's not you at all."*

"*why wont u let me help though?? uve been like the best friend ever and i want to help if u feel like shit"*

I smiled a bit at that. "*You* *do* *help. I would have gone nuts all day if you hadn't spent it with me."*

It was a while before she replied. By that time I'd already taken double the recommended dose of my strongest painkillers and fallen asleep on the couch. Anything, really, to avoid thinking about what had happened with Gemma last night, what I knew it meant about me and what I had to tell Henry about tomorrow.

The clock on my phone said *3:13AM* when I opened her message, and I was too tired to really know how I felt about it.

"*well if u cant figure out how i can help u feel better about stuff maybe ill try to think of something myself............ :) :) :)"*

My head was aching again, and if she was *that* determined to help, I was tempted to ask her to leave codeine by my front door instead of coffee this time. It was too late to reply, though, so I didn't. I just had another sub-par painkiller, tucked myself in bed and hoped I'd accidentally sleep all the way through tomorrow.

FIFTEEN

I knew exactly how I was going to say it. I'd spent all of Sunday morning staring blankly at my laptop while I meticulously chose every word. I was going to open up by saying, 'Henry, I need to talk to you about something important. I did something *awful* on Friday night'. He'd want to take me somewhere more private to talk properly, and then I could tell him everything, all in one go.

So when I'd finally managed to talk myself into a nice dress and some heels and I'd showed up the right amount of early to be relaxed when he arrived, everything went wrong.

Henry was late.

It was weird, because Henry was *never* late, not ever, not unless it was something to do with work. In fact, he was pathologically early everywhere, it was one of the things we'd bonded over when I'd first come to Sydney. He'd say, 'I'll see you at six,' and we'd both show up at wherever we'd arranged to meet at 5:40. So when the clock ticked 12 and he still hadn't shown up, I felt like I was in the twilight zone.

It was a bit too early to worry about horrific car accidents yet—although I won't promise it didn't cross my mind—so I stood on the stairs out the front of the cinemas on George Street and checked my phone.

He hadn't texted me. No one had texted me, actually, although I had a couple of dozen comments from the painting of Bree's childhood creek I'd uploaded this morning. I didn't really have anything to do, so I just stood on the stairs of the cinema and wondered what the fuck was going on. The wait was *killing* me. I was exhausted. Whatever was going to happen, I just wanted it over and done with.

As I stood there, though, I still couldn't help rehearsing the whole thing. *Henry*, I thought, *I ran into Sarah and went for a drink with her. Her friends showed up, and I was really drunk, and one of them kissed me and I let her.* I stopped and made a face. Now that I imagined saying that to him, it didn't sound like anything. If some random drunk girl grabbed Henry and pashed him, I wasn't sure I'd care about it. Okay, I thought apprehensively, I should tell him more. 'I let her and I enjoyed it', maybe? How much, though?

Should I tell him that it really turned me on and I wanted to keep going? Or is it cruel to rub it in his face that much?

I wondered again if I should just tell him about the guy-stuff, too, and immediately dismissed that idea. That really would be the kiss of death for me and Henry. He thought he was dating a nice, feminine woman. How would *any* guy react to their girlfriend saying, 'Okay, so, I enjoyed pashing a woman on Friday night *and* I hate looking like a woman, I hate dressing like a woman, I don't really *feel* like a woman, and, actually, I might be better off as a guy'. Yeah, *no*. Both Bree and Sarah had been great about it, but then neither of them were dating me.

When I heard Henry's voice behind me, my heart started going again. "Min! There you are! I'm so sorry!"

I'd been turning towards him, opening my mouth to say, 'Henry, I need to speak to you', but the words died on my lips when I saw him.

Henry was carrying an enormous rectangular box that had a picture of a pram on the side of it. And not just any ordinary pram, space-age pram that had two stroller-type seats and one canopy-thing where you were probably supposed to put a baby.

Henry set the box down on its end beside me, took me by the shoulders and kissed my cheek. "Sorry I'm late," he said. "As you can see, I had some shopping to do, and when I realised I wasn't going to make it in time I went to text you, but..." He took his phone out of the pocket in his jeans and showed me; it was dead. "I was so tired last night when I got back from Melbourne that I think I forgot to switch the power point on when I plugged it in."

I was still staring at the pram box, distracted from my confession. "That's for Alice, right?" I said confidently, sure that I knew the answer, but *extremely* uncomfortable about it at the same time. There were *three* seats on that thing.

He looked surprised. "No, it was on special. I thought I might as well start investing in baby stuff now." At my horrified expression, he laughed and put a hand on my shoulder. "Oh, Min," he said. "I'm *joking*. As if right after you get a promotion is the right time to even be thinking about a family."

I forced a smile, but for a moment I couldn't escape from the disturbing mental image of myself with a big pregnant belly. Henry wants kids, Min, I tried to tell myself. That means at some point you're going to have to do that. That is, if he doesn't dump your sorry arse for cheating on him. I swallowed.

Henry hoisted the box under one arm and started to usher me inside. "Yes, it's for Alice. I was planning on leaving it in the car, but it was *really* expensive." He patted the box. "So, if you don't mind, it's coming to see a movie with us. Don't worry, I'm sure it won't eat much of the popcorn."

While we were buying the popcorn, people were staring at us. Henry laughed about it a little, but I just felt like everything was completely out of control and I couldn't find anything funny. I saw him look at me with concern, but he didn't comment on it while we were heading to our seats. When we'd sat down by ourselves in the very back of the cinema with the pram beside us, I *still* hadn't told him about Gemma.

Before I got a chance to talk myself into it, though, Henry had already put a gentle hand on my forearm and leant in quietly to ask, "Min, are you alright? I didn't want to say anything in front of everyone out there, but you look *really* run down and really worried. Is everything okay?"

It's happening, I thought, and felt sick. This is it. "No."

He glanced around us; no one was sitting at all near us yet. "Do you want to talk about it?"

Well, I didn't *want* to. Actually, what was I thinking? Yes, I did want to, because then I wouldn't have to constantly worry about how he was going to react. I'd know.

I took a deep breath. "Something happened on Friday," I told him, in the moment completely forgetting my beautifully worded confession. "And I can't stop thinking about it."

He nodded slowly. "Something to do with work again?"

I had been about to say, 'no', when I remembered that Gemma *was* from work, and technically Sarah was my employee.

Henry interpreted my silence as 'yes' and thought twice about asking any further questions. "It's okay, you don't need to tell me details, I know your project is strictly confidential," he reassured me. "So how would you like me to help? It must be *so* stressful not being able to talk to anyone about it. Especially in your first management position."

259

I slumped, and I think Henry mistook that for me relaxing. *No, Henry, it's not my project,* I thought a bit helplessly. I didn't say that, though, because he was already trying really hard to think of ways to make me feel better. Unsuccessfully, but I didn't want to interrupt him anyway.

"Maybe we could plan our next holiday? That always makes *me* relax," he helpfully suggested. "Well, that and having grand visions of staging a really dramatic resignation." He smiled at me, offering me some popcorn. I shook my head and only managed a really weak smile in return as he continued. "How *do* you feel about New Zealand? Because, personally, I'd really like to visit. Maybe we could go right after your project's finished? You could really use the break, and I'm sure you can negotiate a week or two off once it's signed."

He had to stop when a couple made to get past us, because he needed to stand up and hold the pram box in a way that they could squeeze through. The three of them laughed a bit at the box, and Henry said, "Just practising taking the kids to the movies for later," with a big smile on his face.

"Three kids?" the lady joked with him as she edged past me. She was older than we were and she probably actually *had* kids. "I hope you're not planning on ever having any money again."

Henry put his arm around the box. "Just the cost of this pram alone pushed back our plans for another couple of years."

The couple laughed politely and went to go sit up the end of the row. Henry set the box back down against the seat beside us, and then sat down himself. "Actually, that's why I'm doing this for Alice," he told me. "She and Zhang could never afford to spend $1500 on a pram."

I was still stressing about the fact he so easily talked about 'our' kids, completely oblivious to the fact I'd pashed a girl on Friday night. As I was working up the courage to butt in with my, 'I need to tell you something', Henry turned to me and said, "Actually I need your help with this."

My help with the pram? I must have looked confused, because he winced and said, "Yes, I'm not planning on actually telling Alice that I bought it, because they're both a bit iffy about me showering them with presents. So, obviously I can't say I spent *$1500*."

"You're going to tell them it cost less?"

He shook his head, still looking guilty. "I'm going to tell them I asked around work and found someone with a pram they can use. Which unfortunately means I need to assemble it before I drop it off later tonight. I was hoping I could do that at your place...?"

He was looking at me like he actually felt *bad* about that, and, despite how stressed out I was, I couldn't help myself. "Henry, you're a terrible person," I said in a complete deadpan.

He had a pained expression. "You see, this is one of those times that I can't tell if you're joking or not."

I balked. Was he *kidding?* "Of course I'm joking, Henry, why would *anyone* think that was bad?"

He made a face. "I know it's not bad, I know. I just wish I could tell her how lucky I feel to be able to be generous to my little sister. I think part of her would love to be told how much money her big brother is happy to spend on her, you know?" He shrugged. "But I guess everyone always worries if they're doing the right thing or not..."

I stared at him. "Henry, are you fucking serious? I wish you could hear yourself," I said quietly. "Listening to you stressing about *this* making you a bad person is an insult to everyone with *actual* moral dilemmas." Like me, for example. "You're like the perfect guy, I'm still trying to figure out what the catch is. You're too nice."

He laughed wryly, relaxing a little. "You're right, I'm probably gay."

I was glad I hadn't eaten any of the popcorn, because I would have choked on it. "*What?*" I said in the top register of my voice. Around the cinema, people stopped watching the trailers to look at me. I shrank a little in my chair.

He took one look at my expression and *laughed*. "Min, I'm not gay, I promise," he reassured me in a whisper. I must have looked very sceptical, because he laughed a bit more. "Why are you looking at me like that? *You* of all people should know I'm not!"

Except that *he* of all people didn't know that *I* probably *was*. "Because *your* line is that people don't say things out of the blue, so based on your own logic you must have *thought* about it!"

He shrugged, casting a furtive glance around us to make sure there was no one sitting close enough to hear him. "I was actually just following that old trope of 'he's too perfect, he must be gay' that is repeated so often in movies and TV, but in the spirit of full disclosure, I suppose it *has* crossed my mind a couple of times." He touched my hand. "But for me it's one of those things that's better in theory than in reality. I have no particular interest in it. So, yes: not gay."

I had so many conflicting thoughts about what he'd just told me, so many. I couldn't get Gemma and Friday night out of my head, though. If he'd thought about it the way I had about Gemma... "But you've *thought* about it?"

He frowned. "Yes, I frequently fantasise about pushing Sean Frost off the balcony on level 36, as well, but I definitely won't be doing that," he whispered. "It doesn't make me a murderer, does it?"

I raised my eyebrows, sitting back a little. "Okay, that's a really good point."

He took another handful of popcorn. "You seem very invested in my answer, though," he observed, watching me a little too intently. "Why is that?"

My heart stopped. *Now's your chance, Min,* I thought, *tell him about Friday night.*

Before I got there, though, he was already picking through what I'd said with the fine-toothed comb they handed out to him in shrink school. "'But you thought about it'," he said, repeating what I'd asked word-for-word and examining all of them. It made me *really* nervous. "*You've* thought about it," was his conclusion, "being with another woman."

How the *fuck* did he do that? I swallowed. "Actually, yeah..."

The concentration on his face looked like a frown; or maybe it *was* a frown. "We've talked about this before, though," he said. "Recently, actually, right after you were worrying about that painting and the photo that you uploaded. You weren't so upset about it then, you were even joking about it, so this must be recent." He watched me very closely. "Did something happen, Min? In the last few weeks?"

Jesus fuck he was a fucking *mind* reader. How the hell did he zoom in on things like that? I looked around us, even though I knew there wasn't anyone sitting very close. Henry was being *really* discreet about how he was reacting, but *fuck,* it was a *cinema.* I had to tell him, though, and if I didn't do it now I wasn't sure I'd manage to later. God, I was *shaking* again. "Something happened on Friday."

He didn't say anything this time, he was just listening intently so I was obliged to continue. "I went out with Sarah and got drunk, and one of her friends kissed me." I couldn't read him at all. "I didn't let her keep doing it, but I liked it." After some debate, I added, "A lot."

His brow softened and he sat back, watching me. I saw his eyes dip to my shaking knees. "That's all that happened?" I nodded. "You didn't know her before, and you're not planning on seeing her again, are you?"

"No." Sarah's text message was unfortunately fresh in my mind, however: *'You work in the same building,'* she'd said, and *'you're both friends with me'*. I dismissed that thought. I'd never seen Gemma at Frost before, and Sarah and I had been working together for some time. Of course, Gemma hadn't had my phone number before...

He was watching me carefully, and I could see his brain ticking over. This is where I find out, I thought. This is where I find out what's going to happen to us.

His eyes were on my face, my chest and my legs. He was noticing how nervous I was. "It wasn't work upsetting you just before, was it?" he said at last. I shook my head.

Say something, Henry, I thought, anything. When he didn't, I couldn't take it any longer, so *I* did. "I'm sorry," I whispered, feeling like he should really hear it. "Henry, I'm so, so sorry, I didn't mean to—"

He reached across and put a hand on my shoulder, glancing over his own at the other patrons. No one was paying any attention to us. "Min," he said, interrupting me. "Let's talk this through." It sounded like he already had it all figured out. "Here's what happened: another woman kissed you, you enjoyed it, you stopped her, yes?" I nodded. "You can't control what other people do, only what *you* do, so the fact she kissed you is kind of irrelevant. What *you* were in control of was stopping her from taking it anywhere else. And you did that," he said, and let that hang in the air for a moment before concluding, "So realistically, it's the third thing you're worried about, and that you're worried *I'll* be worried about, isn't it: that you enjoyed it?"

I stared at him. My jaw might even be a little bit open. "How the *fuck* do you do that?" I asked him nervously. "Just like that?"

He broke the tension by chuckling a little. "Five years at uni and nearly a decade of working with people," he said, and then he scrunched up his face for a moment. "Although, despite that, I *did* think it was work bothering you the first time around, remember?" His smile faded a little, but he didn't seem angry or upset. "Min, *lots* of women are attracted to other women. It's nothing to lose sleep over. And as long as you're still attracted to me, too, it doesn't worry me, either."

I tried as much as I could to veil my reaction to that so he couldn't read it. 'Still' attracted to him?

"I mean that," he said. "And although you said earlier that you 'couldn't stop thinking' about what happened, it really sounds like you're not planning on doing anything about that, are you?" I shook my head, and he smiled again, relaxing. "Then it's just a nice thought. There's nothing wrong with thinking nice thoughts, everyone does," he said, and then cringed. "Although, if I want to retain some self-respect, *I* should probably think about what you just told me a lot less..." He reached for a handful of popcorn, and it felt like the end of the conversation.

I didn't know if he was being serious about imagining me and a woman or if he was just joking about it to make me feel better, so I didn't comment on it. I just sat there frowning at him. "Why are you okay with this?" I asked him, still not really believing it. Just like that, everything was fine?

He paused before he put the popcorn in his mouth, grinning and saying pointedly, "Because not everything is a crisis, Min." He looked back at the screen. "The movie's about to start."

The movie *was* starting, so I sat back in my own chair, staring blankly forward.

That was it? *That* was what I'd been tearing my hair out over? I mean, I hadn't actually told him *everything*, but he'd homed in like a fucking heat-seeking missile on what had been upsetting me and he didn't seem to mind it at all. I couldn't imagine why it didn't bother him, though. Then again, Henry wasn't actually the one of us who was having a sexual identity crisis, *and* he thought that I was attracted to him *and* women. I made a face.

You also didn't tell him about the guy-stuff, an irritating voice in my head reminded me, and I squashed it down. Henry didn't need to know that. I wasn't going to do it around him or at work or anywhere where it would impact him and therefore he didn't need to know. It was just something I could keep between me and Bree, and maybe occasionally Sarah. It was like his thing with Alice and the pram, I decided. Not knowing will make him happier, and it doesn't hurt anyone.

Fuck, though. It was crazy. I had been *completely* fucking myself up over the Gemma thing all night and morning, and the whole thing had just turned into an enormous anti-climax. What a waste of energy; I don't know why I always expected the apocalypse.

"I think I need to stop being so fucking paranoid about everything," I said vaguely, loudly enough for him to hear.

He looked surprised for a second, but it melted away into affection as he chuckled to himself and leant over towards me. "Well, that is certainly one way of putting it," he said mildly, and then continued to watch the movie.

I pretended to watch it, too, but there was *so much* to think about, I couldn't even get my head around it all. Fortunately we'd chosen an action flick, so I didn't really need to give it much attention. I just watched all the pretty explosions and wondered about the fact Henry seemed to be so unruffled by the idea I was thinking about women. He didn't seem to think thoughts mattered at all, really. At one point I needed to ask him about it, so I said next to his ear, "Do you really just happily think about things like killing Sean and me getting with girls, even if it can't happen? You don't think it's, like, fucked up to fool yourself by imagining things that will never be?"

He frowned a bit, whispering, "There's nothing wrong with any thought unless you don't like it." He kissed the back of my hand. "Think whatever you want to."

I relaxed back in my chair, staring wide-eyed at the screen. Fuck. I felt like I'd just had an epiphany. Especially after years at a Catholic high school and having been brought up by my everything-is-a-sin mother, I felt like someone had just handed me the world and said, 'Here, go nuts', and I had *no* idea what I wanted to do with it.

I took a handful of popcorn before Henry ate it all and stuffed it in my mouth as I tried to cope with the idea.

I really hoped that no one would ask me what the movie was like because I didn't watch it. I could probably have made one or two observations about the environmental design—I had *always* been a bit partial to futuristic dystopia—but other than that, the plot went right over my head because I was paying next to no attention to it.

Henry made a few comments as we left, though, pram box under one arm. "The lead was very unconvincing," he said. "I find it really hard to focus on the story when you can tell the entire crew is more interested in making sure an actress looks beautiful than making sure she's really selling the character."

"Maybe she just needs better marketers," I said, still too stuck on all of the stuff we'd discussed before the movie had started to be too interested in reviewing it.

"I don't think people who sell *women* are generally called marketers..." Henry joked, looking around as we walked up to the lift. He didn't press the button straight away, though, second-guessing himself. "I think I'm on level five, but I'm lost without my phone. I usually make a note of which floor I parked on."

I didn't really care where he'd parked his car, because I was too aware of the fact he wasn't saying anything about what he'd learnt about me. It was like we'd never even had that conversation. It didn't feel right.

He *had* actually parked on level five, but it took us longer to get up there and find his car than it actually took us to drive back to my building and park under it. As we got out and went to walk over to another lift, Henry stopped by an empty parking space, looking at it.

"You moved your car," he noted. "Did the battery go flat again?"

I gave him a look. "How the hell do you need to put a thing on your phone about where *your* car is parked but you know where mine's supposed to be?" He shrugged, smiling, as I said, "No, I was stressing out over all that stuff I told you, and so Bree and I went for a road trip yesterday."

"Ah," he said as we got to the lift.

We then stood there waiting for it to collect us, and he didn't say anything else. It was driving me nuts. "Aren't you going to ask about what we did? Where we went?" I turned toward him. "After what I told you happened on Friday, aren't you worried about what I'm doing with her?"

He looked *really* surprised. "Should I be worried?"

I sighed. "Well, no, not about *that*," I said. "But it's really weird that you're not."

He raised his eyebrows at me, and then looked back at the lift. "Well, then." As we stepped into the lift, he pressed the '*26*' button and watched me again for a moment as the doors closed. "You remember how you said you worry too much?"

I made a face. "Yeah..."

He raised his eyebrows at me. "Mmmm," he said simply and left it at that. He did think further about what I'd said, though, which was at least a *little* comforting. "I've told you this before, Min: I'm glad you're making friends here. I don't know much about Bree, but despite the terrible singing voice and issues with boundaries, she seems very sweet. Sarah and her partner are nice. Do I think you're sleeping with them all because a stranger kissed you on Friday night? No, I don't."

Well, when he put it like that, I felt a bit silly. I supposed he was right, I *was* worrying too much again. I cringed a bit internally about him describing Sarah as 'nice', though, because that was what *she'd* said about *him. Sarah thinks you're nice, too, Henry. She just wants me to break up with you and get it on with girls.*

"How is she, anyway?" Henry asked, changing the subject. "Bree, I mean? You haven't talked much about why she was so upset that other night."

I made a face; I'd forgotten I hadn't given him the update. "That's because I don't *know* much about why she's upset, she'll hardly tell me *anything*," I complained. "Like I texted you: it's something to do with her brother, but she won't say what. I think something to do with money, as well."

He smiled sideways at me, jogging the expensive pram box under his arm. "That sounds very familiar."

I shook my head at him in the reflection. If *only* Bree had a brother like Henry. "Yeah, I think it's a bit different for her," I said. "I don't think it's a you-Alice thing, I think it might be more of a Diane-Sean thing, except Bree is no Diane."

"Well, if she's got a brother like Sean, I really *do* pity her," Henry said with conviction. "She's okay, though?" He looked at me for confirmation, and I shrugged and then nodded. He mirrored my nod and looked forward again. "That's the main thing, isn't it?"

I sighed deeply. I still didn't understand why the hell she didn't want me to know. As we got out of the lift and I was fishing around in the front pocket of my handbag for the keycard, I had to concede I had *no* idea what was going on with her. "I worry about her, even though she doesn't want me to. I wish she'd just tell me everything."

Henry actually found what I'd said quite funny for some reason as he turned his head to look at me. "Coming from you, that's rich," he told me as I let us into my apartment. "She'll get there. Give her time."

I watched him for a second, feeling uncomfortable about the way he'd put that.

Once we were inside, Henry went and plugged his phone in. Then, we pushed the coffee table out of the way so we could sit on the living room floor together and try and figure out how to assemble the pram. It was the first time in a couple of weeks that I'd hung around my house without wearing my boy clothes, and it was fucking uncomfortable, especially in stockings. I fidgeted on the carpet while Henry dug around in the box.

He found the instructions inside, and we lay those out on the floor and examined them. They were seriously intense. I hadn't seen anything that complicated since I'd finished Advanced Statistics. All of the numbered, annotated diagrams made it look like we were building some sort of military-grade drone, complete with detachable baby-capsule for the car. The only thing missing was wings. When Henry emptied the box, there were *hundreds* of parts and most of them were unrecognisable.

"I regret not choosing to study astrophysics right now," Henry said as he held a mystery screw up to the light, trying to figure out how many rings it had so he knew what it was for. He gave up, looking helplessly at me. "I think this calls for wine."

I saluted at him and then went to get us some. Once we both

had a couple of glasses in us, the process was a lot easier. We somehow navigated the diagrams, and by the time I'd offered Henry his third glass—"I'd better not, I'll have to drop this off to her shortly"—we had what looked like a pretty respectable spaceship for three small children. Who designed these things, anyway?

Henry attached the canopy, and we both stood back to examine the finished product. "How does that look?" he asked, tilting his head at it.

I was on my third glass. "Like she's brand new and ready for warp drive."

He sighed, looking from me with the glass in my hand to the pram. "It *does* look new, doesn't it?" he said, and then surveyed my apartment. "Well. Let's find something to mess it up with." He went to go and poke around in my kitchen, and I went straight for my box of old painting supplies.

They were in my wardrobe and Henry didn't follow me, which meant that I could rifle through all my clothes without worrying what I was hiding in there. I could hear him opening and closing cupboards in my kitchen. It reminded me of Bree, actually, and even more so when he said, "Min, just a question: do you have any actual *food* in your kitchen? Any at all?"

I walked in there with my paintbox and looked over his shoulder. "Kids like two minute noodles, right?" I asked. They were the only things in the cupboard, apart from that lonely pickle in a jar up the back.

Henry lifted up the packet and looked critically at it. "I'm not sure what the food content of these noodles is," he said, using his *you-should-really-eat-healthier-Min* voice. "But I'm sure it's not very high."

He crumbled them into the pram anyway, making sure to push them into all the crevices while I asked the most philosophical question of all as I mixed my paints, "What colour do you think baby vomit is?" I held up my palette thoughtfully. "More yellow or more green than this?" I tested out a smear on the canopy-thing, and then stood back to examine it. "More yellow," I decided, and then went about blending it.

He had been laughing, but he stopped for a moment to look at me.

"Fuck, Min, I love you," he said with such gravity, and then he leant over and kissed me.

I didn't stop him, of course, but I suddenly felt *so* uncomfortable. I had been enjoying myself and I hadn't really thought about what we were doing, but now that I was, I felt very self-conscious. As boyfriend and girlfriend, we were drinking, joking and assembling a pram. It was so domestic. Somewhere, Mum was probably popping champagne and drinking to her future grandchildren.

Henry didn't say anything for a second after he pulled back, just hovering close to me and smiling. "I have to go drop this at Alice's, but I'll be back in about half an hour, okay?"

Judging by that kiss, I knew what was on the cards when he got back. I drank the rest of my glass of wine in a couple of mouthfuls.

It took us a minute or two to figure out how to fold it up, but after we had, Henry grabbed his phone and his keys and then carried the pram towards the door.

"Are you sure you're right to drive?" I asked him, because *I* certainly wouldn't have been at that point.

"Two glasses over a couple of hours? Sure," he said, and then smiled at me as he left. "See you soon."

I raised a hand to say goodbye and then dropped it once the door was closed, exhaling. Well, it had been a few weeks, it was probably about time we had sex again. I sighed. There was at least another glass left in that bottle, so I poured it for myself and sat down at the table with my phone.

Now that I had a second, I texted Bree to make sure she was okay. When I unlocked my phone, I discovered I already had a text message and I thought it might actually be Bree beating me to it, but it ended up being from Sarah. "*Hey,*" it began, "*look, I read over that message I sent you last night and it was kind of harsh. I'm sorry if I came across as a bitch.*"

I made a face. She had, a little. I understood why. "*Henry is perfect, Sarah. I'm lucky to have him, and I want to make it work.*"

"*How do you make it work with a guy if you're into the ladies? That's a serious question, I'm not being snarky. Do you close your eyes and think of boobs?*"

I wasn't touching that one with a ten foot pole. "*Just tell Gemma not to expect anything if you really did give her my number.*"

While I was waiting for her to reply again, I finished off my fourth glass. *"She doesn't. I'm pretty sure she just wants to apologise. Is that cool?"*

I thought for a second. There didn't seem to be any harm in that; she had been quite angry at herself on Friday night after I'd taken off. She'd probably feel a lot better if she could say sorry. Those freckles, though... *"I guess?"*

"'Kay, see you tomorrow. Sorry, again. It's your choice who you date and why..."

I read that a couple of times, sighed, and I figured I had absolutely nothing to lose by opening another bottle. I did that and went for glass number five, *finally* texting Bree.

"Hey there," I typed. *"Just wanted to let you know that I'm thinking of you and I hope you're okay."*

When my phone buzzed, I opened it up, again expecting it to be Bree. I was a bit confused by the punctuation and use of capital letters until I looked up the top and saw that instead of saying 'Bree' it was from a number that I didn't recognise.

"Hi, Min, it's Gemma," it said, and my heart stopped for a second. I had to put my glass down to read it. *"Sarah said it would be okay for me to text you, so hopefully it is! I wanted to let you know I was having great time on Friday and I'm really sorry I ruined it for everyone. I was kicking myself all day yesterday over it. I hope you don't think I'm some selfish home-wrecker, because I'm not and I don't want to do that to you xxoo"*

I read the message, and it made me smile. So did those Xs and Os. *"It's fine,"* I typed back. *"And I actually mean that this time. I was having a great time, too, and I don't think you're a home-wrecker. Just please don't tell anyone anything about what happened. Like, anyone at all."*

She didn't reply and I didn't know if she was going to, so I just sat there with a smile on my face.

I could actually barely remember what she looked like—probably because of the combination of alcohol and bad lighting—but I just had this vague sense that she was beautiful. I'd have to be content with that, I decided, wishing I'd somehow taken a photo of her. Part of me wanted to try and look for a photo of her online, but I didn't have Sarah's powerful Facebook analytics tools and I couldn't search for Gemma without a surname. And if I asked Sarah for her surname, it would be *so obvious* what it was for, and Sarah would have a total field day over me wanting one of her friends.

Wait a second. I sat up. 'Her friends'? Sarah had said the girls used Facebook to invite each other out, hadn't she? That meant Gemma probably had a Facebook and that she was probably friends with Sarah on it... which meant I could click through to Gemma's profile from Sarah's.

Feeling like a Bree-grade stalker, I opened the Facebook app and scrolled through Sarah's friends list. I found her quickly, and tapped through to her albums.

The last Facebook album I'd looked through had been Bree's, and Gemma's was *very* different. She didn't have any of Bree's sexuality or naughtiness in the photos, and there were hardly any selfies, either. Instead, they were mostly snaps of Sarah, Liz and Gemma and various other people, some were of Gemma and her family, and some were of Gemma and her cat. In all of them, Gemma had this beautiful shy smile and lovely wavy auburn hair. Her nose and cheeks also had those freckles I remembered, too. She might not have had Bree's 'great rack', as Sarah put it, and she didn't share half her body with the camera, but she was sexy. Maybe *because* of that she was sexy. It was fun looking at her in a slouchy jumper and just imagining what was underneath, more fun than seeing it. Too much fun, actually.

I couldn't believe Henry had given me the green light to imagine whoever I wanted, because *god* it felt good. I felt like I shouldn't be allowed to, as well, and that made it even.hotter.

I didn't get to think much more than that, though, because I could hear Henry letting himself in the front door. *Here goes nothing*, I thought, still glowing a little from what I'd been imagining. I suppose now was my opportunity to find out if I could salvage any sort of attraction I had to Henry by using the powers of red wine. I stood up and leant on the kitchen bench.

When Henry got into my place, he actually had his arms full. Not with the pram, this time, but with some sort of fresh-looking takeaway and a *big* bunch of pink roses. When he saw me looking at them, he nodded his head towards the skeletal flowers that were still in a vase on the counter. "I figured it was time to put them out of their misery," he said, dumping the food on the table in front of me. He reconsidered what he'd said when he got a closer look at the vase, however. "Actually, their misery probably ended a long time ago. A very long time ago."

He laid the roses down on the table for a moment, intending to give me a quick kiss before he put them in water. Just before he did that, though, I said to him, "Shame. I've been enjoying the Silent Hill ambience they bring to my apartment," and he changed his mind.

He laughed openly, cupping my cheek for a moment. The way he was looking at me, it was almost a relief when he kissed me and I couldn't see it any more. He did lean back for a moment after he'd started, though, licking his lips experimentally. "More wine?" he said, and then glanced at the table and back at me. "Is that bottle number two? Because there's not much left of it."

"Mmm hmm," I said, and then, because I didn't want him to start a lecture on taking care of myself, I pushed him back against the counter and kissed him very solidly.

He didn't stop me, but when we broke he gave me an entirely different look. "Not that I'm complaining," he said, breathing heavily, "but who are you and what have you done with my girlfriend?"

"That is a very good question," I say thoughtfully, and then decided to kiss him again.

I can't say I was very surprised, but no matter what I did I got *nothing* out of that kiss. Nothing like I had with Gemma when she'd actually kissed me, and nothing like I had even just by thinking about her a few minutes before. I may actually have tried to imagine I was with her instead, but Henry was taller and bigger than she was. She was small and soft and reaching down to her and feeling a slight body in my arms had been a total turn on. I really liked how it had made *me* feel in comparison. I didn't have any of that to appreciate about Henry.

All I had with him was this big, hard body... and something big and very hard against my hip. I didn't want to feel it against me, so I leant a bit away from him. It was only supposed to be a *bit* away, but I stumbled backwards.

He caught me, and spent a couple of seconds watching me with concern. "How drunk *are* you?" he asked me carefully. "Should we even be doing this?"

I scoffed. "You're my boyfriend and you're worried about taking advantage of me?"

He looked completely serious. "Actually, yes."

I silenced him by dragging him into the bedroom with me. I may not have been attracted to him, but *fuck* was everything a whole lot easier when I was drunk. Before I really knew what I was doing, I was on my back on the bed and Henry had my skirt around my hips and was pulling off my stockings. Because of that, I thought it might all be over quite soon, but I'd forgotten it was *Henry* I was dealing with. Of course it wasn't.

Instead of just sticking it in like any other average guy might have done in the circumstance, he settled down between my legs, hooking an elbow under my knees. Then, he went down on me.

It wasn't like I usually hated it or anything, but I don't really think I'd ever been particularly *into* it, either. He knew what he was doing, I guess, but really I just let him do it because it made him feel like he was being a good boyfriend.

This time, though? I figured I owed it to him to make a serious attempt to enjoy it. I tried to think a bit about Gemma, and then that didn't work, I tried to just focus on how it actually *felt* and not who was down there and what they had their mouth on.

The problem was that when I opened my eyes, I saw a half-open dress, my breasts, and a man between my legs and there wasn't anything that wasn't *very* wrong with that picture. I hurriedly closed my eyes again and tried to get back to what I'd been imagining. This time, though, I avoided focusing on myself. I imagined pushing Gemma's dress all the way up those bare thighs of hers just like mine was now.

I must have made some sort of noise, because Henry stopped, looking alarmed. "Are you okay?" he asked me. "Do you want me to stop?"

I groaned, a bit frustrated at him for ruining my fantasy. "I'm fine," I said, and then caught myself thinking, 'I'm just actually a bit turned on for once, that's all'. I didn't say it though—fuck, I could *never* say something that mean to him. So I bit my tongue and just mumbled, "Keep going."

He looked uncertain, but followed my instructions.

This time, though, all I could think about was how weird this all was. It was distracting. I stared at the ceiling, trying to figure out what to do.

I didn't even need to tell him to stop, though, because he'd already been watching me. "Okay," he said when he saw my expression. "Not tonight, then." He then went to climb over me to get off the bed, but I stopped him. I didn't know what to say, though. I didn't know how to explain it. Nothing looked right or felt right or was right, and my face was numb and my head was spinning from all the wine.

He gently prompted me. "Well, you can always tell me what *you* want."

I want to get it over with for the next few weeks, I thought. I just need to work out how to get through it. Sarah's text message rang in my ears for a bit, '*do you just close your eyes and think of boobs?*' And, with the word 'boobs', the first image that came to mind was Bree. *Bree?*

"Would you like to have a bath together or something instead?" he asked. "Or maybe we could give each other a massage to relax first?"

When I looked over at him and his bare, flat chest and full boxers, I tried to think of anything I'd be happy to do, but all of them ended up in the same place. And the problem was, I didn't want him inside me. I didn't want *anything* inside me. I had a sudden strong conviction that things just didn't belong inside me, and, actually, I didn't want anything to do with anything beneath my bellybutton right now. Or beneath his.

He saw my expression. "Okay, let's just give it a miss tonight," he said, putting a leg over me and getting off the bed. "You've been looking really unhappy since the start and regardless of the fact you keep telling me to go on, I can't go through with it." He sat on the edge of the mattress. "I'm sorry, Min."

As he said that, I groaned and put my head in my hands. Fuck. "No, I'm sorry," I told him, too wasted to try and pretend anything. "I'm sorry, I wanted to..." *...see if being drunk made it easier to deal with sleeping with you*, I thought. And it doesn't, and I can't, and this is bad. I closed my eyes and drew a long, slow breath. I just can't, and it's *worse* now, for some reason.

After he'd taken a few deep breaths of his own, he gave me a big, warm hug. I leant against him as he stroked my back, my head spinning. We stayed like that for a minute or two before he got up, giving me a bit of a pained expression. I looked down; he was *really* hard.

He saw where I was looking and smiled wryly. "I'm going to go have a quick shower," he said without needing to explain himself.

"I'm a bad girlfriend," I said, and sighed, thinking I should have at least offered to give him a hand job, but I couldn't do it.

"Hardly. You're *drunk,*" he pointed out. "I shouldn't even have let it get this far. I'm just lucky you didn't just throw up on me."

I wasn't feeling that great, actually. "Come back. There's still time."

He laughed a bit awkwardly. "It's okay, Min. Really. No harm done." He touched my cheek and watched me for a few seconds, and then went off to the bathroom.

Once I heard the water running, I started the long process of trying to convince myself to do up my bra and dress and put my stockings back on. By the time Henry was done, I *was* dressed and I'd set myself up on the dining table to have another go at a test piece for the project. Henry couldn't see, of course, so I had the screen angled away from him and had to sit so he couldn't see what I was doing on the tablet.

"Work?" he asked as he wandered into the living room, buffing his wet hair with a towel.

I nodded. "You can't see, though."

He made a short, non-committal noise to acknowledge what I'd said, and then went to throw out the evil flowers and put the roses in their vase. My brain still a bit foggy, I watched him over the kitchen counter as he unceremoniously dumped their corpses in the kitchen bin. Bree would have been mortified. She'd probably have wanted to give them some sort of funeral; I chuckled at the thought.

After Henry had spread the roses out nicely and turned the vase to hide a big brown patch in the foliage on one side, he admired his work for a second and then started opening the plastic bags from the takeaway he'd bought. "Feeling sober enough to eat?"

I shrugged, and he put some salad on a plate for me anyway and then walked past me into the living room. As he sat down on the couch, he picked up the PlayStation controller. "I'm going to beat all your high scores while you do that," he informed me with a grin.

I scoffed. "In your dreams," I told him, looking back at my tablet as he settled on the couch and put his legs up on the coffee table.

My canvas stayed blank for a couple of minutes. The last few times I'd painted, Bree had been hanging over me practically salivating all over my tablet. I had a lot more elbow room today. It was also kind of quiet, even with Henry here.

Henry was already scrolling through menus and changing settings on in the game, absently humming the title song that was playing in the background. Every now and then he'd pause the game, lean over his plate to eat some of his salad, and then keep going. I'd seen him do it a hundred times over the last three or four years, and it was as if today had never even happened. As if we hadn't just had really disastrous sex that was so bad he needed to go and jerk off in the shower, and as if I'd never told him about Friday night.

Henry noticed me watching him, and guessed what it was about. "Min, it's fine. These things happen." He smiled.

I managed to smile back, but I wasn't feeling it. Looking back at my tablet, I scribbled a few lines. I was glad Henry was still here with me, but it shouldn't have been so 'fine'.

SIXTEEN

There was no such thing as too hung-over to sneak out of bed at the crack of dawn to avoid an awkward morning after with Henry. I slipped out from under the doona, had the world's quietest shower and then did a spectacular job of getting dressed in the dark all the way up until I stubbed my toe on the foot of the bed. Then I stood in place, clutching my crunched toe and howling silently until I'd recovered enough to hobble out the door. As if my headache wasn't bad enough.

I didn't have any good painkillers left, either, so I ended up ducking into the chemist before work to grab a couple of bottles.

While I was waiting for the pharmacist to run my name on the computer system, I checked my phone. Henry set his alarm for 6:45, and since it was nearly seven he'd probably be getting dressed right now. He wouldn't be too bothered that I'd left, he'd probably assume I had an early meeting I'd forgotten to mention or that I had work I needed to—*shit.* Getting dressed? His spare suit was in my wardrobe, probably hanging *right* over the guy clothes I was trying to hide from him.

Shit, shit... Maybe it was too dark to see anything? I'd tried to push the clothes underneath my winter stuff, so maybe they wouldn't show anyway and I was just—

"Min Lee?" the pharmacist addressed me, reminding me I was in the middle of something. I probably looked completely out of it. "Sign here." He pointed to my account and then handed me my painkillers while I scribbled on it. "Hope you're feeling better," he said as I left. I stared at him for a moment, and then walked out of the shop. Did I look that bad, or was he just being polite?

On the way across the road to Frost and then whole trip upstairs and into Oslo, I worried about those clothes. Then, when I was finally convinced he probably wouldn't have noticed them, I remembered the terrible, awkward, awful sex we'd had yesterday evening and *cringed.*

Dr. Henry would probably put two and two together at some point, I just knew it. He wouldn't confront me, either. That wasn't his style. He wasn't Bree, and he wasn't Sarah, he'd wait for *me* to bring it up with *him.* I had an alarming thought: what if he'd already figured it out and he'd known all along?

As I hooked up my tablet to my work computer, I thought about that. I wouldn't put already knowing past him, actually. I wondered if maybe *that's* why he'd been so calm yesterday? Even Sarah had guessed *something* was up, and not only wasn't she a psychologist, but she wasn't my boyfriend.

Speaking of the devil, the door opened. It was Sarah, of course, and she dumped her handbag and gave me a *very* smug look. She had her hair down again and was wearing a lot more clothes than she had been on Friday night. She also looked like she'd had a much more restful weekend than I had had.

"I *knew it!*" she announced. Then, sitting on her office chair rolling it across the carpet to mine, she placed a Red Bull innocently in front of my keyboard. "I knew you were hiding something!"

I gave her a dirty look as I was waiting for Photoshop to open. "If you think buying me that makes up for anything, you're mistaken."

She snorted, opening her own Red Bull and completely ignoring the fact I was glaring at her. "You're right, only an evil bitch would point out when her friend's settling for a guy she's not into."

I had to look over her shoulder towards the door to make sure there was definitely no one anywhere. "You've got it the wrong way around. *He's* settling for *me*," I said quietly when I was sure we were alone. Then I cringed again as I opened my landscape file, remembering yesterday's failed sex.

Sarah gave me a really tired look. "Yeah, yeah, woe is you. So, anyway, do you think he knows about you?"

"Probably, given that I told him."

She leant forward. "You *told* him?"

I nodded. "Yesterday. About Gemma." I started working on the picture. "Not about the other stuff."

Sarah gave me the once-over. "Hence the I-haven't-slept look you're rocking this morning," she said. "Was it a big fight?" She tapped a fingernail against my Red Bull. "Should I go buy some vodka for this?"

I shook my head and I was about to reply when my phone buzzed. I checked it; Henry had sent me a picture message. It was a photo of his computer screen with 384 unread emails and the annotation, *"Some idiot approved four weeks of annual leave for his assistant manager. Serves him right."*

I showed it to Sarah and she squinted at the screen. "That's not something you say to someone you're not talking to." For a second, she gave me a hard stare. "Are you messing with me? Did you not tell him after all?"

"No, I did, and he's actually fine with it," I told her while I was figuring out how to reply. Since a couple of my reference pictures for the water were beach-related, I took a photo of one of them and sent him the message back, *"I'm painting your assistant manager laughing at you from a beach right now."*

Sarah watched me put my phone away. "Well, if he starts introducing you to random girls and making comments about how the bed's so big it can fit more than two people in it..." I groaned at her and she put her hands up in a yield motion. "I'm just suggesting it's one possibility."

Henry had joked about threesomes before, but I really doubted that had anything to do with why he said everything was fine. I didn't know, though, and worrying about it was exhausting. "Maybe," I said a bit dismissively.

Sarah probably wanted to push the point, but she didn't. She just watched me paint for a minute or two while she was thinking.

It seemed like a good moment to explain what I was up to. "Bree actually had a really good idea on Saturday," I said. Sarah smirked at me when I said her name, but I ignored it. "Instead of spending a million hours looking for the perfect photo for the materials and the slides, I can just spend a few hours painting exactly what I want. That way I can get the dimensions and the colours on point, too, and if there's text I can make sure the composition of the photo doesn't look unbalanced by it."

I zoomed out to show her the landscape; it was only half-finished but it was clear what I was aiming for.

She still looked a bit distracted. "I was wondering why you had your tablet here," she said, "and I know we're *at* work and we've got this super urgent project and about two weeks left to get signed, but I'm really having trouble getting past everything that happened on the weekend and, well..." She gestured at my dress.

I sighed. "Can we play a game where we pretend Friday didn't happen and I'm just a normal, boring project manager?"

She laughed at how I put that. "If you knew how much I sucked at games, you wouldn't ask," she told me, and then continued to stare intently at me in my dress while she drank. "You know how when I met Schoolgirl, she said, 'You look weird' about your work clothes?" I nodded. "Well, I don't know what she's on, because you look like your garden variety office chick to me. No one would ever guess you'd rather be a guy."

"Good," I said, reflecting on how much effort it took to achieve that each morning. The jury was still out on the 'rather be a guy' stuff, though. I knew how I'd rather look, but when it came to what I'd rather be? I had thought 'guy', but it seemed to depend on who I was with. On Friday, I had felt like one.

Something occurred to me, and I looked up from my painting. "You're completely sure Gemma and Liz won't say anything to anyone at Frost about Friday? Not just about me and Gemma, but about how I looked?"

She stopped drinking and nodded. "Uh, yeah," she said. "You should hear some of the wild stuff we've done over the years. But you're not going to, because..." She made a zipping motion across her lips.

She unzipped it after watching me thoughtfully for a few minutes, though. "I get your thing about that other painting now," she said smugly. "If the photo doesn't look right, just paint what you want to see, yeah? Anyway." She slapped her knees. "I did actually come in stupidly early for a reason. There's a truck load of analytics I'm supposed to have ready for my meeting with the other project team this morning which I haven't done. I'm going to try and get them together now and pretend I was a good little Frost marketer and did them all on the weekend when I was supposed to."

She went back onto the main floor to use the networked computers to do that, leaving me alone with my tablet and not doing anything at all that resembled working on the painting. Sarah hadn't meant *this* painting, she'd meant the painting I'd done of myself. I couldn't focus, so I thought I'd just have another quick look at it.

I hadn't opened it for a while, so of course the first thing I noticed was that I'd fucked up the lighting on one of the legs of the table. I managed to resist the urge to fix it.

Looking at this painting now, I understood why Sarah had recognised me on Friday night. I *did* look like this when I was dressed up like a guy, minus the suave suit and funky hairdo. Even how I was holding myself. I looked so fucking cool in it, it was a huge compliment that someone thought I looked like this in real life. She couldn't really be lying about it to make me feel better, either, because then she wouldn't have recognised me. It made me smile. I felt a bit cool, for a second or two.

Then I looked down my front towards the tablet to keep painting, saw my breasts and remembered that I *wasn't* cool. Cool was the last thing I was. The guy-me in the painting probably looked so relaxed because he didn't have twelve feet of elastic bandages wrapped tightly around his ribs to achieve that perfectly flat chest.

Since I'd been meaning to and since I had a few minutes, I decided I'd Google the right way to wrap them so they weren't so uncomfortable. I hoped there was a right way; not that I hadn't managed heels eventually, but it would be great if I didn't have to suffer for months while I was getting used to having my chest bound, too.

I'd typed '*how do I use bandages to bind my breasts*' into Google, expecting to be greeted with friendly diagrams and how-tos, but what I *actually* got were a whole series of dire warnings about health complications ranging from discomfort to broken ribs. A link down the bottom of one of the more militant sites—complete with alarming pictures of technicolour bruises and rants about 'internalised transphobia'—lead to an online store where I could purchase chest binders that were allegedly so comfortable I'd never even know I was wearing them.

"Sold," I told my phone, and then went to buy a couple. The site itself was located in Taiwan and had some really serious Chinglish happening, so when it announced to me that '*with 2 binder bought you have receiving free gift packer for all*', I assumed that was something to do with postage and handling so naturally I selected it. When I got to the checkout screen, though, I ended up paying for postage. I bought them anyway because I was curious about whether or not it was possible to actually be comfortable with flat breasts, and then put my phone away. I sat back over my tablet, wondering about that wording and imagining the package showing up in festive gift-wrapping with ribbons and bows. I chuckled at the thought.

I was midway through adding reflections to the water when my team started to trickle in.

Ian was first. "Oh, you're doing graphics?" he asked as soon as he saw my tablet. He wandered over to have a look, and then ended up standing and watching over my shoulder. "Wow," he said after a minute or two. "I've heard people say you're good for graphics and layout, but that's pretty impressive."

I smiled. John and Carlos weren't that far after him, and before long I had an audience of people behind me watching me paint.

"Is it distracting?" Ian asked. "Having us looking over your shoulder while you do it?"

I shook my head. If I wasn't distracted by Bree buzzing around me and leaning all over me, I wasn't going to be distracted by three men being silently impressed a polite distance behind my chair.

"Well," Ian said after I'd told the three of them what I was planning to do, "if you're going to put that on a five by seven projector, it's going to look amazing," he said. "I reckon do it." There were murmurs of agreement from the other two.

"Now I just have to sell it to Jason," I said, adding some of the finishing touches and then flipping the canvas horizontally to check it wasn't a horrible mess. It wasn't.

"Now might actually be a great time to do that," Sarah's voice commented behind me. It was a bit of a surprise, I hadn't noticed her come back. She hadn't announced herself, either, which was a bit unlike her. "One of the investment teams got signed and he's still high on his prospective bonus from that."

While I hustled the rest of the team back to their desks to work on researching some of the companies Vladivostok had suggested, I saved the image onto a USB and went looking for my boss.

I had thought I would at least need to explain to Jason why I'd decided to paint the images instead of using true photos, but he didn't seem to care. "Looks good," he said, giving it all of a five-second glance in between hunting around for his celebratory cigars. "Make sure you choose a single theme or it's going to look pretty fragmented. Whatever you think is best." With Jason, that was generally code for, 'I don't care now but later I will call you at 3 am and tell you to change *everything*'.

Still, it was heartening that he didn't *hate* the idea, and Bree was going to be totally rapt that her suggestion was popular. I texted her about it before lunch.

The reply was a bit strange. *"haha thats great!!!!! :) :) :) "* it read. Nothing else. That wasn't very 'Bree', but I left it. Maybe she was in class and couldn't talk properly. She'd probably send another one later. I put my phone in my pocket so I'd feel it vibrate when she did.

Before I went to go grab something to eat, Ian asked me if I was feeling okay and since he was the third person to basically tell me I looked terrible, it was a cue for me to go and check out how bad I *actually* looked in the bathroom mirror.

Sarah was in the Women's doing her eyeliner when I walked in there. "Are you lost?" she asked me with a grin as I came and stood next to her at the basin.

I looked down at my dress and then at the symbol on the door, which was a figure *in* a dress. I then looked pointedly at Sarah's legs. She was wearing pants. "Apparently *you're* lost," I told her, returning her grin and checking to make sure there was no one in the stalls before I leant up to the glass to examine the bags under my eyes.

Sarah kept going on her eyeliner. "Like I said before, you don't look that great," she told me, and at my expression, she clarified, "I mean you look *sick*, not anything else. Although, I'm still totally tripping out over Friday. Talk about not judging a book by its Stepford Wives cover." She blinked a few times and then examined her work. "Can I have your girly work clothes when you throw them out? Some of those dresses you have are great."

"If you don't mind that they'll come down to your ankles." I said, fixing my pearls so the catch was at the back of my neck again. "But I think I'll be wearing them for some time yet, so I hope you're patient."

She made a face as she took out her mascara. "Yeah, while we wait for Frost to join us in the twenty-first century."

That, I thought, and the fact Henry was being patient enough about me being into girls. I wanted to leave it there for now and not push my luck.

Sarah brushed some mascara on her lashes, and I think she took my silence as an invitation to elaborate on her twenty-first century comment. "In the meeting just before, I gave my report—which I got done on time, by the way, because I'm awesome—and then I offered to make a chart and a table so the stats were easier to read because some of the team were having trouble following them. It's a small team, so the meetings always feel kind of informal. Anyway, I went to the lead, 'is there anything else you'd like me to make while I'm at it?' and the asshole went, 'Yeah, a sandwich' and the whole fucking team including Jason thought it was hilarious and they all laughed. Then for the rest of the meeting they kept making references to it, and at the end, Jason said, 'I'll expect that sandwich on my desk by lunchtime'."

I had been watching her while she told the story, when I had a Henry moment. "That's why you're fixing your eyes," I said, feeling my stomach drop. "Because of *that*."

She stopped what she was doing and took a breath. "You'd think I'd be used to it by now, wouldn't you?" Then, her eyes welled up. While she was trying desperately to rescue her fresh makeup with a tissue, I just watched her helplessly.

I should have been used to it as well, but I wasn't. Each time it happened it was still fucking humiliating, and it was awful to think of *Sarah* who wasn't exactly a fountain of emotion being so upset about what happened that she'd come in here to cry. It was pretty secluded; there were only five women who worked on the floor. All the rest were egotistical marketing fucks who'd been using women's half-naked bodies to sell shit for most of their careers. It was no wonder they turned out like Jason.

Fuck Jason, I thought as I watched Sarah tilting her head back to stop her tears from falling. Fuck him. I had that fantasy again where I waltzed into work dressed like a boss and just punched the fucking daylights out of him. Why couldn't we have a manager who was more like Henry?

When the immediate threat of tears had passed, she stopped for a second and looked at me. "Just a word to the wise," she told me when I didn't do anything. "When a chick cries you're supposed to hug her."

"I see," I said, and then kind of awkwardly put my arms around her. "Do you want me to tell Henry? Not as a formal report of course, but—"

"No," she said firmly. "I can deal with it. I'm just freaking out because our project pitches in two weeks and this other project I'm on is about a month behind and we have maybe eight weeks' worth of work to cram into four. Rob would normally be really great about everything but he's on the other side of the country at the moment. It's hell." She patted my back, taking a deep breath as she stepped away from me. "Screw everything, I've had enough of today. Want to come and get lunch with me up the road?"

After she'd opened up to me like that, the last thing I was going to do was say no to anything at all she wanted from me, on a personal *or* professional level. So we went a safe distance up George street to a café that definitely didn't have any Frost employees in it and Sarah instituted a No Work Talk rule. It was relaxing, I listened to her chat about Rob while we sat in the sun and waited for our lunch. Around our feet, huge flocks of pigeons and sparrows were also patiently waiting for our food to be delivered.

I laughed at their reaction to lunch arriving. "If Bree was here half her food would be inside them by now," I told Sarah as I threw a couple of crumbs on the pavement to watch them all swarm like piranhas on it. "No wonder she's so small."

Sarah smirked at me. "Is she why you keep checking your phone?"

I stopped chewing for a second. I hadn't realised I'd been doing it *that* much. "No comment." Sarah's eyebrows flickered at me, but she didn't say anything, so I did. "Anyway, since you're convinced there's something going on between me and Bree, doesn't it bother you about Gemma?"

Sarah shrugged. "You kissed her. I'm not expecting a wedding invite. She isn't, either. She just thinks you're really nice and really hot." She took another bite of her lunch and swallowed it, thinking. "Having said that, though, knowing Gem she'd probably still get drunk and jump you again, and if it turns out Henry's up for that threesome..." Sarah looked very entertained by my expression, and then made it even worse. "I told her about that little blonde schoolgirl you're definitely not sleeping with anyway."

"Told her what, Sarah?" I asked suspiciously, closing my jaw and throwing another few crumbs at the desperate looking birds. "There's nothing to tell, remember?"

"I actually just linked her to Schoolgirl's Facebook."

Oh, God. I squeezed my eyes closed for a moment and groaned.

"Yeah, so," Sarah said, getting stuck into her focaccia, "she can draw her own conclusions from it. I don't need to *say* anything."

It wasn't until we had nearly finished lunch that Bree finally texted me. I turned my phone over as soon as I felt it vibrate on the table. *"got something to give u...... what time u finish work???"*

Sarah was smirking a little, so I showed it to her so she wouldn't think Bree was sexting me. It didn't stop her though. "I know what she wants to give to you," Sarah said with a grin. "*It.*"

I sighed at her and messaged Bree back, "*Just come past my work after school and text me when you're downstairs. I'll come down and meet you.*"

As we packed up and headed back to Frost, I asked Sarah, "Why are you so interested in my love life, anyway? Something wrong with yours?"

She snorted. "Hell no, Rob's an Energiser bunny. I'm just nosy." We walked through the big rotating door at the front of the building. "And," she said, looking sideways at me and smiling, "after all those projects where you messed with me and played pranks on me, it's kind of fun to watch *you* squirm for once."

Back in Oslo, I was greeted by Ian. "Where've you been?" he asked. "Jason was looking for you and he won't tell me why."

I naturally panicked and assumed it was something serious, but when I found him smoking on the balcony with a cigarette in one hand and his mobile against his ear with the other, it wasn't. "Mini!" he yelled to me, and then said to whoever was on the phone, "Sorry, mate, secret marketing business." He hung up and walked purposefully over to me. I felt like I was about to get blasted for something, especially given what had happened to Sarah this morning. I should have known.

"Mini, if you're going to do enormous slides, make sure you book the media rooms to deliver. The board rooms have those pissy projectors that won't get the colours right." Then, he held up his phone again, put his cigarette in his mouth and called back whoever he'd been speaking to before.

That's it? I thought, I stressed the fuck out and swept the floor looking for you over that? Did Jason not think I was capable of making that decision myself? It was actually insulting, and I had to stop myself from groaning aloud as he got back into an animated conversation on his mobile.

'You're an asshole!' I wanted to yell, and then I wanted to yell at him for what he'd said to Sarah that morning, too. It bothered me for the rest of the day, and when I needed to go and ask Jason about an email I was planning to send to a prospective contact, I decided to defer it to tomorrow. I could just work on the slides today and relax and *not* brutally murder my boss. I finished another draft painting and presented it to the team. I wasn't sure I liked it.

"I don't really know what theme I want to go for," I told everyone, giving them all copies of the pictures I'd done so far to consider. "It would be great if you guys could have a think about the research you've done and decide which Australian landscapes are going to sell pink diamond distribution contracts to a Russian multi-millionaire."

When I finally got Bree's text to tell me she was downstairs, I was definitely ready for a break and maybe some dinner. Which would give me the perfect opportunity to have a talk with her about her Facebook.

She'd asked me to meet her around the corner of the building off the food court and I wasn't really sure exactly why out the front of it was a problem until she ambushed me in a really tight hug. "Hi!" she said from my stomach. "Don't worry, no one can see us here, you can relax. I'm just collected on that hug you owe me."

I ruffled her curls because, as always, they were at perfect ruffling height. "If this is what you were planning on giving me all along, after the day I've had I may actually strangle you."

She giggled. "I didn't think of that," she said, pulling back and grinning up at me. "But it's not, I promise. I made you something." She bent down to where she'd dumped her bag at my feet and rifled around in it before standing up and giving it to me. It was a coloured envelope thing wrapped in sticky tape. I looked at her for an explanation. "Well, I couldn't buy wrapping paper, so I just went on Google and looked for a graphic of it and printed it out and then wrapped it up like that. Don't open it yet, though! It's for when I have to go home."

My eyes were wide. "Uh, okay, thanks?" I said, and then looked back down at it. It was too small to be anything too crazy, and since she didn't have any money to buy jewellery, it couldn't be that, either. I guessed I'd know soon enough, so I put it in my handbag. "How are you, anyway? Is everything okay?" She looked well, but, then again, she usually did.

"I didn't fail my stats midterm," she said cheerfully like it was an achievement. "So that's good. I even had two points to spare."

I had to laugh at that. Mum would have *killed* me if I'd gotten less than ninety on anything. "Congratulations," I said, making sure I didn't mention *her* parents. "How are you planning to celebrate?"

"Don't know," she said. "Killing people is illegal, isn't it?"

I gave her a pained expression. "I was going to suggest 'by having dinner with Min'. It's not as cathartic, but it's much less likely to get you thrown in jail."

She laughed and wrapped herself around my arm. "Okay, let's do that instead."

I stooped to pick up her bag and then herded her into the food court. "I'm glad you said that," I told her. "Because we need to talk about your Facebook."

While I was ordering us two Souvlakis, Bree was hanging off me and looking very sheepish. "You found my Facebook," she said. "You saw my albums too, yeah?"

I gave her a look.

"I probably should have warned you about that," she decided, accepting her Souvlaki as we sat down. "They're kind of... well, I know you don't really like it when I show skin."

"Show skin?" I repeated before I took a bite. "You show so much skin that I feel like I should be giving my credit card number to someone before I'm allowed to look at them, to be honest."

She looked thoughtful as she considered what I'd said. "Really? You think people would do that?"

Was she *fucking serious*? I swallowed my mouthful way too early just so I could reply immediately. "No, Bree," I told her, abandoning my dinner. "I don't even care what your reasoning is. Just no. *No.*" The more I thought about it, the more abhorrent the idea was, and Bree really didn't look like it bothered her in the slightest. It was unnerving. "Are you seriously thinking of doing that? I swear to god I'll find a way to shut down any site that has pictures like that of you. I cannot let you do that to yourself, and I really wish you'd take down all those photos from your Facebook, as well."

She had been mostly ambivalent about everything until I started ranting at her. Then, she smiled. "I like it when you do that," she said, looking charmed.

"What, give myself high blood pressure by stressing out about you?" My heart was pounding.

She made a face. "Well, not that part, but the rest is nice."

289

She was just sitting there smiling at me as she picked at her dinner. To make matters worse, she'd loosened her school tie so she could undo the top button of her shirt again, as if her tiny skirt wasn't bad enough. It was driving me nuts. I'd had it with her.

"Come on," I said, standing up and taking her by her arm. "You're coming with me."

"I am?" she said as she let me drag her away from the table. "But what about dinner?"

"We can eat later," I said, and led her down the road to the shopping centre.

I took her upstairs to one of the slightly more upmarket and funky clothes stores, and we went inside. Then, just like she'd done when she was choosing clothes for me, I chose a whole stack of clothes for her. She didn't look very impressed by my selection.

The sales clerks had been eyeing us a little cautiously since we'd come in, but eventually one of them ventured over to ask, "Hi, can I help you?"

"That depends," Bree said, giggling at what I was doing. "Does this place sell burqas?"

"Bree," I warned her, and then said to the clerk before he retreated, "Thanks, we'll be fine."

I'd taken a big stack of clothes over to the dressing rooms and pushed Bree into one, but she pulled me in behind her and shut the door. "How do you plan on seeing how they look if you're out there?" she asked, and then slipped off her tie and looped it around my neck.

"You're supposed to open the door and show me the ones you like," I told her as she unbuttoned the rest of her school shirt and shrugged it off her shoulders.

I immediately looked straight up at the ceiling; her bra had *cupcakes with cherries* printed on it, and it was bad enough I had to look at myself in the mirror, let alone her wearing something like *that*. We looked so strange together when I was dressed up as a woman, anyway. Like two people who would ordinarily never have anything to do with each other. I didn't like it, and I wished I could change. We look so much more balanced when I was in my guy clothes.

She laughed at me refusing to look at her. "You are *so* uptight," she told me. "Girls change in front of other girls all the..." she realised what she was saying. "*Oh*," she said, just standing there in her bra as she suddenly understood. "Oh, yeah. Well, you're in here now and it's not like you haven't seen me like this before..."

She put on the jeans and one of the tops I'd chosen for her. The jeans were a bit tight, but the top looked quite nice. It was a loose, floaty shirt in gentle pastels that really suited her pale skin and blonde hair. She looked older in it, and it understated her curves. It was subtle, I liked it. She looked really pretty. Bree, however, did not look impressed.

"This looks like something you would force yourself to wear," she said flatly. "And look how that turned out for you."

She didn't like the next one, either. "Can we save this one until I'm, like, 50? Or maybe 60?"

To the third, she said, "Okay, just a question: whose funeral am I going to?"

She had similar comments about all of the other clothes and in the end she was just standing opposite me in the fitting room looking frustrated. "I'm sorry, Min, but I don't like any of this stuff," she said. "I know what you're trying to do. But don't worry, I've been dressing like this since I was 14 and it's been fine."

I'd really liked her in one of the tops, and I held it up a little mournfully. "You can love your body without sharing it with everyone on the street," I said. "I really think you should wear this one. Are you sure you don't like it?"

"Very sure," she said, without hesitating. "At least when *I* tell you to wear things it's stuff you already like. I don't like any of these." She paused. "And Min, it's really weird to be talking to you and you're, like, looking everywhere else. I get that you're a guy and all but even a guy would totally be looking at me right now. Especially a gay one, a gay one would be like, 'Oh my god, you got your bellybutton pierced, that's *so* 90s...'." She mimicked a stereotypical queen voice.

I did look, but only because I hadn't noticed she had her bellybutton pierced. When I looked, I discovered that she *didn't*.

"Psych!" she said, looking very pleased with herself. "So, can I ask a question? I really don't get why you have such a problem with how I dress. I mean, I kind of get the Facebook thing because in half of them I obviously look like I'm ready for someone to bust on me, but even my school lets me wear my uniform like that." She gestured at it on the floor of the cubicle.

I gave up on the nice top I'd hoped she'd warm to, and put it back on the hanger. "Bree, I would get *fired* if I marketed you the way you market yourself," I said, and then thought about Frost and the people I worked with. "Actually, maybe that's not true, maybe I'd get promoted. But, essentially, the point is you're selling yourself as someone you're not," I told her. "*I* know you're this really sweet, really nice girl who *doesn't* go around sleeping with everyone. But people take one look at you dressed like that, and, well," I shrugged, "at some point you're going to want a job, and—"

She scoffed. "Yeah, in a few years I'll need to get a job, so I'd better start covering up my boobs now in preparation," she said. "That makes so much sense. Maybe I should start waking up earlier, too, so in a few years when I'll need to get to work by eight, I'll—"

"—Bree, this is serious," I said, interrupting her. "You're nice, you should be—"

"Oh my god, nice girls can get their boobs out, too, Min! Watch! No one cares!"

To my *horror,* Bree, who was in those tight jeans she'd been trying on and was still and only wearing that very unsupportive bra, opened the cubicle door and just walked out of it.

My jaw *dropped* and I rushed after her. "*Bree!*"

I couldn't stop her though, and before I had even tried to, she was out on the floor in the store, walking casually over to the women's section as if it was the most normal thing ever. I stood at the entrance to the fitting rooms with my mouth open and my hand over it, watching her. Despite the fact that there were only a couple of other customers in the store and they looked more amused than shocked, the clerks shared my horror and then rushed over to help her.

"If you need another size you can just ask," one of them hurriedly told Bree, trying to usher her back into the fitting rooms.

"Thanks, I'm good," she said innocently, selecting a top from the rack and then walking back past me into the cubicle we'd been in before. She pulled me back inside and locked the door behind us.

I leant against the cubicle wall, my mouth still open. "I

292

can't believe you did that," I said, still shocked. "Who the hell *does* that?"

"I do, and see how no one cared?" she asked me, and pulled the top on over her head. It was another V-neck t-shirt that clearly showed the curves over her breasts. "There," she said, turning around to present it to me. "*This* is more like it. And, actually, I can still be really nice when I wear this, I promise. I don't automatically need to blow everyone just because you can see my cleavage."

I sighed at her.

She watched me for a moment. "Like, okay. I get how with the whole trans stuff you really don't like how *you* look or *your* boobs and—"

"It doesn't have anything to do with me," I interrupted her. "People feel uncomfortable when they look at you dressed like that."

"*Why?*" she asked like it was the craziest comment ever, and looked down her front.

Because you're fucking gorgeous, Bree, I thought, a little shocked *that* was what had come to mind. You're fucking gorgeous. But there's more to you than those 'boobs' you're so proud of and no one would ever fucking know it with the rate you go around presenting yourself like *this.*

"You're actually the first person who's said that," she told me, really confusing me for a second. Had I said that aloud...? "So you don't like the t-shirt, then?" She turned back to the mirror to have another look. "I don't know. I mean, I don't wear red that often, but I kind of like it anyway?"

I shook my head. I gave up, seriously. What the hell do you *do* with someone like Bree? "You drive me fucking crazy," I told her. "Okay, I'll get you the t-shirt."

She turned back towards me. "Really?" she sounded genuinely surprised. "But look how much of my boobs you can see!" She showed me, and I looked. As if seeing that much cleavage on her didn't already make me uncomfortable, those tight jeans hugged her hips and her thighs and when she went to take them off she had to wriggle them down her legs. The rest of her jiggled, too. I looked away and told myself off, but when the t-shirt went over her head I couldn't help but glance at her body in the reflection again.

She was leaning forward to get her school uniform off the floor and that bra *really* needed to be replaced with one that was fit for service. Or maybe it didn't. Fuck, those were *much* bigger than Gemma's, and Bree was hardly more than half Gemma's age. *Fuck.*

When she was all dressed and we went to pay at the register, I was still in a bit of a daze. "Sorry," I said quietly to the clerk while Bree was looking through some of the scarves in a bucket near the counter.

The clerk gave me a secret smile, and then made a surreptitious gesture to her neck. I didn't understand what she meant at first, until I realised she meant *my* neck. I looked down.

I was still wearing Bree's school tie over my dress.

I hurriedly pulled it off, and I can only imagine the deep shade of red my face turned. I was so red that Bree, who hadn't even seen the exchange, laughed at me when I gave her tie back to her.

"You're definitely going to be the death of me," I told her on the way of the store, and then put my head in my hands again as I remembered Bree walking out in her bra. "*Fuck!* God knows what she thought we were doing in there!"

Bree laughed. "Oh my god, your *life is ruined,* they think you're a *lesbian,*" she said dramatically, fixing her tie. Then she completely changed the subject. "So, do you want to get something else to eat? I could kind of go one of those milkshake-juice things they put fruit in."

I got her one, and she walked me back to work, hanging lazily off my arm and appearing very content. "Does this mean you're not going to get on my case about what I wear anymore?" she asked.

I exhaled audibly and was about to reply when I felt her stiffen against me. I looked down; her eyes were fixed on a group of men in suits coming out of Frost. She relaxed as soon as they walked out into the evening sun, though, turning back to me and saying, "Or did you just, like, give up for today?"

"With you, Bree? I just give up in general." As we crossed the road I looked from her to the men who'd just come out of Frost; she didn't seem very interested in them now, though. I wondered who she thought they were. She probably wouldn't tell me, so I didn't ask. "Are you staying over tonight?"

She scrunched up her nose as we stopped out the front of the building. "Nah, I have to go home tonight, but Mum's working Thursday and Friday this week. Can I stay then?"

"Sure," I told her, glancing over her head towards where the men had gone. "Are you... safe to get home tonight?"

"Oh my god, Min," she said. "It's not like as soon as you turn your back every guy in Sydney is going to try and get in my pants..." She gestured around us with the fat straw still in the corner of her mouth. "The *sun* is still out."

That didn't stop you from being worried about those men you thought you recognised, Bree. "Okay," I was all I told her. I gave her back her schoolbag. "Oh," I said. "Did you want me to open the present now, or...?"

She stood up straight. "Oh!" she said, immediately brightening. "Oh, yeah!" She bounced up and down in front of me in that treacherously unsupportive bra as I took the present-thing out of my handbag and turned it over in my hands. "Go on! I spent all yesterday making it!"

I wasn't sure what I expected. With Bree, it could have been anything. I unwrapped it while she watched me intently, worrying that I was going to hate it and I'd need to pretend it was great.

What was *actually* inside was a second-hand 4GB USB, and it was wrapped in a print out. I unfolded the paper while Bree writhed with excitement. It was several long lists, and as I reviewed them, I realised they were all playlists. One of them was called '*happy*', another was '*angry*' and there were several more. The last one was '*my favourites :) :) :)*'.

While I was reading it, Bree couldn't wait any longer. "When you were painting on Saturday you said you listened to stuff while you do it, so I was thinking when you were feeling like shit on Saturday night that I'd download you some really happy songs that you could listen to and feel better," she said. "But then I got a bit carried away because sometimes when you're not feeling great, happy songs are like the worst thing you can listen to, you know? So I thought of all the shit emotions you could be feeling and found songs to go with those feelings." She stood on her tip-toes and pointed to the last list. "And just in case you were interested, those are all my favourites. I also just put a little text file in there explaining why I love them so much. You don't need to read it. But just in case you were wondering." When she finished explaining, she looked up at me expectantly with those big eyes. It was gorgeous.

"Wow," I said. There were easily a hundred songs on there. It must have taken her *hours*.

She could barely contain herself. "Do you like it?"

"No." I concealed a smile.

She shoved me. "Stop it!" she said, actually sounding really worried. "It totally stresses me out when you do that!"

I dropped the poker-face. "Well, what do *you* think?" I asked her, and released the smile. "Thanks, Bree. I will actually be able to use it, I think. I'm a bit sick of my old playlists."

Her face lit up. "Really?" she asked looking absolutely delighted. Before she spoke again, though, her smile wavered for a moment. "Because, like, I know things kind of suck for you right now. And it's just awful knowing you're at home feeling like shit and there's nothing I can do about it. So I thought I'd make you this, and when everything sucks you can listen to it, and it's good on two levels, because you're listening to music that is just right for how you feel," she said, and then paused. "And also because you know that somewhere, there's someone who made it for you and just wants you to be happy."

God. "You're too much," I said to her, and gave her a giant bear hug. Her cheeks were pink when I let her go. "Thanks, Bree," I told her. "And likewise."

She beamed at me, but it didn't last. "I'd better get going, I guess," she said, and slung her schoolbag over her shoulder. "Thanks for the t-shirt, and I'm sorry I like getting my boobs out."

A couple of people gave us *really* strange looks as they walked past. "It's okay," I said to Bree, trying to ignore everyone else. "I'll get used to it. Take care."

After she'd gone it was still quite early, so I went back upstairs to keep working because we only had *two weeks left* before pitch. It was actually scary to think about. Fortunately, half my team were still up there working as well, including Sarah who accosted me at the vending machine. "How's Schoolgirl?" she asked, and then wagged her eyebrows at me over the can as she took a sip.

"How long have you got?" I asked her, torn between smiling and groaning.

I had sat down at my computer and spent half an hour or so trying to focus when my phone buzzed on the table beside me. I checked it, knowing who it was going to be. "*i uploaded something to facebook for u.........*"

I grimaced, immediately imagining some awful appreciation photo of her posing like her other selfies in the red t-shirt. When I opened the app and searched for her, though, she'd just taken a mirror shot of herself in the t-shirt. Of course her cleavage was very visible and she wasn't trying to hide it, but she wasn't bearing it at the camera to be 'busted on' or whatever she'd said before about those poses. That description *still* made me cringe. This photo didn't, though. She just looked sweet and pretty, exactly like she was. It was the nicest photo I'd seen of her.

I was about to comment to that effect on it when I noticed her album looked a bit different. I stopped, and then I tapped through to her mobile uploads. Aside from the mirror shot, there were hardly any selfies at all. She'd deleted *all* of them, and all that was left was tame photos of her and her family, her and some of her school friends and other photos of food and animals. Her latest status update cryptically read, '*now u can stop worrying so much......... ;) ;)*'

I must have been gaping at my phone, because Sarah said, "You right there, Min?" from the other side of the room.

I closed my jaw. "You remember Bree's Facebook albums?" I asked her.

She gave me a look like *are you serious*? "What's she done this time?"

I wheeled my chair over to her and showed her my phone. I don't know what Sarah had been expecting, but I watched her face cycle from concern to confusion to — she looked at me — amusement. "Gee, I wonder who she did that for," she said, smirking at me and then getting back to her computer. "It's a complete mystery."

I'd gone back to my own desk to grin like an idiot at all my emails when my phone went off again. I assumed it was Bree, so I unlocked it. It wasn't, though, it was just Henry. "*There's a new Thai place that's opened up behind the Regent,*" it said. "*I was thinking we could try it out on Thursday or Friday? Or maybe early next week before I fly back to the Motherland?"*

'The Motherland', I chuckled at that. Both our mothers *were* there, and my mum *did* talk about South Korea like it was the cradle of all culture and civilisation.

I didn't grin for long, though. He'd be visiting Mum while he was over there, and I could only imagine what kind of stuff she'd be saying to him. He never seemed to mind her, but that was completely irrelevant because *I* minded her. And I felt really fucking uncomfortable about what they'd talk about without me there.

I didn't even know what to talk about with him at the moment. It had been so weird last night.

Fuck. I frowned down at the message, reading it again. Thursday or Friday, I thought. Bree will be visiting then. Not that it would necessarily be a problem for her to just chill in my apartment while I was out with him, but he'd probably want to come back afterwards and stay the night and then I'd have to stay in my women's clothes and Bree would just be there feeling awkward. On the other hand, it would also give me a fantastic excuse to not have sex with him. Poor Bree, though. Did I really want to put her in an awkward situation just to avoid having sex with my boyfriend?

I sighed. I couldn't deal with this now. We had—I counted—17 days left before that pitch to Sasha Burov, and I'd lose four of those to Easter. I couldn't really expect my team to *not* spend Easter with their families, even if I wasn't planning to myself. Additionally, I had no idea when we'd end up pitching to any of those leads in Vladivostok, maybe even sooner than that.

I really needed to get this project across the line and just not worry about crap until after we had signatures. I could take time off *after* the pitch if I needed to. Before it, I needed to just focus on work.

I locked my phone and put it inside my handbag. I could worry about what I was going to say to Henry after I'd finished with all the stuff I still had to get done tonight.

SEVENTEEN

Bree actually made it all the way to Thursday without showing up outside my work. On Thursday morning, though, she sent me about five texts in a row while I was in a meeting with my team. I had to turn vibrate off, because the four of them were just staring at my phone on the table in front of me and not paying any attention to anything coming out of my mouth.

"Maybe you should get that," Ian suggested.

"Oh, she's already got that," Sarah said innocently, still working on her breakfast muffin. Ian gave her a weird look.

I put the phone in my pocket and kept talking, ignoring both of them. "...So I don't really think using the rainforests or the beaches really works, I was thinking more sort of central Australia, but that's more orange than anything else. I could paint it in pinks, of course. Or a sunset or something. Sunsets over Uluru are a bit cliché, though."

"Still quite iconic," Carlos said. He was tapping his pen against his lip while he held one of the printouts up. "And icons are generally what sells Australia, so if we're trying to use Australia to sell diamonds..."

"'Mined from the heart of a wild country'," Ian tested, and then made a face. "Ugh, I hate myself. Why do I do this? It might work, though. "

"Digging up Uluru might not be the image we're looking for," I pointed out after I'd thought more about it. "In fact, if we put the image of Uluru with anything using the word 'mine', we'll probably be on the front page of the *The Sydney Morning Herald* with 'Frost Plans to Blow Up World Starting with Sacred Aboriginal Landmark'."

"Isn't that free publicity, though?" John asked, completely oblivious as always.

We all winced. Sarah was the one that answered. "Particular campaigns suit that style of marketing. Diamonds don't. Reputation is basically how we get our sales."

For a minute or two the team all sat there, frowning at the Australian landscape printouts in the centre of the table. Eventually, I sighed. "Well, let's move on to Vladivostok. We can think about this in our own time."

After we'd all fried our brains trying to figure out what we wanted to do with the two leads in Eastern Russia who were taking ages to get back to us, we broke for morning tea and so I could see what Bree's drama was.

To be honest, I *had* been a little worried something had happened. So, when I opened the string of messages that started with a keyboard smash, ended in *"sorry i just had to do that im good now :3"* and had *"yeesssss its thurrsdaaayyyy!!!!"* somewhere in the middle, I slapped my forehead.

I also couldn't resist messing with her, so I texted her back, *"Actually I decided to go out with Henry this evening, and he'll probably stay all weekend. I might see you next week. Or maybe after Easter."* I waited for a couple of minutes, and then when I didn't get a reply, I added, *"Bree, I'm messing with you. See you tonight ;)"*

This time, my phone buzzed again. *"i hate u so much.............."*

I was grinning to myself and trying to figure out how to reply, when I noticed Sarah leaning against the door with her second coffee for the day, watching me. I felt a bit self-conscious, especially when she smirked and casually wandered over. I was pretty sure it was obvious who I'd been messaging.

"What are you doing tomorrow night?" she asked.

I glanced up; there was no one within earshot. "Not getting drunk and making out with your friends."

She laughed. "Rats! And I bought popcorn especially." Casting a quick look over her shoulder as well, she corrected herself. "Anyway, I said that wrong. I *meant* to say, 'I know what you're doing tomorrow night. You're coming to movie night at my place'. There will be a few people. Not that many." When I looked sceptical, she pointed a finger at me. "Yes. No excuses. I've had a bad week, you're coming to my thing."

Oh, was that how it was? While I was standing there with my eyebrows up, I remembered some of the stuff that had been going on for her during the week and felt a bit guilty. She *had* had a rough week, especially with the grief her other team had been giving her. That didn't override my discomfort about coming to any more of her social events, though. Something else occurred to me. "Wait, will Gemma be there?"

There was a glint in Sarah's eye that I was a bit concerned about. "Possibly."

"That's a yes, isn't it?" I said, and that made up my mind. I couldn't really be around her again, it would be too awkward. "Sorry, Sarah, I've got too much going on. I'd rather just stay home with Bree and relax tomorrow night."

"Yeah, that's not going to happen," she said easily, tipping the last of her coffee down her throat and chucking the cup in my bin. She sounded pretty confident, it was suspicious.

"Oh? Why not?"

She gave me a very mischievous grin as she turned to go back to her own desk. "Because Schoolgirl's coming to my thing."

I stared at her for a second. No *way*.

Closing my jaw, I followed her to her desk. "You *invited* her?"

"On Facebook," she said as she sat down and hit the space bar a few times to wake up her laptop. "And she accepted. So, I guess you can stay home if you want to, but I'm sure she has a lot to say about you..."

There wasn't enough air in the room for how much I wanted to sigh right then. "This is blackmail," I told her. "You're blackmailing me."

"Yup!" she said, gave me a smile, and then got back to her research while we were waiting for the others to get back. I stared daggers at the side of her head while she pretended I wasn't there. She even started humming softly.

I didn't get to take revenge then, though, because Ian and Carlos returned with their own coffees and then Ian came right up to me and said, "Hey, here's an idea: do we know exactly where the mine's going to be? We could do some shots of the area, you know, dress it up a bit and then sell it like that: capturing a piece of this wild and beautiful country or something."

In the background, Carlos muttered, "That was *my* idea..."

I decided to ignore whatever was going on there. "In Western Australia," I said. "The Kimberley, the prospectus didn't say *exactly* where, but we can look it up by mining lease, I guess. Could you do that?" Ian nodded, and then went to sit down at his PC.

Sarah had stopped what she was doing to listen. She gave me a 'not bad' expression and then took out her phone and started flipping through it while I went to sit back at my desk.

Ian did find the location, and it was somewhere out in the middle of the Kimberley down a dirt track. We hopped along it on Google maps in case there were any interesting locations, but the whole area looked unremarkable.

"There goes that idea," Ian said, and then turned around to Carlos, "good one, mate." The two of them faced off for a second, but neither of them pushed it any further.

I was watching them and wondering how to handle the conflict when Sarah made a noise. I'd been seated at my computer with them around me to look through Google maps and she was still standing over me. "Look at this," Sarah told me, and then held her phone so I could see the screen.

Someone had sent her a photo of a *spectacular* sunset over the ocean. I squinted at it. "That's Australia, yeah? Where is it?"

She grinned. "Broome. Rob took it from his front porch." She pretended to think hard. "Broome's in the Kimberley, right?" She was still grinning.

I had another look at it. "Guys," I called, and gathered everyone back around again to show them Rob's photo. "What do you think?"

"I think I'm moving to Broome," Carlos said as he gave the phone back to Sarah.

Everyone was looking at each other. That was basically a consensus, so I turned back to Sarah. "Rob would be fine for me to paint something from that, yeah? Can you send it to me?"

She did, and for the rest of the morning I alternated between checking my secure email and painting an incredible sunset slightly off to one side to accommodate the Frost logo and some to-be-written text. None of the contacts from the companies we were trying to get a hold of in Vladivostok got back to me, but I did use every colour in the palette on the sunset.

I also finished off the last playlist from Bree's USB, which was her favourite music. It was a mixture of pop and some classics, and even a few Disney songs. Some of them were a bit obnoxious, but it had been *ages* since I'd listened to music and painted so even obnoxious pop music was kind of enjoyable. At one point I was experimenting with a couple of filters and it occurred to me how much money I was being paid for sitting here painting and listening to music, and I felt like I was cheating the universe.

"You're in a good mood," Sarah commented from across the room. I didn't hear her the first time, so I took out my ear buds and she repeated herself.

"I'm plotting my revenge against you," I told her. "It's sweeter than anticipated." I put my ear buds back in and kept going as she laughed.

When I'd finished and shown Jason this particular painting, he actually stopped what he was doing—which was making angry noises while he read the marketing requirements documents of another team—to give my picture his full attention. "You painted that, Mini?" I nodded, and he looked at it again. "Fucking hell. I want that on my wall. Yeah, that's good, use it, and use white text on this side," he said, and then went back to grunting at the MRD without making any sort of infuriating or snide comment either about the fact I was female or that I was Asian. It was disorienting.

"What did he say?" Sarah asked me when I returned to Oslo. The boys were gone. I checked the clock and it was past six so they'd probably gone home. I envied them; I couldn't wait to get these fucking clothes off myself. She spun around in her chair to face me for second. "Did he like it?"

I gave her a confused look. "Yeah," I said. "And he didn't tell me to make him a sandwich, either."

Sarah feigned profound shock and she swivelled back to her desk. "Maybe he *knows* about you."

I probably looked as alarmed as I felt. "Don't even say that," I said, and then started packing up. "Speaking of which, what am I wearing tomorrow? Who's going to be there?"

"Do your guy thing, you'll be fine," Sarah told me as she copied and pasted data between spreadsheets. That wasn't for my project, so it must have been for her other team. "Liz and Gem will be there, but I met everyone else at uni, not Frost. One of them is a gay guy who's bringing his new boyfriend for us to meet."

Well, that sounded promising at least. "And you're sure no one's going to be weird about me?"

Sarah made a face and shook her head. "I doubt it. Not on

purpose, anyway." As I left, she added, "Tell your little schoolgirl I said hi."

I stuck my head back through the door to glare at her. "Tell her yourself, since you guys are now BFFs on Facebook."

"Okay," Sarah said sweetly. "And while I'm at it I'll tell Gem you're looking forward to tomorrow." I gave her a look, and she laughed. "I won't, I promise. Don't worry, it's not going to be awkward at all with the two of you. We're all adults."

I hoped she was right, because I really couldn't handle being there if it was going to be uncomfortable. I hoped Bree wouldn't be upset if we had to leave early as a result.

Later, Bree wasn't waiting for me outside work, which was odd. I checked around the corner where she'd met me last time, but it was empty. When I took out my phone to see if she'd texted me, she had. So had Henry, actually. I checked his first because I felt a bit bad about not replying to his dinner invite from Monday.

"No dinner tonight I assume...? Maybe early next week. I hope you're not working too hard."

I made a face and I replied, *"Yeah, sorry, work is so full on at the moment. Maybe we can do Sunday? Same time as last week?"* I decided not to mention Bree and that she was staying over. He'd probably understand, but I just didn't want to complicate things for now.

He replied with, *"No worries :) Take care of yourself. Call if you need to."*

Bree's text message had an entirely different tone. *"its cold im going to wait at ur place"*

I looked around me, frowning. It wasn't that cold; the sun hadn't even set yet. Then again, I wasn't wearing as little as Bree always was, so maybe that had something to do with it.

On my way back home, I wondered what Sarah and her friends were going to make of Bree. She was lovely, sure; but she was a bit of an acquired taste and liable to do something either infuriating or embarrassing. I cringed, remembering her just walking straight out of the fitting rooms in her cupcake bra with her breasts practically falling out everywhere. God, *Bree.* I hoped she wouldn't do anything like that at Sarah's. That was just about the last thing I could handle right now. Actually, fuck, what was I doing? If something went wrong at Sarah's I really couldn't afford to be fucked up by it over the weekend. We had less than two weeks before pitch, I needed to focus. We should probably just stay home.

When I got back up to my apartment, Bree was seated against my door as usual but jumped up to greet me as I stepped out of the lift and walked towards her. Grabbing one of my forearms, she bounced up and down beside me, excited. "Did you listen to everything?" She had her tie loosened and her top button undone. I could see into it, and her bouncing was not helping me to focus on getting to my front door. I wished she wouldn't do that.

"I'm pretty sure your school doesn't let you wear your uniform like *that*," I commented, nodding at her cleavage.

She stopped jumping up and down and peered down her body. "Oh my god, are we back to *this*?" she asked, laughing at me. "Why, are you going to give me detention or something if I don't do it up?" She didn't make any sort of move to fix it as she trailed along next to me to my door. "So what did you think of my favourite songs? Sorry there was so much Disney, I *love* that stuff. Did you watch Disney when you were a kid, or did you watch, like, Korean things?"

I fished my keycard out of my handbag, giving her a look. "I grew up in Australia, remember," I told her, but neglected to mention that Mum had forced me to watch all the dubbed versions of everything, anyway.

"So, did you like them?" she asked, hanging off my arm as I awkwardly tried to swipe my card in the reader.

I gave her a *what do you think*? look with a slight grin and swiped my card again, finally getting a green light and pushing the door open. "They're not generally my thing, but yes, I enjoyed them."

She released me to take her shoes off. "So what *is* your thing? If you say goth or death metal or something I'm totally going to judge you. My brother likes that stuff."

"Nah," I told her, hanging up my bag and kicking off my own heels. Fuck, it felt good to be rid of them. Now to get all of these other stupid, uncomfortable clothes off asap. "Mainly game soundtracks, orchestral movie soundtracks, that sort of thing. There's a stack of old CDs next my games if you're interested."

Bree followed me up the hallway in her socks, making a face. "That music puts me to sleep."

I grinned down at her. "Note to self..." Oh, that reminded me. My grin disappeared.

She saw it immediately and looked panicked. "What? I didn't mean that I hated that music! It's not boring or anything, I mean it literally makes me tired and sleepy!"

I gave her a hard glare over my shoulder. "It's not that. I hear you've been talking to Sarah on Facebook." She came into the bedroom with me as I took my pearls and my earrings off and put them on my dresser.

In the reflection of the small mirror, I saw her look a little guilty. "Oh..." She knew exactly what I was talking about. "Come on, it'll be fun," she said. "I'd like to meet your friends! I'll be really nice, I promise."

That was a wholly unconvincing argument, because Bree's 'really nice' was just a more intense version of herself. "They're not really my friends," I said. "Sarah's my friend, and they're *her* friends. I actually think we should probably leave it until after my project's signed. I've got too much to deal with at the moment, there's no reason to add to it." I tied my hair back.

"Well, we're going anyway. I promised Sarah."

I stopped in the middle of putting the elastic around my ponytail to look down at her. "Oh?" Actually, it made me a bit angry. "Since when did you decide you were able to tell me what to do?"

She looked a little uncertain, but fired back, "Uh, you constantly tell me what to do. Constantly. And, like, that's okay, but now this is something *you* need to do." I expected her to back off and apologise when I glowered at her, but she didn't. Not at all. "I took those pics off Facebook, and you're coming to this party thing tomorrow night at Sarah's with me."

It was actually difficult to argue with that, because she was right. I just... hadn't expected her to stand her ground like that. I should have, because 'stubborn' didn't even begin to describe her. I watched her for a couple of seconds, and then turned back to the mirror and finished my hair. "I'm not comfortable with doing this kind of stuff in the middle of a project."

"Your comfort zone is the size of a pea, Min," Bree told me. "And like, I get it with the whole trans stuff, like it must be super awful to always have to worry that people might flip out, but Sarah said none of her friends are like that so I don't see what the big deal is." She frowned at me. "And I'd totally threaten to just tie you up and drag you there, but I kind of don't think I'll need to."

Having *Bree* lecturing *me* was... unsettling. I twisted to look down at her. She was waiting for me to answer, and, actually, she looked serious. I felt like a petulant teenager refusing to clean their room. What a *strange* feeling.

I tightened my ponytail. I'd never hear the end of it if I refused, would I? "Fine," I said simply.

She looked stunned. "Really?"

"You just went off at me and you're *surprised* I said yes?"

She made a face. "Yeah, kind of. Guess I won't have to tie you up after all!"

I raised an eyebrow at her on my way to the bathroom. "I'm having a shower," I told her. "I'll be out in a minute." Closing the door, I left her to bounce around my apartment in celebration.

I spent longer in the shower than I usually did because after so much of Bree's cleavage, I noticed mine and got really depressed about it. They might disappear if I lost more weight, I thought as I stood away from the mirror. Then again, *I* might disappear if I lost more weight. I was already so skinny that I didn't even have periods every month as it was. It occurred to me that if I lost more weight I might stop getting them altogether. Tempting, but I seriously couldn't face Henry's patented Looks of Concern, and if I accidentally put myself in hospital for any length of time I was unlikely to get lead on any projects anytime soon.

I bandaged my chest up and then put my jeans and hoodie over everything. The bandages were tight, but it was still such a relief to have everything gone and just be smooth surfaces. Well, except for my ponytail which stuck out a bit, but there wasn't much I could do about that.

When I opened the door to the living room, I expected Bree to perhaps be upside down on my couch with her phone. I *didn't* expect her to be standing at the dining table, elbow-deep in packaging with a *really* guilty look on her face.

She jumped when I came in, looking down at the package and

then up at me. She was holding something that looked like, well, I didn't want to specify what it looked like. "The courier came while you were in the shower," she said, like that explained everything. Then, she went *bright* red. "I-I just thought I'd take a peek, but... but..."

I didn't understand what she was so nervous about until I walked up to the table, about to ask her that very question, and saw what she was holding. The breath caught in my throat. What the fucking *fuck?* "What's *that?*"

She looked like she was about to burst with something. Discomfort? Nervous laughter? I couldn't tell. "It's your new dick." She was cupping it in her hands like she would a baby bird, and it was *so fucking horribly, unbearably* uncomfortable I could hardly handle looking at it.

"It's *what?*" I said, probably sounding like a cut guitar string, as I hurriedly scrambled through the packaging. When I saw the binders, I realised that it was what I'd ordered on Monday, but what the *fucking hell* was *this* doing in the box? "I didn't order it!" I said desperately. I could feel my face *burning*. "I didn't order it... Why the *fuck* would they send something that I didn't order? Maybe it's a mistake? Maybe they mixed up the orders...?"

Just as I said that, though, I saw the packaging for what Bree had in her hands and it had the word 'Packer' on it. It had a picture of a guy slipping it into his undies and then apparently going to a business meeting, and suddenly everything made sense. 'Free packer with two binders ordered?' Oh god... oh god, oh god....*oh god, I did order it.*

"It's okay," Bree said, looking down at it and looking anything but okay. "It's okay, I get it, I shouldn't have opened it, I'm sorry..." I thought she was *finally* about to put it down, but she was looking at it again, brow quivering. "Um, like, are they normally this big? Or did you just choose a big one to look, you know, hung?"

I couldn't even answer her, I just put my hands up in my hair and felt like part of me was dying inside forever. "Why are you holding it like that?" I asked her. "Why are you *holding* it? Why is it out of the *box? Why did you open my mail?*"

She was so red that even her neck and cleavage were red. "I was just wondering what was inside so I thought I'd unpack it for you and then when I saw it I.... well, they're supposed to be really lifelike these days, right? So I kind of thought I wanted to know what one felt like, because I haven't... Uh, yeah. So I was just taking it out of the packaging and then I remembered I read on this website that you're supposed to treat your partner's packer like a bio dick, you know, respect it, be gentle, and so I thought I'd just hold it really carefully," she demonstrated, "like this, and—"

"—and, god, Bree put it away, *Jesus fuck*! You're killing me!"

"Okay, okay! But you should feel it first, because it feels kind of... well..." She looked down and it and then slowly turned it over in her hands, and it was fucking *agonising* to watch. It *looked* like a real dick, and it looked like Bree was playing with it. "It's really soft, here, feel it."

No fucking way. Not in front of her. I put my hands in my hair and did a circle on the spot I was standing on. "Bree!" The whole fucking thing was fucking unbearable. When she opened her mouth to say something else, I cut her off. "Put it away and stop *talking* about it! *Fuck*!"

Mutely, she put it very gently on the glass dining table. I was about to breathe a sigh of relief when she looked up at me for a moment as if she'd just had a great revelation. "I've gone from, like, zero to third base with you in two minutes." Her mouth was open. "I just touched your dick," she said with a really strange expression, and then completely lost it in a fit of something that was a cross between nervous giggling and shrieking, and went and buried her face in her hands on the couch.

I was just about there too. I watched her for a second, still *horrified*. Then I looked back at the table.

As much as I wanted to make it disappear, I... actually did kind of want to see what all the fuss was about. Especially after Bree had made such a show of telling me how soft it was. It looked pretty solid, so it couldn't be *that* soft, could it? Bree was busy wailing into the couch cushions and wasn't watching me, so I took a few steps over to the table and looked down at it.

It looked real enough, I supposed; bigger than Henry when he was just walking around but not comically big. I really had to talk myself into actually picking it up. What eventually worked was reminding myself that if I *did* actually end up feeling better as a guy,

I'd probably need to use one of these. It wasn't a very convincing argument, though, because I could still pass as a guy without one.

When I picked it up it *was* soft. Not really as soft as a real one, but everything else looked real. All the anatomical detail was there, even roadmaps of wrinkles on the balls and a puffy vein on the shaft. I just.... no part of me could conceive of having that *anywhere* near my underwear. I felt wholly disconnected from it. So much so that I wanted to get it very far away from me as quickly as possible because it was making me nervous, but that was a strong reaction to a lump of silicone, or polymer, or whatever the fuck it was, right? Was it *too* strong a reaction?

Maybe my horror wasn't because I knew I really *didn't* want that in my pants, but because some part of me was absolutely terrified that I maybe did? What if I wanted *more* than just a rubber one, too? I literally had no idea. None. The muscles in my jaw were spasming because I was clenching it so tightly.

Bree had calmed down somewhat, but was still sitting on the couch, looking intensely at me with her mouth partly open.

I looked down at my hands and the dick in them and the *complete* absurdity of the situation just hit me. It was funny, almost. I squeezed the packer experimentally, and it stayed limp. Not *that* realistic, apparently...

"See what I mean about it being really soft?" Bree managed.

She left that one *wide* open to be messed with. I couldn't help it. "I'm so sorry," I said to her. "These things happen sometimes. It's not you, it's me."

She snorted, but blushed again.

I put it down on the table, and then went and sat at the opposite end of the couch to her and put my head in my hands for a moment. "*Fuck,*" I said, and then made a pained noise.

Bree looked slightly less red when I emerged. "Are you going to try it on?"

I gave her a look like *are you fucking kidding me*? "I'm going to put it at the bottom of a deep, dark drawer and try to pretend I don't own it," I said. "Either that, or I might mail it express to Antarctica and go on a celebrity breakdown-style bender in hope that I fry all my brain cells and forget it ever arrived."

Bree gave me her own *are you fucking serious* look. "Uh, if you don't want it, you could always just like, you know, *throw it away*?"

I scrunched up my face and shook my head. "But what if the reason I'm like '*no fucking way!*' is because some part of me knows I'll end up wanting it?"

"Then you'll have a really big dick waiting in the bottom of one of your drawers," she said earnestly, and then started giggling again when she looked over on the table. It wasn't malicious laughter; she was just *really* nervous and judging by how red her face was, all the blood in her body was in her cheeks. "I mean, I guess it's not really *that* big? You're pretty tall. Just compared to me, it's really big. I'm so short that it wouldn't even be able to..." I could guess where that sentence was leading, and she knew that. She looked horrified again and let it trail off, clapping her hand over her mouth again as she giggled and looked helplessly at me.

I leant back on the couch and stared at the dick innocuously resting on my glass dining table. There is a rubber *dick* on my dining table, I thought. Then, I started *laughing*. It was all just too, too weird.

When I stopped, Bree was watching me. She still looked apologetic and she shuffled over to me to take my arm. "I'm sorry," she said. "Like, I was telling myself I need to be really calm and really mature about the fact that you ordered a packer, but then I took it out and you came and saw it and you just were like '*what!*' and I just kind of panicked..."

I wasn't bothered, but that didn't stop me from pretending I was. "You'd better be sorry," I said as neutrally as I could manage, and then I felt guilty when I watched her face drop. "You're going to have to be very supportive to make up for it. Make sure you tell it constantly how big and manly it is. Also if you could gasp in awe when you see it, that would be great."

She started thumping me repeatedly with a cushion as soon as she realised I was joking. "Why do you always *torture* me?" she asked. "I always think you're really upset!"

Because you're cute when you blush, I thought. Then, noticing how much she was blushing, I looked somewhere else, and that somewhere else was the table with the packer on it. The part of me that had just died forever continued to die forever as I put my head in my hands and *groaned.*

We both just sat there on the couch for a minute or two. Bree had managed to stop giggling again. She stood up and went to get the packaging, and then brought it back to the couch to have a read of it. She was holding it so I could see it, too. I think it was deliberate, and when she was done she offered in to me.

I must have shaken my head a little too strongly, because she said, "Why are you so..." She gestured at how I was sitting; I hadn't realised how stiff I looked until she pointed it out. "Was it because I took it out? Because I kind of get that I totally shouldn't have."

I grimaced, remembering. I wasn't angry at her, exactly. I'd just been really embarrassed. "It's just... god, Bree, this stuff is so private. It's so, so private. It's something you never want anyone else to know about you or see about you. I mean, *god*, if people knew..." I watched her, realising that despite the fact we were both *so* uncomfortable, she'd never tried to make me feel bad about it. She could have. Easily. "Thanks for..." I struggled with how to word it, though. "Well, for not making fun of me."

She looked mildly surprised. "Why would I make fun of you?"

I shrugged. "A lot of people probably would." I had an *awful* vision of Marketing getting their hands on everything in that box, and I flinched. "A *lot* of people."

She watched me really closely, and I could practically see her brain ticking over. "People are pretty selfish but I don't think many of them are, like, actually *nasty,*" she said. "Why would anyone be awful to you like that? Like, why?"

My stomach knotted. That was a question I'd asked myself many, many times, over and over, every night in bed for six years. "I don't know," I said honestly. I wasn't going to say anything else, but she was listening so intently that I kind of felt obliged to. "I suppose unless I really try not to, I make people uncomfortable."

Bree frowned for a moment, and I actually think she understood. "Well, fuck them," she said firmly. "They can go fuck themselves, I'm not like that. It's totally fine, you can make me as uncomfortable as you like, I don't mind." She paused, cringing at how that sounded. "I mean, I'm not saying you make me uncomfortable or anything, I mean you kind of do, but it's not *bad* uncomfortable." She clamped her mouth shut for a second. "I'm going to stop now before I ruin everything," she told me.

312

That made me grin, a little. "So what you're saying is that I make you *good* uncomfortable?"

Her cheeks went a bit pink again. "Maybe," she said, and then she gave me a coy little smile.

I'd have been *stupid* to miss what that meant, but I was so surprised by it I just stared at her, my eyes darting between hers and the package in her hands. It had a picture of the packer on it.

She saw me looking and misunderstood. "Oh, right. Here," she said, looking quickly away from me and handing me the box. Our fingers brushed as I took it from her.

I looked down at it, but I wasn't actually reading. Really? I asked the universe. After that whole awkward, *agonising* situation, she was doing the exact opposite of running for the hills?

She changed the subject very abruptly. "I actually brought us some dinner from home," she said, standing up and walking over to her schoolbag. She pulled out a big lunch box, her face still red. Those pink cheeks suggested that dinner was the last thing she cared about right now, and wondering what she was *actually* thinking felt surprisingly good. She continued with her ruse, though, saying, "It's just chicken, but I *really* like it cooked like this. You want to eat now, or...?"

I was a bit hungry, so I showed her how to use the microwave and then we sat down to eat. Halfway through dinner, though, I had to get up and go bury the whole postage box under everything in my wardrobe, because both of us kept staring at the packer and it was stressing me out. I needed more time to think about it and having it just out on the table there meant that I couldn't think about anything else. That, and Bree had turned this permanent shade of pink and I was worried she was going to burst something.

After dinner, Sarah had emailed me a couple more photos Rob had taken so I decided to see if I could fix the composition of them. Bree got excited when I told her I was going to be painting, but after two or three hours of watching me work on details in a *huge* landscape, she ended up falling asleep on the couch next to me.

I'd taken the doona from the bed and was tucking it around her when she stirred.

"The couch hurts my back," she said somewhat cryptically as I helped her put a pillow I'd brought out under her head. She was really warm.

"I can sleep out here on it if you want, I don't mind," I offered. "You can sleep in there."

She looked disappointed. "Nah, it's okay, I guess," she said miserably, and then turned to face the backrest.

I watched her for a few seconds. I knew what she was implying, but however innocent it would have been, I knew I shouldn't be sharing my bed with her. After that whole fiasco with the packer today, and afterwards when she'd smiled at me... Yeah, it was probably better if we slept separately. With my hand on my heart, I couldn't really say there was *nothing* going on between us, even if it never went anywhere. That, and I kept worrying about what would happen if Henry let himself in, even though in all the years I'd known him he'd never been that assuming.

My bed was fucking cold without my doona, but when my alarm went off in the morning, I woke up really toasty and warm. I didn't understand why until I looked down my body and saw my doona over me. I groaned, and then felt around on the other side of the bed until I found the culprit. "*Bree.*"

"I'm wearing pants this time!" she mumbled, and then pulled the doona over her head and continued to doze.

I didn't force her to get up, instead leaving her a keycard and a twenty on the kitchen bench on my way to work. There was no reason she needed to get up as stupidly early as I did.

When I got into the office, Sarah was already sitting at her desk even though it was 7:30. She looked really tired and was in the same position I'd left her in yesterday. The only clue that she hadn't just stayed overnight was that she was wearing different clothes.

"Maybe I'll get *you* a Red Bull this morning," I offered, shooting her a worried look as I put my bag in my drawer.

She laughed darkly. "Yeah, I know what I look like," she said. "My other team's project has gone to crap because the arrogant bastard who's running it accidentally insulted our key contact last night. On one hand, I'm delighted to watch him crash and burn, on the other, it's my career and bonus, too, so here I am at the crack of dawn, looking for other potentials..."

I did actually go and grab her a Red Bull, and she took it from me and drank deeply, giving me the once-over as she swallowed. She then asked, "So, how's Schoolgirl?"

The image of Bree cupping the packer surfaced in my mind, and, embarrassed, I blushed a bit. "Still asleep," I said neutrally. "Henry's fine, too. Thanks for asking."

Sarah didn't miss my blush, but instead of saying anything she just smirked. "I'm looking forward to getting to know her better tonight." She then got back to her spreadsheet. The fact she was still grinning was a bit concerning, but I left it.

While my laptop was booting, I stared at the dark screen and remembered that whole incident yesterday. I really wished Bree *had* treated the packer like just a lump of rubber instead of some hallowed object, because her behaving like she was cradling my genitals had been, *god,* at least half of the agony. It wasn't attached to me, and if it had been and Bree had actually put her hands down my pants... wow, yeah, Min, no. *No.* Leave that mental image *alone.* That girl's got god knows what going on at home, and she's made your place her safe haven. You don't go taking advantage of that no matter how nice she is or how pretty she is, or because she's always trying to do nice things for you.

I had a sip of my energy drink, watching the Windows logo swirl on my screen. Those playlists had been a great idea. I'd made some throwaway comment about listening to music while I painted and she'd gone and spent *hours* arranging songs to cheer me up. That was on top of the coffee and the flowers and all the other little things she tried to do because she thought I'd like them. The gender stuff took the cake, though, I decided. It was such a non-event to her. It made it feel like a non-event to me, too, even though it wasn't. It was so easy to be around her. I just wished she'd do up her fucking shirt.

When Windows appeared on my screen, I was a bit startled for a second and I stared blankly at it. I'd completely forgotten what I'd been doing while I was thinking about Bree, and when I looked up from my screen, and I could see my reflection in the window. I was *smiling.*

Fuck.

Oh *fuck,* I thought, watching the smile falling off my face. No, no. *No...*

315

She's *18*, Min, I told myself as I opened Outlook and waited for it to load. 'She' is 18. You are with Henry who is *really* lovely and *really* good for you, who your mum loves and who works for the same company you do... Okay, so you're not attracted to him, but everyone ends up not attracted to their partners, right?

I looked across at Sarah, because she and Rob certainly seemed to be still attracted to each other. There goes that theory, I thought, sighing and getting back to Outlook.

I had been stuck on that thought until my eyes skimmed over the three unread emails I had. Two of them were ones Jason had forwarded, but the third was from an address I didn't recognise. It had the domain *@impressions.ru*, which was a *huge* jeweller in Eastern Russia we'd been courting. I had thought it might just be another request for information, but as I went over it, it became clear it was even better.

I was so shocked I read it aloud to Sarah. "...*Our acquisitions team should be free on either Wednesday or Thursday next week for an info session,*" I read, getting more and more excited. "And it's signed by the director of *Impressions Creation,* Vladivostok."

Sarah gaped at me. "*Impressions* got back to us with a pitch date?" she asked, and then stood up and put her hands up in a 'whoa' position. "Did we just score a pitch to Impressions?" She came rushing over to shake me. "*Did we just score a pitch to the top prestige jewellers in Eastern Russia?*"

"On Wednesday *or* Thursday," I said, and then my stomach bottomed out. How the fuck were we going to put together an *entire* pitch in *five days*? We normally needed at least two to even train the Sales staff!

Sarah saw my expression and clapped me on the shoulders as she read the email from my screen. "Don't think this gives you an excuse to pull out of tonight, by the way," she said. "You won't miss a few hours."

Tonight, I thought, and that reminded me of Bree. God, and Gemma. But whatever, *we had a pitch in five fucking days* and I could worry about everything else later.

As soon as the guys arrived I gave them the news and they reacted exactly the same way I had: with huge, elated smiles that quickly sagged when they heard the timeframes.

"You're kidding," Ian said. "*Jesus*, my daughter's birthday is on Tuesday, I was hoping to get a couple of hours off so I could at least pick her up from school."

"You can just buy her a pony with your bonus from this," Carlos told him flatly.

"Perhaps spend a couple of hours with her on Sunday instead? We'll probably be in meetings with Sales by Tuesday that you'll need to come to."

In the background, John just looked nervous; perhaps from the conflict.

I got the whole team combing all the Impressions stock lists and looking at all their catalogues for the past five years while we tried to decide how we were going to angle it.

"The director is really traditional," Sarah said, reading some page through Google translate. "His daughter married at 19 and had three kids, and now one of *them* is about to get married. He's sixty or something, and there a lot of discussion about which church to have the wedding in, because his granddaughter and her partner are two different denominations."

"Can we use that somehow?" I asked her.

"We're not pitching to the director," Ian called out from the printer. "Their buying team is a pack of corporate sharks. He's not on it."

I sat back in my chair. Fuck. "Better stick to the margins and sales data, then," I said. "I'll get the numbers."

I emailed a few people in Finance for the full profit and sales data from last year; then I had John pick through our rival company's annual reports for *their* data, too, since they had more experience selling pink diamonds.

By the evening, I'd only eaten because Sarah had shoved an old sandwich in front of my face at one point. I'd looked at the sandwich and then looked at her, and she'd rolled her eyes and said, "Don't, okay? It was the only thing left at the café." And otherwise, I'd hardly had time for anything. Finance hadn't gotten back to me, and since it was Friday, I really needed the data urgently or we'd lose two days working on it over the weekend. I checked my phone, it was nearly 5 pm. I was *really* running out of time.

Ducking out onto the main floor, I called reception. "Can you put me through to Finance?" I asked them, and then the phone rang a couple of times.

"Sean Frost's office," a female voice said.

What? "Uh, it's Min Lee from Marketing, reception was going to put me through to Finance but looks like they made a mistake," I said. "Could you do it instead?"

"I could," she said, "but they had a team-building day today, and the few staff that *were* here ran the bank files and then went home about 30 minutes ago. No one's going to answer."

Shit. "There's no one there? No one?"

"I don't think so. You'll have to wait until Monday." There was a pause. "Is it urgent?"

"*Yes.* It really is. I'm on some seriously tight deadlines. Are you absolutely, positively sure there's no one?"

She exhaled. "I'll speak to Sean," she said. "There might be someone down there. Or, if you come down to 35, I have access to the accounting system and maybe I can find what you're after."

I couldn't get down the stairs fast enough. If there was anyone left in the department, I didn't want to miss them.

When I got to thirty-five, though— I'd very expertly taken the long way to avoid going past Henry's office—it was actually Sean who was waiting for me. He was leaning casually against his door frame just in front of his personal assistant. Unlike Diane's assistant, her desk wasn't covered in *mountains* of paperwork and she even had her mobile out.

What was *the* co-*CEO* of Frost International doing waiting to help me with some menial enquiry? It didn't make any sense, but I smiled at him anyway, and he smiled back. "Min," he greeted me. "I understand there's some crisis?"

I stood in front of him. "I'm so sorry about this," I said and he held his hand up and shook his head as a reply, as if to say 'Don't worry about it'. "I just have deadlines," I explained. "Tight deadlines. I emailed Finance this morning for some figures from last year, but apparently there's no one there?"

He nodded. "Yes, bad timing to need anything from them. They played minigolf all day and now they're probably getting drunk. Maybe I can help you instead?"

You can help me by telling me why everyone hates you when you're so *nice*, I thought, remembering everyone's dire warnings about him. I glanced back at his assistant. She seemed relaxed. That meant something, didn't it?

"Um," I said, realising he'd actually required a response from me. There were some specific figures I needed, but I couldn't ask him just for those because it might give the project away. I went long, instead. "I'm looking for last year's full sales figures. The full data ones, not the ones in the annual report."

He looked surprised. "*All* of them?"

Behind him, his Personal Assistant who had been packing things into her handbag stopped and made a face. "It's okay, Sean, I can start doing it for her."

He waved his hand dismissively at her. "No, no, that's fine, Frances, you go and enjoy your weekend. I think Sales management has all that data on USBs that they give out with induction packs," he said, running a hand absently over his five o'clock shadow. "Actually, yes, now that I think about it I'm pretty sure I've seen Omar with a drawer full of them. Come on, I'll take you down there." He gestured at me to follow him. I did, but I wondered if Diane or Jason would be concerned that *he* was helping me. I hoped no one from Marketing would see.

As Frances walked with us to the lift, I surreptitiously cast a glance upward to one of the clocks on the wall. 5:04 pm. Sean let his assistant go home *on time*?

I couldn't leave it. "Something special happening tonight?" I asked her pleasantly as we all stepped into the lift.

She shook her head, a bit confused about why I'd asked. "Uh, no? Not unless you consider a new episode of my favourite show 'something special'." She smiled and took out her phone to check her messages.

Sean chuckled as he selected the fourth floor—Sales—guessing what I was surprised about. "Work-life balance," he said, and he and Frances shared a professional smile. "My employees work a little differently to Diane's. How late are *you* likely to be here tonight?"

I thought about what I needed to do. "Probably seven? It would be later, but I have something on tonight."

"And you're still here?" He laughed pleasantly. "Suddenly I understand why you and Henry work so well together." At the mention of Henry I winced, but I tried not to let him see. "Can you do me a favour, Min? He and I butt heads *constantly* over the fact he never takes his holidays. I think he's decided I'm micromanaging his annual leave, but, really, I'm just trying to get him to take a break once in a while. Could you get him out of here for a week or two? Put him on a beach somewhere and take his phone off him?" Sean put his hands in his pockets. "It's not that I don't appreciate his dedication, but, you know..." He smiled at me.

Henry *hates* you, Sean, I thought, but I smiled back. "Well, he's going to South Korea next weekend."

"And I'm sure he'll find four days with his extended family and his soon-to-be in-laws very restful," he pointed out with a grin. *Soon-to-be in-laws*? I think I nearly gaped at him. He noticed and smoothly changed the subject. I was grateful. "Speaking of extending families, Belinda's due any day now," he said, patting his breast pocket where I could see the outline of a mobile. "Just waiting for the call."

"You must be so excited," I said politely. "Boy or girl?"

The lift stopped on level 31. Sean dissolved into a charmed smile at the question as the doors opened and several people got into the lift. "A girl again," he said, and then started to tell me about his other children.

While he was talking, I glanced across at the people who'd joined us. They were all bunched together talking and laughing about something, but when one of the guys got a little bit *too* loud, another hushed him and shot a worried glance towards Sean. There was a woman with them, but there were men in the way so I couldn't see much of her. What I could see were ballet flats, tights and what looked like a very nice dress suit. She had her hair up, too, in a loose bun with little curls poking out of it. It was red like Gemma's, actually, and I think I'd seen some pictures on her Facebook where she had her hair like...

I realised what I was thinking. Oh, *fuck*. Fuck! That hair isn't red *like* Gemma's, it *is* Gemma's. That's *Gemma*. I panicked. I did *not* want her to see me at work and looking like *this*. With every fibre of my being I didn't want her to even know that I had a 'this'.

She obviously hadn't seen me on her way in, but the whole lift was made of mirrors and at some point she was going to catch sight of me. I looked up at the panel above the door; we were only at floor 29, and there were three other floors on call on the way down to four, as well. I couldn't turn around to face the wall because the wall was a mirror, and I couldn't even get out early because I'd have to push through that group of people with her to press the button. Most importantly, *the co-CEO* was escorting me somewhere, and you don't just bail on the *co-CEO*. I was trapped in here in this fucking dress and heels and makeup, pretending to be the model woman, and hoping desperately that she was too distracted to look over towards me.

I looked up at the display panel showing which floors we were passing: *28... 27...*

"What would you like? A boy or a girl?" Sean asked me conversationally. "If you could choose."

I stared at him, confused. *What?* Had he *really* asked that question?

His eyebrows went up when he saw my expression, and he laughed warmly. "I asked you if you wanted a boy or girl when you have children, but perhaps it's a bit early to be asking that question. Especially while you're flavour of the month in Marketing."

I *winced* when he said 'Marketing'. Gemma knew that's where Sarah and I worked. She hadn't heard him, though. "How's your project going, by the way? I imagine by the urgency, you're pitching soon?"

I couldn't tell him about that, even if all he wanted was a simple yes or no, and I was so distracted by desperately trying to keep someone standing between me and Gemma that I didn't have enough brain power to say anything but, "Uh..."

26...25...

Just as I was saying that, the lift stopped on the 23rd floor, and three of the men with Gemma waved goodbye to her and walked out. When they were gone, she turned and leant against the wall opposite me and took out her phone.

I was standing *opposite* her in the lift, she was literally two metres from me.

Don't look up, I mentally willed her. Don't look up!

The doors felt like they took *eternity* to close, and the lift seemed to be going much more slowly than usual. *19...18... 17...*

"I'm sorry, I shouldn't put you in that position," Sean said to me when I didn't answer. I could hardly even remember what we were talking about. "I'm just so used to asking Jason about his projects and his pitches and all the things he does in marketing that it's just a habit to talk to marketers like that..."

God, please stop saying that word, I thought, glancing between him and the display panel. Let's just talk about kids again, I don't care.

I must have looked pretty stressed out, because Sean asked, "Are you feeling alright, Min? You look a bit pale suddenly."

When he said my name, I felt it like a tonne of bricks and immediately looked at Gemma to see if she'd heard it.

She had.

She looked up momentarily, glancing at us. I pushed back against the wall of the lift, holding my breath. I hoped Sarah was right about how different I looked. She must have been right, because Gemma didn't recognise me at first, but I think my height made her double-take.

When she did look back at me she frowned, I think second-guessing herself. Her eyes swept over me, and when she got to my face, recognition dawned on hers. Her *jaw dropped.*

She gave me a really obvious, really astonished once-over, but it was her tone of voice that really betrayed her shock to everyone else in the lift, including Sean Frost. "*Min...?*"

EIGHTEEN

Gemma's obvious shock only lasted for a few seconds. Then her eyes darted between Sean and I and she straightened, stammering, "I-I'm sorry, I didn't recognise—" She stopped herself before she finished that sentence, though, looking away and blushing deeply. I remembered that blush, but this wasn't how I'd imagined causing it.

I wanted to apologise to her, but I couldn't. I couldn't say anything. Everyone was staring at us—Sean Frost was staring at us—and I couldn't think of anything I could say to her that wouldn't be a dead giveaway, either as to how we knew each other or why she hadn't recognised me. So neither of us said anything, we just both tried desperately not to look at each other while everyone was looking at us.

You could have heard a pin drop over the hydraulics. I could even hear my own heartbeat.

Obviously trying to break the tension, Gemma unlocked her phone to go back to whatever she'd been doing, and in the process fumbled with it and it slipped out of her hands. It clattered across the floor of the lift, under the feet of a couple of the other people in there, and everyone bent down to try and help her retrieve it. She nearly knocked heads with someone in the process and when she stood up again, examining a scratch on the corner of her phone, she was an even deeper red and just looked so humiliated. I could hardly bear to watch it. It was like my own personal horror show.

This is my fault, I thought, feeling the knife twisting in my gut. That she feels that way is all my fault. If I'd just told her that I have to look like this at work, it would be nothing. Why didn't I just tell her?

Even as I asked myself that question, I could see my reflection frowning back at me from one of the panels. I knew why: because I hated that I had to look like this. I felt like a footballer in a tutu. I felt wrong, and exposed, and fuck, I had to be wearing a white blouse today, didn't I? So she could definitely see the shape of my breasts? What a shocking reality check it must be for her. It would be one thing for her to kind of know that I had breasts I was hiding away somewhere, and another to see me dolled up like the public face of Chanel. I cringed. I bet she didn't think I was hot now.

Sean's eyebrows had been up in his hairline as he watched the exchange, but he quickly relaxed. "Old friends?" he asked amicably.

We both looked at him, and then each other, and then I was blushing, too. I sure as fuck wasn't going to answer, and after a few seconds it became clear Gemma wasn't going to either. One of us had to or it was going to sound pretty suspicious, so I managed, "Friend of a friend."

"Ah," Sean said, looking between us. He seemed to accept that, but, boy, was he watching me closely. Very, very closely. Then, just as easily as he had before, he expertly smoothed things over. "This is an enormous company," he began, "I actually went to university with one of the Ops managers up in Queensland. We'd hired him and I'd even signed off on it and hadn't noticed at all until I visited the site and there he was, with his own big office. Hilarious." Remembering, he winced. "Except that he thought I'd been deliberately ignoring him. Less hilarious. Solved by a night out at the local, though." He laughed.

A night at the local, I thought, glancing at Gemma again. She was looking at her feet and her lips were pressed in a tight line. Please don't regret kissing me, I thought as I looked at those lips. I couldn't handle being someone's drunken 'whoops'. Sean was telling some other light-hearted story about someone else he'd bumped into unexpectedly, but I couldn't focus on anything he was saying. I could only focus on the fact there was a girl I'd kissed—that still sounded so weird to me—standing two metres from me and obviously wishing she was a hundred million miles away.

Sean had to take a step towards me before I realised we'd reached the fourth floor and the doors had slid open. I couldn't even look at Gemma as I stepped out.

Sean stopped abruptly just outside the lifts and took out his phone for some reason, so I just stared at the ground between us. How the fuck was I going to go to Sarah's thing tonight, now? There was no way I could be in the same room with her after that, even if I should really apologise.

As soon as the doors on the lift were closed, Sean tucked his phone in his pocket and turned back to me. "Min," he said. I looked across at him, confused. "I hope I'm not speaking out of turn here. Are you alright? You look shaken."

I put my hands to my cheeks, glancing around us to make sure there was no one listening. "Oh, do I?" I asked, feigning surprise. "No, no... I'm fine."

He gave me a look as if to say, 'you don't need to play brave with me'. "Something happened in there, and I don't know what it was, perhaps you two had a falling out? If so, Frost provides our employees with excellent dispute resolution services. Counselling, mediation, you name it. Would you like me to give you some more information about that?"

They can't be that state of the art if you and Diane are still at each other's throats, I thought. I shook my head. "It's fine, really, it's just a misunderstanding."

He directed me a very concerned frown for a good five or ten seconds while he considered something. "Even so," he said. "Look. How about you just go back upstairs and put your energy into those deadlines you mentioned earlier? I'll go and grab one of those USBs from Sales and bring it up to you."

My stomach dropped. That last thing I wanted was for the co-CEO to think I needed extra assistance and special treatment, especially on top of that nightmare lift ride. "No, no, Sean, that's absolutely fine, I don't need you to waste your time, it's just been a really intense project and once it's over, I'll—"

"—Be assigned to another one, if I know my sister as well as I do," he said, chuckling. "I do actually have a personal interest in the profitability of my own company, believe it or not, and Marketing plays an important role in that. If I can do a few things here and there to help, it's definitely not a waste of my time." He put a hand on my arm. "Go on, off you go." When that didn't work and I didn't look convinced, he smiled. "It's fine, Min, really. You're actually doing me a favour. I enjoy helping out." He gave my arm one last reassuring pat, and then turned and walked down the corridor towards the Sales offices.

I watched him disappear around a corner, waiting for his body language to change, or waiting him to throw me an angry glance or shake his head... but he didn't do anything of the sort. He was striding like he was on his way to do something important, and not play assistant to a Marketing Lead. It was so confusing. Henry had fed me a series of vague stories about what a horrible person he was, so I felt like it didn't make sense. But maybe it did, maybe they really just didn't get along. His assistant just seemed so happy. That meant something, didn't it?

I turned back towards the lift, pressing the button and half-expecting the doors to slide open and reveal Gemma. Just to avoid any chance of that, I seriously considered taking the stairs. It was a good thing she wasn't in there when I stepped into the lift again, because I wasn't that fit and I didn't really relish the idea of doing 32 floors in stilettos. I would have, though, and a hundred fucking times over, to avoid a repeat of what happened before.

I closed my eyes as the lift went up. God, how the fuck was I going to survive Sarah's movie thing tonight? With Bree and Sarah going, I really didn't like my chances of figuring out some way to get out of it. Bree might let me overrule her, but then I'd have to deal with those sad puppy dog eyes all night. And Sarah would never let up on me about bailing if I did.

If there were a lot of people, maybe Gemma and I could just... manage to not cross paths. Then I wouldn't have to explain to her why I looked like this at work. Fuck, though, I really should apologise to her for putting her in that position. She didn't deserve to be humiliated just because I had issues going on with my gender that I didn't want anyone to know about.

As I stepped off the lift and walked through Marketing, something occurred to me. If there were a lot of people at Sarah's place... well, Sarah didn't seem like the type to go blabbing about stuff to people, so she probably didn't tell them too much about me. That was a problem because they were going to want to know what my deal was; guys didn't just go around being called 'she' by their friends, and girls didn't look and act exactly like men unless there was something going on...

Fuck. I really didn't want to go. There were just so many reasons why I didn't. I opened Oslo—I had to use my key, which meant that everyone had taken my absence as a great reason to go home— trying to figure out how I could possibly get out of it.

As I sat down at my laptop again, stuck on that thought, I noticed a post-it on my screen. I plucked it off and held it steady to read. 'See you at 7ish. You promised!' I sighed at it, and then scrunched it up and threw it in my bin.

I hadn't even been away from my laptop for long enough for it to go to sleep, so I just gazed at the lock screen. I should start doing some slides, I thought. Which meant picking a colour palette and a design, which meant researching the company we're pitching to, which meant I need to start sorting through those catalogues and then looking at the websites and materials from other companies they purchase prestige stock from...

I tried to focus on all the work I needed to do, but my brain kept cycling back to that whole thing with Gemma in the lift, and I kept looking down at my white blouse, seeing my breasts, and worrying

326

about Sarah's movie night. And the more I looked down, the more I just wanted to run home and take these stupid clothes off as fast as possible so I didn't have to feel this way.

It was only after I'd been staring at an empty palette for ten minutes that I realised working tonight was a completely lost cause. *Fuck it*, I thought resolutely, *I've had it with today. I'm going to go home, take this crap off and put on something huge and baggy.*

I stood up, switched everything off and collected all the materials I'd need to work at home. I'd been opening the door as I fished around in my handbag for the key, when I looked up and saw Sean Frost. His fist was raised where the door had been, mid-knock. He knocked in the air anyway. "Perfect timing," he said, and held out a USB towards me with a big smile.

Fuck... In the space of 15 minutes, I'd completely forgotten he was doing that for me. I'd nearly walked out on the co-CEO doing me a huge favour. God, I could only imagine how that would have looked if I'd disappeared, on top of the thing in the lift and how shaken he said I looked afterward. I accepted the USB but was still completely horrified with myself. I was losing the fucking plot. "Thank you."

He looked surprised by my expression. "You're most welcome, but why the face?" he asked. "Didn't you think I would actually do it?"

I closed my jaw and shook my head as I tucked the USB into my handbag. "No, no, it's not that. I'm really sorry," I told him. "I'm just—" I thought better of actually telling him anything; instead, I just forced a smile. "Thank you very much for this," I said. "I appreciate it."

He watched my whole struggle and jabbed his finger at me. It was more collegial than authoritative. "Burnout," he said, "Google it. And after you've Googled it, both you and your workaholic boyfriend need to use your annual leave days, okay?" After I nodded reluctantly at him, he nodded once back, and then shifted his weight. "Now," he said. "Because hypocrisy has always been a strong point of mine, I'm going to go downstairs and get a coffee to keep myself awake for the next eight hours." He glanced at my handbag. "Would you like to keep me company in the lift again? I gather we're not likely to have a repeat of earlier."

I cringed. Well, I guessed nothing could be worse than what he'd seen between Gemma and I, could it? "Sure."

There were no more embarrassing incidents on the way downstairs, though, unless you counted me being too intimidated by the fact he was the co-CEO and too horrified about how emotionally unstable he probably thought I was to make any useful conversation with him. He didn't seem to mind. In fact, he was happy to fill the space with easy, casual chatter.

Before we parted ways in the foyer, he smiled at me. "Thanks for the company," he said. "And I'm glad you're going home earlier than you expected. Don't work too hard, no matter what my sister says. It's not worth it."

I patted my handbag where I'd put the USB. "Thank you for doing this for me. As I said, I appreciate it."

He nodded, and was about to say goodbye, I thought, when something caught his eye. He looked past me, his brow dipping momentarily. "Another friend of yours?"

I didn't like the sound of that. It could only be one person. Oh, god, no. No… I turned to face the rotating doors, and saw a familiar mop of blonde curls and a big, open smile. "Min!" Bree called out, waving at me and rushing towards us.

She must have gone back to my place before coming to wait for me, because she was holding a Tupperware container and not wearing a school uniform for once. Instead, she was wearing a light blue cotton dress which I was delighted to see actually covered everything. At least, I was delighted until she came rushing over to us and with every bounce I realised how thin the fabric was. God, was she even wearing a bra with it? She looked like, well, like something you'd download off the internet. *Fuck.*

I glanced hurriedly back at Sean, and he raised his eyebrows at me. There wasn't even anything I could say about Bree that would justify her.

"Hi!" Bree said as she got to me. Instead of hugging me though—thank god, Sean was right there—she presented me with the container. "Dinner!" she announced. "I made a wrap so if you were really hungry you could walk and eat on the way home!"

Not 'on the way to your house', but 'on the way home'. Fuck, how all of this must have sounded to him. I was sure I'd gone from pale to bright red in the space of 30 seconds, and it only got worse.

She was looking up at Sean. "Hi, who are you? Do you work with Min?" she asked him cheerfully, extending her hand for him to shake. "I'm Bree."

Instead of looking insulted that Bree didn't know who he was, he just seemed very entertained and let her shake his hand. "Sean," he said. "And I don't really work with Min. I was just helping her do something today."

"Pleased to meet you," Bree said, and then looked him up and down. "That tie is amazing."

To his credit, he actually appeared to have taken it as a compliment. "Thank you, my wife bought it for me. It's one of my favourites, too. Now," he said, straightening a little, "if you'll excuse me, I won't hold you up any longer. I'm sure you two have big plans for this evening."

Was he... implying what I thought he was? He had a completely neutral expression, so I couldn't tell if he just meant the plans I'd mentioned before, or something else. Was I being paranoid again?

"Pleasure to meet you, Bree," he said, remembering her name. To me, he said with a hint of amusement, "Bye, Min." I think he might have been chuckling to himself as he headed over to the café in the lobby.

I watched him go, wondering helplessly if there was any other possible way I could be more of a joke to him than I already was. I groaned, and would have put my head in my hands if they hadn't been full of the Tupperware container Bree had given me a minute ago. The only consolation was that he had seemed genuinely okay about everything. That, and he wasn't actually my direct boss. Maybe I was just worrying too much again.

I sighed at her as we headed out. "Why do you have to be the way you are...?"

She looked indignant. "I was really nice to him," she said. "Besides, Min, I just made you dinner and waited out here for you for nearly an hour." She motioned at the Tupperware container I was carrying. "Go on, have a look!"

At her request, I opened the container and peeked inside. The wrap had completely fallen apart. I closed the lid quickly before she could see. "Looks delicious," I said anyway. I didn't really want to tell her I'd just had a very stressful day and the sight of food was making my stomach turn, so I changed the subject a little. "How did you get all the ingredients?"

She scoffed. "You left me a twenty. There's food for the whole weekend in your fridge. Probably like five or six meals."

I gave her a sceptical look as we walked out onto the street. Twenty had never bought me more than a single meal in the city. Then again, I wasn't exactly a regular in supermarkets. "How did you buy five or six meals with twenty dollars?"

She looked very pleased with herself. "I know all the tricks," she boasted with a smile. "All the ways you get great food for really cheap." She didn't let me ask why that was, though, because she kept talking about how she'd done it all the way back to my place.

When we got there, I waited until Bree was in my en suite to take the mangled wrap out of the container and put it on my plate. I wasn't hungry at all, but I couldn't very well not eat it after she'd put so much effort into making it. She looked disappointed when she came back out and saw the jumble of food it had become, though. "You wrecked it," she accused me.

I shrugged, my mouth half-full. "I've never been great with food. Henry's always the one who cooks if either of us does, and we normally get takeaway, anyway."

The ex-wrap wasn't terrible. It wasn't fantastic, either, but it was definitely edible and probably better for me than what I would have had instead: takeaway and red wine. Bree rested her chin on her forearms at the table and watched me eat it, looking delighted. Afterward, she insisted she was going to wash my dishes while I had a shower.

I didn't get up from the table straight away, though, because after I'd had that shower I'd need to get dressed, and after I'd gotten dressed we'd need to leave, and then after we'd arrived I'd be sharing a room with Gemma again. Not to mention a whole truckload of other people I didn't know and who didn't know what was going on with me. I grimaced. I wasn't sure which was worse; at least with Gemma I had a shot at trying to avoid her all evening. But a room full of people wondering why I looked the way I did...?

Bree saw my expression and lifted her head off the table. "What's wrong?"

"I don't suppose I can convince you to stay in and watch movies with me here, can I?"

I must have looked more stressed out than usual, because she didn't even turn those puppy eyes on me. She was serious. "It's going to be fine, I promise. I asked Sarah like five times if it was definitely going to be okay, and she said everyone's cool."

"Maybe I should just dress up as a girl..." I wondered aloud. Gemma knew the truth now, and other than her, there was only Liz who'd never seen me as a woman. "Because even 'cool' people are still going to be thinking, 'what are you?' and get really shocked if they see me in my work clothes later."

Bree made a face. "It's not shocking seeing you dressed like a girl," she said. "It's just kind of like… 'nope'."

Yeah, I thought as I listened to her, *but you didn't get it on with one version of me, not knowing about the other one.* That must have been a bit of a shock to Gemma. Fuck, and I still hadn't told Bree what had happened last Friday, had I? I didn't really want to yet, to be honest. I'd rather she kept assuming I was into Henry for now. It just made everything a lot less complicated.

"You look way more comfortable and you make way more sense as a guy." Bree told me, and then paused to reconsider her wording. "Or when you're like a guy. Or whatever it ends up you are."

"You see? You don't even know what to say, and you know me."

Bree put her hands on my shoulders and shook me a little. "Min," she said. "People aren't going to be thinking it like that, in that tone of voice."

I slumped back in my chair. "You don't know that."

"Yeah, well, neither do you," she said, taking my arm. "You're just being a stress ball again." I let her pull me up out of the chair and drag me all the way to the bathroom. "It's going to be fine," she told me sternly, and then closed the door and went back into the kitchen, presumably to wash up after me. While I was in the shower, I kept waiting to hear the sound of her breaking my crockery. It didn't happen, but I still decided I should invest in plastic tableware.

After I was done in the bathroom and had managed to get myself to a point where I realised I was going to have to go to Sarah's movie thing, I decided that at least it gave me the opportunity to road test my new binders.

I took one of them out of the packaging, reading, 'So comfortable you won't remember you're wearing one!', and then examined what essentially felt like slab of thick elastic mesh in a tank top. I wasn't sure it would fit, because it was kind of small. Contrary to expectation, though, with a great amount of struggling I did finally manage to get into it. And, when I'd twisted it so it sat right on my chest and on my stomach, the result was fucking impressive.

I was flat. I stood side on to the mirror, and apart from the fact I was wearing women's undies and there was nothing filling them, you'd never have known I was a girl. I quickly pulled my jeans on to hide that. I was going to need to buy some boxers or something.

I didn't realise how long I'd been admiring my completely smooth chest from various angles until Bree pounded on the door. "Miiiiiiin," she said, giving my name about four syllables, "you're taking *ages*."

I looked at myself in the mirror. Well, I guessed technically a binder was underwear, but you couldn't really see anything. "Come in, then."

She opened the door, probably beginning to detail her adventures in breaking my crockery, but stopped when she saw me.

"What do you think?" I said, with a smile on my face.

She looked me up and down. "Wow," she said. "I mean you weren't that big anyway, but wow. Does it hurt?"

I circled my shoulders. It was definitely false advertising because there was no way I could forget I was wearing this. However, it was way more comfortable than the bandages were, and with the tank top part over it, it looked better, too. It looked real. "Well, it's tight," I said. "But it doesn't really hurt." I walked over to the wardrobe and opened it again. "So. Should I wear that shirt you like?"

Bree had other ideas about what I was going to wear, though, and through a systematic process of begging and actual physical force, she got me into one of Henry's shirts. I felt weird about wearing them when he didn't know about my gender stuff, but, really, I didn't see what the harm was. I wore a whole lot of his other clothes. I stopped short of wearing his ties, though, and that was fine with Bree because she had some serious anti-Paisley prejudice. "Here," she told me, retrieving her school tie from somewhere on my floor and threading it through my collar. Somewhat embarrassingly, she needed to teach me how to knot it, too.

When she was done, I stood back and closed my wardrobe door so I could scrutinise myself in the mirror on it. "Not too dressy?" I asked, holding my arms out as she shook her head. Henry was wider than me in general, and the shirt was much baggier than my other ones. It didn't look bad, though, and, most importantly, I felt fucking great. It was a huge relief. I wished I could wear this stuff to work.

"So," Bree said somewhat coyly while I was still checking myself out. "Are you going to wear the packer?"

I watched my eyebrows go up in my reflection. "Nope," I said quickly. She looked disappointed. That was interesting, and it made me want to mess with her. "Why?" I asked, fixing her with a grin and saying at the lowest register of my voice, "Would you *like* me to wear it, Bree?"

She went bright red. "Oh my god, stop it, I was just asking!"

"So was I," I said, enjoying her reaction.

She recovered, giving me a cheeky little smile in the reflection. "If I said yes, would you?"

I watched her for a moment, and during the course of that moment, that smile faded right off her face and she went even deeper red. This was so much fun, this blushing thing girls did. "Sure, if you told me exactly why you want me to."

She was the first one to look away. "Oh my god," she said, fanning her face with her hands. "Oh my god. Okay, that dry-sarcastic-jokey thing you always do works a lot differently when you're dressed like that. Like, a lot differently. Whoa!" She was trying not to look at me. Unlike what had happened in the lift, this type of trying-not-to-look-at-me was something I actually enjoyed. Probably a little too much, actually.

I was still grinning as I filed that thought away somewhere and presented myself to her. "So I'm wearing this, then?"

She gestured pointedly at our reflection in the mirror, like it spoke for itself. "Uh, yeah." Then, she looked down at her own body. "And you haven't even commented on my dress. I spent ages digging through my clothes looking for something that covered everything and you didn't even notice!"

"I did notice," I told her, nodding appreciatively at it while I took my sneakers out and sat down on the bed to put them on. "It's nice, it suits you."

"Then why didn't you say anything?" she asked me, sitting down next to me on the mattress and crossing her arms.

I stopped threading my laces and looked down at her. "Say what? 'Thank you for not advertising your wares?'"

She looked at me for a second and then burst out laughing while I was finishing with my sneakers. When I was done, I stood there over her and pretended to wait impatiently while she got her act together, but that just made her laugh harder.

She did manage to stop for a second, rasping, "'My wares', I'm totally using that. 'Hey, do you like my wares in this shirt? If you're interested in my wares I have a nice pair of jugs you could inspect,'" She could hardly breathe. "Oh my god, are you, like, 70? Because—"

I rolled my eyes, silencing her by pushing her back on the mattress and grabbing a pillow which I held jokingly over her face. "How do I shut you up?" I asked the pillow. In between fits of giggles she was shrieking at me and one of her fists was loosely drumming my side. She did say something back, but it was muffled by a mouthful of fabric. "Sorry," I yelled, leaning down. "I can't hear you. What was that?"

I didn't want to actually suffocate her, so after a little while I tossed the pillow aside and stood up, grinning back at her as I walked out of the bedroom. I did throw a glance over my shoulder to check I hadn't gone too far, but she was just lying flat on her back, laughing. It made me smile.

I left her in the bedroom and went into the kitchen to continue getting ready. While I was sharing my stuff between all my pockets, she crept in and wrapped her arms around my waist. "I didn't want to hug you before because of that guy you were with," she explained.

Yeah, I was pretty glad she hadn't hugged me in front of Sean Frost, because on top of what had happened in the lift, the fact he'd thought I was burning out and the fact I had a small mini-porn star trailing cheerfully after me... Well, I didn't want him *also* thinking I was cheating on Henry with a girl. Henry did work for him, after all. "Good decision," I told her, ruffling her hair and then prying her free. "Come on, let's go."

When Sarah had said she lived miles away, we must have had different ideas about what constituted 'miles' because I'd pulled up in front of her house in less than half an hour, and most of that was spent in traffic trying to get out of the city. That meant we got there really early. Henry would already have been expecting that and been ready by quarter-to, but I didn't think Sarah was used to me yet.

"So we're just going to sit here for 15 minutes," Bree said flatly, looking across at me from the passenger seat like I was crazy.

"Yup," I said, but just as I'd said it, another prestige car pulled up in front of us. Two guys got out of it, and while they were unloading a crate of wine, one of them slapped the other on the arse. I sat up in my seat. "I think they're Sarah's friends."

"They're not waiting in the car," Bree observed, and then before I'd told her not to, she just jumped out to go and say hello.

Of course she would, I thought, and then reluctantly followed her out. They were already shaking hands with her as I walked up. I was taller than both of them; I felt self-conscious. I wondered if they could tell I was female.

"This is Matt," she said, pointing to the white guy, and then she pointed at his partner, who was Asian, too, "and this is Andrew, his boyfriend. And this," she said, presenting me, "is Min."

I took my hand out of my pocket to greet them with a stiff wave.

Andrew didn't look Korean, I didn't think. I shook his hand when he offered it, and it turned out he was thinking the same thing. "You're not Viet, are you?" he asked me.

I shook my head. "Korean."

He nodded, and then stood back and looked up at me like I was a tall building. "Some serious tall genes you got there. Want to swap parents?" was his assessment. "I'm sick being called 'shorty' by this one, here." He scruffed his boyfriend's hair affectionately.

"Well, you're welcome to my mother," I said dryly. "Please, have her."

Both of the men laughed openly at that, which suggested to me he might actually have my brand of mother, too. "Trust me, I've got one of those of my own," Andrew said as he turned back towards the car and took out a crate. "Here, could you grab this for us?"

He dumped a crate in my arms and then turned around to get another one. It was such a subtle confirmation, and as it dawned on me what it meant, I smiled slightly. They do think I'm a guy, I realised. It wasn't surprising given how I looked, but still — it was daylight. I'd spoken to them, and neither of them had appeared to think twice about it.

On the way in, though, Bree pulled me a little to the side. "Does Sarah use male pronouns for you? You know, when you're dressed like this?" I shook my head and she made a face. "Well what do I do, then? They think you're a guy."

On one hand, I would have been perfectly fine for everyone to use 'he', on the other, did I really want to create any more awkward situations where people saw me in my work clothing or found out I wasn't male? 'She' was okay, I was used to it. And really, I didn't care. I just didn't want everyone to talk about it. *I* didn't even want to talk about it. "Just leave it. It will sort itself out."

Bree didn't look comfortable with that at all. "Not knowing which ones to use with these guys is stressing me out," she said, and then walked up the driveway onto the porch and rang the bell.

Yeah, well, this whole thing about needing to choose right now at this second is stressing me out, I thought, following her onto the porch.

Bree had progressed to knocking on the door as I carted the crate up the stairs. It was Liz who opened it though, not Sarah. She gave Bree the once-over. "You must be Bree."

"You must be a supermodel," was Bree's reply as she looked up at Liz.

I came up behind Bree with the crate on one hip, reaching down and wrapping my arm around her head until my hand was over her mouth. "Hi, Liz," I said casually, as if Bree wasn't struggling and mumbling through my hand.

Liz looked very entertained. "You guys are fucking priceless," she said. "Come and bring the grog in to—" She caught sight of the other two guys over my shoulder. "Hey! Matty-boy! Long time no see!" She pushed past us to go and basically jump on him. He swung her around despite the fact his boyfriend was standing right there. They must have been friends from way back.

When he put her down, he held his arm out towards Andrew. "This is my man," he said, and introduced them.

I wanted to hear more of that conversation, but Bree was tugging on my shirt. "Come on, let's go in!"

I left Liz and the boys on the porch and followed Bree inside and down a long hallway which lead to the back half of the house. Gemma's probably in there, I thought, and while I was mentally preparing myself for that, Sarah leant out of a doorway to the side and stopped me. "Hey, Toyboy!" she said, pulling me inside by an elbow. "Fuck, I can't believe you actually came. Bring the wine in here."

Bree followed us into the kitchen. "I told you I'd get her here."

Sarah went and crouched back in front of the fridge where she was playing a game of Jenga with the carefully stacked beer. "You've done well, young Padawan," she said, laughing, and then gave Bree a beer. "Can you go give that to the guy who's got his leg up on a chair in the living room?"

"Sure!" Bree said, and then went to do that.

When she was gone, Sarah looked me up and down. "Fuck," she said. "And now you're a guy again. It's like a magic trick." She squinted at my tie. "Is that..." Leaning forward, she flipped it over to display the Cloverfield emblem on the back. Leaning back, she smirked at me.

"Clearly it's proof I'm sleeping with her," I said flatly.

"I didn't say anything," she told me innocently as Bree's head hung around the doorway again.

Bree looked troubled. "Min," she said. "I kind of need you to make a ruling on this one. The guy with the busted ankle saw you before Sarah dragged you in here and he's like, 'is he your boyfriend?' and I'm like, 'no, just a friend' and then he's like, 'so how does he know Sarah?' and now I don't know what to do, so I told him I needed to ask you something."

Before I could answer, the two boyfriends and Liz came down the hallway and dumped their crate in the kitchen, greeting Sarah and then heading off into the living room. I stood out the way for them, and then for Liz, who came in after they were gone.

"Okay," Liz said to me. "This is kind of a really strange thing to ask, but they think you're a guy. Did you tell them you were a guy? Should I correct them, or...?"

I probably went as red as Bree had been earlier. I did not want to talk about this, and I felt cornered. "Oh, good," I said dryly, "Let's all have a big conference about my gender and talk about it as much as possible. This is great."

Sarah opened one of the beers she'd carefully extracted and reached past me to give it to Liz. "Just pick one and we'll go with it," she said to me, and then went about grabbing another couple of drinks out. "Or we'll try to, anyway."

Bree was still hanging around the door frame. "We could go male pronouns?" she offered. "Like, maybe you could try it and see if you like it? You do really look like one, after all."

Liz looked from Bree to me, eyebrows way up. "Okay, what does that mean?"

I was *so* not ready to school people on gender, because 'I don't know, call me whatever you want' seemed like a perfectly acceptable answer to me, but everyone else was having huge issues with it. Fine, I thought, I'll choose something to keep everyone happy. I was actually tempted to go for Bree's suggestion of male pronouns, but Sarah's 'or we'll try to' was what worried me. I didn't want people mixing them and then thinking they needed to correct themselves and each other all evening. Having my gender constantly coming up was the very last thing in the world that I wanted.

I just went with the easiest option that I thought would cause the minimum amount of discussion. "Tell them I'm a girl, then, I guess."

Liz took a sip of her beer. "Okay," she said. "Killer shirt, by the way. Where did you get it? I should get some ones like that for Chris."

I shrugged. "It's Henry's."

Liz and Sarah shared a glance. "Oh," Liz said. "Okay." She continued to the living room. Bree followed her, presumably to deliver her answer to Chris.

Sarah stood up from the fridge and offered me a beer. I accepted it and as she passed it to me, she said, "I'm glad you said 'girl', because I've been talking about my boss like you're a chick for the last three weeks. That, and Gem isn't here yet, either. I can just imagine her coming into the living room and saying 'she' something about you and then having you both freak out over the scene that would cause. It was difficult enough to drag you out from under your bed, I don't need to do it to her as well." She put her hands on her hips, glancing up at the clock. "Anyway, that reminds me. I don't know where that girl is. She was going to come here after work but she hasn't and she's not replying to any of my texts. She overthinks stuff a bit, but I didn't think she was that worried about you being here."

I grimaced. I knew exactly why she wasn't here. "Um," I began, and Sarah looked suspiciously at me. I scrunched up my face. "I bumped into her in the lift at work," I said, adding, "Also, Sean Frost was in there, too."

Sarah watched me as the implications of what I'd told her settled in. She exhaled, looking a bit frustrated. "Didn't go so well?" I shook my head. She rolled her eyes and said cryptically, "And I can't even outsource this one, either. We really need to find that girl a boyfriend."

Her keys were on the counter, and she grabbed them. "Back in 15," she said, and then rushed out the door. Shortly after that, I heard a car start. She was probably going to go check to make sure Gemma was okay, I thought, guessing that that's what she meant about Gemma needing a boyfriend. That was nice of her, but, fuck, I hoped Gemma wasn't staying away just because of me. Away from her own group of friends... all of whom were probably waiting in the living room to meet me, I realised. With Bree. I winced.

Well, I couldn't just hang out in the kitchen by myself. I took my beer, psyched myself up and went to join everyone in the living room. There were a couple of other people I didn't know in there—both men—and everyone turned to look at me as I came in. Bree had been sitting on the back of couch behind an enormous, muscular guy with his leg bandaged, and instead of letting me slink quietly in she called to everyone, "This is Min! Min: this is everyone!"

"Hi, everyone..." I said, feeling really self-conscious. There weren't any seats left on the couches, so I just stood behind them, taking a sip of my beer.

The huge guy was probably Chris, Liz's rugby-playing husband. He was staring at me, with particular attention to my flat chest. Liz clipped him across the ear. "Stop being a dick and just drink your beer," she told him quietly.

"There's space next to us," Andrew offered, shuffling along the couch to create room. I was okay with standing over here, but I didn't want to seem impolite, so I went and sat down next to them. "Sorry I thought you were a guy before," he said, looking a bit embarrassed.

"It's kind of the look I'm going for," I told him a bit shortly, aware everyone was trying to pretend they weren't watching me. I really, really, really didn't want to talk about it, either. Especially not in front of all these people. "So, thanks, I guess..."

Bree made eye-contact with me from the other couch, and she saw how uncomfortable I was. She looked around frantically until her eyes fell on Chris's bandaged knee. "So how did you fuck your knee?" she asked him. "Is it a cool story?"

Liz groaned. She might have heard it a few times. "Don't get him started," she told Bree, but it looked like she was too late.

Chris puffed out his colossal chest and looked fiercely proud of his injury. "I still reckon I scored the try that won the fucking game with it," he said, and then launched into his story.

I had absolutely zero interest in rugby but I listened politely, so thankful to Bree for distracting everyone from me. People were still casting curious looks in my direction but at least they weren't saying anything. I thought Sarah was probably right: they probably didn't care, but being the centre of attention was something I hated and I just kind of wished I could press a button and become invisible. I figured I'd probably care a lot less if I was loaded up on alcohol, and if I got started early I'd be sober again by the time I needed to drive home. I finished my beer in record time.

One of the other guys I didn't know leant over to me from a chair he'd pulled up, and handed me his full bottle when I was done with mine. "I don't really like this one, you want it? Don't worry, it's not gross or anything, I didn't backwash."

I looked down at myself as I accepted the drink from him. "I think it's a bit too late for me to worry about being infected with guy germs."

He looked relieved for some reason and then laughed, holding out his hand for me to shake. "The name's Matt as well, but these guys call me Smithy because the position of 'Matt' had already been filled by this guy when I rocked up."

Matt, who must have been furtively listening, grinned across Andrew at Smithy. "First in, best dressed, bro."

Both of them were dressed very casually, and because I already had a beer in me, I couldn't just leave that one. "I'm clearly the best dressed out of the three of us," I pointed out. "Does that mean I win the title of 'Matt'?"

They all thought that was hilarious, and that made me relax a little. They can't be that uncomfortable with me if they're laughing at my jokes, I thought. They were okay.

When they were done laughing, we all sat back and listened to Chris waxing poetic about his heroic sports injury. Or they did, anyway. I was just happy they'd all stopped throwing secret glances at me when they thought I wasn't looking.

The topic had shifted to other heroic injuries, and Smithy had started to tell us about when he'd broken his arm—complete with horrifying scar, which we all made faces about—when the front door opened. Shortly afterwards, Sarah came marching into the living room with an open bottle of Sauvignon Blanc. "Did you miss me?"

Smithy mock-glared at Sarah. "I was actually in the middle of telling everyone about when that car knocked me off my bike," he said. "If you don't mind."

Sarah looked properly chastised and grabbed a couple of wine glasses from the kitchen table as she wandered over to where Bree was seated on the spine of the couch. While Smithy got going again, I saw Sarah pour some wine into one of them.

"Can I have some?" Bree asked her.

"Not until you're a grown-up," Sarah told her, but then gave her the full glass anyway.

Bree took a sip from it. "I'm not a kid."

Sarah gave Bree's large chest a very pointed look as she poured another glass. "I can see that."

I had expected that glass to be Sarah's, but she didn't drink from it. Instead, she stood up and walked over to the doorway and handed it to the person who was quietly loitering in it. When I saw who it was, I nearly spat out my beer. It was Gemma. She was dressed in a big floppy jumper, tracksuit pants and Uggboots. She looked a bit embarrassed by that, especially when she spotted me among the faces looking at her. We shared an awkward whoops-I-didn't-mean-to-look-at-you glance. "Hi guys," she said a bit shyly as everyone greeted her. "Sarah didn't give me time to get changed..."

"We're all friends," Sarah said as Gemma took the wine from her. "It doesn't matter what you wear."

I could guess what Gemma meant by saying Sarah hadn't let her change: Sarah had needed to drag her here, and that made me feel awful. These were her friends and because of me she hadn't felt welcome.

I had gone to sit forwards again so it didn't look like I was staring at her, but when I glanced over at Bree, she'd noticed already. She didn't look happy, either, and she hopped down off the spine of the other couch and came and stood in front of me. "There's enough room for me," she told us, speaking mainly to me. "I'm small."

Matt and Andrew looked at each other. There really wasn't enough room. I was tempted to offer Bree my lap, but then I wondered why that thought had even crossed my mind. *No, Min,* I thought, *you're not going there, not with Bree, you know that.* Instead, I stood up.

"Have my seat," I told her, and then went and sat on one of the kitchen chairs.

Bree took it, but when she looked over at me from my spot on the couch, she looked so hurt and disappointed. It was like I'd just rejected her. I didn't know what to do about it, so I just tried to look apologetic.

The boys were still half-listening to Smithy's story, but Gemma saw the whole exchange between me and Bree, and looked like she was liable to just go home again. Before she could, though, Sarah ushered her into the living room. "Pizza's going to be like an hour," Sarah told us all, seating Gemma in one of the kitchen chairs. "It's busy tonight. So," she said, walking over to the TV and turning on her Foxtel IQ. "I've got like a hundred movies recorded. Which one first?" We all participated in scrolling through the list, and the consensus seemed to be a horror movie. While Sarah was getting it all set up, everyone went to go and grab themselves more alcohol.

Bree took that opportunity to come over. "Why don't you want to sit with me?" she asked, although I suspected that wasn't the real question.

"There's actually no room," I said, ignoring what she really meant. "I didn't want to annoy Matt and Andrew."

She looked at the now-empty couch, and then back at me. "Come on," she said mischievously as she took my hand, "there's no one there now!"

This time, I didn't let her pull me up. "That's rude," I told her, but I accidentally glanced over at Gemma again.

Bree saw, and her face cycled through a series of emotions. "Okay..." she said eventually, and then went and sat there by herself. Before I could second-guess my decision and join her, Matt and Andrew returned and sat down, chatting with each other, and with Smithy who pulled a chair up behind the couch to continue their conversation. No one was talking to Bree even though she was wedged up next to them, and I felt awful.

Maybe we should go home early, I thought, worrying about her. It would be easier for Gemma, too. Fuck, I was causing a lot of headaches by being here, wasn't I?

Sarah came up to me with one of the wines. "Hold this," she said, and then poured me a big glass of red wine.

"Whoa, whoa, stop," I told her, and she paid completely no attention to me. "I have to drive home at some point!"

Sarah gave me a look. "Mmhmm," she said noncommittally, and only stopped pouring when the wine was almost at the brim. "It's really nice, trust me," she said, smiling sweetly and then moving on to Chris.

Since I really didn't want a repeat of last Friday, I just had a couple of mouthfuls and put it on table behind me as everyone got seated. Sarah dimmed the lights, and then we got started on whatever horror movie people had chosen.

Gemma was sitting on a chair not too fair away from Bree, which meant I couldn't look at Bree without Gemma blushing a bit and thinking I was looking at her. Obviously, I didn't want

343

to further humiliate her after the whole lift thing, so I tried not to. In the process, Bree looked even more crestfallen.

Towards the middle of the movie, my phone buzzed in my pocket and I took it out; Bree had sent me a message, and it only said one thing, ":(:(:("

I didn't want to look up at her, so I texted back, *"I'm sorry..."*

"ur being weird again...... please can we just have fun....? these guys seem nice... well except for that girl behind me who wont even look at me whats up with her???"

I winced. *"We both work for Frost and there was kind of a situation there with the CEO today."*

"ooooohhh so its a work thing???"

I exhaled, thinking about how to answer that. I really should just tell her what happened between Gemma and I, it was reaching a point where it looked like I was deliberately concealing it from her. And I couldn't hide it forever, because if we were going to keep hanging around with these guys, it would come up eventually. Now probably wasn't the best time, though. *"Kind of, I'll tell you when we get home, okay?"*

She seemed to accept that, and while I was staring down at my messages and ignoring the movie and everything else going on, Sarah said pointedly, "Hey, Min, I'm really comfortable and I could use another beer, would you mind?"

I looked up from my phone, feeling a bit guilty. She was probably trying to get me off it, which was fair enough, because she'd invited me to this gathering with her friends and I was sitting glued to my mobile and texting people. I felt a bit bad, I hoped she wouldn't be angry. "Sure," I told her, and hopped up to head into the kitchen.

I'd opened the door and walked straight in when I realised the kitchen was already occupied. Gemma was sitting on the far end of the counter, all by herself with a glass of wine. She looked just as alarmed as I did.

Sarah hadn't been trying to get me off my phone after all; I was going to kill her.

My first instinct was to apologise to Gemma, turn and walk out again, but I also didn't want to be rude. Fuck. I couldn't just stand there staring at her, either. "I'm, uh—" I gestured at the fridge. "Sarah wanted me to get her beer."

Gemma made a face. "Of course she wants you to get her a beer, I'm in the kitchen," she said glumly.

I opened the fridge, but when I pulled out one of the beers, my hands were shaking and so several others fell out onto the floor. I needed to go chasing one of them at a crouch across the kitchen. As if that wasn't embarrassing enough, the drawer that I'd seen Sarah take the bottle opener out of was under Gemma's dangling legs. I pointed at them, and she blushed. "I know, I know," she said, "they're really old trackies, and I can't believe I still have them in my—"

"—No, the bottle opener," I said, interrupting her before she could embarrass herself. "It's in that drawer."

"Oh..." she said, hurriedly shuffling over so I could get into it. While I was fishing around for it amongst all the whisks, spatulas and other weird implements, I cut myself on something and hissed, holding my finger up to inspect the damage. It wasn't bleeding as far as I could see, but it stung. I ran it under the tap anyway, just in case. Jesus, could I be any more pathetic?

Gemma had been watching me and she started to laugh, putting her head in her hands. "God," she said, groaning. "I am like the Queen of awkward, I'm so sorry. I basically spend my whole life this colour." She indicated her flushed face. She was so red I could hardly see her freckles anymore.

"Well, I'm ruling right alongside you," I said, looking down at the unopened beer and just giving up on the bottle opener. "Fuck." I tried to bang the lid a bit on the sink to get it off, but that didn't work either and I just ended up leaning against the wall and laughing at myself.

We stopped laughing, eventually, and she ran a hand over her face.

"Min," she began, "I am so, so, so sorry about what happened in the lift today. I've been beating myself up over what a total idiot I was in front of the CEO and those other guys in there. And..." She stopped and made a face, straining as if she was trying to remember something. "You know, I had this whole speech prepared about how I was going to apologise to you and I've been rehearsing it all evening, but it's gone now."

That sounded familiar, so familiar it made me chuckle. "Are you kidding?" I asked. "This is my fault. I should have told you I look like a girl at work. None of this would have happened if I'd just been up front about why I wanted you to pretend you hadn't met me."

She was nodding. "You do look like a girl at work," she said. "It's actually kind of incredible. I didn't even recognise you, and then I thought to myself, 'Oh, her name is Min and she's really tall, too...?' and then I realised..." She gave me a really pained expression. "Oh, god," she said. "Sean Frost."

I shook my head. "I don't know, he seemed kind of fine about it, actually? He offered me dispute resolution services or something afterwards. I don't—well, I don't want anyone at work to guess what happened between you and I, but I was mainly worried about what you were thinking."

She laughed once, humourlessly. "What I've been thinking? I've been drinking all evening and celebrating my future as a lonely cat lady," she said. "I'm hopeless in general, but I'm especially hopeless when people are interested in me."

I was just trying to pay her a compliment, but it came out a bit smooth. "Which must happen a lot, right?"

She pretended to glare at me. "Do you want to make me all awkward again?" she asked. "Do you?"

I laughed. "Sorry. Just saying you kind of seem like one of those girls at school that would have had all the guys swarming around her."

She sighed. "Yeah, I was friends with those kind of girls," she said, and jerked her thumb backwards towards the living room. Then, she put her head in her hands again. "And now my apology has turned into a counselling session."

"On the bright side, we are in a room full of alcohol," I pointed out. "There's no better room to get depressed in."

She laughed at that, a little nervously, I thought. When she stopped, she watched me for a moment, as if she was trying to talk herself into something. "Okay, I'm going to do it, I'm going to take a big risk and say something completely embarrassing." I mimed 'come at me'. She took an exaggeratedly deep breath, gathered herself and then continued, "You're totally hot, and I'd kind of go there again, you know? But I'm not sure I'm actually into that, and if it all goes badly and gets awkward, then either you can't hang around with us again, or I can't, and Sarah's been pretty keen to get you to come out with us for years."

"I can't anyway," I reminded her. "I have a boyfriend."

"Yeah, so you keep saying..." she said. "But, yeah... God." She put her face back in her hands again. "I can't believe I just said all of that to you. Of course you have a boyfriend, and then there's that girl you brought tonight... what am I doing...?"

Meanwhile, I couldn't believe I was actually about to say this to someone other than myself. "Gemma, you're beating yourself up too much." I remembered my first impression of her. "You want to know what I thought when I first met you?"

She gave me a pained expression. "Do I?"

I grinned. "I thought, 'That girl can't possibly be being nice to me, she's too hot. She's probably teasing me'."

I wasn't sure that helped. "Oh, god, did I come across as really arrogant, too? Too drunk is what I was. I can't be trusted when I'm drunk, and I can hardly remember half of that evening. I think I called you Sarah's toyboy or something, and she won't let me forget it." She did look a bit charmed, though. "Thanks, anyway. Wow, I was worried you were going to be so angry with me..."

I shook my head wryly, and a much easier silence stretched between us. "So, are we good?"

She smiled. "Yeah," she said, and then hopped off the bench and stood there awkwardly for a moment, looking at me like she wasn't sure if she should hug me or not.

I hugged her, because she was hilarious, and at least as hopeless as I was. "And I thought *I* needed to chill out."

She gave my flat chest a bit of suspicious look as I let her go. "How did you—"

"Magic," I told her, and then we both wandered out into the living room again as she laughed at that.

Sarah was beaming at us as we came back, and I handed her the beer she'd been after. It still had the cap on, and I pretended it was on purpose. "Well, you didn't specify that you wanted me to open it."

Chris was sitting next to Sarah, and took the bottle off her for a second, opening it with his big rugby hands. Sarah rolled her eyes at me. "So you were in there for like ten minutes and still you didn't even open my beer?" she asked us. "What were you two doing, anyway?"

I looked down at Gemma, who was blushing again at Sarah's implication. Instead of saying anything, I just winked at Sarah as I went to sit down.

I didn't get there, though, because as I watched Gemma go back to her seat, my eyes landed on Bree. She had a really strange expression on her face. "No, seriously," she said so everyone could hear. "What were you two doing?"

Everyone shifted a bit uncomfortably in their seats, trying to pretend they were watching the movie. I looked around at them, feeling the blood drain from my face again. There wasn't anything I could say. If I told her the truth, she wouldn't believe me.

When I didn't say anything, she took a deep breath, and even in the low light I could see her eyes were veiled. "I'm sure you guys were doing a lot of *work* in there," she said evenly, and then she stood up and marched out the front door. It slammed heavily behind her.

NINETEEN

For those short little legs of hers, Bree was surprisingly fast. By the time I'd made it to the front door, I couldn't even see the tail end of her so I had no idea which direction she'd gone in. I looked around the side of the house, in the shed, and all through the backyard, but she wasn't anywhere to be seen which meant that she'd taken off up the road. In the dark, in suburb she didn't know, in that flimsy dress, a*gain*.

I shouldn't have put off telling her about Gemma and I. I rushed out onto the footpath and looked both ways. I should have just told her last Saturday, right after it had happened. I'd even told Henry, but not Bree. Why not Bree?

I knew the answer to that question, but I was too distracted by the fact I couldn't see her anywhere. *Shit.* I stood in the entrance to the driveway, trying to figure out what to do.

The front door opened. "Hey, Min, is everything okay?" It was Sarah's voice, and she actually sounded kind of concerned. "I mean, obviously not, but you know..."

I was worried and a bit frustrated and I very nearly had a go at her for sending me into the kitchen while Gemma was there, but I bit my tongue. I was glad Gemma and I had sorted stuff out, and it wasn't anyone's fault except mine that I hadn't told Bree what had happened.

While I was still stuck on what to do next, Sarah wandered down onto the driveway with me. "Well, that settles that," she said with a bit of an ironic grin.

I frowned at her. "What settles what?"

She was still grinning. "The great debate about whether or not Schoolgirl is into you."

I threw a hard stare at her. "If she's running around... wherever the hell we are right now because you decided to teach me a lesson, I'm going to be pretty fucking pissed off." Turning back towards the road, my eyes rested on my car. I should take it, I thought. I can cover more ground more quickly that way. I walked out onto the road.

Sarah followed me out to it. "Do you actually think I'd do that?" she asked me, as I patted down my pockets to try and figure out where my key was. I didn't answer her, and she said a bit indignantly, "I'm not a sadist, Min. The way she was angling herself into your lap earlier, I kind of figured she already knew and was pretty keen on making sure Gem didn't get another shot at you."

"Well, she didn't know," I said, and then opened the car door and went to get in.

Sarah stopped me. "Yeah, I got that much," she said. "Are you right to drive? I saw two beers and some wine go into you."

Wow, in worrying about Bree I hadn't even thought of that. "Yeah, I probably am," I decided. "Just."

She let me go and I climbed in. I was putting on my seatbelt when the other door opened and Sarah swung in the other side. She put her seatbelt on, too. I stopped what I was doing and looked across at her, narrowing my eyes. She crossed her arms. "Oh, come on, Min. All this is partially my fault. Let me help you look for her, at least."

I made a face, and then started the engine. She probably *would* be a help. "Which way's the train station?"

"Left," she answered. "You think she's actually going to go home, though? Because there's a park the other way, maybe she just needed some time alone."

I pulled away from the curb and turned left.

"...Okay, then. Left again up here," Sarah said, pointing to the end of the road. Then, she spent a few seconds looking at me. "I know I've been teasing you for weeks, but what *is* going on between you two?" I didn't want to answer her, so I didn't. I had *no idea*.

Actually, who the fuck was I kidding? That was bullshit, of course I knew what was going on. That little smile she'd given me yesterday had confirmed it, but if I was honest with myself I think I might have known before that. She's into you, Min, I told myself, and, come on, you know she's doing something to you. You're falling for someone who's about five years old, has no concept of personal boundaries and takes 'extrovert' to new and frightening levels. What the fuck is wrong with you? When on earth did you start to prefer *her* company over Henry's, and where the hell do you think this is going to go?

I hadn't answered Sarah, which I think *was* her answer. "They have a Facebook relationship status especially for you and Bree," she told me, looking forward at the road ahead of us.

"It's not complicated," I said. "I'm just a fucking idiot."

She laughed a bit at that. "Well, not to rub it in, but I could have told you where it was all heading the first time I met her. That girl basically has '*I LOVE YOU, MIN*' tattooed in capital letters on her forehead."

I slowed at an intersection. "You did tell me. Constantly," I said dryly and gestured at the road. "This way?"

Sarah looked back at where we were going. "Oh, sorry, yeah. Just up there on the main road," she instructed, pointing. "Well, I like her and I think you two are cute together. I mean, I like Henry, too, but he kind of seems like your brother."

I gave her a tired look. "Can you not?"

She put a hand on my forearm as I waited to turn out onto the main road. "Min, I'm saying this as a slightly drunk friend: believe me, I've been in relationships like yours, myself. Just cut him loose, it's better for both of you."

"It's not that simple, Sarah," I told her, turning out onto the main road and pulling up alongside the train station. "I want to try and make it work with Henry. I really like him, and he's always been there for me."

Her hand was still on my arm. "Min, other people can be there for you." I looked across at her for a second. She wasn't spooked by the fact I was watching her either, she just let me, and then she smiled. "Go on, off you go." She inclined her head towards the station. "Go rescue Schoolgirl."

'Rescue', yeah right. I headed up to the station and awkwardly jumped the barriers to Platform One in my denim jeans.

It was remote enough and late enough in the evening that it was deserted, and that made me worry even more. I couldn't find her in any of the waiting rooms, or along the platform. The toilets were seriously gross but I checked both of them anyway, and eventually walked out onto the platform to have another look out across it. There was no one.

Maybe Sarah was right, maybe she'd just gone to have some alone time in the park? I was half-walking, half-jogging back to barriers when I rounded the corner and nearly collided with her. She looked like she'd only just arrived; she must have come a different way.

My heart lifted. "Bree!" I said, and then went to hug her. "Fuck, I'm really sorry I didn't—" I stopped, because she coldly shrugged me off and kept walking out onto the platform. "Bree?"

"You can go back to your party," she said bitterly; or at least, she tried to. She sounded too sad to pull off 'angry'.

I easily caught up to her. "I will if you come back with me."

She shook her head and slumped on one of the benches. She wouldn't even look at me. "Sorry, but being abandoned by the person who brought me to a party while they get it on with other people kind of isn't my idea of a fun Friday night."

I sat down carefully next to her. "Gemma and I were actually just talking in there," I said, and when she finally looked up at me, it was to give me a look that said 'are you joking?', so I added, "I *have* kissed her. Once, last Friday. She actually kissed *me*. We were both really drunk."

She reacted to that like I'd actually backhanded her. "So you've been keeping this from me *all week*?"

I made a face. "Not keeping it from you, exactly. I just... it was something that happened between Gemma and I. I needed to think what it meant about me. I wasn't sharing it around."

There was hurt visible on her face. "Sarah totally knew. So you told her and not me. And that blonde girl, what's her name? The supermodel one. She knew, as well. *Everyone* knew, but I'm supposed to be your friend and you didn't tell me."

I swallowed. "Bree, they were there when it happened. I didn't really tell either of them. And remember that text message I sent before? I said I was going to tell you when we got home."

"Yeah, I remember. I had to basically drag it out of you." She looked forwards again, down at the train tracks with her lips pressed in a tight line. It was a little while before she spoke. "I mean, I understand, I guess," she said, not sounding very much like she actually did understand. "That girl *is* more your age..."

I inhaled, my heart going again. More my own age than *Bree* was, I knew she meant, and I knew what she was implying. It was one thing to talk theoretically about the fact Bree was into me with Sarah, and quite another to have Bree almost *telling* me. I was so not ready for this, not at all. "Bree..."

"Is that why?" she asked me, turning those huge blue eyes on me. "Is that why you went for her instead?"

Alarm bells went off in my head and I felt deeply, deeply uncomfortable. I was *not* okay with where this conversation was heading. "I don't want to talk about this now," I said. "Come on, come back to my place, we can open a bottle of red and—"

"—and then not talk about it there, either," she said, interrupting me. "'Not now' means 'not ever' with you."

My hackles rose a bit; I didn't want to be forced into talking about how I felt about her, and I certainly did *not* want to hear what she had to say about her feelings for me. "Okay, then maybe I just don't want to have this discussion full-stop," I said shortly.

She watched me with this bleak expression for a few seconds, and then looked back at the train tracks. It was ages before she said anything, and while I was waiting, I felt like I sweat out the entire water content of my body. "I'm stupid," was all she said when she spoke again. "I'm so fucking stupid."

"No, you're not," I said quietly. "I am."

That made her eyes swim for some reason. "Yeah, actually, I am," she said, and then looked up at me again. "Want to hear why?" She didn't wait for me to reply before she started. "Min, I had *such* a great time on Saturday, and on Sunday I spent all day making you the USB, and I was thinking the whole time about how much you'd enjoy it and how I wanted to make you happy. And then today I did all that shopping for you and," she took a measured breath, "it was kind of nice, you know? Being domestic. Looking around at all the food and thinking, 'I wonder if Min would like that?' and planning what I was going to make for us."

I listened, feeling progressively more terrible with everything she was saying.

"While I was making your dinner, I kept thinking it would be really nice if I could do that all the time. Like, make your dinner and your lunches and then give you a big hug when you get home from work. I was doing all these things thinking about you. I *always* think about you. I can't believe this amazing person likes spending time with me and having me over. It's like a dream come true." When she stopped this time, those tears spilt down her cheeks. "Only it's not really, is it? It's not really. Because all this time you were thinking about *her*."

God, my *heart.* I tried to take her hand, but she batted it away. "Bree, no, no, no, no, it's not like that," I said. "It's nothing like that. Gemma and I were both drunk, she kissed me and today we agreed it was an accident. It doesn't have anything to do with how much I enjoy your company or how much I care about you."

"It was an accident? Like, how does that even work? How do you *accidentally* pash someone? Did you slip and fall on her face?"

"Bree..."

"Okay, okay," she said, quietening down a little. "I just... I thought you were gay, you know? Because of Henry. And because you weren't into girls I was like, well, I can still spend time with her and still cheer her up, that's okay. And it was okay. More would have been nice, but I couldn't have it, so what we had was okay." She swallowed. "But you're not gay, and you *are* into girls... and, well, what does that other girl even want? Does she want to make you happy? Does she—"

"—I met her on Friday, Bree. We were both drunk, she seriously

353

doesn't want anything from me, and I don't understand why you're—"

"And yet *she's* the one you kissed," Bree interrupted me. "You went there with *her,* despite all the things I've been doing for you and—"

I couldn't deal with a confession. I didn't want to hear it, so I cut her off. "Yeah, I did," I said a bit harshly. "And just doing nice things for someone doesn't entitle you to anything more than 'thank you'." I regretted it immediately after I'd said it, because I could see the heartbreak on her face.

"I didn't say that," she said in this tiny voice, with more tears welling in her eyes. "And I didn't mean that, and Min, I just want to be the one making you happy, and you know what?" she asked me. "You don't even say 'thank you'. You act like it's some huge gift that you tolerate me."

I wanted to snap back at her, but I also didn't want to hurt her again. "That's not fair," I told her. "You know I do—" I nearly said 'love', but I didn't want to use that word, "—enjoy your company."

"But you never *say* it," she said. "You never *tell me.* I don't know if you expect me to be psychic or something—"

"Bree, you're not being fair—"

She was shaking like a leaf. "No, *you're* not being fair!" she said. "You're acting like this is no big deal that you pashed this girl, but it *is* a big deal, it's *so* not fair, and so you clearly just don't understand what this feels like—"

Okay, *what*? No, I was *not* leaving that one, so I stopped her. "Excuse me, Bree, but I 'don't understand' what not fair is like? *I* don't understand 'not fair'? Are you *high*? Are you *actually high*?"

She looked obstinate, even though her eyebrows were almost touching and she had her arms folded tightly across her stomach because she was so nervous. "Like, okay, there's the trans stuff, but you have a normal family, and this great job and you're really successful and have lots of money and you have this guy who totally loves you and all these other people who want you, and so *of course* you don't get what it's like to be someone like me—"

That made my blood rise. I couldn't sit down for this, so I stood up. What the *fuck* was she on? "Are you fucking kidding me,

Bree? *I* don't understand what 'not fair' is like and everything is just so fucking great in my life? You must be fucking blind Bree, because *look* at me! *Look at me!*"

I presented myself to her, and she sat back in the seat, stunned at how loud I was. In the distance, I could hear the horn of a train blaring.

I imitated her for a second. "'*Okay there's the trans stuff*', do you even fucking *know what that means?* What the *fuck* am I, Bree? *What is this body?* I've hated it for as long as I can fucking remember and all the way through high school, Bree, *all the way*, I was teased half to death because of it. It's not even my fault. It's not even my fucking fault. I used to shout at them, 'You think I like looking like this? You think I chose it?', but it didn't matter. And it doesn't matter, because life *isn't* fucking fair, and I can't believe you're telling me I don't understand 'not fair' and saying all these people are swarming around me when *not a single fucking person* looked twice at me until Henry, and then there's you, who ticks all the right boxes with how a girl should look and feel, and—"

"—and where has it gotten me?" she interrupted me, "Look at where it's gotten me. Here. Being shouted at by the one person in the world who I think is amazing. No one fucking wants me anyway—"

I made a frustrated noise. "*Fucking hell, Bree*! Do you even *ask* people if they want you before just telling them they don't? Or do you just bulldoze people like always and completely disregard what's actually going on for them?"

"I don't need to fucking ask them, Min, because I can just tell they—" She was cut off by the train thundering into the station and throwing a wall of air against the side of us. Her curls blew everywhere and she had to hold her dress down, but it didn't distract her even a bit. She just yelled over the top of it. "—Well, people would tell me if they were into me, wouldn't they? Or maybe not, like, say it, but they'd try something! But they don't! I'm 18, and no one has seriously—"

I took a step towards her, throwing out my hands. "That's exactly fucking it, Bree! You're *18!* Maybe that's more of an issue for people than you think! Maybe people don't want to take advantage of you because you're so young—"

"Apparently I'm not too young for *you* to take advantage of!"

My jaw dropped. "You fucking take that back, Bree," I ordered her. "I've never laid a *finger* on you!"

"Yeah, but you let me do all this stuff for you. You totally let me, and you don't even say thank you! You just act like letting me do it should be thanks enough!"

"You don't take no for an answer, Bree! What the fuck was I supposed to do? Take out an intervention order? *Move house*? Assume a secret identity?"

She narrowed her eyes at me and she fixed me with a really hurt, really solid glare as the train slowed on the edge of the platform. "Fuck off, Min, you already have one of those, and you can blame me all you want but we both know you don't need any help to run away from things you're not okay with. You're already pretty fucking good at it."

I *was going to fucking strangle her*. I put my hands up to my head, breathing heavily. "You drive me *fucking crazy*, Bree," I told her. "What the fuck do you want? Do you want me to be sorry that a girl kissed me last Friday? Well, congratulations, because I am! Fucking believe me, I am!"

As the train came to a complete stop and the station PA system announced its arrival, Bree just watched me. "There are two things in this world that I want," she said bitterly. "I want my shithead brother to go to jail and never get out, but he won't. And I want this one person. Like really, I really, really want them, but they're not interested in me like that."

I sighed at her. "How the hell do you actually know that person isn't interested? Do you have any actual evidence or have you just decided it for them like you always do?"

One second I was looking down at those big hurt eyes of hers, and the next, she'd gotten a hold of my tie—her tie?—and pulled me down on top of her. I threw a hand out to brace myself on the back of the bench so I didn't crush her, but it looked like she wouldn't have cared if I had. She wrapped her arms around my neck and hooked her leg behind my knee, and for such a tiny person she was really strong. She was so close to me, I could smell her vanilla shampoo and I could feel her body pressed all against mine and feel how fast and shallow her breathing was... and how warm and soft she was, and how smooth her skin was... and I responded to that. I couldn't *not* respond to that. She was gorgeous, and infuriating, and I cared about this gorgeous, infuriating girl so fucking much, and yet I was *so angry with her* and *so full of adrenaline* and I wasn't sure if I *wanted to fucking tear her to pieces* or just *fuck* her. I didn't do either; of course I didn't, no matter how much I wanted to. I just froze.

As a result she nearly managed to kiss me. Nearly. But this time I wasn't drunk, and my reflexes were better. Determined not to cheat on Henry *again,* I managed to pry myself away just in time, with my blood still pumping and my skin still humming from her touch. I stood back, weak. I was shaking even more violently than she was.

Finally, those tears that had been swimming in front of her eyes for last minute spilt over her cheeks again. "There's my evidence," she said to me, sounding so, so hurt, and pushing roughly past me to walk towards the open door of the train.

I tried to stop her. "It's not that simple, Bree!" I told her. She shrugged me off and stepped into the carriage, standing in the doorway to block me from getting on, too. She was actually going to go home, I realised. She wasn't bluffing. Even though I was an inch away from killing her, that made me panic. "Come on, get off the train and come back to my car, it's late, you shouldn't—"

"I wish you really *did* care about me," she hissed, interrupting me. "Instead of just *saying* all this stuff."

God *fucking damn it!* "Are you fucking kidding, Bree? Are you serious? Do you *actually* think I don't? After everything?"

"Yeah, I don't, because just saying something over and over doesn't make it real," she said, and then paused, teeth almost grit. "You 'care about me' like you 'love your boyfriend', right?"

I had it in my head the whole time that I wasn't going to go where she was going, I *wasn't* going to sink to her level, but that... that just *sealed it.* "Adult relationships are complicated, Bree," I yelled at her, "I wouldn't expect someone *your age* to understand. Just following people around and waiting for hours for them and opening their mail doesn't constitute a relationship." I watched her jaw drop and the heart-break spread across her face. "It's called stalking, Bree, so forgive me if I don't *thank* you for it."

She didn't say anything else, because the transparent doors shut and she leant against them, staring open mouthed at me for a second. God, the hurt on her face. The *hurt on her face*. I was watching the one girl that fucking twisted me inside out *breaking* in front of me and *every single part of it was my fault*. As the train began to pull away from the station, I watched her collapse on the steps just inside the door and curl into a little ball as she began sobbing.

No, I thought, as the train pulled away. No, no, no, this isn't supposed to be how this fight ends. This isn't where we leave it.

I ran after the carriage for a few metres, and then it was too fast and I gave up, staring at the back of it as it disappeared down the tracks.

'...It's called stalking, Bree, so forgive me if I don't thank you for it.'

Did I really say that to her? Did *she* really say those things to me? God, I... Did I really just...?

Her *face.* That final expression was *burnt* onto my retinas. She was looking at me like she just couldn't understand it. Like she couldn't believe I was saying that to her. But I was.

Fuck. I'm a *monster,* I thought fiercely, crumpling on the bench Bree had been sitting on. I was *shaking.* How could I hurt her like that? On *purpose*? Like... it was one thing to accidentally hurt her by kissing another woman. But... saying those things to her when I didn't even really feel like they were true, *knowing* how much they would hurt her? *So* they would hurt her?

I took out my phone, my hands shaking so much and my palms so sweaty that it was almost impossible to use. "*I'm sorry,*" I texted her. "*Fuck, Bree, I'm so sorry, I didn't mean any of that.*"

She replied quickly. "*yes u did*"

"No, I didn't!" I told my phone aloud, and tried to call her. She rejected the call, and then once more when I tried her again. "Answer the phone, Bree!" I yelled at it when I rang her a third time, and when she rejected the call and her cheerful voicemail recording began, I nearly *threw* my phone at the train tracks.

Resting my elbows on my knees and my head in my hands, I just stared at the asphalt between my sneakers. Why did we just *do* that? I couldn't answer that question. I should have just kissed her, I thought. Then she wouldn't be on that train, we wouldn't have *said* those things. She'd still be safe and here with me and not *bawling her eyes out, alone.* God...

I didn't really know how long I sat there—whatever the time between trains was, I guess, since the next one was apparently due—when I heard heels clopping along the platform. I didn't look up so I didn't have to make eye contact with whoever it was. I just kept staring down at the asphalt on the platform.

"I'm guessing this means the rescue party didn't go too well," Sarah's voice said, and there was a swish of fabric and the bench shook as she sat down beside me. I sighed heavily as I felt a gentle hand touch my shoulder. "Are you okay?"

I shook my head. I still felt weak.

Then, to my surprise, she put her arms around me and rested her head against my shoulder. Even more surprising was the fact that I *did* find it comforting. It was just nice to have someone do that, even if I didn't fucking deserve it. I wasn't going to cry, I wasn't...

"Is it too soon to ask what happened?" She said, leaning away from my shoulder and giving my back a rub.

My throat was dry, and so were my lips, and it took me a couple of seconds to say anything. "I don't know," I said. "But she didn't deserve it." I sat up, swallowing. For once, Sarah didn't push me. She waited for me to speak. "It all started off like a conversation and..." I shook my head again. "I don't know what happened. I've never done *anything* like that before. The things I said..."

Recognition dawned on Sarah's face, and she smiled a bit. "Been there," she told me. "Not with Rob, he's a big teddy bear. But my last boyfriend... We had the cops called on us once just because of how much we yelled."

I watched her carefully. "And he wasn't right for you in the end?"

She shrugged. "Well, he might have been, and we were together for nearly five years, but he took a job in England, and I got a job with Frost, so..." She rubbed my back. "Don't worry about Bree. She's crazy about you, give it a few days to settle and then tell her you're sorry."

"If she'll ever talk to me again."

Sarah gave me a look. "What, did you like *hit* her or something?" At my horrified expression she said, "Okay, okay, I was just asking because you're acting like you've never had a nasty fight with anyone and you're just..." While she spoke to me, she was watching my expression, and as she said that her eyebrows went up. "Are you kidding me? You've *never* fought with Henry?"

"Henry doesn't really fight."

Sarah was shaking her head as she thought about what I'd said. "I think you're dating a robot," she told me. "Because the way Bree reacted tonight? That's the way Henry *should* have when you told him about you and Gem, and you're not even officially dating Bree."

I know, I thought, but my head was in too much of a tangle for me to be able to think any further about it. Bree, I thought. *Bree.* How could I do that to her?

"Come on, Toyboy," Sarah said, and gave my back a motivational pat. "You can't sit here all night. Let's get you home." She walked me arm-in-arm back to the car and then put her hand out to me when we got there. "I'll drive," she said. "You're a mess. I say that in the nicest possible way."

I wouldn't let her take the keys. "I'm going home afterwards," I said. "I'm right to drive."

She gave me this appraising look. "You sure?" she asked, "I'm not going to find out on the news tomorrow that star marketing lead Min Lee drove off the end of a bridge last night, am I?"

I rolled my eyes at her. "*No.*"

"Just checking," she said as she got into the passenger seat. "Okay."

We drove in silence back to her house, and I pulled up to the curb beside her driveway and stuck the car in Park. We sat there for a minute or two.

"So... this is a bit left field, but what are you doing for Easter?" Sarah asked me, eventually. "I know Henry's going to Seoul, but what are *you* doing?"

I shrugged. "I assumed I'd be working."

"And it doesn't matter where you do that from, right?" I shrugged again, and she grinned, leaning forward and putting both hands on my arm. "Awesome. You're coming up to Broome with me, okay? I spoke to Rob about it already, and he's hooked on the idea of having someone to play video games with." I must have looked a bit hesitant, because she patted me. "Oh, come on. You can't just sit around at home and feel sorry for yourself at Easter. We can eat ourselves sick on chocolate and then you can listen to me cry about how terrible I look in bathers afterwards."

I had to smile a bit at that. I wondered what Bree would be doing, and then I felt another stab in the chest.

"I know it's controversial, but I'm interpreting your silence as consent and booking your flights on the same plane. I hope that's cool."

"I actually don't really like chocolate," I told her, chuckling.

She looked aghast. "Well that's it," she said. "You're clearly *not* a woman. Fine, I'll just eat all the chocolate by myself and you and Rob can cane each other on... whatever game he's obsessed with at the moment. The one with guns that you need to shoot everyone else with."

I laughed at her. That described half the games on my shelves. Before she got out of the car, though, I remembered one of the things Bree had yelled at me and stopped her.

She turned back to me, eyebrows up. "Hmm?"

I struggled a bit even though I knew what I wanted to say. "Thank you."

She broke into a smile. "Don't think I'm too altruistic," she said, eyebrow twitching. "I'm actually only offering because I know I'll really enjoy having you up there, and so will Rob. Drive safe." I nodded, and she shut the door behind her and waved as I left.

I had been feeling a little better after that. Unfortunately, that mood wore off and by the time I got home I'd already started to go over everything Bree and I had said to each other in fine detail and the knot in my stomach was back. The worst thing was how I'd last seen her: curled into a tiny little ball, sobbing her eyes out on the train. How could I *do* that to her? Even after what she'd said to me? She was alone, crying on a train in the dark. I couldn't have put her in any *more* danger.

As soon as I'd parked under my building, I took my phone out and texted her again. *"Please just tell me when you get home, so I know you're okay..."*

Again, she replied quickly. *"no"*

I deserved that, I thought, sighing and slipping the phone back in my pocket as I got out of the car. When I got upstairs, I opened my door to Bree's school shoes and her schoolbag. All her stuff was still here, and as I was looking down at it, I saw her tie was around my neck. *That means I have to see her again*, I thought, feeling both heartened by that and really terrified at the thought of her not wanting any more contact after she'd retrieved her stuff. Really terrified, actually, terrified enough that it made my heart race. She's the only one who knows all about my gender stuff, I realised. Some of the stuff Bree knows I'd *never* tell anyone else. Not even Sarah.

Fuck, what if she *didn't* want to see me again?

That thought drove me to the pantry in search of wine, and when I opened it, expecting to see two empty shelves and a whole lot of bottles on the third one, I got a surprise. The top shelf had a cut loaf of fresh bread — bakery bread, I thought — a jar of Vegemite, a packet of pasta and a packet of long grain rice. There were even two apples in a bowl and a can of something beside them. I inspected it; it was pasta sauce.

The fridge had food in it, too, and worst of all, *worst of all*, there was a little can of Red Bull. I could see something stuck to the back of it, so I lifted it up.

It was a post-it note with a familiar lopsided smiley face. '*Surprise!*' was written underneath.

I let the fridge fall closed while I was looking at it, feeling like I'd been punched in the stomach. She'd done all this for me, I thought. Thinking of me, imagining how I'd react when I found it. And I called her a stalker and told her to stop deluding herself. After everything she'd done for me, after how good she made me feel about myself and how open and accepting she was of me, *that's* how I repaid her? 'Bree, I tolerate you because I don't have a choice'?

I put my hand on my chest, over where it was *aching. It's not true, Bree*, I thought. It's not true. That's not how I feel about you.

I couldn't deal with any of it, so I had a couple of codeine for the hole in my chest and I just took one of the bottles of red wine to bed with me.

As a result, I woke up some time on Saturday with a pounding fucking headache that even two more codeine wasn't likely to make a dent in. I pulled the covers back over my head and probably would have just stayed there for the rest of the day if I hadn't been busting to go to the toilet. It was the only thing that got me out of bed, and then I spent the next two hours of the early afternoon staring at my unread work emails and not opening them.

Instead, I found myself on Bree's Facebook page, wondering if she'd posted something that would at least confirm she got home okay. She hadn't. There had been no activity on her account since yesterday, and that made me worry. It was stupid, I know; Sarah was right, and Bree was right: Bree *was* an adult. But after what I'd done and how I'd left her, I still worried. She'd been so upset, and so tiny curled up in that little ball.

The last photo she'd uploaded was that lovely one of her in the red t-shirt I'd bought her, and I looked at it for a while, wondering what had possessed me to be so cruel to such a sweet person who thought the world of me. She *had* been rude, but she'd been hurt, and rightfully so. *Fuck*, and I'd just gotten *stuck* into her. Seeing her gorgeous smiling face in the photo and remembering how destroyed she'd looked when she'd left me was too great a contrast for me to be able to deal with.

It ended up getting on top of me and I texted her again, "*Bree, I'm so sorry. I hope you're alright...*"

This time, she didn't reply quickly. In fact, by dinnertime she *still* hadn't replied, and because I kept checking my phone while I was trying to cook dinner, I basically turned the rice into glue. Mum would have disowned me if she'd seen it. Actually, she'd probably just disown me if she found out I didn't have a rice cooker. If she ever found out about the person who caused me to ruin the rice...

I waited until midnight and then gave up. She was probably holding up to punish me, and I definitely deserved it, but part of me couldn't help but be *really* worried. I couldn't decide which scenario troubled me more: that she'd never reply because she didn't want to see me again, or that she'd never reply because something had happened to her. Only three-quarters of a bottle of red finally put me to sleep.

I woke up the following morning... or afternoon... or whenever it was, to the sound of knocking on my door. I sat up in bed, listened, and then lay back down again. It was probably room service, because Bree wouldn't knock, and Henry only came around when he was... invited. *Shit*! What day was it today? Was it Sunday? I checked my phone and I had two messages. I hurriedly unlocked it, hoping desperately that maybe Bree had finally replied, but neither of them were from Bree, just Henry. Both of them asked if midday was still okay, the second one also asked if I'd gotten the first. Shit. It was nearly 12:15.

I couldn't be bothered, I really couldn't. I *really* didn't feel like getting into my *nice* clothes and putting on makeup and being a good little girlfriend... but I couldn't just ignore him, could I? He was just being his lovely self. I tapped on the handset icon and put the phone to my ear.

The knocking stopped. "I promise I'm not trying to beat down your door," he answered.

"I'm sorry, I was asleep," I said, and then I groaned. "Fuck, Henry, I'm sorry, I totally forgot."

He laughed gently. "It's okay, I don't blame you, you have *so much* work at the moment. I'll wait for you to get ready."

Get 'ready'? I didn't feel like getting out of bed. I felt *so* physically ill and so emotionally drained that going back to sleep seemed like the best option. I rubbed my face in one of my hands; I *couldn't face stockings*. I couldn't even face pretending that I didn't feel really *wrong* in them. I had to, though, didn't I?

"Min? Are you okay?"

"No," I said, letting my nausea win. "I'm in bed. Can you just come in?"

He paused. "Uh, sure, I'll be right there."

He was, too. It took him the space of about ten seconds—it would have been five, but I heard him shout as he nearly tripped over Bree's schoolbag in the hallway—to get into my bedroom. The look on his face as he walked up to the bed... "Min, you look..." Like a guy, I thought, you can say it. It wasn't what he was thinking at all, though. "God, are you alright? Is everything alright?" He sat down on the edge of the bed and felt my forehead. It wouldn't have been hot. I couldn't pretend I was sick.

"This is how I look without makeup," I said miserably.

That made him look even more worried. "Min, I've been with you for three years, I have happened upon you not wearing makeup before. I can pretend to be horrified if you want, but I'm not," he told me as he stroked my cheek. He was about to say something else when he noticed the empty wine bottle on my bedside table. His eyes rested on it for a second, but he didn't comment on it. Instead, he just watched me at length, his brow knit. "Min, I think you should take the week off work," he said. "You've landed that pitch after Easter, you'll be ready for it, you need a break."

"I've got a pitch this week, too. On Wednesday."

He winced. "*This* week? When did you find out about that?"

"On Friday."

There was a little 'ah' moment visible on his face. "No wonder you're so stressed out." He bent down and kissed my forehead, looking a bit relieved. "Well, I guess there go my dinner plans for us tonight. Can I do anything for you instead?"

I looked up at him smiling warmly down at me. He's really handsome, I thought. Handsome and kind. It was such a pity that it was wasted on me. "You can stop being so wonderful," I suggested. "That would help."

He looked surprised, and then he laughed. "Because it makes you feel guilty about being a grump?" he asked, and then leant down a placed another firm kiss on my forehead. "Sorry. That's not how I work." He stood up. "Let me get you a glass of water. If you're feeling as hung-over as you look, that should get you on the road to recovery."

He got up and went to the kitchen, and handed me a glass of water when he got back. I accepted it from him, sitting up against the headboard and taking a few sips.

He climbed up on the bed next to me and sat on the other side, his long legs stretched out in front of him on top of the doona. He looked down at them from a second, and then at me. "There's food in your cupboard," he observed.

I'd forgotten about that. Bree. My stomach knotted at the thought of her cheerfully buying it for me. "Yeah."

"You don't like Vegemite."

The knot tightened. "I forgot to tell Bree that," I said. "And she's the one that bought it."

He nodded once, slowly. "Okay," he said, and then appeared to completely accept it. "Well, that's nice of her. It's nice to know that even when I'm not around you're eating something other than greasy takeaway." I finished the water, and put the glass on the bedside table, next to the empty wine bottle. He was still watching me. "Would you like me to make you something? I saw some pasta and some sauce in there. Perhaps you feel like that?"

I shook my head. "It's okay, Henry, I'm not hungry. Thank you, though." He was still watching me, and it was unnerving. I felt like he could read my mind when he looked at me like that, and I didn't want him to know what was in there. I changed the subject. "How did Alice and Zhang like the pram? You never told me. Were they fooled by the beautiful masterpiece of fake baby vomit I smeared all over the canopy?"

It worked, and his eyes lit up as he remembered. "Oh, that's right!" he said. "Yes, actually, and their two oldest insisted on being pushed around in it while I was there, so Zhang and I somehow ended up racing them around using the old pram. The spaceship pram would have won, but that sneaky bastard *cheated.* I should never have lent him *Grand Theft Auto...*"

He started telling me what had happened, and I pretended to listen. No, that wasn't true, I *was* listening, it was just that I kept being distracted by how indulgently he talked about the kids and their family and how animated he looked when he was telling the story.

Halfway through it, when he was talking about how exhausted Alice was and how delighted she'd been when they'd found out they were going to have twins this time, he took my hand, absently turning it over in his as he spoke. When he saw me looking down at it, he smiled, and there was so much gentle patience in that smile.

And, fuck, it *hit* me what it meant. Like a tonne of fucking bricks dropped from the Empire State Building. He had all these plans for us; he never talked about them, but I knew they were there. He wanted to give *me* massages and soak *my* swollen ankles while I was pregnant with his twins. He wanted the white picket fence in the suburbs and the seven-seater four wheel drive full of children. He wanted Christmas stockings over the fireplace, and Easter egg hunts on crisp April mornings, and preschool and theme park holidays and graduation dinners. He wanted to grow old with me on our front porch, watching the street change over the years. He gave me space and he gave me time because this is where he assumed we'd end up if he was patient: together, holding hands on our matching rocking chairs and watching our children's cars pull up with *their* children inside.

And I couldn't do it.

I can't do it, I thought, feeling tears well up in my eyes as I looked at him. Henry, I can't do this. This isn't what I want, I can't ever be the mother of our children. I'm not a woman, I can't ever be a mother. I would be *miserable*.

No, I corrected myself: I *am* miserable, and I want to be happy.

I just want to be *happy*.

He stopped talking and the smile fell off his face when he saw my eyes fill with tears. He leant towards me, putting a hand on my leg over the doona. "Min? Fuck, are you alright?"

My hand flew up to my mouth and for a second I couldn't say anything, I could only shake my head as my eyes brimmed. "I love you," I breathed through my fingers. "Henry, I love you."

He didn't know how to take it, because I was obviously about to cry. "That's the first time you've said it," he told me eventually, looking like *he* was going to cry. He hugged me so tightly, and I stared over his big shoulders wishing they were smaller shoulders, softer shoulders, and knowing who I wished they belonged to. Remembering what I'd done to that person, the tears spilt down my cheeks.

He wanted to cuddle a bit after that, and I was *so* not up for it. I let him anyway, feeling hollow and disconnected and like I was absolutely the worst person in the world in every possible way. He was so lovely, and so gentle. He was so wonderful to me. And I loved him, I knew I did... but not in the way he wanted me to, and I never would.

Afterwards, Henry lay next to me, lacing our fingers together and just looking so, so happy.

I lay beside him and *ached*, just *ached*, wishing I hadn't said those awful things to Bree, wishing I loved him like that, wishing I *could* love him like that, and that I was the woman that he thought I was. But no amount of wishing, or pretending, or going through the motions was going to make any of it true. It was all crap and I just *ached.* I was going to have to tell him, and I didn't know how. But I couldn't leave it like I had with Bree. I had to tell him. I tried to put the words together in my head as I lay there, but none of them seemed right. What was the right way to break someone's heart?

"Well, I imagine you've got a lot of work to do," he murmured next to my ear, interrupting my thoughts. "And I don't want to be responsible for you not getting things done. I've been here for a while…"

I nodded, relieved.

He kissed me briefly. "I'll head off now," he said. "Would you like me to make some reservations on Wednesday night, instead? Or will your team be celebrating after the pitch?"

"I think we'll all actually just go home and die in our beds after it," I said honestly. "It's going to be *so much work*."

He chuckled. "Well, let me know, then. If you're not up for it, we can just have a quiet night in before I fly off to Seoul." He made a noise. "Oh, that reminds me. What do you want me to pick up for your mother? More of those weird Coogee jumpers she likes?"

The knife twisted in my chest. "Sure," I said mechanically. "I'll pay you back, just let me know."

He waved his hand at me as he climbed off the mattress. "I make twice what you do," he said. "It's fine." He stood at the end of the bed and went to fix the doona; he'd messed it up while he was sitting on it. While he was doing that, a sock fell out of it and he bent down to pick it up, probably thinking he'd drop it in the clothes hamper on his way out. When he picked it up, though, he stopped for a second.

It was a knee-high school sock, and the step was *tiny*.

His mouth opened a little, and he looked from it to me. "She sleeps in your bed?"

The colour drained from my face. "Yeah, the couch hurts her back."

He nodded slowly, looking down at it again. He didn't seem satisfied with that answer.

Please ask me, I thought. *Please* just ask me. Ask me how I feel about her. I am *so, so* tired.

For once he didn't, though. He didn't get out his Masters and use it to pick me apart. He just nodded again, resolutely, and said, "Well, that's nice of you to let her take the bed. The couch must be even more uncomfortable for someone as tall as we both are." I sighed.

I did get out of bed to show him out, though, in my old, ugly t-shirt and his tracksuit pants. He laughed a bit at that. "I can't believe they fit you," he said, and then gave me the once over. "It's kind of nice seeing you dressed-down. You don't have to always look perfect in front of me, you know. You're already perfect."

My *heart*. I put my hand to my chest from the discomfort, and that served to remind me that my breasts were unbound and visible. It made me self-conscious, even in front of Henry. "Apart from these, I look like a guy," I said flatly. "If that's what you think 'perfect' is."

He grimaced at how I'd put it. "I don't know, there's something a bit attractive about women when they're dressed boyishly," he said, his eyes twinkling. At my expression, though, he opted not to keep flirting. "Look, don't worry so much, you're not in high school anymore," he said. "And don't work yourself too hard, okay?"

He walked me down the hallway to the front door, kissing me as he said goodbye. Just before he left, though, he gave me this long, measured look. "I love you," he said, and then left without waiting for me to reply.

I stared at the door after it fell shut, and then down at Bree's schoolbag. I was so sore, and tired, and drained, and I'd had enough of today. I couldn't face my laptop or anything related to work; but I also couldn't face lying in bed and having to think about Henry and I. *That* worried me more, so I sat down in front of my laptop and used every ounce of resolve I had left to turn it on and address the steady stream of emails from my team.

They started on Friday night with queries, and together the four of them managed to answer most of their own questions but they'd formed this annoying habit of appending everything they wrote with, 'Better just wait for Min to give us the ok'. That habit meant that by today — Sunday — they were all getting pissed off about the fact I hadn't replied to any of them. Ian had even CCed Jason in a, 'has anyone heard from Min?' email and Sarah had replied to it by saying, 'Yes, actually, I have, and she's working on the templates right now'.

Fuck, I thought, staring at my completely blank templates. Fuck, I'm screwing up, I've got to do this now. I looked up at the clock: 2 pm. If I really knuckled down, I could have the templates for all the material ready for content by tomorrow morning and just pretend I'd been working solidly on them all weekend and hadn't wanted any distractions. But *fuck,* I'd need to get my act together.

I usually put music or cartoons or something on while I was doing graphics, but as soon as I thought 'music', it reminded me of Bree and that USB she'd spent hours making for me and I felt like *shit*. I put it on anyway, partially to torture myself because I deserved it, and partially because she'd made a playlist called 'cheer up' and I wanted to see if it worked. Most of the songs were okay, I guess, but I wasn't completely sold on it until I got to *Things Can Only Get Better* and saw my head nodding along to the music in the reflection of the balcony doors.

I was making some progress and feeling markedly less shit about everything when I felt the table vibrate under my tablet. I stopped immediately, looking up. That was my phone. *Bree,* I thought, and yanked my ear buds out, feeling around under print-outs spread out around me for where I'd put it. When I finally found it, it was from a landline number I didn't recognise and my heart lifted. I really couldn't think of who else would call me from a number I didn't have saved.

"Bree?" I answered, worried she was going to be *really* angry.

Instead, there was a laugh down the receiver. "Yeah, *you're* not smitten. Guess again," I recognised that voice, and it wasn't Bree's. "Actually we don't have time for that. It's Sarah. Are you on your computer?"

I looked across my tablet at it. "Uh, yeah?"

"Okay, good, I need you to get onto Facebook right now. As in, right now. There's something you need to see."

TWENTY

As soon as Sarah had said the word 'Facebook', the only thing I could think was: *Bree.*

"Fuck, has she posted something?" I asked Sarah, immediately reaching across my tablet to the keyboard and switching to my browser.

"Schoolgirl? Not this time," Sarah said, and then paused. "And by the way we'll talk more about why you immediately thought of her later, but now you need to type John's name into the search field."

Wait, *John*? As in, work John? "I'm typing *John's* name in here? Why?" I asked, but followed her instructions.

"You'll see," she said cryptically. "Is his profile loaded yet?"

"Yeah..." I said as it did. "But I don't see what—" I stopped talking as soon as the images loaded, because even without clicking on the thumbnails, I recognised them. They were three of the pictures I'd painted—all test landscapes that we'd decided not to use—along with the text '*The best thing about working at Frost is being surrounded by all these talented people! Check out these pictures that my lead painted! I can't tell you what they're for, though, because it's confidential...*'

I could hardly believe what I was seeing, and I had to click on each one to check I wasn't mistaken. Was he *fucking serious?* First he's sending unencrypted emails, and then *this?* I almost couldn't believe it. Could someone actually be *that* stupid? "Yeah, John, and what the fuck do you think 'confidential' actually means?" I asked aloud.

"Apparently it means 'upload graphics to Facebook so that my friends-of-friends can all see our theme'," Sarah said. "I only saw them just now because I haven't been on Facebook for a couple of days."

I checked the date on them: *Thursday.* "Fuck, they've been up for *four days*," I realised, and then I went to take a look at who he had friended, hoping it was just friends and family. Unfortunately, there were several faces I recognised from Marketing. More than several, actually. "And he's got *half of Marketing* on his friends list. *Fuck!*" I said, sitting back and running a hand over my hair. "*Why*, John?"

Sarah made a sound like a vocal shrug. "He probably thought we're not using them anyway, and there's no specific details on them, so...?"

"Yeah, but who uses Australian landscapes to broker deals with Australian political parties?" I asked, only realising the gravity of what was happening as I actually said it. "Fuck, that's it, isn't it? No one would use landscapes to sell interest in Frost to *any* Australian political party. This is basically a big neon sign saying, 'Hey, guess what! We're not doing a political pitch after all, everyone!'. And with half of Marketing following him, it's only a matter of time before one of the boys tells Jason he's done this, and people start asking what we're *really* doing."

"On the bright side, at least now you know, you can get in first, before anyone else tells him," Sarah pointed out.

"Yes, I'm looking forward to *that* conversation," I said. "'Hey, Jason, you know how I said I've got security in my team under control? Well, turns out I'm full of shit'." I took a deep breath. "How the fuck was I supposed to have guessed John would do this, though?"

Sarah made a noise. "You weren't. It's not your fault, he's always been kind of dense. I mean, don't get me wrong, he's a *genius* at analytics and there's no way I could even get close to the stats he burns through in like five minutes, but you know all that stuff he was always saying about marketing? It's like he read the books cover to cover and went to all the lectures, but no one ever taught him how to apply that stuff in real life."

"Well, he hasn't been in marketing for very long, has he? *Frost* is probably supposed to teach him all that he..." I realised what I was saying. Frost was supposed to teach him all that stuff, management at Frost. *I'm* his management, I realised as my stomach bottomed out. Fuck. *Fuck!* "Sarah, it was probably *my* job to be *really* specific about this stuff to him, wasn't it?"

"Uh, you can't teach common sense, Min."

God, I felt sick. I *knew* he was like that, though, didn't I? "Did you ever hear me say not to show the pictures to anyone, though? *Should* I have? Especially when the boys know I have old ones up all over my house, and various places online?" I stared down at my tablet. "Fuck, Sarah, it probably actually *is* my fault he did this. With the stuff he says, we all knew he had heaps to learn."

"You're being *way* too hard on yourself. Besides, you have *heaps* going on at the moment, so it's not like you had all that extra time to watch over him and make sure he wasn't—"

"--*should* I have, though? Ignore all the fourteen million reasons I didn't, *should* I have? This shouldn't have been so left field, should it? Fuck!" I leant back in my chair. "I haven't been focusing so much on work recently..."

"Oh my god, Min, seriously: you're *way* too hard on yourself. You work harder than *anyone* I know, including me, and that's an understatement."

Regardless of whether or not I should have paid closer attention to John, it was definitely going to be *me* that Jason *killed.* "I'd better call John," I said. "And tell him to take them down right now. I'll figure out what to do about him tomorrow, if Jason doesn't behead me."

"Okay, then. Sorry to be the bringer of bad news, even though you've had a terrible weekend. I just thought this couldn't wait, even though I know you've got heaps to do..."

"Yeah, it couldn't, good call." Fuck, though, that 'heaps to do' meant these templates I was already *very* behind on because I'd spent all weekend lying in bed and feeling sorry for myself. Sorting this out was going to get me even *more* behind, and on top of everything, I just couldn't be bothered with this shit right now. "I'll thank you properly later," I told her as we said goodbye. "I promise."

After I hung up I sat back in the chair for a second, staring at John's profile pic smiling back at me. It was his employee ID which was a bit of a strange choice, but it wasn't a bad photo. Fuck, though: he looked *really* young in that picture, and that actually reminded me of Bree. Bree would have done something like this, I thought, and I'd expect it of her. I'd even tell her several times not to and check later that she hadn't. Why didn't I expect it of *him?* Was I *really* taking my eye off the ball? Or was this something that I never could have predicted, even if I *had* been focusing on work?

I'd usually call Henry if I had questions like this. But I couldn't, not now. I just had to attempt to fix this somehow, and that started with getting John to take the pictures down immediately before anyone else saw them.

I tabbed through my phone and selected John's number, putting it to my ear while it rang.

Just stick to the facts and don't get angry, I told myself while I waited for him to answer. 'Take the pictures down off Facebook, this is a serious problem that I need to speak to you about, meet me first thing on Monday morning and we'll deal with it'. Yeah, that was okay, I could say that. Focus on the facts. Henry always says that—I winced. *Henry* again.

I was so busy worrying about me and Henry that it was actually a surprise when the phone rang out. I took it away from my ear to look at it for a moment, and then tried again. John didn't answer a second time, and he didn't even have voicemail.

I put the phone on the table. If I couldn't speak to John right now, I couldn't get him to take down the pictures right now. Which meant more people would see them, and which potentially meant that when I needed to speak to Jason tomorrow, they would *still be up*. Fuck, fuck, I needed him to answer his fucking phone. I tried again: nothing. I texted him, emailed him and messaged him on Facebook to take them down and just *hoped* he'd fucking check at least *one* of those platforms.

I left it a few minutes and then tried calling him again, but he kept not answering, and while I was waiting for him to get back to me and trying to get the graphics done, I just couldn't focus. Everything was taking me twice as long because I was fucking stressing out.

Jason was going to *kill* me. Diane was going to *kill* me. They were going to fire me and use me as an example of how *not* to run a team. All my fucking hard work over the years was going to mean jack shit if I screwed up the one opportunity they gave me to shine. I was basically relegating myself to the Marketing floor for decades. Fuck, after all my work, everything. I gave my fucking *soul* to this company. I picked up my phone and tried John *again*, and he didn't answer. It was *hours* after I'd first tried him, and it was starting to feel like he was actively avoiding me.

I probably finished the templates at midnight or maybe a bit after, but I stayed awake for ages in bed, refreshing Facebook to see if John had taken the paintings down. I wasn't sure what time I fell asleep, but it wouldn't have been earlier than about two.

As a result, when my alarm went off three or four hours later, I was *so* out of it that I almost didn't hear it. After I finally figured out what the noise was and sat up to silence it... fuck, I caught sight of myself in the wardrobe door. I looked like something out of *The Walking Dead.* I didn't have time to worry about that, though, because I needed to get into work and figure out what the fuck I was going to do about John without losing my job.

Before I did anything else I checked Facebook and *thank god*, the paintings weren't there anymore. Thank fucking god. At least there was that, I thought, and went to get ready. I managed to wrangle myself into a dress I hadn't worn for a few weeks and when I was inspecting myself to make sure I looked as uncomfortably female as I was supposed to, I noticed it was hanging off me more than usual which meant I'd lost weight again. Whatever, I thought. That was the last thing that mattered right now.

I had been rushing out the door so I could beat Jason to work when I nearly fell over what was still in the doorway.

Bree's schoolbag and her school shoes.

It's Monday, I thought, looking down at them. It's Monday, and Bree doesn't have any of her school stuff, and she hasn't tried to contact me about it.

A knot started to form in my stomach, and I pushed the feeling aside. She might have called in sick, I thought, wishing I could do exactly the same. *She's probably fine, Min.* Fuck, though, I hoped she *was* fine. It would be my fault if she wasn't. I fought against texting her again as I left for work; I didn't want to end up looking like the stalker I'd accused *her* of being.

I hadn't eaten much over the weekend, and as a result of that and all the pressure I was under, I was a bit light-headed on the way to the office. Enough to force me to stop and actually buy breakfast which I basically never did. When Sarah arrived at Oslo before eight and saw me eating, she raised her eyebrows. "Real food?" she asked me. "Food someone else didn't get for you?"

I shrugged. "Photosynthesis wasn't working for me," I said after I'd swallowed. "Turns out I'd need to get some actual sunlight for that."

I expected her to laugh, but she didn't. "Min, I know you're joking, but you look pretty terrible. Like, *pretty* terrible."

"Gee, thanks," I said dryly, trying to brush it off. "You're too kind."

She looked wholly unconvinced. "I'm getting you about five Red Bulls," she told me, and then put her bag away and went back out into Marketing.

I watched Sarah go, and then looked back at my laptop while it booted.

Bree's school uniform being still at my house... In amongst all this shit with John, I kept thinking about it. Even though she'd been *so upset* on the train, she'd still replied to my texts on Friday, hadn't she? She hadn't replied to them since then, though. I didn't feel good about it at all. It was really unlike Bree, and—

"*Mini!*" The door to Oslo *flew* open and slammed violently against the wall behind it, scaring the living daylights out of me.

In the doorway stood Jason, red-faced and *fuming*, as he *stormed* into the office and marched right up to me, the toe of his shoes almost against my chair legs. "Mini, for fuck's sake, what the *fuck* is this?" He waved a piece of paper in my face, so close that the corners of it actually touched me. I had to squint my eyes shut as he did it.

Normally I was taller than him, but when I was sitting down he towered over me. It was really intimidating, especially when he was *shouting*. I felt light-headed again. We were alone, and while I was reasonably certain he was at least professional enough to not *actually* hurt me... god, I didn't believe it right then.

"I need to talk to you," was all I managed to say. "About John."

"About John? I already *know* about John!" he bellowed, slapping the printout loudly down on the table in front of me. The whole desk shook. "What the *fuck* is this, Mini? Did you give this idiot the impression that *this* was okay?"

I picked up the printout, aware my hand was shaking.

It was an email, and I had expected it to be from someone in Marketing to Jason about the Facebook page, but it wasn't. When I looked at the 'from' address, it was John's, and it was an email saying that he'd been struck down with a terrible bout of food poisoning and was unlikely to return until after Easter. He apologised for missing the pitch to Vladivostok.

Fuck. This made me look *even worse*, and it also meant that however angry Jason was about a week's sick leave at a very critical point in the project, he was going to be *even angrier* about the information leak.

"*Well?*" Jason prompted, at a volume that made my ears feel like they were going to burst. "What were you going to tell me about him? It had better fucking me that he's so sick he's basically in a coma. Because otherwise there's no excuse for missing a pitch."

I took measured breath. "Actually, it's worse..." I began, feeling his eyes *boring* into my skull. "He uploaded three of the test-paintings I did for the slides to Facebook. They were up between Thursday and last night. The only information about them was that they were for this project. I took screen dumps so you could see what—"

"He did fucking what?" Jason interrupted me, and then started *blasting* me again. "*He did fucking what? How the fuck did this happen?*"

I wasn't sure if he was asking me rhetorically, and so I didn't answer for a moment because I thought he was going to follow up. He didn't.

"I asked you a question, Mini," he prompted me, leaning up close. "You do speak *English,* right? *Speaky Eng-rish?*"

I flinched; did he *really* just say that? "I'm sorry," I said in perfect English. "I tried to be really specific to him about the need for confidentiality."

He stood back, taking a breath as he narrowed his eyes at me. "Obviously not fucking specific enough, were you? Jesus Christ, Mini, he's a brand new employee from fuck knows where, some third world country where they probably don't even have Facebook. He needs more fucking guidance than that and you've obviously been ignoring him," Jason told me, rubbing his head for a second. "I am going to get my fucking ass handed to me over this," he told me, and then jabbed his finger in the air down at me. "Mark my fucking words. Diane is going to fucking eat me alive—"

Behind Jason, movement caught my eye and I saw Ian standing in the doorway with his briefcase, eyes as wide as saucers. He was listening.

"And to think I *recommended* you for this project, Mini. What the hell was I thinking? Just because someone can throw some colours and shapes together doesn't mean they can lead a fucking team. I should put you back out in administration where you can just paint pretty pictures all day and not fuck up people's projects!"

Ian's jaw *dropped*, and he looked at someone else I couldn't see. I shifted a little in my chair to get a better view; it was Carlos. They were watching and whispering about what was going on, and then when Jason straightened like he was getting ready to leave, they rushed off somewhere before they got caught eavesdropping. My face was bright red, I could feel it. Fuck, I thought, they will *never* respect me after this, and neither will *anyone* in Marketing when they find out Jason was blasting me. I just sat there trying to hide how much I was shaking.

"Jesus fucking Christ. I'd better not lose my quarterly bonus over this," he finished. "I need a cigarette. When Diane gets back from Vancouver she's going to *kill us both*." He took a deep breath like he was trying to decide what to do. Eventually, he shook his head. "Just bring those screen dumps to my office," he ordered me as he left, "I want to see what the damage is. *Fuck!*"

After he was gone, this heavy silence hung in the air while I sat there and tried to digest what had happened. I should have been angry, but I wasn't; not with him. I felt sick. Sick, and humiliated, and disgusting, and, *ugh*, just *so useless* and *wrong* in every way. It was such a familiar feeling.

I could hardly breathe. I had to, though, because I had to somehow get from here to Jason's office with the USB that had the screen dumps on it. My legs were weak as I made my way there, and, embarrassingly, I nearly rolled my fucking ankle on those stupid heels on the way there. I was pretty sure at least one or two people saw me stumble, too.

Jason didn't take long with his cigarette. In fact, he finished it in record time and came back to scrutinise the screen dumps. This time, he didn't yell at me. What he did do was even worse: he stared at the screen, silent, with his heavy eyebrows low over his eyes and his tree-trunk arms crossed.

I sat there waiting for him to say *anything* for a good ten minutes, terrified that at any second he was going to stand up and start *shouting* at me again, or worse, that he was going to say very calmly that I was fired and I could collect my personal belongings and leave immediately. My head was spinning and I was *so* spaced out. I did *not* feel well.

"Diane is going to rake me over the coals for this," he told me eventually, shaking his head. "That's it, that's the project blown. It's fucking obviously not a political pitch now, is it? Look at all these employees he's got friended, fucking hell. There is *no way* Sean won't get wind of this. God fucking knows what Diane is going to do about it. She's going to *kill us both* when she gets back tonight. What kind of lead *are* you? You need to *spell everything out* with new employees. They're not psychic, *someone* has to teach them how things work. Good fucking job with that, Mini. Great work."

He spent a few more minutes shaking his head at his screen. "Get out of my sight," he said when he was done. "You'd better fucking teach those Sales boys everything they need to know to nail that fucking pitch, because if we don't get this contract signed, I'm betting at least your job is on the line."

I felt that last thing he said like a punch in the stomach. I wandered out of his office, dazed, and completely fucking sure it was my last day at Frost. I'd worked *so hard* on that project, but all anyone was going to remember, all that *Diane* was going to remember, was that I left some rookie to his own devices and he posted confidential material on Facebook.

Fuck. I didn't want Diane to get back. She was fucking terrifying. At the same time, though, I actually *did* want her to get back—and as quickly as possible—because waiting for my sentence and having that axe hanging over me was making it impossible for me to think about *anything* else. Unfortunately, she was on a plane somewhere so I had to spend the *whole day* imagining all the terrible things that might happen while I tried to be productive. Even the five Red Bulls Sarah had actually bought me weren't taking the edge of my exhaustion or my stress.

We only had the morning to get the materials ready—which we did, somehow—and then we sent them off to print while we had a meeting with the Sales team who were delivering the pitch for us. The Sales boys were pretty frustrated about the fact that they only had *one full day* to learn the material and work out how they were going to play it, too, which meant that I needed to deal with a lot of whinging, egotistical men the whole meeting.

"Well, just don't blame us if we blow the pitch and don't get a signature," one of the Sales boys said, ignoring that I'd explained to him we ourselves had only found out the pitch date last Friday. "You're giving us basically no time to prepare, that's all I'm saying. It's going to be a shit couple of days for us."

'Oh, it's going to be a shit couple of days *for you*?' I nearly said.

'Would you like to hear the sort of shit that's going on *for me* at the moment?' I kept my mouth shut though and just forged through it, packing up at the end of the day when we couldn't do any more.

On my way out, I saw Jason had his door shut and his blinds closed, which he never did. That was over me and my team, I thought, and felt guilty about what that meant for the team. What was going to happen to us?

I took my mobile out in the lift; Bree *still* hadn't texted me, and as I was heading downstairs I wondered if maybe she'd be waiting for me outside like she often did, instead. I got out of the lift, looking around the sea of people for blonde curls and a big smile... but I couldn't see her anywhere. She wasn't inside the building, or outside the building, and no one jumped on me and gave me a big hug on the way home. I could have *really* used one about now.

I had thought maybe she'd be waiting for me at home, and when the lift opened and I saw a shadow there in front of my door for a second my heart lifted and I smiled and it... was my clean clothes hamper left there by room service. I carried it inside and just left it in the doorway because I couldn't be bothered dealing with it right now; half the clothes in it were Bree's, anyway.

There really wasn't much left I could do for either of the pitches. I suppose I could have painted graphics for the one to Sasha Burov, but it seemed a bit ridiculous to spend hours searching for references online now when I could just walk outside this coming weekend *in Broome* and do it. That was supposing, of course, that I still had a job this coming weekend.

I switched into my boy clothes and just lay back on the couch.

It was quiet. Really quiet.

Fuck, I couldn't deal with this. I couldn't just sit here remembering Jason *blasting* me or worrying about what Diane was going to say and do. I went and turned on the PlayStation and settled down on the couch with the controller and a bottle of red to play *Call of Duty*. For the rest of the night, I alternated between drinking and checking my phone in case Bree had messaged me. She didn't message me, but Sarah did a couple of times just to check I hadn't jumped off my balcony.

By bedtime I still hadn't heard from Bree, and I was worried enough about the fact she hadn't even come back for her school uniform that I decided to try calling again while I was waiting for my codeine to kick in. Who was going to care if I looked like a stalker, anyway? I was worried about her.

I lay there under the doona and put the phone to my ear. I had been expecting to hear ring tones, but instead I got three beeps and an automated message saying, "*Your call could not be connected. Please check the number and try again.*"

I double-checked that it *was* Bree's number I had selected, and then *did* try again. I got the same message.

...What?

I put the phone beside me on the pillow, feeling sick. Why was her number disconnected? That seemed like a rather extreme reaction to being angry with me. Not that Bree wasn't capable of extreme reactions, but... no. Deep in my gut, I knew that this wasn't a result of her throwing a tantrum and changing her number because of me. *Seriously, Min*, I told myself, *you know something's going on with that girl*. No one wants their brother to go to jail and never get out without good reason. That was what she had said, wasn't it?

Fuck. Why jail, though? Why jail? Had she been lying about not being in danger to me this whole time? Or what if she was so upset by everything that she *had* tried something stupid, or whatever Sarah was worried that *I* was going to do to myself? I shouldn't have yelled at Bree, I thought, messaging her on both Facebook and Deviant Art. I was trying to figure out what else I should do when the codeine must have kicked in and I passed out.

Bree hadn't messaged me back on any medium when I woke up groggy the following morning, and her number was *still* disconnected. I tried desperately to come up with other scenarios that didn't involve anything having happened to her; I wondered if maybe she hadn't paid her phone bill or bought credit or whatever and *that* was why it was disconnected and she hadn't replied. Her family did have money problems, right? But even that didn't explain why she hadn't contacted me on Deviant Art.

Nothing explained it, unless something *had* happened to her. That thought just churned my insides. I had to have another couple of painkillers because of it, and I couldn't even get myself into stockings until they were working, either.

Despite the fact Jason and Diane were so worried about Sean's apparently sinister desire to tank the project, Jason was having a smoke with him on the balcony when I got to work. Jason jogged to the door when he saw me inside. "Mini, get in my office!" he called across the floor, holding his cigarette outside the door so he didn't set off the sprinklers. "I want to speak with you immediately."

Through the glass, I could see Sean's eyebrows go up. He finished his own cigarette, and then patted Jason on the back and slipped past him through the door. "Coffee time," I think I heard him say, shooting me a warm smile and heading inside and off towards the lifts. Jason *scowled* after him. I had *no idea* what to make of that; why the hell would Jason choose to be *friends* with him—and maybe doing whatever else they might be doing—if he was *that* much of a problem?

I followed Jason's instructions to go into his office, where he left me by myself to contemplate my fate for twenty minutes while he went to speak with Diane's assistant. When he finally came back, he just told me Diane would be in the office shortly and we'd meet with her straight away and find out how fucked we both were. On that note he released me to go wait for them both in Oslo, telling me absolutely nothing about whatever conversation he'd obviously had with her overnight.

I wandered back to my office feeling completely overwhelmed, but that didn't prepare me at all for what was waiting for me.

As soon as I got in the door, Sarah spun around towards me with a really intense look on her face. She didn't even greet me. "You're white as a sheet, Min," she told me, "are you alright?" I shrugged as I dumped my handbag in my drawer. She looked concerned about me, but she clearly was on a mission to tell me something else, so she pushed it aside for now. "Sean's looking for you."

I looked up at her. "*Sean* is?"

"Yeah," she said, still with the same expression. "Min, how does Sean know Bree?"

What? That got rid of my disorientation. "Uh, they shook hands in the foyer on Friday afternoon?" I said. "What the hell do you mean 'how does Sean know Bree'?"

Sarah shook her head. "I don't know, he just said to tell you 'a young friend' of yours was downstairs and to go see him, and then he said he had to leave quickly before Diane spotted him here."

"Bree's downstairs?" I repeated.

Sarah looked completely blank. "Yeah, that's what he said, I think."

Fucking hell, and I was supposed to wait here for Jason to come and get me to meet with Diane. Fuck, fuck. I couldn't leave her down there, though, could I? And *goddamnit* I *really* wanted to see her and just make sure that she was okay. I could be quick, I thought. Very quick, Jason didn't have to know. "If Jason comes looking for me can you tell him I went to the toilet or something?" I asked Sarah, who only got time to nod at me before I took off across Marketing towards the lifts, hammering the button and willing one to hurry up and arrive.

If she was downstairs, that probably meant she was okay, right? She *wasn't* lying in a ditch somewhere. That was the most enormous relief, just knowing she was at least physically okay. But, then again, why would she be waiting downstairs for me before work...?

Maybe she just wants to get her school uniform, I thought, wondering if I should run back to Oslo and grab my keycard. I decided against that because I was in such a rush, and because I could just tell reception to code me another if we needed to go back to my place for anything.

The lift took *eternity* to arrive, and even longer to get down, because it was stopping on basically every single fucking floor to collect people who wanted to go and get real coffee. Next to the ride down on Friday with Gemma, it definitely topped my list of the Longest Trips of My Life.

About four years later when the lift finally delivered us all down to ground level, I had to wait for the dozen or so other people to get out first before I could rush out into the foyer. When I did, I couldn't see blonde curls anywhere. Not in the café, not waiting in the atrium and when I rushed outside onto the street to see if she was waiting out there, I couldn't see her there, either. I craned my neck down the road and then checked around the side of the building briefly, but she wasn't anywhere.

I stood outside the front of the building for a moment as peak-hour traffic rushed past, wondering what next. Maybe Sarah had been mistaken about the message Sean had meant to give me? Maybe he'd wanted to say something about meeting Bree on Friday, instead? Fuck, I *really* should go back upstairs in case Jason was already looking for me.

While I was trying to figure out what I should do, I noticed someone who'd pulled over in a loading zone watching me. That made me really self-conscious, especially when I looked like *this*, so I pulled nervously at the hem of my dress and went to walk calmly back inside the foyer. It was no wonder people were staring at me, the way I'd been running like a nutcase a second ago.

As I approached the rotating door, though, the person in the car stopped the engine and got out, looking like he was going to come inside Frost, too. For some reason, that got the adrenaline pumping. There were a million reasons someone might have come into Frost—and even if *he* did want to speak to me, there was no reason it was threatening. Maybe he just wanted directions.

The guy ended up changing his mind and going back into the car instead of following me in. As he did so, I noticed he was wearing a very sharp suit. That got my attention. Hadn't Bree been a bit weird about guys in suits? I watched him through the reflective glass of the atrium, trying to figure out why that was. He didn't seem like a businessman at all, despite the suit. He carried himself like a big, burly security guard or something. The logo on his car read Fischer Mercantile. I'd never heard of them.

The man didn't hang around for long. When nothing happened, he ended up driving slowly down the street with his window wound down. It was creepy as *fuck,* and it made me worry about Bree.

I turned away from the glass, frowning. The guy *had* been kind of old, though, and he was white. Maybe he was a family member? An uncle? Someone else looking for Bree? I didn't like that possibility, because if someone from Bree's family was looking for her, it probably meant *they* hadn't heard from her, either.

Sean might know what was going on if he'd met with Bree. Actually, this might even be what he'd wanted to see me about... but Jason might be waiting for me on level 36 already.

I scrunched my face up. Fuck, *what to do*? It had only been like five or ten minutes that I'd been gone, I thought. If I made it 15 by going to see Sean, it was still plausible that I'd just been taking a long time doing my makeup or something in the toilets. And that's if Jason was even waiting for me from the second I left, which he probably wasn't.

Okay, fuck it, I decided, I'll go and ask Sean why he wanted to see me. I'll just have to be quick.

I took the World's Slowest Lift back up to level 35 to find Sean on the phone in his office with the door closed. His assistant smiled at me and offered me a seat to wait for him, but I shook my head and decided to wait in the hallway instead. I was too worked up to sit down, and I didn't want to just pace around in her office.

I had been wringing my hands and worrying about the time, my job, Bree and that guy in the suit when I heard a familiar voice that was too gentle to be Sean's. "Min! What a nice surprise."

Henry. God, I just couldn't do this right now. I couldn't, but I tried anyway. "Hi..." I said, turning towards him.

He was going to kiss my forehead I think, but when he saw me front on, he stopped leaning towards me and gave me the once-over.

"Min, you look really unwell," he said. "*Really* unwell. Please tell me you're down here submitting a sick-leave form." I shook my head. He gave me one of his Looks of Concern, and then rubbed my arm. "Well, at least it's not long to go until it's all over," he said, not even knowing how true that might be, "and then you can just lie back and relax for a couple of weeks."

I exhaled. Or longer than a couple of weeks if they fire me.

When I didn't say anything, his frown deepened. "You look really unwell, though. Maybe I should cancel my visit to Seoul and just stay back here and take care of you."

"Judging by that expression on her face, Henry, I'm guessing she'd prefer you didn't do that."

I twisted to see Sean leaning out of his office. He had his hands casually in his pockets. "I'd prefer you wouldn't do that, either. Accounting keeps getting on my case about how many banked annual leave days you have." He chuckled and took a few steps towards us. "Min, I'm glad you came so promptly. I need to speak to you about Bree. Please, come in."

I closed my eyes for a second as he said her name, and then glanced up at Henry. Henry looked from me to Sean with a *really* strained expression. It only lasted a second, and then he forced a smile for Sean. "Take care of Min," he said faux-pleasantly. "As you can see, she's not feeling that well."

Sean smiled. "She's a capable adult, Henry. I'm sure she'll tell me herself if she needs anything," he said and then gestured at me. "Come in."

I wanted to apologise and explain myself to Henry, but I couldn't. There wasn't anything I could say in front of Sean, and there really wasn't anything I could explain in general. Whatever he was thinking, he was probably *right* about it. I did give him an apologetic glance as I followed Sean into his office, though, feeling *awful*. The shock and surprise on his face... *Fuck.* Poor Henry. He didn't deserve *any* of this.

Sean showed me into his office at a leisurely, relaxed pace and closed the door. Meanwhile, the clock was ticking.

I couldn't help myself, even if he *was* the co-CEO. I was in such a rush, and on top of that I was *desperate* to know what happened with Bree. As soon as the latch clicked, I asked him, "Is she okay? Was she here before?"

He looked surprised, and then before he answered, he walked slowly around his desk and sat down in his chair. He gestured for me to sit opposite him. "She was here before," he confirmed. "Please, take a seat."

I didn't want to take a seat, I wanted him to confirm she was okay, tell me what happened and then let me go back upstairs and wait for Jason and Diane. I followed his direction anyway, because he *was* the co-CEO. One of my knees was jittering, and I had to consciously stop it.

"I'm worried about your friend," Sean said eventually, leaning back and watching me. "Do you know if everything's okay for her?"

This conversation was already taking too long. "Everything *isn't* okay for her," I said. "Did she say something to you? What did she say?"

He nodded, and let another *agonising* silence stretch between us while he considered how he was going to reply. "She said quite a lot to me."

I was practically bursting, but I couldn't say what I wanted to: 'What did she say? Just tell me what she said!'. I just sat there and pushed down on my knee so it wouldn't jiggle.

"She thought I was one of your teammates, actually. She was desperate to see you, she even asked me to go and get you. Naturally I told her that I knew you were in a very important meeting with your manager and that I wasn't able to interrupt."

Fuck, why was she desperate to see me? If she was that desperate, it shouldn't have waited; as if sitting by myself in a room while my boss stomped around level 36 in a mood constituted an 'important meeting'. "I wish you *had* interrupted Jason," I said kind of bitterly in reply, and then *immediately* regretted it.

I must have looked horrified with myself, because he laughed gently. "Oh, trust me, I know what he can be like, he's a good friend of mine," he said. "Okay, if it happens again I promise I'll impose."

He leant back and watched me again, and I hoped this time, *this* time he'd tell me why Bree was downstairs, what had happened and what she'd wanted.

He didn't. "I just wanted to let you know that if either or both of you need counselling, I can pull a few strings and bill her on the Employee Assistance Program as a family member," he offered. "After all, we bill people's partners on it. Why not... very close friends...?"

Any colour that had been left in my face drained from it. Was he implying what I thought he was?

"That's why I wanted to speak to you in private," he said simply. "If you tell EAP I sent you, you don't need to get approval from HR."

Fuck, I think he *was*. What on earth had Bree said to him? Or had she just simply been crazy and over the top and he was just guessing based on how desperate she'd been to see me?

While I was trying to figure that out, he spotted where I was looking. Or, where he thought I was looking, because I was actually just gazing into oblivion while I worried about what he knew and who he might tell about what he knew.

"Oh, do you like it?" he said, spinning his chair to look at the wall. On it there was an impressionist-style painting of a busy day on Bondi beach. He smiled appreciatively at it. "I received it as a gift for a Fundraiser I attended. It's not ordinarily my style, but it was a nice gesture," he said, and then turned back to me. "Of course, it's not as good as *your* work. I've come across some of it online: very impressive. Anyway," he said, slapping his hands lightly on the desk and standing up. "I can see you're obviously busy, so I won't detain you any longer. I just wanted you to know that my door's always open. Okay?"

I stood automatically because he did, but I could hardly breathe. He'd seen some of my work online? Online on John's Facebook? Or online on... fuck, not Deviant Art? He didn't mean Deviant Art, did he? I almost *hoped* he meant Facebook, partially because I couldn't really believe that he'd have any sort of motive to sabotage a project that would be making his own company money, regardless of what Jason and Diane said. And partially because, fuck, I *really* needed to take that painting of me *off* Deviant Art right away. If he already thought there might be something going on with me and Bree and then he saw *that*...

"Okay," I repeated, and I was *so* distracted by what he'd inferred that I completely forgot to ask him all the questions I'd wanted to about Bree. I managed to get one in at the last minute before he ushered me out of his office. "She was okay, though, wasn't she?"

He pressed his lips together. "She was upset."

The evoked images of when I'd left Bree on the train and the residual codeine in my system didn't even fucking touch how much *they* hurt. God, my *chest.* I felt like I was having a heart attack. "Thanks," I told him a bit vaguely as I left.

When I got out into the hallway, I stood in place for a second, reeling. I didn't know what *any* of that meant, or what the point of it had been—well, no, he'd said he'd wanted to let me know that he'd pulled strings to make counselling available to Bree—but why hadn't he just told me everything that had happened? Surely there was a reason, right? Or maybe Bree had told him something *really* private or *really* embarrassing and he didn't want to intrude...?

I didn't understand. Nothing made sense. Nothing about any of this made any fucking sense and when Diane got in, I'd....

..*Shit.* Jason would be waiting for me!

I rushed into Oslo, hoping desperately in the 25 or so minutes I'd been gone that Diane hadn't arrived. But when I opened the door to the office, I nearly crashed into Jason who was sitting in a chair right near the doorway and obviously waiting for me.

He looked—and I wasn't exaggerating—*furious*. Absolutely like he was ready to string me up by my neck and beat the stuffing out of me. "I've just about had it with you, *I told you to stay here so we could meet with Diane*," he said, and then encircled my wrist and physically *dragged* me out of Oslo. "Diane has been waiting for 15 minutes and we're both going to cop it. What the *fuck* was Sean Frost doing looking for you, anyway?"

Maybe I've started smoking, I thought bitterly as we reached Diane's office and he roughly shoved me inside.

I had expected Diane to look just as angry as Jason did, but she was in the middle of some paperwork and just looked up neutrally when we entered. "Please, take a seat," she said in the most professional tone I'd ever heard. From that tone of voice, I had no idea if Jason had even told her anything.

I sat down in a chair beside Jason and opposite her, feeling him *glaring* at the side of my head. At least he couldn't tower over me while he was sitting down.

Diane took a few moments finishing what she'd been reading, and then set it aside, laced her hands together on the table and looked across at us. "How has the project been travelling, Min?" she asked, and it sounded unassuming. It was delivered like a question she'd have asked me any other day of the week.

"Up until yesterday, very well," I said. "We're on track with all the pitches, and the materials are ready. Sales is learning the content as we speak."

She either feigned interest or *was* interested. "These materials?" she asked, sliding a familiar brochure across to me. I picked it up, it was one of the sales brochures we'd done yesterday for Vladivostok, and... well, it wasn't some of my best work, but it looked passable enough. Professional, and that was the most important thing. I picked it up and flipped through it as she continued.

"There's just something I wanted to clarify with you on the second page," she told me. I looked up and her for a moment, and then flipped through to that page. Jason was fidgeting next to me, and it was distracting. "Just a small question," she asked as she watched me, "is that, there, on the second line, is that how you spell 'relevance'?"

My heart practically stopped. *What*? I looked down at the text, and sure enough, I'd missed that one of the team had spelt it 'relevence'. *Fuck,* I'd *trusted* Ian and Carlos with this. I mean, I knew I should have checked it myself, but did I really have to go over everything with a fine tooth comb like that? They were *professionals,* and they were making me look wholly *un*professional.

I swallowed. "Just a typo," I said. "I should have checked it. I'll get it reprinted immediately."

"Mmm," she said, accepting that. "Tell me about John."

I glanced across at Jason. "He's excellent at analytics," I said. "But he was sending unencrypted emails a couple of weeks ago—"

"—which you reprimanded him for, of course?"

"—of course, which is wh—"

"—what makes it very interesting that he thought it would be appropriate for him to post those landscapes on his Facebook page," Diane finished, still sounding very mild. Too mild. She looked far, far too calm to be heading the conversation in the direction she was. I felt weak again. "Whatever you said to him, it didn't seem to get the message across that this sort of behaviour is unacceptable. Perhaps, given that he's such a new employee, you should have double-checked that he really understood."

I didn't have anything to say to that. She was right.

She took a measured breath, watching me carefully. "This is a concern for me, Min. A big concern. I'm a hundred percent certain my brother has already seen these."

I swallowed.

She was watching me like a hawk. "And he was looking for you, and you were with him a second ago, weren't you?"

I opened my mouth, and then closed it. Jason was *constantly* with Sean and Diane didn't seem to be going off at *him* for that. I'd spent ten minutes with him and now *I* was the bad guy? "It has nothing to do with the project," I said as respectfully as I could.

She and Jason shared a glance. Diane's lips tightened momentarily. "I want to believe you, Min," she said. "I really do. But the timing doesn't look great for you, so I think we're in big trouble."

I looked across at Jason, and he *glared* back at me. "Timing?" I asked, almost afraid to.

Diane took the piece of paper she'd been reading when Jason and I had entered and passed it across the desk to me. It was a printed copy of an email. I looked from Diane to Jason and then at the print-out, and read over it. Then, I read over it again and again, almost not believing what I was reading.

It was an email from Vladivostok, and it was cancelling the pitch.

My jaw *dropped.* "When did this..." I looked at the time on the email; 15 minutes ago. "But, why did they—?" God, all the team's hard work. All *my* hard work. Everything we'd busted our guts over... and one of the pitches had collapsed. I could hardly fucking believe it. I mean, these things happened from time to time, but... they were right, the timing just looked *really* suspicious.

Fuck, the team were going to be *devastated,* and Sales was going to *kill* me.

"I was hoping you could tell me more about the 'why', Min," Diane said, and then directed her full attention to me, waiting for me to speak.

I couldn't tell them anything. I had *no idea* what had happened, but it had to be something to do with Facebook and John and the timing must just have been a massively unfortunate coincidence. Just as I was trying to haphazardly put together some scenario in my head about what could possibly have led to this, there was a knock on the door and whoever was on the other side didn't wait to be told they could come in before they entered.

It was Diane's assistant, and she looked worried.

Diane looked annoyed momentarily. "We're busy, Cadence," she said firmly.

Cadence looked nervous. "I know, I'm sorry to interrupt, but it's an urgent phone call."

Diane sighed. "It had better be," she warned the girl. "Fine, put it through."

The assistant's eyes darted between Diane and me. "It's actually not for you," she told Diane uncertainly. "It's the police. They want to speak to Min."

TWENTY-ONE

"You can put the call through to my office, Cadence," Diane instructed her personal assistant. The girl glanced nervously between us, nodded and then went back out to her desk. As soon as she was gone, Diane looked directly at me. "Why do the police want to speak to you, Min?"

I shook my head; my jaw was still open. I had *no* idea.

"Someone had better fucking be dead, I swear to god," Jason muttered next to me.

Bree, I thought, panicking. It couldn't be anyone else except her. And *fuck* I hoped Jason was wrong; it had only been... 20 minutes, maybe half an hour since she'd been here. Surely that wasn't enough time for something terrible to have happened to her? Something that would get the police involved?

Diane looked like she might say something to Jason, but then her phone rang. Instead of picking up the handset, however, she just hit the 'conference' button.

"Putting the call through now," Cadence's voice said to us over the speaker, and then there was a beep.

"Hello, Diane Frost speaking," Diane said. "I believe you're after Min Lee?"

"Yes, I am," said a woman's voice. "This is Constable Garrett, can you put her on the phone?"

"She's listening now," Diane told her in a don't-argue-with-me voice.

There was a pause. I was pretty sure even the police weren't going to mess with Diane Frost. I was right. "Min Lee?"

My voice crackled at first; my throat was dry. "I'm here."

"Do you know a Briana Dejanovic?"

Any colour that might have been left drained from my face. It *was* about her. "Yes," I said, and even though Jason and Diane were listening, I couldn't help myself. I had *awful* mental images of things that could have happened to her. "Is she there with you? Is she okay?"

"She's here with us. We'd actually like to speak with you in person about her," Constable Garrett told me. "Are you able to come to the corner of Essex and Harrington immediately?" It didn't sound like a request.

Jason and Diane glanced at each other and then back at me; they recognised the address. It was close to the hotel where Frost permanently leased some of the apartments to relocated employees: my building. What had *happened* there? And why did it involve Bree? My heart was racing. I looked at Diane for permission before I answered.

Diane narrowed her eyes at me, and then leant a little towards the phone. "Is it really necessary?" she asked. I think I was holding my breath. "We're in the middle of a very important meeting. Can it wait an hour?"

A *whole hour*? To find out if Bree was okay or not?

"We'd actually appreciate it if she would be able to come down here as soon as possible."

"Is that right?" I couldn't believe how direct Diane was being with the police; I supposed when you were a multi-billionaire the average police officer was of little concern. "You'd appreciate it, Constable Garrett, or it's an order?"

"We would very much appreciate it."

"Thank you," Diane told her resolutely. "Min will be down there in due course." She reached up and hung up the call just as the Constable was saying something else.

I stared at the phone, gaping, as Diane turned away from it. I couldn't focus on anything other than what I'd just heard. If they wanted to speak to me in person that was bad, right? Didn't they have to deliver the news of someone's death in person? That seemed ridiculous, though. I wasn't Bree's next of kin. Why would they call *me* if something happened to her?

"I believe we were about to discuss the fact you were in Sean's office when the Vladivostok pitch was cancelled," Diane prompted me. I looked from the phone to her, distracted.

Jason butted in with, "And the fact that when I told you to stay put, you went straight to his office." Diane didn't look like she welcomed his input, but she didn't say anything about it.

I didn't know how to answer. I could hardly think. Everything was just nuts and I was *shaking*. All these different scenarios were racing through my head: Bree had had an accident and asked for me, maybe Bree's brother had done something and they wanted to know what I knew about him? After all, Bree did say something about jail, didn't she? Wouldn't crimes generally involve the police? Or maybe she'd done something crazy and been arrested and she needed someone to post bail for her and her family couldn't afford that? And while I was grappling with a million questions about Bree, I was completely aware of Diane *staring through me*, wanting me to answer *her* question about Sean and the lost pitch.

I didn't have the answers, not to any of it. Everything was completely over my head, and I forced it out of my dry lips. "I don't know."

Jason looked like he didn't believe me, but Diane was more difficult to read. She just sat there in her high-backed office chair, watching me closely. I didn't think she believed me, either, but after a good few seconds she gave up. She leant back in her chair and crossed her legs. "Go on," she told me shortly. "Obviously you think whatever they want is serious. Jason and I need to have a word about what's happened anyway." The way she looked at him, I think *he* might have been sweating as much as I was. He then turned that same severe glare on me as I left.

I should have been more worried about that, but right now, all I could manage was a mumble of thanks as I rushed out.

Sarah had been loitering around the corner, and as I jogged past she caught up with me. "Oh my god, Min, are you okay?" she asked as we headed for the lifts. "What happened? And why are we practically running?"

I could barely say it. I could hardly believe it, really, but I needed to tell the team as soon as possible. "Vladivostok cancelled the pitch."

She looked at me like she thought she might have misheard me. "*What*?" she said, probably much more loudly than she'd intended. "*Why*? We were solid with them!"

We got to the lifts and I pummelled the button, shaking my head. "I don't know why," I said honestly. "Except Diane and Jason seem to think it has something to do with the fact I was in Sean's office ten minutes ago, but obviously it doesn't, and *now* the police have called—something to do with Bree—and I have to go meet them."

The lift dinged and the doors opened. Sarah just kind of stared at me. "All this happened now? Like in the last five minutes?"

I nodded and as I stepped into the lift, I made a face. "I know this is a big ask, but could you tell the team about Vladivostok for me?" I was cringing even as I said it.

Her brow had a deep line through it. "Yeah," she said a bit vaguely.

The doors slid closed on her gaping at me.

It normally took me about 15 minutes to get home, door to door, but I swear to god right then it took me five minutes to get to the corner of Essex and Harrington. When I turned down the side roads there were *three* police cars all pulled up along the curb of Harrington Street with their lights flashing. I had absolutely no idea what was going on until I saw a familiar man in a suit arguing loudly with two policemen. It was that guy who'd nearly followed me into Frost, and behind him was the car I'd last seen crawling down George Street. It looked different now, though: the windscreen was smashed and the side of it was covered in dents. Its hazard lights were going, and on the road all around it there were little cubes of safety glass *everywhere.*

"Excuse me, are you Min Lee?" a woman's voice asked me.

I turned towards it. "Yeah?"

It belonged to a short woman in a fitted police uniform. She was fully kitted out: gun, baton, high visibility vest and walkie-talkie on her shoulder. She was also holding a notepad in her hand. "I'm Constable Garrett," she said. "Sorry to interrupt your meeting, I hope it's not too much of a hassle."

I shook my head. I was very out of breath. "It's okay," I said. "Where is she? Is she here? Is she okay?" I surveyed the area around us, looking for curls.

The officer made a gesture for me to follow her, and started walking towards the hairdresser's on the corner. "That's what I wanted to discuss with you. We actually need her to come down to the station and make a statement about what just happened."

We passed the Fischer Mercantile car with the dents in it. "Did she do that?" I asked. They were *big* dents.

Constable Garrett cringed. "Allegedly," she said. "And that's what we need her to make a statement about." She stopped on the footpath. "Look, normal process is just to forcibly arrest people who refuse or resist. But she's not doing that well, and probably it would be better for her mental health if you could convince her to come of her own accord. We have a duty of care to make sure she has support if she needs it."

Arrest her? Not doing that well...? "I'm not her next of kin," I told the officer, in case it was relevant.

She shrugged. "We asked her if there was someone we could call for her, and she said you." She was looking pointedly over my shoulder, and I turned to see what was there.

The street had a pretty steep incline, and flights of stairs were spaced along the length of the footpath. Beside them were garden beds that hid them from the road. A police officer was standing a short distance from them, and at first I thought he wasn't doing anything. I was wrong, though, because he kept looking over his shoulder at the stairs beside the hairdresser. In the shadow of a garden bed, I could see Bree on the stairs. She was all curled up in that same foetal position I'd left her in on the train, with her arms around her knees and her head resting on them. There was gravel and dirt *all* over her.

My heart practically stopped and I completely forgot about the officer. "Bree!" I shouted, and ran across the road towards her. I was lucky there was no traffic.

When she heard my voice, she looked up, surprised. From the state of her, it looked like she'd been crying all weekend. Her eyes were puffy and her nose was bright pink, and she just looked *so* lost. I wanted to give her a big hug, but the last time I'd done that she'd pushed me off. So I just stood in front of her at the bottom of the stairs, unsure about what I *should* do.

"What are you doing here?" she asked, her voice croaky.

What am I... "Bree, you *asked* for me," I said, confused.

"I know," she said and just stared at me, stunned and still breathing a bit raggedly. She'd stopped crying, though.

I was so taken aback that I had absolutely *no* idea what to say to that. Didn't she want me here?

Constable Garrett came up behind me. "Worked like a charm," she said, giving both of us a smile. Then she looked at Bree. "You want to come down to the station now that you seem to be feeling better?"

Bree looked from me to the officer, and then pulled herself up and walked past me, following her into the patrol car. I watched them, wondering what the fuck I was doing here if Bree was just going to ignore me, and then followed them into the car anyway.

When I stooped to climb inside, Bree had already barricaded herself all the way across the back seat against the other door, and was gazing out of the window. After I'd buckled myself in, I spent a while worrying about the fact she was too angry to even *look* at me. When I heard her sniff, though, I realised why she'd turned away: she was trying to hide the fact she'd started to cry again.

What's happened, Bree? I asked silently, watching her. *What did you do that ended with us both being in a police car?*

It would have been insensitive for me to ask her what was going on while she was so upset, and the two police officers in the front of the car were obviously preoccupied. The hiss and static of the comms radio kept cutting in and out as we drove; I couldn't really understand what anyone was saying through it, but Constable Garrett and her colleague were in serious discussion about it for most of the way.

The back seat was quiet. Bree didn't say anything to me, and the more silent she was, the more I wanted to ask her why she'd told them to call me. She wasn't making any attempt to talk to me, or ask for comfort, or anything. I wondered if maybe this 'duty of care' or whatever the officer had said they were bound by forced them to contact someone, and Bree didn't want her family to know she was in trouble.

Well, regardless of whether she wanted me to be here or not, it was still painful listening to her crying. I would have apologised about Friday if the police weren't able to hear everything we said, and I would have hugged her if she didn't look so much like she wished none of us were there.

The police car came to a stop and the officer who was driving twisted in his seat. "Here we are," he said to Bree. "Just follow Garrett inside, she'll sort you out."

We bundled out of the car and into the station; it was on the south side of the city, and it was nerve-wracking how close we were to all the Korean shops on Sussex Street. Not that I'd had anything to do with the Korean community in Sydney other than Henry's family, but Mum always seemed to know people who knew people, and if I'd had my phone with me I'd have expected to get a call from her along the lines of, 'What are you doing at the police station with a little white girl when you should be at work!'. *I really don't know, Mum*, I thought, looking down at Bree as we followed Constable Garrett inside.

Constable Garrett took Bree behind the counter straight away, and as she was ushering her into an interview room and promising her everything would be over soon, Bree gave me this frown and then the door closed.

She definitely doesn't want me here, I thought, and then felt a surge of emotion about that. I'd rushed out of a critical meeting because I thought something had happened to Bree and I was so, so worried about her, and she didn't even want me here.

I turned towards the empty waiting room; *everything* was turning to shit. Work, at least, I could probably still do something about. I should call Jason and let him know what was going on, I decided, looking around to see if there was a phone anywhere. The only phone I could see was behind the desk and I didn't have the guts to ask the policeman doing reception duty if I could use it. Part of me was thankful it looked so inaccessible anyway, because I *really* didn't want to speak to Jason right now.

I sat down in one of the chairs. I was in two minds about whether or not I should have left the meeting for Bree at all; on one hand, it was good to see she was alright, even if she was upset and didn't want to talk to me. At least I knew nothing had happened to her. But on the other hand, now Diane and Jason had yet another reason to think I was a screw-up.

Secretly I think I was relieved, though. If I was honest with myself, I was getting extra time to try and make some sort of sense out of what Diane was accusing me of. *Sabotage*, I thought, remembering her drawing a connection between me being in Sean's office and the Vladivostok pitch being cancelled. *Surely* all my hard work made it obvious that that suggestion was outrageous, right? And conspiring with Sean? Why would I want to ruin my marketing career by going behind Jason and Diane's back? And why did Diane have one set of rules for Jason, and another set for me?

None of it made sense. Nothing made sense. And now I was sitting in a police station while Bree was being hauled up for some mystery crime.

I'd grabbed one of the old magazines from a table nearby so I could flick through it and distract myself, when an officer came through the internal door and leant across reception. "Hey, any interview rooms free?" he asked his colleague. "I need to make a phone call."

The guy on reception was in the middle of typing something and pushed a thick exercise book at him. "Check for yourself, mate, I'm not your secretary," he said gruffly, but he was grinning. They were speaking so openly they probably thought I couldn't hear them from all the way over here.

The other officer did check, flipping through the pages and reading the contents. "Whoa, we've got *Fischer* in here again?" he asked, holding the book open so he could read the entry. "What's he done this time?"

The policeman on duty shook his head. "Nah, not him, some kid got sick of his crap and threw a flower pot at his car, we've got her in room three."

"Fair dinkum," the other guy said, and then borrowed a pen to scribble in the book. "Well, I guess he'd better learn that if he ignores the debt collection guidelines, he's going to have people ignoring all sorts of laws in return, yeah?" He laughed. "And room 11 is free. Thanks."

That suited guy was a debt collector? Well, that fit right in with my guess that Bree's family had money problems. I would probably have asked more about this Fischer person, but I had a feeling I wasn't supposed to have heard that conversation and I didn't actually think they'd tell me any more about it.

Bree threw a *flower pot* at his car, though? It explained the dents in it, but I agreed with the assessment that officer had made: Bree didn't look big enough to have caused them.

"Thanks, Briana," I heard a voice say as Constable Garrett walked through the dividing door, holding it open. Bree emerged, walking out past her into the middle of the waiting room where she stood uncomfortably, refusing to look at me. Constable Garrett noticed, but I think she assumed it was over the flower pot incident. "We're all done here. Nothing to worry about, we're not going to charge her," she told me. "I'll sort you out to get home."

The constable organised for one of the units on patrol to ferry us back up there since they were headed up to the Quay anyway, and we got into the back of the car, sitting in silence as we were driven.

Bree was still silent. I watched her as she stared miserably out the window at the pedestrians on George Street, desperate to take her hand or say something comforting to her.

The police dropped us off outside my building in the valet circle. Bree waited besides me as they drove off, hunched with her arms crossed. She was still wearing those dirt-stained clothes.

"You want to come up and change?" I asked her quietly, and she nodded. That was a relief at least. I got a spare keycard coded by reception and led her upstairs.

Once we were inside my apartment she just kind of stood in the hallway.

"Your clean clothes are in the hamper in my bathroom," I told her, because I didn't know what else to say. "You can have a shower if you want, your towel's still on the rack."

She exhaled, and then turned and looked at me with a really forlorn expression on her face. "I can't believe you're even talking to me after Friday."

That felt like a kick in the gut. I deserved it. "I know, I know I don't have any right to," I said. "I just... well. You needed help, so..." I swallowed. "You can leave, if you want."

Her face cycled through a series of emotions: surprise, panic and finally horror. Then, it crumpled up again. "I fuck everything up," was all she said, blinking back fresh tears. With that, she took off and shut herself in the bathroom. I could hear her crying over the sound of the water.

Join the club, Bree, I thought, walking into my bedroom. I'd run out of energy to try and guess what was going on for her. I was exhausted.

I glanced at the clock; it was nearly lunch time. The responsible thing to do would be to go back to work now the police stuff was over, but, then again, Bree was *sobbing* in my bathroom. It would probably be more irresponsible to leave her while she was feeling like this—regardless of how much she didn't even want me to talk to her—than it would be to take the rest of the day as sick leave. With the Vladivostok pitch cancelled there wasn't anything *urgent* that needed to be done. I mean, I should have been there to debrief the team after a failed pitch, but... fuck, they probably all thought I was hopeless, anyway.

The more I stared at my reflection, the more I decided that with all the shit going on, I didn't have enough energy to look like *this*. Fuck it, I thought. I'll take the rest of the day off. I changed into my guy clothes and washed my makeup off in the kitchen sink.

Then, because Bree had turned the shower off, I went and sat on my bed and waited for her to come out. I didn't know what was going to happen when she did, she might just have wanted to go straight home, anyway. She'd stopped crying; that was good, at least.

She didn't come out, though. Five minutes went by, ten minutes.... and she was still in there, silent. It was unnerving.

I stood up and went and knocked lightly on the door. "Bree?" I asked through it. "Are you okay?"

Silence.

I knocked again; maybe she had a towel on her head or something. "Bree?" When she didn't answer, I went to open the door just a fraction so I could talk through the gap. The door wouldn't open, though; she'd latched it shut. I rattled it. "Bree?"

Putting my ear against the wood, I listened. The bathroom usually had really loud acoustics, but I couldn't even hear her breathing. I had this awful vision for a second of discovering Bree in the bath like that scene in *The Virgin Suicides*, but when I rattled the door again, I heard her sigh.

"Why did you even come today?" she asked me in this little voice; it came from just below me. She was seated against the door.

I sighed with relief that she was still alive enough to resent me. "Because I was worried about you," I told her. "Especially after Friday."

"So you just came because you felt guilty."

I groaned and leant my forehead against the door. It was true, but it was only a tiny part of the reason. "No, Bree," I said. "That's not why. Look... I don't know why you asked them to call me. I did come, even though you—"

"Yeah. I thought you wouldn't."

"Why *did* you ask, then?" I said through the door, wondering if I wanted to hear the answer.

"Because I'm stupid," she said. "Even though you think I'm this total screw-up who just follows you around and makes you buy me stuff, I don't know, I just kind of hoped..." She didn't finish the sentence. "I'm stupid."

I sighed. "I don't think those things, Bree." I traced a pattern in the wood on the door with my fingernail. "I was just angry."

"I know, and it's because you're sick of me. And, like, I don't really blame you. You're this giant introvert and I've just kind of been forcing myself on you, it's no wonder you don't like it."

I shook my head against the wood, but then I remembered she couldn't see me. "I *do* like it, Bree," I told her. "It's just... well... it takes me a while to get used to stuff."

"If you like it, why did you say those things?"

Because there's *huge* consequences if I say anything else, I thought. I turned and slid my back against the door until I was sitting against it, too. "I don't know," was all I told her.

We sat there for a couple of minutes. I still had basically *no* idea what had happened today. "Did you really throw a flower pot at that guy's car?"

"Yeah."

That was such a weird image. "*Why?*"

"Because he keeps telling me to get my brother to call him about the money he owes, and my stupid fuck brother never *does* call. And so the guy was like, 'Even though he knows I'm following you around? Jesus, kid, normally when I lean on the little sister the big brother comes out of the woodwork, but not with you. He's still nowhere. He really must not give two shits about you'."

I winced. That was a sore point for her. "Your brother..." I exhaled, deciding not to push her for more information. She'd already ruled that topic off-limits.

It was another minute or two before she spoke again. "I did want to tell you what was going on," she said quietly. "I really did, but you already have so much to worry about with work and stuff, and I didn't want you to feel like I was just dumping my shit on you. I wanted us to have fun together, you know? But sometimes I just really, really wanted to say it all, and then you could hug me and tell me everything's going to be okay even though it's not. Like, some nights I'd be lying in my bed at home and everything would just be *so awful* and I'd have my phone and I'd be like, 'I'm going to call her and tell her', but I didn't."

"I wish you had called me, Bree."

I didn't really think this conversation was going to lead anywhere, because the cops had spent nearly half an hour trying to get to her to describe five minutes, and because I'd asked her *so many times* before and been told nothing. That's why when she said, "Ring, ring," I sat straighter, surprised.

"You're going to tell me?" I twisted towards the door.

I could hear her swallow. "If you promise not to say 'oh, is that all'."

"You just threw a flower pot at a guy's car. I'm pretty sure I'm not going to say that."

The door rattled a little as she sat heavily against it. I could hear her inhale deeply, and then sigh. "It's so weird because Andrej used to be normal," she said. "Like, I mean, he was always annoying because he's a dick, but everything was fine until he turned eighteen. Then he was out heaps but I didn't care because he was an annoying dick." She paused. "Anyway one day this guy came to the door—"

"--that flower pot guy?" I interrupted her.

She made a noise that contradicted me. "Nah, just some guy. He looked like a courier and he had a big A4 envelope thing. I just thought it was something one of us had ordered off the internet so I opened the door and took it off him, and he said, 'Do Mr and Mrs Stefan Dejanovic live here?' and I was like, 'yeah' and he was like, 'You're being served with *bankruptcy* papers on their behalf. Do you understand?' and I was like, 'what the fuck, no? I don't understand! Why would you be serving us with *bankruptcy* papers, we have plenty of money!'. He didn't say anything else, though, he just left."

"Your brother did something," I said, feeling rising dread.

She didn't answer that directly. "Mum and Dad went *crazy* and phoned all the banks. They found out they had something like a hundred thousand dollars in credit cards in their name, and someone had signed to withdraw another two hundred grand against the house. And then Dad completely tore both our rooms apart, and found like seven credit cards in my bookcase. And then he just pushed me against the wall and started *screaming* at me."

She was saying all of it so mechanically, as if she was telling me someone else's story. It was hard to listen to. I didn't know which part of what she was saying alarmed me more. Credit cards? Someone trapping and *screaming* at little Bree? "Your brother put them in *your* bookcase?" I asked for confirmation. I could hardly fucking believe a brother would frame his sister like that.

"Yeah, and when Dad was going nuts at me, Andrej didn't even try to tell him the truth. He just let Dad keep screaming at me about what a useless, stupid, life-ruining brat I was." Her throat was getting tighter, now. I could hear it. "When the statements came in they could see the withdrawals had been while I was at school or at home, Andrej even said, 'Oh, maybe Bree's got some boyfriend she's giving money to' and Mum and Dad believed him at first, *they believed him*, even though I've never had a boyfriend. But all the withdrawals were from pubs Mum had picked Andrej up from before, and it ended up being obvious he'd done it. He still says it wasn't him though, even though we all know it was."

It was just so much to process. "What did he need all that money for? What does *anyone* need that much money for?"

I heard her draw a ragged breath. "I don't know," she said in this tiny voice. "I don't know. Three hundred thousand dollars, he took. *Three hundred thousand.* I can't even imagine that much money, but it's probably all gone now." Her voice was so quiet. "And when Dad called the bank and told them what had happened, the banks all said, 'You need to press charges against him or there's nothing we could do'. And, like, my parents were angry with him and everything, but Mum was like, 'Well, my precious Andrej will have a really hard life if he has a criminal record,' and Dad was all like 'everyone will know, it will be on the news if we press charges'. So they didn't. They just took extra jobs to pay the arrears. And now no one is home ever, and when they are they're really angry, and Mum and Dad fight all the time."

I didn't think she'd been crying until that point, but I could hear from how much she was struggling to talk that she was now. The door was even bulging against my back every time she drew an uneven breath.

"And it's just fucking *awful* there, Min. It's awful. Andrej always goes through my room and pinches things to sell and Mum and Dad are so sick of dealing with it that they don't even do anything. Sometimes he even just comes into my room and takes things in front of me if I don't hide them. And I'd only taken off your bracelet for a couple of minutes while I got changed so I didn't think I *needed* to hide it..."

The bracelet she'd loved so much...

"I'm so stupid, I know what he's like. I should have hidden it. He steals everything, even my mail. And we're always getting final bills in the post and the phone never stops ringing because of debt collectors and Dad constantly *yells* at me that I'm really expensive and that I'm stupid and useless and sending me to private school is a waste of money because I'm dumb and I just hate it," she said. "I hate it, and it's not fair. It's *so* not fair, because none of it's my fault."

I had my shoulder against the door, she was sobbing just on the other side of it. "It *isn't* your fault," I told her quietly. "Bree, *god*, I wish you'd just told me."

"I don't really tell people, anymore. They always think I'm going to say that I'm being abused or something and then when I say what it is, they're always like, 'Oh, is *that* all?' Even Courtney thinks I'm being a drama queen. I don't even think she actually believes me."

I felt *really* guilty, because abuse had been my first guess, too, and I'd been relieved when I found out it wasn't that. I wasn't relieved now. I was *anything* but relieved now. Bree was sitting two inches away from me, crying against the door. It was such a lost, despairing sound. I didn't know what to say.

I didn't think there *was* anything to say. "Please, Bree, *please* let me hug you."

She was silent for a moment, and then I heard fabric switch and the latch click. The door opened slowly with me still sitting against it, revealing Bree in her clean clothes. Her cheeks were wet, and her hair was a bit wet, too.

I'd been about to stand up, but she got down next to me before I was able to and just crawled under my arm and cuddled up against my side. I let her; of course I did. I just shifted so I was sitting against the door frame instead.

She rested her head against my collarbone, and I rested my cheek against the top of her damp curls and just hugged her. She cried a little bit more into me and her tears soaked through my hoodie and through my t-shirt and through my binder. It was different crying now, though, not the helpless, inconsolable sobs from earlier. She was just sad. She was just *so* sad.

"Don't ever cry without me, okay?" I murmured into her damp hair. "Even if it's my fault."

"The problem is that when it's your fault I *still* don't want to do it without you."

Fuck, Bree, I thought, *I don't want to do anything without you, not ever*. I didn't say it, but I *did* hug her fiercely against me. She was so tiny and she fit right there, under my arm. I wasn't just tall and awkward for once. Everything just felt so right.

"Can I just stay here forever?" she asked me quietly, tracing the pattern on the front of my hoodie with her fingers.

I didn't think she meant it seriously, but I responded anyway. "Here, as in my-apartment-here?" I asked her, looking out towards my bedroom. "Well, I don't like the idea of you staying with your family at all, but with the way things are going at work I'm probably going to move out of here soon..."

"Why would you have to move out because of work?"

"This place belongs to Frost, it's part of my package. If I get fired I have to move out." She looked up at me from my chest, eyes wide, so I explained, "Things haven't been going so well at work. It's complicated."

"Oh," she said, and then thought about that. "No wonder you look like you're about to die. Did you even sleep in the past four days?"

I laughed bleakly. "Not really. But that's partly your fault, too." She looked surprised, so I explained, "I was feeling awful about Friday, and then I was worried about you when you disconnected your phone and disappeared."

She put her head back against me. "I didn't disconnect it. Fucking Andrej took it, and there aren't any computers left at home now. He pawned Dad's last week. Besides, after what happened, I didn't think you'd want me to bother you."

I grimaced, remembering what I'd said to her.

She saw my expression. "It was kind of my fault, too. You were right, you can kiss whoever you want. I just thought that..." She sighed. "I don't know, that it was leading somewhere even though you're with Henry. I'm just stupid like that, I guess."

It is *leading somewhere,* I thought, peering down at her snuggled up against me. Look at us. Tell me it's completely platonic when two people end up cuddling with each other in the bathroom doorway after a fight. And that wasn't all, I'd missed her like fucking crazy over the weekend. I'd been wanting to hug her all day. I think I was maybe even about to leave someone who was potentially the most wonderful, perfect man in the world to be with her. The only problem was that I was still *in* a relationship with that wonderful, perfect man, and he didn't deserve to keep being cheated on. She was wrong about what she said.

"I *can't* kiss whoever I want," I said cryptically. She lifted her head from my shoulder, and with the way I was looking at her, she understood.

Her lips parted, and she took a hushed breath. "No, you can," she murmured. "If you want to..."

"Wanting to isn't the issue," I told her. "Or maybe it *is* the issue." Her face was so close, and her lips were so pink from how much she'd been crying. "I *shouldn't*, Bree."

She wet them with the tip of her tongue. "I know," she said, her breath warming my lips. "I'm just saying you can if you want to."

Fuck, I *did* want to. Especially after all that stuff she'd told me. She was gorgeous and sweet and fun and she just had this lovely gentle heart and I wanted to kiss her. And when she looked up at me with those big blue eyes that were puffy from how much she'd been crying... *god*. She deserved so much more than the way her life was right now.

She could see the conflict on my face, and her eyebrows met. "Please, Min," she whispered. "Please, even just once. Just once..."

That sealed it. I was going to make *another* bad decision. I bent my neck and touched my lips to hers, so lightly at first. I think that was only because Bree was too shocked to respond straight away. It didn't last long. She exhaled and reached up to me, slipping her arms around my neck and just pressing her mouth so desperately against mine. I don't think she'd kissed many people before, because it took a couple of seconds to negotiate a rhythm with her. She settled into it quickly, relaxing peacefully against me with a happy sigh.

I could feel her smiling. There was nothing like that feeling. She was smiling, and I was smiling, too. And, god, it... well, it wasn't *hot* like Gemma's kiss had been, but it was something. It was warm, and she was soft, and I could feel with each kiss how much she wanted me and how much she cared about me. She was making these little sounds, and when she did, *fuck.* It was *working.* She was making me breathless. I had no idea what to do about it because of my stupid body, but, *fuck,* I wanted to try and figure it out. She was so *gorgeous.*

The only thing that stopped me from doing anything else was that I tasted salt. She was *crying*? I pulled away from her immediately, even though she didn't want to let me go.

When she took my face in both hands, I thought she was just going to kiss me again. She didn't. "I know I said just once," she whispered. "But please don't marry Henry. Please don't marry him. Please, I'll be so good to you. I'll make you happy, I'll try really, really hard..."

She was upset, and I wanted to pay attention to that, but I was confused. "Huh?" I said, "Bree, I'm not marrying Henry."

She stopped pleading with me, looking as confused as I was. "Yes, you are," she said, sounding uncertain.

I squinted. "I'm pretty sure I need to agree to that," I said. "I mean, Mum's traditional, but she's not *that* traditional, and I haven't agreed to anything."

Bree sat back on her heels beside me, her hands dropping from my face. "But Sean said..." *Sean* said? "He was just talking to me to try and make me feel better, and he asked if I'd picked out something nice to wear to your wedding, because he said that he thought talking about all that pretty stuff would cheer me up."

"And it didn't," I said, for confirmation.

"I kind of ran off."

"I see," I said, and groaned. No *wonder* Sean had figured out about us. But why did he think I was marrying Henry? I didn't know *anything* about that, and it wasn't the type of thing Henry would just spring on me. He knew what I was like. Besides, how would *Sean* know before me? Henry *hated* him, and I couldn't imagine Henry confiding in him. Unless... Henry had needed something from Sean. But the only thing Henry could need from Sean that would have anything to do with proposals and weddings was time off work. Then again, Sean *had* been talking about us taking time off, hadn't he...? But, fuck. *Fuck!* Henry wanted to *propose* to me?

I leant heavily against the door frame and squeezed my eyes shut. My wonderful boyfriend was going about his day imagining marriage and kids and growing old together with me... And I was up here dressed as a guy and getting it on with a *teenage girl. Ouch.*

I stood up so I wasn't tempted to keep going with Bree. "We can't do this anymore until I have everything sorted out," I told her. "It's messed up, and I've messed up enough already."

She didn't seem upset by that. The opposite. "'Until you get everything sorted out'?" she queried. "You mean Henry?"

I gave her a look, straightening slowly because the position had made my back stiff. *Yes, 'Henry',* I thought, and then grimaced again.

"Maybe you're getting old," she told me, thinking my expression was to do with my back as I stretched.

"You watch it," I told her, helping her up. She giggled and followed me out into the living room as I added, "Don't think I won't smother you just because things suck for you at the moment. So, are you hungry?

"Things are looking *unbelievably fantastic*, actually," she corrected me. It seemed a bit ironic she was saying that because she still looked like she'd been crying for four days straight. "And yeah, I totally am hungry. You want pasta? I'll cook it for you." She stopped for a moment and shifted her weight a little uncomfortably, making a face. "Um. In a second, anyway. I just need to fix something. Be right back." She rushed off into the bathroom. When I realised what she was planning on fixing... I could have given Gemma's deep blushes a run for their money.

I was busy trying to ignore everything beneath *my* bellybutton as I got myself a glass of water when there was a knock on the door. I swallowed my mouthful, frowning at it. It was the middle of the day, who'd want anything right now? I went over to take a look through the peephole; it was just room service. I opened the door.

"Hi, Miss Lee," the attendant greeted me, and then gave me a strange look as soon as she'd said that. She was holding my handbag which she passed over. "Someone left this for you at reception."

I thanked her and went inside, immediately feeling *really terrible* because it was probably Henry who'd returned it. He was being a lovely, considerate boyfriend and I was *making out with girls behind his back*. While I was torturing myself over that, I went straight for my phone to check to see how many missed calls I had.

There was a post-it stuck to the screen, and it wasn't Henry's writing.

"Hey Toyboy, you're not missing much. Your absence started a leadership coup, but everyone's too terrified of Jason to go as far as declaring themselves lead. Next week's pitch is fine, don't worry about it. I don't think I need to tell you to have fun... ;) See you in Broome."

Sarah. I half-laughed, half-groaned at her message, crumpling it up and throwing it in the bin so that no one would see it. I texted her a quick thanks and put my phone back in my handbag where I couldn't see or hear if it was ringing or not. I decided I didn't want to think about work right now. Not after the day I'd had, and not while Bree was here.

Speak of the devil, she returned from the bathroom and banished me out of the kitchen, putting on the house apron that was way too big for her and then getting started on the pasta. I watched her from the couch, a bit worried that she'd burn something and set the sprinklers off.

She noticed and guessed what I was stressing about. "I'm not going to set your kitchen on fire!" she called over the bench, from behind the wilted roses. "I cook all the time! Also, how much cheese do you want?"

"All of it," I told her, thinking that I couldn't remember the last time I'd eaten something.

"Okay!" was her cheerful response, and then I heard the fridge open and her bustle around in it. ...all while I was sitting here on the couch, doing absolutely nothing.

Despite the crap day she'd had, she was still cooking for us. And despite everything that *always* was going on for her, she still made time to do nice things for me. All that stuff she'd said on Friday about me acting like my gift to her was just letting her do nice things: I remembered it with a painful level of detail.

"Bree…" I began, and my tone of voice made her stand on tip-toes behind the counter so she could see me properly. "I…" I swallowed. "Well, thanks. Thanks for cooking for us."

She looked *delighted*, and even blushed a little. "It's my pleasure, Min."

We held eye contact for a little too long, because she was giving me this cheeky little smile.

And, wow, it gave me butterflies. I turned back at the TV so she couldn't see the big stupid grin on my face, and decided to leave her alone to cook. She seemed happy again, she was going to feed me, and maybe everything would be okay after all.

TWENTY-TWO

I definitely *should* have gone into work. I woke up at the crack of dawn when my alarm went off, like it was any other day. As I was feeling around my bedside table for my buzzing phone, however, all the events of yesterday slowly started coming back to me. I groaned, tapped the snooze function, and turned over.

It took me full three rounds with snooze to actually manage to get myself out of bed. I washed and dressed and got as far as checking my outfit and worrying about how it looked when I realised what I was doing.

I was wearing clothes I *hated* to go and be yelled at by someone I hated even more, and I was actually worrying about whether or not this stupid blouse my mother bought me went with this skirt and what she'd have thought about it. It didn't *matter* what she thought about it, she wasn't here to see it. Jason wasn't going to give a fuck about my mismatched fabrics while he yelled at me, and it didn't even matter what *Diane* thought about it. She wasn't just going to *not* fire me because I'd picked the perfect outfit.

The whole thing just seemed completely messed up and none of it fucking mattered. But if it didn't matter, why was it all so critically important to me? I sat down on the bed to talk myself through it, but just ended up with my forehead resting on my palm, wondering about the logistics of *actually* jumping on a plane and running away.

I'd been trying to be quiet because Bree was still asleep, but when I sat down on the bed I must have woken her up anyway. I could see her yawn and stretch in the mirror behind me, but she stopped mid-yawn when she saw what I was wearing. "You're not actually going in to work today, are you?" she asked, propping herself up on an arm and rubbing her eyes. "I thought you said you didn't have anything urgent that needs doing because that Russian-pitch-thingy got cancelled."

I exhaled. "If I'm not there for my team to take their disappointment out on, they'll all bitch about me behind my back," I said. "And the last thing I want is for Marketing to decide I'm a hot topic, because they kind of know that I was made lead of a confidential project and everyone loves to tear down someone who got promoted above them. So there's that. Plus Jason and Diane weren't done with having a go at me and I should let them finish."

Bree just stared at me. "Where do you actually work?" she asked me. "Hell?"

I laughed once. "Well, the pay is good," I said, and stood up. "How do I look?"

She couldn't have given me a more tired expression. "Min, take those clothes off and get back into bed. You're being *totally* ridiculous. If people are going to talk shit about you, it's way better if you're *not* there to hear it because it's probably all bullshit anyway." She put the doona over her head and turned over.

I looked back at my reflection, decided she was right, and just put my comfy clothes back on and got back into bed with her.

Bree sat up for the express purpose of returning some of the doona to me and tucking me in. "You care too much about what people think about you," she told me for like the hundredth time, and then before I was able to stop her, she lay down against my side, put her head on my shoulder and draped an arm across my stomach.

I stiffened. I could feel her breasts against my ribs. "Bree, we shouldn't be—"

"Relax, Min, I'm not starting anything, I promise. I just need to make sure you don't sneak off to work the minute I go back to sleep," she told me, and then snuggled into me and did exactly that.

Sneak off to work? She made me sound like a heroin addict. I lay there for a moment, not really sure what I should do. While I was trying to figure that out, I ended up accidentally falling asleep again, too.

I woke up way too late to call in sick. If I called now, I either risked getting Henry when I was put through to HR, or risked getting Jason if I got put through to Marketing. I peeled Bree off me—somewhat reluctantly, actually, she was really warm—and then went to go write work an email, instead.

When I sat down at the laptop to try and figure out what I should say, I didn't know where to start. I *knew* I should have gone in.

I still hadn't written anything when Bree wandered out into the living room in her thin pyjamas. I double-took; she wasn't wearing a bra.

I hadn't even written a subject. "Maybe the fact I can't write this email is a sign that I'm supposed to be a mature, responsible adult and face the shit that's waiting for me at work," I said to her as she walked past.

She didn't look at all convinced. "Or maybe it's a sign that place is fucking awful and you should quit before it kills you," she helpfully suggested, and then went and opened my living room blinds... to a miserable, rainy day outside.

"Oh, well," she said brightly. "We can stay inside and watch movies or something together." She bent down by the bottom shelf where all my DVDs were to go through them while I just typed out some flimsy excuse with the word 'police' in it and sent the damn thing.

When I was done, I went and sat on the couch near where she was crouched. She'd taken some of the cases out. "You have heaps of Disney movies," she observed. "All the old ones. I never picked you for that type of person."

"Because I'm big and tough, you mean?" I asked her neutrally. She rolled her eyes at me, so I explained, "When I was a lot younger I really wanted to be an animator for Disney. I used to put those movies on repeat, rewind all my favourite scenes and imagine that I was watching something I'd helped create."

413

Bree looked absolutely charmed. "That's so beautiful," she said. "You could still be one, you know. If you really wanted to. You're only 25."

I scrunched my nose and shook my head. "Nah," I said. "I'd need to retrain, and to be honest, animation isn't my forte anyway. It was just nice to think about." That wasn't the only problem, either. "Besides, Mum would kill me if I quit my job. She just loves to tell everyone her daughter is in marketing for Frost International, and I'm actually pretty good at it most of the time, so it's not that bad."

Bree's smile faltered a little. "You should have seen yourself yesterday when the police called you, Min. You looked *so* sick. I'm sure your mum wouldn't want to see you like that, no matter what she likes to say about you." I shrugged, not really wanting to go into the intricacies of my relationship with Mum.

Bree watched me intently for a moment, and then shuffled forward a little, DVDs momentarily forgotten. "If you could be anything, like if someone gave you a wish or something, what would you be? I bet it wouldn't be a marketer."

I snorted. "If I could be anything? I'd be a dragon. Or maybe invisible, I don't know."

She laughed. "That's not what I meant!"

"I know," I said, but I didn't answer her *real* question.

She selected a few boxes and came to sit next to me on the couch. "Let's watch some of these," she said, and spread them across her lap. "Which one's your favourite?"

I was about to answer her when my mobile rang. Bree casually picked it up from the coffee table to give to me, but her face fell when she glanced in passing at it and saw what was on the screen. For a second I thought she might be about to reject the call. She didn't, though. Instead, she just passed it over. Our fingers brushed as I accepted it and looked down at the screen.

'*Henry*' was flashing on it, and my thumb hovered over the red handset symbol.

Just seeing his name, I felt all the energy I'd built up from relaxing and sleeping in drain out of me. I didn't want to talk to him. I wanted to pretend he didn't exist and just live in sick day land forever.

"Are you going to pick up?" Bree asked.

I pressed my lips together. "I don't want to."

"Okay, just leave it, then. Let's watch Disney movies all day and order pizza."

I looked between Bree and the phone and *groaned.*

I *couldn't* ignore Henry just because Bree's suggestion sounded *perfect,* and I felt really guilty about that. A month ago, a perfect evening would have been spent playing Black Ops with Henry. I would have had fun, too. I always did, except when he was being all romantic. He didn't deserve for me to ignore him just because I felt *really* guilty, though.

I scrunched my eyes shut and swiped the screen as I put it to my ear. "Hi, Henry."

Beside me, Bree slumped.

"Hi," he said gently. "How are you feeling?"

"Better," I told him. At least it was true.

"You *sound* so much better. Wow, I was so worried about you yesterday, and when I saw you in the corridor you looked *so* pale." I kept waiting for him to mention Sean, or ask what Sean had to do with Bree, but he didn't. It felt like a really deliberate omission. "I'm so glad you took my advice and are using some of your sick leave for once."

I made a non-committal noise.

"Anyway, I know you're probably not up to going out tonight, but I was hoping I could drop around in my lunch break? I'd like to show you what I bought your family, and since you're not feeling too well, I thought perhaps I could bring you some healthy food. Pasta and bread are great for energy, but when you're running yourself down you'll need greenery as well as the carbs."

Bree must have been able to hear the conversation, because she looked very indignant. "I bought apples," she muttered. I patted her, but I was too distracted by the fact he wanted to come over to be very comforting.

I *really, really* didn't want to see Henry right now. I'd been looking forward to a nice, relaxing day with Bree, and I couldn't imagine how any day with both Bree and Henry together could ever be described as 'nice and relaxing'. I was *sure* Henry suspected something, and even if he didn't, I was worried that either Bree or I would say something while he was here that would give it away.

Henry was going to find out the whole story because I was going to tell him, but it had to be while we were both alone and not in any sort of rush. And I wasn't sending Bree home now, that was certain. I wanted to keep her out of her own house as much as possible. Fuck. That meant I was going to have to let him come over, didn't it?

I looked apologetically across at Bree. She had a really strange expression on her face.

"Min? Are you still there?" Henry's voice startled me a bit.

I was just going to have to suck it up and deal with the discomfort. It was all my own fault, anyway. "Sure, that's fine, come over."

Bree made a face and then flopped backwards on the couch, groaning. Disney DVDs scattered everywhere.

He sounded relieved. "Okay, that's great," he said. "I'll be there in about ten minutes. I can't wait to see you, Min."

"Me, too." I stopped him before he hung up, not looking forward to what I had to say next. "Henry..." I began.

"Yeah?" he sounded like he thought he knew what I was going to say. There was a smile in his voice.

He thinks I'm going to say, 'I love you' again, I realised, jamming my eyes shut. I didn't. "Bree's here."

There was a long pause. "Oh..." he said. He sounded *so* taken aback, and even in that one single syllable, I could hear such disappointment. He quickly disguised it. "Oh. That just means I need to buy more food, I suppose. See you soon."

We hung up and I exhaled, still grimacing.

Bree was still lying supine on the couch. "He hates me, doesn't he?" she said flatly.

I shook my head, taking a deep breath and releasing it slowly. "No, he's not like that," I told her, and then stood up to get changed. Even though he'd seen me dressed down without make-up last time, I think seeing me in a binder was one step too far.

Bree followed me as I walked into the bedroom. "He *should* hate me."

I opened the wardrobe and sighed at all my tight, frilly clothes. "He should hate *me*," I said. "But he doesn't."

Bree sat down on the bed, looking troubled as she watched me.

I took out a very feminine blouse, thinking I could probably get away with these jeans if I was wearing a nice top. I felt depressed even just looking at it, but twisted around to Bree. "Would you mind...?" She obediently lay back and put the doona over her face so she couldn't see me change as I began to. "You know what the most fucked up thing is about all of this?" I asked her as I pulled off my hoodie and t-shirt and began trying to wrestle myself out of my binder.

Her voice was muffled by the covers. "No?"

I wondered if I should even tell her. "I was about ready to get an intervention order against you when you found out where I lived, but Henry thought the coffee was a cute idea and told me I should get to know you, because I need more friends."

"*Oh*," Bree said. I was *still* trying to get out of my binder even after she'd had few seconds to consider that. "Wow, that makes me feel really bad. I mean, not the intervention order stuff. You were pretty upfront about that in the beginning. But like, that your nice boyfriend was just looking out for you and helping you make friends with me and then I end up going behind his back and stealing you from him."

Once I was done, I stood in front of the mirror for a second, feeling weird. "Is it okay?" I asked Bree as she emerged from under the doona. "Are the jeans too 'guy'?"

She shrugged. "You're asking the wrong person," she told me. "Because if you want my honest opinion, I *prefer* you as a guy."

I grimaced, looking back at my reflection. *That* wasn't a guy. Sighing, I went to sit on the bed beside her and put my head in my hands for a moment.

Bree gave me a comforting pat on the back, but it was weird having people touch me when I was dressed like this. Even Bree. I didn't shrug her off exactly, but when I stiffened, she got the message and snatched her hand away. "Sorry."

That made me feel even more guilty. "No, Bree, don't be sorry, it's just..." At least it was easier to sigh deeply without the binder on. "This is my reality." I gestured to my chest. "Even if you'd kind of prefer it wasn't."

She glanced at my breasts and her cheeks went a bit pink. "Oh, no, that's not what I meant," she told me. "I mean, you're completely different when you're being a guy. Like seriously, when you're wearing menswear and walking around like that, you're just funnier and nicer and *way* more relaxed. *That's* what I like more. I don't even care about how your body is. I mean, obviously *you* do, but to me you're still the same person whether you have boobs or not, you know? It doesn't matter to me."

I smiled at that, and exhaled at length. It was so comforting to hear that from her. "Sometimes you really *do* say the right things," I told her quietly.

She flipped her hair smugly and then went to put her own clothes on.

Henry was definitely less than ten minutes away; I didn't even think it had been five when he knocked on the door. I stood to go and answer it, but Bree stopped me. When I looked back at her, she had that weird expression again. "Don't make out in front of me, okay?" she asked a bit forlornly. "Please."

I understood what she meant; I wouldn't want to see her making out with someone else, either. "Henry and I have never been like that. I was never into it anyway."

She followed me out into the main room as I went to let Henry in. Before I did, I took a deep breath, pulling myself together, and opened the door with the biggest smile I could manage.

Henry was standing there in the doorway in his suit with one hand full of grocery bags and the other with a *big* bouquet of crisp red roses. "That's a beautiful smile," he said warmly, and then pecked me on the cheek and walked past me into the hallway on his way to the kitchen.

Bree watched the display from living room.

He unloaded his arms onto the kitchen bench, drying his hands on my tea-towel. "I figured the other roses would be getting a bit tired by now, so I bought you some new ones." As he straightened again, he spotted Bree standing there. Rather than look angry or disappointed or any of the things he should have, recognition just passed over his face and he smiled. "Bree, isn't it?" He walked over to her and held out his hand. "I've heard so much about you. It's a pleasure to finally meet you."

Stunned, Bree shook his hand automatically. I didn't know what to make of it, either, but I supposed it made sense. This was Henry, 'nice' was his MO. I shouldn't have expected otherwise.

"Hi," she said up at him when they were done shaking hands. "You're as tall as Min."

He laughed. "Thanks, I think." He looked between us as I wandered cautiously out of the hallway. "It occurred to me that I've never actually had much of an opportunity to get to know Bree. Maybe I could fix that by cooking you two lunch?"

My stomach was already beginning to knot, but I very carefully tried not to let that show. Behind Henry, Bree was looking *really* uncomfortable. I didn't want to put her into another stressful situation when she had so much going on at home, but being cooked for by my boyfriend wasn't really something I could say no to, was it?

"Sounds great," I managed.

He beamed at me, and then nodded once. "Great," he repeated. "I was thinking I might cook something a bit traditional today, so I bought the ingredients for *Japchae.*" For Bree's benefit, he added, "A Korean noodle dish."

He didn't need to explain what it was to me; it was probably my *favourite* Korean food, but only when Henry cooked it. He knew that, too.

"Oh, right," Bree said, trying to sound excited. "Sounds yum."

Henry asked us to sit down on the couch, and we all made polite conversation while he was preparing all the ingredients. When he actually had to cook it, though, he needed to turn around to the stove. The range hood fan plus the splattering sesame oil meant that the noise was too much for us to hear each other. It was a relief, but it was over too soon.

"So, ladies," he asked, plates out and spatula ready, "How big a serving would you like?"

I didn't know how I made it through that lunch. Stress always made it basically impossible for me to eat, and even though I *loved* Henry's cooking, the taste alone wasn't enough to break through the discomfort so I could enjoy it. I did succeed in getting all of it inside me at least, and created enough of a fanfare that Henry must have been convinced that I thought it was delicious. He sat back when we were all done and looked content.

"Anyway, I'd better get moving," he said as he stood up and

cleared our empty plates, taking them back to the sink and turning the tap on. "People are going to start asking where I am if I'm not back at the office soon. Thanks for having me, though. It was great to learn more about you, Bree."

Bree looked at me, confused. She'd said a few things, but for the most part she'd been silent.

When he was done washing up the plates, he threw out the old roses and filled the vase with the lovely new ones. I could smell them from where I was sitting; they must have been very fresh. He stood back after he'd spread them in the vase to admire his handiwork, asking, "What do you think?"

I thought that I didn't deserve them. "They're beautiful."

He smiled fondly at me. "Well, they've come to the right person."

It felt like a knife twisting in my gut. When I stood up to show him out, he walked me up the end of my hall where Bree couldn't see us and I was worried he was going to kiss me. Fortunately, I was wrong.

"I didn't want to spend ages talking about your family in front of Bree and make her feel excluded," he said, picking up a plastic bag he'd dropped in the doorway. "Anyway, I bought these for your mum and grandma. What do you think?"

He'd bought them each one of those godawful Coogee jumpers they loved, and he held them both up so I could inspect his purchase. I could even tell which one he'd got for which person, because he knew them both and guessed their colours. It just hurt. Even the sizes were right.

"They're lovely," I told him, feeling empty.

He noticed my expression. "It's not too late to come with me to Seoul," he offered. "My family would still love to have you stay."

I shook my head. "I'm going to Broome with Sarah. I can't say much."

"Work?" he asked and I nodded, and then I saw something pass over his face. Disregarding it, he asked very casually, "Sounds fun, is Bree going, too?" When I shook my head, he may have tried to hide it, but I saw relief.

A silence stretched between us. Tell him, Min, I thought. Just say it. Say *anything*. I kept thinking about Mum, though. She *loved* him.

She would have been spending the last week cleaning the house to make sure it was perfect for him. She would have been planning what they'd eat for a month and have half of it cooked already. She'd have told *everyone* he was coming, and be so looking forward to it. I clenched my eyes shut for a moment.

"Well, I suppose I'd better head off..." Henry said, when I stayed silent.

This time when he leant in to kiss me, I stopped him. "Henry, no," I murmured, and then sighed.

I saw his throat bob as he swallowed, and then he took a breath. "It's probably for the best," he said carefully. "If you're sick, you don't want to give it to me so I can give it to your grandma." I let him lift his hand and tenderly cup my cheek. "I'll be waiting for you to feel better, though," he told me. "Okay? You just let me know when you do."

His hand dropped and then saluted me, the same way I'd done to him a thousand times. "See you soon," he said, and then turned to walk toward the lift.

I watched him leave and then shut the door after him, leaning on it for a second.

If I had *any* doubt that he knew exactly what was going on between me and Bree, that exchange laid it to rest. I squeezed my eyes shut, feeling *sick*.

I'd just listened to the man whose emotional acuity usually *amazed* me make a decision that was *so* unhealthy I couldn't even believe it had come from him. It was so unlike him, and it was *my* fault. *I* was doing this to him. I was so, so bad for him; we were bad for each other, and I'd wasted so many years of his life.

Bree padded gingerly up the hallway in her socks to check on me. "Are you okay?" I shook my head. She didn't try to touch me, though, not until after I'd gone into the bedroom and changed back into my guy stuff. Then, as we were sitting on the bed, she wrapped her arms around my shoulders and rested her head against mine.

"Wow," she said bleakly. "He's really, really nice."

I nodded slowly.

After a minute or so she took another breath, lifting her head from mine to look towards me. "I know you always take ages to tell everyone everything, but can you please not do that and tell him quickly this time? Because he's really, really nice and it just kind of *really* hurts to think about him assuming everything is okay when it's not."

I made a pained noise. "He knows."

She looked like she didn't understand. "But he was so nice to me."

"Yeah. That's Henry." I put my head back in my hands and swore. "Fuck. I wanted to tell him, but of course he's going to Mum's this weekend and if I break up with him now, I'm probably ruining Grandma's last Easter." Bree sat up, silent. She had her hand on my back. "They *love* him. Mum's been telling me to marry him since day one. She's convinced he'll leave me as soon as he realises he's making a big mistake. She thinks he's way too good for me." And she was probably right. Look at how I was treating him, after all.

"Your mum isn't very nice to you," Bree commented.

I waved my hand dismissively. "She's just strict, maybe it's a Korean thing. Or maybe it's just my mum. She loves me, though."

"Really?" Bree asked after some thought. It was a genuine question.

I looked up at her. "Yeah, of course."

She had those big sad eyes again. "Because you keep telling me all this stuff she says about you or all these things she's pressured you to do—"

"—She doesn't *pressure* me these days. Well, not like she used to. I just know what she'd want for me."

Bree scoffed. "It's the same thing. Maybe you should talk to her. I mean, do you really think she'd want you to marry Henry, even if she knew you weren't in love with him?"

I knew the answer to that question. "Yes."

Bree looked surprised by that, and it took her a couple of seconds to get over it. "But doesn't she know you're *miserable*?"

I shrugged.

Looking aghast, she touched my face with light fingertips, and it was such a delicate, affectionate gesture. Her voice was quiet when she spoke again. "But if she really loves you, like really, why doesn't she just want you to be *happy?*"

I hadn't expected that, and it felt like a fucking sword through the chest. I put a hand over my mouth as sudden tears welled in my eyes.

It was a question I'd *felt* my entire life, every time she disapproved of something I'd done. Every time she'd told me I was doing things wrong. Every time she'd dressed me in the clothes she thought I should be wearing, and cut my hair the way she thought it should be cut, and put me in 'the right type of school' so I could get into a course she'd chosen in her preferred university. I'd made friends I thought she'd like in uni, and I could still hear that phrase she always muttered when she disapproved of something, 'If only your father was here to see how the daughter he wanted *actually* turned out...'

Why *didn't* she want me to be happy?

Bree looked really distressed. "I'm sorry," she said desperately, throwing her arms around me and obviously about to cry, too. "I'm sorry! I didn't mean to make you upset!"

I shook my head, but I couldn't say anything straight away. Bree was so caring, and so sweet and she wanted to help me so much. But Mum wasn't something she could do anything about. I still wanted her to understand, though. I wanted her to understand. The trouble was, I didn't even know where to start. I'd never told anyone before, not even school counsellors, and Henry had just quietly understood.

I took a breath. There was one memory I still thought about, sometimes.

"When I was in high school, something that used to comfort me through all the shit was lying awake in bed at night and imagining what would happen if I was made dux of the school. It would be my biggest triumph. I used to imagine how proud Mum would be of me, how it would feel to have her look at me with real actual pride in her eyes." I smiled faintly. "And then it happened. I got top marks. I walked out on that stage and was presented with the diploma by the principal and the *whole* auditorium stood one by one in their seats and gave me a standing ovation. It went on and on, all these people clapping and cheering for me. When I found her face in the audience, though, she was looking down the front where all the popular girls who made my life hell were standing, slow-clapping and pretending to yawn. Later, after the ceremony, she said to me, 'Of course none of those girls like you, you're too arrogant. Nails that stick out get hammered'.”

Bree looked appalled. “Min, that's so awful,” she said. “Why would anyone say that to you?”

I shrugged. “She was just raised like that, I guess. To her 'strict' is the opposite of 'neglectful'. She's not a bad person. She's just...” I took a deep breath and let it out slowly. “She's just how she is.”

Bree stroked the hair at the back of my neck. “At least she's all the way over in Korea now...”

I laughed once, darkly. “Yeah, I thought I was going to be free, too, when I got moved up to Sydney and she decided to go back to Seoul. But I'm not. The worst part is, no matter where she is in the world, I *still fucking care* about it all. I still care. Even about tiny little things, like I put on my fucking blouse this morning and I was asking myself, 'Would Mum like me in this?'. Nothing I seem to be able to do stops that from being true.” I paused, looking down at my flat chest and jeans. “And if she knew how I feel about myself, and the way I'd rather be...”

“Oh...”

“Yeah, 'oh',” I said, copying her. “She didn't even like me wearing sneakers because they made my feet look big and unfeminine, *especially* after I started getting teased at school. She threw out all my comfortable clothes. ” I exhaled. “So, yeah. Maybe she does want me to be happy, in her own way. Or maybe not. Maybe she wants me to be miserable like she is. I don't even know. I don't think I ever will.”

Bree's thumb brushed lightly across my cheek, over where some of my tears had spilt. She was so gentle. “Well, *I* want you to be happy,” she said quietly.

That got another tear out of me. I smiled wryly, and pushed a couple of curls behind her ears. She had tears on her cheeks; she'd been crying because I was. “I want *you* to be happy, too.”

Leaning her head into my hand, she said, “I am right now...” and gave me a little smile.

I just wrapped my arms around her shoulders and squeezed the life out of her. “Stop it, Bree, you're going to make me cry again.”

When I pulled back she was still smiling up at me, so I skimmed one of her rosy cheeks with the back of my knuckles. I wanted to kiss her. I wanted to do more than that, but I wanted to start by kissing those gentle lips of hers again.

Almost like she could read my thoughts, she said, "I really want to just kiss you, but Henry's too nice. I would feel like such an awful person."

Sitting back, I nodded. "I know." I ran my hands over my face.

She began to look sad again and that reminded me of all the crap we'd been talking about. I was *exhausted.* "Come on," I told her, standing up and offering her my hand. "Let's go overdose on Disney." I led her back out into the living room to do exactly that.

I didn't stop thinking about the stuff that we'd talked about as we watched the movies, though, and I kept remembering that I was leaving for Broome tomorrow and Bree would have to go back home to *her* messed up family.

"What are you doing for Easter?" I asked her. "Anything particular?"

She shrugged, looking from the screen to me. "Everyone usually comes over, which is just *great*." She sounded heavily sarcastic. "There's nothing I love more than being in a house with my whole fucked up family, all together."

"Your brother, too?"

She made a face at the mention of him. "Yeah, probably, because Grandma will bring a cake over and they're awesome." She reconsidered that, scowling. "Who the fuck am I kidding? He'll be over because Grandma always carries cash and leaves her handbag by the front door."

I couldn't get that image out of my head: her brother just coming into her room and stealing that bracelet she loved from right in front of her. Or the image of her lying alone in bed wishing she was somewhere else, like here.

Actually... "Don't go back there for Easter," I found myself telling her. "Stay here and look after my apartment while I'm in Broome. If you won't be too lonely, that is."

She unfolded her arms, her face relaxing out of the frown it had been in. "Really?" I nodded. "You're trusting me to stay here by myself?" She sounded completely incredulous, like she didn't believe anyone could ever have faith in her.

"Well if I get back and my apartment is gone, I'm going to be very upset."

She wrapped her arms completely around me and the strength at which she was crushing me threatened to break a couple of my ribs. "Really?" she said, just checking again. "You're not joking, are you? Like, seriously?"

I managed to get an arm up despite the vice-like grip she had me in, and I ruffled those curls. "Stay here, Bree. It's fine. I'll leave you some money for food and emergencies."

I didn't get her off me for the rest of the movie, but at least she obediently stayed on the other side of the bed all night.

The following day after I'd packed and showed her how to use the Smart TV—"You can use the internet *on your TV*? That is *so cool!*"—I put my mobile number beside the phone and three hundred on the kitchen bench. I'd originally been planning on leaving five, but then I worried that given her family's situation it might look like showing off.

"Let me know if you need more," I told her, worrying anyway. "I can arrange it via the hotel."

She picked up the six fifties and fanned them like a suit of cards in her hand. "Are you *kidding*?" she asked. "What the hell am I going to need all this money for?" As I was checking I had everything I needed, though, I noticed her surveying the apartment and gave her a questioning look. She had a pained expression. "It's stupid," she told me. "Like, as soon as I picked up the money, my first thought was, 'Oh, god, where the hell am I going to hide this?'"

"It's safe here," I promised her, and then pat myself down, trying to figure out which pocket I'd put my phone in. I hadn't been wearing these jeans long enough to have routines about them.

She looked me up and down. "You're going as a guy?"

I shrugged. "Who's going to recognise me in Broome?"

She held her hands up. "I'm not having a go at you, I think it's great!" she said. "Take lots of photos."

I gave her a look that said 'in your dreams'. "I'd better go or I'm going to miss my plane."

She grabbed my sleeve. "You didn't hug me. I'm going to be by myself for like four whole days and you didn't even hug me."

"Oh," I said, and very pointedly put down my handbag and my suitcase before holding my arms out to her. She giggled and jumped into them, throwing hers around my neck. I had to hunch so much to let her do it that after a few seconds it started to hurt my back. For a moment I considered just picking her up. I could, I thought, if I wanted to. I didn't this time, though, I just hugged her tightly.

She pulled away from me with this elated expression on her face. Her cheeks were glowing and that made me want to kiss them. "That was a good hug," she told me. "You're getting much better at them."

"Well, I'm learning from the master," I said, shooting her a wink. Then, I picked up my luggage. "Have a nice time, Bree. Call me whenever you want."

"Don't say things like that to me," she called down the hotel corridor as I wheeled my suitcase to the lift. "Because I *always* want to call you!"

I gave her a little wave as the lift doors closed, a giant smile on my face. Fuck, and to think I almost hadn't gone to dinner with her that time. I'd never been so glad someone had stolen my handbag as I was on the way down to the basement car park.

As it turned out, I didn't miss my plane. In fact, there was next to no traffic because it was school holidays and only Thursday and half of Sydney still had to work. I got to the airport in no time and found myself pathologically early, as usual. I decided it was a good time to check my work email, and when I did I wished I hadn't.

Ian couldn't have been any more passive aggressive about the fact two of the team were on sick-leave, reminding us that he'd missed picking up his daughter from school on her birthday for the failed pitch. And as if that wasn't bad enough, the clerks Diane had picked out from Sales were getting shitty about the failed pitch and were dragging their feet about learning what material was complete for the Sasha Burov pitch, too. The end of their email read, "*We're just concerned we'll put a lot of unnecessary effort into this one, too. Some sort of assurance it's worthwhile would be nice.*" Jason had replied even more passive-aggressively with an attachment that contained the Sales Clerk job description, and asked them if they could kindly locate the section that referred to 'if we feel like it' with reference to learning materials and delivering pitches.

The most concerning email was the one Jason had forwarded me from Diane which simply said, "Make sure you set up a meeting when she returns to work. And please ensure that everything is complete and this pitch is delivered impeccably. I need that signature on a contract before 4pm Friday or the finance won't go through and we'll lose the lease."

That one, I replied to. *"I'll get it done,"* I promised Jason, adding a couple of timeframes and forwarding him some information showing that we were on target for that pitch.

He replied immediately. *"You'd better hope that's true or someone's going to be out of a job next Friday."*

I worried about that for the rest of my tense stay in the airport lounge, wishing Sarah had been able to get us on the same flight. Because I was alone, I had expected to sit and worry about it on the plane, too, but mercifully I ended up falling asleep. I woke up to the hostess tapping me on the shoulder.

"Sir?" she asked, shaking me lightly. "Sir? You need to put your window shade up for landing."

I was half-asleep, and it took me a couple of seconds to realise she was talking to me. When I did, I couldn't help but smile up at her; I'd forgotten I was dressed as a guy. She looked a bit confused by my reaction. "Your shade," she said, leaning over me and showing me what to do in case I didn't speak English.

"Thanks," I said, and followed her instructions.

Broome International Airport was *tiny* compared to most of the places I'd flown to, and that was really a statement because I'd been in regional airports in Canada. It looked like it consisted of basically one building surrounded by palm trees and luscious, thick lawns. Because it was so small, though, they got us off the plane and out the door pretty quickly.

Sarah had caught a much earlier flight and was waiting for me, leaning against a big four wheel drive that was covered in orange dust. She was also wearing denim shorts and a loose tank top, and I don't even think I'd seen her dressed so casually. It made sense; it was *really* humid.

She looked like she had similar thoughts about me as she walked over to help me with my luggage. "Aren't you *dying* in that hoodie?" was the first thing she said to me, thankfully relieving me of my tablet which felt like it was *breaking my arm*. "It's 35 degrees."

"Now that you mention it..." I said, and stopped for a second to pull it off. I was wearing a t-shirt underneath, and even though she'd already seen me with a flat chest, she still looked incredulously at it. I chuckled at her reaction as we loaded my stuff into the car. "I have a spare binder in my luggage," I told her. "If you're *really* curious about what they do, you can try it on. No guarantees you'll be able to get it off, though."

She gave me a look. "Isn't that like asking a magician to explain his tricks? I'm sure it's against some code or something."

"Yeah, I've joined a secret society of trans men and they'll all gang together and vanquish me if I ever betray their secrets."

She *laughed* at that. "Min, you're a riot, I am *so* glad I invited you," she said, giving me a big hug just before we both got into the car. "And I don't care what the rest of the team says, you look *so much* better after a couple of days off. I was really worried about you on Monday."

"Yeah, I saw what they said. I read all the emails." I fastened my seatbelt, still surprised by how comfortable it was to wear one while I had the binder on. Seatbelts were apparently not designed for people with breasts.

Sarah inhaled through grit teeth as she pulled out of the car park. "Yeah, it's been pretty intense in the office. We had a couple of meetings with Sales about the failed pitch and they were all seriously, excuse my French, *fucking assholes*. Diane even came to speak to us about the need for security and she basically said if any of us step out of line at all we'll only get one more paycheque."

I closed my eyes for a second. "That does *not* bode well for me."

Sarah shrugged, turning out onto the main road. "Well, they would have taken you straight off the project if they were *really* worried. But Jason's still CCing stuff to you and Diane kept naming you, so I guess you're not gone yet. Plus, everyone knows you're coming up here to paint amazing graphics for all the material and no one's told you not to." While I was thinking that she had a really good point, she glanced at me. "You really started the rumour mill going, though."

My stomach dropped. "What?"

She looked confused by my horror. "Oh!" she said, guessing what I was worried about. "Not about your..." She waved her hand at my clothes, "Everyone is *completely* convinced you got arrested on

Tuesday and that the reason you're not at work is because you're in lock-up somewhere. I heard one guy say that the only reason 'Mini' would miss work is death or jail. There are some pretty interesting theories about what you got arrested for. My favourite is drugs. People have decided that obviously you're on amphetamines and that's why you get so much done."

I listened to her, shaking my head. "Jason and Diane don't believe that stuff at all, do they?"

She shrugged. "Well, you're still on the project, aren't you? Anyway, the whole team was Googling you yesterday when you didn't come in. I think some of the department didn't know you're an amazing painter. They know now."

My Deviant Art, I thought, feeling sick as I remembered what I had featured on my profile. "Fuck, that painting of me as a guy." I took out my phone to hurriedly put that picture in storage where it would be hidden. "*Everyone* will have seen it by now."

Sarah shrugged. "Yeah, but I saw it and I didn't think anything. I just went, 'Oh, she looks pretty boyish there. Maybe she's doing some Salvador Dali-Van Gogh-artsy reality-bending thing or something'. Because at work, you look *really* girly."

I didn't feel better until I'd hidden it, though. And for good measure, I hid that awful photo of me from the last wrap party. "Yeah. But it just takes one person to ask, 'Why is Mini painting herself as a guy?'..."

"You worry too much," Sarah told me. "Anyway, speaking of you worrying too much about stuff, how's Schoolgirl? You never said what happened."

I remembered that last image of Bree waving jubilantly at me from my doorway. From my secret smile, Sarah gasped openly and reached across the car to push me. "*No!*" she said, laughing. "*You didn't!*"

"I did," I told her, knowing exactly what she meant. "Just some kissing, though."

She laughed openly. "I am *psychic*, I swear to god!" she announced, taking her hands off the wheel for a second so she hold them up to the sky in triumph. She quickly put them back as another car passed us. "Not that I'd really have needed to be. Schoolgirl basically has heart eyes every time she looks at you."

I told her some of the details as we continued the rest of the way to Rob's house, but stopped abruptly as she took a sharp turn off the end of a road directly into loose orange sand. I could see the top of a roof nestled in some trees just ahead. I would have liked to appreciate the lovely quaint picture that might have made, but I was too busy worrying about my tablet cracking because of how much the car was lurching around. "You call this a driveway?"

"You know, I said pretty much the same think the first time Rob brought me here," she told me, and reached over again to pat me firmly on the back, imitating Rob's broad Australian accent. "Welcome to the *real* Australia, babe."

We passed another much newer four wheel drive as we parked outside the house, and Sarah made an excited noise. "Rob's home from work early!" she told me, and then leapt out of the car almost before she'd parked it to jog up the stairs.

The door swung open before she made it there, and Rob came out with the hugest, most genuine smile on his face. He held his arms out to her and she jumped into them and they kissed soundly on the porch, interrupted only by Rob telling her how much he loved her and how much he'd missed her.

It was beautiful. They were *so* happy. I could have watched them for ages—honestly, I kind of wanted to paint it—but it probably looked creepy, me just sitting here staring at them. I climbed out of the car while they were greeting each other and went to get my luggage out of the boot.

"Welcome to my humble abode!" I could hear Rob booming from the porch as I pulled my suitcase out. I'd been here for about three minutes, and I was already glad I'd come.

TWENTY-THREE

The problem with feeling comfortable looking like this was that I *completely* forgot that Bree was the only person used to seeing it. As it was, I had so much going on that it didn't even occur to me that Sarah wouldn't have told Rob everything about my gender stuff, until he stopped halfway down the front stairs when I emerged from the boot of the car.

"Jesus, you weren't wrong!" he said to Sarah with complete astonishment on his face, "That *is* different!"

Like Sarah, he had a barrage of questions. Unlike Sarah, though, he wasn't as diplomatic in how he worded them, which made me nervous. I was still *very* uncomfortable talking about this with people, even people who were sympathetic.

After I'd mumbled something about maybe being transgender and Rob had very openly asked all the usual questions that I didn't have answers for like, 'when did you know?' and 'how did you know?' and 'are you going to get surgery?', he looked over his shoulder at me as he carried my luggage into the house. "Sorry," he said amicably, clearly just curious. "No offence. I don't know any of this stuff."

I shook my head. "I don't know any of it either," I said. "It's all just kind of happening to me. Sorry my answers are mostly 'I don't know'."

Sarah held the door open for us as we went inside, and Rob dumped my suitcase inside a door off the tiny hallway and then gave me the *strangest* look. "I don't get how you cannot know, though. Can't you just," he waved his hand vaguely at my jeans, "check what's in there, or are you one of those people who has both or something?"

I felt *deeply* uncomfortable about the part of me he was referring to, and I didn't think I was going to be able to explain the disconnect I had with it.

Fortunately, Sarah came to my rescue. While Rob was showing me around his house—which was basically like a large run-down bachelor pad complete with pool table and a bar in the living room—Sarah explained the difference between someone's physical sex and their gender identity. The things Sarah was saying I already intrinsically kind of knew just from my own experience, but it was all brand new information to Rob who looked like we'd just told him the Earth actually was flat.

"How the hell do you know all this?" he asked her when she was done. "Did you sneak off and do *another* degree while I was busy up here?"

Sarah laughed. "Nope," she said. "I asked Google."

"Huh," he said, and then looked at me with the most baffled expression. "Well, I need a drink after that," he said. "And I bet *you* need one."

I sighed. "Just one?"

He looked delighted with that answer. "Now you're talking, I bought a whole slab!"

While he went and stuck his head into the enormous fridge he had behind his bar, Sarah leant over to me. "I love that guy," she told me with a big grin on her face. "Even though he works with hardcore bigots I *knew* he'd still be fine with it."

She was right: it hadn't gone so badly, even though Rob was, in his own words, a country boy. I should have been feeling good about that, but I was still shaky and tense and uncomfortable. The whole coming out process was stressful. I wished there was something I could say that would make people just nod and get on with their day instead of asking a million questions. Maybe I should make brochures, I thought, since that seemed to be what I specialised in these days. I could hand out beautifully illustrated, high-gloss material with a FAQ titled, 'Everything you need to know about why Min looks like a boy now'.

While I was imagining what Jason would do if I came back from Broome with those brochures instead, Rob returned with three stubbies, twisted the lids off with his hands and passed each of us one. "Here you go," he said. "Want to go sit on the back porch? Pretty nice afternoon outside."

There was an old couch and a classic rocking chair out the back, and since Rob and Sarah obviously wanted to sew themselves together at the hip, I took the rocking chair. I was itching to make an 'it rocks' joke, but I was still a bit rattled from our previous conversation so I didn't say anything. I just looked out towards the sea.

It was a great view; Rob's orange backyard opened up onto a sugar-white sandy beach and the water was just as blue as the sky. It was probably not quite atmospheric enough to paint yet, but sitting here *was* relaxing.

Sarah took a swig of her beer and settled into the couch as Rob draped an arm across her shoulders. "What are you doing home so early, anyway?" she asked him. "You're not normally back until at least seven or eight."

"Yeah, well," he said, as if Sarah had just asked a really big question. "I've got no fucking idea what's going on up at the Waterbank site. We'd had dramas on and off for a month and today the boss put us all on standby pending some court case." He had a sip of beer, looking unaffected. "I don't really care. Standby rates are shit, but having free time isn't."

"How long are you off for?" she asked. "Just today?"

Rob shook his head. "No idea. There's a directional meeting-thing or some shit on Wednesday next week, so I guess we'll find out how long we're off after that. Means I don't need to work Saturday, though," he said, giving Sarah a squeeze. "More time to spend here." They kissed briefly.

I felt a bit like a third wheel; I'd forgotten how all over each other they were. Since I had my phone in one of my pockets, I thought I might as well check to make sure Bree hadn't burnt down the hotel yet. I hadn't even turned it on since I got off the plane, and when I did, a message came through from a number I didn't have saved.

I opened it, bracing myself in case it was someone from work.

It wasn't. *"so uh... u would be surprised the type of mobiles you can get for 300..............."*

I groaned audibly. Really, Bree? She'd blown all of it in *six hours*? *"That money was supposed to be for food and emergencies,"* I replied, saved her number, and then checked my bank account balance to see what I could tell the hotel to debit from me. I didn't *really* have a problem with her using the money for a phone, but I wished she'd told me because now it was going to be annoying to get more to her. I should have left her that five hundred after all, I thought.

"yay u didnt die in a plane crash!!!! also ur tv is totally amazing. it can do aaallllll this cool stuff!!"

I was still annoyed about the money. *"I never really used any of the extra features."*

I didn't exactly invite an explanation, but she gave me one anyway. *"well it has this thing where u can get it to tell u when a show u like is on so u dont miss it..... and the manual says u can like wave at it or something and get it to do stuff but i havent figured out how to get it to do that yet.. u can apparantly skype from it too but all i can do so far is take bad pics of myself...........also.......... it has this messaging function where u can send people text messages without even having a mobile....................;) ;) ;)"*

I stopped trying to scroll through my address book for the external hotel reception number. Was she...? *"You actually didn't buy a phone, did you?"*

"haha nope!!!!!!!!! im way too lazy to go anywhere ive just had room service and now im about 1000000kg and i cant get off the couch ;) ;) ;) haha i cant believe u fell for it!!!"

Bree, I thought, shaking my head and chuckling to myself. I was going to have to get her back for that one.

I was replying to her text when I realised I couldn't see Sarah or Rob moving in my peripheral vision. I looked up. They'd stopped kissing—some time ago, by the looks of it—and were waiting for me to notice they were watching me. They laughed at my expression.

"Is that Bree?" Rob asked with a big grin.

I looked from him to Sarah. "You *told* him," I accused her flatly.

She looked guilty. "I thought you were going to ask if you could bring her up, too, so I had to say *something*!"

My eyebrows went up. "I didn't know that was an option," I said, wondering if it was too late to fly her up now. It probably was; it was Easter, all the flights would be full. "I kind of wish I had. Bree loves watching me paint."

Sarah snorted. "That sounds like a euphemism."

I gave her a look. "It's not," I said, taking a sip of beer as I looked back at the view off the porch. "Anyway, I should really start thinking about what I'm going to do, I guess. This is a beautiful place."

Rob practically puffed up his big barrel chest. "Yeah, nice backdrop, isn't it? What do you reckon?" he asked me. "Will you be able to do something with that?"

I considered it. "Yeah," I decided. "Not right now, though. I need specific colours, so I'll probably do most of my paintings at sunrise and sunset. I should get some variety in the images, too. I've got seven to do, and it would be fantastic if they were all really different." I looked back toward him. "Do you know any picturesque places I should go?"

A big smile grew across Rob's face.

I'd asked exactly the right question. Rob was fiercely proud of his new hometown, and couldn't *wait* to take us on a tour of the area. He went inside and brought a big map out onto the porch, holding it up and spending a good half an hour going over possibilities about where he could take me. By the time we had a route mapped out, Rob was keen to start straight away, except we'd all had a few beers by that point and no one was driving anywhere.

"I'll stick to the beach here tonight," I reassured him. "You can drive us around tomorrow."

Later, as the sun set, I took my laptop, tablet and two deck chairs down to the beach and set up camp on the sand facing the shallow red cliffs on the edge of the shoreline.

Sarah and Rob were quite helpful and I thought they were just being really nice at first, before I realised that me being this far away from the house for a couple of hours was going to give them the opportunity to get reacquainted, so to speak. I accepted the deck chair from Sarah and then rolled my eyes at her. "Go on," I told her, inclining my head towards the house.

She grinned. "Sorry," she said a bit bashfully. "It's been two weeks since I've seen him and I'm pretty up for it right now."

"Just make sure I don't walk in on it or you'll scar me for life," I told her as she hiked up the embankment towards where Rob was waiting for her on the porch.

She laughed at that, turning around and shouting, "Lies! I've got a great rack! You'd be completely turned on!" Rob didn't look like he was going to disagree with that as they disappeared into the house.

I chuckled, settling down on the deck chair and turning all my equipment on. It was so weird to think of them tearing off each other's clothes in there. It wasn't like the mental images were terrible, though, just foreign. That's how relationships normally were, I guessed. When half of the couple wasn't secretly dealing with gender stuff and both partners were actually attracted to each other. I sighed, opening a blank file and plotting out some of the shapes I could see in front of me.

I got the outline of the landscape and spent a few minutes

setting up a colour palette for the sky, the sea and the cliffs. I'd sat back to just double check I'd got the hues right when it struck me where I actually was. I was *looking* at these cliffs, I wasn't just squinting at a screen with reference pictures on it. I was in the middle of fucking nowhere, painting *beautiful* scenery and, at least for now, someone was paying me to do it. I wasn't sure how long this would last with all the crap that was going down at work, but it was nice while it did.

All of that felt so far away, though. Henry would be landing in Korea shortly; Jason and Diane and the rest of the asshole Marketing department were still in Sydney. Out here, with the gentle sound of waves breaking, it was easy to pretend none of it mattered and none of them existed. I briefly considered just chucking it all in and moving up here forever, but quickly dismissed that fantasy. Mum *wasn't* pretend, and she would *never* leave me alone if I did something so impulsive. I couldn't do that to Henry, either. I owed him an explanation of what was going on. And then there was work. I'd *never* find another job like Frost, ever. Every marketing student in every Australian university would *kill* for my job, and if I quit, I'd never get a reference and that was it for my career.

I couldn't leave Bree, either. Not now.

So while all of that was nice to think about, none of it was realistic. All my problems were still real, they wouldn't just disappear because I moved up here.

I sighed. I'd been enjoying the peace right up until that point, but now all this quiet time to think was making me miserable. I stopped for a moment and looked down at my pocket where my phone was.

It took me the space of about three seconds to decide to call Bree. She didn't pick up straight away, and I wondered if she wouldn't because I was calling the hotel phone. In the end, she did. "Hello, Min's phone?" she said, trying to sound mature. I found it endearing.

I altered my voice so it sounded really feminine. "Yes, hello, I'm looking for Min Lee."

She hesitated. "Um... sh—Min's not available right now. Can I take a message?"

437

I smirked, propping the phone between my shoulder and my ear and filling in some of the colour of the cliffs. "Actually I'm downstairs in the foyer. I have a package marked for Min Lee. Perhaps you could come down and collect it?"

"Uh, I guess? Okay, I'll be right there." She hung up.

I waited several minutes, and then finally I got a text message from her. *"oh my god i know that was u AND UR TERRIBLE!!!!!"*

I laughed outright, and called her back. "That's for tricking me about spending three hundred on a phone," I told her.

"Oh my god, I *hate* you," she said, and I could hear her giggling. "I was running everywhere down there and then I went up to reception and said, 'Did you see a woman with a package down here?' and they all thought I was *crazy!*"

Imagining her doing that made me smile. "...*Thought* you were crazy?"

"Oh, shut up, it was all your fault," she said, and I heard the sound of the couch groan as she lay back in it, the handset still against her ear. "So how is it? Are you having fun? Where are the others? Weren't there other people up there with you? Wasn't *Sarah* up there with you?"

I didn't know which question to answer first, so I just picked one. "Yeah, it's Sarah's boyfriend's place that I'm staying at," I told her. "They're... *busy* right now."

"Busy?" She realised what I meant. "*Oh. Oh!*" She sounded smug. "So naturally you called *me.*"

I... hadn't thought of it like that, but I supposed she was right. "Yeah."

I could almost *feel* her smiling through the phone. "Well, I wish I was there, then..."

I stopped painting for a second, smiling myself. I wished she *was* here, too, but I doubted I'd be painting if she were.

"So what's it like? Is it pretty?"

I looked around me. "Would you like to see? If the TV can get MMSes, that is." I took a photo with my phone and sent it to the number Bree had been texting me from.

I heard a chime in the background, and Bree said, "I guess it can." There was a pause. "Oh, wow, you're actually *on the beach*? Is it hot?"

"Mid-twenties, now. During the day it was 30-something."

"Hot, mid-20s..." Bree said, and then giggled. "If I was there, I'd totally be wearing this bikini I have. My cousin got it for me in Brazil, it's not like a G-string or anything but there isn't much to it. Oh, and if you think my boobs look big in a bra, you should *so* see me in this thing." I could hear the grin in her voice. It faded. "Dad won't let me wear it, though."

"Well, you could wear it up here," I told her, fixing the opacity of the brush I was using.

"That's bullshit, you'd never let me wear it, either."

I looked up from my tablet. "I wouldn't?"

She was smiling again. "No way. You'd be all like, 'Oh, Bree, it makes me *uncomfortable* when you show that much skin. Please put your habit back on'."

She actually probably had a point. Although... I looked around me at the beach. Far up the other end of it near the centre of Broome I could still see some people swimming. Up this end, I was the only person. There were some other houses, but they appeared to be empty so Bree could have probably have run around here wearing whatever she wanted. I stood by my previous comment that I wouldn't have gotten any painting done, though. "I'm by myself at the moment, so maybe not."

"It wouldn't make a difference, though, you'd still be *uncomfortable*."

I frowned, bleeding some colour from the sky down onto the water while I waited for her to continue.

"Just so you know, I get *why* you're uncomfortable, and half of it has nothing to do with other people." I opened my mouth and began to contradict her, but she interrupted me. "Maybe if you just looked, you know? Like, if you didn't keep saying 'oh, I shouldn't' and just actually did it because you want to?"

When I was staring blankly at my tablet and trying to process what she'd just said, she quickly added, "Actually. Call me back later, okay? I'm going to figure this TV out," and hung up.

The dial tone beeped in my ear. I took my mobile from between my jaw and shoulder, blinked at it, and then put it back in my pocket and kept painting while I thought about what she'd said. It seemed important and I had a feeling I should have paid attention to it, but I also really needed to paint as much as possible before the sun set and I was running out of time. I took a couple of photos with my phone just to preserve some of the detail, and then blocked in as much colour as I could before it was too late.

After the light I needed had gone and I was packing up, I heard the back door to the house open and shut and Sarah emerged with something in her hand. She saw me looking at her and raised it so I could see: it was a bottle of alcohol. Her hair was wet from the shower and she looked *much* more relaxed as she staggered down the embankment and offered me the bottle.

I smirked at her, showing her my hands were full of my electronics. "Feeling better?"

"I'm feeling *great,* thanks," she told me, drinking from the bottle since I couldn't take it. "A bit guilty about the fact you were down here working while I was inside getting my rocks off, but I figured Johnny Walker will make me feel a lot better about that if I came out here and shared him with you."

I laughed. "Now that's my kind of threesome," I told her. "Can you help me get these onto the porch, though? I don't want to get sand in them."

She did, and then we both sat down on the edge of the embankment with the daylight fading, passing the bottle between us as the sun disappeared over the ocean.

"I can't believe you're actually here," Sarah said eventually, after a minute or two of quietly regarding me. "A month ago I could hardly get you out of your house, and now you're here in my boyfriend's backyard in the middle of nowhere, drinking with me."

It really hit home when she put it like that. "Yeah." Even I could hardly reconcile myself with the person I was a month ago; with the *woman* I thought I was a month ago.

Sarah chuckled at my one-word answer. "So eloquent." She took the bottle from me and had a couple of mouthfuls. "You should have brought Schoolgirl. It would have been a riot, she's great."

I smiled at that. "Yeah," I repeated, and then realised I still wasn't pulling my weight in the conversation. "I was talking to her before. It would have been nice to have her here, even if I'm still with Henry..."

Sarah poked me with the bottle as she was passing it back. "Just call him up and tell him it's over, Min," she said as I took the whiskey from her and had some more. "Trust me, the bandaid method is the only way, it hurts like hell if you peel away at it slowly."

I grimaced, half because I'd had a really big mouthful of straight whisky and it *burnt*, and half because of what she'd said. "He's actually visiting my mother in Korea over Easter."

She made a face. "Ouch."

I nodded. "Yeah. You see my dilemma? My mum personally invited him because she *loves* him. And she will never, ever accept me dating Bree. Or me as anything else except her daughter. I'm not exaggerating, either. She will *never* accept either of those things."

Sarah watched me. "So you're not going to do them?"

I sighed at length. "No, I guess I *am* going to do them," I said. "But I just haven't figured out how I'm going to handle her yet." I thought more about it and shook my head. I didn't even know how I'd broach the subject with Mum. It didn't really make sense to me, either; I couldn't figure out how Bree and I had become so involved with each other, and so *quickly*. Too quickly, maybe?

"What if I'm making a giant mistake?" I asked, and Sarah looked quizzically at me, so I elaborated. "With Bree. She's so young, and I can't even figure out if we have anything in common."

Sarah snorted. "Yeah, I know that argument. Not so much the young one, but Rob and I literally have *nothing* in common." She grinned ear to ear. "And I love that big, stupid beefcake. He's the nicest, most down-to-earth guy I've ever met and the sex is fantastic. I hope I end up marrying him."

I looked across at her. She and Rob *were* different. Sarah was the type of smart that approached actually being intimidating, and Rob... well, he wasn't. "Don't you worry about that, though?" I really struggled to put it nicely. "That you'll miss having really intellectual discussions with someone?"

"Nope," she said resolutely, and then looked sideways at me. "I know you've kind of walled yourself in at home with Henry for the last three years, but you actually *don't* have to just choose one person for the rest of your life and you're not allowed to talk to or have anything to do with anyone else. Rob's my partner. We do partner-y things together, and what he can't give me I'll just come to you guys for."

I sat back and thought about what she'd said. "That's actually really deep."

She looked at me for a second, and then laughed. "I love how this is a totally new concept for you. 'I can talk to more than one person? *Really*?'." She took the bottle from me and had another drink. "I bet you were one of those people who had just *one* best friend all the way through school and barely talked to anyone else."

I didn't say anything, I just pressed my lips in a tight line.

She looked across at me. "No? Did I get that wrong?"

"Yeah."

Her eyebrows went up. "Wow, sorry," she said. "I just couldn't really see Uptight Girl Min relaxing and socialising with a group of people, my bad." That actually really hurt, and she panicked when she saw it in my face. "Wow, okay, that sounded *really* nasty. I didn't mean it as an insult. I meant it as a genuine observation."

I *knew* she didn't mean it as an insult, but it was really close to the bone and it took me a few moments to recover from it. 'Uptight Girl Min' didn't relax and socialise.

"You're right, though, Sarah."

Sarah spent a few seconds frowning at me. "I feel like there's a lot more to this," she said. "If you want to tell me, that is, especially after I was just accidentally a total bitch. It's okay if you don't."

I wouldn't normally have said anything. I actually was tempted to joke about it, but I didn't. The alcohol was starting to get to me, and Sarah was giving me her full attention, too. Against my better judgement, I ended up just saying it. "I didn't have any friends in high school," I told her. "I used to be friends with this boy in primary school, but a couple of years into high school he stopped hanging around with me."

Sarah was at least careful about treading more lightly this time. "Why? Did you just kind of... you know, drift apart?"

I shook my head. "I was *really* unpopular, and I guess it's hard to be associated with someone like that."

She sat back, blowing a stream of air through her lips. "Wow..." she said. "That really, really sucks."

"It did."

I took a deep breath and exhaled, and Sarah very pointedly

passed the bottle to me. I took a few mouthfuls from it.

When I swallowed, she asked, "Did they pick on you for some specific reason? Like, were they jealous because you're really smart or something? I had some kids tease me at the beginning of high school because I skipped a grade and I was younger than them."

I wished it had been something like that, I thought, remembering what had happened. I never talked about it, though. I could barely even bring myself to think about it most of the time. The only reason I could come up with as to why I was doing either right now was that I'd had far too much Scottish whiskey and it was interfering with my ability to know when I should keep my mouth shut.

"It wasn't jealousy," I said, handing the bottle back to her. "Nothing like that. I mean... it kind of makes sense now when I think about it now. On my first day at high school, I wore my PE uniform because my dress was too big. I've always been pretty tall and I guess I was a tomboy, so yeah... one of the girls in my class thought I *was* a boy, and she kept slipping me notes and making loud comments to her friends about how cute she thought I was. I was *way* too shy to correct her."

Sarah was listening so intently she had forgotten it was her turn to drink. I felt like my only option was to continue, so I did.

"Anyway, after Mum had taken in my skirt and I came to school in it..." I shook my head. "Her face when I walked into the classroom... She was *so* angry, and all her friends were laughing at her and teasing her about it."

"And so *she* started teasing *you*," Sarah finished, finally taking that drink. "What stuff did they do? It must have been really terrible, right? I just used to get called Doogie Howser. I hated it at the time but it didn't scar me or anything."

I *wished* it had only been light name-calling. It hadn't been. "Well, it started off as really juvenile stuff, like teasing me about the fact I liked my uniform baggy, or saying I should join the Chinese basketball team. The original girl really homed in on the fact I was a tomboy, though, and she and her bitchy friends would tape coupons for push-up bras, ads for breast augmentation and things like that to the outside of my locker. One time after swimming my bra went missing, and I found it on the skeleton in the science room, and then as I was taking it off someone said, 'that's not Min's bra, there's no *way* that surfboard girl is a B-cup'. I didn't want to go to PE after that. I always got into heaps of trouble for skipping it, but I didn't care. I just couldn't take all that crap anymore and I was sick of hiding and crying and *everything* and I just couldn't do it."

I *never* said this much about it. I hated talking about this kind of stuff, but I could remember it all so clearly and the alcohol made me feel like a dam had been breached and there was nothing I could do to stop the words from *pouring* out of me.

"I couldn't walk into a classroom. I couldn't answer a teacher's question. I couldn't do *anything* without people leaning together and whispering. I just couldn't handle it, it was *hell.* I hated waking up in the morning knowing I had to go to school, every morning on the way to school I felt sick. I hated everything about myself and how I looked and I just wanted to disappear into nothing. There wasn't any part of me they didn't pick at or make fun of, and even when I tried to fit in I just felt so *different* and wrong. I begged my Mum to let me change schools. I *begged* her for six whole years. But she said I should just ignore people who said bad things about me because St. Mary's was the best school and I belonged there."

After I stopped, a silence hung in the air. All I could hear was the sound of the waves breaking on the beach, Sarah didn't say anything.

I slowly realised what I'd said. How *much* I'd said. I'd never told *anyone* that much. And when I looked across at Sarah, she had her jaw *open*. She had no idea what to say.

My stomach clenched. Fuck, I should have kept my mouth shut, I thought, I've said too much. I've said *way* too much. *Why* did I tell her all that stuff? She was one of the last remaining people on the planet that still retained some modicum of respect for me, and here I was, pathetically blubbering on about how I'd been bullied in high school. She invited me up here thinking we were going to have fun, and instead I'd dumped all my crap on her.

"Min, that's *awful*," she said finally, still shell-shocked. "I don't know what to say. You're great and you look great, those kids were full of it."

I was spaced out, and I couldn't say anything. I didn't want her to feel sorry for me, and I didn't want her to think I was fishing for compliments, but it sounded like I was, didn't it?

Sarah could see my expression and she looked like she was panicking just as much as I was. "At least that's all in the past, right?" she said, trying to reassure me. "I mean, you look great now. I've always thought you were really pretty and you've got a great body, you know? People would kill for a body like yours."

I flinched when she said 'pretty'. She was simply trying to be nice, but the very last thing I needed right now was to be reminded about my female body. I couldn't even face *thinking* about it, let alone *talking* about it. Honestly, whoever would kill for it was *welcome* to it. I didn't say as much to Sarah because she was really, honestly just trying to make me feel better. There wasn't anything I could do. I just wanted to mumble some excuse and rush off back to the house and shut myself in the bedroom *forever*.

I didn't, though. We'd gone past the point where I could run off on her.

"Sarah," I said shakily, putting my hand on her arm so she didn't say anything else. "I appreciate you trying to make me feel better. I just... Can you give me a few minutes?"

"Yeah, sure, of course," she said immediately, but she looked upset.

I've done it again, I thought, feeling my throat tighten. I've wrecked her night. "Thanks."

She smiled a bit and held up the half-full bottle of Johnny Walker, saying with exaggerated casualness, "Plenty left of this, so I'll be right here."

I worried about the fact she was waiting for me, and then turned and left, staggering ungracefully up the embankment and falling over several times in the loose soil.

Inside, Rob was completely engrossed in the TV, a beer in one hand and a bowl of chips in the other. He waved at me with the beer as I went past him. I smiled, and then went straight into the room he'd dumped my bags in and closed the door. It had a little key in the lock so I turned that, too, and then sat on the bed.

I couldn't *believe* I'd told her all of that pathetic crap about myself. Especially not when she'd brought me up here to have fun with her and Rob over Easter.

I was about a thousand miles away from 'fun' right now. I kept thinking that maybe Sarah was just feeling sorry for me and being patient right now, but pretty soon she'd be sick of my bullshit. And then she'd get frustrated and angry and regret ever inviting me up here and the further I went with that thought the more certain I was that I shouldn't ever have come because by the end of this weekend Sarah and I wouldn't even be able to talk to each other and I'd be avoiding both her and Henry and everyone else at work and I was breathless and my ears were ringing.

I didn't want to freak out here. I wanted to have a good time. Why the *hell* did I tell her all that depressing stuff?

While I was sitting there on the edge of the bed trying to take deep, slow breaths, my pocket buzzed. *Bree*, I thought, and while clambering to get my phone out, I nearly dropped it.

When I'd finally opened the message, it was a picture of her waving brightly at the TV, dressed in her pyjamas with the text, *"so guess who got picture messages to work.........?? :) :) :)"*

That smile... I turned my phone over in my hand for a few seconds, and then just hit the redial function.

"Hello, Min's phone?"

"Hello, my phone," I said. I could hear the waver in my voice. I wondered if she could.

"Hey!" she said, and, *fuck*, it was so nice to hear her being so cheerful and imagine that matching smile. "Did you get my message?"

"Yeah."

"Your TV is *so* amazing. It's like something out of a sci-fi movie. I've been playing with it all evening! Did you know it has games, too?" I could hear her walking across the room and flopping down into the couch.

"So does the black console next to it," I told her. I lay back against the mattress of the bed and closed my eyes, trying to focus on her happy voice.

"Yeah, but that's *supposed* to have games. This is a TV, it's supposed to do TV things, but it does *everything* and it's totally amazing!" She paused, and when it was silent, she said, "Min, you seem kind of... off? Are you okay?"

I opened my eyes; I hadn't realised it was that obvious. No, Bree, I thought. No, I'm not okay. Please just keep talking.

She understood. "Anyway," she continued, "So, I was just trying to figure out how to get Skype to work and it turns out there's this *whole* section on video calling that I needed to read..."

I listened to her explain the virtues of my TV with more animation than someone trying to make commission off the sale of it. The highlight for her was the part where she discovered that the camera on the TV actually *followed you around the room* when you walked across it. She was *so* excited about it, and by the time she'd finished, all that whiskey I'd had a quarter of an hour ago was starting to make me feel like I was floating on my back in the sea.

"And you can set the zoom so that no matter where you are in the room, it always has exactly the same amount of your head in the shot!" she finished.

"That actually sounds creepy," I told her, feeling pleasantly drunk. "Are we one hundred per cent certain it hasn't been sent to exterminate mankind?"

She giggled, and then ended with a sigh. "Do you feel better, now?"

I exhaled. "Yeah."

"So what was it? Work again? Because those guys can seriously get fucked."

"No..." It took me a little while to figure out what I was going to say while Bree waited patiently on the other end of the phone. "Sarah invited me up here to have fun, and instead she accidentally brought up stuff from high school..."

"And now you're hiding somewhere and you feel like crap?"

That was surprisingly acute. "Yeah, actually."

She chuckled once. "Yeah, well, welcome to my life." We lay there for another minute or so, silent. Eventually she said, "Can I say something really weird?"

"You're asking for permission now?"

"*Min*," she said, but she giggled a bit. "You told me a while back that you locked yourself in the graphics lab at school every day for six years, and I think about that a lot. Like, a lot. And you've told me other stuff about how much school sucked for you and how other kids made you feel really bad about yourself, and like... okay, no, I need to start somewhere else, sorry," she said. I had to laugh a bit at that. "Okay, okay. So there's a really big colour printer at school, and only the art students are supposed to use it, but whatever. Sometimes when everything sucks, I look around the internet for really beautiful pictures, like of beautiful landscapes and beautiful creatures, and I just print them all out and cover my wall in them," she said. "So when I'm at home and lying in bed, everywhere I look it's so beautiful, and so colourful and, like, magical."

My paintings, I thought.

"And one time I decided to message the person who made them, and, well, that person was *so* nice to me. And, like, really funny. And after that when I looked up at the pictures on my wall I remembered that, and it made them even more beautiful. And then I decided eventually that I really wanted to meet that person... and I did, and you were *nice*, and so generous, and I know I'm kind of intense and you were pretty good about that too, and when you bought that bracelet for me... I can't even tell you what that felt like. So, yeah. Here we are. I think heaps about those kids chasing you into the graphics lab, because as much as I hate them for making you hate yourself, look at the *amazing* things they helped you create."

I'd never thought of it like that. It had never even occurred to me to think of it like that.

"So, I kind of feel like that other stuff, all the body stuff, I want to help you with that. And I know I can't do everything because I don't have a magic wand and can't magically make you a guy, but... I feel like if I try hard enough, I can help."

I opened my mouth and closed it again. "Bree, you do help. You know you help."

"Then I'll keep going," she said, and then added, "I have this idea that one day you'll be able to see yourself the way I see you."

I couldn't even *imagine* thinking like Bree spoke about me. "I think that's an impossible goal."

"Well," she sounded cheerful. "I won't know unless I try, will I?"

I smiled to myself. Bree's 'try' rarely left room for fail, and there was so much comfort in that, so much. "Thank you."

"My pleasure," she said warmly, and then changed the subject. "You want to Skype for a bit? I can show you the creepy camera."

I made a face. I would actually have liked to, but I couldn't. "No, I'd better wash all this red soil off me and then go back out to

Sarah. She's waiting for me."

Bree made a noise. "I should have a shower, too. My hair looks like a pom-pom. We can shower together." She paused. "I was also going to say 'Whoops, I didn't mean that!', but I kind of do."

I chuckled. "Thanks, Bree. I'll call you later." I hung up. I was grinning as I grabbed my toiletries and went to have a shower.

Rob's bathroom was cursed with a full-length mirror on the back of the door, and for most of my shower I managed to expertly avoid seeing any of myself in it. Unfortunately the exhaust fan was really effective and the mirror didn't fog up, so when I stepped out of the shower and reached across to the far wall for my towel, I ended up in front of it, towel in hand.

I didn't see myself naked much, maybe that was the reason I hardly recognised myself. The mirror framed me perfectly like a photo, and I'd been painting and doing graphics for work so much recently that my first instinct was to think 'Okay, where do I start? How do I retouch this photo so it's fit for the purpose I need it for?'.

I would have taken the liquify tool and just flattened my chest, leaving nothing. I'd have straightened all my curves, and sharpened all my round edges, but when it came to my crotch, I faltered. Should I add something there? Did the image need a dick to be complete? I couldn't answer that, not at all, and even just asking the question made me feel art-blocked. If I'd had a deadline on submitting this image and needed to make a decision *right now*, I would have just taken the same tool as my chest and smoothed the whole area over like the pants of a Ken doll.

There was something comforting about the idea of my body just being a blank canvas. Being nothing. With nothing I needed to feel uncomfortable about or hate or hide under baggy clothes.

I chalked *that* thought up to a third of a bottle of Johnny Walker. Laughing darkly at how weird I was being, I staggered around and dried myself off, nearly dropping my phone in the bathtub while I was getting dressed again so I could go back out to Sarah.

She was where I left her. I wasn't sure how I expected her to react when she saw me, but she just smiled and patted the patch of hard red soil beside her. "I wasn't sure you were going to come back," she said. "I'm glad I waited, though. It gave Johnny and I the opportunity to spend some quality time together." She held up the bottle; she'd had another good chunk of it while I was gone.

I chuckled at that as I sat down beside her.

She had her phone propped on her knees and she'd obviously been playing with it. All her attention was on me now, though, and she passed me the bottle. "You look better," she observed.

I nodded, and had a drink.

"Sorry if I said the wrong thing before, I'm always worried I'll say the wrong thing when people are upset. You'd tell me if I said something that really hurt you, right?"

I frowned at her. I wasn't sure I would, actually. "I think you'd figure it out," I decided. "But you didn't say anything like that. Sharing personal stuff stresses me out, that's all, and I'm also kind of not okay with talking about my body, so..."

"Yeah, okay, noted," Sarah said, and scrunched up her face. "I *should* have figured that out." I shrugged and handed her the bottle. She gave me the once-over before she drank any more. "So you're okay, now? We're cool?"

"If you don't mind the fact that every time you try to have fun with me I freak out and wreck everything."

She snorted. "I don't know what you thought I expected," she said. "I actually thought inviting you up here would be a really great way to get you out from under your rock and get to know you." She waited for me to process that before she added, "Also, occasionally you're absolutely hilarious so I was hoping for some of that, too. And," she said, "I've been *dying* to prank Rob because he's the most gullible person in the world. I suck at it and you're the master, so I was thinking we could team up and do something diabolical."

She was smiling across at me, and because I was reaching the really affectionate level of drunk, I had this moment where I was *really* glad she wanted to be friends with me. I put an arm around her and hugged her a bit clumsily. "Thanks for putting up with me."

She laughed as I let her go. "I seriously don't know what goes on in your head, Min," she told me. "Most of the time you're just walled and silent and sometimes you say funny things. I don't think anyone's going to give me a medal for 'putting up' with you." She tilted the bottle to her lips and drank the last of the whiskey. "Well, that's it," she said, putting it down beside her. "Johnny's spent. Both

450

of us are going to be *sore* in the morning."

I grinned. Hangovers were such a common occurrence for me they were a non-event. "So did anything particularly exciting happen in my absence?" I nodded at the phone in her lap.

Something occurred to her. "Oh, wow! Actually!" she picked up her phone and unlocked it. "Yeah. Since you were taking ages I thought I'd snoop around a bit about what's going on with Waterbank, right? I didn't actually expect to find anything because all my great web analytics tools are on my laptop. But anyway, Rob said that the court case was listed on Wednesday, so I went through all the different courts and..." she passed the phone to me.

I accepted it from her. "...and you found something?"

She leant over to me and we nearly knocked heads as she pointed at the screen. "That's it," she said, showing me a listing. "Click it." I tapped the screen, and then waited for the details to load on the crappy slow data connection out here as she continued, "It might be nothing, but I kept thinking about the fact Diane was totally obsessed with making sure Sean didn't find out anything about our project, and Diane has nothing to do with Frost Energy because Sean does all that..."

The details loaded, and the Federal Court case for Waterbank was listed as: *10:15AM (Directions) Frost International v Frost Energy.*

TWENTY-FOUR

I had no memory of how I got to bed, but when I woke up I was itchy and topless and there was a ring of sand around me on the bed sheets. I also had a terrible headache which was nothing new, so I popped a couple of painkillers, had a shower, and then wandered out onto the porch where Rob was busy barbecuing *eggs*. Sarah was hunched on the couch trying to eat them as she was reading her phone.

"Morning, Sunshine," Rob said with exaggerated cheer as I emerged. He handed me a plate with bacon and eggs that he'd royally fucked up by burning to a crisp. "Aussie breakfast," he explained, and then held a blackened oblong towards me. "Sausage?"

My stomach turned. "I'm good, thanks."

He shrugged. "More for me."

I sat down next to Sarah. She glanced up, and I expected her to comment on how terrible she felt—but instead she just said sagely, "Sean and Diane will destroy Sydney *ala* Tokyo in King Kong versus Godzilla."

I gave her a weird look, and she laughed gently and showed me the screen of her phone. On it, there was a whole list of theories the two of us had apparently come up with about *Frost International v Frost Energy* last night while we were wasted. Some of them weren't half bad, but most of them were ridiculous and you could only have found them funny if you were *extremely* drunk.

"I don't remember *any* of that," I confessed, and let her go back to reading them while I tried to do something about the plate of 'food' Rob had given me.

"Which means you don't know the *great* news," Rob told me, turning off the gas to the barbecue and flopping down on the rocking chair with his plate of charcoal.

"Great news?" I asked.

"Yeah," he said, taking a bite of his sausage. "The Swans trashed the 'Pies, 100-79. It was beautiful. I haven't cried so much since I was five years old."

Sarah groaned. "*Football.*" She ran a hand over her face. "I can't cope with football right now. I have the worst headache in the history of alcohol. I will *never drink again.*"

"I have a box of painkillers that says otherwise," I told her, and then ducked into my bedroom to grab a couple and returned to give them to her. She dry-swallowed them which was impressive, and then got back to her breakfast.

Rob finished his with a very loud, guttural burp. Both of us stared at him and he just grinned. "So, when shall we hit the road, girls?" he said, remembering too late and then looking with panic at me. "...people."

I waved my hand dismissively at him. He was trying. "We've missed the opportunity for me to get a sunrise today, I think. I wouldn't mind seeing..." I glanced towards Sarah, wanting to say 'the proposed mining site' but also not wanting to give away *anything* to Rob after that whole John saga. "Confidential...

things."

Sarah just squinted at me as she stood stiffly. "That makes it sound like you're taking me out into the desert so I can give you a private show."

I deadpanned. "Isn't that why I'm here?"

I expected Rob either to realise I was joking and laugh at me or have a really strong opinion about that not happening, but he just looked very confused about what to think.

Sarah laughed. "Sure, Min, just put on about 50 kilos of muscle and we'll talk," she said as she yawned and stretched. "Maybe 70. Okay, I'm going to go and have a shower, maybe that will make me feel less like crap." She hung on the doorway before she went back inside, though, swinging on it. "Oh, and just a question, in the event that you and I *do* actually hook up, should I wear a school uniform, or...?"

That was what made Rob burst out laughing. Blushing, I stink-eyed them both.

After Sarah had jumped in the shower, Rob rocked backwards and forwards in the chair playfully. "You got a photo of her?" he asked. "Your girl? Sare's never showed me."

'My girl'? I kind of liked that. "Yeah." I patted down my pockets to find my phone, and when I unlocked it I discovered I had a new message. I thought it might be from the girl herself, so I opened it. It wasn't.

"*Just landed in Seoul,*" Henry had sent me last night. "*I hope you arrived safely in Broome and aren't working too hard! ;)*"

I cringed, but disregarded that message so I could find the photo of Bree in the red t-shirt I'd bought her. I passed the phone over to Rob who stopped rocking to look at it. His eyebrows went up and he nodded appreciatively. "Nice," he said as he got up and drummed his full stomach. "You should've brought her."

Now you all tell me, I thought, and stood as well. "I'll wash up," I said, holding my hand out to him so he could pass me his plate.

I spent the whole time I was doing our dishes wishing I *had* actually brought Bree. She'd be hanging over the countertop talking to me while I did this, I thought. Actually, who was I kidding? She'd be *doing* this while *I* leant on the countertop. She probably wouldn't even have let Rob cook breakfast, she'd have insisted on doing it herself. Then she'd have stood by with a delighted smile on her face watching while we ate her food. Thinking about those big smiles of hers made *me* smile.

She'd have loved it here, I decided. The temperature this morning was a really sort of pleasant early twenties, and the sun wasn't too harsh yet. It was great weather for swimming, but I personally wasn't going to be seen in anything less than a big t-shirt and jeans. If Bree had come, I could have just sat on the beach and watched her in that bikini she mentioned yesterday. I tried to imagine what Bree's definition of 'not much to it' in reference to the bikini meant, when there was not much to anything she wore even when she considered herself fully clothed. It was a *very* pleasant thought.

"Geez, Min, I wonder who *you're* thinking about," Sarah said as she emerged from the bathroom, damp and grinning ear-to-ear.

I ignored what she'd said, looking her up and down. She was really relaxed. "Yeah, but why are *you* so happy?"

She kept grinning. "I don't know what the hell is in those painkillers you gave me," she said as she finished towel-drying her hair. "But I feel like I've just shot up or something. They are *strong*."

I shrugged, drying my hands on a tea-towel. "Well, you said you had a bad headache."

She draped her own towel over the back of a kitchen chair so it could dry. "Yeah, but I think I could pop two of those and not notice I was missing a leg. Anyway," she said, yawning. "You want to go take the Range Rover out now to see if we can find the proposed site? It's actually not that far out."

Of course I wanted to, so I put all my electronics in the back of Rob's big four wheel drive and we headed off. Rob waved us off from the front stairs, looking a bit miserable he wasn't allowed to come with us today.

"Maybe it would have been okay for him to join us," I suggested, trying to figure out where the blinkers were on Rob's car, and turning on the windscreen wipers instead. I would have preferred that Sarah drive this big monster of a car, but I wasn't going to let her behind the wheel while she was high on my painkillers. "At least then he could have driven."

"It's that kind of thinking that got you in trouble with Diane and

Jason," Sarah told me, and when I opened my mouth to have a go at her, she smirked at me. "Don't worry, Rob'll be fine. I'll make it up to him tonight."

"By cooking him dinner?" I asked innocently, and then turned out onto the road.

Sarah found that really amusing. "Didn't you say Schoolgirl cooks for you a lot...?"

I ignored her, because she was terrible. "You're supposed to be telling me where to go," I reminded her, and she sobered and started to actually give me directions.

The site really *wasn't* that far out of town — maybe half an hour up the highway towards Derby. We had to leave the main road to get to it, and I had expected there either to be no track or something really makeshift because the site hadn't been constructed yet. But it was a raked gravel road and it looked well-travelled.

To make everything even more confusing, there was an *Approved Vehicles Only* sign and the Frost snowflake, but it had the clear blue flame behind it which meant it was a Frost Energy logo and not the Frost International one.

"Weird," Sarah commented as we drove past it. I agreed with her.

We had to drive off the gravel road to get to the proposed site which was just over the hill, but before I turned off the road, I pulled over and we looked up it. "I'm kind of inclined to go to the end and see what's there." I looked across at Sarah, and when she didn't disagree, we continued up the road until we got to an enormous boom gate.

At least the signage was better at this end. On a big black placard beside the gate, the print read *Waterbank Hydraulic Fracturing Well* and had a whole list of facilities beneath it and ended with *Frost Energy: Powering the Future.*

Sarah leant closer to read the rest of the sign. "So this is where Rob works."

I twisted around behind us to look back at the hill we should have turned off at. It wasn't far away at all. "...*Really* close to the proposed Pink mine."

Since we couldn't get in and probably shouldn't have anyway, I chucked a u-turn and we went and drove back up the hill. I'd been hoping to take a look at the site in case it was pretty and I could paint it later—but it was just rock-solid orange soil covered in skinny trees and shrubs. It was also on the side of the hill and gave us a great view of Waterbank. We leant out of the car and looked down at it.

"Okay, I'm totally convinced that the court case is to do with project Pink," Sarah said eventually. "I could throw a rock down onto that site from here, it's so close."

"Well, *you* couldn't," I corrected her and shot her a sideways grin. "But I take your point." I spent another minute or two looking at it. "Not that I didn't take that confidentiality stuff seriously, because I did, but *wow*, I really thought it was over something petty, like Diane eating the last Tim Tam or something."

"Yeah, I know what you mean. I felt so bad not being able to discuss any of it with Rob, but now I'm pretty glad I kept my mouth shut."

I didn't say anything to that, because while I hadn't breathed a word to Henry, I'd chatted about it with Bree. Who would Bree tell, though? She had nothing to do with Frost.

"Well," I said, and then sat back and buckled my seat belt. "Fuck. I wish I *had* been assigned to some boring investment project, now."

We drove back to the highway. Neither of us had any ideas about how everything knit together; I didn't know anything about law that didn't relate to marketing and Sarah, despite being one of those people who seemed to know lots about everything, didn't either.

"There's heaps of really complex laws about mining leases and stuff," she said. "I think we got told about that stuff in induction, but I don't remember any of it."

"Would Rob know?" I wondered. "He works out here, after all."

She shook her head. "Nah, he's a work-with-his-hands type of person, in case that didn't come across."

I nodded, and then we spent another few minutes in silence. When Sarah spoke again I thought she was going to have another theory, but instead she just said, "Well, I'm hungry and I need caffeine. Want to go grab something in town?" When I was about to remind her that we'd had breakfast, she scoffed at me. "Please, tell me *you* ate anything he cooked. I love him, but he torches metal for a living."

I wasn't all that keen on walking around the centre of Broome in broad daylight like this when Frost employed half of Western Australia. However, Sarah managed to coax me out of the car by promising me most of the FIFO employees would have flown back home for Easter and there would only be tourists.

Because I wasn't wearing my hoodie, either, I didn't have anything I could put over my ponytail. It wasn't even that I wore the hood up most of the time, it was just that I liked having it there in case I wanted to hide. Without it, I felt really exposed. "Do you have a baseball cap in here somewhere?" I asked Sarah, looking over the driver's seat into the back.

She groaned. "I told you, the hair just looks like a bad fashion decision." She hauled me out of the car and closed the door before I could get back inside. "It doesn't make you look like a chick."

"It makes me *feel* like a chick," I told her, but she ignored that and dragged me toting all my electronics into a little café. It had been freshly painted and freshly furnished, by the look of it. Everything looked new and bright.

"Just cut your hair off," Sarah said as she walked up to the counter. Whoever owned the place was out the back in the kitchen and not serving in the empty café. "Heaps of chicks have short hair. Get the hairdresser to give you something you can make look feminine or masculine depending how you style it."

"Heaps of chicks aren't as tall or as boyish as me," I told her. "Can you imagine how much I'd cop it at work if I chopped all my hair off? They're all weird about the fact I'm taller than them as it is. That, and Mum would *kill* me."

The owner came through the double-doors, wiping his hands on his apron. "Good morning!"

"Good morning!" Sarah greeted him, and then turned back to me. "Your mum's in *Korea*," she pointed out, as if that solved everything. It didn't solve jack. She had *no* idea what my Mum was like.

The owner was in his early sixties, had greying hair and the look of a cashed-up retiree. "Take a seat if you like," he said, and when we did, he brought us out a couple of menus. We ordered breakfast and coffee and then he ducked behind the counter to deliver our caffeine fix. After that was sorted, he went back into the kitchen.

Sarah tested her latte. "He's nice," she decided. "The coffee's not bad, either."

I had a sip of mine, too, but because I wasn't really a coffee drinker I had no idea if it was good or bad. I was happy as long as it contained caffeine.

Sarah still had that far-off gaze of someone who was lost in thought. "Maybe Diane's angry about Sean for something else and just put the mine right there to spite him or something?"

I shrugged. That whole dynamic between Sean and Diane was a total mystery to me, and the more I thought about how fucked it all was, the more I really wished the project was over.

I must have looked a bit dismissive, because Sarah frowned. "Aren't you interested in finding out what's going on with those two?"

"I would be more interested if I wasn't in the middle of it, Sarah," I told her shortly. "I really, really just want to get these graphics done, get the pitch delivered and get the contract signed. Knowing what's *really* going on would be great, but it's not going to help me keep my job."

She winced. "Whoops," she said, looking very guilty. "I forgot about that meeting you had with Diane before you left work. Wow, sorry, that was really insensitive." She changed the subject. "So how are you going to handle the graphics, anyway? Did you finish that one last night?"

"Yeah. It's a bit rough, I'll add detail this afternoon, maybe. You want to see?"

She did, so I set up my laptop and tablet to show her what I'd done. I was busy going over what I thought about the placement of text when the owner came back with our food and I had to hurriedly close everything.

He looked amused. "What *were* you guys looking at in my café?" he asked with a grin, obviously assuming it was porn or something. I probably would have joked about it, but I didn't know this guy and I didn't know if he'd get my sense of humour.

"Oh, Min's an artist," Sarah told him. "But sh—he's working on some confidential stuff right now."

To my discomfort, the owner sat down beside us. "You're an

artist?" he asked me, immediately interested.

I shot Sarah a look. "I'm not an artist," I told him. "I work in marketing. I just enjoy painting and I sometimes do the graphics for our campaigns."

He leant forward on the table. "Is that right?" he asked. "Would I have seen your stuff anywhere?"

Sarah laughed briefly. "Probably, we work for Frost."

"So, can I see?" He gestured at his walls. "I'm in the middle of decorating, and I'm on the lookout for some good work to put up."

Sarah and I glanced at each other. I couldn't show him the project paintings, but there seemed to be no good reason *not* to show him my general pieces. I had some of them saved in folders on my laptop so I opened them up and passed him the tablet. "They display better on that," I explained, and then tabbed through them for him.

He looked very impressed. "These are great," he said. "Would you do a request? I want to get a big beachscape for this wall. No people, just a long sandy beach, maybe with some driftwood or a palm tree or two or something like that. Nice and relaxing. How much do you think you'd charge for that kind of thing?"

It sounded like something I really didn't have time for, to be honest. The wall was a good six or seven metres long, and that was a *lot* of work, probably at least a full week. I didn't want to say that, though. "I normally just do graphics for work," I told him. "I've never thought about what I'd charge."

"Well, can you think about it and give me your card?" he asked. "I think it would look great."

I wouldn't have given him my work cards anyway because they had 'Miss' on them, but fortunately I didn't have any with me. I just scribbled my private email on a serviette with an old pen he leant me, and then put my computer away and got stuck into my breakfast as he left.

Sarah looked pleased. "You could get quite a tidy side business going if you did stuff like this," she told me. "I reckon that guy's got a lot of money. You could probably ask for a few thousand."

I scoffed at her. "Yeah, I'll do it in all the stacks of free time I get by working at Frost." I had a bite of my toast. "Besides, freelancing sucks, you never know where your next paycheque is coming from.

I stress out enough as it is, I don't need to worry about not knowing how I'm going to pay for my next meal." Or how I'd explain to Mum why I no longer had anywhere to live, which was a much bigger problem.

"I didn't say anything about freelancing," Sarah pointed out smugly. I sighed at her and kept eating.

We headed back home when we were done with our *real* breakfast, and just as I was pulling out of the car park, my phone rang from my laptop bag.

Sarah dove on it. "If it's Schoolgirl, I'm answering," she said, unlocking it and then looking surprised. "Okay, I'm *not* answering."

I glanced over at her and saw 'Henry' on the screen. Fuck. "Yeah, just leave it. I'll call him later."

She looked uneasy as it kept ringing in her hand, and only put it back in the laptop bag when it fell silent. A few seconds later it chimed to let me know I had a voicemail. I made a face at it, but didn't say anything. Sarah didn't bring it up again, either.

When we got back to the house, Rob was waiting for us on the porch like a Labrador and showed us inside where he'd rearranged the furniture so there were three comfortable positions in front of the TV. "I'm going to induct you into the wonderful world of *AFL Live*," he announced, to which Sarah put her head in her hands. It was an Australian football game for consoles. He looked unaffected by her reaction as he told me, "You might *love* it."

I very much doubted I would love it because sports games were *not* my thing, but I was willing to give it a shot because Rob was very excited and I wanted a good reason to avoid calling Henry back.

Rob sat me down to explain the rules and the controls, and Sarah sat politely with us but spent the first quarter messaging people on her mobile and the second quarter dozing off in the armchair.

I didn't actually get the hang of the game, and Rob had to keep pausing it to explain the rules to me when I screwed up.

Before we gave up and switched to shooters, though, I took a photo of the living room with footy on the TV and Sarah asleep in one of the armchairs and sent it to Bree. "*Highlights of the wild adventures you're missing out on up here.*"

As we were changing the discs, I got a reply. "*haha.... if ur bored....well that chair looks like there might be enough room for both of us in it.........??? maybe i could keep u busy??? ;) ;) ;)*"

I was a bit stunned she'd send me something so suggestive, but on the other hand, this was Bree. Bree who freely posted those 'bust on me' photos of her cleavage on *Facebook.* Suggesting sitting on my lap in an armchair was comparatively pretty tame. And yet, it had far more of an effect on me than her raunchy photos ever did.

I looked over at the armchair she was talking about and imagined playing the whole game with Bree sitting on my lap. That would have been infinitely more fun, I thought, flushing a bit as Rob put *Halo* in the Xbox.

I spent all of *Halo* imagining Bree straddling me and kissing my neck, kissing around my ears, pushing the controller aside and just making out with me in earnest... I died *far* too often for Rob to not notice I was distracted. It was almost a shame when we had to quit so he could drive me to the first of the 'grouse' places he thought I might like to paint as the sun set.

The shallow canyon was nowhere near as entertaining as imagining Bree, but I *did* have work to do, so I tried to focus on it.

Keeping me company while I painted, Sarah had been trying to read up on mining law on her phone when my own phone rang.

"It might be Schoolgirl," Sarah commented, looking pointedly at my ringing pocket. We both knew it wasn't.

I shook my head, focusing on my tablet. "She'd message first. I'll call him back later when I'm not in the middle of something."

Even though I told Sarah I'd call Henry back twice today and had planned on doing it after dinner, Sarah, Rob and I took fish and chips down to the beach after the sun had set and we didn't get home until late. I probably still could have called him at ten or eleven because he would have answered, but I didn't. I just lay awake in bed and imagined what it would have been like if Bree had come up with me here, and kept thinking back to pashing her on the floor outside my bathroom. The way her lips had felt, the way the blade of her tongue ran along mine, and those desperate little sounds she'd been making...

It was such a great feeling, just lying there and indulging those memories in all their glorious detail. And when I thought back to the sweet things she'd said last night and how affectionate and open she was and how good it had felt to imagine her on my lap in the chair... wow, yeah. This was all working for me, in a way that Henry never had. I *wanted* her, and the urgency of it was actually painful. I lay there torn between how good it felt to think about her, and how much it physically hurt she was four thousand kilometres away. I wanted her here in this bed with me.

Shortly before midnight I couldn't take it anymore and texted her, "*I can't stop thinking about you.*"

I wasn't sure if she'd reply because it was so late, but she did. "*dont stop then....im not going to......*"

That gave me one of those stupid smiles again, and I had to put the phone down for a minute or two and grin like an idiot. I picked it up again when it buzzed on my stomach. She'd sent another message. "*what are u thinking about exactly.......???*"

It wasn't cheating just *talking* about it, was it? I hoped not, because before I could talk myself out of it, I replied, "*Kissing you.*"

I held the phone over my face and waited for her to reply. It felt like eternity before another text came through. "*ur making me blush so bad.........*"

That mental image got me. It was hot, imagining her flustered. "*If you think you're blushing now, just wait til I get back...*"

"*......oh my god min ur giving me butterflies...................*"

My stomach was full of them as well, and I wanted to reply, 'I want to give you more than that', but that was *way* too bold for me to convince myself to say to anyone while I was sober. Instead, I decided we'd probably gone as far as I was comfortable going given that I wasn't actually single, so I replied, "*And there's a lot more where they came from ;) Goodnight, Bree.*"

As I was trying to get comfortable in bed, she sent me one last message. "*great how am i supposed to sleep now???????*"

She didn't actually sleep for a while I don't think. I did, though, and when I woke up to my alarm at 5:30 am the following morning so I could go somewhere and paint the sunrise, there was a message on my phone. I rubbed my eyes, yawning, and opened it.

It was a picture message, and it was of Bree sitting on the couch in the doona—in *only* the doona—holding it to her chest with one hand while she pointed the remote towards my magic TV with the other. Compared to some of the photos she'd put on Facebook, you couldn't really see much. It was more her bare shoulders with her curls falling over them and the *knowledge* that there was apparently nothing between her and the doona that made it sexy. And it *was* sexy. She was hardly showing anything, and she didn't have an over-the-top O-face, or a duck-face, or any of the other weird expressions she'd been making in her other photos. In fact, all she had was this shy little smile and those bare shoulders and *fuck* I was going to need a very, very cold shower. I wanted to rip that doona right off her.

The text underneath read, *"wish u were here.............(this one is tasteful right???)"*

I had to laugh at that. She was gorgeous.

I did have a quick shower while I tried not to think about *why* Bree might have been naked in the doona and what she might have been doing, and when I dressed and rushed out into the living room, Sarah was slumped in a kitchen chair looking half-dead. "God, what time is it?" she asked in a croaky voice. "Why couldn't you use stock photos for our materials like everyone else does?"

"Everyone else's careers aren't riding on this one pitch," I reminded her, and tried to figure out where I'd ditched my sneakers.

Rob came out of the master bedroom in his boxers and a dressing gown. "You ready?" he said, apparently having decided he was. At Sarah's expression, he looked down his body. There was nothing self-conscious about him at all, despite the fact he was half-naked and had a sizable beer-belly to go with his muscles. "I'm going to come back here for some more shut-eye while you two are working. What's the point of getting dressed?"

He seemed a lot chirpier than Sarah did, so on the way to wherever Rob was driving us, I asked her, "Couldn't sleep?"

She shrugged. "I could have if I'd tried. I was just reading common law court cases between mining companies to see if I could find anything."

I raised my eyebrows at her. "You see, that would *put* me to sleep, not keep me up. Did you end up finding anything?"

She shook her head. "I probably would have come and told you if I had."

This time Rob dropped us along a rocky creek. The landscape itself wasn't that impressive, but the still water perfectly reflected the sunrise, and it turned out to be a great choice.

Unfortunately, I was distracted. Not by what I should have been distracted by, which was the prospect of fucking up and losing my job or all the infighting going on at Frost, but by the text conversation Bree and I had had last night and that photo she'd sent me.

"Min," Sarah said neutrally at one point, finishing the muesli bar she'd been eating. "You can't *will* the painting onto your tablet. I think you have to actually use the stylus." I'd just been sitting there staring at it.

"I knew I should have read the instructions," I told her in the same flat tone, and then got back to copying the scene in front of me. I was actually a bit embarrassed.

Sarah laughed. "I think someone else was up late," she observed.

"Not that late."

"Late enough to have stuff to think about," she fired back.

I grinned a bit, and she whooped and pointed at me. "I knew it!" she announced. "Probably best I didn't find anything in those court cases, right? Who knows what I would have interrupted if I'd come rushing into your room?"

It was a rhetorical question which was good because the answer was 'nothing'. I didn't want her to know that, though, because I was kind of aware that anyone else who'd been thinking the things I had been would have had their hand down their pants. Everyone else was happy with the contents of theirs, though. I wanted as little as possible to do with mine—I didn't even want to *think* about it—and I didn't want Sarah to guess that. I didn't want *anyone* to guess that.

So, instead, I said, "Pity you didn't. You could have joined in," and winked at her. She groaned and threw her scrunched-up muesli bar wrapper at my head. It missed, and I chuckled and kept painting until I had what I needed.

Since Rob had far more places he wanted to show us than the number of paintings I had scheduled, Sarah and I let him drive us around for the better part of the day. We finished on the beach again with a six-pack of beer, and only came home well after the sun had gone down. After we got there, Sarah and Rob went mysteriously missing together, so I had a quick shower and then switched on my laptop with the intention of finishing off a painting while they were busy with each other. However, I was still a bit drunk and thinking about what Sarah and Rob were doing meant I ended up wanting to message Bree.

Before I did, though, I opened up that picture message she'd sent me to have another look.

It had the same effect the second time around; maybe a bit more so because I was tipsy. Those bare shoulders coupled with that coy little smile... She looked so sweet and innocent—and she was, about some things—but when it came to her body and the effect it had on people, I suspected she knew exactly what she was doing. Her pose was too deliberate, and the angle was too staged. She'd done it on purpose. That made it hotter, though; there was something so deliciously illicit about her spending ages trying to take the perfect photo so I'd be turned on when I looked at it.

She *wants* to turn me on, I thought as I stared at that smile, and she wants me to touch her. She *wants* me to imagine pulling down that doona so I can get to what's underneath. And boy, was I ever doing exactly as she intended.

It made me think other things, too; snapshots, not even whole thoughts. Moving on top of her, skin-to-skin as we kissed deeply... or her rocking back and forth in my lap as she straddled me on the armchair... or even me bearing her down against that hard bench when she'd tried to kiss me at the train station. And, as *hot* as each of those thoughts was and as much as I wanted to indulge them and linger on them and imagine whole scenes and whole stories around them until I was *desperate* for her to be enacting them with me... when I started to think about them, when I started to imagine how they'd begin or how we'd get there.... I got stuck.

I *wanted* her to be straddling my lap, but what was that really going to achieve, with my body? I *wanted* to be on top of her with her legs wrapped around me, but, again, how would that actually work? And in the scenarios I'd been imagining, the movements I wanted to make on her just seemed so easy and so natural. I had such a clear, almost primal expectation of what I was supposed to do, but I didn't have the right body to do it with. It was so

465

disorienting.

And while I was perfectly aware of the fact there were *other* things we could do—and I quite liked the idea of them, actually, at least the idea of doing them to her—they weren't the main course for me, not even close. Trying to pretend they were felt forced. I caught myself thinking, 'Well, I suppose I could *pretend* I'm happy with just head so that I don't upset Bree...' and I *stopped myself dead in my tracks.* I wasn't going to do to Bree what I'd done to Henry. I wasn't going to pretend I was completely happy with something when I wasn't.

I was doing it already, though, wasn't I? When I'd started dating Henry, I'd really, really worried about needing to have sex with him. I'd ended up doing it anyway because I didn't want to upset him, and before I knew it I was stuck doing something I wasn't into. And now here I was worrying about sex again, this time with Bree.

I had an awful thought that maybe I just wasn't supposed to have sex at all, that no matter how much I desperately wanted to, it was never going to work and I was always going to be unhappy.

That was a really confronting, really fucking terrifying thought. I didn't want to think any more about it, because I was going to stress myself out again.

I put my phone away without messaging Bree after all, and tried to focus on completing the paintings.

After a little while Sarah and Rob came back from wherever they'd been, pink-cheeked and glowing. I hated them both a little bit, but I didn't say anything. It wasn't their fault everything just worked for them. I think Sarah noticed something was wrong because she asked about me, but I muttered something about work and she left me alone to finish.

When I was done with one of the paintings, I checked my phone out of habit, and Bree had sent me a message. *"....soooooo......u want me to show you the cool things your tv can do for video calls.............?? ;) ;) ;)"*

I slumped. I *did*, but at the same time, I didn't. I didn't want to be reminded about the crap I'd been worrying about earlier. And if Bree thought were going to give each other private stripteases... I was so at odds with my body right then that if someone had offered me the technology to bond my clothes to my flesh, I would have paid just about anything to do it.

I didn't want to leave her hanging, though, so I messaged back, *"Sorry, Bree, I'm in the middle of working right now."*

I felt guilty about that, but I did call the hotel phone before I went to sleep.

She yawned. "Hey...! I thought maybe you'd gone to sleep already, so I did, too..." From the way she spoke, I could tell she'd been asleep. I could also hear the clock ticking, which meant she was in the living room.

"Wait, are you sleeping on the couch?"

She finished her yawn. "Uh huh."

"Uh, why?"

"Well... it's where the TV is," she told me in a little voice. "Just in case you changed your mind and decided you *did* want to video chat with me, I didn't want to miss the call."

Ouch. I lay there in my own bed, staring up at the ceiling. I wanted to tell her about that stuff I'd worried about earlier, but I couldn't imagine ever talking about things that were so private with someone. I didn't even want to *think* about it, but it was stuff that wouldn't go away, wasn't it? Bree was going to notice if we weren't having sex.

"Min, are you okay? You want to talk again?"

I exhaled. "Yeah. But I don't know how to."

She giggled. "So *that's* why you're so quiet all the time..."

"Oh, *shut up*," I told her, but I was smiling. It didn't last long.

She was yawning again. "Well, I'll give you a big hug when you come home again, okay? I've been eating so many Easter eggs I'll be ball-shaped by then, and you can squish me like a stress ball. It will be very therapeutic."

I smiled briefly at that image, but since she was obviously half-asleep I let her go. I had to have another couple of painkillers before I could get to sleep myself, though.

It would have been nice to spend Easter Day actually relaxing, but I had six half-finished paintings that needed to be formatted, laid out and sent to the rest of the team before I flew back to Sydney on Monday. So, instead of sleeping in and relaxing and celebrating the spirit of Easter or whatever, I had my nose to the grindstone, sitting on the porch and trying one-by-one to complete

467

the detail in all of the paintings. It was a *mammoth* task.

My phone had also been ringing since about nine in the morning, so I left it in my bedroom in order to concentrate on work. A bit after lunch, Sarah, who had been sitting inside reading up on mining law again, came marching onto the porch with my phone. It was vibrating in her hand.

"Min," she said sternly as she stood in front of me and held it out, using my actual name for emphasis. "This thing has been going non-stop for the past two hours. It's stressing *me* out and he's not even my boyfriend. Can you just answer the damn thing and have a conversation with him?"

I accepted the phone from her, feeling guilty. She nodded resolutely and then walked back inside, but as soon as she was gone I just rejected the call, turned vibrate off, and put it in my pocket. I couldn't focus on painting if I had to think about what Henry and my mother were saying to each other while he was visiting her. I'd call him later when I had the energy to pretend everything was fine.

I did actually get all the graphics finished, cleaned up and laid out on some pretty flash looking templates before I went to bed that night. I texted Bree goodnight, and when I woke up in the morning she'd replied, *"im so excited ur coming back tomorrow!!!!!! :D :D :D"*

I smiled at that, rolling onto my back and stretching.

I wasn't excited to go back. I just wanted to stay here, fly Bree up, and leave no forwarding address for ninety per cent of the people I knew. I couldn't, though. I couldn't even lie in bed and feel sorry for myself because I was leaving on the morning flight. Sarah hadn't been able to get me on the afternoon one with her, and that meant I needed to rush around at the crack of dawn to make sure I'd packed everything that belonged to me.

Rob was hardly awake as I left, but he did wander stiffly over and gave me a big bear hug. "Thanks for coming," he said. "You're great. Bring the PlayStation next time, yeah? We can try some of your games as well." I agreed to, clapped him on the back and said goodbye.

Sarah and I drove to the airport in silence, partly because the sun wasn't even up and we were both semi-conscious, and partly because neither of us was looking forward to going back to work tomorrow.

When we got to the airport, we both just sat in the car and looked at it before I climbed out.

I broke the silence. "So, Bree suggested running away to Canada."

She laughed shortly. "No way, I'm not letting the bastards win," she said. "They're not driving me out of their chauvinistic hell-hole, I'll go on my own terms. Maybe after I've paid off my house."

We got out and she helped me get my suitcase out of the back. I was going to see her tomorrow so there was no point in a big goodbye, I just hugged her briefly when it looked like she wanted to. "Thanks for inviting me, Sarah. I had a great time. Sorry if I was a bit stressed out."

She shoved me. "Stop apologising!"

I made a show of being thoroughly chastised, saluted her and went to check in.

Sitting at the airport was a depressing experience. I had taken my laptop out just to double-check and triple-check the graphics and templates before I emailed them off — I didn't want any clipping issues or something embarrassing like the typos Diane had pointed out on the Vladivostok materials — when my phone buzzed.

It was too early for Henry, so I felt around for it, assuming it was Bree. It didn't stop buzzing, though, which meant it was ringing. Who'd ring me at seven o'clock on a public holiday?

I made the mistake of answering it. "Hello, Min speaking."

"*Now* you answer your phone, Jesus Christ," it was Jason, and he was *really* angry. All the colour drained from my face the second I heard his thundering voice. "You *know* we've got a pitch on Thursday and yet you couldn't find it in you to answer your phone even once yesterday. You sure know how to get me in shit tonnes of trouble, don't you?" He took a breath. "Diane wants running updates on the graphics in case you flake out like you did last week. Did you flake out this weekend too? Or did you actually do some fucking work for once?"

My throat tightened. All I did was work, that was *all* I ever did. "I've finished the graphics, I'll send the templates out to the team in about five minutes and cc you."

"You'd better. She wanted them last night. I'm fucking sick of this, pick up your fucking game, Mini." With that, he loudly hung up in my ear.

I stared at my phone for a second, my heart pounding. Shaken, I finished looking over the graphics and sent them out.

Since I had my phone out, I just thought I'd double-check how many times *Henry* had actually called me, since it obviously wasn't him trying yesterday. I scrolled through the log and found his number three times. He'd left a voicemail each time.

I decided now was as good a time as any to empty my voicemail, but since I had seven and only three of them were from Henry, I had to talk myself into listening to them because I knew the rest were from Jason and he'd be yelling at me. I wasn't wrong; they were painful to listen to. Not as painful as Henry's, though.

The first one was before Easter. "Hi, Min," Henry began pleasantly. "Just thought I'd let you know my family says hello and they wished you could be here visiting, too. Give me a ring when you have the chance, and don't work too hard!"

I deleted that one, and moved onto the next. "Hi again Min, you must be pretty busy with all those paintings you need to finish. I just want to let you know that I spoke to your mum and she's pretty keen on me accompanying her to Church on Sunday morning for the Easter service. She wants to introduce me to all her Church friends." I *cringed.* I could only imagine how Mum would be introducing Henry to them. "Anyway, I'll be at her place from nine or so on Sunday morning. She'd love it if you called. Maybe we could all Skype together? Hope you're having lots of fun despite all the work you need to do. Love you."

I could barely bring myself to listen to the last one, but I managed to press '5' to continue, anyway. "Hi, your mum was pretty upset that you haven't called. I had a quick look on the internet and noticed Telstra's the only carrier with good coverage out there, so I explained to her you probably had no reception and you'd call when you got back. Church actually wasn't so bad after all, your mum's friends were all nice and asked how you were. Your mum and grandma loved the Coogee tops we bought them, too." He paused, and his tone sobered. "Your grandma's not doing so well these days. I know you're not that close, but you should really try

470

and visit her as soon as you can, Min. They all want to hear about how you're doing. Your mum is really excited about your promotion. She couldn't stop talking about how *proud* she is that you're 'going places', I think her words were. She understands it means you can't talk as much. But she misses you, Min. Everyone misses you."

I took the phone away from my ear for a second, listening to voicemail operator give me a list of options about what I could do with that message. My thumb hovered over the delete option, but I decided against it at the last second, and saved it.

Fuck. Just fuck.

I sat back in the airport lounge chair, trying to process what I'd just heard. I couldn't, and I didn't have the energy to deal with it. Trying to give me a headache as well, so as my flight boarded I popped a couple of painkillers and then just settled down to try and nap as much as I could on the way back to Sydney.

At least once I landed it was cold enough to put my hoodie back on, and because I was feeling particularly crap I put my hood up on the way back to the car park. It was only once I sat in my car that I remembered Bree was waiting for me at home, and that cheered me up. Before I exited the car park, I texted her to let her know I'd landed and I'd be home soon. She replied with an excited keyboard smash.

It was a public holiday, and that meant the traffic back to the city was light. I half-listened to the radio while I drove, wishing I'd checked to see if I had any emails from the team before I'd left the airport. I tried a couple of times to check on my phone, but the encryption software wouldn't work properly on the app and trying to figure it out was making me miss lights and get honked by the people behind me.

Back in my building, I'd parked and wheeled my suitcase into the lift, and was having another go at syncing my phone when a pretty, petite Asian lady got her own suitcase stuck between the car park floor and the gap to the lift. I leant forward and helped her lift it clear, and she laughed and thanked me. I didn't miss her glance up at me and self-consciously check her reflection to see how she looked.

I'd gone back to my phone when she reached over to press her floor on the number panel, and then retracted her hand at the last moment. "Oh, you're going to 26 as well?" she asked in a very cultured, feminine voice. "Isn't that the floor for Frost employees, only? You must work for them, too, then?"

A knot formed in my stomach, and I tucked my phone into the front pocket of my hoodie.

Shit.

"Mmm," I said noncommittally, and was glad I had my hood up. I looked towards her just to check to see if I recognised her, and I didn't. I couldn't place her accent, either, but she wasn't Australian.

"Would I know you?" she asked me as the lift doors slid closed. "I haven't started working with any of the employees, yet, but I had my orientation last week."

I smiled and shook my head. "Probably not," I said as quietly as I could, because I sounded more like a guy when I spoke quietly. "I was away most of last week."

"Ah, well, it's nice to meet you. Cecilia," she said, and extended her hand for me to shake, so I did. "I'm down from Singapore. Just doing business development consulting for a couple of months, working with management mostly. But we might cross paths."

I nodded. She hadn't noticed I hadn't introduced myself, thank *god.*

"So what department do you work in?" she asked.

I didn't have enough time to think of a good lie. "Marketing."

Recognition crossed her face. "Oh, *that's* who you remind me of!" she said. "That tall Korean lady from the end apartment, I've seen her a couple of times, but she's always in a rush so I never said hello. What's her name? Minnie, or something?"

"Min Lee."

She nodded, "Yes, that's the one. You must be related to her...?"

Now was my chance to correct her this time. It was simple, 'Actually, I *am* Min Lee', and it was on the tip of my tongue. But as I looked down at her crisp dress and perfect hair, I faltered. She looked conservative. She was from somewhere conservative, I just knew it. I felt sick, and glanced nervously up numbers rising on the display panel. What I actually said was, "That's one way of putting it."

She laughed sociably as if I'd said something funny. "I have a sister myself, I know what they're like," she said, lightly touching my arm. It was flirtatious, and I flinched. I *hated* lifts, and I couldn't get out of this one fast enough. I watched the numbers rise and felt around in my pocket for my keycard so I could make a quick escape.

"This is my first time in Sydney," she continued, batting her pretty eyelashes. "Well, my second — I went back to Singapore for a couple of days for Easter. Can you recommend any must-see places for me? Or any good restaurants around here?"

She was angling for a dinner invite, and that was the very last thing in the world she was going to get from me. We were only one floor away from 26, but it felt like *eternity* before the lift stopped and the doors slid open while I pretended to be trying to think of good places for her.

Before I was able to mutter something and run off, I heard a squeal. "*Min!*"

To my abject horror, Bree had been waiting for me outside my apartment. When she spotted me, she came zooming up the hallway in her socks with her curls and everything else bouncing and wrapped herself tightly around my middle. In the process of attaching herself to me, she pulled my hood back and my long hair was visible. "Oh my god! I'm so happy you're back!"

The look on Cecilia's face was hauntingly familiar. "*Min?*" she repeated, shell-shocked. "*You're* Min Lee?"

Bree didn't notice. "Sorry, but I need to steal him right now," she told Cecilia. "He's been gone for *four days.*"

Cecilia's eyes darted between mine and my hair, and her lips formed 'him'.

It was surreal, like none of it was happening to me.

"Come on!" Bree said, grabbing my case and my hand and pulling me out of the lift. I was too paralysed by what was happening to stop her. "I made you lunch! I hope they didn't feed you too much on the plane, because you're going to *love* this. I used *real* salmon!"

As Bree dragged me up the hallway, I cast a glance back towards Cecilia. She was still staring, but just as I walked inside my apartment, I saw her jaw close and her cheeks flush.

Shit.

TWENTY-FIVE

Had that really just happened?

I stood in the centre of my hallway, my hand over my mouth... I kept seeing Cecilia's face when Bree had shouted my name. The culprit herself had been busily chatting to me while being completely fucking indiscreet and oblivious, but when she turned around to see why I wasn't following her up the hallway, her big smile disappeared.

"What's wrong?" she asked, looking genuinely confused. "Are you okay?"

I shook my head tightly, and then let my hand fall from my mouth. I felt numb. "Bree," I said shortly, "that woman you just outed me to was from work."

She watched me for a few seconds, and at first I don't think she knew who I meant. It dawned on her, though, and then her face cycled through a series of emotions and settled on remorse.

I gestured towards the closed door. "That woman, who clearly lives in this hotel, on this floor, who you thought it would be an excellent idea to 'he' me to and hug me in front of." The more I kept going, the worse it sounded. "Bree, this floor is a work floor, I've told you that. Why do you think I wear my hood up in here?"

She looked *mortified.* "But you usually like to be called 'he' in public..." she said hesitantly, as if she was trying to piece together why she'd done it, too.

I sighed heavily and passed a hand over my face for a second.

"I'm sorry, Min," she said in one of her tiny little voices. "I didn't mean to, I was just really happy to see you!"

"I know you didn't mean to, but you did it anyway." I shook my head. "Jesus, Bree. Fuck. I need to think." I walked briskly down the hallway, and when I passed Bree she tried to catch my hand, but I held it out of her reach. I don't know why I thought I'd be able to think better in the living room, but I couldn't stand still, so I didn't.

Someone at work had seen me like this. Someone who was likely to be working with both Henry and Jason. How the *fuck* was I going to deal with this?

"Maybe she won't tell anyone," Bree suggested meekly from the mouth of the hallway. "Not everyone goes blabbing stuff around."

"She doesn't even need to 'go blabbing'," I told her. "She just needs to ask someone, 'Hey, something weird happened yesterday, do you know Min Lee? She works in Marketing and I—*shit*, I told her I work in Marketing! Like I need to give her *any more* invitation to have that conversation with *Jason!*" I flopped into the couch and put my head in my hands.

Bree came over to slowly and gingerly sit next to me, but she didn't look very relaxed. From the crinkle in her forehead, I could tell that she was worrying.

I was worrying, too. I was sitting there and imagining Cecilia chatting with Henry, or Jason, or anyone in Marketing... Just one innocent question to them about me, and I was *fucked.* I needed to make sure that one innocent question never happened, somehow.

As I sat and tried to figure out what I was going to do, I knew I only really had one option. And as much as I *loathed* the idea and how uncomfortable it made me, and as far away I wished I was right now: I had to do it. "I've got to tell her everything so she doesn't need to ask," I realised aloud, hating every word of it. "Before she *does* say something to someone."

I stood up, both to go and unpack and also to try and figure out how the fuck I was going to tell a conservative woman from a conservative country that *I* wasn't a woman. I also didn't know how to find her to even start that conversation.

Door-knocking and ringing around the building looking for her were out of the question—the *last* thing I wanted was 40 to 45 Frost employees asking questions about what was going on with Min—so I decided that what I needed to do was to get ready *really* early tomorrow and sit and wait by the lift for her to leave for work.

Bree, who was teary and guilt-ridden, had a whole host of creative alternatives, like calling reception and pretending we had something to return to Cecilia. None of them would work, though, because I didn't know Cecilia's surname.

In the end, the only solution that made sense was getting up early and waiting.

After I'd unpacked, Bree and I both ended up on the couch with those Disney movies and a bottle of red wine, trying to make the stress go away. Nearly a full bottle later it still hadn't, and I still had no idea how the *fuck* I was going to tell a stranger something incredibly private about myself.

Bree had stopped waiting for me to officially forgive her and had crept over and passed out adorably across my lap. I didn't push her off, although I probably should have. Actually, while she was unconscious, I probably should have just taken the opportunity to *smother* her before she could wreck more havoc. I didn't, though. I just stroked her hair and worried about work tomorrow. As caring and supportive as Bree was, she did possess some uncanny ability to seek out things to spectacularly fuck up. My life, for example.

After we went to bed, I set my alarm for five in the morning just in case Cecilia had a breakfast meeting she needed to leave the hotel for. When my alarm went off and I got up, even two codeine barely touched my headache. I didn't have any choice, though, I had to get ready.

It was near fucking impossible to put a skirt on, especially after having been able to dress the way I felt comfortable for nearly a full week. I soldiered on through the wrongness and self-loathing anyway to do my hair and makeup, and then went and camped in the foyer by the lift to wait for Cecilia.

I sat facing the lift so I couldn't miss her when she came down.

I had to get this right, I only had one shot.

'I need to talk to you,' I mentally rehearsed while I watched the numbers on the display panels light up. 'I'm sorry about the misunderstanding yesterday, it's a really embarrassing issue for me...' Should I say 'embarrassing', I wondered? Maybe 'sensitive' is better?

I spent a good hour agonising over the exact wording before the lifts started to empty quite sizable numbers of people from the tower each time they arrived at ground. The vast majority of people who walked past me were tourists — it was a prime spot in Sydney, after all — but one or two of them were Frost employees and one of them recognised me.

"Morning," he said cordially as he walked past. I smiled tightly at him and kept practising.

Should I say 'transgender' to Cecilia, though? I still felt kind of uncomfortable with that word, although I couldn't explain why. The problem was that there didn't seem to be any other way I could accurately describe myself that wasn't going to raise even more questions.

I watched another lift-full of various people empty and disperse, again without Cecilia. *Where was she?*

Up until that point, I hadn't worried at all that I would miss her. I started to now, and checked my phone: it was nearly 7:40am. Management mostly started at 8am, and if she worked with management, where the hell was she...?

I suddenly had an awful thought; maybe as a consultant she was one of the lucky people who got a company car and a parking spot under Frost HQ. In that case, she would have left from the basement car park and wouldn't have come past me at all.

My stomach dropped. Fuck, what if I'd missed her? What if she was sitting down with management right now? With *Henry*?

I stood up, panicking, and just ignored my headache and powered all the way to work in case I was wrong.

The lift to the basement car park at Frost wasn't the same one as those that led up into the building, and there was a café in the atrium. I could just pretend I was grabbing a coffee and sit in a chair that faced the lifts. I'd see her if she swapped over between them.

The problem was when I did that and sat down facing the lifts, it meant that *everyone* getting into the lifts had to walk past me. I got some very weird looks from my co-workers for not being my usual hard-working self, but I ignored them and focused on watching the people on their way to their offices, looking for a petite woman with dyed brown hair.

I did actually see one, but she wasn't Asian or the person I was looking for and her hair was *naturally* brown. It was good to see this one, though.

Sarah walked up to me with a big smile on her face. "Okay, I'm getting more of Bree's 'whoa, weird' vibe about you in chick clothes," she said, glancing around us before she did.

My eyes kept darting over towards the lifts, and she noticed. "You waiting for someone?" she asked, turning around to look where I was. "Henry?"

I winced as she said his name, but shook my head and looked

around us again to make sure no one was in earshot. "Bree accidentally outed me to someone at the hotel, so I'm waiting for her," I said in a low voice. "Cecilia someone, a new consultant who—"

Sarah's eyebrows went up and she interrupted me. "Cecilia Yeo? That new Business Development person?" I nodded, surprised Sarah knew her. She explained why. "We got an email about her. She's going to be working with all the departments on streamlining procedures. Mainly with the managers, though."

I sat up. They had her details in an email? I hadn't checked my generic Frost email account for at least a week. "Did the email mention where her office is going to be?" I asked Sarah, thinking maybe I could go straight to her office and speak privately with her there. My heart lifted.

Sarah frowned. "Maybe," she said, and we both took out our phones and started flipping through our emails.

"Yes!" Sarah announced, sounding triumphant as she showed me her screen. "Here: level five, in the temporary suites, and it has her mobile number, too. I'll forward it to you so it's easy to find."

"*Thanks*, Sarah," I told her, sculling the last of my coffee as I stood up. "You're a life-saver. I'll head up there right now."

I expected Sarah to be supportive of that idea, but she looked hesitant. "We've got that 8am meeting Jason told us about last night, though," she said. "In like..." She checked her phone. "Six minutes."

I hadn't read my project emails last night because I was too busy worrying about what had happened. I was *still* worrying about that, but the real question was if I was worried about Jason's wrath at me being late *more* than I was worried he would find out about my gender stuff. My indecision must have shown on my face.

Sarah put a hand on my arm. "Min, you can't be late to this. You should have heard the stuff Jason was *already* saying about you."

Fuck. But what if Cecilia had a meeting with Henry this morning? Or a meeting with Jason after ours? I looked over Sarah's shoulder towards the crowd of people waiting to go upstairs.

"Come on," Sarah said, taking my arm and leading me towards the lifts. "You'll probably have a couple of seconds to email her before the meeting starts."

I grabbed my handbag and let her lead me into the crowd, and all I could think of was what each and every one of these people would think of me if they knew about me. I could almost feel them looking at me now.

Sarah leant up towards me as we got into the lift. "It'll be fine, it probably won't even come up," she whispered. "She's new. Most people don't randomly gossip with strangers."

"Yeah," I said glumly, remembering high school. "'*Most*'."

The lift emptied before we got to 36, which gave Sarah the opportunity to ask me, "So what happened, anyway?" I told her briefly, watching her look more and more concerned. "She actually *hit* on you when she read you as a guy? *Whoops.*" She exhaled. "Well, that must be serious *déjà vu* for you. Was she angry when she found out you're not the kind of guy she expected?"

I shrugged. "Bree had dragged me away by that point."

Sarah pressed her lips into a thin line for a second. "Mmm, okay," she said. "I get why you're worried."

That wasn't very comforting. "Yeah."

The lift doors opened, and we walked out into Marketing. Thankfully there weren't very many people in yet, and even though we had an 8 am meeting, the rest of my team weren't in, either.

Well, at least it gave me the opportunity to write a quick email to Cecilia. While Sarah ran back to the lift to grab a couple of Red Bulls for us, I decided to compose it on my phone so that no one could look over my shoulder if they came in. I was just in the middle of trying to figure out how to make the email as benign as possible in case someone else read it, when Ian and Carlos arrived with matching coffees, distracting me.

"Oh, you're here today. That's a nice surprise," Ian said passive-aggressively as he walked casually past me. Carlos didn't say anything, but he didn't greet me, either.

"Good morning," I said neutrally to them both anyway, and didn't engage Ian in whatever argument he was trying to start with me. "How are you going with populating content into the templates?" He gave me a tired look and didn't answer, and that made my blood rise. "I was just asking. It's my job to ask."

He put his coffee on his desk and then turned back to me. "If we're talking about what your job is as lead, it's not to call in sick when things go wrong," he said. "I missed my daughter's birthday party because of this stupid project, and I'm not even lead of it." He turned to sit at his desk.

I did *not* have the energy for office politics right now. Especially right now. "No, you're not. They put *me* on lead, and—"

The door burst open and Jason came thundering in. "—And then 'they' realised their huge fucking mistake and took you straight off lead," he told me loudly. "You forfeit when you fucked up and then didn't show up. I'm taking over before you fuck anything else up and putting you back doing the things you're good at."

Across the room, Ian gave me a pointed look.

Jason wasn't done with me yet, either. He picked up the complimentary Frost notepads and a pen, and walked over to hand them to me. He was my boss, so I couldn't do anything but accept them. When I did he said in a very sarcastic Playschool voice, "Why don't you just sit there and draw a nice picture, Mini? Wouldn't that be fun?"

I took a deep breath, jaw set.

He straightened, swore and shook his head. "I'm sick of this bullshit," he said. "I lost my quarterly bonus because of you, Mini. Nineteen thousand fucking dollars because when Diane asked, 'Tell me about Min Lee', I said, 'reliable employee who keeps her trap shut and basically lives at work' instead of 'neurotic woman who crumbles disastrously under stress'. You can imagine the level of respect Diane has for *me* at the moment." He put his hands on his hips and shook his head with disgust as he looked down at me. "Anyway, like I said, I'm taking over from here. At least maybe I can reclaim some of that if I can fix up your mess and get this project signed."

I sat there looking at the floor at his feet. The Sasha Burov pitch *wasn't* in a mess, I wanted to say. It was right on target and it looked great. I couldn't say anything, though. I couldn't talk back to him.

Sarah returned with the Red Bulls, and stopped for a second when she saw Jason towering over me. He almost paid *no* attention to her as she came around him and passed one of the cans to me. I was scared to open it in case the hiss of the can set Jason off again, so I just put it quietly on the table beside me.

"Sit around here," Jason said, leaving me and walking over to the central meeting table which he slapped with a hand, making my heart jump. "We've got some business to attend to."

It wasn't until he started going over the templates that I recovered from what had just happened and realised I hadn't actually emailed Cecilia yet.

My phone was face down just beside my hand on the table. It would only take me a few seconds to flip it over, type out the perfectly vague wording I'd decided on and send it. Jason turned his back a couple of times, first to grab some of Vladivostok materials to tell us what *not* to do, and second to write a couple of things on the floating whiteboard. Each time, my hand hovered over my phone.

Ian gave me a sharp look, though, and I ended up feeling guilty and not doing it.

Jason had just been going over security measures—Sarah and I glanced at each other, remembering the *Frost v Frost* listing—when the door opened and *Diane* walked coolly in. We'd all been slouching until that point. Not anymore.

"Good morning, Pink," Diane said, remarkably authoritative despite her impassive tone. We all smiled in greeting. At least, everyone else smiled. I just felt sick, especially as she glanced at me. "We need to have a little refresher about information security, it seems."

She stood in front of us and reminded us of all the things I'd initially told the team — docs saved *only* on password-protected USBs, not leaving laptops unlocked and lying around, not speaking about the project to *anyone* other than people on the team, and, "Most importantly," she finished. "Most importantly, *do not speak to my brother*. There are legal proceedings in place. Do not speak to him, irrespective of the reason." She was looking *directly* at me as she said that. I swallowed. "Is that crystal clear? There will be severe consequences for anyone who is not able to adhere to that."

We all nodded. I did, too.

"Good," she said as she left. "I have another meeting to head off to, so I'll hand you back to Jason."

She did, and then Jason went on, and on, and on, and *on* about timelines, attention to detail, and periodically inserted thinly veiled jabs at me for the poor quality of the Vladivostok materials. I knew they weren't my best work, but I'd done then *in three days,* what did he expect?

As the clock kept ticking and the likelihood that Cecilia would have an opportunity to tell someone about me kept getting greater and greater, I must have looked very distracted because at one point Jason put his hands on his hips and said impatiently, "Sorry, Mini, are we keeping you from something?" I shook my head mutely.

When *finally* the meeting was over and Jason left us to check on another team, the first thing I did was flip over my phone to write that email. Before I'd finished it, though, Sarah put a gentle hand on my arm and *scared the fucking life out of me.* I jumped, startled everyone in the room, and then felt like an idiot.

Once the boys had gone back to what they were doing, Sarah passed me her phone. I looked quizzically at her, and she just nodded at the screen. On it, there was the room-booking calendar for level five, and the board room was booked out for 'Business Development Consultation' for an hour from nine until ten. I checked my watch: *9:52am.*

"You could probably use some *real* coffee from downstairs after that, right?" she said cryptically and then turned away. "That was pretty awful."

That was clear enough for me. I cast a glance over at Ian and Carlos, and then put my phone in the side pocket of my skirt and exited Oslo. Marketing had filled up while we were in that long meeting with Jason, and as I walked across the floor towards the lifts, various people called out to me. I ignored them.

While I was waiting for a lift, though, one of them came to grab an energy drink from the machine. However, despite that ruse, he was obviously coming here for the sole purpose of talking to me, and because he was smirking, that was really, really concerning.

Did people *already* know?

"Hey, Mini," he said conversationally as he took his can out of the dispenser tray. "How was jail?"

Oh, *that.* I would have sighed with relief if I wasn't alarmed at how quickly *that* rumour had spread, and how much it had escalated out of a simple phone call from Constable Garrett in that time. How many work days had I been away, one and a half? Two? I gave him a look and just hammered on the lift call button. At least he didn't hang around to ask more questions. He just opened his drink and wandered back out onto the floor as I got into the lift.

As soon as the doors closed, I forgot about *that* rumour and remembered the one I was trying to prevent, and how I was going to prevent it: I was about to go and tell my most private secrets to a complete fucking stranger and beg her not to tell anyone. My heart began to pound again and the request I'd been practising started circling around my head. It was surreal rehearsing coming out to someone as transgender while I stared at my ultra-feminine reflection.

I'd never been on level five before, so when I stepped out into it I felt like I'd walked into another dimension. The temporary and consulting suites were mainly used for boring stuff like auditing, so there'd never been any call for a marketing clerk to be down here. The only way I could figure out where to find the boardroom was by referring to the Fire Exit map by the lift.

I did eventually find the room, and went to wait up the other end of the corridor. I checked my watch: *10:01am.* I was probably just in time, and it gave me a few minutes to stress a bit more about *how* I was going to actually do this.

I didn't know how I was going to get Cecilia by herself—I decided I could be direct about that, couldn't I? 'Cecilia, mind if I have a word with you for a second?', that would work, if I didn't 'crumble disastrously under stress' or whatever Jason had said, anyway. It should be fine, she had seemed like the type of person who'd be polite and not make a scene. I'd just have to wait for the meeting to end.

And I did wait, and I kept waiting. The time ticked past: *10:10am, 10:13am, 10:21am...* Fuck, I was going to have to go back upstairs soon, or people were going to notice I was missing for longer than coffee, and Jason was going to literally kill me with his bare hands.

While I was fidgeting and trying to decide how much longer I could stay down here, the door to the conference room opened, and *Diane* walked out, phone in hand.

I swung around the corner, inhaling sharply.

She hadn't seen me. But if she *did* see me hanging around down here where I shouldn't be, I'd get in a lot of trouble for not being upstairs and hard at work on the project instead. I jogged back up the corridor and waited in the staff kitchen on the other side of the lifts for her to leave.

I could hear footsteps and the hum of several simultaneous conversations, which meant the meeting was over and everyone was leaving, and while I kept checking around the corner and waiting for Diane to get into the lift, I finally saw Cecilia.

...and she walked right up beside Diane at the lifts and they made polite small talk.

You had to be *fucking* kidding me. Diane was right here, right now? Just when I needed to speak to Cecilia?

While I was watching them and mentally willing Diane to get in the lift without her, a group of other senior execs started to arrive and mill around the lift.

Then, everything took a whole further detour into *terrible*. Another manager who I didn't recognise had asked Cecilia a question and she was answering it, and then a tall man wandered over to congratulate Cecilia on something, butting into the conversation. From the back of his head and his shoulders I knew exactly who he was the second I laid eyes on him: *Henry. Fuck.*

God, *why? No,* I thought, *don't talk to her!*

I felt around in my pocket for my phone and took it out, turning it over in my hands for a second. Then, on impulse, I called him. *Answer it*, I thought, *walk away from her and answer the phone.*

I saw him reach up and pat his breast pocket, slipping his phone out and casually glancing at it while he was still talking to her. When he saw it was me, he double-took and actually paused mid-sentence to concentrate on it for a few seconds. Then, I saw him exhale, reject the call and put it back into his pocket.

The execs standing around him had actually been waiting for him to continue what he'd been saying, and I realised at that point that I'd made a *grave* error. Someone asked him who it was, and Henry shook his head dismissively, but he looked veiled. Cecilia noticed.

She wants to ask him about that phone call, I thought. Fuck, why did I do that? I just gave them both an actual *reason* to talk about me. *God, everyone, just stop talking, get in the lift and go all your separate ways!*

That didn't happen, of course. The lift arrived and everyone got into it without me, and as the doors closed, it began to settle just how very fucked I was. I'd been down here for half an hour waiting to beg someone not to out me. She was in the lift with my partner who had no idea about my gender issues, and from how friendly everyone was being I just knew they'd all have lunch together. Even if that phone call *didn't* come up, all the usual questions would: 'Are you from Sydney?', 'Are you married?'. I swallowed. I could imagine how that conversation would go. If Cecilia showed *any* sort of hesitation when it came to me, Henry would notice, and he'd get the truth out of her.

"*Fuck!*" I said aloud, and went to go and get a lift, myself.

Well, that was it, wasn't it? It was about to be all over. There was no way out of this, would there even be any point in emailing her now? I didn't know if consultants could get email on their phones like regular employees could, but even *if* she could, would she check them before Henry got the truth out of her?

While I was in the lift I wrote her one anyway, just in case.

The wording was important, not only because our emails were monitored from time to time, but also because I didn't want her to be able to show it to someone and have them guess the matter was personal. It had to sound like business. "*Hi Cecilia, Great to meet you yesterday but please make sure you don't share any of the contents of our meeting with any other employees as it is highly sensitive information. Come and see me with any questions. Regards, Min Lee.*" I read it a few times, decided it was impersonal enough, and then sent it.

As soon as it had gone, though, I went to the sent box and re-read it a few times, second-guessing myself. I hoped it wouldn't be *too* cryptic for her to have no idea what I was on about.

I arrived in Marketing again and walked briskly across the floor to avoid as many felon and jail jokes as I could. Once I was safe in Oslo, the team had clearly noticed I was gone, but none of them commented on it. Ian just greased me off as I sat down at my desk and turned my laptop on. I was too busy focusing on this being-outed crisis to pay any attention to him.

If Henry managed to tease the full story out of Cecilia, he was going to be *so* upset I hadn't told him, even if he understood. I imagined the expression on his gentle face and my chest tightened. He was so lovely, and he'd been so good to me. Fuck, and all those things he'd done for my Mum in Korea, not to mention for me... he'd been patient, and generous, and kind, even though he knew something was up with me and Bree. There were so many ways he could have hurt me over that, and he didn't. It wouldn't have even occurred to him.

What the *fuck* was I doing, seriously? What the fuck was I doing to him? I should have told him, I thought. I really, really should have told him. Ages ago, before I started to have feelings for Bree. He shouldn't have to hear about this from a complete stranger.

While my laptop was booting up, I took out my phone.

I should do it as soon as possible, shouldn't I?

I mulled over the idea, trying to decide whether or not I thought Cecilia would say anything to him. In the end, I decided that even if she didn't tell him about my gender stuff, *I* should. The way his shoulders had slumped before he'd rejected my call downstairs... god. Poor Henry, I was a fucking monster. I still didn't know how I was going to handle breaking up with him, because there was *so much shit* attached to that I didn't even know where to start. But my gender stuff, I should really tell him about it right now.

I opened messaging and just stared at it for a second. I had no idea how to start this. I spent a minute or two typing a few things, but nothing seemed appropriate so I deleted the whole lot.

This was really the type of stuff I should do in person. *"Henry, I need to talk to you asap."*

He didn't reply immediately, leaving me to languish over the slides I was supposed to be laying out. When he did, it was just, *"Sorry I missed your call before, Diane and a Whitman's Sampler of all the scariest managers at Frost were surrounding me. Is something wrong? Are you okay? Do you need me to call you back now?"*

It was a bit worrying that Henry's first impression of why I needed to talk to him was that I was freaking out and needed someone to calm me down. That was very telling. I felt a knot form in my stomach. *"I'm fine, but there's something really important I need to discuss with you as soon as possible. Today, if we can. Lunch? Dinner?"*

This time, he replied much faster. *"Oh, I'm glad you're fine, I've been worried about you. Today is no good for me, unfortunately. I'm booked out for the next couple of days, and if it's very important, wouldn't you like to sleep on it and think about it before we discuss it? Perhaps I could come around on Thursday night. Your project is finished by then, isn't it?"*

I sighed, hoping that would be soon enough. *"Okay, Thursday night is good. See you then."*

After I'd taken a few deep breaths and tried to refocus, I opened up the Sasha Burov slides and started to lay out the data and text that Ian and Carlos were emailing me.

While I was trying to decide how to politely tell Ian that he'd sent me *way* too much text for a single slide without sounding like I was trying to get back at him for our argument, there was a knock on the door. Sarah had been working solidly on charts beside me, and we looked at each other. She got up to answer it and had a brief, quiet conversation with someone on the other side before turning back to me. "Phone for you."

That was weird. "Are you sure?"

She shrugged, and went to sit back down as I stood up and went over. The guy who'd come to get me was just a regular clerk from Marketing, not the floor admin or Diane's assistant or anyone who I'd normally expect to be transferring calls to me. I followed him over to his desk on the other side of the floor. "Who is it?"

He was giving me a *really* strange expression. It made me nervous. "Alan someone. Paton, I think?"

I shook my head, I'd never heard of him. "Can you double-check it's definitely for me?"

He tried to give the handset to me, but I refused it so he just stuck the phone on speaker so we could bother hear. "Hi, what was your name again?"

"Alan Pattern," the voice said, and it sounded vaguely familiar. "Look, he won't know me, I didn't introduce myself. I'm no good at this email thing, I'd just like to have a quick conversation with him, that's all. Can you convince him to speak to me? I'll explain."

The second I heard 'him', all the blood drained out of my face. The clerk looked to me to answer so I did, but too quietly for the phone mic to pick it up. "Obviously there's some mistake."

At my expression, another clerk whose desk was nearby swung around to listen. I felt sick.

"Are you definitely sure it's 'Min Lee' you're looking for?" the clerk asked, leaning towards the phone as he spoke.

"Well," the speaker said, and there was the sound of rustling. "His email address is M-i-n-l-e-e, and I'm pretty sure I heard his colleague call him 'Min', so that's probably it? Why, is there no Min Lee there? Has Frost got another Marketing department by any chance? Perhaps I've called the wrong one."

My heart was pounding, and my legs were starting to feel weak. There were three people watching me, now. One of them I'd worked extensively with on the last project and he knew me quite well. We didn't really like each other.

While I was gaping, unsure what to say, I heard a familiar voice behind me. "Hey, Jason is looking for you." It was Sarah, and she put a hand on my arm before frowning at us standing around the phone. "What's going on?" she asked. "Who's calling?"

"I think it's the wrong number," I rasped, still too quiet for the phone to hear. Sarah didn't look like she believed me.

The clerk did, though and he leant towards the phone again. "No, there's only one Marketing department," he said. "Are you definitely sure the person you're looking for is a man, though? Can you describe him? Maybe you're thinking of someone else in here."

There was a silence. "That's a *really* weird question," was the response. He answered anyway, if hesitantly. "Of course I'm sure he was a man. Very tall, I guess. Asian guy, fantastic artist. Really fantastic, he showed me a self-portrait that was Archibald Prize material, I'm telling you. Came into my café in Broome on Good Friday with a smaller brunette who apparently also works there. Look, why are you asking me these questions? Is he there or not?"

As it dawned on me who the guy was, three Marketing clerks looked between me and Sarah, and their jaws all dropped.

I felt Sarah's hand on my arm as I stared at them, my ears ringing like I was about to faint.

Before the man could say anything else, I stepped forward and said hurriedly, "Sorry, you've got the wrong number," and just pushed two fingers on the cradle so the call dropped. I stood there for a moment, frozen, while three pairs of eyes bored into me.

The clerk who'd taken the call cracked a smile, and then laughed. It was more confused than malicious, however. "Mini, *what the fuck* was that?" he asked me. "What the fuck? Why did he think you were *a guy*?"

"Mind your own business, Ryan," Sarah said shortly, and then took my arm to lead me away. "Come on, Min, we've got *heaps* of work to do..."

'Ryan' didn't stop there though. "Because that's obviously you, Mini. Tall, Asian, great artist..."

I didn't let Sarah drag me away just yet, though. I stopped for a moment, willing myself to speak. "Please don't say anything to anyone," I asked him quietly. "Please."

I think on some level when I looked him in the eye and said that, he understood that it was important to me. He still seemed a mixture of interested and confused, but at least he nodded. Unfortunately, his colleague behind him had already stood up and bent double over the divider to talk to another clerk on the other side. The third guy was just smirking at me like he'd just learnt something *really, really* juicy. He picked up his phone to start texting someone.

No.

Fuck, *no*, this couldn't be happening. No. No, no. I wanted to stop them, but I couldn't. It was too late. My chest felt tight as if I was still wearing the binder, and there wasn't enough air in here. I couldn't just stand here gasping for breath while Ryan stared at us, so I shook Sarah free and ran—ironically—into the women's and just shut myself in one of the stalls.

It was over.

It was only a matter of time before the whole Marketing department knew about that phone conversation, and with them, Jason. The clerks were bad enough themselves with stuff like this, but Jason? God, I didn't want to think about what he could do. I just didn't want to think about it.

But I didn't need to just think about it, did I? Pretty soon it would be *happening*.

And I couldn't get away from it. I couldn't take any sick leave or any time off work because of the pitch on Thursday, not unless I wanted to be fired on the spot and be homeless with no employment prospects.

I leant against the cubicle wall and put my head in my hands. It was over. I knew how this stuff spread, I remembered it in HD 1080 detail from living it as a teenager and from all the nightmares where I was trapped back at high school. It was happening again.

The door burst open and heels clicked around the tiles. "Min!" It was Sarah. The footsteps stopped, and then there was a tentative knock on the cubicle door. "Min, are you okay?" She sounded worried. "I mean, obviously not, but, yeah. Open up!"

I sighed, and turned the lock. After I'd actually opened the door, though, I didn't know what to say, and she didn't either. She just leant a shoulder against the door frame and watched me.

I closed my eyes for a moment. "This is it, isn't it?"

She didn't say anything straight away. "Well," she began when she finally did speak. "On the way in here that guy who had that irritating smile on his face throughout the whole phone call stopped me and asked me if you had 'junk' and if I'd seen it."

"What did you say?"

She shrugged. "I didn't say anything. Because if I joked about it, it would be clear you didn't have any, and I don't know who you want to tell the truth to, so..." She laughed once, humourlessly. "You know, I was actually *sure* Schoolgirl was going to be the one to accidentally out you to everyone at work. At least for being... gay, or straight, or into women, or whatever your sexuality is that isn't Henry. Maybe for being a guy, too."

I exhaled. "She did. Yesterday. And if that phone call hadn't happened, who knows? Maybe Cecilia would have said something anyway." I thought more about that, and put my head in my hands again. "*Fuck,* what the *fuck* am I going to do? I can't get through this shit *again.*"

Something occurred Sarah. "Then don't."

I looked up at her. "What?"

She shrugged. "Don't. Like, the way I see it you've really got two options. Rumours happen because people love talking about stuff they're not supposed to. Secrets are interesting. If you just rocked up in a suit tomorrow and announced, 'Yeah, I'm a guy, whatever', and then got on with life... well, it would probably suck at first because people would ask you a lot of questions, but then it's over."

In a million years, I could *not* imagine myself doing that at Frost, no matter how sound her logic was. This place was *way* too fucking conservative for me being a guy to ever be considered 'over'. They'd never leave me alone. Gay guys, they could handle. But someone who was transgender? "What was the other option?"

"Well, rumours always go away eventually, don't they? Just don't say *anything,* don't engage anyone at all on the issue and people will get sick of talking about it all the time."

I made a face. "Yeah, but they'll still tease me about it *forever.*"

"Yeah, that's true," Sarah acknowledged. "But you can't really escape that now no matter what you do."

I deflated again. "Like I said, I'm fucked," I told her. "Plus..." I didn't really know how to say it. "I'm not... one hundred per cent on being a guy, you know? I don't really want to come to work and announce I'm a guy and then later find out it's not true."

"You reckon you're going to end up being a chick after all of this?" She didn't look like she thought that would be the case at all.

"No..." I said, and then exhaled at length. "But you see what I mean? I don't know *what* I am, and I just don't know why or how to explain *why* I don't know. So I guess this is it." I felt sick. "I'm fucked. I'm *so* fucked. If one of those guys comes up to me and asks me any questions about it..."

"Just joke or something," she told me. "You're, like, the master of deflection. Just do something like that." Even if I forced myself, I didn't think I could joke about this. Sarah took a step forward and pulled me out of the cubicle. "Come on, let's just go up the road and have lunch like we did when I was pissed off at Jason for being a sexist bastard. You can chill out and we can figure out what you're going to say when people confront you about it."

I let her drag me out of the cubicle, but I was still shaking. It was noticeable even to her. "If people confront me about it...? I can't do this again, Sarah," I told her, my throat tight. "I can't go through all of this again. I can't do it. High school was..." I swallowed. It had been a *nightmare*, and even thinking about it now made my heart race. "I can't, I just can't."

She rubbed my back and led me over to the door. "Well, you're here, aren't you? Which means you survived it, so you *can* do it again. Come on. Let's get out of this place for a bit," she said, pulling the door open...

... to Jason, standing in the doorway with a *very* strange expression on his face and his arms crossed. I wasn't sure how he knew we were in here, but from the way he was looking at me, I knew he'd heard *everything*.

TWENTY-SIX

Jason didn't speak quietly. He didn't even close the door. He didn't do *anything* to protect my privacy in any way when he said at the top of his voice, "What the *fuck* did I just hear you two talking about?"

The Women's was over the other side of the floor to where most of Marketing sat, but a few of the clerks stood over the partitions anyway, frowning and trying to figure out what was going on. If it had been anyone other than Jason, they wouldn't have been able to hear what he was saying. The problem was that it *was* Jason, and he had this booming, thunderous voice like a coach who needed to shout across a football field.

I was past the point where I thought my secret was salvageable, so I just stood there with my eyes glazed, *shaking.* This is it, I thought.

"Jesus," Jason said after a few more seconds of stunned silence. "Jesus. Fuck, I don't even know where to start. You," he said, presumably to Sarah, because he didn't prompt me when I wouldn't look up at him. "'Sexist prick'? Are you joking? If you've got a problem with me not going easy on you because you're a girl, Presti, take that shit to HR. And *you*," he said, and this time I knew he was looking at me. I could *feel* him staring at the top of my head as I focused on his Italian leather shoes. "*Jesus.*"

He was talking *so* loudly that all of Australia could probably hear.

"Jesus. Okay, Mini, okay. Here's the 101: You work in *marketing.* This isn't some desk job where you lock yourself in an office forever, you need to be fucking presentable to clients and I'll be *fucked* if you're going to blow this fucking pitch by rocking up looking like anything other than that," he gestured at my dress, "in front of a *Russian.* You know how conservative they are. And 'not one-hundred per cent on being a guy?' *What the fuck*? Look at you. You are *zero* per cent a guy, and trust me, I know about guys. Maybe you've got some weird Asian ladyboy shit going on under there but I don't want to know about it, and I don't want the clients to know about it. You're completely free to do whatever tranny make-believe dress-ups or crap you want at home, but you don't bring that to work. Especially not in marketing. Not on Frost time. Got that?"

I couldn't move. I couldn't even think. 'Tranny'? 'Make-believe dress-ups'?

"I said *got that*?" he *yelled*, and I could feel tiny drops of spit on my bowed forehead.

I forced myself to nod because I was worried what he would do if I didn't, but kept hearing all the things he'd said and I was so sick to my stomach that I *shook* with it. It must have been obvious, because I felt the back of Sarah's knuckles brush mine.

He didn't stop there, either. He kept shouting. "Fuck. I can't even deal with you two right now. Fucking unbelievable. Okay, so, here's how it's going to be, ladies. You're both going to arrive at that pitch looking immaculate, looking delighted to be there and acting like two women who are on a hundred-a-year-plus salaries. None of this wah wah woe is me bullshit, okay? You don't even know *half the fucked-up shit* I have to do in this job to keep it, but I'm not carrying on like my life sucks because of that. And we all have a part to play here: *I'm* going to talk about Burov's teenage wife and sexy women and act like I give a fuck about either. It's going to take two hours tops and it's worth a shit tonne of money so *suck it up, ladies*."

He let that sink in for a second while we both stood there.

"And Presti," he said, turning a bit towards her. "You're going to come out with me and Burov tomorrow night to the casino. A couple of the Sales boys are coming, too, and Burov will probably want some eye-candy to go with his chit-chat. Wear something low cut, yeah? I'm getting one of the Sales guys to get us a pink diamond on loan from *Oxford's*, and it will sit right between those huge tits. And, Mini..." From his legs I could see him turning back to me. "Get back to work. Those slides and materials better be perfect, I swear to god. Both of you, just do your fucking jobs.

Diane's already breathing down my neck at the moment because of you, and if I lose my job on top of the nineteen grand despite *everything* I had to do to get it..."

He stood there for a couple more seconds, as if he still couldn't believe what he'd heard us say. Then he made a really frustrated noise, threw his hands to the ceiling and marched off, swearing to himself.

Sarah and I just stood frozen there for a moment, silent.

The people who'd been watching us glanced at each other and sat back down at their desks. I wondered how much they'd heard; I guessed I wouldn't have to wait too long to find out.

"*Fuck* that prick," Sarah murmured to me, breathless. It was still jarring to hear her swear. "*Fuck* him. What was he doing standing at the door and *listening* to us, anyway? I don't care if he's our boss, he can't do that and he can't talk to us like that. What the hell?"

The sad thing was he *was* our boss and he *could* talk to us like that, I thought. I was still too shaken to speak, though.

She noticed. "Come back in here," she said, and we took a couple of steps back into the bathroom, letting the door fall closed. She leant against the basins, thinking. After a moment, she shook her head angrily. "What the fuck, using my rack as a display case, though? That's *so* messed up. 'Please go and stand there and be pretty with the diamond'. Yeah, because Burov definitely won't be interested in having an actual conversation with me, but ogling my boobs? *Sure*. That's what chicks are for, right?"

I wanted to be angry for her, but I was numb. I felt like I was somewhere else. Nothing felt real and I couldn't believe any of this was actually happening. I felt like any moment I might wake up from this and discover it was a nightmare.

If only.

Fuck, I'd been saying that a lot lately, hadn't I? If only, if only. If only things were different, but they weren't different. This was my life, this was really my job, he was really my boss, and I'd just been spectacularly outed in *every possible way*. I felt naked, and stupid and I had this moment of clarity where I imagined how I must look to people. Ultra-feminine and claiming that I didn't feel like a woman? *Fuck*. They probably thought I was one huge joke.

"And that stuff he said to you?" Sarah said, bringing me back to the conversation. When I didn't say anything, she looked worried, taking a step towards me and putting her hand on my arm. I gazed down at it; at my pretty pearl bracelet and delicate, feminine wrists; I couldn't believe it was attached to me. I couldn't believe *any* of this was attached to me. Jason was right. He was *right*. Who the *fuck* was I kidding? *This* was my reality.

"Are you okay?"

I shook my head.

She pressed her lips together. "This is crap, Min. He can't do this."

My throat was dry. "Watch him."

"I mean, he *shouldn't* be allowed to. You know what? *Fuck* this." She dropped her arm so she could put her hands on her hips. "I don't want to keep working in this department with him as a boss. Just before you came up from Melbourne they had this old guy who retired and he was okay. I mean, he wasn't fantastic, but I don't think anyone could be worse than Jason. I think like four people quit when Jason got promoted."

"Are you saying we should quit?" There was *no way* I could do that, no matter what happened. Mum would *kill* me.

She gave me a weird look. "Hell no," she said. "I'm saying we should stop him."

Like it was that easy. "Well, then, just let me get my magic wand."

She chuckled once, but ignored what I'd meant. "Come on, Min, let's go to HR and lodge a formal complaint against that bastard for discrimination and bullying. The law forces them to take it seriously."

She looked so determined that for a fraction of a second I considered it. Not really because I thought it would achieve much— I had any expectations of complaint systems working beaten out of me in high school—but mainly because Sarah wanted to.

Then I remembered whose boyfriend ran HR. "I can't."

She realised what I meant. "Oh, right, *Henry*," she said. "Well, there's got to be someone else. What about that other guy? The assistant manager?"

The more I thought about it, the more I realised it just wasn't going to happen. "Yeah, about that," I said, still feeling sick. "He's taking all his annual leave at the moment. The other HR people are just paper-pushers, according to Henry. I wouldn't trust them with something like this. And I guess we could always report Jason to his boss... except his boss is *Diane*."

Sarah groaned. "Well, who's the next person above Henry in HR? We could report it to them."

"Sean Frost," I said flatly.

Sarah's eyebrows went up. "Oh."

"So yeah. Not only did we just get told we're *expressly forbidden* to speak to Sean because of Pink, but Sean and Jason are obviously giving it to each other. So that complaint's not going anywhere, either." I shook my head. "Anyway, maybe if we wait until—"

The door to the toilet burst open, scaring the life out of me. It was Ian, and he didn't look too happy to be there.

"You'd better come back to Oslo," he said, sounding tired. "Jason's in there, timing how long it takes you two to get back, and Carlos and I can't concentrate on anything while he's sitting behind us and huffing."

Sarah and I looked at each other. "Thanks," Sarah said, and Ian left. To me, she rolled her eyes. "There's got to be some way to complain about that bastard asap," she said. "I seriously can't wait for this stupid project to be over." She then coaxed me out of the toilets back towards Oslo. It took some doing, because I *really, really* didn't want to see anyone who'd just overheard Jason *yelling* at us.

On the way back, Marketing had returned to what they'd been up to before Jason had distracted them: being hunched over papers on their desk, parked in front of shared monitors or busy on phone calls... but in addition to those things, they were all *staring* at me.

I tried not to look at anyone but I could feel their eyes. As I passed between the desks, it wasn't so much what people were doing; no one was whispering or shouting stuff out at me. Not yet, anyway. It was just that the usual laughter and chatter than happened on the floor during work hours was conspicuously absent. There was oppressive silence, and that was how I knew for sure that Jason's voice had carried all the way over here.

This was how it had started at school, before the other students had begun to gang up on me: I'd walked down corridors and into classrooms with everyone *staring*. That's not where it stopped, though. The staring was just the beginning. It was only a matter of time before the emails would start to circulate, people would start asking me questions and making 'funny' comments, and everything would become four hundred million times more awful than even the staring was. We didn't have a skeleton at Frost for people to hang my bra on — but these men were older and obsessed with their own creative genius. They'd find something else to do to me because it was oh my god *so* funny to tease co-workers. It was only a matter of time.

Jason *was* waiting for us back in Oslo. He didn't comment on our short absence, though, thanks in part to Ian who I think *really* just wanted to get the project finished and get his bonus.

Unfortunately, Jason didn't leave. He sat there for the rest of the fucking day, making snide comments and jabs at me and sighing heavily whenever he looked at any of the updates I was sending around it. It was unbearable, except that I had no choice but *to* bear it. The alternative was going somewhere else, and that meant running the gauntlet of silent, staring marketing clerks.

Despite everything Jason was doing, the materials *were* finished by the end of the day and they looked fucking *fantastic.* They were definitely the best work I'd done, and the colours and text balancing looked amazing.

I must have been smiling at them in the evening when they came back from Printing, because Jason snatched the one I was holding off me to inspect it. He didn't compliment it, though. He just said, "Better than the mess that was the Vladivostok ones, at least. I'm almost glad the pitch was cancelled so you didn't embarrass Frost by handing out sub-par information packs."

The rest of the team glanced at each other, but no one said anything. They didn't say anything when Jason pulled me aside as we all left for the night, either. "Don't you even think about not showing up tomorrow, or you'll end up like John." I obediently mumbled something to agree with him, and he let me go.

I didn't even know what had happened with John, so I asked Sarah at the lift. I'd just assumed he was still off sick. "Oh!" she said looking stricken. "No one told you? You knew he was still on probation, right? After the Vladivostok pitch failed, they decided they were going to fire him, but only after the Burov pitch so that he doesn't try to sabotage it."

I gaped at her. There were *firing* him? For one fuck up when he was brand new? Wow, that was... God. This was partially my fault for not mentoring him better, wasn't it? My actions had just gotten a young man fired.

Sarah had been carefully watching me. "You don't look like you're doing too well, you want company tonight?"

I smiled bleakly as we stepped into the lift. "Why? Are you afraid I'll throw myself under a bus?"

She gave me a look. "Min, work was so terrible today that *I'm* about ready to throw myself under a bus, and I'm otherwise pretty happy with my life." She sobered. "Seriously, though. I can't leave you alone like this. You look like a zombie."

I wasn't sure I liked the idea of her taking care of me, to be honest. It made me feel emasculated, somehow. Luckily she didn't need to. "Bree's at my place." She made an 'oh' shape with her mouth. "What about you?" I asked her. "Are *you* okay?"

She shrugged. "I'll be okay. Rob and I have a Skype date later tonight, we'll probably watch a movie together or something." I nodded at her and when we walked out of the building, she gave me a big hug. "Jason's full of it," she told me. "Don't let him get to you. At least not before we figure out how to report the bastard."

Easier said than done. "Okay, I'll forget about Jason," I told her, and watched her relax before I added, "it gives me more time to focus on what crap the other thirty marketing clerks have in store for me."

She didn't laugh, she just hugged me again after she'd wagged her finger at me. "No buses," she said sternly as she left.

Lucky for me, there weren't any running at this time of night anyway. That meant that as I made my way home I wasn't tempted to throw myself under anything while I reflected on how well today went and looked forward to more of the same tomorrow.

Tomorrow, which was the last day before the pitch.

The last day to make sure everything was on track so we were ready to deliver smoothly and hopefully get that contract signed. All the materials were done, the slides were ready and all that remained was training the reluctant Sales team. I worried about that. I knew they were hesitant to properly learn the materials because the last pitch had fallen apart at the eleventh hour, and I didn't really blame them for that. They blamed *me* for that, though, and so did most of my team.

At least there wasn't anything Ian and Carlos and the Sales boys could say to the rest of Marketing about my role in the failed pitch right now, but after the project was over they'd tell everyone what their theories were.

And once people knew about my catastrophic foray into leadership on top of the fact I was a 'tranny', or whatever the hell Jason had been shouting across the Marketing floor... well, at least in high school I'd had fantastic grades. It was something else to be the butt of everyone's jokes *and* a fuck up.

How on earth was I going to get through this? I had *no* idea how I was even going to manage to show up at work, let alone pay any attention to it at all.

I hadn't eaten all day—thank god—or I might have actually thrown up with how much that question stressed me out. Instead, my stomach just clenched and I just wished I could get home to Bree faster. As much as I hated her indiscretion, she did always make me feel better. I thought about her all the way up to my level in the lift, and hoped she hadn't cooked me anything to eat because I was *not* in a place where food was going to work for me.

As I let myself into my apartment, I expected Bree to be jumping all over me like an excited terrier, but she wasn't. In fact, I found her on the couch hugging a cushion. She looked like she'd been crying, but she completely forgot about whatever was making her upset when she saw me.

"Oh my god, Min, you look *terrible*!" she said, distracting me from asking about her tears. Abandoning the cushion, she rushed over to me.

I couldn't be touched right now, though. Not looking like *this*. "Let me change," I said stiffly, and she released me to let me go have a quick shower.

When I was getting dressed, though, I was just standing there in my bedroom holding the binder and trying to decide if it was too late at night to bother wrestling myself into it, when what Jason had said hit me. Dress-ups, I thought, and looked up at my reflection with breasts in the mirror. It *is* just dress-ups, isn't it? It's not real. I'm kidding myself. Look, Min, you might try to pretend you don't, but you do have breasts because you're *female*.

As much as I fucking hated Jason, that didn't mean he was automatically wrong, did it? Was I *actually* kidding myself? I wondered if I *should* just give up on this whole gender thing and all the shit it was getting me into. Even though I'd be comfortably invisible again if I did, the thought of going back to being a woman full-time was so depressing that I threw my binder in a corner, pulled my hoodie on and just sat down on the bed with my head in my hands.

I felt like there was no way out of this. I was trapped in every possible fucking way; with my boyfriend, in my job, by my family and in this *stupid* body. There was no way out, and tomorrow I had the churning rumour-mill to look forward to at work. There was no escape.

I heard a gentle knock on the door. "Min...?"

Bree. "Come in. I'm dressed."

She opened the door slowly and spotted me slumped on the bed. She didn't say anything at first, she just came and knelt next to me on the bed and put her arms around my shoulders. I leant into her, and she hugged me tighter.

"I'm a mess," I said quietly.

"Me too," she said beside my ear. "Why are you so upset? Did everyone find out after all?"

I nodded slowly, and told her what happened. "And tomorrow," I finished, "I have to put up with *all* of that again, and then after this pitch is finished and confidentiality is lifted someone will tell the Marketing boys how much I fucked up, so I won't just be *tranny* Min," I said, my lip curling on the slur, "I'll be useless tranny Min. That's if I even have a job by then. If not, I'll just be disowned, homeless, broke, useless tranny Min."

In the mirror, I could see Bree frown. "Don't talk about yourself like that," she said. When I just shrugged, she said, "Because, okay, you can be a total pessimist, but you're like this super smart, super talented *amazing* person *and* on top of that you're completely gorgeous. If *you're* useless, what the hell does that make me? I'm kind of dumb and I can't do anything special. I don't have any talents. I'm just cute and I've got big boobs, but it's never gotten me anywhere, no matter what they say about looks."

I put a hand up beside her head and hugged it against my shoulder. She *could* be 'kind of dumb', but there were so many good things about her. "You shouldn't be so hard on yourself."

"Hypocrite," she muttered.

I chuckled at that and ruffled her curls, even though I felt like *crap* about everything. "I wish it would all just end," I confessed. "Sarah's got her heart set on complaining about Jason, but I don't realistically see that doing anything except getting us in the shit with him."

"Aren't you *already* 'in the shit with him' after that whole John-Vladivostok-thing and taking time off, though? Maybe Sarah's right, maybe you *should* complain. I mean, it's not like it can make things *worse* than they already are, can it?"

"With Jason? Probably not," I said. "But then there's Diane: if we did complain, she'd *kill* us when she found out. Which she would, by the way, because it's Sean Frost we need to complain to." At Bree's confused look, I clarified, "Sean Frost, the other CEO."

Her eyebrows went up. "Sean? Like, that guy who tried to make me feel better when the debt collector was hassling me? *He's* a CEO?" I nodded. "He was so nice to me, though! You'd never know he was a mega-billionaire or whatever."

I shrugged. "Well, if you listen to anything Henry, Diane and Jason say, he's the root of all evil."

"Bullshit," Bree said simply. "Jason's root of all evil. I haven't met him, but I can already tell he's a fuck."

I exhaled audibly. "Yeah. And he's my boss, and Diane and Sean are CEOs, and at some point in the near future Henry, the manager of HR, is going to be my ex... Sounds like a fantastic place to work, what do you think?"

Bree was quiet for a few seconds, her fingers were absently playing with the wisps of hair at the back of my neck. "I know you say you can't quit because of your mum, but you're going to have a heart attack and die when you're like thirty," she told me. When I frowned at her in the reflection, she added, "Seriously. Stress kills people. Everyone knows that."

I sighed. "Well, what do you suggest? I quit, get turfed out of here and just be homeless on the street with my career over?"

Bree made a face. "Can't you just withdraw some money and rent somewhere? You'd have savings, right?"

"Sure, if you consider my Mum a savings account."

"Your *mum* has all your money?" I nodded, and she gave me a look. "Whoa," she said. "Fuck." She thought about that a bit more. "You couldn't even ask her for any, could you? Because if she's like what you said, she'd be really nosy about it."

I agreed with her, exhaling. Everything was just *so* fucked up, and literally, there was no escaping it. I had *no* idea how I was going to get through this, it was all so much that I didn't even know where to start. "Well, I need a drink," I said, and went to stand up, but Bree didn't let me go.

"Isn't this relaxing?" she asked, hugging around my shoulders.

I squinted at her. "Not as relaxing as a glass of red."

She pursed her lips, and didn't take her arms away. "Not that drinking heaps isn't fun, but I'm still feeling kind of sick after all the wine we had last night."

I was, too, but given the choice between being physically ill and emotionally unstable, well, there were always painkillers. "You don't have to drink with me. I'm perfectly capable of drinking alone."

"Yeah, you are," Bree said pointedly. That stung a bit, and I think it showed on my face, because she quickly changed the subject. "I read heaps of stuff on the internet today about all sorts of alternatives to drinking to help you relax. Maybe I could run a bath for you, or we could watch a really happy movie, or I could give you a massage or something?"

I looked across at her, about to tell her that none of those things contained as many antioxidants as red wine, but the words never got past my lips. She looked so earnest with those big puppy eyes. I ended up looking at them longer than I'd intended to while I tried to think of some polite way to decline those suggestions, and I think she mistook that as me asking her for something completely different. She drew a little breath and put her hand on my thigh.

"Or," she said, her cheeks a bit pink, "you know, I could do something else..." She looked up at me from underneath those long

502

lashes with her other arm still slung around my shoulder. Her face was really close to mine again. I could feel her warm breath on my lips.

On some level I definitely wanted to at least kiss her, but all I could think of was those failed fantasies I'd had in Broome. On top of all the shit that was going down in *every* part of my life, I didn't have the energy to try and overcome the wrongness of my body and let her touch me anywhere, no matter how much I might end up enjoying it if I could.

When her hand on my thigh moved up a fraction, I inhaled sharply, alarmed. "I wouldn't find that relaxing, Bree." I said quickly, pushing her hand off in panic. She broke eye contact and nodded. I exhaled at length, feeling *really* guilty. I didn't want to make her feel unattractive, because she wasn't. She *really* wasn't. It was just that I was a complete head case right now. "I'm sorry. It's just that I'm—" I didn't know where I was going with that one, so I tried something else. "I mean, I can't—"

"It's okay," she interrupted me when she could see I was struggling. "No pressure. I just offered because I thought that was what you wanted."

I groaned and rubbed my face with my hands. What I wanted? What I wanted was a Golden Ticket out of this fucking existence to somewhere where anything in my life went right. *In your fucking dreams, Min,* I thought. *You're stuck here. Get used to it.*

"How about I just get you a glass of orange juice?" Bree offered, changing the subject again. "I got some really nice organic stuff."

She went off to do that, and I left my face in my hands. My head was one giant tangle and I was *exhausted* just thinking about everything, but when she returned I still managed a few sips of her organic juice to humour her since she'd got to the effort of getting it for me.

She looked very happy about that, and there was something really gratifying about making her happy. "I bet after all of this crap, this pitch doesn't get cancelled and goes really well and everything will be okay," she said, I think just trying to comfort me. "And if not, maybe Jason will get hit by a car or something."

I snorted orange juice through my nose and coughed. "I mean, I hate him, but that's a pretty awful thing to wish on someone," I said, spluttering. I couldn't say I didn't secretly like the idea, though.

"That fuck makes me want to learn to drive."

When I looked across at her, I realised she was completely serious and I had to laugh a bit and hug her. "Thanks, Bree," I said, kissing her forehead. I could see her delighted smile in the reflection of the mirror. There is no way this girl was capable of harming anyone, despite what she'd said. She got emotional over rescuing *flowers* for fuck's sake. "Thanks for listening."

"My pleasure," she said, blushing.

I was finishing my glass of orange juice when I noticed her blush had faded and she was frowning. "There's just one thing I don't get about all that stuff you said," she told me when I looked across at her. "If the CEO is on your team, why are you scared to say anything?"

It was a bit of a weird question, I thought. "Diane's not really on my team. This project is just really important to her for some reason. And she's scary in general."

Bree looked blankly at me. "Not her, Sean."

I put my glass on the bedside table and frowned at her. "Sean's not on my team."

Her brow lowered. "He's not?" I shook my head. "But I thought..."

A knot began to form in my stomach. I felt uneasy about where this was going. "Why, did I say something to make it sound like he was?"

She was staring at me, confused. "I just saw you together that time, before the party. And then when he came down to make me feel better and we were talking... So, wait," she said, piecing everything together and looking more and more worried, "if he's the other CEO, that means *he's* the one that Diane didn't want to know about project, isn't he?"

My heart practically stopped in place. No, it couldn't be, *no*. I turned and put a firm hand on her shoulder. "Bree, did you say *something to him*?"

Recognition passed over her features, and she looked *mortified*. "I thought he was on your team. I even said 'since you're working with Min' and he didn't contradict me!"

The timing of the cancellation fell into place; Diane and Jason had been right: it *hadn't* actually been a coincidence after all. *God fucking damnit*! *Bree*! "Jesus, Bree, how much did you tell him?"

She flinched at how loudly I was speaking. "I'm *sorry*, Min!" she said, which basically meant she'd told him everything. "He said he wanted to know what you'd told me! And then he said not to worry and not to mention it to you because it would just stress you out and you were so stressed out already and *he was right*!"

I released Bree only to put my hands to either side of my head. *Bree* had been the leak, *not* John. Which meant a whole lot of things, mainly that Vladivostok pulling the pin *had* been my fault, and that an innocent young man was getting fired as a result.

Fuck. I couldn't even... I couldn't even deal with this. On top of everything. I could have had two supply contracts signed instead of being the focus of Jason's ire, and then maybe everything would have...

And I couldn't... well... I had to say something, didn't I? That it was *my* fault, but... then again John maybe had done other things wrong.... *Fuck,* I couldn't fucking think straight.

Sean wouldn't do that, either, would he? Maybe it *was* a coincidence?

Nothing made sense. I couldn't think. I could hardly breathe. "Bree, someone's getting fired because of that," I managed to say to her. "Maybe two people, if I do as well."

She looked really upset. "But I didn't mean to!" she said, as if that made one ounce of difference.

"You *never* mean to do things!" I told her. "But you still always *do them anyway,* intentionally or not!"

I shook my head at her, trying to figure out what the fucking fuck I should do. I should turf her out of here, I thought. I should yell at her, tell her *everything* that the failed pitch and her being arrested by the police and me needing to chase Cecilia all day today had caused. Two careers were potentially over because of this. I should delete her number and block her on Deviant Art and never talk to her again...

...but as I looked down at that nose of hers that went pink when she was about to cry, I couldn't. I couldn't. I *knew* what she was like, *I* shouldn't have told her anything. It was just as much my fault as it was hers. And who was I kidding, anyway? She was fucking infuriating, but I would have gone nuts if she wasn't here to hug me and comfort me and bring me organic fucking orange juice.

I didn't know what I should have done, I didn't know what *to* do. Everything was too fucking much and this was just *one more thing* I needed to worry about. It was too much. "Fucking hell, Bree…" I said, exhausted, flopping back on the mattress and draping my forearm over my eyes. "Why the hell do you do this stuff, *and* exactly when everything is already complete shit? *Why…?*"

Bree still looked like she was bracing for me to blast her, and was surprised when I didn't. "You're not going to yell at me and throw me out for completely wrecking *everything*?" I shook my head, I was too tired to explain. Cautiously, she lay down beside me, as if she thought I'd change my mind. We stared up at the ceiling for a minute or two. I felt the doona move as she turned her head towards me. "I *am* sorry, though. Like, really, I know I'm completely fucking hopeless. Dad always says it, and he's right, I am hopeless."

I just sighed. I want to murder you, I thought, and I probably would, except I'd miss you far too much.

She was still looking at me. "I know what you meant about everything being total shit right now."

I glanced towards her, still angry. I'd forgotten she'd been recently crying when I'd arrived home. "Yeah?"

She exhaled heavily. "My family is really angry at me for missing Easter. Like, grandma and my aunt and uncles and stuff. They don't know about what Andrej did and what it's like at home so they just think I'm being bratty and ditching Easter for sex and drugs or whatever." She shifted her weight on the mattress. "And, like, I don't really care about that, but then Andrej sent me a message on Facebook and all it said was, 'So Courtney told me where your friend lives'."

I considered that. "Do you really think he'd do anything with my address?"

She thought about that. "Maybe. Not like anything violent, but maybe something dodgy if he thought there was anything in it for him. It's not about me, I'm just his scapegoat."

I touched her hand because I just had no emotional energy left to say anything comforting. "'8' on the phone is security," I told her. She nodded, and we just lay there together, holding hands.

I was so exhausted and so conflicted about what to do about Sean and John and what Bree had said that I must have fallen asleep like that, because when I woke up in the morning I was lying the wrong way on the bed with a pillow under my head and wrapped in the doona. The culprit was still asleep, cuddled up against my side. For just a moment I smiled at how peaceful she looked, gently stroking her cheek with the knuckles of my fingers. Then I remembered *she'd told Sean Frost about Russia*.

That opened the floodgates. I just lay paralysed for a couple of seconds as *everything* came back to me: Jason's constant bullying, the entire marketing knowing about my gender stuff and all the torment that would come from that, the fact I kept fucking *everything* up and, oh, yes, someone was getting *fired* because apparently I didn't understand the meaning of 'confidentiality agreement'.

I couldn't lie here and stress, though, because my heart was starting to race and if I freaked out I'd never make it to work early enough to avoid everyone and barricade myself in Oslo.

I dressed in something Jason would probably consider appropriate and hated every second of it, threw on the rest of my costume and high-tailed to work before everyone else could arrive. I did actually buy myself an energy drink because unlike Sarah, I couldn't dry-swallow my painkillers, but I thought better of drinking most of it. If I needed to go to the toilet too often, I'd have to leave Oslo and face the rabble on the Marketing floor. Even *with* Jason it was safer in here.

Then I watched the clock nervously and reviewed every tiny millimetre of the materials to make sure everything was perfect while I waited for my team to arrive.

When the door opened I expected it to be Sarah, so I swung around and was in the middle of saying, "Hi—" when I saw it was *Jason*.

I went *bright* red, and he gave me a really suspicious look. "Just for your information, sucking up doesn't help your cause, Mini. Not unless it comes backed up with nineteen grand and the renewed respect of Diane Frost." He looked me up and down, and when he didn't say anything about my dress, I knew I'd chosen the right one.

He seemed a bit more subdued today, I observed, and I wondered what had caused that. I turned back to my desk to keep working. It was hard, though, because as he moved around the room, despite the fact he wasn't saying anything and didn't *seem* like he was going to yell at me, I could *feel* where he was. The hair was standing up on the back of my neck, especially when he was right behind me.

"What are you doing?" he asked, after he'd been standing there for a few seconds. It sounded like a loaded question.

My clammy fingers slipped on the ruler. "I'm checking the dimensions of the material to make sure it was printed correctly and it will fit in the packs we ordered."

He stood there for another minute or two watching me check and make note of the measurements; it was *fucked up*. He had *no reason* to be scrutinising me. At least no work-related reason. I realised he was probably waiting for me to make a mistake so he could yell at me. I didn't, and after a while he got bored with standing over me and went to do something productive. I released a breath I didn't even know I'd been holding.

The rest of the team trickled in, and today Sarah was last. She arrived looking unslept with giant bags under her eyes that she'd failed to effectively conceal with foundation. I gave her a questioning look, but there wasn't anything she could say because Jason launched us right into a meeting and soon after that, the Sales boys Diane had chosen arrived to learn the material.

Jason wasn't their boss, and it showed. They checked their phones, whispered to each other, and interrupted him from time-to-time while he was introducing himself and the project. It pissed him off, and you could see the rising frustration on his face. That worried me. I didn't want him to get angry again and go off at us. I had a sudden thought about what he might do if he found out that I'd told Bree about the project and Bree had told Sean. He'd have fired me on the spot, wouldn't he?

I had no idea what happened during the rest of the meeting, because my head was swimming around that question. I wondered if what I'd told Bree about *this* pitch was enough for Sean to cancel it—except it wasn't cancelled so it mustn't have been, right?—and I wondered what would happen if the whole department found out how much I'd fucked that up *on top of* knowing about my gender stuff.

When Jason called a break and went to check on a couple of the other teams, and our boys went to grab coffee or food, Sarah came up to me. "Min," she said, glancing behind her to make sure they were all definitely gone, "I couldn't sleep last night because I was thinking about what happened in the toilets. What he did was *so* not okay, and we shouldn't let him get away with it. We need to report him."

I shook my head. There was no one to report him *to*, not before the assistant manager of HR got back from his leave, and especially not after what Bree had revealed last night. "We can't report it now," I whispered to her.

She made a face. "Sure we can, Sean's in the office today, I checked on his—"

"Sarah, Bree told Sean about Vladivostok right before they cancelled."

She hadn't been expecting me to say anything like that and for a second she frowned at me like she didn't know what I meant. *"What?"*

I swallowed, elaborating. "She was always around when I was painting for the project, and that time when I was looking for stock photos, she helped. And then the other day when she was downstairs, just before the police thing, Sean managed to get the story out of her. Straight after that, the pitch was cancelled."

She took a few seconds to process that. "You *told Schoolgirl* about a *confidential pitch*?" she asked, incredulous, and then followed straight up with, "Are you *sure* about the timing, though?"

I scrunched up my face. "I think so."

Sarah stood back. "Wow," she said. "*Wow.*" She thought about that for a second. "Then again, okay, let's go through this carefully. The withdrawal came at open of business for Vladivostok, so I actually don't think anyone *blames* you really, apart from Jason. But I think he'd blame anyone right now, he's just angry in general. And since it came at open of business, it's possible the boss decided the night before and then emailed us the following morning. We normally find out in the morning if pitches flop. So, are we *sure* it was Sean? I mean, how much did you actually tell Bree? Did you tell her it was to *Impressions*?"

I shook my head. "I just called it 'Vladivostok'."

She made a *tada* motion with her hands. "Are you still sure? Sure enough to not report really serious bullying to management?"

I watched her. "Regardless, we can't be seen talking to Sean, anyway. You know that."

She was about to say something else, but she couldn't because the Sales boys came back in with their coffees and muffins. They were speaking quietly, but I was sure I heard one of them griping about Jason micromanaging them. They stopped when they saw us, though, all looking at me and then at each other. They didn't say anything — I didn't know them well enough for them to risk bringing up anything personal with me — but I guessed someone on the floor had told them about what Jason had said yesterday.

I looked through the crack in the door as Ian and Carlos came back in and recognised a few familiar faces outside. Someone spotted me and grinned. I turned away from the door, inhaling.

For the rest of the meeting, I tried to imagine what was going around the floor about Jason's tirade and what was going to happen to me as a result. The stuff that had been done to me in high school was pretty awful, and they'd just been immature kids. What could immature *adults* do?

When the meeting was over, I'd been so lost in thought that I didn't notice Jason coming to stand in front of me with his arms crossed. When I finally did and I looked up at him, confused, everyone except Sarah laughed at how distracted I'd been. Jason shook his head in disgust at me, and then he and all the boys went out to lunch together. They invited Sarah, too, but she had something she needed to do for her other team. She told me later privately that she wouldn't have gone without me, anyway.

"Are you going to be okay?" she asked as she left. "You want something to eat? I can go out there and get it."

"No," I told her, "Thanks, I couldn't eat anything anyway, but I need to go down and set up the media room." I actually didn't need to do that *right* now, but it gave me an excuse to be somewhere private by myself.

Getting down there meant five minutes of psyching myself up to leave Oslo and brave whatever was waiting for me outside, and then bursting out of our office at a brisk walk so I looked really busy and fewer people would try and talk to me. Luckily, most people were at lunch and the odd person who'd stayed back was hard at work with whatever task he hadn't finished.

I went down the internal stairs anyway, just to avoid any more uncomfortable lift rides.

The media room had been left in disarray from the last pitch; there were chairs everywhere. I counted how many chairs I'd need on my fingers: there was Diane, Jason and the four of us in Pink, and then the four Sales boys, and Burov's entourage. He'd said he was bringing that PA of his, a 'good friend'—Russian code for 'bodyguard', I was told—and another guy from his business.

I set them all up, checked that the screen was working and that the computer was working and then sat down at the back. Marketing didn't normally sit in on Sales pitches, but because the Sales boys didn't have the usual three days to learn the materials, they'd insisted on it in case there were questions that needed answering.

There were a lot of questions about this pitch in general that were unanswered, but we had so little time to get everything done. Aside from Vladivostok, this was definitely the most tenuous pitch I'd been on; normally the time-frames from concept to contract were sort of arbitrarily set by management as a performance indicator, but in this one, they actually mattered. No signature meant no mine, and that was at a cost of millions to Frost.

A bad pitch came at a greater personal cost to me, though.

I was completely certain that if we didn't get a sale, Jason would make sure I didn't have a job on Friday. And that meant on Saturday, I'd be homeless unless I could cough up the several hundred a night for the hotel casual rates. I could for a few nights, but not for long enough to find somewhere else to live. I'd always thought if something happened at work I could stay with Henry... but I couldn't now. Not anymore.

Well, I just had to make sure it didn't happen and that we made this sale.

While I was trying to convince myself to go back upstairs, my phone buzzed in my pocket. I assumed it was either Sarah or Bree so I took it out to glance at the screen. It was a hidden number, and since I didn't want a repeat of that situation where Jason had *yelled* at me for not answering my phone, I took it. "Hello, Min Lee speaking."

"Min! You answered!" There was only one person on the planet who'd call me and speak Korean. "Why don't you ever call your poor mother?"

Fuck. This was the absolute *last* thing I could deal with today. "Hi, Mum," I said in English. "Didn't Henry tell you how busy I am with work? Really busy, actually, I—"

"Too busy to call your own mother?" she interrupted me. "Henry wasn't too busy to *visit* me. You're too busy to even call."

This was an argument that I couldn't win, so I didn't try. "How's Grandma?" I asked, knowing it would get her started on long hospital visit stories. I thought I'd succeeded, but she only spent a couple of minutes talking about Grandma before she got stuck right back into me again.

"You should visit, Min. Spend some time with your grandma in her winter years. She'd like to get to know you."

She's heavily demented, Mum. She wouldn't even recognise me from photos. "I can't just take time off like that, I told you," I said. "Look, maybe if something unexpected happened soon and I wasn't able to keep working at Frost, then—"

"You're *pregnant*?" she said, completely misunderstanding me. "That's fantastic! Well, it's a sin, but I'm sure He will forgive you because I know Henry will propose to you soon, I just know it. I tried to get Henry to tell me when he's going to do it while he was here, but he's very tight-lipped. That's a good quality in a man, you don't want someone who will broadcast your private affairs. But if you're going to have a baby then you should definitely get married soon, because—"

"Mum, I'm not pregnant," I cut her off. I'm potentially about to be fired and homeless. Also I'm transgender, I like women and I will *never* be pregnant.

She ignored me as if I hadn't spoken at all. "I'm sure the two of you can live on Henry's salary. And doesn't the Australian government pay for maternity leave now? You can send that back to us, instead, if Henry's still working there. I'm sure your grandma and I will be able to manage on that, even if it's a lot less than you normally give us." She sighed peacefully. "I'm so happy for you, Min. Henry is going to make such a wonderful husband and a great father, and someone like you needs all the support they can get with motherhood. Everyone at Church loved him, and we all can't wait for the wedding. It makes me so happy to know when I'm so far away from you that you have someone like him taking care of you."

I had my lips pressed in a tight line as she kept gushing and gushing.

"And it's so lucky that Frost decided to hire you, even though you're much too shy and really antisocial. The salary means I can stay at home and take care of my mother in her dying years. She took such good care of me when I was a child, after all. I'm glad I don't have to abandon her just as she's leaving us."

I closed my eyes. There was nothing I could say to that. If there was no more high salary, I wouldn't be able to send money back and Mum would have to work and either put Grandma in a home or get a nurse to look after her during the day. That stuff was expensive.

Fuck. I *had* to get this pitch signed.

"Anyway, it's lovely to talk to you. Don't eat bruised fruit, okay? That's bad for babies. I'm going to send you a book about what to eat when you're pregnant. Call me as soon as it's confirmed, okay, I'm going to buy that book now, bye!"

She hung up, and I sat there for a second staring at the phone.

I had *no* idea if she actually thought I was pregnant, or if Henry had said something — recently he'd been talking a lot about family and children, after all — or if this was just her very subtle and manipulative way of pushing me along to get married and have babies.

I had no idea about anything, and I just felt *like shit*.

I'd also overstayed my lunch and should probably go back upstairs so I could continue getting picked on by Jason into the early hours of the afternoon. I tried to reassure myself that if I'd made it through two days of being victimised by him, I could make it through the couple of hours I had left of him today before he had to go get Sasha Burov from the airport.

Despite that, I struggled to leave the room.

There were several floors between the media suites and thirty-six, but I took the stairwell again so I wouldn't bump into anyone anyway. It meant that by the time I got upstairs I was puffed and I needed to stand behind the door and wait until I'd caught my breath again. I listened to make sure no one was waiting for a lift and only came out when it was silent.

I had thought people probably wouldn't be back from lunch yet, but when I walked out onto the Marketing floor, I discovered I was wrong. Most of the department *was* back from lunch, but they weren't working yet. They were chatting, bunched together watching video clips on each other's computers, or finishing off their food.

I tried to sneak around the side where people looked the busiest and hoped no one would notice; no such luck.

"Hey! Mini!" someone called. I recognised the voice, it was the old lead from my last pitch. I pretended not to hear him, but he just shouted louder and made *everyone* look. To stop him from drawing so much attention to me, I turned and gave him a wave. However, as soon as I'd acknowledged him he made a 'come here' gesture. My heart pounded.

I hurriedly shook my head. "I have work to do."

"Two seconds!" he shouted back.

Everyone was starting to watch us and I wanted them to *stop* so I just decided to do what he said.

Walking over to his desk pod, I felt eyes on me and as I passed people, they leant their heads together and whispered behind me, turned to smirk at their colleagues and someone smothered laughter. *They think I'm a joke*, I realised. I desperately wanted to go back to being invisible to them, someone whose name only came up when they wanted to talk graphics.

The snickering behind me was too much. It was too much to deal with, and so awful that I was numb.

"Dave," someone said to the lead and passed him a stack of printouts. "Here, ask Mini about those."

Dave looked down at them and then up at me. "So," he said, and I expected every second for him to make some comment about what he'd heard Jason shout. "We're about to send these back to our graphic artist for changes, could you take a quick look and tell me if anything stands out?" He pulled out a chair at his desk for me to sit in and held the printouts at me.

Cautiously, I took them and sat down. As soon as I'd done that, the rest of his team came over and crowded around, probably to hear what I had to say. It was claustrophobic with all these men standing over me, but there was nothing I could do.

I tried to focus on the materials. It was difficult, but as I flipped through them, a couple of things looked off and I pointed to them and told Dave my suggested changes. Everyone nodded and when I was done, I handed the printouts back to him and went to stand up.

I couldn't, because there were too many people around me and my chair wouldn't move at all from under the desk. My pulse started to race.

"Thanks," Dave told me, "you're a lifesaver. None of us have any idea about materials." He looked like he wanted to say something else and mentally I *begged* him not to. It may or may not have shown on my face; he'd never been that perceptive anyway. None of them had. "So..." he began conversationally.

Panicking, I looked up at all the men above me, trying to figure out if I could just force my chair back and stand up.

"Is it true what Jason said?" he asked. "Are you...?"

I must have looked like a deer in headlights.

One of the other boys finished his sentence. "A tranny," he said. Not cruelly; at least, not *intentionally* cruelly. When someone elbowed him and told him to shush, he said, "What! That's the word for it, isn't it? 'Tranny'?"

"Transsexual," one of his colleagues corrected him. "The word is 'transsexual', 'tranny' is really fucking rude, man, it's like 'faggot', you don't say that shit, at least not at work."

The original guy shrugged. "I don't know, I kind of like it," he said. "Mini the Tranny, it has a ring to it. Sounds like a kid's book or something."

They were all talking to each other over my head while I sat there, paralysed and struggling to breathe. I couldn't do anything. I couldn't say anything. It was like a nightmare where the monsters were chasing me but I couldn't run away.

"Mini," someone clapped me on the shoulder. I jumped. "You never really liked being called that, did you? Well, I've got a new nickname for you. How about 'Manny'?" The men around him laughed and I had a few more people clap me on the back.

"Does this mean you'll come to strip clubs with us now?" someone asked me. "Or do we need to wait until after surgery? How do they do that, anyway? Do they get a donor dick off some guy in a motorcycle accident, or what? I've always wondered."

"Dude, you need to learn to use Google, that's not how they do it," someone called over the partition.

They weren't going to stop; I couldn't deal with this. "I need to work," I rasped. When it was clear no one had heard me, I said it louder and forced my chair back directly into a few legs and feet so I could stand up. "I need to go back to work!"

I stood up, taller than most of them, and they all stopped talking and gaped at me. The guy who I'd nearly run over with my chair bent down to rub his thigh. "Jesus, Mini, you could have just *asked* me to move."

They were all watching me, quiet. I *hated* having all these people *staring* at me, and a couple of them seemed offended that I'd ruined their fun, light-hearted conversation about my genitals. They just had *no* fucking idea. I turned and went back into Oslo, pulling the door shut behind me.

Jason was sitting at my desk, apparently waiting for me.

I glanced around the room; there was no one else in it. I stood in place because I wasn't sure what he was going to do, but I felt apprehensive about it.

He didn't say anything off the bat. He just tossed me the Employee ID tag that I used to get into the building and I caught it, confused. He nodded at it, and when I looked down, I saw someone had printed off that picture I'd painted of me as a guy, cut the face out and sticky-taped it over my photo on the ID.

While I was reeling from that, Jason said, "You know what the problem with that is, apart from the fact that no one in here is ever going to call you '*Mr* Min Lee'?"

I shook my head, because there were a *lot* of problems with that.

"The problem is that someone had to get in here, open your

drawer and spend several minutes actually *doing* that. And do you know *how* they did it?"

I swallowed.

"Because you didn't lock the fucking door when you left, Mini."

I flushed. *Fuck*, had I really done something *that* stupid...? All I could remember when I left was just being *so* worried about what people were going to say about me once I was out of this room that I... I must have forgotten.

"I'm sorry," I stammered, "I've just got a lot on my mind."

He stood up from my chair and went to leave Oslo. I was still standing by the door, and he stopped next to me on the way out. He looked tired and angry. "Mini, every single person on this project is stressed out. *None* of us are sleeping. We *all* have a lot on our minds. You're the only seasoned rep who's fucking up, though, did you notice?"

I just looked at the ground.

He wasn't done. "When you crash and burn on team projects, Mini, people crash and burn with you. I told you yesterday: if that tranny shit is what's distracting you, *leave it at home*, okay? Pull yourself together, I'm fucking sick of this. You've already made me look like a total idiot in front of Diane, and I spent *years* trying to get her respect." He shook his head in disgust, and then left.

I stood there for a moment after he'd gone, looking down at my ID with the painting taped to it.

I was losing the plot. But how was I supposed to 'leave it at home' when it was here, haunting me, every second of every day? How could I leave that conversation with the Marketing boys I'd just had out there at home? How could I leave Jason shouting at me in the toilets over what he'd heard at home? How could I leave *seeing myself in a dress in every reflective surface* at home?

I swallowed. I'd fucking 'pull myself together' in a heartbeat if I could, you *asshole*. If I had the option, I'd just do it. But I didn't have the option, did I?

I felt like everything was slipping through my fingers. Everything I'd worked so hard at my whole life: I'd worked myself half to death at high school and uni, all to get this amazing, high-flying job, and then I'd slogged my guts out at this job, too. And now it was slipping away from me. No matter how I tried, I felt like I couldn't hold onto it and it was getting further and further away, and it was so unfair, *so fucking unfair,* because it was over something I couldn't control.

A lump formed in my throat. I didn't ask for this, Jason, I thought. I didn't *ask* for this. I don't *want* this. It just is, and I just am, and I can't help it. I don't *want* to look in the mirror and feel wrong and bad and depressed about what I see. I don't *want* to lie in bed *wishing* things were different and *wishing* I just knew what's right and how I'm supposed to be... I just do. That's how it is for me. And I can't control it or turn it off when I feel like it, or don't you fucking think I would have already fucking done it, Jason? *Don't you fucking think I would have already done it?*

I was tearing up, and I couldn't do that here. I didn't want Jason or Ian or Carlos or any of the Sales boys to see me like this.

I left Oslo—stopping long enough to lock it this time—and made a break for the Women's toilets. I didn't care who saw me run or what they thought. I was already a fucking laughing stock, it couldn't get any worse.

Once I was in there I went right to the far wall and leant there, looking upwards and trying not to blink so my tears wouldn't spill down my cheeks. In the end it was a lost cause. Like everything else, I couldn't stop them.

Hunched against the wall, with my arms tightly folded across my stomach, I just stood there and *wept* for all my wasted effort, all my hard work and the giant mess me and my 'perfect' life had become in a short two months. It just wasn't fair.

Sarah found me.

I didn't know how long I'd been in there when she did. She walked over to the hand basin near where I was standing and leant against it, reaching out and putting a comforting hand on my arm.

We stood there for a few minutes. Eventually, she said, "You know it'll all be over soon, right?"

"Not soon enough." I was sniffing, and she went and grabbed me some toilet paper out of one of the stalls so I could blow my nose.

While I did that, she rubbed my arm. "Okay, though, I have a dilemma. Men normally like to be left alone when they're sad and women normally like hugs so I'm not sure how to comfort you?"

I laughed bleakly. "Are those the only two choices I've got?"

She shrugged. We stood there for a minute while I tried desperately to stop *crying* over all of this. "You've got to report him, Min."

I closed my eyes and shook my head. The *last* thing I needed was Diane to find out we'd spoke to Sean and for her to get angry with us, too.

Sarah guessed what I was thinking. "I am *so* over this mortal-enemy thing Diane and Sean have got going. It's not *our* fault they can't play nice. Why are they making it our problem? Come on," she said, and then took my arm. "Let's go find Sean, I don't even care what he has or hasn't said or done anymore. *Anything* is better than this."

When she started to drag me out of the bathroom, I got as far as the door before I panicked. I dug my heels into the tiles as my heart pounded. "I can't," I told Sarah, "I can't, I can't go out there and I can't talk to Sean, please..."

She let go of me as soon as I protested, but she looked worried. "Min, in like an hour I have to go get ready to meet Burov tonight and I am literally going to be sitting there stressing about you unless I know this is taken care of. And even if Sean *was* somehow the cause of the Vladivostok pitch flopping and he and Jason *are* involved, he's still required to obey the law and do something about Jason and the crap work environment he creates." She paused. "Plus he's less scary than Diane and she's the other alternative."

I didn't move.

She held her hand out to me. "Come on, Min, *please.*"

In the end she did manage to convince me because she was so determined and I just didn't have any sort of fight left. Maybe we were making the right decision, maybe we weren't. But Sarah was right about one thing: I couldn't go on like this.

She led me out of the Women's and down the stairwell to 35, and then into Sean's office. His assistant greeted us, and I saw recognition flash over her face when she saw me.

"Oh..." she said about the state I was in, and then intelligently didn't add anything else. "He's on the phone right now. Let me get him."

She excused herself and slipped into his room, returning

immediately and holding the door open for us. Sean was hanging up the phone as we entered, and as soon as he saw me, he stood up, looking deeply concerned.

"Min," he acknowledged me, and hurriedly nodded at his assistant. "Thanks, Frances." She quietly excused herself and closed the door behind her.

He rounded the table and, in a way that was much more 'brother' than 'CEO', received me from Sarah and put a warm hand on my back as he ushered me to sit down. "You look like you've been in the wars. Can I get you anything?" Before I'd even answered, he retrieved his tissue box from behind his computer and placed it directly in front of me on his desk. "They're aloe vera," he said, indicating them. "Please. If you need to." He leant on the edge of the desk in front of me as Sarah sat down.

"We need to talk to you," she said cryptically.

He laughed shortly, but it wasn't a harsh sound at all. "Yes, I can see that," he said, and then held out his hand for her to shake. "Sarah, isn't it? Sarah Presti?"

She looked impressed. "Yes," she said. "And you pronounced it right. Thanks."

He smiled. "So. What's up?"

Sarah and I looked at each other. I was still acutely aware that he might have been responsible for Vladivostok failing and a good chunk of why Diane and Jason were angry with me. It made me nervous and made me doubt we were doing the right thing, being in his office. Sean looked between us as we hesitated, but he didn't say anything.

It was Sarah who spoke. "We shouldn't even be here," she said. "Is there some way Diane and Jason cannot find out about this?"

He sighed theatrically and crossed his arms. "Well, I can't control who saw you coming down here, but my staff won't tell her or Jason. Everyone's a little bit afraid of them." We both smiled at that. "If this is about that confidential project she has running, I'm going to say something a bit shocking: I don't care about it."

We both frowned at him.

He shrugged. "Diane and I have our differences about how to handle operations. I would be perfectly happy to sit down and have a discussion, but the first thing *she* does is get the lawyers out. I'm so sorry both of you were caught up in this."

Beside me I could see Sarah relaxing. I was still nervous. "But Bree...didn't she tell you?"

He gave me a look. "She told me *a lot* of things," he said. "And I have done exactly nothing with that information except try and offer you both support, if you recall." I must have looked a bit sceptical, because he added, "I know what you're thinking because Jason's already had a go at me. I was still looking for you when the pitch was cancelled. They wouldn't even have had time to write the email if I'd had anything to do with it."

I wracked my brains trying to figure out if that could be true. It might have been; I didn't have too clear a memory of events on that day because I'd been feeling really sick and been doped up on codeine. Everything did happen in a very tight sequence. Maybe me being stupid and telling Bree hadn't ruined everything for me, after all. It was a relief, hearing that. I didn't want to be angry at her, and I was already angry enough at myself.

He waited for us to process that, then he said, "Now that that's out of the way, you want to tell me what the real problem is?"

Sarah looked towards me. "Do you want to go first?"

I did tell him. As soon as I'd opened my mouth everything just came *pouring* out. He was warm and kind and he gave me his full attention and listened carefully to everything I was saying, occasionally taking notes. Sarah chipped in with her story too, but when it came to the really private stuff about me, I spent a good two or three minutes stuck on the point of coming out to him, even if everyone upstairs knew.

"Jason outed you?" Sean prompted me. "You mean as bi? Or *gay* even?"

I took a deep breath, then released it, and then tried again. "No," I said. "As transgender."

His eyebrows went *right* up, which at least meant Bree had kept *that* much to herself. "Well," he said carefully. "I can certainly see why that would be a problem in Marketing."

I nodded, and then remembered being trapped at that desk while the men all discussed my genitals, and being yelled at to stop kidding myself with the 'tranny make-believe dress-ups' in the toilets, and then how I couldn't even fucking *walk around the building* without worrying who I was going to bump into and what they were going to say and how I was going to react. It was like high school all over again. Even my nightmares weren't as awful.

"It's hell," I said, and to my horror my voice wavered. And now, I wanted to add, because this crap occupied a hundred per cent of my brain space, I was fucking things up, too.

He bent down and put a hand on my shoulder. "It sounds like it," he said quietly. "I don't want you to have to work somewhere like that, Min."

He had a gentle and caring voice just like Henry's. It was a comparison that made me unexpectedly emotional, because I didn't know if I'd ever hear Henry speak to me like that again. Henry was wonderful and lovely and had spent *years* supporting me and what was I doing? I was leaving him for a schoolgirl who specialised in screwing things up. He didn't deserve that. He deserved to be happy with someone who was actually in love with him.

I didn't ask for this, Henry, I thought. *I didn't ask for this. I'm sorry. I'm so sorry.* Tears filled my eyes, and I panicked again. *No, no, please no. Don't cry now, you can't cry now, not in front of the CEO.*

"It's okay, Min," Sean said warmly, nudging the tissues towards me. "Just let it all out." It was such a small movement, but there was so much quiet acceptance in it. In a few seconds I *was* crying again. Why couldn't I have a boss like Sean instead of Jason? *Why?*

Sarah put an arm around me, and when I glanced over at her, her brow was knit.

Sean was rubbing my shoulder, too, and it was probably very unprofessional, but it was caring and friendly. I didn't mind. "How about both of you take a few days off," he suggested. "I'll take care of Jason."

"No," we both said in unison, and then looked at each other.

"We're kind of busy right now," Sarah clarified.

Sean narrowed his eyes at us. "Okay," he said slowly. "At least tomorrow, then."

Neither of us answered, because we weren't supposed to say *anything* to him about the pitch, whether or not he cared or was involved or whatever. It was pretty obvious from silence, though.

He smiled and shook his head, apparently not picking up on it.

"Workaholics, both of you," he said with a wry smile, and then went around his desk. "Are you planning to make a formal complaint about Jason?"

It sounded like a completely unloaded question, but I kept remembering Jason and Sean and how buddy-buddy they were with each other. Sean was so considerate that I felt bad for not being just as considerate as he was.

"I'm sorry, I know this puts you in a difficult position," I told him.

"Please," he said, holding up a hand to silence me. "I've been expecting to have this conversation with someone ever since Diane introduced me to Jason. I enjoy spending time with him, but I'm not blind to what he can be like." He sat down in his office chair. "Don't let that be the reason you don't complain about something this serious."

Sarah leant forward in her seat. "And Diane won't find out we came to you?"

He pressed his lips together and shook his head a little. "No," he said. "Of course I'll document our meeting for HR and performance management purposes which is why you came to me, but you make formal complaints using the Intranet Portal because we need them all in writing. I'll send you the link. Diane will never know you were the one who did it, I promise. The complaint is de-identified and only delivered to the employee's manager once the investigation is complete."

"Investigation?" I said, worrying about that.

"Not as scary as it sounds," he reassured me. "We don't haul you in front of a tribunal like the Fair Work Ombudsman would or make you stand up in front of a court like you would perhaps need to if you went out on WorkCover. Internal complaints are discreet and painless. Anyway, I'll get you that link."

Sarah and I watched while he swivelled to his computer and shifted the mouse a bit to wake the screen up. After he typed a couple of things in, he sat back in his chair. "Done," he told us. "That should be in your inboxes."

I relaxed a little.

Sarah had probably made the right decision to drag me down here, because I *did* feel better. Sean seemed like the kind of person who understood people, and he was so much like Henry that I trusted that he'd make good decisions about who to speak to for this 'investigation' and what to say. At least now there was a light at the end of the tunnel with all this awful work drama. Maybe I could begin to look forward to working somewhere that *wasn't* awful.

I turned and smiled a bit at Sarah, and she understood and put an arm across my shoulder. "Told you," she said quietly. Then, she sat up. "I'll do the complaint-thing later, because I'm really sorry, but I have to rush off and get ready to meet—" She nearly said, 'Sasha Burov', but she stopped herself in time. "To meet a really good friend of mine I haven't seen in ages."

I saw Sean's eyes dart up to the clock on the wall — it was nearly 3pm, definitely still work hours — but he didn't say anything about it. "Thank you," he said to her. Before I stood up though, he said, "You don't have to rush off as well. I'm going to go grab myself a coffee, you're welcome to sit in here until you feel a bit better."

I smiled appreciatively. "Thanks."

Sarah hugged me as she stood up. "Are you going to be okay?" I nodded, and she hugged me again. "You were killing me before," she said quietly. "Seriously. You're like the funniest person I know and when I walked in on you in the toilets..."

I didn't want Sean to hear, because I already felt a bit pathetic about crying in front of him even if he'd been really gracious about it. I shushed her and then said goodbye.

While Sean was out getting his coffee, I spent a few minutes trying to get the mascara off my cheeks using my reflection in the window. He chuckled when he snuck back into the room and saw me doing it. "I bet you wish you never had to wear that again."

I had to laugh at that. "Exactly." I stopped cleaning it off, though, because it was weird doing that in front of someone. I probably should have just thanked him and left at that point, but when I remembered what was waiting for me back upstairs, I got stuck by the door with my fingers on the handle.

Sean saw my difficulty. "Jason's already gone," he reassured me. "I saw him leave while I was getting my coffee. And you don't look like you've been crying, except that you have no eye make-up and one of your eyelashes is coming unglued." He smiled slightly.

I quickly peeled them all off my lids. "Thank you," I said, and then when he smiled at me, I really felt a flood of gratitude for him.

Bree was right, he was *so* nice and so easy to talk to. Additionally, he'd been that way with me even though I was complaining about his friend and potentially forcing him to fire someone he cared about. "I mean that: really, thank you."

"You're welcome," he said simply, and turned back to his computer as I left.

Because I felt better, I managed to make it back to Oslo without ending up in the Women's toilets again.

Ian and Carlos weren't anywhere to be seen, and since the Sales boys were missing, too, I figured they'd probably all gone on a long lunch together prior to meeting Burov, both to learn the materials and drink expensive wine on the Frost credit card. I didn't miss any of them.

Just as Sean said he had done, when I sat down and pulled out my phone, he'd sent me a link to the complaint form. I forwarded it to my private email so I could open it on my Pink laptop, and then clicked on it.

When the form loaded on my page, I sat there for a second, my heart racing with what I was about to do. This was official. This was it. If I put all this stuff in writing, I couldn't take it back, and I couldn't hide the fact I was transgender from anyone, either. Not that it was likely to be much of a secret soon, the way the Marketing boys all gossiped like teenage girls. But this, this was so *final.*

I put my fingers to the keyboard, unsure about what points to focus on, and then spent the better part of an hour and a half making sure *everything* was there. I debated whether or not to click the 'submit' button. Before I could talk myself out of it, I did.

And then it was gone. I'd formally complained about my racist, sexist, bigoted boss. I'd finally complained about the bastard after years of wanting to.

I reclined back in my chair, my heart still going. I've done it, I thought. I mean, I was worried about whatever this investigation process was, but I was glad it was happening. I was *so* glad once again that Sarah had dragged me to complain to Sean. He'd just been great. It felt good to know that there were actually people in this company I could trust with my welfare and that it didn't *need* to be the awful godforsaken hellhole it had become. And maybe I could focus a bit on work now.

I double-checked all the materials again, checked the PowerPoint, made sure we had everything ready for tomorrow and then sat down in my chair again. My pulse was still a bit jumpy — probably from lack of food as much as everything else — so I'd sat down and closed my eyes and was just taking a few deep breaths, when the door to Oslo *burst* open.

I gasped audibly and sat up straight, my eyes flying open. I was already shaking, because with that kind of movement, I expected it to be Jason and the thought of him terrified me.

But it wasn't Jason. It was much, much worse.

Diane Frost came striding into the room with a series of printouts in her hand. Not in five years working at Frost had I *ever* seen her so angry.

"You," she said, making a sharp gesture at me. "My office. *Now!*"

TWENTY-SEVEN

"Sit," Diane said sharply, shutting her office door behind me. I obeyed as she walked around the desk and sat across from me in a neat, practised movement.

It was so quiet all I could hear was the ticking of the ornate clock on her desk and the distant hum of traffic far below. She didn't need to scream for me to be able to *feel* how angry she was. The air was thick with it.

For what seemed like *eternity* she stared across at me, lips pursed. I've disappointed someone else, I thought, waiting any second for her to crack and *blast* me like Jason did.

Eventually she drew a breath. "Let me ask you a question, Min."

I waited, stricken. This must be about Sean, I thought. She knows Sarah and I went to see Sean.

She didn't say anything about him, though. She just held the printouts towards me, and I accepted them. She sounded cool and impassive. "How did you expect me to react to this?"

She obviously intended me to read them, so I ran my eyes over the first page. I didn't get two lines in before I recognised what I was holding, and all the blood drained from my face.

This was the complaint I'd written about Jason.

But that didn't make sense, how did *Diane* get it? She wasn't supposed to get it until it had finished being investigated! As I flipped through the pages to see how much text was there, my heart was racing, and when I glanced back up at her, I realised she'd been waiting the whole time for me to reply.

All I could think was, 'How did you get this?' but that wasn't the reply she was looking for. I just shook my head, because I didn't understand.

She made a non-committal noise. "May I ask who suggested a formal complaint was the best course of action?"

Sarah, I thought. But she was just looking out for me. I gave her the same courtesy. "It was my decision."

Diane leant back in her chair, her elbows relaxed on the arm rests as she considered me. "Do you know much about industrial law and how it influences our internal policies, Min?"

I shook my head again.

"When a serious harassment claim is made, the employee accused is immediately suspended with full pay pending investigation. Additionally, all disciplinary action is suspended against the complainant, and this is especially true in circumstances where the complaint is about a superior."

She let that sink in, and it only took me a second to understand exactly what her implication was. Jason was going to be suspended *right now*, and Frost was unable to take any disciplinary action against me until the complaint was dealt with. I can only imagine how that looked to Diane; I'd been in big trouble last week and I was in big trouble right now. This looked reactionary. The only problem was that it *wasn't*.

"Given that, Min," Diane continued. "What do you think my first thoughts were when I read this?"

Fuck, it looked *bad*, didn't it? Very bad. My voice wavered. "But it's true."

She scoffed. "*This*," she said, gesturing at the copy of the complaint in my hands. "Is true?"

"*Yes*."

She watched me closely for a few seconds, and I saw her eyes run over my pretty dress, and my pearls, and my loosely curled hair. I looked down at it myself, and my stomach clenched. I know I look very feminine, I thought. Believe me, I know. But the complaint is still true.

Something passed over her face for a moment, and she frowned slightly. Her tone changed. "And you just decided to make it yourself, and right now?"

Well, Sean had sent me the link, but Sarah and I had *asked* for it. I wasn't trying to cause trouble. "I thought the complaints process was discreet and that you'd only find out the verdict at the end of the investigation."

She didn't say anything. She held her hand out towards me for the printouts, and when I passed them to her, she leafed through them until she found what she was looking for. She handed that sheet to me, indicating where I should read.

I looked down at it. '*A copy of this complaint had been CCed to the manager of the employee(s) selected, as per Frost Group performance management policy*'.

That knocked the wind out of me. Sean had said the *exact* opposite. I read it again and again while Diane watched me. Eventually I managed to ask her, "Is this always what happens?"

She nodded once. "A manager is likely to notice if one of their employees is suspended."

My blood ran cold as the gravity of that hit me: he'd *lied* to us, and now I was sitting in here, across from Diane. God, he'd *lied* to us. To our faces, and with a smile on his. I felt *sick*. God, I felt *sick*.

While I stuck on that thought, Diane had been looking through a pile of papers in front of her, and she held one of them at me. I could see it was a copy of the Vladivostok materials before I'd even taken it from her. I winced. I'd been handling the Burov ones all day and these looked vulgar and slapped together in comparison. I thought that's what she meant. "I know they're not my best work," I began, "But I didn't—"

"—the numbers, Min," she interrupted me. "Look at the sales figures you've quoted there."

I looked up at her. "Did John get them wrong?" I asked, confused. "We extracted them straight from the raw data files."

She gave me a considered look, and then slid open a drawer in her desk and went through it until she found a copy of last year's full annual report. She opened it at the gross sales page and lay it on the desk in front of me, one perfectly manicured fingernail pointing to a figure on the page. I looked from that number to the same one on the Vladivostok materials.

They were different. Very different.

But we'd had the financial reports extracted straight from the system, and, well, maybe John *had* got the numbers wrong, but I'd quickly double-checked his calculations and hadn't seen anything that I was worried about. The numbers in the materials matched the numbers in the data files that Sean had...

I swallowed. That *Sean* had extracted for us.

Oh, shit.

Oh, *shit.*

Fuck, I'd been so messed up over the Gemma-lift-thing that I... oh, my *god.* How could I have been so *stupid?*

I sat back, my jaw wide open as I looked across at Diane. Oh my *god.*

Diane gave me a few moments to sit with that before she added, "And let's not forget who you were in a meeting with when Jason and I wanted to speak to you about John and the Vladivostok pitch falling over."

With Sean, I thought. With Sean. I'd been so worried about Bree that I'd decided to risk it. And boy, was his door wide fucking open for me when I did.

Oh, my god.

Fuck, I'd *cried* in front of him. I'd let him *comfort* me. He must have thought I was *pathetic.*

"So," Diane said, lacing her fingers in front of her. "The IT contractors cost me $13,700 to set up an external secure network in Oslo. The encryption was a further $650, and then to set up all the security software was another couple of thousand on top of that. I got them to come in and start at 3am. I spent *days* talking over who to put on this project with Jason."

And I'd completely disregarded all of that, her specific advice to stay away from Sean, and now look at what had happened. I'd thought he was nice. I'd thought he was supportive and professional and warm like Henry was. And I'd thought that even though Henry himself had warned me about Sean.

Fuck.

Diane had warned me about Sean. *Jason* had even warned me about Sean. Everyone had warned me about him, and *still* I'd been in his office letting him offer me tissues.

Fucking hell, I was *an idiot*. I was a prize fucking idiot. In front of *both* of the CEOs of a multi-billion dollar corporation, I looked naïve, pathetic and *stupid*. I'd just had so much other stuff going on in my personal life that I hadn't... I swallowed. I hadn't been paying attention. I'd let myself be a fucking *puppet*. Sean was probably laughing over how easy it had been to use me.

Diane didn't speak for some time. "Don't think I don't know what my brother's like, Min," she said eventually. "And don't think I'm not onto Jason for not giving you the managerial support you should have been provided. But despite that, you're an intelligent woman who's been working here for five years, and yet we still find ourselves in this situation."

I could barely speak. "I know. I'm sorry."

She didn't address my apology. At least not directly. "So. What do you recommend I do with you?"

I know what *I* wanted to do. I wanted to throw myself through one of those big windows behind her. That was stupid, though, and I couldn't say that to her, even if I felt it. I'd got everyone into this mess and the mature, appropriate thing to do was to get everyone out of it, too. Even if I was so disgusted with myself that I was *sick* with it.

"I'll fix them," I said. "The Burov materials, I'll fix them. The pitch isn't over yet."

There wasn't even a hint of smile on her lips. She just glanced at her clock. It was 4:19pm. "Printing closes in 41 minutes," she observed. "You'd better hurry up."

41 minutes? 'Hurry up' was an understatement of the century, I wasn't sure how I was going to lay out *one* new page in forty minutes, let alone fix and proof *three* in that time. I wasn't even sure it was possible, except it *had* to be, didn't it?

She was clearly dismissing me, but I knew the conversation wasn't even close to being over. We'd just resume later. I stood, worrying about that, my treacherous fucking legs weak and knees locking as I tried to walk briskly out.

She stopped me just before I left, and I turned towards her as she said mildly, "This is your last chance, Min. Any more mistakes and it would be irresponsible of me to continue to employ you."

I swallowed, and then left her office and made a beeline for Oslo and let myself in.

I didn't have time to think. I didn't have any time to sit and reflect about what had just happened or what was going to happen or what was currently happening because I literally needed *every fucking second* to get these hard copies fixed before Printing closed. At least the text I needed to fix was laid out across a solid colour background, so it was just a matter of fixing the figures, resizing everything and checking the balance. Which meant *focusing,* and not thinking at all about Sean or Jason and what they'd *done* to me and, *fuck, what* time was it? How long did I have left?

Every time I finished a page I looked straight up at the clock: *4:31pm*, *4:44pm*, *4:55pm.* When the last one was done and I'd frantically checked over it to make sure not only did everything fit but that it also looked *great*, it was nearly on the dot of five and I had to rush out into Marketing and call Printing.

"He's just left for the day," their admin informed me when I asked for my contact.

"Then run out there and get him," I told her. When she hesitated, I said, "It's urgent!"

After I'd made sure that my contact *had* returned and the materials *would* be printed, I moved straight onto the presentation materials.

I didn't even have a second to spare because unlike the printed materials where the text was across a solid background, in the presentation slides there *were* figures across the graphics. That meant that when I'd corrected the numbers, the composition was off and two or three of them were really hard to read. I tried resizing the images a little and changing the font but that threw the balance off further, and in the end I realised I was going to need to edit the images if I wanted this to look at all professional and presentable. I tried to do it with my mouse but it was twitchy and imprecise and in the end I sat back.

It was a lost cause trying to do this on work computers with work software. Fixing them properly meant getting my tablet, which was at home, where I was forbidden to go until this was finished. Which meant I needed to ask Diane.

The prospect of needing to talk to Diane again was literally making me sweat. It took a lot of rationalising to convince myself to walk up to Diane's office; I kept telling myself that Bree was at home and she'd be able to do something with how *crap* I felt so that I had enough emotional energy to come back into the office and finish these.

It was okay, I told myself, Diane was going to let me, she wanted this done as much as I did.

When I let myself out of Oslo, Marketing was quiet. There was one guy still left up the other end of the floor, bent double over his monitor while he analysed something. Other than him, no one was left. The clock outside Diane's office said *8:17pm,* and her assistant had gone home.

Diane's light was on, though, but her blinds were drawn.

I took a deep breath and lifted my fist to knock on the door, when I heard Diane say, "...what is *this* bullshit?" I heard the sound of rustling papers like she was shaking something. It was weird hearing her swear.

I dropped my arm and held my head close to the door to listen.

"Well, Di," that was Sean's voice, and he was patronising her, "it looks like a formal complaint. But I'm not certain, since you *won't let me read it."*

All the hair stood up on the back of my neck and I was flooded with emotion. *Sean.* You *bastard,* I thought. You *fucking bastard. How could you?*

"Don't bullshit me, Sean. Stay the fuck out of my department and stop meddling with my assets."

Assets?

"Your assets?" Sean said in an amused voice. "You mean your *staff*? They're people, Di, people who—"

"Who you need to learn to stay away from."

I moved to a place on the interior window where I could see a tiny gap in the blinds. I peeked through it; Sean was sitting casually on the edge of Diane's desk, tinkering with the desk clock while she sat 'calmly' at her computer. I'd seen him do the same to Henry, and Henry had looked just as annoyed as Diane did right now.

"Oh, please," Sean said casually. "I never seek out your staff, they come to me like children in need of a big hug because Mummy is *so mean.*" He twisted towards her. "By the way, how about the ones you actually send to me, should I stop 'meddling' with those, too?" He was clearly baiting her.

She took a measured breath. "See you in court, Sean," she said, attempting to be dismissive.

That got a reaction out of him, and he put the clock down on the desk. "This is fucking ridiculous, Di, you're actually going to go ahead with this? Just because of *one dispute* I lodged? You're going to be *that* anal about it?"

"The directions hearing today found grounds to sue, so I will."

"*Why*? It's going to put Waterbank out of commission for *12 weeks*. If you have this head for business, or whatever you like to think about yourself, you'll know that means tens of millions of—"

"—Reputation, Sean, is worth *at least* that. I would have thought that was something you'd understand, given how *you* like to present yourself to *my staff.*"

"Gee, I'm so sorry that people actually *like* me, Di, I know that's difficult for you to understand because fear is a poor substitute for—"

She cracked. "—oh, *fuck off*, Sean. No one likes *you*, they like this bullshit nice guy persona you invented. Everyone who knows who you *really* are hates your fucking guts. And you *really* think your wife doesn't know? Really? Because she's a smart woman, Sean. I can't wait until she actually has the courage to leave you."

He laughed openly. This time, it was a really harsh sound. "Oh, Di, you can be so funny sometimes."

Diane smiled tightly at him, lacing her fingers together on the table in front of her. "Yeah. Must be pretty funny to hear about how much your own parents *hated* you. I bet you lie in bed every night and laugh about it."

"At least there's someone lying next to me. No one would come within ten k's of *your* bed."

Diane didn't look the least bit bothered by that. In fact, she smirked. "Well, it's that far up the driveway," she paused, "of Mum and Dad's estate."

He directed her a heavy stare. "Which I'm sure is going to be really comforting when you're alone on your death bed. Maybe you can hire some top grief professionals to expertly cry for you."

Diane just gazed calmly at him, and then feigned surprise. "Oh, *that* was it? I was expecting you to finish with something actually insulting."

He didn't sound as relaxed when he spoke this time. In fact, he sounded very serious. "Drop the fucking court case or I'm going to stuff up your pitch tomorrow. I don't even care how much our share price drops if I do. It'll be worth it to watch your face when you miss out on getting finance for your pet mine."

She pretended to turn back to her computer. "See you in court, Sean."

"Did you even hear me? You can't piss me off by blocking access to Waterbank if your mine doesn't exist."

She glanced towards him and smiled again, repeating pointedly, "See you in court, Sean."

"Well, then, see you at your pitch tomorrow, *Diane*," he said, slipping back into his super-professional, super-calm tone, and hopped off the table to approach the door near where I was standing.

My heart pounded, and I backed into the corner of the room and hoped it was as badly lit as I thought it was. When he opened the door, slamming it so loudly the windows all shook as he left, he didn't notice me.

I stood there for a second trying to process what I'd just heard, but the clock was directly across on the other wall from me and it read 8:*26pm*. I had no idea how long it was going to take to fix the images, but it was going to take me at least twenty minutes to get home and back and that was time lost.

Stunned and numb, I knocked on Diane's door. She didn't answer—probably because she thought it was Sean—so I just entered. Her jaw was still set when she peered over her monitor at me. "Are you done?" I couldn't read her.

My heart was still pounding, and as I opened my mouth to speak I could feel it against my ribs. "The printed materials are done and I got them in on time," I told her. "I need to alter two of the images on the slides, though." I took a breath. "Which means I need to go home and get my tablet."

She watched me intently for a few seconds. "30 minutes," she said finally. There was an implied threat in that. I knew something bad would happen if I wasn't back in the office and working hard by minute thirty-one, but she didn't specify what that was.

I swallowed. It would probably only take me twenty, anyway, which left a couple of minutes for Bree. "Okay."

She nodded, and I showed myself out and went to grab my handbag and head downstairs.

The muscles in my legs were weak and I had to be careful about how I walked. All of me was *shaking*, and I honestly felt like I was just about to pass out.

Fuck, I could barely make any sense of what had just happened. What I'd discovered about Sean, what a *fucking idiot* I'd been, and then that conversation I'd overheard. The details just hung in my head and didn't fit together. Now that I had a second, I needed to tell Sarah about this. She was incredibly fucking switched on and not a human mess like I was, she'd figure it all out.

I took my phone out of my handbag and dialled her number while I was waiting at the lights. I held my phone to my cheek and waited. I needed to remember to ask her if she'd known that Jason would be suspended when we complained, too.

It didn't ring, though, it went straight to voicemail, and as her upbeat voice told me to leave a message, I pulled the phone away from my ear and frowned at the screen. Why wasn't she— oh, of course, *that's* right. It had been ages since she'd left, and by now she'd be entertaining Sasha Burov in the Star. There was no way Jason would let her get away with having her phone on, let alone answering it.

I put the phone back to my ear anyway to leave a message. "Hey," I told her, forgetting to say who it was. "I need to talk to you. Ring me as soon as you get this." I put the phone back in my bag.

I'd been looking forward to speaking to her and the anticlimax of not being able to do it was disorienting. It made my pulse race, and I tried to walk a little faster to burn off the adrenaline. Bree was at home, anyway, and I'd have at least a couple of minutes to spend with her. She'd sort me out. She always did.

The lift in my building took *ages* to arrive, and then it felt like it stopped on every fucking floor on the planet before it got to twenty-six. I paced restlessly in the lift, I just wanted to get home, get my tablet, and get these slides done so I could get at least *one thing* right for Diane and my team after I'd royally screwed everything else up.

When I finally got to my level, I strode down the hallway on shaky legs, trying to figure out how I'd brush out part of one of the cliffs in the graphics. I was thinking about the best way to do that, fishing my keycard out and fitting it into the reader when I noticed the surface of my door had fresh marks on it.

I stopped, frowning.

I put a couple of fingers to the wood to touch them; they were sunken and crescent-shaped as if someone had struck the centre of my door with an object that had a round edge.

Worrying about that, I swiped my card and stepped inside. I had begun to say, "Bree?" when I noticed there was something large missing from the hallway. I didn't trip over a schoolbag as I walked inside and dropped my Jimmy Choos, and there weren't school shoes or thongs discarded randomly en route to the living room. My apartment was cold, and empty and silent.

I let that sink in as I walked into the living room, dumping my handbag on the kitchen counter. Bree was gone, and I had absolutely no way to contact her, and those pock-marks in the door could only mean one thing: Andrej.

I stood in the centre of the living room, worrying about her in that toxic house. She'd specifically said Andrej *wasn't* violent but she must have been a *bit* afraid of him, right...*shit*, is that the time?

My eyes passed over the clock on my wall: *8:49pm.* I worried about her. I worried a *lot* about her, and I also worried about *myself* that she wasn't here to give me a hug right now but I didn't have time for this and I—take a deep breath, Min, take a *deep* breath and focus—I've just got to get my tablet and get back to work in ten minutes and finish those slides and *then* I can come home and have a drink and worry about Bree. Then, I can.

I took a slow, steadying breath and turned to grab my laptop off my...

...my empty dining table? I frowned at it. Well, maybe Bree had been playing with my laptop again. I went into the bedroom to see if she'd left it there, but the bed was neatly made and there was nothing in it. The only three things on the bedside table were an empty glass, the painkillers and the phone charger. No laptop, and no tablet.

No, I thought, my heart *thumping. No, no...* this can't be happening. I went all over my apartment, out on the balcony, feeling a sinking, grinding feeling in my stomach and a tightness in my chest and, *god*, I couldn't breathe and I couldn't think and *this couldn't be happening* and in the end I just had to accept that it was, it was happening, this was happening and, *oh, god...*

My laptop was missing. The case with my tablet in it was missing. They were gone and Bree was gone.

Time stopped still for a second while *everything* converged on me. It was gone, my tablet was *gone.* The item I needed for the *one last chance* Diane gave me was *gone.* My ears began to ring and my head spun and I had to *brace* myself against the wall and try and make sense of this. I can't breathe, I thought, I can't fucking breathe and I have *five fucking minutes* to get back to work and be in Oslo or Diane will *kill* me and I'm not going to make it and the slides aren't going to get finished because my tablet is gone and the pitch is going to fail and *fuck* this can't be happening this can't be happening *this can't be happening*!

My chest *ached* and *clenched* and I pawed at it, trying to get enough oxygen into my lungs. I couldn't *think straight* with the pain of it and the room was spinning and everything was starting to feel far away and through a tunnel so far away... and *fuck, no, Min, take some deep breaths you're not going to pass out...*

What I needed were some fucking painkillers and I half-staggered and half-jogged into the bedroom to grab the bottle from the bedside table but as soon as I lifted it I could tell there was nothing left in that one and I just threw it somewhere as I tried to breath and tried to remember where I'd left the other bottle.

While I was hunched there and trying to recall the last time I'd had any codeine I caught sight of my reflection in my wardrobe mirror and it was just so shrunken and slumped and *pathetic and female* and I *hated* it *and I couldn't deal with anything right now and fuck everything* and before I knew it I had the empty glass in my hand and I'd *hurled* it at the wardrobe.

The mirror didn't even give me the satisfaction of shattering into a million pieces on impact; the empty glass I'd thrown just bounced off the door and rolled across the carpet, leaving a long crack through the mirror. I could still see that woman in it and I *hated her*, I hated those breasts and that long, beautifully curled hair, those hips and that dress and *I just hated everything god fucking damnit* why was this happening why did this shit *always* happen to me it wasn't *fucking fair* and why the *fuck* did I look like *this*? Why did *I* have to look like this? Why *me*? Half the fucking world was born with the angles and lines that I wanted and through some fucking mistake of nature I was *that, that female person* in the mirror.

I shook. I shook so much I could barely stand up. No wonder Diane didn't believe I was transgender and thought the complaint was vexatious when she first read it if *that* pathetic woman in the mirror was what she saw.

I couldn't look at the mirror. I couldn't *look at that thing that people thought I was*, and within *two steps* I'd wrenched the wardrobe door off its runners and hurled it across the room and this time, *this time*, the mirror smashed. It smashed everywhere, all over my bed and my carpet and my wall and my room but it wasn't enough. It wasn't enough for how much I *hated* this. I hated this. I *hated this*. I hated everything about myself and this and *everything* and my wardrobe was open and I wrenched each of my fucking *stupid* dresses and blouses and belts and skirts and frilly jackets and lacy shirts and tights and *fuck everything* and stockings and underwear *out* of their drawers and *off* their hangers and *out of* their covers and scattered them with the glass on the floor and then I... my chest... my chest... I clutched at it as it *hurt... I needed those fucking painkillers.*

I staggered into the bathroom and the first thing I saw was my red face and pearls and earrings and long hair in the mirror and *all of my makeup* on the vanity and *fuck it all* and in one clean movement I'd *swept it all onto the floor* and listened to things *smash* and *clatter* across the tiles.

As I looked around my stockinged feet at the debris, I realised how many *thousands* of fucking dollars I'd spent on everything, and those clothes in my other room, thousands and thousands and thousands spent on them and it was *all for nothing* because it was thirty-one minutes and Diane was going to fire me and I was going to be homeless and everything that I'd fucking worked at my whole fucking life was about to fall apart and Mum was going to kill me and all those kids in high school were *right* and I... just couldn't ever seem to fucking breathe.

I could never seem to catch my breath. Never, and all of this was never going to end, was it? This was never going to end. I was always going to feel fucking *crushed* under the weight of everything, and *everyone* wanted a piece of me.

Henry thought I was this tortured genius who he'd liberate and make a fulfilled wife and a great mother. Mum had all these elaborate fantasies about me having a brief, successful career before settling down with a nice man like Henry and having babies. Sarah wanted me to be this fun prankster at Frost with her. Even Bree, even Bree saw me as her saviour, but I just *wasn't. I* was the one who needed rescuing and even with all these people desperately trying to, I still couldn't succeed, and I was beginning to drag them all down with me. Henry. He used to be so funny and so cheeky, and now... fuck, I'd turned him into the long-suffering apologist for me. Sarah was getting sucked into my bullshit at work. I was about to get fired and that meant Mum would have to go back to work and hire a nurse for Grandma. And Bree... she had such a beautiful girl with a beautiful heart and she deserved a *proper* first love. Someone to be giddy with. Someone to hug and kiss and make love to and feel like the sky had opened up and sun was finally shining and, god... I just couldn't. I couldn't. I couldn't be that for her. Not like *this.*

"I can't do this," I realised aloud, and watched my lips move. "I can't do this. I can't, I can't..." I repeated it to myself like a mantra, clutching myself and slipping against the wall until I was curled on the floor surrounded by my makeup and cosmetics and tweezers and shavers and tiny bottles of crème and moisturiser and toner.

So much fucking effort. So much effort, so much care, so much time and so much money just to ultimately *fail*. And there was *no way out*. There was *nothing* I could do.

I was a failure. I was a fucking failure. I was *nothing,* and there was *nothing* left of me. Five whole years of my life working my *guts* out to just fail when at last I had the opportunity to shine.

God, I'd been so happy, hadn't I? A few weeks ago when Diane had smiled at me, it had made my day. And then, *then* when I'd first sat in Oslo and looked out across all of Sydney, promoted to *lead* of a top secret project, I'd been so elated and so on top of the world and I'd wanted to dance and skip and smile ear to ear. I'd been *getting* somewhere. All my hard work and suffering had paid off. The universe worked, Karma was finally delivering me the reward I deserved. After all the *shit* in my life, something great had finally happened to me, and *Diane Frost* had smiled at me, had promoted me, and was so impressed by me that she wanted to move me into management and everything looked *so bright.*

And now...?

My throat tightened.

Now I was *nothing.* I was *ruined, and* I was about to be jobless and homeless and broke, and I was about to *fail* all the people I loved. And I couldn't stop myself. No matter how I tried, I couldn't stop myself.

Curled up in the corner of my bathroom with my knees to my chest and my hands over my head, I *sobbed.* I clutched at my hair and my face and *wrenched out my beautiful pearl earrings* until there was blood on my fingertips and I *sobbed.* My chest ached and I couldn't breathe, but I didn't care. I didn't *care* if I couldn't breathe because it *didn't matter.* What was the *point* in me breathing? There *was no point.* There was just no point to anything anymore. I ached and ached and everything just *hurt.*

I'd been lying there for a few minutes, feeling hot tears on my cheers and gazing helplessly at the bathroom floor, when I noticed something tiny and oval-shaped on the dark tiles. One of my painkillers; *that's* where they were. I must have knocked the bottle off when I'd thrashed the vanity.

I leant forward to pick it up, and noticed another one beside it, and another one beside that, and pretty soon I had a palm full of them. Kneeling on the floor, I looked down at them, my hand shaking as I remembered Sarah's comment about how strong they were. She'd only had two; I had at least 15 right here.

I counted them: 17.

I could just do it.

Just one move and all these little pills would be in my mouth, and there was a tap right there for water to swallow them with. They kicked in quickly, *very* quickly. It was one of the reasons I bought this brand. It wouldn't be long before I wouldn't have to deal with any of this.

I was so tired. I was *so* tired and my chest *ached* and I was so, so sick of being *suffocated.* But I didn't have to be, did I? There was another option here, in my palm.

Shaking, I pushed myself up and went and sat on the edge of the bathtub. I counted the pills again. Was seventeen enough, I wondered? I didn't want to not finish the job. The worst thing I could imagine was waking up in hospital with Henry and Mum bent over me.

The bottle had to be around here somewhere, so I crawled around on the floor and found it, turning the label to the light. *Daily total dose should not exceed six tablets*, it read. I had nearly three times that, but was that really a lethal dose? I wasn't sure, so I kept reading. It was when I got to the *DO NOT USE IN CONJUNCTION WITH ALCOHOL* in bold text and capital letters that I had a way forward, because I had *plenty* of alcohol.

Standing, I walked mechanically into the kitchen with my fistful of codeine and opened the cupboard in my pantry where I kept it all. I took out a fresh bottle, reasoning that a whole bottle of wine mixed with *anything* would be pretty dangerous.

I put it on the counter and stared at it. The label had a little wine glass with the number of standard drinks printed inside it: *9.1.* I'd drunk a whole bottle of wine in an hour once and literally passed out, so this plus the codeine was probably going to be enough to kill me.

Okay. Where should I do it, though? I surveyed my apartment. My bed was covered in glass and women's clothes. I supposed there was always the couch, but someone walking around my apartment might not actually see me lying there. Realistically I should probably just do it in the hallway to make sure that my body was found before it started to decompose.

I wondered who would find it, and for one panicky second I thought it might be Bree. She had a keycard, but if she'd only just left she'd probably spend a day or two at her parents' house before coming back here. No, tomorrow was the pitch and if I wasn't at that, Sarah would worry. I wasn't sure whether she'd come straight here if I didn't show up, though. She could be pushy, but she generally knew when to give me space so she'd probably leave it a day or two.

It would be Henry, wouldn't it? We had plans tomorrow night. He'd never let himself in before without me giving him permission to, but I'd answered my phone or answered the door before. If I didn't do that, he'd worry, and in his worrying, he'd probably let himself in. Well, at least he'd probably tell Mum it was an accident.

That was *if* it even worked, I thought, counting the pills again and then looking between them and the wine. No. No, I couldn't take any chances. I should just do something that would *definitely* kill me, and preferably something that actually looked like a real accident.

Maybe I could have a few pills and drink a bit of wine and just climb over the balcony? I could put something slippery on the surface and make it look like I'd just toppled over. I was tall, it was probably possible.

I slid the balcony door open and went and stood out there, leaning over the railing and trying to decide if the fall would kill me outright. 26 floors, how many metres was that? And what if I fell on one of those buildings down there? They were.... seventeen or eighteen stories, I thought. Eight or nine floors might *not* kill me. I'd probably be seriously injured, though, and at that height I'd probably die before help got to me. That was enough. I could spill some sunscreen out here on the floor or something and pretend I slipped in it.

Well, I'd better take *some* of the pills now so that if that happened I wouldn't be in excruciating pain before I ultimately died. I went back into the bathroom with them.

I don't know how long I stood over the bathroom sink, looking down at the pills in my palm and arguing with myself over whether I should jump off the balcony or whether I should try and overdose and what the exact chance of both of those working was.

Additionally, the logistics of who was going to clean out my apartment was stalling me. I had that packer in my wardrobe, and my binder and my boy clothes in my bedroom. Henry was going to find those, wasn't he? I had the idea that maybe I could just put my binder on before I did it. I could put on all my boy clothes, and dying in them would be my way of coming out to him. It would be such a shock for him, though, on top of finding me dead. He loved me, did I *really* want to do that to him?

While I was watching the mirror, the absolute absurdity of that statement *hit* me.

I was about to *kill* myself. As if Henry was going to give a *fuck* about my binder.

Henry was going to rush into the hallway and see my lifeless body on the carpet, and his first thought was definitely *not* going to be, '*Oh no, my girlfriend is transgender!*', it was going to be about the fact the person he was in love with had taken her own life. He wasn't going to give a *fuck* about the fucking binder as he scooped my body into his arms, desperately shouting for help and cradling me in his lap. All he was going to do was whisper to me and cry for me and beg me to wake up and then spend the rest of his life blaming himself and wishing he'd done something differently. He wouldn't give a *flying fuck* about the fact I was trans, except to blame himself for not noticing and blame himself for *everything*.

Shit. This was going to really hurt him, wasn't it? *More* than the fact I'd been cheating on him.

And fuck, who was I kidding about Sarah? I'd seen cracks in that easy-going exterior before. I knew there were emotions in there, regardless of how she presented herself, and if I thought me doing this wasn't going to impact her, I was fucking *dreaming*.

And Bree, god, *Bree*... Sarah was right, she *loved* me. She wanted so much to take care of me and be taken care of by me. The *joy* she got out of making me smile and cheering me up... she'd spend her whole life wondering what she'd done wrong.

In the mirror, I saw my eyes were swimming. I'd been fine a second ago; calm, collected, ready to do what needed to be done and I didn't *want* to have to *feel* any of this again. I didn't *want* to. I didn't want to hurt and ache and *deal with this, I couldn't deal* with this again! I didn't *want* to think about all the people who cared about me and how this would affect them and how their lives would be ruined and, fuck, I couldn't go through this again and *why, why* did I have to think about everyone? I loved them all and I didn't want to *do this to them* but there *just wasn't any other way*. I couldn't live like this. I couldn't *live* like this. *I couldn't live like this.*

"Why do people even love you?" I asked my reflection. Why did people love her? How could anyone love *that?* She was pathetic, and *stupid*, and useless and pretty soon she'd be dead.

I had a sudden, surreal realisation that I was about to kill that woman I was looking at, and because I felt so completely divorced from my reflection, that made the *hair stand up on my neck.*

It was a shocking reality check to really *see* her.

The woman I was staring at was *shaking*. She was shaking like a leaf, and she was crying. Her eyes were sunken. Her skin was sallow. She was so weak because she hadn't eaten in days, and her whole life was unravelling while she tried desperately to grab at the frayed ends of it. She was lost, and hurting, and so, so trapped and instead of *loving* her, instead of caring for her and forgiving her and being gentle with her, I was *hating* her. I was insulting her. I was mechanically plotting all these violent things and violent ways I could kill her.

But none of this was her fault. She couldn't help it. She wasn't me, I thought. She wasn't me, but it wasn't her fault.

She was doing the best she could, wasn't she? In a loveless relationship, in an organisation where employees were just *assets* to be used and milked and bled dry until the last ounce of productivity was taken from them. Played like a tennis ball between two CEOs who would hardly notice and definitely not care if she *did* die. She'd just be more collateral damage in the civil war they were waging on each other.

She was trying to make the best of a mother who cared more about her own dreams for her daughter than anything about the person her daughter wanted to become.

She was trying to make the best of a body she didn't connect with and didn't understand.

She was doing the best she could in every area of her life. She was trying, trying so, so hard to be everything she was supposed to and everything people wanted her to be until she couldn't breathe and couldn't move and instead of loving her, instead of *forgiving* her, I wanted to *kill* her.

I wanted to kill her for things that weren't her fault, for goals and wishes and dreams that had been set for her because they interfered with *my* wishes and *my* dreams. But they weren't mine. It was like we were two separate people. It was like I was looking at a stranger in the mirror and punishing myself for not being her.

And that's when I realised it. I wasn't failing at living *my* life, I was failing at living *hers*. And was it any wonder? Look at her. No part of her was really me. And not being able to be *me*, not being able to *not* be her was *killing me.* She was killing me, and I was killing myself.

It wasn't *me* who I wanted desperately to kill, it was *her.*

That broken and spent woman in the mirror, with tears running down her cheeks and the weight of a thousand expectations on her shoulders, this had to be it for her. It had to be. This was the end of her stressful, miserable existence. After all her suffering and all of her struggling, it was finally time to lay her to rest.

I watched her face crumple in the mirror, fresh tears spilling down her cheeks as I reached out to the glass to touch her fingertips. It wasn't her fault. None of this was her fault. She didn't ask for this, and she'd done the best she could. "I'm sorry," I told her, our voices shaking. "I'm so sorry."

I dropped the pills on the counter and had to brush them off my palms where they'd stuck, and bent down to retrieve my scissors from the floor.

This was it. No turning back now, unless I actually felt like pitching myself off the balcony or choking to death on my own vomit.

Goodbye, I told that woman, and then held the scissors to our hair.

Goodbye.

The blades were dull and as I squeezed and dragged them through my hair, the strands crunched and tore between the shears and I needed both hands to get through it all. My thick hair got caught in the join and it *pulled* and I seethed and endured it as I kept cutting.

I watched my reflection transform as that woman disappeared, taking with her the dreams so many people had for her. White wedding dresses. A private honeymoon on a tropical island somewhere with beach sex and skinny-dipping and laughter and kisses. A blue cross on a pregnancy test, maternity wear, baby showers and one final push and the sharp cry of our first born. Henry's joy as he held our baby, Mum's delighted smile as she held her grandchild for the first time, a *grandmother*, and family portraits of four generations of Lees on the wall of her house in Seoul. Promotions. Presentations and pay rises. Upsizing to four bedrooms in the suburbs, and then school and graduation and downsizing to a little cottage in the hills. Retiring together to sunsets and slow walks through fields paved with wildflowers as we reminisced about our happy, domestic life and held our *own* grandchildren.

As I cut, all of this fell away. All of that disappeared, and as I lay that woman who'd been my reflection for twenty-five years to rest, I laid her to rest with the shattered dreams of the people who loved her. I ended them, and I ended her stressful, dutiful life.

So I could finally start *mine.*

When I was done cutting, I had a fistful of hair like a severed limb in my hand. It weighed maybe a hundred grams at the most, but I felt like a thousand, million, billion tonnes had just been lifted from my shoulders.

And even though I'd well and truly fucked up my hair, and even though I was still wearing a dress, when I looked in the mirror I finally saw something of a person I recognised. And all the money and all the accolades and all the promotions in the world couldn't compensate for how much of a relief that was: to finally look in the mirror and see someone *familiar.*

Tears *poured* down my cheeks, but I was smiling as I dropped that handful of hair into the bin where it belonged. 25 years. 25 years, I'd wasted. But now, *now* I still had the remainder. There would be consequences for this, I knew, but *fuck* them. I was alive to face them.

I was still shaking when I walked out into the kitchen and checked the time; *9:42 pm.*

Wasn't that little hairdresser on the corner open until ten? It couldn't take that long to do a men's cut, could it?

For the last time ever, I took off a dress and tossed it onto the mess that I'd made of my bed. I pulled on my binder, my jeans and my hoodie and then grabbed my purse and headed down onto the street. People stared at me because of the frighteningly bad job I'd done on my hair, but I just smiled right back at them.

The city lights were so bright and so colourful and as I looked upwards towards the night sky I imagined painting them spiralling around me. I felt like I was seeing them for the first time, and they were *beautiful*. Everything was beautiful, and the night air was crisp and fresh and I breathed it deeply into my lungs and smelt all the pizzerias and the salty harbour and burnt diesel fuel from the cruisers. Couples walked arm in arm, laughing with each other, and I was *so happy* for them.

Frost HQ loomed over the skyline, the big snowflake-diamond logo lit against the dark sky. I stopped to look at it before I went inside the hairdresser, and for once I didn't feel heavy. I didn't think about my deadlines, or my workload, or my mother. I didn't feel anything.

Diane was probably riotously angry about my disappearance right now, and I was pleasantly surprised by how little that actually bothered me. It was tempting to *never* go into work again after all the pain and suffering they'd caused me, except that I think I actually *wanted* to. I wanted them to meet me, and I wanted to see their reactions. After *everything* those assholes had put me through, there was something satisfying about the thought of arriving at that critical pitch dressed as something Jason had expressly forbidden me to be.

I smiled indulgently at the thought of his red face and all his veins popping out, and then pushed the door of the boutique open.

The woman behind the counter was already packing up for the night, but she froze when she saw me. "Oh, dear," she said, her eyes fixed on my head. "Should I ask what happened?"

My own eyes were so puffy it was probably obvious I'd had a breakdown and hacked off all my hair. As if I was going to say that, though. Instead, I deadpanned. "If you think *this* is bad, you should see the other guy."

She snorted and gave me a mock stern look. "Let me get my gear out," she said, and then started to unpack everything again.

I sat down in the chair, surprised to see a grin on my face in the mirror. I was *excited.* And as the woman asked me what I wanted and showed me pictures in men's magazines, I had butterflies in my stomach. It felt like I was about to get my very first haircut, and just in time for the pitch.

I'd been terrified about this stupid pitch tomorrow for so long, but this was the first time I'd felt any type of excitement about it. Because it didn't matter what happened now. Signature or not, it didn't matter. I'd chosen. I'd lose my job. I'd get evicted, but it was okay.

Because I was going to do it all on *my* terms, as *me.*

TWENTY-EIGHT

As I lay on the couch, I thought long and hard about whether or not I *should* actually go into work tomorrow. On one hand I didn't want to expose myself to another second of being treated like a pathetic fuck-up, but on the other, that wasn't how I wanted them to remember me, either. Calling in sick, making mistakes, crying in bathrooms. That was *not* who I was. If I left now, I left as that person. I didn't want it to be like that.

The couch was uncomfortable and with that one question circling in my head I found it really difficult to sleep. So, after a few hours of trying, I decided to just lie awake and do some more research on Sasha Burov, thinking that maybe I would figure out a solution.

We'd already researched his work and his collections to death, and I'd already read interview after interview. I read them again, focusing on how he responded to questions. I already knew he wasn't put off by flattery and was impressed when people showed good knowledge of his work, but I wanted to know more about what type of interviewer he engaged best with. He was overconfident and very forward in just about everything I read, and by the early morning, I'd already decided how I was going to play this. I was going to take a *big* risk, and that was in *addition* to showing up dressed as a guy and hoping he didn't recognise me.

I was going to try and pull off a *Grand Theft Pitch*.

Diane and Jason were *obsessed* with everything going smoothly and according to plan because that's how they saw this contract getting signed. Jason had emphasised again and again that we had to appear like a well-oiled machine to Burov, and despite all our differences we had to come across as a cohesive team. Well, if that was the case, there was *no way* either of them would try and fight with me in front of him, no way. And they wouldn't let him guess I was female, either. I actually disagreed that 'conservative' was the best way to interact with Burov, but as long as Diane and Jason believed it was, there was a possibility I was going to get away with attempting a heist.

Fuck, though. This was so unlike anything I'd done before. I wasn't cocky. I wasn't super-confident. And the thought of doing something brash and naughty was both terrifying and exhilarating and I couldn't sleep. I just lay there with my stomach fluttering, hoping I could pull it off.

The following morning I disregarded the expensive dresses spread all over the glass-littered floor of my bedroom and put on Henry's spare suit. It fit me, right down to the same weathered belt notch. Even the Y-fronts Mum had bought him 'on sale' that he hated fit me. I hardly needed to touch my short hair—except I did anyway because I *loved* it—so I stood back to admire myself.

I looked *great*. I *felt* great. Every little detail was perfect, from the top of my head to my Windsor knot, all the way down to... the sagging crotch of these fucking suit pants, I swear to god. I made a face.

Maybe I could fill it with... I turned slightly towards my bedroom, second guessing myself. I probably shouldn't use the packer, though. It was big, it might look a bit pornographic, like I was casually walking around Sydney with a semi. I stood there arguing with myself over it, and then eventually decided that the only way I could settle this was to try it.

I did, taking it from the bottom of my wardrobe and slipping easily into the Y-fronts. I zipped everything back up and looked down my body to the new bulge and felt... a bit weird about it, actually. It didn't look pornographic at all, it looked completely natural. I didn't feel natural about it, though. It made me feel self-conscious and I would have preferred not to be able to see any sign of it on the smooth planes of my front.

I sighed at my new bulge. *Whatever*, though. I was *so* over stressing about my body and what should or shouldn't be part of it. The important thing was that I passed as a guy and the packer completed the picture, so that was enough. I let myself out of the apartment with nothing but a few cards and my phone in my pocket.

I was leaving a lot later than usual this morning—the pitch was at ten and I didn't need to arrive early—so the crowds of business people in suits had already dissipated into their offices. In their place, there were hordes of tourists around Circular Quay. That made me a bit conspicuous in my sharp suit. I would normally have hated standing out, but I didn't anymore. Not dressed like this. And the looks they were giving me weren't because I was only an inch or two shy of being a human skyscraper or because I was different, not at all. They were, 'hey, check *him* out'. By the time I'd walked into Frost HQ, I'd already decided I *really* needed to buy a few suits of my own. I liked this.

No one recognised me as I swiped my card at the security gates or as I got into the lifts. Everyone was on their phones, anyway, so I took mine out as well to check the time again. I noticed I had a message from Sarah.

"Hey, are you okay? I only just got your message—last night was totally crazy. Burov is so full of himself, his ego is bigger than Jason's. He put a $5k bet down and when he lost he was like, 'Guess I better work an extra 15 minutes today!'. Anyway, I haven't seen you yet, are you in? Jason is about ready to decapitate you if you are and he's going through all your USBs. He won't say why, might be about the complaint. Or it might be because he's a dick."

I guessed Diane didn't suspend him like she was supposed to, I thought. *Good.* I wanted him to be part of this, too. I texted back, *"Yeah, I'm here. Tell Jason I've finished the presentation and I'll be up with it in two seconds."* I hadn't, and I was going to take longer than two seconds, but that wasn't the point.

I checked the time: it was a bit too early to go in yet. I needed to be late. I was just staring at the lift panels and wondering how I was going to kill ten minutes when my eyes fell on '35'. On impulse, I pushed it. Maybe I'd regret it, but I wanted Henry to see me like this before anyone else did. It was the least I could do since these were his clothes.

I was the last one out of the lift, and 35 was quiet, *really* quiet. I went straight to his office, my heart *pounding* every step of the way, only to find it empty. All the offices were empty.

"If you're looking for HR, they're doing orientation in the auditorium right now," a familiar voice told me. I knew that super friendly, super warm tone, and it belonged to someone who wasn't either. My hair stood on end as I turned towards the voice.

Fucking Sean had his suit jacket on and was clearly heading somewhere — our pitch probably — when he'd bumped into me on his way to the lift.

He didn't recognise me at first, and I didn't tell him who I was. I didn't do anything, in fact. I was so surprised to see him and so fucking *angry* and so *betrayed* that I just stood there paralysed while he double-took and looked delighted.

"Min!" he said, standing back to look me up and down. "Wow, you certainly look different! It must have taken so much *courage* to come to work dressed like that." He flashed me a smile. "You look great."

I *didn't* smile. Shut the fuck up, you *lying, psychopathic asshole,* I thought, internally seething. I wanted him to burn in the fires of hell for what he'd done to me, and I opened my mouth to say exactly that to him in probably just as many words, when something occurred to me: he was being nice to me because he didn't know I knew he was a lying two-faced fuck. I closed my mouth.

He thought I was the same person as the one who'd cried in his office yesterday and that I was fragile and upset and stressed out of my brains. And while I was staring at him, I had an idea. If I wanted to *really* get revenge on him, it wasn't by telling him to go fuck himself right here and right now, as satisfying as that would be. No, that wasn't how I was going to get him. I had a better idea, and one that stopped him from sabotaging the pitch.

I could use this.

I forced what I thought was a bit of a shy smile. "Thank you," I said, and then pretended to look self-consciously down my body. "Do you think it's a bit much, though? I don't want to look overdressed."

The bastard had the gall to put a warm hand 'comfortingly' on my shoulder. "Don't worry, it looks great," he said. "And anyway, even if it didn't, it's a bit late to go home and get changed now, isn't it?" I pretended to be clueless, and he chuckled. "You don't need to hide it anymore. I know, I checked room bookings. You've got that pitch on now."

"Oh!" I said, trying my absolute hardest to look like I suddenly realised what he meant. "Oh, yes, that's today. It's not now, though. The clients had a big night last night and opted to delay an hour, so I thought I'd come and visit Henry and get his opinion on this suit."

From Sean's expression, he bought my story. And why wouldn't he? The Min Lee he knew was a diligent, hard worker. She'd never be late for a pitch. "I'm sure he'll be disappointed he wasn't able to give it," he said. "I'll give you mine instead, though: you're not overdressed. Russians are less casual than Australians in business so I think you'll find you fit right in."

I smiled appreciatively at him. "I hope so," I said. "I did hop onto the *Impressions* website to take a look at the publicity shots to see what they all were wearing," I said, brushing my front down. "Good, I'm glad I made the right choice. Okay. I guess I'd better go pour over the materials one more time to make sure everything's perfect. Thanks."

Sean didn't miss my 'slip', I saw something pass across his face when I said *Impressions*. He also didn't draw any attention to the fact I'd said it, either. "You're welcome," he said, and then watched me leave.

I stood waiting for a lift, expecting at any second that he'd come and stand alongside me and follow me anyway. He didn't, though. He'd gone back to his office, probably to call his contact in Vladivostok and ask *what the hell was going on*. That made me smirk... until I remembered how quickly he'd gotten onto his contact on the day the pitch was cancelled. I probably didn't have much time.

Well, that just meant I had to do a really good job, didn't I? I got into the lift and headed down to the floor with the media rooms.

As I walked out onto it, it really sank in what I was about to try and do, and my heart was *pounding*. I felt like I was about to rob a bank. I cycled through a series of 'I can't do this's and 'sure, I can!'s until I finally settled on 'too late to back out now just keep walking'.

This is it, I thought. This is it. Take a deep breath, Min. There's no reason to stress out: you have *nothing* to lose.

As I approached the suite, the door was open and I could hear talking inside. I walked straight in the room, shut the door and very subtly *locked* it. Then, I turned around to face all the people seated in front of me.

It was everyone. Diane, Jason, the rest of my team including Sarah, and Burov and his entourage. The Frost employees all looked up with curiosity, wondering why some guy had just walked in here.

And one-by-one, *all* their jaws *dropped.*

Hi, guys, I thought, and took advantage of their shock.

"Thanks for waiting, everyone," I said in the most gender neutral voice I could manage, bustling confidently over to the projector and fitting my USB into it. Once I'd done that, I stepped around the lectern and over to Burov, focusing intently on him and extending my hand. "Min," I said as he shook it. "It's great to finally meet you, Mr. Burov. I've been admiring your collections for years. Particularly the ones you hand-picked for the Royal wedding. And that necklace you commissioned last week for Isnakov's daughter?" I nodded appreciatively. "Beautiful. Was it all your idea to choose baguette cuts?"

I stole a glance at Jason. His face and neck had gone *bright red,* but he couldn't say anything about what I was doing. Not in front of Burov, not without ruining the 'cohesive team' illusion.

Burov didn't recognise me or my name. And, just like he had in the video conference, he looked impressed and a bit flattered by my knowledge of him. "Of course I chose the cuts," he said, and then inclined his head towards my shocked compatriots. "What's wrong with them?"

Jason looked like he was about to explode, and Diane... if looks could kill, she'd have landed a critical hit on me. She staged a short, polite laugh at the very suggestion something was up. "Nothing's wrong," she said easily. "We were expecting someone different to arrive in time for—"

I interrupted her. "She couldn't come, which is *fantastic,*" I flashed a grin at Burov, "for me, at least. It gives me the chance to network with one of the most prestigious diamond brokers on the planet, so it's absolutely my pleasure to fill in for her."

Diane's eyes darted over to Burov as she spoke. "And we thank you so much for doing that," she was as good at 'pleasant' as her brother was when she needed to be. "But it's fine, we've invited—"

She was gesturing at the Sales team when I cut her off again.

"Much appreciated." I went back over to the computer and entered my password for the USB before opening up the presentation file. "It's fantastic how supportive this organisation is. You don't need to worry, though, Diane. I'm happy to help."

The Sales boys actually looked somewhat amused, and I didn't know why until I realised they were just as entertained by Jason's reaction as I was. No one knew how to handle what I was doing. Ian and Carlos were just sitting up the back, sweating, and Sarah had *the biggest* smirk. I doubted there was any sort of training on how to handle a Sales heist on a pitch, and everyone had turned to look at Diane as if to say, 'Well, what do we do now?'

Diane didn't have an answer for them, she just *glared* at me while she tried to think.

The multi-billionaire co-CEO of one of the world's richest mining companies was glaring at me. And guess what? I didn't care. I didn't need her approval. "Shall we get started?" I asked brightly.

"You don't need to worry, Min," Diane said calmly. "We're all ready. You can just take a seat and let our experienced team of—"

Burov made a gruff noise. "Let the boy talk," he told Diane. "He's got spunk. I like that. I was like that when I was his age."

I hadn't actually been expecting Burov to side with me, even if I'd heavily researched how to impress him. Hell, I wasn't even sure I'd get away with convincing him that I was a guy. That I'd somehow managed to achieve both of those things in under a minute was *fucking incredible.*

Holy fuck, I thought, grinning at everyone. I'm actually getting away with this. I'm using a client to steamroll Jason and Diane, and it's *working.*

After a few seconds of revelling in what I'd done, I turned towards the screen, dimming the lights and activating the presentation. "Well, let me tell you exactly why you're going to want our diamonds for your collection, Mr. Burov," I said loudly and clearly.

The presentation went well enough, and I certainly knew every inch of the material since I'd supervised the majority of the research and strategy. I didn't skip past the slides with the incorrect Sales figures in them, though, and when they flashed up on the screen I could hear the collective gasp of several Frost employees.

I didn't shy away from it. "You might notice this figure up here," I used the laser pointer to indicate it, "is different from the ones in your brochure." I upped the lights a bit so Burov could refer to his information kit materials. "The figure in the brochure is the one you need to refer to."

Burov was nodding. "Why's that number there?" he said, indicating the screen.

I tried to look charming. "Because it turns out I'm not a great accountant," I said openly. "But that's okay, because believe me, I know my diamonds. And that's what we're all here for, right? The highest quality, highest clarity diamonds in the world?"

Burov and his friend shared a knowing glance. I must have looked interested in it, because his friend said something in Russian, and Burov laughed and translated. "He said, 'Sasha is the same as you. He does the diamonds, I do the books'." Burov sat back in his chair and gestured at me to continue. "Okay. Tell me more about how long I have to wait to get actual pink diamonds from this mine."

And that was it. That mistake that Diane had made such a big deal out of: it didn't matter. It was over in twenty seconds, and Burov didn't care. He didn't care about most of the presentation, either, but he *did* remark on one of the paintings in the background.

"Where's that?" he asked, interrupting me.

That was actually something only Sarah and I could answer. I let her, because she hadn't said anything yet, she'd just been sitting up the back with huge smile on her face. "That's from right up close to where you're getting the actual diamonds from," she told him. "When you sign this contract, we'd love to take you on a tour of the location. There's some spectacular scenery out there." As Burov looked appreciatively at the painting, Sarah added, "Min did a pretty good job of capturing it, didn't he?"

She looked smug about dobbing me in. I wouldn't have said anything about it myself.

Burov took a closer look at the painting. "*You* did that?" I nodded and pretended to dust off my shoulders. He responded to that, turning to look at both Diane and Jason. "Where did you find this guy?" he asked them sociably. "He must make a fortune for you. I want one for *my* business."

Jason was *seething* at me. "How do you feel about just taking that one?"

Burov understood him literally, and sounded interested. "He'll be the one giving me sales support if I sign?"

I looked pointedly at Jason and Diane. Both of them were trying not to appear angry, and it was *beautiful*. "Diane? Jason? Will I be the guy giving him sales support?"

"We can discuss that once the contract is signed," Diane said diplomatically. "Those smaller details are by negotiation, but we're certainly happy to consider accommodating all your requests."

Burov and his friend shared a brief exchange in Russian while the rest of us just stood there and waited. The Sales boys couldn't have looked any more entertained than if they were sitting in the front row munching popcorn. Since they had nothing else to do, they'd been very surreptitiously texting people under the table throughout the presentation, and while Burov was busy I saw one of them take a cheeky photo of Jason. Neither he nor Diane noticed, but I had a feeling that photo was going to circulate Sales and Marketing within the hour. They took one of me standing up the front, too, and I smiled for it. I hope they emailed those two photos together.

While I was watching them, Burov said something to his assistant who hurriedly reached into her briefcase and passed Burov a bulldog-clipped stack of paper. He put it on the table in front of him, taking a pen from his pocket and clicking out the nose of it.

It took me several seconds to realise that *that stack of papers was the contract*. The contract that had been the centre of my world for nearly two months. My heart was racing as the nib of the pen descended to it.

"I think I've seen enough," Burov said, sounding satisfied. "I like these diamonds and I like how you do business. I like a good excuse to come to Australia, too." He laughed. "We can work together."

All our eyes were glued to the dotted line and everything was dead silent as he signed on it. You could even hear the scratch of the pen on the paper. When it was done, he closed the document and pushed it across the table to Jason.

Jason took it, too stunned by the suddenness to remember to be angry at me. "It's great to have you on board," he said automatically

556

to Burov, and then looked at me with an expression that said *what?*

I grinned. I grinned directly at him. Fuck you, I thought, enunciating each syllable in my head. Fuck you, Jason. Fuck you, fuck Diane and *especially* fuck Sean. Fuck all of you, and fuck your toxic bullshit workplace. I'm *not* nothing. I'm *something.* I have skills and talents and value and *look at what I just did.*

Look at what you're losing, Jason. Sit down there and look up at the person you've been calling a fuck-up.

He knew what I was thinking, but there was *nothing* he could do. It was over.

The rest of the team, all their eyes were on me. And in all of them, every single one, I could see something I never dared to hope for after everything that had happened: *respect.* I was up here dressed like a guy and it didn't matter. Every single one of those people was just in awe of me. And I *deserved* it.

Dreams were made of moments like this.

Burov clapped the table with his hands, missing all of this. "Tell me you people have a yacht," he said. "Let's hire a yacht. I want to see this city."

Burov had more to discuss with Jason and Diane, and as much as they kept glancing at me, they were stuck in conversation with him. The Sales boys didn't know me well enough to say anything about what I'd just done, but Sarah, Ian and Carlos did. Sarah practically danced over.

"You look *great*," she said, "and that was *incredible.* I was ready to give you a standing ovation when Burov passed the contract to Jason!"

Both Carlos and Ian looked like they'd run a marathon. "You scared the hell out of me," Ian said quietly. "I was thinking, 'there goes my performance bonus'. I can't believe you did that." He stole a quick glance at Diane and Jason. "You know they're going to fire you anyway, right?"

I shrugged. "They were going to before I came in."

Sarah leant in. "Min made a formal complaint about Jason because of..." She gestured at my suit.

Ian and Carlos both looked scandalised. "You *complained* about him?" Carlos asked for confirmation. "Wow, I've wanted to do that for *years,* but I never had the guts." He watched me for a moment, considering that.

I think he was about to say something else, but he never got the chance to. Over everyone's shoulders, Burov and Diane looked like they were winding up their little talk and I did *not* want to be around to take a dressing down from anyone. Not while I felt on top of the fucking world.

"I have to go," I told the three of them.

They all glanced behind them at where I was looking. "Are you coming back?" Ian asked. "I mean, assuming they let you in the building."

"Dude, she just single-handedly sold a multi-million dollar contract," Sarah told him. "I'm sure they'll let her in." She paused, squinting. "Erm, *'him'* in?"

I didn't have an answer for Ian, and the pronoun question was too big to answer right now. "I don't know," I said to them both, starting to walk towards the door. "I'll think about coming in, I guess, but right now I think it's time for me to make a quick exit."

Burov actually called out to me as I left, but I pretended not to hear. I closed the door behind me and stood there for a minute to just absorb what I'd done.

I just fucked over Jason and Diane. Like, actually fucked them over. A CEO and a senior manager had been in there, and I'd well and truly rolled them. Wow. When I'd decided I was going to take over the pitch, I'd never dreamed it would go so smoothly. But it had, and everything was *awesome,* and *fuck,* Diane and Jason's expressions! A lot of how well that had just gone could be chalked up to good luck, I'd admit that. What I was happiest about couldn't, though.

It wasn't luck I'd put on a suit and come into work today. It wasn't luck that I'd held my head high and marched in there and taken a *giant* risk. None of *that* was luck. *I'd* done that. Quiet, shy, obedient Min Lee had said fuck it all and walked in there, and, not knowing how it was going to turn out, had done it all anyway.

And nothing, *nothing* can describe how that felt. I was *so* proud of myself. I was so, so proud of myself.

My feet hardly touched the fucking floor on the way to the lifts, I was on cloud nine. I had no idea what I was going to do now, but it didn't matter. I could go shopping for some new clothes, or I could go have lunch by the harbour, or I could just do a victory lap of Sydney and feel people looking at me and enjoy not worrying about it.

I'd stepped into the lift with a couple of other people and had pressed 'G', when the doors of the lift on the opposite side opened.

Sean Frost was standing in it, and he spotted me immediately. His usual easy smile was absent, and when I glanced at my phone to check the time—*10:35am*—I realised he was too early for an 11am pitch. That meant that he'd figured out I'd lied to him, and he'd come to try and crash the party. *You're too late, Sean*, I thought indulgently. *Looks like Diane's building that mine you don't want after all.*

As my doors slid shut, I gave him a little wave and a big, bright smile.

His expression. God, it was *too much.* Suck it, I thought as the lift began its descent, and laughed to myself despite the fact I was sharing the lift with several other employees. In the mirrors, I could see them all trying to avoid eye-contact and smother grins. I didn't try and hide mine. I just stood there with it across my face for the rest of the lift ride.

The clouds had parted by the time I walked out of Frost HQ, revealing a beautiful sunny day. I didn't want to go home for once. I wanted to be out in it, and I couldn't imagine how the day could get any better until I heard a stunned voice behind me.

"*Min?*"

Bree...? Bree was waiting for me *already*? I turned towards her voice, spotting her on the shallow staircase outside the building. She'd been sitting on one of the stairs, I think, but when she'd seen me, she'd stood up. She was gaping, too.

Her eyes were a bit puffy, but she wasn't crying now, not at all. In fact, a big smile was growing on her face, and *that* was way better. Especially knowing I'd caused it. "Whoa," she said as she came over to me, disregarding whatever had upset her as she looked me up and down. "*Yeah!*"

Her timing couldn't have been any fucking better. I was really glad to see her, and because I was still high on rolling Sean, Diane and Jason and everything was *fucking awesome*, I grabbed her, pulled her up to me and kissed her right in the middle of fucking

George Street. I shouldn't have because of Henry, I probably shouldn't have because of *a lot* of reasons. But holding her just felt so good, and it had been *so long* since I'd felt like this. I wanted to enjoy that feeling.

After a few seconds she pulled away, though. "I'm really sorry," she said, as if she was desperate to get that in. "When Andrej was like, *whacking* your door, I didn't—"

I shushed her. "I've had the most amazing morning. I don't care about what happened last—"

"—But you don't understand!" she said, interrupting me. "I couldn't sleep all night because I'm so sorry, it's so fucked up that you got dragged into all of my shit and it's *all my fault* that he took your—"

"Bree," I said, gripping her shoulders. After nearly killing myself, the *last* thing I cared about was *stuff*. "It's okay. It's really okay. I just took a big risk at work, it paid off big time, and right now I don't care about *anything*." I smiled at her. "Look! I'm taking *the whole day off*. If you could do anything right now, what would it be?"

I think she was expecting me to be more upset about the things Andrej had stolen, and she just blinked at me, taking a few seconds to process my question. When she did, she leant against me. "What if I'm already doing it...?" Almost immediately, though, she stood back and looked downwards, distracted. "Oh my god, you're wearing it, aren't you?" she asked in a strange voice, eyes fixed on the crotch of my pants. Her cheeks were a bit pink, and I knew exactly what she meant.

She looked up at me, and I nodded.

She went bright red and dissolved into giggles. "Sorry," she said after a couple of seconds, trying to compose herself. "Sorry, that's really fucked up of me, of course you're wearing it. I just can't get the image of it out of my head and it's *in there*. Oh, god. I'm good. I'm totally good." She tried to be serious for a couple of seconds, and then lost it again.

I stood there while she giggled helplessly, amused. "Just out of curiosity, how old did you say you were?"

She smacked my arm. "Oh, shut up! It's hilarious. That thing is *enormous*."

"Thanks," I said, and winked at her, which made her burst into another fit of nervous giggles.

She tried to compose herself again, and this time she managed to. "Seriously, though, Min, you look great. That suit is like the sexiest thing on the planet and your hair looks *so cool*." She bounced on her tip-toes, looking hopeful. "Can I...?" She pointed at my head, and I bowed it a little so she could feel my hair and fuzz the shaved sides with her fingertips. I liked how it felt, and so did she, apparently. "What made you flip and do it, after all that?" She looked a little worried. "It wasn't because you were angry, was it?" The implication was 'with me'.

I didn't want to go into details of last night with her right now. I didn't want to ruin my mood. I'd tell her the full story eventually, but right now the best answer was, "No, I wasn't angry with you. I'd had enough of everything, especially Frost. I'm quitting." I stood back up, looking at the building behind me. "Fuck this place. Let's go celebrate my freedom with the rest of my money before I'm flat broke."

"You want to spend some money?" she asked. "We can go have lunch at that place I dragged you to the first time. Oh my god, I *love* that place. I'm salivating just thinking about it. It can be like our Last Supper or something."

I rolled my eyes. "I said 'spend' not 'waste'," I told her, but she'd already taken my hand and was towing me along the footpath. "You're hopeless."

"I know," she said over her shoulder. "But can you think of a better way to celebrate? You can tell me all about that thing you said you did today and what happened to your hair and we can look across the harbour, eat stupidly expensive food and have well-paid waitresses call us 'madam' and 'sir' and show us wine lists and we can pretend we actually have any idea what all of the names and years mean."

I *did* have some idea what the names and years meant, but she had a point. It *was* a nice place, and I *did* want to celebrate. "Okay," I said simply.

She actually stopped pulling me along. "Like, 'okay, yeah, let's do it'?" she asked for clarification. I nodded, and her eyebrows went up. "Huh," she said. "Well, I guess it's lucky I don't need to steal your bag this time, because you don't have one."

This time *I* took her hand. "Let's go get called 'madam' and 'sir'," I said neutrally. "But I think I might give the wine a miss, if you don't mind."

She knew exactly what I meant, and another big smile grew on her face as she watched me for a moment. "I'm so glad you decided to quit that stupid job," she said. "Like, really, really glad. You don't know what it feels like to look at you and see you *smiling.*"

She was wrong about that. "I think I do," I said, and brushed my thumb across her own smiling cheeks. Despite all the shit going on for her, she looked *so happy* right now, and her happiness was contagious.

Hand-in hand, we headed down to Darling Harbour.

I still couldn't believe what I'd done at work; I don't think it had really sunk in yet. I kept remembering little details of the pitch and being stunned that *I* had said those things and *I* had done those things, having spent basically my entire life with my mouth glued shut. It was liberating to discover I could surprise myself like that. Yes, there was going to be fallout and yes, it meant I'd shortly be looking for a new job, but *whatever.* Right now it meant I could walk along the harbour in the middle of a beautiful day with probably the cutest girl in Sydney. I kind of thought I didn't look that bad, either.

I didn't have to look away from reflective surfaces anymore as I passed them, and every window of every building became an opportunity to admire my hair, admire how the suit fit me, and admire how natural Bree and I looked together.

We looked like any other young couple, and both of us had these *huge, stupid* smiles plastered across our faces. Her curls bounced as we walked and the pastel sundress she was wearing blew against her front as we walked, suggesting what was underneath. I wanted to kiss her. I wanted to touch her. It was *exhilarating.* I felt like a teenager again, except that I'd never actually felt like this even when I *was* one.

She caught me stealing glances at her while we were crossing the foot bridge, and flipped her hair for my benefit. There was no one on either side of us, so on impulse I pushed her up against the railing and kissed her soundly. She made this groan at the back of her throat, reaching up around my shoulders. It was really hot right up into the part where my back started to hurt.

"You're too short," I told her, standing away and stretching out my spine. Secretly, I liked the contrast.

"Only if we're standing up," she said, eyes twinkling. "Want to go somewhere where we don't have to...?"

I feigned innocence. "I'm pretty sure they'll let us sit down at the restaurant. No promises, though."

She smoothed her dress. "They have booths there, you know."

She was actually right. The restaurant *did* have padded booths along the back wall, and because we were really early for lunch, all of them were vacant. Bree led me right up to the one in the corner and then sat very demurely and patiently with her hands folded in her lap while the waiter recited the specials of the day.

"I'll be back shortly for your orders," he said. "Would you like something to drink in the meantime?"

"Whatever coffee takes the longest to make," Bree said with a completely straight face.

I was the one who actually laughed at that. "Two lattes will be fine."

The waiter nodded and turned to leave. Bree watched him intently as he very slowly walked down the stairs and very slowly went into the kitchen. The second he was gone, she ignored the fact we were in a classy restaurant and slid across the long padded seat, grabbed my tie, and pulled me on top of her.

I'd never made out with someone in public before; I'd always been kind of grossed out by it, especially the sound of it. But the sounds we were making now were about a million miles away from grossing me out, and the sounds *she* was making as we were kissing... *fuck*. They were *hot*. All of it was hot, and lying half on top of her with our bodies together...? Yeah, we were both lucky my Y-fronts were full of 100% silicone and not anything else.

It actually took a considerable amount of willpower to convince myself to sit up and a bit away from her in time for the waiter to come back with our lattes. We probably looked extremely suspicious—Bree's cheeks were pink and I was breathing heavily—but if the waiter noticed, he didn't say anything.

"So," he said, taking out his notepad with his pen poised. "What did you decide on?"

Bree and I looked at each other. Our menus were unopened.

We did eventually decide on what we wanted; 'eventually' was the right word because Bree needed to discuss the pros and cons of *every fucking item* before settling on ordering a bowl of gourmet ice cream. Fuck that, though, I was getting that million-dollar steak. I'd hardly eaten anything in three days. They seriously could have just led the whole cow over to the table and drizzled gravy on it and I would have been good to go.

When we were done with our food and I'd cashed in all my Mum's term deposits and sold a kidney to pay the bill, we walked out on the harbour and looked around us.

"We could go shopping," Bree suggested. "And like get you some funky new clothes to go with your awesome hair. That's not a waste of money."

"It *would* involve taking off this great suit, though," I pointed out, stroking the lapel. "And that's not going to happen."

Bree put her hands on her hips. "Okay, then. So, like, where do people go to have fun in the middle of the day, anyway?" She looked down towards the harbour, where there was a patch of grass and several people just relaxing in the sun. There was a couple making out there, too. She looked up at me with a cheeky grin.

The idea was pretty appealing, but I didn't want to ruin Henry's clothes. I shook my head. "Suit," I reminded her. "Plus, I can do outdoor things when I'm pov, and they don't really say 'celebration', do they? I'm kind of feeling like saying, 'fuck it all' and spending a few hundred on whatever while I still can." Something occurred to me. "Do you need a new phone?"

She made a face. "Not until Andrej stops taking stuff."

I hummed. "Okay, so I can't buy you *things*. I don't really want to buy stuff for myself either, because I'll have to move soon and it will be just more things to put in boxes."

She still had her nose scrunched up. "So if you're not buying, like, food, and you don't want to buy things, how can you spend money and celebrate?"

Even before she'd finished that sentence I knew the answer, mainly because Burov and my team had been there all night. "The casino," I said. "Actually, *The Star* is really close to here, isn't it?" The more I thought about it, the more I liked the idea. They'd all been having fun there without me, hadn't they?

"What's with that grin?" Bree asked me, mirroring it.

"My team were there last night and I wasn't invited, and it was *me* who closed the contract today. Going there after rolling everyone is kind of poetic."

"Maybe you'll win a million dollars, too," Bree added. "*That* would be poetry."

I laughed and took her hand again. "In my dreams. Come on, let's go have some fun," I told her, and we headed off to *The Star.*

I'd had been there a few times myself over the years to entertain clients, but I'd never arrived during the day. I expected inside to be different than it was at night, but I was mistaken. As soon as we set foot in the casino, there was something about the lighting and the sounds and colours that was frozen in time. As soon as we were away from the door, I'd never have been able to guess whether the sun or the moon was up outside. There were no clocks anywhere, either.

"I've never been in a casino before," Bree told me, looking charmed by all the machines. "Is it usually this busy?"

I shrugged. "I'm not sure I'm here often enough to make 'usually' statements about it," I told her. "What do you want to do first?"

Bree didn't know, so we just wandered around the floors arm-in-arm, looking at all the different things people were doing. We got stuck watching a *very* exciting game of Blackjack where the player was clearly every bit as knowledgeable and skilled as the dealer, but in the end, the house won. The man who'd been playing mopped his brow and laughed.

"How much did you lose?" someone asked him.

"This time? A grand," he said, and then sat back down again. "What the hell, I brought two grand with me today. You game?" he asked the dealer, who smiled and set about shuffling the cards.

"Two thousand dollars," Bree said later, when we were walking around looking at all the different flashing, musical pokies. "That's so much! I can't believe someone would just *blow* that."

"Maybe he feels as lucky as I do," I told her with a smile, hugging her against my side. "Everything's so great that I don't think I'd miss a couple of grand right now."

Bree looked unimpressed. "That much would replace your

laptop, though," she said. "Or get you a new tablet. It could buy you a lot of things that are better than just handing it over to a casino."

We'd reached the end of the aisle and I was looking around for what else we could do when my eyes rested on an advertisement on the wall. It was a helicopter flying over Sydney, and the text read, *Scenic Helicopter Flights—Let The Star take you on a tour of Sydney you will never forget!*

I couldn't think of anything more perfect right now. I *already* felt on top of the world. "I know what's better than handing money over for nothing," I told her with a grin, nodding at the advertisement.

She twisted to read it, and then turned back to me with a *huge* smile. "Oh my god, are you *serious*?" she asked, bouncing up to me. "Like, *yes!*"

Bree had never been in a helicopter before—something she must have told me a total of ten times on the way up to the rooftop. I hadn't, either, but I was getting a lot more enjoyment out of *her* excitement than I was out of my own.

We had to read a whole stack of documents about crashes and emergencies, and then we needed to fill out some indemnity paperwork before they'd let us even see the helicopter. That was all fine, except there was one question I got stuck on and left until last. *Sex:* it said, and the two options were M and F. I chewed the pen in thought.

Technically I was female, wasn't I? It should be a no-brainer, and this *was* for medical purposes. However, with the way I was a dressed and acting, if I circled 'F', I was going to draw a lot of attention to myself. Even despite that I was tempted to circle 'M' anyway, and my pen hovered above the question while I wondered if I could be sued for falsifying documents if I did. I wished there was an 'other' option like on Deviant Art, or an 'it's complicated' option like on Facebook. Fuck, how was I supposed to answer this?

Bree saw my difficulty. Giving me a little smile, she pushed my hand against the paper and circled 'M' like it was no big deal. And it wasn't, because the lady took our documents without even looking at them and then showed us out onto the rooftop.

The helicopter was in the middle of the helipad with its door slid open, waiting for us. I couldn't help but smile, I was a little bit scared and it just made it more exciting.

The pilot greeted us, gave us some safety information and then we climbed into the helicopter and belted ourselves in.

There was this moment when the engine powered up and chopper blades began to turn that my stomach was full of butterflies—Bree grabbed my hand and laughed nervously — and then the helicopter lifted into the air like it was *weightless*.

In no time at all we'd pulled *way* up above the harbour, and way up above all of the graffitied alleyways that I'd walked through hundreds of times on the way to work. I could see the Frost snowflake across the tops of the buildings, and pretty soon we were above that, too, and up into the sky.

It was a beautiful clear autumn day. The water in the harbour was glistening with reflected sunlight and out on it, yachts with sails of a million colours were flitting in and out around the cruise ships. The city was full of people as small as ants, chatting and walking and sitting in the rich green parks that were tucked in amongst the skyscrapers. Out on the horizon, the iconic arc of the Harbour Bridge and the many wings of the Opera House were in silhouette against the bright blue sky.

I'd been living here for four years, and every day I looked out on that city and those landmarks. But looking at it now, I felt like I'd never seen any of it before. It felt all new. This is where I live, I thought. This is my city. And it's *beautiful.*

As if echoing my thoughts, Bree leant towards me and shouted over the sound of the engine, "This is *incredible!*"

You're incredible, was my first thought as I smiled at her. I felt fantastic already, but I was so glad Bree had come to wait for me; I didn't think I would have done this by myself. Having her here with me was like the cherry on top of the perfect day, and even though she was about as far away from perfect as someone could be, she still *was* perfect. She was perfect, and she was as beautiful as the shining cityscape behind her.

Watching me, she smiled and reached up to touch my cheek. Her eyes swum a little.

"Are you okay?" I asked her, referring to the tears.

She nodded, her fingertips tracing my cheekbones. "You look *so happy*."

That's because I am, I thought, and then kissed her.

She laughed a bit afterwards. "You didn't spent six hundred dollars just to look at me the whole time!"

I kissed her nose. "I would, though."

Despite saying that, I didn't. For the rest of the half an hour flight, we had our arms around each other and sat back to let the pilot take us on an aerial tour of Sydney.

When the helicopter landed again on top of *The Star*, my face hurt from smiling so much. It didn't last that long, though, because Bree got her sundress caught in the seatbelt and kept making jokes about just leaving it there while the pilot tried to help her untangle it. She ended up leaving with the dress still on her, and we walked back inside the casino, laughing about it.

"I think my bra's only on one hook now, though," she said as we walked up to the lifts. "It feels weird."

"Shit," I said flatly. "I *really* hope it doesn't fall off."

She giggled. "Yeah, I bet you do," she looked around us. "And, like, I totally wouldn't care about fixing it right here but I think we'd get thrown out if I just randomly took my top off..."

I snorted. "With *those* hanging out? They'd offer you a job serving alcohol." When she stopped laughing and gave me a thoughtful look, I squinted at her. "*No.*"

She giggled. "I don't know," she said wriggling her shoulders uncomfortably. "It might be worth it to earn the money to buy your stuff back."

I gave her a look. "Fuck my stuff, keep your top on."

She stopped fiddling with her straps, groaned and gestured at her back. "Can you...?"

I spent a few seconds unsuccessfully trying to help her before I gave up. Over her shoulder, there was a pub-bar-club thing in the background. I pointed at it. "If you're that uncomfortable, that place probably has toilets you can fix your bra in." She was, so we headed in there.

Given that we were in a casino, I should have guessed it was Sports Bar. There were *huge* screens with every different sport playing on them, and groups of men drinking, chatting and periodically cheering at the big TVs. We edged between them, looking for the toilets.

On the way down the back, we passed an area that didn't have crowds of people in it. In fact, it only had one. There was just one solitary young guy standing alone with his back to us, clutching a paper ticket like his life depended on it and leaning up towards a TV screen. It was playing a horse-race, and with how intent this guy was on the TV, you'd have thought it was *his own* horse competing.

It was winning, too, because the guy kept saying, "Yeah, *come on!*" as we walked past, and then suddenly burst into a triumphant, aggressive shout of, "*Yeah*, you *motherfucker! Yes, fuck you, fuck you!*" behind us when the race ended.

My eyebrows were up in my hairline, but Bree stopped dead in her tracks with a strange expression on her face. She paused for a moment, listening, and then led me back to the room. I followed her, not really sure what she was up to.

The guy was still dancing around, pumping his fists and cheering for himself *by* himself in the middle of the empty area. I watched him as Bree stood frozen beside me, and when the guy realised we were staring at him, he stopped jumping around and looked at us. I suddenly recognised him from the photos I'd seen on Facebook.

Oh, *fuck.*

"*Andrej*?" Bree asked him, and in that one word I could hear her heart breaking.

TWENTY-NINE

"What are you *doing* here?" Bree asked in a tiny little voice. I could hardly hear her over all the conversations and cheers from the other sections of the enormous Sports Bar. "Andrej, what are you *doing* here?"

It was obvious: he was in a casino, surrounded by dozens of screens showing dozens of sports, holding a ticket. I was guessing it wasn't the first time he'd done it, either, because like the high-roller playing Blackjack, he'd looked quite at home watching the race a moment ago. Bree had said he'd had stolen nearly three hundred thousand dollars from their parents; looking at him here, I could see we'd clearly solved the mystery of what had happened to all that money.

I couldn't even *imagine* how it felt for Bree to learn that all that money had been spent on *gambling,* but I could see every single one of those emotions playing out across her face.

He didn't answer her, though. He didn't even look at her. He just walked straight past her and up to me, like she wasn't even there. "Hey, buddy," he said casually, holding out his hand for me to grasp in greeting. "Andrej. You want to go halves on the next race?" He nodded back towards the screen. "It's paying out big time today. You won't be disappointed."

Past him, I could see Bree gaping at his back. "What have you *done*?" she asked him, looking between the television and the piece of paper in his hands. "Andrej..."

I withdrew my hand so it was *very* clear I wasn't going to be his 'buddy'. What the hell was he thinking? "I know who you are," I said clearly over the ambient noise. "Bree told me all about you."

Andrej watched my reaction to him, and then he sighed. "Oh, man, not *you too.*"

Me too? I watched him warily.

He rolled his eyes. "You must be Bree's flavour of the month," he said, explaining like he was doing me a favour. "She gets really obsessively into people and then completely ditches them when she finds someone better. Just ask her last best friend. Bree stopped talking to her about a month ago. Courtney was *so* upset, she really thought they were soul mates—"

"—that's *bullshit!*" Bree interrupted him. "You *stole* her from me!"

He didn't look at her. "It's funny, Courtney tells quite a different version of that story," he said. "One where Bree's completely forgotten about her and is spending all her time with *cool rich person who has a luxury apartment.* I guess that's you this week." He clapped his hand on my shoulder. "Sorry to break it to you, buddy, but she'll be done with you pretty soon. She's got a short attention span."

Bree's jaw *dropped.* "*You're* the one who has, like, a million girlfriends!" When he didn't pay any attention to her she threw her hands up. "Oh my god, *stop ignoring me, Andrej!* This is *so* fucked up! I *hate* it when you do this!"

I must have looked extremely sceptical about what he'd just told me, because he sighed again. "Come on. You think you're the first person she's done this to?" he asked. "I bet she *begged* you to take her to that expensive restaurant, yeah? She always makes people take her there."

I... closed my mouth. I didn't have a response to that.

"You like going there, too, Andrej!" Bree protested. "There's nothing *wrong* with wanting to eat there!"

He smiled wryly at me. "Except when you force other people to pay for you, am I right? I bet she's done that a lot, hasn't she? It's kind of her MO. Bree likes spending other people's money."

I frowned at him. Bree *had* done that a lot, and she *had* dragged me there and forced me to pay. How did he know all about it, though? Was she *really* the kind of person who did this so often that her brother was saying things like, 'yeah, that's just what she does'?

He noticed my reaction and looked sympathetic. "So you did take her there, yeah? Did she do the whole, 'Oh, I can't get home, help me!' or the 'I have *no food*' thing, too? Come on," he said. "She lives in Bellevue Hill. She goes to Cloverfield, and you don't actually think someone like *Bree* is there on a scholarship, do you?"

No, I definitely hadn't thought she was there on a scholarship, but I was too distracted by what else I'd just learnt to pay attention to it: she lived in *Bellevue Hill*? I hadn't been in Sydney that long, but even I knew Bellevue Hill was a *really* expensive area. She'd never told me, and the only reason I could think of about why she wouldn't say anything was exactly that: because it was an expensive area and she didn't want me to know. I felt uncomfortable.

"Oh my god, that's such total bullshit, Andrej! We *don't* ever have food around!" Bree was saying desperately behind him. "We don't! And we haven't even paid my school fees yet this—"

Andrej didn't even wait until she was done as he started talking over her. "No food around? Yeah, right. Did you like that great cake she *stole* from our fridge? Our grandma spent *ages* making that for the whole family to celebrate her birthday, and she just took off with it. After all that effort, Grandma didn't even get to light the candles. Maybe that's part of the reason there's no food. If people steal it out of the fridge because they don't want to share it, it stops being there, doesn't it, Bree?"

He half-glanced over his shoulder at her. She didn't have a comeback for that. She *had* done it, and her exact words had been something like, 'No, I don't want to share it with *them*'. I'd felt a bit bad about that, myself, but I also did *not* like how Andrej was speaking over her right now.

"Look, the thing is," he continued while I frowned at him, "Bree's one of those girls who likes attention. She likes being this little pathetic victim people want to protect and take care of. So she comes up with all these stories and all these lies about who did what and why, but you only have to look at the hard evidence to know what's *really* true," he told me, and then counted on his fingers. "One: at home, we all know what she's *really* like and she doesn't get the attention and pandering she thinks she deserves. So she's all, 'I'm so neglected, no one loves me', to whoever she's obsessed with until they take her in. Courtney's parents even felt sorry for her and bought her a bed there a week before she just ditched them all."

"That's *so not true*!" Bree said, coming up to me. "That's not true, Min!"

Andrej *sighed* and looked over his shoulder. "Are you going to *lie* about this now, too? Did Court's parents buy you a bed or not?"

Bree looked taken aback. "No, I mean, they did, but—"

"See?" Andrej said, turning back to me. "And now it's empty. Probably because she's sleeping in *your* bed, am I right?"

He *was* right, and that was very, very disconcerting. She had ended up there very quickly, too, which did kind of suggest that she might be quite practised at this 'obsessive friendship' thing, like he said.

He kept counting. "Two: she always has new clothes and new phones and all that, and she doesn't have a job because she fucks everything up and can't focus for more than five minutes. So either Mum and Dad bought them for her and she's not poor and destitute like she wants people to believe, or she's got a lot of people who she gets to buy her stuff, you know what I'm saying?"

He was about to move onto number three, whatever that was, when Bree piped up with, "No! That's *so* fucking not true! It's not!" She gave up trying to argue with him and turned to me, taking a handful of my jacket. "He always twists everything! He's so full of shit! I'm not going all over Sydney with a tonne of guys and I'm not lying to you, don't listen to him! *He's* the one who's had heaps of girlfriends!"

He refused to acknowledge anything she'd said. "She takes things, too, did you notice?" When Bree began to contradict that, he just kept talking and ploughed through her. "The neighbours' mail goes missing and then mysteriously shows up in her room, opened and empty."

I *had* sprung her opening something addressed to me before, hadn't I...?

He saw my expression. "Yeah, *see*?" he said. "And did things go missing from your house, too? Because Bree's always pinching things. And if you catch her, she'll be all, 'Oh, my brother did it! He magically showed up here and took it! My brother is *so awful!*'" he imitated her voice for a moment.

"He *did* show up last night, Min!" Bree was pleading with me. "He did! Ask reception! Ask anyone! I know it sounds really, really bad, but he *did* come! I promise! *Please!*" She turned around to him and yelled, "Andrej, this is so fucked up! Stop! Stop it! Why the fuck are you *doing* this!"

I wanted to believe Bree because I had feelings for her, but... fuck, she'd had plenty of time to pack up all her stuff last night before she left, and there was no sign of a struggle or anything...

He paid absolutely zero attention to the fact Bree was *yelling* at him. "And, get this: she's absent-minded, yeah?"

Yeah, I thought. She definitely is.

He nodded. "Mm-hmm. And because of that she's *always* losing things. Jewellery, her phone, *everything,* and then the second she can't find it, she's like, 'Oh, my brother must have stolen it because he's such a bad human being who always steals everything', it's fucked up." He gestured to himself. "And, hey, I'm a big boy now, I can deal with it. But it's kind of fucked up that my own sister wants to spread lies about me, yeah? And it's so weird at home now, because Courtney's parents told Mum and Dad all the awful shit Bree says about us, and Mum and Dad are naturally pretty angry with her."

"Shut up!" Bree shouted at him. "Shut up! *You're* the reason it sucks at home now, you *fucking asshole*! It's *awful* at home since you took all the money! Mum and Dad just work all the time and everyone is angry!" She turned to me. "Please, please, don't listen to him, Min! Please!"

He rolled his eyes exaggeratedly, and turned to address her like he was addressing a child. "We don't have money problems, Bree," he said, enunciating each syllable as if he didn't think she'd understand otherwise. "Mum and Dad work because, unlike you, they're not layabouts who just leach off other people. I know money's a difficult concept for you to understand because you are only good at spending other people's, but *we don't have money problems*."

Bree looked *so angry* and *so frustrated* that she was on the verge of tears. It was a stark contrast to how calm Andrej was. Bree was so angry she was *shaking*. "How can you fucking say all of this with such a straight fucking face? What fucking planet are you—"

He turned back to me before she'd even finished her sentence. "*If* we had money problems," he said, talking over her again, "it would be because Bree goes to a *really* expensive school. Which she hardly ever shows up at, mind you, even though she knows how much Mum and Dad are spending on it."

It *did* bother me how little she seemed to care about her education. If her parents were paying for her schooling and she happily told me she'd hardly passed a test, that *did* kind of suggest that she didn't appreciate all the money they were spending on her to go there. Which made me wonder about all that other money stuff she'd said.

Fuck. *Fuck.* Had Bree been *using* me for my money? Even just in the beginning? Had *that* been why she'd been so hell-bent on anchoring herself in my life?

He patted my arm. "So, anyway, like I said. Sorry to be the one to break this all to you, but at least there are plenty of other cute and actually *sane* chicks in Sydney, am I right? Come sit down and have a drink with me, I'll tell you some of the other stuff she's done, it's *crazy*. There's another race starting soon, too. Maybe I'll have another big win."

For a second I just stood there staring at him, piecing together what he was saying and matching it up against what Bree had told me. What he was saying made sense, it made *chilling* sense, more sense than what Bree had said. I couldn't explain why she wouldn't tell me where she lived. I couldn't explain her expensive school or the fact she had nice clothes and allegedly no money. And *if* Andrej had shown up at my apartment, she'd packed her things before apparently willingly going home with him. She could have called security, but for some reason she didn't. It seemed much more likely that *she'd* taken my stuff. And three hundred thousand dollars *did* seem a bit far-fetched...

Fuck, after that whole Sean thing I just didn't know what to think about *anyone* anymore.

I squinted, trying run through what Andrej had said. And that's when I noticed I could see through the carbon paper he was holding.

Printed on it in bold font was *$1500.00*. On *one* race. I ran my eyes over it several times, thinking maybe I'd misread it backwards through the paper. He was spending $1500 on *one race?* Who even put down that kind of money on *horse* racing, except people like Sasha Burov who were worth millions of dollars? That didn't seem right. That didn't seem right at all, especially when Bree literally didn't have five cents in her pocket.

Other things he was saying about her didn't make sense, either, when I really thought about them. Bree hadn't taken off with *any* of the money I'd given her, not ever. She could easily have spent the residual from all those taxi rides on things for herself, but instead she'd spent it on things for me or things for us. And when I'd given her money for food she'd spend it on actual food—and *lots* of it— with all these elaborate explanations about how she knew where to get very cheap, good quality produce. People weren't just born knowing the tricks to getting cheap food, that stuff was learnt through extensive experience. And rich families didn't generally spend hours going from shop to shop for the chance to get a few cents off the price of their apples. No, Andrej hadn't been telling the truth: money *was* a problem for the Dejanovics.

And if money was a problem for them and Andrej cared so much more about them than Bree did, why was he spending *fifteen hundred dollars on a single horse race*?

All his other arguments unravelled, too. Bree hadn't 'ditched'

Courtney. If I remembered correctly, she had been *really* upset and hurt when Andrej had moved in on her best friend. And all these alleged people Bree had gone around Sydney with, there was absolutely no sign of them. Not on her Facebook. Not on *Courtney's* Facebook, she hadn't been texting anyone at all at my house. The only other people I'd heard Bree talk about were her cousins. Bree wasn't *abandoning* her family to come stay with me, either, not at all. They never called.

And, most importantly, she wasn't 'spreading lies' about her brother to make herself look like a pathetic victim. She had fought so hard to *not* tell me what was going on and *not* have me think of her like that.

She *was* a bit tragic, and she was a bit of a fuck-up and, yes, she did lie occasionally and I did buy a lot of things for her, but he was *twisting* that. He was taking little pieces of the truth and *twisting* them beyond fucking recognition and it was *sick,* and I felt a bit sick for even *considering* that Bree might be using me.

Jesus fucking Christ, Andrej was *full* of it. We'd sprung this bastard in a casino betting *$1500* on the horses, how the fuck did this become about *Bree?*

"I'm not like that, Min, *please,*" Bree was desperately begging me through her tears, "please, please, please don't listen to him! Please, I couldn't deal with it if *you* believed him. He always says all this stuff about me, he always says it and *everyone* believes him and *everyone* always ends up thinking that I'm some crazy liar. No one believes me, it's why I never tell anyone ever, because *no one* believes me—"

I put an arm around her and looked back up at him. He was standing there defiantly in front of us with his ticket, looking a bit restless as he waited for me to give him an answer about drinks. Before I did, he glanced a bit impatiently over at one of the TAB machines and then at his ticket.

No *fucking* way. He was thinking about his money despite the fact his sister was hanging off my arm and crying, and despite the fact we were right in the middle of a very serious conversation.

I had to say it. "You put fifteen hundred dollars on a single race."

He looked back at me and shrugged nonchalantly. "So? I had a win before."

"Fifteen hundred dollars...?" Bree said, distracted from how upset she was by the large number. "Fifteen hundred? Where the hell did you get all that money? That's enough for a whole mortgage repayment!" He ignored her. "So, what do you drink?" he asked me. "Light? Dark? Or maybe—"

I wasn't playing. "Your sister asked you a question," I prompted him.

He scoffed. "Yes, but if she'd actually been listening to anything other than her own voice, she'd have heard me say, 'I had a win before'."

"But you had to have money to start with!" Bree interjected, even though he still wasn't looking at her. "Is that from what I think it is, Andrej? Did you take that from—"

"—Come on, buddy," he told me. "Come take a seat. I'm pretty good at this stuff, I'll help you pick horses if you've never—"

She didn't give up. "—is that from hocking Min's stuff? Or Mum's rings? Or did you—"

"—put money down on the field before. There are some really strong long shots today and they're all bolting the field and making me a mint. Have you done much punting in the—"

"—or did you forge *another* credit card application and Dad owes another ten grand to one of the major—"

"—past, yourself? Because once you get into it—"

I could hardly follow the conversation with them both talking, and I threw my hands up. "*Stop!*" I said to Andrej very firmly. "Stop! Bree is trying to *say* something to you. Are you going to actually listen to her?"

He looked annoyed. "With the way she's been carrying on and accusing me of shit? What would *you* do if someone was talking to you like that?"

I stared him down. "What would *I* do? Well, I wouldn't treat my sister the way you do in the first place, that's for sure. Especially when *she's* not the actual reason we're—"

"Well, you don't know her as well as you think you do, then," he interrupted me. "Because if you knew what she's actually like, you wouldn't be saying—"

"Bree isn't in question here! As she's *trying* to point out, you have a ticket for fifteen hundred—"

He talked over me, just like he had been doing to her. "She's not the angel you think she is, buddy, believe me! If you had to live with her for—"

"Jesus Christ, Andrej!" I had to yell, because there seemed to be no other way to get him to listen. Over at the bar in the centre of the room, we'd got the attention of the staff who then surreptitiously watched us. I lowered my voice a bit. "Listen, this is not about Bree! *You're* the one putting fifteen hundred dollars on the horses like it's nothing! This is about *you*!"

"Only because you actually believe that shit she spins about me for some reason!" he fired back at me. "Maybe you think you're in love with her, I don't know. If you are, that's *really* fucking sad. But the fact of the matter is that we *don't* have money problems, so yeah, I put a couple of bucks on the horses and I won big, and now I've got some credits to play with. It's not evidence that I'm *anything* except good at the fucking horses so how about you tell your girlfriend to stop accusing her own brother of things she's got no proof of?"

I stood back, at a loss as to what to say next. I didn't even know where to *start*. There seemed to just be no fucking way to penetrate his thick skull, and I finally understood exactly what Bree meant when she said her parents had given up arguing with him.

While we were standing there, there was a muted gunshot from the TV behind us. Andrej glanced up, and then dramatically groaned. "Fuck! And now Bree's sucked me into her stupid shit *again* and I've missed the start of a race," he said, perfectly illustrating his priorities. "Look, if you want to tell yourself that Bree can do no wrong and I'm the evil bad guy for pointing out she's not perfect, whatever. Just stop hassling me."

With that, he actually turned away from me and headed over towards the TAB machines to cash his winning ticket. Like nothing we were discussing was important, and like Bree wasn't really upset, and like the whole discussion was just a waste of his time.

I shook my head at him as he walked away from us.

Bree sighed deeply, and I looked down at her beside me. She bowed her head, defeated. "Let's just go," she said tiredly to me. "There's no fucking point. There's *never* any fucking point with him."

I tilted her chin up so I could brush some hair off her face, and she looked up at me with those big puffy eyes and a pink nose. Fifteen minutes ago we'd been on top of the world and she'd been laughing and smiling and bouncing along beside me and talking excitedly about the future... and now? Now she'd just shut down.

Fuck, what was *wrong* with him? The way he was talking over her, talking down to her, saying *awful* things about her. Who could say those things about their own sister like it was *nothing*? Bree was *such* an easy target. And instead of being a proper big brother and protecting her, instead of standing up for her against anyone who *dared* to hurt her, and being a safe haven for her against the world, *he* was the one hurting her. His own little sister. And as much as she desperately wanted to imagine things could be different, she'd just given up. She'd given up on having a big brother.

It was *messed up*. He *shouldn't* be able to do this, and I couldn't let him. "No," I told her emphatically, and she blinked at me. "No. There is a fucking point to fighting with him. There *is* a point, and I'm looking right at her." I touched her cheek. "What he is doing to you is *not* okay, Bree. It's not. And I'm not going to just stand here and let him get away with it."

She swallowed, but she didn't say anything. She just looked sad, like she'd abandoned all hope that standing up to him would achieve anything. Fuck him for taking that from her. *Fuck* him.

If I could stand up to my senior manager and two billionaire CEOs, I could stand up to Bree's messed up brother.

Riding high on my ballsy pitch heist from earlier, I straightened and marched after Andrej. "Hey," I said, calling out to him. "We weren't done."

He hardly glanced at me as he kept walking. "We are if you were going to try and convince me Bree is anything but a liar."

I pulled up next to him, hands in my pockets. "Actually, I'd like to talk about the stuff you stole from me."

He rolled his eyes and kept walking. "I don't know what you're talking about," he said. "But whatever it is, I had nothing to do with it. You should ask Bree, she's the one who took it."

"You know it interfered with my work, right? And I got in a lot of trouble?"

"Well, maybe you should have backed up your files before you took in strays."

Oh, *yes.* Yes, yes, *yes.* "Why should I have backed up my files, Andrej?" I said clearly, stopping him. "I didn't tell you what had been stolen. How did you know it was a computer?"

He faltered for a moment. "Yes, you did, you said it was a laptop."

For about a fraction of a second, I started to go over what I'd said before I realised he was bluffing. Well, two could play that game.

"You know we have security cameras up at my place, yeah?" I asked him. "What do you think was on mine? Would you like me to show you?" I went to take my phone out of my pocket and go to my gallery as if I had a video of it. "Let's watch you damaging my front door and stealing my stuff, shall we? Or do you want to keep pretending everything is Bree's fault?"

He refused to look at my phone, and started walking briskly away from me. "I don't know what you *think* you saw," he said over his shoulder. "But harassment is a crime, too, and *this* place is *also* full of cameras. And you following me around like this, that's stalking."

I didn't buy in to his deflection. I just jogged up next to him and waggled my phone. "What I have is a video of *you* damaging my property and taking my laptop and my tablet. That is a fact. I have that. What is *also* a fact is that *you* said just a minute ago, 'Ask Bree, she's the one who stole it'."

We arrived at the TAB machine, and he took out his wallet. It was completely empty except for his ID, and he looked flustered by me being there. "Leave me alone," he said. "I'm going to call security if you keep harassing me."

To hammer the point home, I stepped in between him and the TAB machine, blocking it. "Bree didn't steal my stuff to bet on the horses, did she, Andrej?" He tried to step around me, and every time he did, I moved so I was still blocking the machine. "And Bree didn't sign those credit card applications either." I shook my head at him. "She's your *sister*, Andrej. And she has debt collectors chasing her around Sydney and strangers have to give her money to get home."

He didn't react to anything I'd said. "Get out of the fucking way," he demanded.

I didn't. "She doesn't even have a *phone* anymore because she 'lost' that, didn't she? And I bet it slipped right into your pocket and fell out again at the pawn store...?"

"Get *out* of the fucking way," he repeated, looking me in the eyes.

He was shorter than me, and it was my absolute pleasure to look down on him. "I'd buy Bree a new phone, but it would end up in here, wouldn't it, like all the other money?" I tapped the machine behind me. "So the way I figure it, I should just cut out the middle man and give it straight to you now." I took a few notes out of my pocket and thrust them at him. "Here," I said. "Go on."

He kept trying to get around me to the machine, and there was something a bit desperate about his movements. "I will call security and have you dragged out of here if you don't get out of the way."

I just pushed the notes at his chest. "Go on, take all my money. It saves me from needing to waste time buying your sister nice things so you can steal them and gamble the proceeds."

He took a deep breath and was about to *blast* me, when instead he double-took and shouted, "Hey!" and there was a flurry of movement beside us. It was Bree who'd darted over here for some reason and now was *running* full pelt across the floor of the bar.

I didn't know what had happened until Andrej took off after her, yelling, "You fucking *thief*! Give that back to me, it's *mine*!" His hands were empty as he ran after her, and Bree had his ticket clutched in one of hers.

Shit. That was a bad move, this guy was *not* in a balanced frame of mind.

"Bree!" I shouted, taking off after both of them. Over at the door, I could see the bouncer on his radio, his eyes fixed on us. He was calling for backup.

Andrej easily caught up to her because his legs were longer and when he did, he roughly swung her around and began trying to pry her arms open. "Give it back!" he shouted, "Someone call the police! This girl *stole* my ticket!"

Bree looked *terrified*. "It's not yours!" she was shrieking as he wrenched at her arms and grabbed at her hands and she curled around the ticket so he couldn't get to it. "It's not your money! It's

Min's! It belongs to Min! Stop saying it's yours!"

When he couldn't get it from her, he just *shook* her really aggressively, his voice *raw* with desperation. "Give it back to me!" he *screamed* through her. "Give it back to me!"

I caught up to them and grabbed him, trying to use my weight to pull him away from her. Unfortunately he was stronger, so he shoved me away and I stumbled.

Other people were turning away from the TVs around the bar to see what was going on, and I heard a number of voices shouting in alarm. All I could think about was Bree, though.

Bree was trembling, and as I came back to try and free her again, she scrunched up the ticket and threw it on the floor away from us. For just a second Andrej and I stared at each other, and then we both *dove* on the floor and scrambled for it.

I was faster and stood up with it in my hand, triumphant. "You want this so much?" I yelled at him. "You want this enough to hurt your sister and send your family to *ruin? Here! Have it, then!"*

I held it up between us, and then very slowly and very deliberately, I tore it right through that precious bar code. I didn't stop there, either, I tore it again and again until it was nothing but confetti in the air.

For a second I was looking into the eyes of a wild animal who'd just watched his last meal escape, and then he lunged towards me and I heard a really loud, dull thump and I... I wasn't sure what happened next.

My face hit something, then my back hit something, but I couldn't see anything and all I could hear was loud ringing and whistling in my ears. My head was spinning like water draining down a plughole. Somewhere in the distance Bree was screaming, but right up close all I could hear was my laboured breathing and my pulse hammering in my ears. I tried to get up, but I couldn't. The whole side of my head was *throbbing.*

He must have punched me, I realised. He must have punched me *really* hard.

"Shit, look at that blood, call an ambulance!" someone was shouting, and, actually, I *could* taste blood in my mouth.

"What have you done, Andrej?" Bree was wailing. I could feel her draped across my stomach. "What have you done...? No! No, no, no... *Min...*"

"Good fucking work, mate," A gruff voice shouted. "You might have just killed someone over a punt." Then, I think he spoke to someone else. "Put that idiot in one of the interview rooms and call the cops, I'll get management. Jesus, that guy's hardly breathing, get that girl off him and do CPR."

It was only when I felt someone undo my jacket and start to unbutton my shirt that I remembered my binder and pushed the hands off me. Then, I turned onto my side and *coughed.* My mouth was full of blood and it was getting up my nose and down my throat and making me gag. When I opened my eyes and looked down at the plush carpet and my blood dripping onto it, though, I discovered it was coming from the side of my face and not my mouth at all. I put my fingers to my cheekbone and looked at them: yup, I was bleeding. That was probably something I should have worried about, but my first thought was 'oh no, Henry's suit!'

Whoever had pulled Bree off me let her go, and she came crawling across the carpet to me, *sobbing.* "Min," she said, looking aghast as she touched my face, presumably where the blood was coming from. "I'm sorry," she said raggedly. "I'm sorry, I'm *sorry...*"

I went to shake my head at her, but when I moved it, it *swam* and I nearly passed out again.

"There, look at what you did," one of the bouncers who was restraining Andrej said to him. "Look at what you did to two people over a few hundred bucks, mate. You need *help.*"

I looked at Andrej, expecting to see defiance, or derision, or *pleasure* at the fact my face was all smashed up and Bree and I were both cowering on the carpet in front of him, but that wasn't the case at all.

It was shock.

Complete shock, as if he'd suddenly snapped out of a drug-addled high and was finally grasping the enormity of what he'd done.

After we'd watched him be carted off, someone gave Bree a tea towel from the bar, and she held it against my cheek to stop the bleeding. She was still a bit teary. "Are you okay?" she asked, her eyes running over my face as if she was looking for *more* injuries. "*Really?*"

I touched her hand on my stomach. "Yeah. I'm not the one who was being *shaken*." I looked her up and down; she *seemed* alright. "Did he hurt you?"

She laughed through her tears. "Oh my god, you're lying on the carpet and there's blood pouring out of your face and you're like, 'hey, Bree, are you okay?'."

I chuckled very gently, because my head was *killing* me. "Well, I'd like to think I sacrificed myself for a noble cause."

Her smile faded. "Gambling..." she said, eyes glazed. "It's just... like, I can't even get my head around it, you know? I mean, you always see those 'think about what you're *really* gambling with' ads, but... I don't know if I really thought people do that. But they wouldn't spend money on those ads to warn people about it if it didn't happen, would they? And Andrej *did* do it. And it's just... it's *gambling*. I don't *get* it. I thought for sure it was drugs or crime or something seriously hardcore." She shook her head, looking overwhelmed. "Like, sometimes when I stay up late I hear Mum crying quietly in bed because we might lose the house and she *loves* it. It's her *dream* house. He hears that, too."

I stroked the back of her hand, and tried to mimic the way Andrej spoke. "But don't you know, Bree? She's crying because she can't believe what a bad daughter she has."

She sighed deeply. "Well... at least you know what he's like now," she said. "I don't want to go home."

"I don't want to go back to work, either. Canada's looking pretty great right now. Let's do it."

She hugged me. "You're crazy," she said, and then immediately looked upset again when she remembered why she was holding a cloth against my face. "Fuck, I can't believe I dragged you into this," she said. "This is all my fault. I *always* do this. I'm so sorry, Min. Like, I'm really, really sorry."

I didn't want her to worry about me. "Nonsense," I said. "That was my first proper fistfight in a bar. By Aussie standards, I'm a *real man* now. I should send your brother a thank you card and shout everyone in here a round."

We were laughing about that, when a gloved hand touched my arm and someone put a huge medical kit beside of me. The person who knelt down had a green paramedic uniform on. "Hey, there," he said. "Min, isn't it?" I nodded, and then winced at the movement. He noticed. "That looks nasty. Can you tell me what happened?"

I was a bit confused about what *had* happened, so Bree told them instead: Andrej had punched me out like a light, and then when I'd fallen I'd smacked my face on a table and ended up on my back on the carpet.

The paramedics were particularly concerned about the fact I'd been unconscious for a short period of time, and had to run through a whole series of questions I needed to answer and actions I needed to do while they repeatedly shone torches in my eyes just to double-check I wasn't dying.

The whole assessment process lasted for a few minutes—I needed to quietly inform them I was female when they went to undo my shirt—and in the end, after they'd patched up my cheek and stopped the bleeding, they actually gave me a choice about whether or not to go with them to the hospital for head scans, MRIs and proper stitches.

I was trying to figure out how to avoid going to hospital when a pair of uniformed police officers came over to me. I think they'd been speaking to Andrej first, because they were talking about him under their breath and when I was telling them what happened, they kept looking at each other.

When I was done making a statement about how I ended up bleeding on a casino floor, the police officer who'd been leading the interview sat back on her haunches. "So, here's the question," she began. "Do you want to press charges? If you do, we'll have to pull the security footage, and you might need to testify in court if he pleads not guilty. Are you prepared to do that? Court can be very stressful and you'll need a lawyer."

My immediate response was that I didn't want to make that big a deal out of it. All that hassle on top of everything else that was going on for me? And I wasn't actually sure how I was going to afford a lawyer in the future, either. I'd opened my mouth to say exactly that when I looked across at Bree. She was waiting with bated breath for me to answer.

'He belongs in jail', she'd told me. She's said that a few times, and when I thought about her descriptions of what he'd done to her, how he took her stuff and bullied her and terrorised her and stole her things and forged her parents' signatures... Her parents probably thought they were doing the right thing by Andrej trying to keep it private. Maybe they thought he'd get over whatever was going on, I didn't know. I didn't think addiction really worked like that, though, did it? It just escalated until something terrible happened or the person got help.

In any case, her parents didn't know what to do with him, and they hadn't done *anything* to protect Bree so far, anything.

But *I* could.

"Yes, I'll press charges and do all those things," I said resolutely. "And he also stole property that belongs to me. Can I report that to you guys now, too?"

Looking across at Bree as the officers got ready to take another statement from me, I could see her lip quivering and her eyes swimming with *gratitude*. She was going to cry.

It was over. Andrej's reign of terror was starting to crumble, and they could finally start to rebuild their family.

I hugged Bree. "Come on," I said as she and one of the police officers helped me up. My ears rang a little now that I was upright, but I didn't fall over again and I was feeling vastly better than I had been twenty or so minutes ago. "Let's get me stitched up and then go home. I need to get this so-called power suit off before it gives me any more bright ideas."

THIRTY

Short of me actually *being in the process of dying*, nothing in the world was going to get me into one of those transparent hospital gowns. So instead of going into the hospital to get stitched up, Bree and I just dropped past a medical centre and got the doctor on duty to do it. Bree spent the whole time profusely apologising for everything and it got to the point where the doctor asked me, "Did *she* do this to you?"

"Basically," Bree had said darkly.

"I think to punch me in the face, you probably need to be able to actually *reach* my face," I pointed out with a grin.

Bree shoved me and interrupted the doctor's work on my cheek.

"It's not funny, Min! This is *all my fault!*"

She'd mostly run out of steam by that point, though, so afterward she just sat and held my hand and watched the doctor finish stitching me up.

I had a pretty nasty headache, so the doctor wouldn't let me go straight home. She sent me upstairs to get a CT scan beforehand, but the clinic was packed and there was some ridiculous wait time.

This place *smelt* like a hospital. "Let's just go home," I said to Bree as we sat on one of the long benches in the corner of the waiting room. "I'm obviously okay."

Bree gave me a stern look and stuck her hand out, making a *'gimme'* motion. "Phone."

I took my phone out of my breast pocket and placed it in her palm. She held it up, took a picture of me, and then showed me the screen.

All around one of my eyes was swollen and bright red, and on my other cheek I had a big white gauze pad that the doctor had taped to my face to cover the stitches. There was blood all over the collar on that side, and you could still see blood caked around the corners of my nose and eyes and places I hadn't managed to clean properly in the dark toilets at the casino. Actually, I looked a lot worse than I felt. I looked like I'd been well and truly beaten up.

"I see what you mean," I told Bree, who then started to play with my phone. "I feel fine, though."

"I don't care," she said. "This is all my fault, and if you go home and die I will *never* forgive myself, so you're going to get all the test things that the doctor says. The reception in here is terrible." She'd already moved on from telling me to stay put and was holding my phone up in various directions looking at the signal strength icon. She then turned and lay on her back on the bench with her head on my thigh, engrossed in whatever she'd needed data reception for.

I surveyed the waiting room. No one looked particularly appalled by the fact she'd decided to make herself comfortable on me. While looking around, I made eye-contact with a guy probably about my age on the other side of the room; his girlfriend was inclined towards him, showing him something on her phone. She'd been talking the whole time we'd been in here, and he was trying really hard to look interested.

She ignored my tone. "You normally treat them like gold."

I stopped trying to explain myself. "*Bree*," I warned her.

She turned her head against my thigh to look around us. There probably wasn't anyone who could hear, so I didn't really mind that much when she probed. She was very gentle about it when she quietly asked me, "You were going to take them all, weren't you?"

I froze. I *never* expected her to get there so easily.

At my silence, she guessed what the answer was, and she looked *absolutely* aghast. "Min..."

I pulled myself together, knowing exactly what she was thinking. "It's not your fault."

She scrunched up her nose in silent disagreement with me. She *had* been thinking that, apparently. After she'd done that, though, her eyes glazed as she was lost in thought. I watched wrinkles grow across her forehead.

"It *isn't* your fault," I repeated, in case she still didn't believe me.

She shook her head dismissively, and I realised she was probably thinking about something different now. But if she was thinking about what I'd just said and she *wasn't* worrying that it was her fault, what *was* she worrying about? I watched her for a little while, reflecting on what I'd told her. It occurred to me how fucking quickly she'd jumped to the right conclusion. That was too quickly for it to be a coincidence, wasn't it?

"Lucky guess about the pills?" I softly asked her. She shrugged, eyes glazed. There seemed to be more she wanted to say, but I didn't really want to push her in the waiting room of a medical clinic. "You don't need to tell me in here if you—"

"I took the rest of my anti-depressants in one go once. Heaps of them."

That was a *lot* of information to take in at once. *Bree* took anti-depressants?

"You tried to *kill* yourself?" I asked quietly, probably sounding every bit as shocked as I was.

She shook her head. "No..." she said. "I was just tired of being miserable all the time. I thought taking that many would make me really happy for a bit, you know? But it like literally didn't do *anything*. Like, I felt a tiny bit sick but that was all. And then I needed to pretend I'd lost them and ask Mum for some money to get some new ones because I couldn't just say I'd taken them all in one go, could I? Mum got *really* angry and then Andrej went on this tirade about how I didn't respect people's money..."

"Wow," I said, and took one of her hands, holding it tightly in mine. "Wow." I thought about that. "You're on anti-depressants?"

"Not anymore," she said. "They're like $40 a month. I'd rather eat."

"I just never would have picked you for someone who'd be on them," I said, and then reconsidered when I thought about the last couple of weeks. "Well, at first, anyway. I know you have some seriously awful stuff going on for you, but you always seem quite cheerful."

"Yeah, because who wants to hang around with someone who's whinging all the time? No one."

Ouch. I wanted to give her a big, warm hug, but I couldn't in the middle of this waiting room. "I wished you'd told me all of this much earlier," I said quietly to her, squeezing her hand. "I would have paid for them for you. I would have been there for you."

Her eyes swam a bit. "*I* wanted to be there for *you*. And you were so stressed out already..."

It was crazy to remember I'd thought she was this vapid, insane, hyperactive teenager when I first met her. And she definitely could be from time to time, I supposed. I don't know why I'd thought that would be all that she was. Of *course* that wouldn't be the whole story.

I stroked her hair. "No matter how stressed out I seem, you don't have to pretend to be happy around me, okay?"

"I don't pretend anymore," she said simply, and then gave me a big, warm smile. She *looked* happy.

Fuck, and she was gorgeous. I wanted to kiss her. I glanced around the waiting room and *actually* considered doing it despite all of the various people in there. I never got there, though, because I was worrying about whether or not people would notice and find it *really* inappropriate.

It wasn't long before we were called anyway, but then the imaging-radiologist-person or whatever you called someone who operated the CT equipment couldn't actually find me on the system once he'd shown us into the lab with the machine.

"Are you a new patient?" he asked, and I nodded. He groaned. "Okay, wait here," he said. "I'll run downstairs and grab your file. They probably didn't put it online yet."

With that, he ran out and left us alone in the white lab with the CT machine. It was an enormous creepy capsule-looking thing with a long platform poking out of it that I thought I was probably going to end up lying down on. The mattress on it looked quite comfortable and was made up like a hospital bed. It was too narrow for two people to lie side-by-side, though...

Bree had been looking right at it, too, and then we glanced at each other. She had a cheeky grin, and when I looked down at it, my eyes didn't stop there.

Throwing me this coy little glance, she wandered up over to the bed and turned back. "Look," she commented innocently. "I think sitting up here might make me taller." Her eyes were twinkling.

"I don't think the CT guy is going to care how tall you are."

She was giving me eyes. "Good, because it's not him I want to get it on with."

I glanced back at the door. We'd probably have some time up our sleeves; the reception desk was *not* close. I took a couple of steps over to her and boosted her to sit up on the bed.

"Just for a couple of seconds, okay?" I breathed across her cheek. "He'll be back soon."

She *was* at a better height like this and I could kiss her without hurting my back. Fuck, she was getting so much better at it, too. So much better. We could only do this for a few more seconds, though, because how long had we been here? Just a few more... I'd been focusing on how much I was enjoying having her catch one of my lips when she leant against my freshly-stitched cheek and I flinched and sucked air through my teeth.

"Sorry, sorry," she said quickly, and then pulled me back in.

My hands were still where they'd been when I'd lifted her: around her rip-cage with my thumbs under her cleavage, and I could feel the pull of fabric under them every time she heaved a breath. My fingertips were *so close* to her breasts and I couldn't think about anything else as I kissed her. Just a tiny movement upwards and I could run my hands over them and feel them and feel the weight of them in my—

"We have fertility services if you're interested," a very amused voice said from the doorway. "But they're actually in another part of the medical centre."

"Oh my god!" Bree said as we pushed away from each other. Then she started giggling.

I must have been blushing, because *everything* on my face began to throb a lot more powerfully and my vision was narrowing in time with my pulse. It *really* hurt, but I was too distracted by the fact I'd been caught making out with Bree on a CT machine to pay too much attention to my discomfort. I just stood there awkwardly.

The guy was probably in his thirties and looked entertained rather than disgusted. "So," he said as he approached me. "Your girlfriend's going to have to wait over there." He pointed at the chair on the far side of the room. "Unless you *are* in the wrong room."

"Sorry," I just said quietly as Bree hopped down off the machine and went to sit obediently in the corner. She was bright red and bit her lip against more giggling.

He laughed. "That's okay, Mr..." he glanced down at my medical file. "Oh, sh—shoot," he said, rescuing himself from swearing. "I'm so sorry, *Ms* Lee." He winced. "I hope I didn't offend you."

I wasn't sure why he thought I'd be offended, I thought it was pretty obvious that 'Mr' was the look I was going for.

Bree opened her mouth to correct him and I just raised my hand a little and shook my head. I *really* didn't want to enter into a discussion about it. "It's okay," I told him, and gestured at the bed. "I'm supposed to lie here, right?"

He nodded. "Head facing that way," he said, pointing towards the machine. He reviewed my notes as I climbed onto it. "'Head trauma, check for intracranial haemorrhage'," he read aloud. "That explains the glorious shiner you have on one side of your face. Got a glorious story to go with it?" he asked, and then went and put my file down.

"My brother did it," Bree volunteered from the end of the room.

The guy looked from her to me with his eyebrows up. "Right," he said. "That *does* sound like quite a story. And you must have *quite* a headache."

I deadpanned. "Yeah, and you know what they say cures

headaches…"

He paused for a second and then *laughed*. It was such a sudden sound that it actually hurt my ears, especially after that punch. He made a few notes on my file and then said, "You two are a riot. Most people come in here and just repeatedly ask me if the CT is going to hurt them."

He then gave me some instructions on what I was supposed to do with the machine and then explained what he was going to do. Then, as he was heading behind the glass shield and I was lying flat on the bed, his eyes passed over the crotch of my pants and lingered there for a second. He didn't say anything about what he saw there, though, he just went and sat down at the computer to operate the CT. Trying not to feel awkward about that, I relaxed and lay still while he took the images and then came back into the room to discuss them with me.

"I'm not really supposed to interpret the images, your doctor is," he said after he'd had an opportunity to look at them. "But to be honest, we mainly tell the doctors what they're looking for, anyway. I don't see any evidence of bleeding. But it might be too minor to see yet, so go straight to hospital if anything changes." He looked uncomfortable, his eyes dipping down to the packer again. "Look, sorry about the fertility comment before."

"It's fine," I said, hoping that would end the conversation.

It didn't. "Although, I guess our services *are* available to lesbian couples, too, so I suppose if you two were ever interested in starting a family, you could—"

I *cringed*. "It's fine," I repeated, and then tried to wind everything up. "Thanks for your help."

Bree was trying not to laugh the whole way out, but as soon as we were walking up Harrington, she blurted out, "We're a lesbian couple," and then dissolved into giggles.

I was busy trying to walk slowly and smoothly so I didn't jar my pounding head, and I didn't answer fast enough.

She read too much into my silence, and looked alarmed. "Shit, Min, I didn't mean that you're a—" She pulled on my arm, which hurt my head. "It's just that you let him 'she' you, so I thought that you wouldn't mind me joking about it!" She paused. "Did it bother you, though?"

"What, being called 'she'?" Bree nodded, and I made a face. "It probably wouldn't if I wasn't wearing the packer."

She stopped us. "So, wait, you *didn't* just transition? Because I thought this whole change thing," she gestured at me, "was like a final fuck you to being a woman."

"It is," I said, turning around to face her. "I think."

"But you don't mind being called 'she'? Trans guys don't usually take female pronouns."

'Usually' wasn't something I traded much in. Trans guys probably didn't *usually* want to have bodies like a Ken doll, either.

Honestly, I got that pronouns were incredibly important to a lot of people, but for me they kind of felt like an afterthought. After all the changes I'd made and was going to make to myself and to every single aspect of my life, whether or not someone called me 'she' or 'he' was like... well, whatever? As long as they didn't see me as the old Min, the passive, shy, feminine Min, and *never* treated me like that or brought her back in any way, it was okay, maybe.

...Maybe. I thought twice as soon as I had decided that, though. Did calling me 'she' kind of do that, in a way...? Remind me of *all* that complete bullshit I'd been though as *Ms* Min Lee? Or was it *actually* fine as long as I could be like I was now and free of all that pressure? I expected to know the answer to that, but I didn't.

All I knew was that both Sarah and Bree 'she'd and 'he'd me in various situations, and as long as they were the *right* situations, it didn't bother me and it felt comfortable. But that was kind of weird, wasn't it? Did it mean something? Ugh, what if it meant that I *wasn't* a guy, after all of this? After everything that had happened...?

Just for a couple of seconds I had that panicky I-need-to-run-away feeling that was far too familiar, my pulse began to race and fuck what if it *was* all a mistake and I began to feel light-headed and *no,* no. No. I didn't need to do this. I just needed to relax and not worry.

It was okay. It *was* okay. None of that mattered. It didn't matter who I was or wasn't like or what other trans people did or didn't do. It wasn't about them, it was about me. And, besides, there was no deadline on making that decision, it wasn't like I had an anvil hanging over my head and an executioner shouting, 'Make up your mind, Min Lee!'. The way things were right now was fine, and if they weren't fine later, I could just change them then.

"People keep asking me about pronouns..." I sighed as we kept walking again. "I honestly don't mind what you call me. Or what Sarah does, or any of the people who know me do. Just don't out me to strangers, okay? The last thing I want to do is be hosting an info session about my gender *every* time I meet someone. I don't want people to even think about it."

Bree linked arms with me, processing all that. "It's kind of weird that I don't know whether to call you my boyfriend or my girlfriend," she said eventually. "I mean, I was *assuming* boyfriend, but..."

"Go with boyfriend," I said, and then with a pained expression I clarified, "I'm still someone's girlfriend at the moment."

Bree made the same face I was making. "Oh, yeah," she said, her eyes dipping to the bloodstained collar of his suit. "Henry." She looked *really* guilty.

When we got home, the first thing I needed to do was take his suit off, hide it somewhere where I couldn't see it and have a shower. Bree had followed me into the bedroom, probably with designs on 'helping me' out of the suit, but she stopped in place when she saw what I'd done last night.

"Whoa," she said, her eyes travelling over all the strewn dresses, lacy scarves and frilly blouses that were mixed in with shards from the broken mirror. "You flipped out properly."

I chuckled. "Yeah," I said. "Actually, I need to get room service to hire someone to clean all that up and throw everything out."

Bree walked carefully around the debris, making me nervous because she was only wearing socks. She turned back to me. "You're really going to just chuck all of this?" I nodded, and she looked scandalised. "But some of those are designer!"

I shrugged. "Well, I did promise Sarah I'd give some to her, but I'm not sure she'd want them now."

Bree gave me a look. "The glass is mostly on that side," she said, pointing. "The rest of them are probably okay."

I left Bree to be horrified by my wastefulness and went for that shower. I did actually have some weak paracetamol painkillers left, so I took the recommended dose. I was pretty sure they were going to be useless after how much codeine I'd been popping recently, though. Oh well, I thought, struggling to get my binder back on over damp skin.

When I'd changed into my jeans and that big floppy t-shirt, I opened the bathroom door. I'd only taken *one* step into the bedroom before I realised Bree had been working on it. There were three piles of neatly-folded clothes along one wall. I gaped at them while she *beamed.*

She presented the stacks of clothes to me. "This one's the pile of clothes that are full of glass, or that are like your personal underwear or something," she said, and then moved along. "And this one's the pile of things that might fit Sarah. And this pile," she said, presenting the biggest one, "is the stuff that we can make a shit tonne of money selling on eBay."

I had to laugh. "You're wonderful," I told her. I never would have been able to deal with any of them, and I think she knew that. "Thank you."

I beckoned her over and she trotted up to me, looking delighted as I wrapped my arms all around her and gave her a *big* hug, burying my nose in her curls. They smelt like vanilla; I was starting to associate that smell with her. I stood there with my arms around her for a minute or two, inhaling that scent and enjoying how we fit together.

After a little while she pulled away a bit, looking up at me. She looked serious; while I'd been relaxing, she'd obviously been deep in thought.

"I wanted to do something for you, because... well... No one's ever done something like that for me," she said. "What you did with Andrej."

I grinned. "You mean, take a punch for you?"

She smiled a bit. "Well, I guess... but I mean, like, you didn't just go, 'Yeah, he's a fuckhead, let's go and enjoy our day', you were like, 'no, screw him, he's not going to do this to you, Bree'." Her eyes shone. "And then I watched you walk right up to him, and even though he's, like, *fucked*, you stayed there and you yelled at him, and you didn't take any of his shit," she said. "And it was for me."

I smiled. "Yeah."

There were tears in her eyes. "And that's really *nice.*"

"Well," I said, looking directly at the three piles of clothes against the wall, "after all the things you do for me, you deserve it."

I think she liked that answer, because she took a handful of my t-shirt, pulling gently. "I preferred it when you were wearing the tie," she said sheepishly. "I want to kiss you, but this," she tugged on my t-shirt, "isn't really cutting it."

I led her out into the living room, and because my couch was still covered in big jumble of blankets and pillows, I had to shove them all aside before I could sit down on it and pat my lap. Her cheeks went a bit pink as she came and sat sideways across it and put her arms around my neck.

"That's better—" she'd begun to say, but then she made a surprised sound and slid back down my thighs, reaching for the bottom of my t-shirt. I let her, because I figured out what she was doing. "Whoa," she said, giggling. "You're still wearing the packer."

I shrugged. "Well, I'm still not sold on it, but I figured I should give it the opportunity to prove itself over a few days before I tuck it away in a drawer somewhere forever."

She looked up at me. "You don't like it?"

I made a face. "I don't *dislike* it. I like it a whole lot more than I like my chest but... I feel like people shouldn't be able to see it, either. But they can."

She snorted. "They really can. Especially in these jeans, oh my god. Look," she held the t-shirt back to show me. "It looks like you have a boner in there. You're going to give people the wrong idea."

"I have a beautiful girl sitting in my lap, Bree. What makes you think it's the wrong idea?" I looked her in the eye, grinning, and she went *bright* red.

"Whoa," she said after a few moments, breathless. Fuck, I loved to hear her like that. She was still looking at my crotch. "Whoa. You know, there's something really hot about the idea of you being hard for me?" As soon as she'd said the word 'hard', I would have been. That very second.

I'd never seen myself as the kind of person to flirt like this, but, then again, I never thought I'd be the kind of person to do the other things I'd done today, either. And having Bree on my lap blushing *furiously* made my heart race. I *loved* imagining what she was thinking. But, fuck, it was *terrifying,* because I knew where this was going.

Still high off the other bold things I'd done today, I brushed her hair aside and leant over next to her ear. "You'd make me hard," I whispered. "If it was real."

She inhaled sharply. "Oh my god," she breathed, and then wouldn't let me lean back again. "I like that..." she said about my lips beside her ear. "Keep doing it."

"Bossy," I murmured, and then kissed down her neck, her head lolling to the side and tilting to give me better access as I did. The skin on her neck was soft and delicate, and there was something so incredibly intimate about her just trusting me to have my lips there. Under them, I could feel her pulse, and it was fast.

I know where this is going, I thought. I know where this is going and for fucking once I *want* it. I want it so much. Fuck, though, we *shouldn't,* I'm still in a relationship. But I didn't want to stop, I wanted to search her body and find other soft places where I could feel her pulse under my lips.

While I was reflecting on how much I really shouldn't have been doing it, I pushed aside the shoulder of her sundress and a pink bra strap to kiss along her collarbone, and seeing the skin there reminded me of that photo she'd taken of herself when I was in Broome. Naked, with the doona covering everything but her shoulders. I wanted her like that, I just wanted to be under the doona with her this time. Fucking hell, I wanted it, I wanted *all* of it, and my fingers hovered over a button on her dress, but I managed to get myself to drop them.

"Stop, stop... *Fuck,*" I said, sitting back from her. "We've got to stop, I'm still with Henry."

Bree nodded, breathless. "I know, I know..." She said, and then we both sat watching each other for a moment. Bree didn't look convinced. "Like, how is this different to what we were doing in the restaurant, though? Didn't we already do this stuff?"

She had a point, but we were in my house this time. It was private. It was dangerous. "It just can't go any further than that, okay?"

She looked pretty pleased with that answer, and she leant forward towards me with a cheeky grin on her face. "But lots more of the same stuff is okay, right?" she asked, kissing my bottom lip for a second before grinning mischievously at me.

"You know, I used to think there was something a bit angelic about how you looked," I told her flatly. "But, hey—" I parted the hair on the top of her head and pretended to be looking for something, "—oh, look. *Horns.*"

She giggled and kissed me once. "It's nice to finally be allowed to kiss you, that's all, so I think it's normal to want to do a lot of it," she said sweetly, dismissing my concern about potentially being employed by Satan. "I wanted to for ages, but I thought you were in this happy relationship..."

I winced as she said that. The movement hurt my soon-to-be black eye. "So did I."

"So... I don't even want to ask because I'm afraid of what you'll say," she told me, pulling back to look at me. "But you *are* going to break up with him, right? And then you're going to officially go out with me? Like, definitely...?" She was trying to sound casual, as if she was just seeking clarification on a point she already knew the answer to. She was watching my answer far too closely, though. Was she *really* afraid I'd say no?

I kissed her. "Bree," I told her, stroking across her cheek. "Of course I am. Of course."

She blushed, delighted. "I'll be really good to you," she promised me. "I will. You'll see!"

I nuzzled each of her pink cheeks with my good one. "You already are. Better than I deserve, sometimes."

I kissed her, taking my time to let her relax into my arms and against me. The way she arched back to let me, completely open, completely unguarded, just letting me set a slow, passionate rhythm... moving with me, sighing into each kiss... it was beautiful. *She* was beautiful, and she was right here on my lap, kissing me, touching me, pressing that soft body up against mine. It was a gentle, pleasant feeling. God, it was a pleasant feeling. I loved that just kissing her could turn me on.

The problem was, I wanted more. I wanted to undress her and kiss more than just her lips and her neck. I wanted to find out what other noises she made, and really, what I *really* wanted to do was show her what it was like to have someone make her feel the way she deserved to feel. She'd spent so long having people discard her and ignore her... I wanted to make her feel the opposite. I wanted to show her that there was someone who was here with her, just for her, and that she was cared for, cherished and *wanted.*

We were both breathing heavily when she sat back from me and swung a knee over me so she was straddling my lap. She didn't explain that, she just sat there for a couple of seconds with a big, nervous smile on her face. Eventually, she worked up the courage to look up at me and say, "I want to show you..." Her fingers toyed with the buttons at the front of her dress.

My breath caught in my throat. Oh, god, *yes.* "Come on, Bree, I shouldn't..."

She shrugged lightly. "I know. I just..." She blushed. "I just want to show you. You know, if you want to see..."

If I want to see? *If I want to see?* "We can't do anything else," I said, desperately hoping she'd find a loophole in that.

She did. "There's nothing wrong with window-shopping, right?"

Fuck. "Okay," I breathed.

She slowly, *slowly* undid all of her buttons one by one, revealing the skin underneath inch by inch. As she got down to her bellybutton, her dress fell open to display her cleavage spilling out of her bra. I helped her unthread her arms from the dress and then just sat there for a moment, looking down at all that skin.

I'd seen this much of her before several times, but there was a big difference between a girl whipping off her top to put on another one, and taking off her top because she wanted to show you what was underneath.

And it was worth showing. It *really* was. The curve of her hips, the fall of her waist, even the little swell of chub she had underneath her bellybutton. It was all gorgeous. I wanted to fully appreciate all of it, but it was difficult to not just stare at her breasts. And it wasn't only because they looked so *good;* her bra was at the very end of its apparently long and painful life. It was small and her breasts were *big*, and it looked like it was in a world of suffering trying to hold onto them. I wanted to put it out of its misery.

It was Bree who did; she reached around behind her in a very familiar movement, and the material went slack as she unclipped it. Watching me with that same coy little smile as before, she shrugged the straps off her shoulders and let the fabric fall away from her.

I'd seen breasts before, lots of them. I had my own. But Bree was *showing* me hers because she wanted to turn me on, and *fuck,* with them right there in front of me, was she ever achieving her aim.

They were *nice*. They were soft and heavy and full; too big to sit up on her ribcage, now that her bra was off they fell a little. Her nipples were so light they were almost the same colour as the rest of her skin, and they were taut with the circles around them. With her curls dropping over her shoulders and those pink cheeks and pink lips... *fuck*. She was *so* beautiful. And she was sitting across my lap. Oh, *god*. I wanted her. I *wanted* her.

"Window-shopping is a real challenge right at this second," I said through grit teeth, eyes glued to what I wasn't allowed to touch.

She blushed again. "Well... They're all yours when you want them..." she said, looking up at me from underneath her lashes.

She was *killing* me. *When I wanted them?* I wanted them *now!* I wanted to reach out and *grab* them. I wanted to lift her off the chair with me and lay her down on my couch and touch and kiss and explore every inch of her. I wanted her back arching and her hips pressing against me, I wanted her legs around my waist and, *fuck*, I wanted more, didn't I? I wanted to be *inside* her. I wanted to be inside her, moving against her, showing her how that felt...

I didn't want to focus on the fact I couldn't do that, because imagining it felt *so* good. I'd almost managed to dismiss the impossibility of it when I felt her hands at the bottom of my t-shirt. She was going to lift it up, and *that* halted everything.

My automatic response was a very powerful *no,* but it wasn't because of Henry.

I stiffened. "Don't..." I said shortly, and put my hands on hers to stop her.

Then, I felt *guilty*. She was topless, she had every right to want *me* to be topless, too, didn't she? But when I thought about what that meant and the fact my binder would come off and I'd be able to look down my body and see my own breasts, it made me remember sex with Henry. And I didn't like it, and I didn't want it, and I had this horrible, sudden feeling of wrongness. I shouldn't have breasts, and I didn't want to see them.

And I didn't know how to say it, because it wasn't fair to her, was it? "Sorry, I— I can't have my..." I took a breath. "I mean, I don't think I can..."

She silenced me. "It's okay, I get it," she said gently. She didn't sound disappointed or upset at all, it was such a relief. "Can we just take the t-shirt off, though...?"

That was okay because my binder was set in a singlet anyway, so she helped me lift the t-shirt over my head and drop it somewhere behind the couch. She traced my shoulders and my bare arms with her fingertips, but stopped at the hem of my binder. I had been worried she might try and put her hands inside it anyway, but she didn't. She was very careful not to touch me *anywhere* that might remind me what I had underneath it, and I was so grateful. She was trying so hard to make me feel comfortable, and it was working.

When she was done exploring all my newly exposed skin, she dropped her hands again and we just sat there for a minute, looking at each other.

She was *gorgeous*, and she was half-naked in my lap and her cheeks were flushed with a mixture of shyness and excitement.

"Oh my god," she said, giggling nervously. "I can't believe we're doing this. I used to imagine what it would be like..."

"You imagined it...?" I prompted her, interested. I hoped she'd tell me *all* the details. In *full* detail, while I looked hungrily at that body of hers and visualised all of it.

She looked embarrassed. "Yeah, so I've been talking to you online for a while, right?" she said. "And, so, your name is Min Lee, so I figured out you were Korean, and then..." she scrunched up her nose, giggling. "Oh my god, I can't even say it, you're going to laugh."

"Believe me, I am not going to laugh," I said, worried about what I'd do instead. Her body was so close to mine...

She was the one who ended up laughing. "So, like... I don't know, it never occurred to me that you weren't a guy? So, yeah, I kind of Google Videoed Korean guys with the SafeSearch function off..."

That did actually make me laugh. "You *didn't*..."

She crumpled up her face. "I did," she said. "Are you horrified yet?"

"A bit," I said, still chuckling. "Were you disappointed when I posted that photo of me as a woman?"

She pressed her lips together. "Um," she said, grimacing. "I kind of just changed my search parameters...?"

I *laughed*. *"Bree...!"* I said, squinting and making my bruised eye *ache*. "Jesus Christ!"

She stopped laughing, looking down between our bodies. "And, yeah," she said. "This is pretty much what I imagined." She looked up at me. "Only with a *lot* more touching... A lot more."

That sounded *great*. I was up for a lot more touching, and I was so close, *so* close to just doing it. *Fuck*, I was in trouble.

She shifted on me. "So," she began, "like, we can still do the same things we did before, right...?"

I made a non-committal noise.

She leant up to me and kissed my chin, and as she did that, her naked breasts brushed the front of my binder. She sat back. "That was okay, right?"

I could barely nod.

She took a deep breath. "I like it when you whisper in my ear," she said. "And kiss my neck... we did *that* before...?"

I lifted her hair, bending down beside her ear so my breath tickled it. Her own breath was fast on my shoulder, and down between us, I could feel those breasts heaving against my front every time she inhaled. When my fingers trailed gently up her arm, they found goose bumps. *God*. She was practically quivering. She *wanted* this, she wanted *me*. It was all I could do not to just *take* her.

I managed not to. *Somehow* I managed not to. "I'm so into you," I breathed into her ear. "Bree... I want to *do* things to you..."

She stopped breathing for a moment. "Then *do* them," she murmured. "Do them..."

I didn't. I just kissed down her neck, listening to each and every breath she struggled to draw. I found a spot under her ear that made her *groan*, and I kissed it over and over, pressing my chin into it and dragging my lips across it. She moved in my lap, leaning into it, leaning into *me*, her hands restless on my thighs.

Eventually she sat up from me, flushed from exertion, and so, *so* turned on and said, *"You're* not allowed to touch me," she said. "But *I* can touch myself, can't I?"

The mental image of that was almost too much. She was *killing* me. "No," I said. "Please don't, I—*Fuck.* This is hard enough as it is..."

We were staring at each other. God, I was losing my resolve, she was driving me crazy. I was *salivating.*

"I want you so much, Min," she said, breathless. "I'm, like, *dying.* And, like, I know about Henry... I know... but I still want you to do *everything* to me. And I feel *terrible* that I want that, but... I can see how much you want it, and I don't see how not having sex with me changes that you've already been cheating on him." She made a face. "Does that make me a bad person?"

No, I thought. God, Bree, you're fucking *anything* but a bad person. "I just feel like there should be one line that isn't crossed..."

"I'm topless," she pointed out. "And I'm on your lap. And we're both so up for it... I don't really see what the difference is. If you were doing this with someone else I'd be upset whether or not you went through with it. And I want you, Min, I want you so much..." She double-took and made a face. "Oh my god, listen to me, that's an awful thing to say, that's awful. I'm sorry, I'm so sorry, I shouldn't have—"

I shushed her, feeling *terrible* that she felt guilty about it. *I'd* let it get this far, every bit of this was my fault, Bree was in *no way* responsible for what was going on, but she was still sitting across my lap, and I'd got her to a point where she was begging me. If I said no here, she was right. I was hurting *two* people, both Henry *and* Bree. I'd already done the wrong thing by Henry, I was already a fucked up person for it. No small technicality was going to rescue me from that, no matter how much I wanted it to. Whether or not I went through with it now, I'd already cheated on him. And Bree was right here, ready for me, waiting for me... At least I could make one of them happy.

That just happened to be the answer every part of me *wanted* to come to, as well. I didn't second-guess it in case I came to a different conclusion.

Exhaling forcefully, I pulled her right up against me. "This is *my* fault, not yours," I breathed, and then I *kissed* her. Hard. She made this tiny little sound and then pressed all up against me, wrapping her arms around behind my head and writhing into me.

605

My hands were around her for a second, feeling her naked back and the hair falling onto it, and then they were around the front of her *grabbing* and *kneading* those breasts and her tummy and her thighs and everything I could hold onto. I couldn't kiss her deeply enough. I couldn't hug her tightly enough. I couldn't be pressed firmly enough against her, I wanted more of her, *more* of her, and my head throbbed and my eye *ached* and my cheek hurt but I just *didn't fucking care.*

I let her pull me down on top of her, and she fell back onto the blankets on the couch, her breasts spread across her ribs and her legs splayed and wrapped around my thighs. Leaning over her I kissed her: first her mouth and those lips and that neck and those collarbones... then I moved down her body. I kissed her skin, I licked across it, I buried my nose in her belly and kissed along the hem of her underwear. I could go further, I thought. I could keep going. I could take a mouthful of what was underneath and have her writhing and squirming and *crying out* as I did it.

She didn't want me to right now, though, she hooked her hands under my shoulders and pulled me up again. "Not yet," she said. "It's just... I don't know, isn't it, like, really full on for your first time with a girl? Do you *really* want to do that to me?"

What a question. "Yes," I said without hesitation.

She laughed. "Okay," she said. "It's just that I'm *really* wet and I didn't want you to be grossed out or something..."

I kissed her briefly. "I would *love* to go down on you," I told her.

She *blushed* a deep, deep crimson. It even spread down her neck. "Oh my god," she said, and took a moment to recover before stretching up to kiss me, pulling me back down on top of her.

When I got there, though, she made a face. "The jeans are a bit..."

"Scratchy?" I finished, and she nodded, and helped me take them off. As soon as I'd settled back down against her, she *gasped* and then smiled, and then laughed helplessly. I didn't know what she meant until she pushed her hips up into mine; the packer was pressing against a key point on her. A point that made her jaw slack and her eyes heavy-lidded. She rolled her hips into me, and when she pushed upwards, she drove the packer against a key point on *me.* I couldn't put something this soft inside her,

606

but, *fuck*, if this wasn't the next best thing we could do with it...

So, yeah, *yeah*, this was going to work. This was going to work, and I let her pull me down into another kiss, her naked calves wrapping up around my now-naked thighs. The feeling of skin-on-skin was *sexy*.

I bore down on her, pushing into her, rocking against her, moving our hips together and, *fuck*, appreciating how *good* it felt. It wasn't just all physical, either. These movements, *these* ones, *this* was right. It felt right. I felt like I was making love to her the way I wanted to, and watching her face every time I reached the end of a thrust... *this* was what I wanted.

Her breathing was erratic on my lips, and she broke away from me to whisper, "Faster..."

I did what she said. Her eyes fell shut and her mouth dropped open, but no sound came out of it. She just froze there, poised against me as I moved on her and it was hot, it was *so* hot, watching her teetering on the brink of letting go and watching her parted lips as she gasped and struggled to breathe and grabbing at the blankets, the couch, at *me*...

"Don't stop," she told me urgently, "*Please* don't stop..."

And then she was gasping, holding her breath, begging me to keep going and finally she *cried* out, her thighs shaking and her hips *driving* into mine and I was watching her face, watching what I'd done to her and all the joy and pleasure and *release* I'd given her as she laughed and *groaned* and arched into me...

When she finally relaxed back into the couch, panting like she'd run a marathon, she pulled me on top of her and kissed me gently.

"Min..." she murmured into my lips. "Oh my god, that was like...." She never finished her sentence.

This is what it was always supposed to be like, making love to someone. With Henry I'd be checking the clock, but this? I never wanted it to stop. I could spend forever bringing her to the edge and then basking in the afterglow. I just lay against her and listened to her breathing slow.

Her hands stroked my hair, and between kisses she nuzzled my cheek, careful to avoid the gauze and my stitches. I smiled against her lips.

The position was a bit uncomfortable, so I shifted to lie on my side next to her, propped up on an elbow. She traced one of my arms, watching me. I smiled down at her.

"What about you?" she asked.

"What about me?" I repeated.

She gave me a look. "I want to make *you* come."

I made a face. I wasn't sure how that was going to work. "I'll take a raincheck on that," I told her.

Her eyes darted up to the eye Andrej had punched and the gauze pad on my cheek. "Oh... because of your head?"

I'd actually completely forgotten about it, and I was tempted for about a quarter of a second to lie to her the way I had done to Henry. Then I realised how *fucking stupid* that would be.

"No," I said, and then struggled with how to explain why. "I don't know..." ...how I want you to touch me.

I had been looking down my body, and I think she guessed what I meant. "Oh," she said, and reached down me to cup the packer, massaging it into me. "Maybe like this?"

I winced. The actual physical sensation of her pushing that packer against me wasn't too bad, but... unless I was using it on her, it didn't feel... right? And looking down my completely smooth and flat body to the *big* bulge in the Y-fronts was just... no. It was no. And that seemed like a *really* weird thing to try and explain. All of it was so weird: I had these really strong feelings about what was and wasn't right and what should and shouldn't be part of me, and the feelings didn't seem consistent and they didn't seem to make sense. How could I *expect* to have a dick, and feel right about the movements and the actions and yet when it came right down to it, not really want one? Or maybe I *did* want one, and was just in some serious fucking denial about it?

It was weird. It was all so weird. How did people ever navigate these feelings?

"That's not working?" Bree asked, noting my distraction. She stopped.

It wasn't. I reached into my Y-fronts and pulled out the packer, putting it on the coffee table. Bree looked at it, and then at me, and then snorted and started giggling.

I probed the empty cup of the Y-fronts to test how they felt without it, because I wasn't sure *this* was right either. It wasn't, but I thought maybe it might be better than the alternative. The fabric had a couple of thick layers at the front, and when I put my fingers there, the thickness hid the details underneath. It just felt smooth and featureless, and I preferred it like that.

We could try this, I thought, but I felt really uncomfortable about asking her for it. In the end I didn't need to, because she reached downward again and said, "Show me?"

I led her hand to my underwear and placed it on top, using my fingers on hers to gently show her the movement I needed. She nodded, a little smile on her face. "Okay."

I rested my head beside hers on the blankets, and sucked in a sharp breath when she started to do what I'd shown her. It felt *good*.

She could have looked down at what she was doing, but she didn't, and that made me feel even more comfortable. Her head was next to mine on the blankets, and she was watching my face. And when I gasped, she smiled, and when my breathing got ragged, she looked *so* happy to be the cause of it. She hung on every nuance of my expression, and it was so, so intimate.

And it felt good, it felt good, it felt *so* good, someone was touching me and I didn't hate it, I didn't hate it at all... I *loved* it. I loved how it felt and that it was her hand down there and that when she moved it rocked her breasts on her ribs, and how when I started to heave each breath, *she* started to heave *her* every breath...

"I love watching you," she murmured. "I love imagining how you feel..."

"I feel good," I whispered. "It feels *really* good..."

And it did. The circles she was drawing on me, such tiny, innocuous movements, but at that second, my whole world centred around them. The way the fabric dragged on me, the warmth of her fingers and the friction against my skin... I was wet, too, and I didn't really want to focus too much on that because it seemed wrong, and it *did* seem wrong, but it felt *good*. All of those things together, and... god, I....

I took a handful of the couch, bracing myself against it. If she just kept going, I was going to.... *Fuck*.

"Fuck, Bree..." I whispered. "Bree..."

I pushed into her hand, the breath catching intermittently in my throat. My arm underneath me was shaking from strain, but *fuck* I didn't care. I didn't care about any of that. All I cared about were those circles she was moving me in and those beautiful blue eyes I was staring into and her ragged breaths and *my* ragged breaths and, fuck, *fuck,* I...

I was right on the edge, unable to breath, feeling it all building in me and swelling in my chest and in my hips and...oh, *fuck...*

And then I was *there, shouting* and pressing into her and *shaking*, shaking as my muscles clenched and my thighs closed around her hand and I curled up and into her, laying my own hand over hers on my underwear and *mashing* it against the fabric and the skin underneath. It didn't stop, it *didn't* stop, I kept having wave after wave of it and she pushed back against me and kept moving and *fuck*.... fuck, it was so... it felt so *good*.

I didn't have to *pretend*. I didn't have to act. I didn't have to do any of those things and none of it was duty or obligation or because I thought I was supposed to. It was because I wanted it, and she wanted it, and, god, I wanted her.

I relaxed back against her, my arm still shaking as I tried to catch my breath. My blood *hummed* and my body *sang*, and... God...

Fuck. Just... fuck.

Wow.

I laughed into her neck. She withdrew her hand, and in my peripheral vision I could see her shaking out her wrist as she made a pained noise. I laughed at that, too.

"Did I do good?" she asked brightly, knowing the answer.

I groaned because I didn't have any words yet, and when I searched for them, I only found one. "Wow," was what I managed.

Bree wrapped her arms around me, and I could feel her smiling against my forehead. She didn't say anything. She just laughed with me. I snuggled into her, listening to that sound. She was warm, and we were both a bit sweaty, but I didn't care. I loved her half-naked with her arms around me, us lazily reclined over each other. *This* was how it was supposed to be.

I couldn't breathe properly with my nose under her neck, so when my arm had stopped tingling, I propped myself back up again, drawing shapes on her torso with my fingertips.

She watched me with a *big* smile on her face.

"What's this for?" I asked, leaning down and kissing her smile.

"You," she said simply. "Us." She gazed thoughtfully up at me. "You know, sometimes I feel like you kind of shut me out," she told me. "Like you have this particular place you get to and then you're like, 'nope! Shop's closed!'. And when you do that I kind of wonder if I did something wrong or if you don't really like me after all or whatever... but today, it's like you've just... I don't know. You just let go of it all. You're, like, *here* with me."

I knew the reason for that. I could remember every detail of cutting off my hair and watching it fall away from my scalp as I *cried and cried* over what I was letting go of, and that I was still alive to be able to.

"Last night..." I reminded her. I think she'd already guessed.

She nodded, and tenderly touched my cheek. "I know," she said, tracing my chin and my shoulders. "How are you now, though? Like, right now?"

There was only one answer for that. "Happy," I said, and kissed her. "Today..." I shook my head. "Today was the kind of day that you *dream* about. It's the kind of day you lie on your death bed and remember every wonderful detail of. I didn't have *any* respect left for myself, but after today..." I smiled. "Well, I fuck up, I know that. We all do. But I did stuff today that I would never in a million years have thought I was able to do." I smiled. "But I did it, I *did* it. And last night... well, last night I never thought that I could."

She nodded, a bit teary. "And just think," she said quietly. "If you'd killed yourself, you'd never have done it and you'd never have had today."

She kissed me, and I kissed her back, and we pulled the blankets over us and lay together in each other's arms.

We'd been cuddling there together for god knows how long when I heard my phone chime from the kitchen counter. I nearly didn't get it, but my curiosity won out.

"Hang on a second," I told Bree, slipping out from under the blankets, hauling myself off the couch and padding across the floor to it.

I noticed my headache was gone as I pulled the slider to unlock my phone; I wanted to attribute it to sex, but it also could have been the Panadol I took earlier. I thought about that as I wondered who'd texted me. Sarah might have guessed what I was up to, I thought. I wouldn't have put it past her to send me a cheeky text message about it.

When I opened it, though, it was from *Henry*.

"*Be around in 10 if you need to get ready xoxo*," it said. I put my face in my free hand and groaned.

Of course, it was *Thursday*. In all the day's commotion I had completely and utterly forgotten that I'd made plans with Henry for tonight.

I looked back at Bree spread on my couch, and then down at my own body. Ten minutes, hey? *Shit*.

This was it, wasn't it?

THIRTY-ONE

In reality, there was no way I actually had a full ten minutes to get Bree out of my apartment. Henry was as bad as I was, he'd probably arrived fifteen minutes ago and had been waiting in his car for an appropriate, non-creepy level of early to text me. That meant I really needed to get Bree out *now* or risk them meeting in the corridor, and the very last thing I wanted was for Henry to invite her in and have us all sit together and sip tea and talk about the weather. To avoid that, 'right now' was almost too late to be kicking her out.

"I need to go home anyway," Bree said miserably while we were both trying to frantically fasten the ten million buttons on the front of her sundress. "Andrej's probably already there and making up some twisted, crazy story about how you attacked him and he was only defending himself but *of course* the police believed *you*..."

Meanwhile, I was alternating between swearing repeatedly and feeling *terrible* for kicking her out *now* of all times. "Fuck him," I said, finishing with the last button and then trying to smooth down her hair. "Come back here tonight. I'll give you some money for dinner while I'm busy."

Her hair wasn't cooperating, but she stood patiently and let me wrangle it anyway. "Trust me, once I've lain on it, it's a lost cause," she told me as I tried and failed to smooth it into a less spherical shape. While I was doing that, she reached up and gently tested the skin around my eye. I flinched, because it *hurt*. "I'm sorry," she said again. "I still can't believe he *punched* you. He's never done anything like that before."

"Well, I was standing in between him and his ability to bury his head in horse-racing," I pointed out, bustling her over to where she'd taken her shoes off. "And then I tore up his ticket to that."

"I know, but I *still* can't believe he punched you." She said, sitting down against the wall and pulling one of her shoes on. I knelt down next to her and got the other one. "Like, not that it's great that you've got this huge painful bruise on your face, but it's awesome that you can press charges against him." She stopped for a moment in the middle of tying her laces. "It's just weird that he punched *you*. Like, he goes around telling everyone *I* ruin his life and blaming *me* for everything he does, and some of it I seriously think he believes. I mean, about taking your stuff, he was like, 'Your friend owes me for Easter, do you know how fucking shitty it was with everyone angry at you not being there, Bree? *I* had to endure that because you were too selfish to come home. Your friend *owes* me', and I swear to god he was serious. So I'm pretty sure even though he's *full* of it, he actually does think I'm this terrible person. But he's never, like, actively tried to physically hurt me before."

Something occurred to me while I got the shoe she'd abandoned. I looked up at her. "Wait, do you think he's going to try and do something to you now because of what happened?" I still had that image of him *shaking* her fresh in my mind.

She shook her head, still looking thoughtful. "Nah, that's not what I meant."

That wasn't good enough for me. "Come on, at least let me take you home myself. I can probably ask Henry to wait for twenty minutes while I do that. He'll understand."

She rolled her eyes. "Min, I've been doing this for ages, remember? I'll be okay." She pushed me with her foot. "And nice try."

I looked across at her, pausing in the middle of double-knotting her laces.

Her arms were crossed. "I'm *so* not giving you *another* reason to put off breaking up with him. He's probably right outside and you're all like, 'Oh, how about that, Bree needs to be taken home so I guess I can't do it after all, bye'."

Ouch. "I will do it," I said, bracing myself on my bent knee and standing up. "I promise."

I held out my hand and pulled her up, too, and she looked charmed by that. "Did you just help me get dressed and put my shoes on?" she asked me. "What am I, like, six?"

"Well, it seemed a bit rude to throw you out here half-naked," I said neutrally.

"Says Ms. Would-Dress-Me-Like-a-Nun-If-Possible." She stopped giggling abruptly and said, "Wait, wait, '*Mr*'? I can't call you my boyfriend if I'm going to 'she' you, can I? It should match."

"I should match, too," I told her, "But I don't. Come on." I caught sight of the clock and shooed her towards the hallway. Before I opened the door, I put a 50 in her hand and checked Henry wasn't already waiting in the corridor.

Bree had gone back to looking wistful while I did that. "You know," she began, "I used to have this dream all the time that I came home from school one day and everything was back to normal. Like I'd walk in the door and everything was the way it always used to be, my parents were relaxed and happy and Andrej was locked in his room on the Internet, and I could smell dinner waiting for me in the kitchen. Mum would nag me to do homework. Dad would be clearing the gutters or fixing a tile on the roof or something, singing shitty 70s songs at the top of his voice. And now, every time I leave somewhere to go home, even though I *know* it won't be... this tiny part of me hopes that *that* will be the home I'll go back to."

Oh, Bree. I touched her cheek. "Maybe one day it will be."

She shook her head, resigned. "Nah, I know it won't. Not even with this police thing, because he has to be found guilty of fraud for that three hundred thousand to not be owed and there is *no way* my parents are going to charge him. Like, no way." She sighed. "And I know that, I do. But, like, even now as I walk through this door," she stepped out of it, "that tiny little part of me still hopes there's a home like that waiting for me."

I couldn't go out into the corridor with her because I was still in my binder and Y-fronts, so I just leant on the doorway. I caught her hand through the open door, though. It was on the tip of my tongue: 'if you can't have a happy home there, *I'll* give you one', but I didn't say it. She knew it, but it wasn't the same. It wasn't the same as having her happy family back.

"I want things to work out for you," was all I told her.

She sighed. "Yeah, I want things to work out for you, too," she said, changing the subject. "Are *you* going to be okay? Like, telling Henry? Is there anything I can do to help?"

I squeezed her hand. "Not unless you've got a time machine you can lend me."

She brightened. "I *wish*." She pulled me down for a kiss before releasing me. "And now I have to go before you get out of telling him!" she said, and jumped up and kissed me again, and then left.

I closed my front door and watched through the peephole as she went. Someone got out of the lift when it opened and Bree nearly collided with him. She apologised profusely and they had a brief conversation before they stepped around each other and she hopped inside the lift herself. The guy walked away from that exchange smiling, and she was smiling too as the doors to the lift began to close. She must have guessed I was still watching her, because she gave me a cheerful wave through the gap before she disappeared.

My face felt like it was about to crack down the middle from the smile plastered across it, starting with my taut stitches. I gingerly touched them, wincing. I didn't have time to dwell on that now, though, *because in like five seconds Henry was going to be here*. I quickly cleaned around the couch, stashed the packer and rushed off towards the bathroom.

I wanted to have a shower before facing him, because I probably smelt like Bree's vanilla shampoo and god knows what else and it seemed *really* disrespectful to have any of that on me when he showed up. So I texted him to let himself in and then shut myself in the bathroom.

I couldn't really wash my hair because of the gauze on my face, but I washed everything else, and just as I was putting the t-shirt back on and making my hair symmetrical, I heard my front door open and close.

My heart started pounding. *This was it.*

He's here, I thought. Here's here, I have to do this *Jesus fuck* I have to do this.

Every part of me kept hoping he would just get sick of my shit and take this fabulous opportunity to be the one to dump *me* instead. I made a face as soon as I realised how ironic that was; I'd been worrying for years that he would dump me because I wasn't good enough for him and now I actually *wanted* him to?

I rested my hands on the vanity and just stood there staring at myself in the mirror. He's going to finally see me like this, I thought. I wondered what his reaction would be, and then, imagining all the possibilities, I couldn't bear to face it. What if he was upset?

I heard the cupboards open and close, and then the tap turn on... I could hear sounds of him moving around my apartment too. He was whistling. He had no idea at all what was about to happen. *Fuck.*

Oh, god. Fuck. *Fuck!* How the *fuck* was I going to do this?

He'd been supporting me for four years. He'd done nothing but be completely available and there for me when I needed him. He was generous and kind and he'd just gone to visit my *mother* and she *loved* him, for fuck's sake...

How the *fuck* was I going to do this, really? This was *Henry.*

There was a gentle knock on the bathroom door. "Are you alright, Min?"

His voice was so familiar; I'd forgotten what that sounded like and how comforting it was. It brought back sudden, unwelcome memories of yelling at the PlayStation together, chatting over dinner and the peaceful sound of him breathing next to me in bed at night. And, of course, the first time someone at Frost had smiled at me. That friendly face, and then his laughter when I'd joked with him. He'd looked twice at me then, pleasantly surprised, with a smile that lasted a bit too long. Four years too long.

"Yeah," I called back. "Just give me a second."

Well, I couldn't just hang around in the bathroom all evening, could I? I'd promised Bree I was going to do this now, I'd promised *myself* I was going to do this now, and doing this now was the right thing to do, and it was about fucking time I did the right thing by Henry.

I pushed myself up from the vanity and turned to open the bathroom door, expecting him to be standing there. It was a bit of an anti-climax when he wasn't.

Where I actually found him was reclined on the couch in the living room beside all the blankets and pillows—which he'd folded neatly, of course—wearing a nice suit and waiting patiently for me to emerge.

When I did, hesitantly and waiting for his shock and surprise and whatever other emotions he might have, *I* was the one that was surprised.

As if I didn't look at all different from usual, he pushed himself up from the couch with a calm smile. "There you are," he said, approaching me. "I was beginning to think I'd need to send in Search and Rescue."

I stood there, my heart *pounding*, waiting for him to comment on how I looked. Waiting for that smile to fall.

It didn't. In fact, when he stood back and considered me with exaggerated concentration, I could tell immediately that he wasn't being serious. "You've changed something," he said light-heartedly. Then he clicked his fingers and pointed at me. "I know. New lipstick?" He was grinning.

I wasn't wearing any makeup. "Henry..."

He pretended to swear under his breath. "Okay, it's not the lipstick. Different hair colour?"

Unsurprisingly, what was left of my hair was black and that was his point, he didn't want to talk about what *was* different. Of course he didn't. And, *fuck*, it was *so* tempting to just go with it, just one last time. I loved sparring with him. We *couldn't*, though. Not now.

My expression must have troubled him because his smile wavered. The minute I saw that, I panicked. I just couldn't bear it. I couldn't bear to see him falter like that, and it was almost a reflex to rescue him.

I deadpanned. "You don't have to pretend, I know how it looks. I mean, I told the hairdresser one or two inches off the ends, and..." I gestured at my head. "Do you think anyone will notice?"

He looked *so* relieved I could see him visibly relax. "No, it's very subtle," he said. "I think you're safe." He leant in to kiss me, and I turned my head away so he couldn't. He did *not* miss a beat as he stood back. "Worried I'll take out the other cheek?"

"You *do* look sharp today, I couldn't take any chances," I shot back, and then *cursed* myself; what are you *doing,* Min? I took a deep breath and opened my mouth to shut down our banter, but he was already speaking.

"Are you alright, anyway? What happened?" he asked me in a more sober tone as he reached up like Bree had done to touch the skin around the eye. I let him. "I heard there was some commotion at work today. Did you get into a fight as well?"

"Yeah, with Diane and Sean Frost," I said. "Oh, and my senior manager. Unfortunately, none of *those* people was the one who punched me or I'd be a millionaire by now."

"Who *did* punch you, just out of curiosity?"

I winced. "Andrej."

He recognised the name and his eyebrows went up. Because of whose brother he was, that answer stopped him asking any more questions about my face. He just nodded and tilted my chin so he could survey the damage.

"Well," he said, while he was considering my injuries. "I heard along the grapevine that your fight with Jason was quite intense." His hand dropped and, with the straightest expression in the world, he added, "Maybe even... a boss fight."

I *groaned.* "You *didn't,*" I accused him, and gave him a shove. "That's *terrible.*"

He laughed, looking pleased with himself. "Reservation's for seven. Let's go eat."

As he walked towards the door, I remembered what I was supposed to be doing, and the smile dropped right off my face. Now's your chance, Min, I thought.

I didn't follow him and he noticed, half-turning towards me. "You still want to go to dinner tonight, right? To celebrate a successful pitch? I booked somewhere *really* nice, you'll love it."

"Henry..." I sighed.

He persisted. "I think they even serve that gold label red wine you really like," he said. "Or maybe we could do champagne this time, now that your stressful project is over and you can finally relax?"

I closed my eyes briefly. "Henry, please. Look at me."

He opened his mouth, hesitating for a moment. He was struggling and it was *so* painful to see him do that. Eventually, he said, "Well, if you'd feel more comfortable we can always go somewhere more casual."

It was *awful* listening to him doing this. "Aren't we going to talk about how I look?"

"We did, Min," he pointed out. "You've cut your hair. Look, it's quite dramatic, but a lot of the celebrities are starting to get rather masculine haircuts, so I suppose it must be in at the moment. Just don't Skype your Mum until it's grown out a bit, okay? You'll give her a heart attack."

It was so tempting to just leave this conversation. To agree with him, to go to dinner, to relax and pretend everything was fine. I couldn't, though, not anymore. I *had* to do this.

I bit my lip, and pulled my t-shirt flat across my front. I was wearing the binder, so there wasn't much to look at. "And this," I said. "This is pretty masculine, too, isn't it?"

His eyes dipped to my smooth chest, and then returned to my face. He asked very carefully, "How are you expecting me to respond to that, Min?"

I dropped my hands, sighing heavily. "I don't know, Henry. Hurt? Confusion?" I said. "*Something*?"

As soon as I'd said that, I realised *exactly* what was so wrong. He *wasn't* responding. If Henry had arrived here in a dress with long, curled hair and make-up, I would have been *shocked* by the suddenness of it. I would have been confused and hurt that there was apparently this big part of him that he wasn't sharing with me. And I may not actually have shown him either of those things, but I sure as hell wouldn't have been able to act like everything was perfectly normal. He was, and I couldn't figure out how or why.

"You think I should be confused because you got your hair cut?" he asked, as if I was overreacting. He walked back over to me, his face in a gentle smile. "Don't be silly," he said. "I know why you've done it, and if you find it liberating, then I'm happy for you."

Somehow, I couldn't believe that he *did* know why I'd done it. "Why do you think I did it, then?"

He put his hands on my shoulders. "What happened to you in high school has always stayed with you, and I know a big component of that was the fact people had trouble distinguishing whether you were a boy or a girl. With things being so difficult for you at work at the moment, I imagine there's a certain freedom in just reclaiming that and owning it so you can feel like you triumphed over that part of your life." He paused. "And I'm not sure I should be saying this: but to be honest, Min, I think that's what Bree's about, too. Didn't you tell me right after you'd met her that she reminded you of the girls who teased you?"

I just frowned at him. I'd never thought about it like that, and that worried me.

He clapped my shoulders and dropped his arms. "So, no, Min, I'm not confused. I *am* hurt, because wouldn't you be if your partner was sleeping with someone else?" I flinched. "But I understand you're still deeply affected by the events from high school, so if doing all this helps you heal and close that part of your life so you can let yourself be happy..." He smiled. "Then I'm happy."

My heart was already racing, but I started to be able to feel it hammering against my ribcage.

Fuck, was he *right*? I hated doubting my judgment, and I hated this feeling of not knowing and not understanding myself, and—no, that wasn't it. I hated *caring* that I didn't understand myself. I'd been fine all day with no desire to figure everything out straight away and had continued to be fine until this very moment.

And now I was just standing here with my jaw open and with absolutely no idea which one of us had a clearer head about my gender issues. We both had such a deep investment in being right that it was the same tangle of feelings I'd had earlier in the day when Andrej and I were...

I swallowed. No, I'd been right, then. And I was right about *this* as well.

I *wasn't* trying to reclaim anything by transitioning, that wasn't what it was about. The feelings were deeper than that, and if I thought back to *why* I'd always wanted baggy uniforms in the first place and *why* I'd wanted my hair cut short at twelve, all of this went back to before I was teased. It just became a problem in high school when I didn't look how people expected me to.

Being with Bree wasn't about making peace with my bullies, either. Bree was about the fun I had with her. She made me happy, and even though she was so screwed up and prone to *terrible* decisions, she still tried to the best of her ability to be good and do good. There was so much to admire in that. When I kissed her, when I held her, I was doing those things for the same reasons other couples did, and for reasons that were *never* present when I let Henry touch me.

Bree and I clicked together like pieces in a jigsaw. I was big and she was small. I was quiet and she was loud. Her body had curves and mine had edges, I looked out for her and she took care of me. It was *right*, and I had never felt that with Henry. Never. I enjoyed his company, I really liked him as a person, I even loved him. But he and I were the same piece of the puzzle, we had the same gaps. We didn't complement each other.

He wasn't right about this one, and I'd deferred to his wisdom about things so often in the past that actually hearing myself think 'Henry's wrong' was *jarring*.

And it was jarring, too, hearing him dismiss the things I'd done to him so easily. "Henry," I said, "that's fucked up. You're *happy* about the things I've done?"

He made a face. "Poor wording," he conceded. "But I understand why you're doing them."

I shook my head slowly. "I don't think you do," I said. "I'm not using Bree to come to terms with high school, and I'm not dressed like this because I'm 'reclaiming' my past. It's more than that."

He didn't look convinced, but he tried to be kind in the way he explained himself to me. "Min," he said gently. "It's been one, maybe two months—only the duration of this incredibly stressful project—that you've even known Bree or had any interest in changing yourself."

The implication, of course, being that none of it was genuine, just a result of me being fucked up over work. "Henry, it doesn't matter how long it's been. I'm not using Bree, and I know how I feel about myself."

He made a face. "It *does* matter how long it's been. For the first one to three months of a relationship, your body is flooded with chemicals that give you a natural high, and so I can understand that—"

I interrupted him. "—Henry, I'm not using Bree."

He calmly continued. "—And I've watched you for the last four years consume hefty amounts of red wine, pain killers and whatever synthetic chemicals are in energy drinks. I know you self-medicate, Min, and I understand it's—"

No. I threw my hands up. "Henry, stop!" I told him. "Stop. We're talking about a person, here. A real person with real feelings, and I am *not* using her. She's not a drug to me. I'm not sleeping with a bottle of red wine, I'm sleeping with another person. I've cheated on you. Doesn't that *mean* something to you?"

I watched his throat bob. He put his hands on my shoulders again. "Min, I love you," he said, "and I *know* you. I've watched you cycle in and out of enough bad patches to know that things will get better for you and you'll be happy again. Of *course* it means something to me that you're sleeping with someone else, but it makes sense, so I forgive you for it. And I'd much rather you do something like this now than later when we have children to take care of."

I shrugged off his hands. That was the most hurtful thing: he wasn't *listening* to me, he wasn't trusting my judgement. I knew his reaction was coloured by years of taking care of me when I was really struggling, and he was only doing what he thought was right, but still. *Still.* It hurt that he didn't believe me when I said, 'I'm sure'.

There was no use arguing with him about this. I just needed to cut to the chase.

I took a breath. "Henry, there is no 'happy again'. I haven't been actually *happy* for years." I said it as kindly as I could, because he had to hear it. "And there's not going to be any children."

The look on his face… he hadn't been expecting me to say that, and it *hurt* him. "Maybe if you tried anti-depressants again you might feel differently about having—"

"No." I watched him. "I know enough about myself to know I'm not supposed to carry children, and I—"

"—well, there's always adoption," he interjected, desperation audible. "It's quite popular these days, and what with our work, it would mean that—"

"—Henry." He stopped talking and we stood there watching each other for a moment. "I need you to hear this: the past few weeks,

I've realised that my body issues aren't because I was bullied in high school. They're because I'm *transgender*, and I don't really know what that means about where I'll end up yet, but—"

"Then don't you want to wait until you *do* know what it means before you do anything rash?" he asked me. "Before you throw the baby out with the bathwater?"

"I know enough to know the changes I'm making are right," I told him, "and Bree's been supporting me and—"

"And I understand why it would have been so hard to come to me about this," he said, his hands up as he tried to placate me. "These topics are very difficult for people to raise with loved ones, and so it all makes sense that you'd need to find someone else to confide in and—"

I stopped him. "Can you stop minimising this?" I asked him. "Can you just stop? I *cheated* on you, and I've been hiding this very big personal issue from you, and you've somehow reduced this to a matter of me going through a 'bad patch'."

"I recognise that, Min," he told me. "But *why* people do things matters. I don't believe for a second that you don't care about me, so I know you didn't do any of this because you don't care about my feelings. You did all this because you were in a very bad place with compromised judgement, and so I don't blame you for—"

"—can you *stop* that?" I cut him off. "*Stop* making excuses for me! *Blame* me, for fuck's sake! I deserve it! I've done something awful to you, my judgement *wasn't* compromised when I did it, and I did it anyway!"

"And I forgive you for it, Min!" he said, his voice wavering. "I forgive you, because you're the woman I want to spend the rest of my life with, and in *every* relationship there are ups and downs!"

I couldn't bear it. "I'm not, Henry," I told him. "I'm not the woman you want to spend the rest of your life with. I'm not even a woman!"

He was beginning to fray around the edges. I could see him clench and unclench his hands, straighten his suit jacket. "You said you didn't know if you were—"

"I know that much!" I told him. "And I'm trying to tell you something here, I'm trying to tell you that I've been cheating on you and I have feelings for her, and I'm trying to tell you something *deeply* personal about me and who I am and you're *not listening*. You're not listening to me! It's like you just want to carry on as normal and pretend everything's fine and nothing's wrong and—"

Something in him *broke*. "—You want to know the *truth*, Min?" he asked, and his voice snapped like a cut guitar string. "You want to know what's *really* going on in here?" He tapped his head. "It's like this: if I take what you're saying at face value, it means," his voice caught, "it means that this woman I'm in *love* with, this woman I've spend the last few years of my life supporting, loving and imagining my future with, the woman I want to marry and raise a family together with and grow old with *doesn't exist*. And you're just standing here demanding I accept that without thinking about the last few years we've had together, and accepting that—"

"—you *have* to accept that, Henry," I told him. "You *have* to, because it's—"

"*Think about what you're asking me to accept*, Min!" he said, raising his voice. "Think about the reality you're demanding I face! Could *you* face it? *Could you*?"

I gaped at him. I'd never heard him shout at someone before; he'd shouted at cooking, the PlayStation, he'd shouted when he was angry with Sean, but he'd never shouted *at me.*

It didn't last long. He cupped my cheeks in his hands, careful to avoid my stitches. "Min," he pleaded with me, "Min, it's been four years. *Four years*. Do you really want to throw that away after a single month? It feels self-destructive, it feels like you're doing all these terrible things to try and push me away because you want to fulfil the prophecy you've always been afraid of: that you don't deserve anyone. I don't want you to push me away just because you want to punish yourself—"

"—I'm not punishing myself, and I know it's only been a month, but—"

"It *has* only been a month," he said. "Can you *really* know in a month? Is that really enough time to undo four years of knowing someone? Three years of a relationship with them? Is one month really enough?"

Unexpectedly, my eyes were swimming. "Yes," I said simply.

His were too, and each of his breaths was ragged. "I don't

believe it," he said shortly. "I don't believe it. I don't want to let you throw everything away, everything you've worked so hard for, everything we've done together—"

"Please, Henry," I said quietly, "Please..."

He shook his head tightly. "No," he said. "No, I can't believe it."

My throat was so tight. "You have to," it was barely more than a breath. "Henry, it's *over.*"

He released my face, taking a step away from me, and... *god*, I watched him crack. I watched my pillar of strength, the man who'd supported me and loved me and been there for me *shake* and crumble in front of my eyes. I watched all of it, knowing it was my fault.

His face crumpled, and tears spilt down his cheeks, and from deep within this chest he made this strangled noise and when he looked at me he wasn't hiding it anymore. It was all there, in every line on his face: *despair.*

I took a few steps towards him with the intention of offering him comfort, but he stepped away from me. "No," he hissed, his voice loaded with emotion. "No, please don't."

I didn't. I stood away from him as he struggled to breathe, stepping this way and that, clutching at his hair... eventually he collapsed on the couch with his head in his hands and *cried.* Deep, open sobs, his throat raw and his chest heaving and, *god,* I'd never heard a man cry like that before.

The worst part was, the man was *Henry.* My funny, light-hearted, patient Henry. He'd held me when *I'd* cried. It was *his* soothing voice that talked me down from panic attacks and comforted me when *I* was struggling. We'd talked houses, children, growing old together and for the past three years, when he looked at me I could see those dreams in his eyes.

He was the first person to love me unconditionally. The first person who wrapped his arms around me and made me feel safe and grounded and loved. There was security in him, he'd always been like a lighthouse to me while I tried to figure out where to sail.

And I was letting go of that. I was cutting the rope and pushing out to sea. I was letting go of him and setting off on a voyage without his guiding light.

As much as it hurt, as much as *he* hurt, it was *right.*

"Can you give me a minute?" he asked, not looking at me.

I opened my mouth, but I didn't know what to say. I just closed it again and left. The only place to go sit was out on the balcony, so I went and slid the door open, closing it behind me and walking out to the railing.

The beautiful day had turned into a beautiful evening, and as the sunlight faded all the city started to glow against the sky. The opera house was lit in multi-colours again; cycling through greens and blues and reds as I watched it. Peak-hour traffic was beginning to slow on the bridge, and below the hotel, out on the street, couples walked hand-in-hand towards restaurants. Families arrived fresh from the airport to check in the hotel. Out on the balcony of an adjoining building I could see a woman sipping a glass of white and turning the page of her book. There was a dog barking somewhere.

Henry and I had broken up, and everywhere, life went on.

I turned one of the chairs out to face the view because I didn't have that much time left to appreciate it. From memory, I recalled hearing that employees were generally given a week to clear their belongings after their contracts finished; I was assuming it was the same if I was terminated. Either way, I should really start packing.

That's when it really hit home for me. 'Packing' meant leaving, leaving the place I'd called home. It meant leaving the company I'd absolutely sacrificed myself to for the past five years, and venturing out into an unknown job market and with nowhere to live yet. I'd always assumed that if I left Frost I'd move in with Henry—and he'd said several times I was welcome to do that—but I'd left him, too.

I was leaving everything, everything I believed and thought I knew about myself behind. The person who was going to walk out of this apartment didn't even resemble the person who walked into it, and that was *terrifying.* Despite the fact it was terrifying, and despite the fact I had *no idea* what I was going to do next with myself, I was doing the right thing. And because of that, I knew that somehow I'd be okay.

I'd been sitting out in the fading twilight, trying to picture what my life was going to look like now when I heard the balcony door slide open and closed.

There was a scrape of a metal chair leg against the concrete, and Henry appeared beside me. He flopped down into one of the chairs, facing out towards Sydney. He didn't look at me.

I didn't say anything to him, either. His eyes were bloodshot from crying, and there was a tightness in his jaw and a pull in his lips that suggested he was still on the cusp of starting all over again. It was hard to look at. He'd done nothing but care for me, support me and love me, and *this* was how it ended up for him. It just wasn't fair.

I'd been looking at his hand on the armrest because it was just a short distance from mine, and he noticed. He turned it over and opened his palm to me, and I put my hand in his. It was warm and familiar, and when I laced our fingers together, he squeezed them so, so tightly.

Closing his eyes for a moment, fresh tears ran over his cheeks. I wanted to dry them.

"I love you," I said quietly. "I know it's hard to believe."

His eyes were still closed and when he nodded, it was this tiny, almost imperceptible movement. "Just not enough," he murmured. There wasn't anything I could say to that. After a few seconds he opened his eyes. They were glazed. "I keep going over what happened in the last two months and wondering what I could have done differently," he began. "That night you left the restaurant early with Sarah and Rob, should I have stayed over? Maybe you'd have told me about what was troubling you. I knew it had something to do with Rob's 'bloke in a skirt' comment, I just assumed it was because of high school." He drew another deep breath and then released it. "Or maybe I *should* have been more upset when you kissed that other woman, or when I realised there was something going on between you and Bree... I keep trying to figure out what I could have done differently."

I stroked his hand with my thumb. "Probably nothing."

He shook his head. "But you're leaving me," he said aloud, finally looking towards me. "Min, what did I do wrong?"

My heart broke for him. "Henry, you know you didn't do anything wrong."

He turned his head back towards the view, exhaling. "Intellectually, I know that," he said. "Intellectually, I can tell myself that relationships don't always work out despite the best efforts of the people involved in them. But I don't *believe* it. I have this voice

627

in my head reminding me how well we get along, how perfect we seemed for each other and how much we have in common..." He trailed off.

I smiled bleakly. "Too much, in fact," I said, looking down at my flat chest and men's jeans.

He looked across at me again, and for the first time this evening, he spent a while considering how I looked now.

"Is it a mistake to ask what you think?" I wondered aloud.

His face softened and shook his head. "You want to know the first thing I noticed?" he asked, and I nodded. "It really struck me how relaxed you seem. You're normally really on edge, but..." He looked at me. I was reclined in the chair with one leg on the bottom of the railing. "Now, you just look comfortable."

I smiled slightly. "I am, like this."

He drew a deep breath and exhaled at length before he spoke again. "I should have known when you showed me that painting you did," he decided, shaking his head. "No so much that you did it in the first place, but because of how much it bothered you. I should have known."

"*I* should have known. But I didn't. I still kind of don't."

"Are you taking male pronouns now anyway?" he asked. "Even if you're not certain yet?"

The *pronoun* question... "It's up to you," I said honestly. "I don't mind."

He spent another period of time considering that. "I think I *will* use them," he said eventually. "And I don't want you to be upset about what I'm going to say, but," he struggled, "you *are* Min Lee. I understand that, and I know some things will be the same. But you're not the Min Lee I thought I knew, the Min Lee I wanted the white picket fence and children with, and, well, she's gone, isn't she?"

I nodded, remembering holding scissors to her last night in the mirror.

"She's gone. I feel like I've just been told she's passed away. And, Min, I need to lay her to rest. I need to *grieve* for her. I need to grieve for how much I loved her and the dreams I had for the two of us. She was my world, and she's gone. That's easier for me to do if you're a him."

He had his hand on his chest, and I had thought it was because he was hurting, but after a few seconds he reached inside his jacket and pulled out a little black velvet box with a white satin ribbon.

It was a Frost gift box.

I knew it from the posters; I'd designed them. He held it out to me and I looked up at him, alarmed. He shook his head at my expression; eyes downcast. "I'm not proposing," he said. "Take it." I did, letting go of his hand to receive it.

I'd seen so many soft-lensed ads of this moment. The young couple would be sharing a tender moment, and just as the music would drop off, the man would step away from her, and slowly lower himself onto one knee. She'd know immediately what was going to happen, and her lips would part. Smiling up at her, he'd hold out a box just like this. Hesitating, she'd take it, and her hand would make the same motion mine was making now to undo that pristine white ribbon. As soon as she'd seen what was inside, crying, she'd pull her new fiancé off his knee and throw her arms around his neck. Through her laughter and her tears and her disbelief, she'd whisper, '*yes*'.

There were tears in my eyes, too, but I wasn't laughing. I wasn't hugging him, and I wasn't saying yes. I was just staring down at a stunning solitaire diamond and feeling *empty*. The text he'd had embossed on the inside of the box... It read, '*to my best friend and soulmate: will you be my wife?*'.

I could hardly see it, I was crying so much. "A Frost Diamond..."

In my peripheral vision, I could see him nod. "So if things changed and we left Frost, it would remind us of how we met."

I looked down at the diamond for a moment, and then closed the box and passed it back to him.

He shook his head and pushed it back towards me. "What am I going to do with it? Keep it."

I frowned. "Return it," I said. "That's got to be at least *twenty-five thousand dollars* right there."

He didn't change his mind. "27," he said. "And I need the dignity of not having to return it more than I need the money. Keep it, or sell it, or do whatever you want with it. It was always for you anyway."

I could tell he wasn't going to budge on that one, so I put it in the pocket of my jeans and felt it dig uncomfortably into my leg.

"I've been carrying it with me every day for the past few months," he confessed. "Just in case the time was right. I wanted to have it on me so I didn't ever miss the opportunity."

Something occurred to me. "Wait, at work, too?" he nodded. "Did Sean know?"

He turned at looked directly at me. "Why?" he asked flatly. "Did that fuck *tell* you?"

I winced. "He told Bree."

Henry's eyes were narrowed. He took a moment to process that. "And he knew about you two as well?" I probably looked as guilty as I felt, and Henry sat heavily back in his chair, shaking his head quite aggressively. "*Fuck* that man," he said. "Frost is divided on what they think 'Mini' did to piss him off, but whatever it was, *good on you*." His jaw was set. "That fuck just cannot help himself when it comes to the joy it gives him to ruin relationships."

"He didn't really ruin our relationship," I said. "*I* did that."

Henry looked back at me, and I could tell he was trying to decide if he wanted to continue or not. In the end, he decided to. "Just before lunch today, I got a quick call from Sean to say he had a few reports he wanted me to look at, but he couldn't get to his office because he was reviewing something with the security personnel. So I went all the way down to ground floor and into that security room to get a stack of printouts from him. When I got there he didn't give anything to me, he just stood and talked about his wife and his kids and a whole host of other things I really don't care about right now, and that's when I realised that some footage that had been looping directly next to his head wasn't random. It was two people kissing out the front of the building. I recognised Bree first because of the angle, and then I realised that the other person was *you*."

My mouth opened. *That* explained why he hadn't been surprised to see how I looked. *Fuck.* "I'm sorry," I said. "Even though I kind of know that's a poor substitute for not doing fucked up shit in the first place."

"You *did* do the wrong thing," he finally acknowledged, "but Sean Frost cashed in on it because he's a psychopathic *bastard*. You didn't do any of that with the intention of hurting me. *He did*." I watched him practically foam at the mouth with how *angry* he was.

"So," I said, pretending to be deathly serious, "I have a business proposition for you." He listened as I continued, "Since money isn't a problem for you and it's about to be for me, if you give me a hundred grand I'll take him out and make it look like an accident."

Henry was squinting at me. "You see, I know you're joking, but I still want you to do it," he said in the same tone I'd spoken in. "Tell me, do you take cheque?"

We laughed a bit over that, and then ended up gazing across at each other again. We've broken up, I thought, remembering that and feeling crap all over again.

He was thinking the same thing, and his eyes shone with tears. "I don't know how I'm going to get through this," he said eventually. "I'm going to *miss* you, Min."

My stomach dropped. "We can't stay friends?"

"I don't know," he said honestly. "It might be too painful for me."

That made me feel like I was going to cry again, and he saw it, reached between us and put a hand on my shoulder. "Can we just sit here and talk for a bit now, though?" he asked, his voice breaking a little. "You know me so well, and I'm not going to have that again with someone for a *long* time."

I smiled at him and nodded, and as we let go of 'us' and all the dreams and plans we'd shared, we sat side-by-side on my balcony together for the last time.

THIRTY-TWO

It was nearly midnight when Henry left my place. I'd made the mistake of offering him some of my red, and despite the fact he was normally a very moderate drinker he did the full bottle in about an hour. That didn't really change anything except the fact that when he got up to leave he needed to transport himself along surfaces to get to the door. I followed him at a safe distance, and then caught him when he tripped over my shoes in the hallway. He was much more solid than I was and I nearly went over with him, but we somehow managed not to fall in a heap.

"I think I may have drunk a little too much," he observed mildly as we stood back up.

I didn't let go of him straight away, because I was worried he'd just fall over again. It was difficult for me to see him like this. "I'm still good," I told him. "I'll drive you home."

He shook his head. "You're too tired. I'll just grab a taxi." He was probably right, so I didn't argue the point.

We stood there for a moment, arms awkwardly around each other. He didn't look at me.

"So this is it," he said eventually. "This is goodbye."

That word felt like a punch in the stomach. "I hope we can stay friends," I said quietly. "You know, when you're ready to."

He still didn't look up at me. "Me too," he said. "It's just in those situations someone usually gets hurt, so even though I want to..." He let the sentence trail off.

"Then I hope it's me," I told him. "I'll deal with it. I probably deserve it, anyway."

He didn't look like he agreed with me. Another silence fell between us.

He spent a while grappling with what he was going to say before he spoke again. "Listen, Min, I have a really big favour to ask," he began, looking up at me. His eyes were still bloodshot. "Can you... not tell your mum straight away? I know she's going to call me repeatedly and try and get me to change your mind when she finds out." He looked pained. "And as long as I wish I *could* change your mind, I just can't deal with that. I need some time."

I hadn't been planning on telling her immediately. There was absolutely no part of any of the changes I was making that she would *ever, ever* accept.

I nodded. "I don't really know what to say to her, anyway."

He smiled faintly. "Thank you. I'm sorry. I know it's wrong of me to try and control who you do and don't tell now that you feel like you're able to—"

"—yeah, and *how dare* you ever ask for anything from anyone? After all the things you do for other people?" I finished with a grin. "You *selfish bastard*!"

He laughed a bit at that, and when he looked up at me there was such affection in his eyes. It might have been because he was drunk, or he might have done it anyway, but before he'd second-guessed himself, he leant in and kissed me. He froze immediately, probably expecting me to push him away. I should have, but I didn't. This was the last time he'd get to do it, and honestly? It was *Henry*. I wasn't attracted to him, but kissing him was okay.

When he inhaled and stepped in against me, though, I did push him gently away. I didn't want to lead him on.

He staggered back, his hand flying up to his mouth. "Sorry," he said quickly. "Sorry, I was... Fuck, I'm *drunk*," was how he finished that thought off. "Fuck. Well, at least that's a very clear illustration of why I need some time without you." This time he *did* reach for the door, bright red and looking *really* embarrassed.

"It's okay," I said, helping him open it.

He didn't say anything else. We did hug again, probably for too long, and then he turned and walked haphazardly down the corridor towards the lift. Like I had Bree, I watched him leave through the peephole. He didn't give me a little cheerful wave from the lift like she had, though. His face just crumpled again as the doors closed with the finality of leaving here for the last time. He was wiping away tears as he disappeared.

I closed my eyes for a moment, resting against the door. *Nothing* prepared you for what it felt like to cause someone you loved that much pain. And knowing he was going home to an empty house... I hated the thought of him crying alone. It wasn't my business anymore, though.

When I went back into the living room, the empty wine bottle was still on the kitchen table.

We'd sat at that table so many times together, eating, chatting, drinking. This apartment whole was full of memories of him, everywhere I looked. There were even pictures of us all over the place. We'd played all my games together. We'd watched all my movies together. I almost expected to look into the kitchen and see him doing the dishes while he hummed to himself, grinning at me over the counter when he noticed me watching.

It was *so weird* to know that that part of my life was over. It was such a disorienting, empty feeling. He'd *always* been here, and he'd never be here again.

I hadn't been there very long—maybe five minutes—when the front door opened again and startled me.

"Uh, Min?" that was *Henry's* voice. Had he forgotten something?

I spun in place to see him standing in the open door, and I was about to ask what was going on when I saw who was standing half-behind him: *Bree*.

She had a *really* guilty expression on her face.

"Delivery for you," he said simply. "And, actually, that reminds me..." He held something out towards me and I accepted it from him; it was a keycard to my apartment. He didn't wait around after I'd taken it, he just nodded at us and then laboured back down the hallway in an impressively straight line for how drunk I knew he was.

"Henry!" I called after him. "Henry, wait!" He didn't answer, he just got in the lift again and left. I put my head in my hands for a moment and *groaned*. "*Fuck*!"

Bree at least looked *really* apologetic. "I'm sorry," she said, sounding it, too. "I thought he'd probably be gone by now or I wouldn't have been *banging* on the front doors when they wouldn't open. I would have waited."

"You need a keycard to get into the hotel after twelve," I told her, exasperated, "*which I've given you*!"

She shrunk. "I know, but I put it somewhere and now I don't know where it is."

I sighed heavily at her. "Come on," I said, and stood aside so she could walk into my hallway. I wanted to text Henry to apologise, but I wasn't sure it was appropriate. *Fuck*.

She took off her shoes by the door, still looking *really* guilty. "I kind of don't want to ask, but you broke up with him, didn't you?" she said, asking me anyway. "I mean, he was crying when he came out of the hotel. Or, like, he was trying not to let me see that he was, so I guess you did it?"

Henry crying... "*Bree*," I said, trying to imagine how it must have felt for him to come across her, looking like that. "Yeah, I did it. Which is why you're the last person on the planet he should ever have bumped into on the way out. *Fuck*. How could you let that happen?"

Her face was still stuck in a grimace. "I didn't *let* it happen! When I saw it was him, I ran off so he wouldn't feel like he had to force himself to be nice to me. I even hid in the laneway down there with all the skip bins, but he followed me down there and he

634

found me. And then he insisted on taking me upstairs."

A tiny laneway in the middle of the night? *I* would have followed her and escorted her back, too.

"I'm sorry," she said. "I'm sorry, Min, it was an accident. You *know* I'd never do anything to—"

I hugged her, because there was really nothing else to do with her. When she tried to speak again I pushed her face into my middle to smother it. "Yeah, I know."

It was only when I went to stroke her hair that it occurred to me that her hair was actually curly again and not frizzy like it had been when she'd left. She was also wearing a different dress and different socks, and that suggested she'd been home and had a shower.

"You *did* go home," I observed as I released her. "But you're back. Did it go badly with Andrej?"

Her eyes were veiled for a moment. "It didn't go at all with him," she began. "I went home and told Mum and Dad what happened and we all waited for him to come home, but he didn't. Dad even got into the car and went looking for him. But he's nowhere. It's so typical. *Of course* he wouldn't come home, would he? I was sitting there on the edge of my bed for *hours*, waiting for him to come back so I could finally hear Dad scream at him for what he's done."

I stroked her hair. "And he didn't come back."

She exhaled. "And he didn't fucking come back. He never has to face *any* of the stuff he does, it's not fair." She leant against me miserably. "And I couldn't sleep because I was really angry at him and because I had this thought like, 'what if Min's breakup with Henry went *really* badly and she's just lying at home crying and there's no one to comfort her?'. So I came back."

I kissed the top of her head. "I'm okay."

She nodded, and looked comforted by that. "I'm *so* tired," she said, exhaling. "Can we just go and cuddle in bed? I didn't sleep much last night because after Andrej stole your stuff I was really fucking angry at him and worried you'd never talk to me again, so I'm *wrecked*."

I hadn't slept much last night either, so it didn't take a lot of convincing to get me to agree to that one. Since my bed still had glass on it, though, we ended up on the couch. Bree had high hopes of being my little spoon, but I needed to be on my back because I wasn't wearing the binder and it was the only way I felt flat. She ended up snuggled up against my side with her head on my shoulder and wrists curled under her chin. She was wearing one of my old t-shirts, too, so when she had her knee bent across me, I knew it was bare. It was pleasant to think about what was at the top of it, but I was too tired to do anything and so was she.

It was comforting to have her there, though, and she was warm. I worried a bit about Henry not having anyone to cuddle, but listening to Bree's steady breathing was relaxing. Before I knew it I was dozing off.

"Min?" I made a noncommittal noise in answer. "Do you think he hates me?"

"Who?" I asked, thinking maybe she meant Andrej.

"Henry," she said. "Do you think he hates me because I stole you?"

I patted her. "It takes a lot for Henry to hate someone. I doubt it."

She exhaled. "But it was pretty selfish of me, wasn't it? I was just thinking about how much I want you and I let you do all that stuff with me, and—"

"I'm 99% sure he doesn't hate you," I told her. "It's fine. Let's sleep."

I closed my eyes and put my head back on my pillow. I'd been on the cusp of falling asleep when I felt her lift her chin again.

"But when you think about it, I *am* selfish and I *am* a thief, aren't I? Like I was getting really mad at Andrej for stealing Courtney, but I just went and did the same thing to you. So maybe when Andrej's like, 'You're selfish, Bree, you're a thief', there's—"

"Bree," I said, pushing her head back down on my shoulder. "You're not selfish, you're not a thief, and Andrej probably just wants to find reasons that quote-unquote 'prove' you're a terrible person so he doesn't feel so bad about doing those things himself. You are *not a bad person*."

She was quiet for a minute, and I thought maybe she'd actually decided to go to sleep.

I was wrong. "I am, though," she said quietly.

There was enough gravity in what she said that I opened my eyes and looked down at her.

"Can I tell you something awful?" I nodded. "It *is* awful, and I'm such a terrible person for it, are you sure you want to hear it?"

I frowned at her. "If you want to tell me, I do."

She looked pained. "It's such a fucked thing to want, and I know that. But sometimes I wish Andrej would just die. Like, be hit by a car one day or something. I don't think I'd be upset." At my silence, she said, "I told you it was *terrible*."

It *was* unexpected, especially from Bree. It was wholly understandable, though, just really sad that his death was the only escape route she could imagine. I'd thought something similar about myself last night. "You're *not* a bad person, Bree," I told her, and hugged her tightly against me. "And I'm sure things will be better one day, and you'll be glad he's alive."

She sighed, and lay her head back down against my shoulder. "I used to tell myself that all the time, 'things will get better'. And, like, part of me remembers when we used to set up the backyard into, like, this killer assault course and play with super soakers together in summer, and how we'd always sneak down early at Christmas time together to look at the presents before Mum and Dad woke up. And this one time I accidentally killed the goldfish because I didn't know blue food dye was toxic and Andrej tried to scrub the blue from the bowl so I didn't have to tell Mum..." She was teary again. "And when I was like eight or something there was this guy down the road from us who used to tease me about my hair and Andrej ran up to him and pushed him off his scooter for it. Andrej always let me get the big part of the Christmas crackers and when we had roast chicken he'd always let me have the legs." I could feel tears on my t-shirt. "It used to be different. Everything used to be different. And I keep hoping and hoping things will go back to that, but they just never do. And now I don't know if I even want him back or I want him to die."

"Things will get better, Bree," I told her, still cuddling her "I promise. It won't be like this forever."

As I said that, though, I thought of Diane and Sean. He was still a *nightmare.* I wondered if Diane had ever been like Bree.

That was a really interesting thought, and despite the fact we'd been in the middle of a really serious conversation and I wanted to think more about Sean and Andrej, I was peacefully drifting off to sleep when Bree woke me up *again*.

"Well, at least nothing else can happen today," she reflected. She sounded less miserable.

My eyes flew open. "Jesus Christ, Bree!" I said, briefly tickling her. "There's this thing called *sleep*. I thought you said you wanted it!"

She squealed, pushing my hands away from her. "I'm sorry!" she said. "My brain won't switch off!"

"Your *what*?" I asked her sarcastically, and she shoved me.

"Don't be mean!" she told me as we settled back down again. "I was just saying that nothing else can happen today."

"No?"

"No," she said, pausing. "Because it's tomorrow already."

I *groaned*. "You dag," I told her, and ruffled her hair. "I can't believe you woke me up to tell me *that*."

I could feel her smiling against my shoulder. "And you broke up with him," she confirmed. I made some sort of vaguely affirmative, sleepy noise. "And that means you're single."

Wait, that was news to me. I opened my eyes again. "I am?"

"Well, you didn't ask me out yet," she said, looking up at me from under her hair. "Not properly."

"It's the twenty-first century," I pointed out. "You can actually ask *me* out, you know."

"I know," she conceded. "But I kind of like all that traditional stuff."

Since my eyes were open, I rolled them. "Fine," I said flatly. "So, Bree, do you come here often? Can I buy you a drink?"

She shoved me in the stomach again, giggling. "Do it properly!"

What did that even mean? I'd never asked anyone out before. "How?" I asked her. "'Will you go out with me?' Is that 'properly'?" She nodded. "Fuck, this is awkward. Bree, will you go out with me?"

She was giggling, and instead of giving me an answer, she just said, "April 29." I gave her a strange look, and she smiled up at me from under her lashes. "April 29," she repeated. "That's today's date. You have to remember it, because it's going to be our anniversary. Here," she said, and reached across me down to the floor, feeling around in my jeans for my mobile, which she retrieved.

"I'll put it in your phone."

I pushed the phone aside. "You don't have to," I said, taking it from her and putting it back on my jeans.

She looked a bit worried. "Why not?"

I smiled. "Because there's no way I'm going to forget it, Bree."

Bree's smile was so big it squeezed the last of the tears from her eyes. "You always make me feel really good about myself," she said. "Even though I'm totally hopeless."

I put a hand gently behind her head and guided her lips down to mine. We lay there for a little while, softly kissing and gently touching each other. After the evening I'd had it was comforting, and there was no pressure in it. No urgency. We were both so tired it never would have led anywhere, anyway. It was just nice to be close to her and cared for, and finally, *finally* I felt her relax.

It was such a relief, everything that had happened in the last couple of days. The bandaid had nearly been ripped off, it was all nearly over. All that was left was work; I'd have to go back in tomorrow so I could cut those last few threads away and just be finally *free* of it all.

Since Bree and I were both *exhausted,* it wasn't that long before we stopped and lay down again, cuddled against each other.

Then, for the first time ever, I went to sleep wrapped in my girlfriend's arms.

Bree was a restless sleeper. At several points in the night I had to rescue the doona, or shift her elbow out of my ribs, or battle through her hair to find oxygen. I was a little under-slept as a result, but it was worth it: I had a pretty awful dream about Henry and waking up to Bree drooling peacefully on my shoulder was the perfect remedy.

Despite my dull headache, I probably got about six hours in the end. That was all *I* needed, but Bree was one of those people who looked dishevelled and disoriented all morning unless she got a full eight. So while I was rushing around trying to figure out if I could make any of the shirts Bree and I had bought together look at all good with Henry's suit pants and the ties he'd left here, Bree lay on the couch and *grumbled.*

"Isn't that Henry's suit?" she asked about my pants. "Didn't he want it back?"

The blue shirt looked kind of okay with the black pants, I decided. And at least there was a tie that matched it. "He told me there was no point in giving it back to him, because he wouldn't be able to wear it again."

"Because of the blood?" I gave her a look, and she made a face. "Oh."

"Yeah." I presented myself to her. "I feel bad about wearing it, too, but I don't have anything else. How do I look? I can't wear the jacket until it's been dry-cleaned, but this is okay by itself, yeah?"

She looked me up and down, but didn't say anything about the actual suit. "Why are you going back?" she asked, clearly not impressed that I was. "Do you think anyone's *actually* expecting you to go back after what you did yesterday?"

I shrugged, ducking back into the bathroom to check the knot on the tie and make sure my hair didn't look like something out of a cartoon. "Probably not," I called back to her. "But I don't want Sean to think he's wrecked my life, and I messed up a couple of things on the project I want to set straight." John's career, for example. I still felt *really* guilty about that. "So, I might as well go in and resign properly."

Bree continued to disapprove of me going in, and I continued to ignore her, leaving a 20 and my keycard on the kitchen counter. "Don't lose that one, okay?" I told her, and then headed off to work.

They hadn't disabled my security pass, so I swiped myself in and went up in the lift with everyone else. No one recognised me until I got to 36, and then as I walked out of the lift, someone shouted and the next second I was surrounded by a group of men.

"Jesus, it *is* true," someone said and clapped me on the back. "Fuck. Hey, Mark, check it out, it's Mini! *Can you believe it*?" "Hey, guys, Mini actually came back!" someone else said, and then they were all talking to me at once and I couldn't understand them.

"Min," I corrected everyone as I kept walking. "And I'm not here for long."

"Were you always a guy the whole time?" someone asked, and then other voices said things like, "Nah, mate, I swear she has boobs in there somewhere," and, "Well, where are they now? Maybe they were fake," over the top of all the gossip about my body, someone was yelling, "Shut up, you idiots, I want to know what she did to Sean Frost!"

It was actually pretty funny, but I wasn't going to answer any of those questions. I just kept walking until I left them all at the door of Oslo and shut it behind them. Sarah was already in, of course, and she looked from the loud door to me and burst out laughing.

"What are *you* doing here!" she said with a big grin, spinning her chair around to face me. "Not that it's not great to see you! I'm still enjoying second-hand glory from that stunt you pulled yesterday."

She stood up to hug me briefly and then leant away from me to examine my eye. It was patchy and bright red, I'd spent a minute or two this morning inspecting it myself. "Did you go pick a fight as the final test of your manliness or something?"

"What, I'm not man enough already?" I asked her. She gave me a look, and I chuckled. "Actually, Bree's brother and I had a disagreement. It's a long story."

"'A disagreement'," she repeated sceptically, "grown-ups normally disagree with their words, Min. Not their fists."

"Hey, *I* used my words," I protested as she finished disapproving of my injuries. "Like I said: long story."

"It *sounds* like a long story," she agreed, and then got straight back to why I was here. "Anyway, are you back here to beg for your job or something? Because don't bother. I know they can't actually fire you right now because of the formal complaint, but Jason will dedicate his life to making yours *hell*." She leant in, clearly about to say something juicy. "Diane had to put Omar as Acting Marketing Manager while the complaint is investigated against Jason, so Jason's just a marketing clerk for now. He applied to take his annual leave for the next couple of weeks so he didn't have to slum it with the rest of us, but, get this, *HR said no it wasn't enough warning and wouldn't give it to him*. Can you believe it? They're going to make him serve out the investigation as a regular clerk."

It took a couple of seconds to process that. Wow; Jason as my peer? It *was* almost worth begging for my job just to experience. I considered actually doing that for a least a few seconds before dismissing the idea. I didn't want to be hanging around bumping into Henry, and there was still the matter of Sean Frost lurking around, waiting to strike. Jason being temporarily demoted didn't change my mind about wanting to leave Frost.

Besides, if I stayed here, I had a feeling Bree would find some way into the building for the sole purpose of dragging me out by my ear.

"Fuck, I wonder if Jason will get demoted for good," I said aloud.

Sarah shook her head. "Probably not," she said. "As much as that would be the best thing to ever happen in this department." She paused. "Actually, scrap that, the best thing to ever happen here was when Ms Min Lee rocked up dressed as *Mr* Min Lee and just *rolled* the whole of management and sold a multi-million dollar contract in 20 minutes." She shook her head incredulously at me. "Aren't you worried that by coming back Diane's going to eat you alive?"

I shrugged. "I actually came in to resign."

"*Oh,*" she said, and then her smile faded. "Oh. Of course."

I made a face. "I'm sorry, Sarah," I told her. "I feel bad about leaving you here, but I can't do this."

She blew a stream of air threw her mouth, and nodded. "No, I get it," she said. "But yeah, it's going to suck around here without you..."

"You were okay before I arrived," I reminded her.

She laughed once. "Yeah, because I didn't know what I was missing!" She beckoned me over to her computer. "You want to see what *you* missed yesterday? It's *great*. I kept all the best ones just in case they fired you and disabled your email."

I pulled a chair up next to her and she showed me a string of emails that had the two photos the Sales boys had taken in the meeting yesterday: the one of me looking triumphant up the front of the media room and the one of Jason looking red-faced and *furious*. The first email was just the raw photos, but, in the grand tradition of Marketing, all the ones that followed had been altered. Some of them had text, some of them had other places and people transposed on them, and my favourite was one that had a speech bubble next to my head saying, '*who da man*?' and a speech bubble next to Jason's head saying, '*U*'.

"I hope you saved that one," I said, pointing at it. "I want to use that as my wallpaper."

"You bet," she said, and kept scrolling through them. "Jason actually sent around a memorandum telling us to stop sharing photos but the second Omar introduced himself as Acting Marketing Manager it all started again. Jason disappeared as a result. So either he discovered the joy of hiding out in toilets or he went home early like you did. Either way: *score*!" When we were done looking at the photos, she leant back in her chair. "So what did you do yesterday, anyway? Or should I say... *who* did you do?" She was smirking.

"Am I that predictable?"

She tilted her head. "Yes. But you also said Andrej punched you, so..."

I told her the abridged version of what happened after I left yesterday, minus why I had a go at Bree's brother. I wasn't sure Bree would be happy for me to tell anyone the details. Sarah probed a bit about why I was so angry at him, but left it after I asked her to. From her expression, I think she was going to try and get the story out of Bree herself, anyway.

"It's good that you finally broke up with Henry," she concluded when I was done. "I mean, obviously it's terrible because he's a great guy, but, yeah. You met Gem and ten minutes later you two had more chemistry than you and Henry probably ever had. And, honestly? I don't know Bree that well, but you've been different since you met her."

"I think it was probably a long time coming," I said, and then winced, remembering Henry's expression when he'd 'delivered' Bree. "He's a *really* nice guy, though. Really nice. I still care about him."

"Are you two going to stay friends?" she wondered, and I shrugged. "Yeah," she agreed. "It's hard to know right afterwards." She slapped her thighs. "Anyway! It sucks you're leaving and I totally don't forgive you for it, but do you need help getting your stuff home? I don't have my car with me, but Gem and I can help you carry stuff back in boxes at lunchtime if it's not too heavy."

We were discussing the details when the door opened sharply. I saw Sarah's expression and guessed who it was before I turned around, myself.

Word had obviously spread like wildfire that I was here, because Diane was leaning in the doorway with her eyes fixed on me. "Good morning," she said to us both, and then gave me a look that said, *'get in my office this very second'*.

I shared a tense glance with Sarah who immediately tried to look busy and productive, and then followed Diane out of Oslo, down the corridor and into her office.

"Close that outer door, too, Cadence," Diane instructed her assistant, who hurriedly followed her instructions.

Even though I literally had nothing to lose and I'd been expecting this to happen anyway, being ushered into Diane's office and having both doors shut was intimidating. Everything about Diane was intimidating. And even though she could fire me on the spot and it would have exactly the same effect as what I was actually planning to do, my heart was pounding. I may still have been a bit afraid she would make me feel like an idiot again. She was certainly capable of making me feel *terrible* if she wanted to.

"I think by now you're familiar with how this goes," she said, gesturing at the seats opposite her desk. I sat in one, and she sat opposite me.

She considered me for some time before she spoke. "I'm surprised to see you here after what you did yesterday."

It looked like I was getting that dressing down, after all. I didn't say anything to her, I just nodded.

"Tell me, Min," she said. "How do you think I should react to what you did yesterday?"

There was no point in pretending I didn't know where this was going. "I think you should fire me on the spot for gross insubordination."

She had *not* been expecting me to say that. To her credit, she managed to look only mildly surprised. "Believe me, I would," she said impassively. "But there's a formal complaint pending and by the looks of things," her eyes dipped, and that was her only subtle reference to how different I looked than I had on Wednesday, "it's not vexatious after all."

She didn't elaborate, she just sat and watched me closely for what felt like eternity. I had *no* idea what she was thinking, and fuck, she was good at being terrifying. There was *seriously* nothing she could do and *still* she was making my knees shake.

"So as not to cause you the distress you've been experiencing in Marketing," she said eventually, "we've had you transferred down to Administration. They have a very large Data Entry job they need extra hands with at the moment, so they'll definitely appreciate the help."

Very diplomatically put, I thought, for what was essentially a forced demotion just like Jason's. "Thank you," I said. "I appreciate the consideration. But I actually came into work today for the sole purpose of formally resigning."

Her eyebrows went up a fraction. "You'll give the customary four weeks' notice, I presume?" I didn't think for a second that she didn't know how I was going to answer that.

I took a deep breath, and shook my head.

She sat back in her chair, resting her elbows on the arms of it and lacing her fingers. She didn't bother telling me my pay was going to be docked for it; she'd probably checked my file and seen I had nearly three years' worth of annual leave banked. Losing a month of it wasn't that big a deal for me.

I didn't wait for her to speak this time. "Also," I said, "I need to talk to you about John." She didn't answer me, she just waited for me to continue, so I did. "It wasn't his fault Sean found out about Pink, it was mine. So if he's been stood down because of that, I'd like to ask you to reconsider that decision. It's not fair otherwise. I don't want him to be held responsible for something that's my fault."

She looked somewhat amused, like she'd entertained the impassioned request of a five year old. I didn't understand why, until she asked for confirmation, "We fired him because of the Facebook leak?"

I was confused. "Isn't that what happened? I thought that was why he's not here."

"I hadn't heard that one, to be perfectly honest," she said with a humourless smile. "Usually I do have some idea what's going around the floor." She looked me in the eye. "Min, shortly after the leak, John resigned because he decided marketing wasn't for him. He's working in Canberra for the Australian Bureau of Statistics. You can apologise for him and to him if you like, but according to HR, he was delighted to get the job."

"Oh..."

"Mmm," she echoed me. There was a certain finality in her voice when she told me, "And while I'd love to accept your resignation verbally, it needs to be in writing, especially given the complaint that's being investigated. An email will suffice."

She was probably dismissing me, but I didn't get up and leave. I wanted to say something about Sean as well, but at this point in the conversation I wasn't sure where to start. Since I had nothing to lose, I just started anywhere.

"For what it's worth, I also wanted to apologise for leaking information about Pink," I told her. "I didn't do it intentionally, but I definitely could have been more careful." I wasn't sure how relevant it was, but I also added, "My girlfriend is struggling with a very difficult brother, and before Wednesday and the meetings with Sean and yourself, I don't think I really understood what that meant."

Diane didn't look very impressed by my apology. "You can be sorry about your actions," she told me, "but unfortunately that doesn't undo the lasting impact they've had on the organisation and people within it. By some miracle you actually sold that contract and you don't need to apologise to your team for missing out on their bonuses. If you did, they'd probably feel much as I do right now. You took an unacceptable risk, *unacceptable.* Of course I'm pleased we sold the contract, but with regard to your behaviour, the outcome is irrelevant."

The lasting impact my actions had on people. "I know," I said. "I'm aware of that. But I think it's still important to apologise."

She looked even more unimpressed. "I think after your dealings with my brother you'll have some idea how little value I place on empty words," she said. "If you break something, fix it. Apologies are useless."

"I thought I did fix it," I said, thinking of the pitch.

She exhaled. "You're in the wrong industry," she said, almost as an afterthought. This time, she didn't leave any opportunity for me to think I was still welcome to remain in her office. "Now go and write me that email you promised," she instructed me. "And afterward, collect your belongings and exit the building. Surrender your security pass on the way out."

That seemed to be it. As I was standing to leave, reflecting on the fact that despite all expectation, she *hadn't* really dressed me down or made me feel particularly stupid, she stopped me. I wasn't sure what else she was going to say to me at first—maybe I was about to be burnt after all—but that wasn't what happened.

She didn't look away from her computer screen, and from her tone of voice I'd never have guessed what she was going to say. "Tell your friend to count her losses and give up on her brother right now," she said impassively. "So that she doesn't waste half her life hoping he'll change."

I gaped at her for a moment. I wasn't given the opportunity to seek clarification about what she meant, because she immediately bent over towards the phone and pressed the pager. "We're done now, Cadence," she said, and then the door behind me promptly opened and I was shown out.

Sarah had been called off to some meeting while I was with Diane—as had most of Marketing, including Ian and Carlos—which meant I was able to sit down at my desk in relative peace and write Diane my resignation. I wrote about 15 versions of it, because now that I had some time to think, I regretted not standing up for myself in how inappropriate Jason's behaviour had been towards me. Eventually I wrote a version that encouraged Diane to seriously consider the complaint, because even in my absence Jason's behaviour would continue to negatively impact the department. While I was wondering if that was bitter and unprofessional, I just hit 'send' anyway. Whatever, it wasn't like I planned to work in marketing again and needed a reference.

While I was clearing out my desk and trying to decide which materials and prints I really wanted to keep and which I could shred, there was a gentle knock on the door. That was a bit weird; Marketing boys weren't generally known for their mild manners.

"Come in," I called while I was elbow deep in one of my drawers. Now that the project was over there was probably no need for confidentiality.

When the door opened, I noticed the red hair before I noticed anything else. The maroon stockings were pretty obvious, too, especially under a black skirt. There was something a bit charming about them. "Gemma," I acknowledged her, and then stood up from my drawer.

She let herself in and closed the door behind her. "Sarah said you might need some help with—" Her eyes dipped to my crotch when she turned to face me again; I forgot she hadn't seen the packer before, even if Sarah had definitely told her about it. She was surprised enough by it that she lost her train of thought momentarily.

"With packing up?" I finished, my word choice deliberate. When she gaped at me for it, I winked. I shouldn't have, because she flushed that glorious deep red that only someone with skin as light as hers could. I didn't let her suffer for long, though. "Yeah, I've got a few boxes I want to take back to my place. Maybe three or four, depending on how ruthlessly I cull this pile." I gestured to the stacks of old marketing material samples that I'd kept.

Gemma tried to pretend she wasn't blushing so much her freckles had disappeared, and came over to inspect the materials. She picked one up and flipped through it. "Why are you keeping all this stuff?" she asked. "If all the things that happened to you here had happened to me, I wouldn't be able to even look at them. I'd be too angry."

I continued to sort everything into two piles. "I think I've run out of emotions for this place," I said. "I literally feel nothing. Almost like it wasn't even me who worked here and I'm cleaning up for someone else, as weird as that sounds. I'm not even angry at Sean."

"Which pile for this one?" she asked about the brochure she was holding, and then put it on the one I indicated. "Why would you be angry at Sean?" she asked, reminding me that I *hadn't* told them about what he was like yet. "He paid for my coffee this morning for no reason, just because he was in the line behind me. He's really nice."

Of course he did, I thought, remembering when we'd crashed into Gemma in the lift. "I'll tell you guys in a minute," I said. "Not at work, though."

She leant on the partition and watched me cleaning out my drawers. "Well, not that we ever hung out much, but it's sad you're leaving. And Sarah probably won't tell you because she's not like that, but she's really going to miss you."

I looked up at her. No, Sarah didn't tell me that, and, yes, probably wouldn't have. "Thanks for letting me know," I said, and then went back to packing and worrying about it.

I didn't have to worry for long, though, because Sarah arrived pretty quickly after Gemma did. "Sorry about bailing on you," she said as she came up to me, "I wanted to be here when Diane was done with you, but..." She stopped talking as soon as she saw Gemma, turning back to me sternly and putting her hands on her hips. "Min," she said. "What did you do. Why is she blushing?"

That only made Gemma blush *more.*

"Exertion, probably," I said in the most innocent of voices. "She was just helping me work through some stuff that I wasn't sure about."

"Oh, *god*..." Gemma mumbled and put her burning face in her hands. "I hate you *both.*"

Sarah mimed beating me up. "You!" she said, "I swear to god I will take out your other eye if you start drama with my friends. Stop *flirting* with her! You have a girlfriend!" She then turned around to Gemma. "And you, she has a girlfriend, Gem!" She stopped for a second and twisted back to me. "I can still say that, right, 'she'? Or is it 'he' now?"

I was never going to escape *fucking pronouns.* "'She' is fine, just not in front of people who don't know me."

Gemma abruptly stopped pretending to cry. "Wait, you're *not* a guy now? But you got your hair cut and you have the..." She looked at my crotch again.

I blinked at her. That was a very difficult question to answer on the spot, especially when I didn't really know the answer.

At Gemma's expression, and despite the fact she had been telling *me* not to tease her, Sarah said, "Well, I guess that means you *will* have to question your sexuality after all, Gem."

Gemma's face scrunched up and she put it in her hands again. "*Sarah,*" she said, but it came out as a pained whimper. "Why are you *doing this...?*"

We had to stop messing around, though, because the door opened again and Ian and Carlos came in. They weren't surprised to see me; apparently word spread fast.

"Is it true Diane just *fired you?*" Carlos asked, eyes wide.

After I'd explained everything and after I'd sorted everything into shred and keep piles, Ian volunteered to do that shredding and then Sarah, Gemma and I shared the other boxes between us to carry them back to my place.

I hadn't been out of Oslo for *five seconds* before people started jogging over to talk to me. I wasn't fazed by that at all until Sarah nudged me and made a frantic noise.

I saw where she was looking; one of the people approaching me was Jason.

Shit, I thought, and kept walking as if everything was fine and normal. Gemma didn't recognise him and pressed the button when we got to the lift. "So, is it far to your place?" she asked. "Not that this box is that heavy, but I made the stupid mistake of wearing heels this morning."

Because Jason was coming up to me, the other clerks held back apprehensively. Technically Jason was their peer now, but he had been their manager and was likely to be their manager again, so their hesitation was understandable. It didn't make me any more comfortable, though.

I pretended to very casually answer Gemma as Jason stopped right next to me, his eyes boring holes through the side of my head. "I can't tell you what a relief it is to wear flats," I said. "These are a tiny bit big, though. I should probably go shopping for ones that actually fit."

When I didn't immediately acknowledge him, Jason cleared his throat. "Mini." He still *sounded* like my manager.

Gemma glanced at him, but double-took when she saw his expression and looked surprised by how harsh it was.

"If those are marketing materials, that's Frost International property and you need to leave them on site."

To be honest, closed marketing materials were a bit of a grey area. There was no real reason for me not to take them as long as I wasn't handing them out on the street, and that wasn't why he was saying it. He was just trying to flex his muscles because he was angry with me about the complaint and the pitch.

I'd had it with him, though, so when the lift dinged at that moment and the doors slid open, I said very politely, "Do I?" and from the tone of my voice it would have been clear to him I was humouring him.

He stepped directly in front of me when I went to walk into the lift.

Around me, people edged away from us. Even Sarah was too afraid to say anything to rescue me, and Gemma just looked really stunned. People down the other end of the floor stood from their desks, watching. *Everyone* was watching. Even the people in the lift were holding the door open for me under the guise of trying to be helpful.

"Excuse me," I said to Jason as if he was anyone else, and went to step around him. He didn't let me.

"I said: those marketing materials need to remain on site, Mini," he enunciated clearly.

When he definitely wasn't going to let me pass, I looked down at him. Being tall definitely had its benefits. "And when I get instructions *from management* to leave them behind, Jason, that's what I'll do."

There was a hum from the floor as people shifted uncomfortably and whispered to their neighbours about that. It was like being at a very polite wrestling match.

He shook his head and chuckled dangerously. He was trying to start something. "You're lucky you quit, Mini."

So he wanted to have it out here, did he? *Really?* In front of everyone? I understood why he thought it would work: two days ago I would have been *terrified* of this very situation. I would have been sweating and panicking and desperate to get away. Not anymore. If he thought I was still a shrinking violet, he was about to discover how mistaken he was.

"Why, Jason?" I asked him openly, jogging the heavy box in my arms. "Why? What else were you planning to do to me if I didn't quit? Were you going to move past yelling at me and insulting me to actually beating me up, or...?"

His expression hardened. "If you'd responded to simple instructions I never would have had to yell, Mini," he told me. "But everything goes in one ear and out the other with you, because you think you know better than everyone else and the world revolves around you and your problems. Your carelessness nearly tanked a critical project. I think that warrants some—"

I cut him off. "Well, I think it warrants some performance management, personally," I said. "Not my manager belittling me and bullying me. But I guess it doesn't matter what *I* think, the

651

internal investigation will determine what should have happened."

I went to step past him again, and he actually took a hold of the box I was carrying to prevent me from leaving. "So that's it," he said, "you're just going to get in one parting shot at *my* career because you're bitter you weren't able to—"

"Let go, Jason," I told him calmly.

He didn't. "—bitter that you weren't able to cope with the pressure that these sort of jobs entail. If you knew the sort of pressure *I've* had to endure daily and the sort of things *I've* had to do over the years to get my job and keep it, you'd—"

You know what? I really didn't care about his problems, especially since he'd shown nothing but callous disregard for mine. I couldn't be bothered listening to him rant on about them, either, so I talked over him. "—Diane's instructions were to get my belongings and leave. Do you think that, on top of all the other difficulties she's having with you, she's going to thank you for obstructing me?" I raised my eyebrows at him.

For a split second I saw something snap in him, and I actually thought he might punch me like Andrej had. He managed to contain himself, though, just aggressively shaking my box before he released it, instead. I wasn't intimidated by him.

"Thank you," I said pointedly, and stepped around him, nodding at Gemma and Sarah, who were staring wide-eyed at me. "Let's go."

Tailed by the other two, I went and stood in the lift. As marketing *gaped* at me, the doors closed.

There was oppressive silence as the lift descended; everyone *inside* it was staring at me, too. Jason's reputation obviously preceded him.

Sarah glanced around at everyone in the lift, smirking. "So, I hear it's going to be really warm this afternoon," she said conversationally, to draw attention to the fact everyone was silent.

Gemma accidentally snorted, and then looked horrified she made such an inelegant sound in public and blushed again, and then then the three of us ended up trying to smother laughter for the whole rest of the trip down.

"I can't believe you did that," Sarah whispered to me as we walked through the atrium, carrying the boxes. "I have been *fantasising* the whole time he's my boss of just shutting him down just like you did. Oh, my god. The level of vicarious triumph I get just by being around you is *amazing*. I think I'm just going to follow you around with pompoms forever."

I grinned at her. "You going to wear those leotards and little skirts, too?"

She gave me a tired look. "Ugh. Down, boy," she said as we walked through the rotating doors and out onto the street.

Sarah may have been joking before in the lift, but it *was* warm today, and the blue sky was reflecting off the mirrored surfaces of all the skyscrapers. I stopped for a moment and looked up at Frost International Headquarters and the black and white snowflake mounted on the top.

I remembered the first time I saw this building; I'd looked up at it, filled with terror and excitement and completely unable to believe that a company had valued me so much they'd paid to relocate me to another state. I'd thrown myself into the work—I could still hear the compliments people paid to my graphics and layouts when they first discovered I could do that stuff—and had enjoyed feeling important and part of something when people had asked me to stay back late. I'd spent four years in there. I'd met *Henry* there, and he'd gone on to be so important to me. I'd met these two there. Working for Frost had consumed me, and I'd put my blood and sweat into everything I produced for them.

And now, right now this second, I was walking away from it. I'd resigned. That part of my life was over, and I wasn't looking up at my work anymore, I was looking up at another generic skyscraper.

Goodbye, I thought. I didn't regret any of it.

"I can't believe you're abandoning us," Sarah said with exaggerated tragedy. "Who the hell am I going to buy Red Bulls for now? Everyone else sucks."

"Gee, thanks," Gemma said with a smile, even though it was obvious Sarah was talking about Marketing.

"Maybe they'll hire a really nice, really cute guy to replace me," I suggested, and then started walking again. They followed me.

"There's already plenty of cute guys in Marketing, much cuter than the ones in Risk," Gemma pointed out. "It's just that they're all either married, or gay, or egotistical bastards."

Sarah laughed once. "So, exactly your types, Gem." She leant over to me. "Gemma likes guys she can't have."

Gemma groaned. "Shut up, Sare, that was *one time*. I didn't know he was married until it was way too late!"

Sarah didn't stop there. "He was older, too, what was he?" She squinted. "She was twenty-four and he was... forty? And *rich*..." She elbowed her friend as they walked. "If that's your type, word is Sean Frost gets around a bit..."

I made an angry noise, and both of them looked at me. "If a married, gay and egotistical bastard is your type, Gemma, then Sean Frost is *definitely* up your alley."

They both frowned at me, and I spent the rest of our walk home detailing all the fuckery Sean Frost had exacted in the last several days, including his parting swing at Henry with the security footage. We were in the lift at my hotel before I was done going over everything.

They were both silent for a few floors, and then Sarah said, "Okay, it's not that I don't believe you because I absolutely do, but *I can't believe he'd do all that*. God... and all over this stupid brother-sister-rivalry thing they've got going." She was frowning. "That conversation you overheard, did you find out what was going on with the Waterbank court case? Because I look at the listings every day and there's never any more info. It must be really important, though. Otherwise they wouldn't be so angry at each other and so secretive about it."

I shook my head. "Maybe something about a shared road, reputation... I don't know. It didn't make much sense. Sean thought Diane was doing it to piss him off, but it seemed like she was doing it because she was sick of his crap."

Sarah shifted the box she was carrying to under the other arm, chewing her lip as she thought. "Well, the case is being held in an open court, so we're going to find out eventually," she said. "Meanwhile, Waterbank's closed, so Rob's bored and hanging around my house. And, don't get me wrong, I love the big oaf, but I swear to god if he paints another room or rearranges the furniture again, I'm going to kill him."

I tried to remember the exact words Sean and Diane had said to each other, but I couldn't. There had been too many other things going on for me. "To be honest, I'm getting to the point where I don't really care about what's going on," I told them. "I'm just curious, because that all that crap was why Pink needed extra security and that caused all of this in the first place, but..." I shook my head. "Whatever. I hope they sue each other into bankruptcy. I'll bring popcorn to their estate auction."

Gemma had been mostly silent, and as we arrived at my floor, Sarah looked over to her. "You right, Gem?"

Gemma grimaced. "Okay: confession," she said, "after Sean bought me that coffee this morning I *did* spend the whole team meeting imagining bumping into him alone in that pub we go to..."

Sarah *groaned,* and put her free arm around Gemma's shoulders. "We need to get you a boyfriend," she said as we approached my front door.

I knocked. Footsteps ran over to the door. "Who is it?" Bree called, reminding me she was too short to reach the peephole.

"It's me," I told her.

Gemma froze. "Oh, no," she said, looking alarmed. "*Bree*'s here?"

I didn't realise what the problem was straight away, because I had *totally* forgotten what happened last time Gemma and Bree had been in the same place. It hadn't even occurred to me to leave Gemma at work as a result of it, either. *Fuck*, I hoped Bree wasn't going to be too upset. She had *not* been happy about Gemma last time they'd been in a room together.

Gemma clearly hadn't forgotten, because she put the box down and turned to leave, mumbling something about needing to get back to work.

Sarah caught her with one hand. "Oh, no, you don't."

The door opened and Bree appeared. Embarrassingly, she was still only wearing my t-shirt, but because she was much shorter than me it was probably longer than any of her skirts anyway. Still, it was dead giveaway that she'd been in bed with me, just in case either Sarah or Gemma weren't completely clear about the fact we were sleeping together.

Bree was oblivious to all that. "Oh, hey!" she said to me, and then spotted Sarah. "Sarah, I didn't know you guys were..." She stopped when she noticed Gemma loitering in the background.

They stared at each other for a moment, stunned. Predictably,

Gemma went bright red.

Bree looked up at me, and back at Gemma's terrified expression. Then, she darted past me, taking a hold of Gemma's hand. "You've never been here before, have you? You *have* to see the view from Min's balcony. It's *awesome*." She towed Gemma past me and out onto said balcony. Gemma threw a look back over her shoulder that was equal parts surprise and relief.

I watched them as Sarah kicked the box Gemma had set down so it was inside the door, and placed her own down on the floor next to it. I followed suite and then we stood and watched Bree leaning double over the balcony and pointing at landmarks. Gemma looked a bit overwhelmed.

"Should I rescue Gemma?" I wondered.

Sarah shook her head. "Nah, it's good for her. Where do you want these boxes?"

I was about to say in my bedroom, but then I remembered the state that my bedroom was in. Which reminded me... "Oh!" I said to Sarah, "You know how I promised you my old dresses a couple of weeks ago? Bree sorted through them and found the ones that might fit you. Want to have a look?"

She gave me a look that said *duh*, and so while Bree was busy with Gemma on the balcony, I led Sarah over to the pile of folded clothes for her in the bedroom.

She gave the glass-ridden ones, the bed and my door-less wardrobe a lengthy stare.

"Redecorating," was my flimsy excuse. I grinned at her as I said it.

From her expression, I think she guessed exactly what happened to the mirror and to the clothes. She didn't say as much, though, she just went straight over to the pile I showed her.

"Wow, you're getting rid of *all* of them?" she asked, picking up the blouse on the top of the pile and holding it up to the light. "Not that I'm complaining! But *wow,* it feels like Christmas!"

There wasn't anywhere to put the clothes in my bedroom for Sarah to sort through them, so she took them out into the living room to select the pieces that she liked. While she was doing that, Bree and Gemma came back inside, and Bree bounced all the way up to me.

"Did the mail come yet?" she asked, wrapping her arms around my middle. "What do they do when it gets delivered, do they bring it up, or do you have to go down and get it?"

"Why, what are you expecting?" I asked her suspiciously, remembering her standing over an opened package with my packer cupped in her hands.

"I was just wondering," she said. "I thought I'd go and grab it for you if they didn't bring it up."

"You can go and check if you want," I told her as I draped an arm around her, "but put some actual clothes on first, okay?"

Just as I'd said that, Sarah pulled her top over her head, reaching for one of the work blouses I was giving her.

All three of us gawked at her. She gave us a weird look. "Oh, come on, I'm wearing a bra." She fussed with the sleeves on the top she was about to try on. "Besides, I want to make sure everyone gets a chance to see how great they are before a have a tonne of kids and ruin them."

Bree looked up at me with a twinkle in her eye. "I'm totally using that one."

While Sarah tried on all the clothes and the rest of us found all sorts of great places to look other than straight at her breasts, Gemma came across a picture of Henry and I. She picked it up, gazing at it for a moment, and then looking up at me. It made me feel uncomfortable, I didn't want anyone to think of or remember me like that. I needed to put those in a box somewhere.

"You guys looked really happy here," she said thoughtfully. "Did you always know? Not about the fact you might actually be a guy, but that you didn't like guys?" I shook my head. She watched my response, and then put the picture frame back down and considered it quietly for a while in the corner of the room.

When Sarah had chosen the pieces she wanted to take home with her, she picked up soft blue blouse that didn't suit her and marched over to Gemma. "Here," she said. "I think this one would look good on *you*."

She was probably right, but when Sarah reached for her buttons, Gemma *panicked* and looked directly at me. Sarah glanced over her shoulder towards me, and the little smirk on her lips suggested she was just teasing Gemma.

Not to be outdone, I leant casually on the kitchen counter and I was about to say something slightly suggestive, when *Bree* went for the kill. I had a feeling she was 100% serious, as well.

"Is it true people with freckles have them all over their boobs, too?" she asked us. "I've always wondered that."

Gemma wrestled the top from Sarah and pretended to strangle her with it. "Now I get why you wanted to be friends with Min," she said, returning to her usual shade of red. "You just wanted *an accomplice to torture me with*."

Since we were done with the clothes, Bree offered everyone lunch. Despite the fact both Sarah and Gemma were probably going to get in trouble for disappearing in the middle of a work day, both of them were happy to stay for food. While Bree was cooking, the three of us went and sat out on the balcony in the late morning sun. Sarah and I had our sleeves rolled up, but Gemma backed all the way into the corner where there was a slither of shadow so she didn't get *more* freckles.

"This view is pretty spectacular," Sarah said, crossing her ankles on the railing. "Are you going to stay here?"

I laughed once. "Hah. It's nearly $3000 a week if you don't work for Frost," I said, "which is ironic because the only people who could afford those rates *do* work for Frost. I've got a week to get out."

"Where are you moving?" Gemma asked.

I shook my head. "I don't know," I said. "My final pay is going to be a few thousand, but I have a feeling it has to last me for quite a long time. I haven't really thought about where I'm going to live, yet. I don't really know Sydney that well."

"The East is nice," Gemma volunteered. "It's a bit expensive, but it's close to the city for work."

"I don't even know what I'm going to do for work," I confessed. "I'll probably follow up with that cafe guy in Broome, but other than that..."

"Well, I saw those paintings inside," Gemma said. "They're incredible. Especially that Great Barrier Reef one. You should do something arty."

"That's what Bree says," I told her. "Honestly, though, I don't know where to start. I don't have any training. I'm sure artists figure out this stuff on their own all the time, but, yeah, I don't know."

Sarah had been watching Gemma and I speak, looking thoughtful. "What do you think about North Shore?" she asked me. "Would you consider moving there?"

I looked across at her. "Yeah, I guess?"

She grinned. "Because all I'm saying is that I've got three bedrooms and I only use two of them, so..."

I wasn't sure I heard her right. "Pardon?"

"I said move in with me, you dag," she told me. "You can play Xbox with Rob and stop him from constantly bothering *me* to do it." At my silence, she added, "Bring Schoolgirl, too, if you want. The more, the merrier."

I just stared at her; I didn't know what to say. It was too good to be true. "*Really*?"

Her smile was genuine. "Yeah."

"Food!" Bree announced from the doorway, distracting us from the conversation and carrying plates and cutlery out for us to eat with.

As usual, Bree's food wasn't award-winning, but it was at least edible and today's pasta had more than the usual concentration of vegetables and was probably very healthy.

"Definitely bring Schoolgirl with you," Sarah told me, helping herself to the olives I'd picked out and put on the side of my plate. "I hate cooking. Rob likes it, but he's *terrible*."

Gemma and Sarah stayed until after lunch, and then Sarah got an angry text message from someone in her other team. Both of them left after that, Sarah with about five Coles bags full of my old clothes.

"Are you sure about this?" she asked, swinging the bags. "You won't regret it?"

"Definitely not," I said. "And besides, even if I did, they're just going to your house a bit earlier than everything else, right? Less to pack up."

Once they'd gone, Bree sat herself down in the hallway with the boxes containing my director's cut of marketing materials to go through them. I watched her from the couch, where I was reclined nursing an overfull stomach. Before she started on the brochures, she fished out my security pass and examined the photo on it. It was me looking really feminine. "Oh, yeah, that's right... I almost forgot."

And I'd completely forgotten to surrender it like Diane had asked me to. "Shit, I should take that back, can you leave it out?"

Bree looked disappointed, but put it aside and opened the box instead. She liked most of the materials, but there was a period from 2010 where a lot of the things I produced contained very aggressive colours. She held up one of them and made a face. "Like, *why*?"

"All the major companies were using really bold colours when I made that," I told her. "I wanted to strike a balance between classic and progressive, and giving the diamond and the text lime green shadows achieved that, I think."

She made a face. "You sound like you're writing an essay," she told me, and then went back to the materials.

"I *could* write an essay on those," I said as I watched her go through them. "People at Frost never really understood that I don't just close my eyes and point to the colour palette. A lot of planning goes into the layouts and the colours and it's part of the sales and marketing process. People are subconsciously affected by colour, so it's important to get it right for the right impact."

Bree listened to me, looking down at a poster she'd unrolled. "Did they teach you that in your degree?"

I shrugged. "Not really. Marketing departments usually hire designers for that. There's no design subjects in the undergraduate marketing degree."

"And you didn't study art in school?"

Not unless you counted shutting myself in the graphics lab to escape the fuck-heads in my grade. "Only by myself."

Bree considered that, and then went back to the materials.

She'd been staring at the same one for a little while when she began, "You know how you had a really bad time in high school?" I made a non-committal noise. "Well, you know the treatment for, like, arachnophobia is slowly introducing people to spiders? And for acrophobia, they take you slowly further and further up until you get used to it and it's fine?"

I squinted at her. "Are you suggesting that I should slowly re-introduce myself to high school until I become un-fucked up over what happened to me when I was a teenager?"

"Well, when you put it like that it sounds silly, but yes? Maybe if you went back to one and saw everything can actually be fine you would feel better? I could go with you, we could go to Cloverfield. Today, maybe?"

Really? There was *no way*. I'd spent six years when I was in one wishing I was anywhere *but* there, and I wasn't going to voluntarily put myself in locations that were going to trigger really awful memories for me. "That's a really nice idea, Bree, but it's not going to happen," I said more firmly than I'd intended. "I've only just started to get over all that stuff now and it's been nearly eight years."

She looked unexpectedly crestfallen. "Oh," she said, getting back to the boxes. "Okay."

She'd only been looking again for a minute or two when she made an excited noise and held Mike aloft from one of the boxes. "Who's this?" she asked me, flicking the souvenir's horribly misshapen head so it wildly nodded.

"Michelangelo."

She laughed about the name. "He's so cute!"

She had to be kidding me. "He is definitely *not* cute. He's so ugly the vendor sold him to my friend at half-price, and then she gave him to me as a joke."

Bree looked really stricken by that. "That's awful," she told me, and then cradled him. "Can you imagine what it would feel like to be sold at half-price because *no one wants you*?"

"Bree. He's a *plastic figurine*. I'm pretty sure he's doing fine without therapy."

She didn't get to elaborate, because there was a knock on the door.

She looked across at me with a blank expression. "Why would they come back so quickly?" she asked, and then since she was already in the hallway, she put Mike down and pushed herself to stand up.

"It might be room service," I said. "I don't think they've been all week."

"Or it might be the mail!" Bree suggested, and pulled open the door with a big smile on her face.

As soon as she saw whoever it was, her smile disappeared. She stood in the doorway for a moment, looking like she was torn between shouting and crying, but she didn't do either. Without saying anything at all, she *slammed* the door and then went running into the bathroom and shut herself in there.

I sat up on the couch, stunned. "Bree?" I called to her as whoever it was knocked insistently on the door again.

I hadn't even got up off the couch before I heard a guy's voice yell, "Bree! Stop fucking running away, you're not fucking five years old anymore! For fuck's sake open the door, I need to talk to you!"

Andrej.

THIRTY-THREE

Andrej was still yelling, "Open the fucking door, Bree!" when *I* pulled it right open. He looked from where he'd been expecting Bree's face to be up to mine, and the words slowed on his lips. He looked *very* surprised to see me. "You're not at work."

"Sorry," I said flatly, probably sounding just as unapologetic as I felt. "Guess you'll have to come back and rob me later."

He wasn't as neat and preened as he had been yesterday; he was bleary-eyed, dishevelled, and still wearing the same clothes. There was something unstrung about him, too. It made me uncomfortable, especially since his eyes flew straight to the injuries *he'd* caused me.

"That looks painful," he said about my eye. It was an observation and nothing more, and if I hadn't already had my hackles up over how he was speaking to Bree, *that* would definitely have been the clincher.

I was in *no* mood for his bullshit. "What do you want, Andrej?"

He took a breath. "I need to speak to Bree."

"Yeah. I think the whole floor got that much. *Why?*"

He looked a bit guarded. "It's kind of private," he said, shifting his weight.

"Then I guess you'll have to wait until she wants to speak to you," I said dismissively, and went to shut the door.

He stepped out in his sneaker and stopped the door open. "Look, I'm sorry I punched you, okay!" he said, as if that was the only reason I wasn't letting him in. "You tore up seven grand, so you can understand why, plus I didn't know you're a girl!"

That was unexpected. I stopped pushing on the door, and I must have looked surprised, because he said less defensively, "It had your sex on the list of charges. Look, I won't tell Mum and Dad, but I need to speak to Bree."

I felt like there was an implied threat in that. "And what happens if I don't let you talk to her?" I asked. "You'll out her? And me?"

"I did *not* say that!" He sounded really frustrated. "Can you stop this shit? I get it, I punched you. I'm on charges because of that. This isn't about that, I just want to speak one-on-one to my sister! I'm not going to have a go at her!"

Somehow, I didn't believe him, even if he believed himself. "Here's what's going to happen," I said in no uncertain terms, "either you're going to tell me what you want to say to Bree, or I'm going to shut the door right now and call security, and—"

"It's okay, Min," Bree interrupted me. She'd come out of the en suite and rounded my bedroom doorway while I was having it out with Andrej. She'd changed clothes.

Andrej tried to step past me so he could see her, but I blocked him and looked him right in the eyes. *Punch me again*, I mentally willed him. *I'll put you in jail.*

Bree came slowly up the hallway toward us, but needed to spend a couple of seconds gathering herself before she faced him.

He was standing on the other side with his arms crossed. When she came up to the door, though, he looked uncomfortable and uncrossed them. Neither of them said anything, they just stood there, watching each other uncertainly for a few seconds. At least he was acknowledging her like another human being. It was something, even if it wasn't much.

"You look terrible," Bree observed with her usual diplomacy.

I wasn't sure if he'd have a go at her for that. He didn't. "You would, too, if you hadn't slept."

Still looking really wary, she prompted him, "You wanted to talk to me?"

Andrej glanced up at me and then back at Bree. He was clearly unhappy with me being there, but I wasn't going anywhere. After what he'd done to her *and* me, I wasn't leaving Bree alone with him. He obviously realised that. Instead of telling me to go away, he just reached into his pocket and took out a crumpled, rolled up sheet of paper and passed it to her.

She cautiously accepted it. After unrolling it and reading it for a few seconds, she said, "Okay..." like she didn't understand what his point was.

"I got a job," he told her, sounding a bit proud of himself, "as an apprentice motor mechanic."

Bree gave him back the sheet of paper. "Yeah, I saw." After another silence, she said, "I thought you told Dad you were going to go to university and do law." She sounded a bit cynical.

He shrugged. "Well, I had a long think last night and decided that we could probably use a bit more money so it would be better if I was working."

Bree swallowed. "You thought we could probably use a bit more money," she repeated.

"Yeah. It would be great to have internet at home again, wouldn't it? I bet it would make it easier for you to study, too. And maybe we could all go out to the movies on Tuesday nights again like we always used to..." For just a second, I saw a glimpse of someone who reminded me of Bree. This was how *she* talked about the home she so desperately missed.

Bree glanced across at me, visibly deflating. I understood why: despite giving her some tiny shred of hope, Andrej's 'let's all go to the movies again', felt like Henry's 'reservation's for seven' from last night. It went zero percent of the way to addressing the real problem. I could see her dilemma: Andrej was obviously *finally* acknowledging things weren't great at home. He was *finally* speaking to her. It must have been *so* tempting for her to agree with him and leave it.

I knew that feeling so well, and that's why I was so proud of her when she said, "But what's you getting a job going to do?"

He didn't expect that response. "What do you mean? It's three hundred a week. I'd thought you'd be happy about it."

She spoke really carefully and her words didn't come straight away. "There's no point in having internet at home if none of us have computers or phones to use it on," she said. "And, like, we can go to the movies, but are we even going to have a home to come back to afterwards? You have a gambling problem, Andrej, and because of it Mum and Dad owe half a million. What's three hundred a week going to do?"

As she was saying that, I watched his face harden. The kid who wanted to help his sister and have movie nights with his family disappeared. "Well, Bree, maybe if *you* got a fucking job instead of mooching off other people, we'd be even better off!"

She exhaled, eyes veiled as what he'd just said about her rang in our ears for a moment.

"You know what?" she eventually said. "Forget it. Maybe it's okay for *you* to pretend everything's fine, but I'm sick of it." With that, she just closed the door in his face, and it slammed shut to a pronounced *click* of the lock.

I had *not* expected her to do that, and I don't think she expected herself to do it, either. We both stood there staring at the door, listening to Andrej's furious breathing on the other side. He was shocked, too, so it took him a few seconds to respond.

"Pretend? *I'm* pretending?" He yelled through the door with a desperate, raw edge to his voice. "I'm not walking around in a dress and telling people I'm a girl. You'd better take a good hard look at your alleged *boyfriend* if you think *you're* the one living in reality here!"

That knocked the wind out of me.

Honestly, I was more shocked that he'd tried to be so cruel than I was hurt by what he said. It was fortunate he'd said it to me now, though, if he'd said it even just a couple of days ago, I would have had the pills in my hand much faster. Now, I was just *appalled* at him.

Bree mistook my stunned silence for a sign he'd hurt me and looked horrified. "*Fuck off, Andrej!*" she yelled over him as he went to talk again. "Just fuck off, or we'll call security!" He did actually leave after she'd shouted at him, probably taking threat of security seriously as he was *already* in trouble with the police.

For several seconds after he'd gone, we both stood in silence behind the closed door, trying to process what had just happened.

Bree looked up at me, and instead of being proud of herself, instead of being happy she'd stood up to her brother, her face crumpled and she burst into tears. Gingerly, I put a gentle had on her shoulder. In a tiny, bitterly disappointed voice, she said, "I just wanted it to be like your pitch..." as she cried.

I scooped her up into my arms, hugging her tightly against me. Andrej was... I shook my head. I wanted to say 'delusional', and I thought that was probably an apt description, but he'd been *really* stressed out in the beginning and I couldn't help thinking I knew why that was: there was a real person in there, a real person who'd once been a member of a close-knit family. Somewhere deep inside him, deep, deep down, buried in the recesses of his mind, I think he knew what he was doing. He knew, and it made him sweat at my door and lie awake at night. But how the fuck did you even access that part if he lashed out so aggressively whenever you tried to?

Ironically, Henry would have been a great person to ask that question of. He'd know how to approach Andrej, this kind of stuff was what he used to do for a living. I hoped I'd get a chance to ask him one day.

"I feel really stupid," Bree confessed. "I was thinking, 'maybe he'll say sorry', 'maybe he'll stop' and I had this hope inside me that everything could go back to normal and I *hate it*. I hate it, I hate it, because everything's *not* going to be okay and *I hate* that he made me think for a second that I could have my family back. It's worse than having no hope. It's worse than anything."

My heart ached for her. "I kind of thought things would change, too," I told her. "After he punched me and police arrested him. I just assumed it was the start of things going back to normal for you..."

"Maybe this *is* normal for me now," she said, leaning against me. I kissed her head. "Maybe he'll never change and this is it." As soon as she said that, she sighed. "But then, like, he talked to me just then. That's different. Maybe if he's an addict and there's rehab or something, he can do it and then we can all go back to the way we were."

That reminded me of something else I'd heard today. "Diane Frost gave me some advice earlier," I told her. "Sean's a fucking bastard, and when I mentioned that you had trouble with Andrej, she said something like, 'Just give up, he'll never change, don't waste half your life hoping for it'."

That upset her again. "It's just so awful, though, to think that," she said. "We used to do everything together when we were little.

Everything. It's just so awful to think that's over. There won't be any more fun Christmases or Easters or birthdays. We'll never sit around the dinner table again. If that's the truth, then I'll *never* get my family back."

"Henry told me he needed to grieve over losing me," I said gently. "Maybe that's what you need to do: just let go of that wish. The Andrej you had fun with is gone. Grieve for him, grieve for the fun you had together and grieve for the fact you *won't* have that same happy family again, so you can finally move on."

That made her cry again. "But I want one," she said. "Min, I *want* one so much. I *hate* feeling this all the time. I just want to not care anymore."

I hugged her close to me. I want to give you one, I thought, knowing it wasn't the same. I still wanted it, though. I wanted Bree to have her happy family and her Christmases and her Easters and her birthdays and all the other things she wanted. I just wanted to give her everything that would make her happy.

"You want to do something nice today?" I asked her, hoping I could cheer her up. "We still have the rest of the afternoon. Maybe we could go for a drive, or go lie in the sun somewhere, or go shopping? Would that make you feel a bit better?"

She exhaled, shaking her head against me. "I've got a thing at school this evening. I need to go home and get changed."

Oh, right. "Is that what you were talking about taking me to before?"

She nodded. "Yeah, but you'll probably find it really stressful because all the girls in my year will be there. I just thought maybe it would help you see that things are different now..."

"I'd be happy to come."

She laughed once. "You're only saying that to try and cheer me up."

Was it that obvious? "You know, I *used* to think that I was kind of mysterious."

I could feel her smiling against my middle. I liked it. "Nah, it's okay," she said. "I'll just catch the train, it's not very far and it's a nice day, so..."

I held her away from me so I could make her look at me. "I'm not happy about leaving you like this."

She'd stopped crying. "Then don't. Walk with me to Circular Quay." She made a face. "When I walk past that hairdresser in the daytime, I keep thinking the woman in there will recognise me and be angry about her flower pots. And I haven't seen that debt collector guy for ages but he can't be gone..."

Well, I knew what *I* was going to lie awake in bed and worry about for the next few nights. "I'm driving you," I said firmly.

I didn't end up driving her, though, because she was surprisingly stubborn and was already out of the door and down the lift before I could figure out where I'd left my car keys. I caught up with her in the lobby, and we walked hand-in-hand out into the street.

"This is nicer, anyway," she said, looking at out clasped hands and swinging them a bit. "Don't you think?"

I thought whatever she liked was fine by me. I was just glad she looked a bit happier.

There wasn't any sign of Andrej, and there wasn't any sign of the debt collector. There were just a king's ransom of tourists and a whole lot of business people, and none of them gave us a second glance. I loved it.

I did worry what was going to happen to her when she got back to her house, though. "Is Andrej going to be at home waiting for you?" I wondered aloud.

Bree shook her head. "He's never home during the day." At the mention of him again, she frowned. "It's so fucked what he said to you, by the way. Not everyone thinks like that. That you're pretending, I mean."

I grimaced. "I know..." I said, and then thought about that whole guy-in-a-dress comment he'd made. I wasn't pretending, not anymore. At least, not in the way he'd meant it. But I still felt a bit off about it, and it was difficult for me to try and pinpoint what caused that.

Bree stopped me. "Why did you say it like that?" she asked, as if I was being insecure and she was comforting me.

It wasn't that, though. I wasn't being insecure about it. I looked down my front at the packer inside my pants. "It's really hard to explain," I said, and then presented myself. "This is how I feel comfortable. That, I'm sure of. I feel right and, well, *safe* when people think I'm a guy. But I still say 'think' and 'assume', don't I? I mean..." I swore. "Fuck, Bree, this stuff is *really* complicated."

She just looked up at me with those big eyes, waiting for me to continue.

I exhaled, checking around us in the street to make sure no one could hear. "When I was with you three girls earlier I was definitely the odd one out, and did you see how Gemma looked at me when Sarah went to take her top off? People can tell I'm not a woman. And I know I look like a guy, in some ways I *feel* like I am one, but... that's not the whole story, is it? I never fit in with the boys at work, *never*, and I'm not like Rob or Henry. I don't feel like I'm the same as any of them." I sighed. "So, I guess I'm fucked. I don't know whether I'm a man or a woman. Sometimes, I don't feel like I'm either."

Very matter-of-factly, Bree said, "Well, maybe you *aren't* either."

I laughed, but it sounded a little bleak. "Fabulous. I'm stuck in limbo *forever.*"

She squinted at me for a moment, and then in the middle of the street she felt me up for my phone. Once she'd got it, she turned away from the sun and started flipping through it and then held it up for me to see.

There was a long list of words on the screen, and I took the phone from her so I could read them. They were adjectives, but I'd never heard of any of them before. I could clearly see they were related to gender, though, because they were words like 'agender' and 'transmasculine' and 'androgyne'.

"Where's this?" I asked her, checking the site and wondering if the words were just made-up by someone.

"Wikipedia," Bree answered.

My eyebrows went up. "Oh," I said, and then read them more carefully. "What are they?"

"Other genders," she said, like this was common everyday knowledge that everyone had. Then, she laughed at my expression. "It's so weird how you're going through this and you're not all over the internet about it," she told me. "If I felt like I wasn't a girl, the first thing I'd do is Google it."

"I did a couple of times. But only for stuff related to being a guy. I didn't even know there *was* anything else." I stopped for a second, and then looked down at her. I seriously had never heard of these words before in my life. "People use these words for themselves?" I asked for clarification.

She nodded. "Heaps. There's heaps of sites and blogs and stuff. Google them."

That was a novel thought. I kept reading down the page for a second, because I was so spun out there was a whole section of the community that I'd never heard of. The page all the info was on was headed 'Genderqueer', and then the section underneath had another list of about a million different types of pronouns that I'd never seen. *Pronouns*, I thought, and hated them all immediately. English overcomplicated things so much sometimes.

"I bet my mother would die of pride to hear me say this," I told Bree, putting the phone back in my pocket and taking her hand so we could keep walking, "but Korean is *way* better for these things. In Korean you can seriously go a whole conversation without using a single pronoun and that's completely normal." I sighed. "That's what I kind of wish I could do. Just let people assume whatever they want and never have to clarify."

"I could learn Korean," Bree offered. "You could teach me."

I squeezed her hand. "Thanks, but since we're in Australia I don't think that's going to solve the problem."

When we walked under the bridge and across to the station, Bree looked a lot more cheery than she had up in my apartment. It was a relief to see her more relaxed.

"You look better," I said, reaching down and tucking her hair behind her ears when she turned around to say goodbye to me.

She smiled. "I feel a bit better," she said. Then, because I was wearing a tie again, she gave it a tug and pulled me down to kiss her. I did, soundly, in front of everyone coming in and out of the station. Someone made a disgusted comment about us and we both ended up laughing to ourselves about it.

I gave her my Opal card again, and tried to give her a twenty, too. She wouldn't take it. "Are you sure you don't want me to come to your school thing?" I asked her. "If it's an awards night or something, wouldn't it be nice to have company?"

She shook her head. "Nah. It'll be boring. It's not worth it to stress you out."

I appreciated that. Being around judgemental high school students brought back things I'd rather not remember. "Okay," I said, and hugged her. "Are you coming back tomorrow?" She nodded. "Good, because I've got something *really* fun we can do: pack all my stuff into boxes. Wild, right?"

She pushed me. "Dag," she said, and then gave me a little smile and tapped through the barriers.

I watched her go with a grin, but I could see her smile was gone by the time she reached the top of the stairs. I wanted to run up there and hug her again, but she had my card. While I was looking at her platform above my head and trying to decide if I should just buy another card and go with her, the train came and left and it was too late.

I sighed and then headed home, thinking about all those genders and pronouns she'd just shown me.

I'd moved on to worrying about Bree and Andrej as I walked back into the hotel lobby, and thinking about Bree reminded me how excited she'd had been about getting mail. With that in mind, I went up to the front desk and collected mine, half expecting there to be a dick-shaped package or something equally humiliating waiting for me there. Fortunately, there wasn't. There was just a stack of nondescript envelopes.

I started opening them as I got into the lift. One of them was my licence renewal, which was well-timed for a brand new ID photo. The others were an assortment of other random things, including a hand-mailed envelope containing a brochure for a law firm. I flipped it over, and there was a note on the back. "We'd like to speak to you," it said. "Please call us on the number below."

I would have been much more interested in how this arrived in my mail if I didn't know how many people *hated* Jason and probably wanted to make sure he suffered. Well, I didn't want to dredge up and relive all that crap I'd just gone through and suffer, either. I put it at the back of the pile.

The last envelope had something inside it. I felt it through the paper; it was probably a USB. Opening the envelope, I discovered I was right. When I took it out, I saw a little black and white snowflake on it, and it took me a couple of seconds to realise that it was *my* USB, and someone was returning it to me. That was weird.

I unfolded the letter, and the first thing I noticed was the letterhead. It was the red crest of the University of Sydney, and underneath it had the words, *Sydney College of the Arts*. What?

I froze. It took me a couple of seconds to bring myself to read it.

"Dear Mr. Lee," it read in beautiful, crisp print, *"It is with great pleasure that we wish to inform you that your portfolio has been accepted and we would like to extend you one of our early placements for midyear entry into the Master of Fine Arts..."*

I couldn't read any further. It was like one of those dreams where you open your bank statement and unexpectedly there's a million dollars in it. Or a dream where you've won the lottery even though you haven't even bought a ticket. I nearly missed my floor staring at this letter, but I somehow made it out of the lift and into my apartment, letter and USB in hand.

I went straight to the Smart TV and stuck the USB in the side of it, trying to figure out how this had happened. I had my art all over the internet, so it was possible someone had found it. Or maybe this USB wasn't mine after all, and someone at Frost — maybe Sarah? — had sent it in to them.

The USB was full of image files of my work, and whoever had put the portfolio together clearly had an eye for composition because they were well-chosen. The last file was a PDF, and when I opened it, it was an application letter. It wasn't professionally worded enough to be something Sarah had written, and I would certainly have done a much better job, but it was polite, enthusiastic and explained how important the course was to... me? It was signed Mr. Min Lee, and *that* was *not* my signature. The second page was blank like it had been accidentally scanned double-sided, except for two stick figures right down the bottom of the page. I had to zoom right in to see them. One was tall and one was short and they were holding hands. And they both had big, lopsided smiley faces.

Bree.

I sat back, gaping at the letter. *Bree* had done this. Okay, so she'd *forged my signature*, but she'd also obviously spent hours and hours choosing examples of my work. She'd made a portfolio for me. She'd filled in the application forms and written an application letter for me. And because of that, I now had an acceptance letter in my hand. I read the letter again, unable to believe that's what it actually was. Master of Fine Arts, I read, again and again, Master of Fine Arts.

When I was a teenager, while I was lying in bed and trying not to cry over school, I'd imagine opening a letter like this. I used to imagine working hard on my painting and creating beautiful, magical, and exotic places... And one day *seeing* my places somewhere. In a gallery. In a movie. Turning on my PlayStation and seeing them in one of my favourite games. Somewhere where I could look at them and think, '*I* did that, that's by *me*!'.

Mum had never let me apply for those courses, she'd insisted on something practical. But here I was, having quit the practical job that nearly killed me, holding a golden ticket in my hand.

My hand over my mouth, I looked up at the Great Barrier Reef painting through a sea of tears. This letter is real, I thought. This is *real*. It's happening.

I was going to be an artist, like I'd *always* wanted. I was going to *finally* do it.

I wanted to jump right up and wrap Bree in a big, suffocating bear hug for doing this for me, but I had no way of contacting her. Well, at least I knew where she was going to be tonight, right? At that second, I didn't give a fuck how crap it made me feel to be surrounded by a sea of high school kids again. I'd weather them to thank her. I'd do fucking *anything* to thank her right now. I couldn't believe she'd done this, and I *couldn't believe* I was *finally* going to be an artist.

I took out my phone and hopped onto the Cloverfield website, figuring that details of whatever Bree had on would be on there. I was tabbing through the calendar, thinking their website could use some redesigning, when I got to today's date. There was only one event listed, and it was *Year 12 Formal, 6pm, auditorium.*

I sat back, letting that sink in. Of course, I thought, Bree had been talking about this in the restaurant when I'd first met her, and I'd *completely* forgotten. She'd tried to segue into inviting me to it today, as well, which meant that she wasn't going with anyone. She was going alone to her Year 12 Formal because she didn't want to trigger me, and probably hadn't even asked me so I couldn't feel bad about saying no. She'd applied to art school for me. She was *constantly* trying to do nice little things for me. Fuck all those judgemental high school students, I was *going* to that fucking formal for her.

I looked up at the clock; it was mid-afternoon. That was enough time. I left my apartment and went into the city, looking for somewhere I could buy a clean suit with a jacket that *wasn't* blood-stained. Once I'd bought one and then hopped in my car and sat in peak hour traffic *forever*, I found a park nearby Cloverfield and got out of my car just as the sun was starting to set.

Everyone else was entering the school via the main gate. Rather than running a gauntlet of prestige vehicles and sobbing parents taking a million photos of their precious daughters, I entered via the side gate, shutting it carefully behind me.

Cloverfield Ladies' College was a big historic school, just like mine had been in Melbourne. Huge, thick-trunked trees were planted all around the grandiose colonial buildings, and their leaves were turning reds and oranges with the approaching winter. I walked through the leaves, kicking them up with my new shoes.

The grounds were quiet, except for the commotion at the other end where the auditorium was. I opted to lay low until everyone was inside, so that I didn't arrive *before* Bree and have to stand around looking like an idiot while I waited for her.

Since I had some time to waste, I went over to a building and put my face up to the windows. It was so strange looking at these empty rooms. There were familiar things still written on the whiteboards: quadratic equations, chemistry formulae, even some Chinese characters. In another room, there were Japanese posters everywhere. The only languages at my school had been French and German.

While I was looking through the corridors at bathrooms like the ones I used to hide in, and lockers like the ones I'd get backed up against, I noticed something different.

On the walls, there were a series of posters. They were bright and colourful, showing all sorts of people of various races, and on one of them, two girls were hugging and had big smiles on their faces. Above them were two interlinked women's symbols and a rainbow flag. Another poster had what looked at first glance like a teenage boy holding up a dress in front of her in the mirror and smiling at how it made her look. '*Celebrate Our Diversity,*' they read, '*Be Yourself!*"

That *hit* me. There had never been posters like that up at my school. The word 'lesbian' was something you called sporty girls behind their backs or anyone you wanted to insult, and I hadn't even heard the word transgender until I was an adult. Even then, it was only in art house movies.

Here, on these walls, there were posters about them both. Attractive posters, and they weren't defaced. Every time a kid walked down this corridor, *every time*, they were reminded that it was okay to be like this. The school accepted that. No, the school *celebrated* that.

There was no need for anyone to shut themselves away in graphics labs or hide in toilets, and there was no need for anyone to cry themselves to sleep at night for six years.

It was a lot to take in, and I had to stand away from the window for a moment because I felt like I was going to cry. Just the thought of a twelve year old with a baggy uniform and a unisex haircut being able to look at these posters and see different possibilities for themselves celebrated was *incredible*. It was everything I never had, and it would have changed so many things for me. I was heartbroken that this wasn't *my* experience, but *so* happy for the students for whom it was. For the kid that got to look up at these posters and know they belonged here, even if they were different.

While I was pulling myself together, the noise down the other end of the grounds was dying down as all the students moved inside the auditorium. I decided I should probably go look for Bree now, and my heart started to pound at the thought of all those students. This is for Bree, I reminded myself, and then headed across the grounds to the auditorium.

I had been standing at the bottom of the stairs trying to will myself to walk up them inside when a startled voice said, "*Min?*"

I looked over towards it, and Bree was sitting off to the side of the building on one of the schoolyard benches. The first thing I noticed was how completely astonished she was to see me, the second was how *beautiful* she was. She was wearing a baby blue satin dress and matching shoes, and she'd done her hair so the curls were larger and tighter than usual. The dress was probably a bit too small for her, but she wore it well.

"What are you *doing* here?" she said as she took a few steps towards me, still looking stunned.

I smiled at her. "Surprise."

"No, really," she said. "I thought you said this would be really difficult for you!"

I nodded, and then walked up to her, taking the letter out of my breast pocket. I passed it to her, and she read it. Very quickly, a smile grew across her face and then she looked up at me. "You got in!" she said, and then looked shocked again, grabbing my arms. "You actually got in, oh my *god*!"

"I didn't get me in," I said, briefly stopping her. "*You* got me in."

She looked a bit sheepish. "Well, I didn't want to tell you in case you didn't make it. Like, I did it last Thursday after you'd gone to Broome and you were feeling really bad at the time so I was like, 'no, I'd better not tell her in case it doesn't work...'" She stroked lapels on my jacket, and straightened my tie. "I just really wanted you to quit that awful job because it was really fucking you up, and so I thought if I could show you that you *could* be an artist if you really wanted to, it would give you something to think about..."

I smiled down at her. "Thank you," I said. I hoped she could hear how much I really meant it.

I think she did, because she beamed up at me. "My pleasure, Min."

Between those rosy cheeks and that big smile, I just had to lean down and kiss her. She giggled and wrapped her arms around my shoulders. "I'm going to rip my dress apart if I put my arms up like this," she said against my mouth.

"Shit," I said sarcastically between kisses. "I really hope that doesn't happen." My hands slipped down her body just a little; *completely* unintentionally, of course...

She was still giggling as I stood up again, and pulled her dress up at the armpits. I was obviously wondering about why she'd chosen it, because she sighed and said, "It's the same one I wore last year and I've put on like five kilos since then. It looks shit, I hate it. But I had to wear it anyway because formal dresses are really expensive and we couldn't afford a new one."

"I would have bought you one," I told her.

She nodded. "I know." She didn't say anything else about it.

I looked around us. "Anyway, not that it's not a lovely night to be outside, but isn't the formal in there?" I pointed inside.

She made a face. "Courtney's coming with Andrej," she said. "I was just trying to convince myself to go in, anyway." She then turned a frown on me. "And look who's talking! You were standing at the bottom of the stairs like you were about to walk the plank."

That was a pretty accurate description of how I felt. I could *hear* the number of students inside. I looked towards the door apprehensively.

She saw my expression. "If it's too much we can just go have dinner somewhere or something," she offered. "Like, we look really nice, we could go to some really fancy restaurant."

For a couple of seconds, I considered that. This wasn't about me, though. I wasn't here for myself. I was here for Bree. Instead of answering her on that, I just offered her the crook of my elbow. "Come on," I said with a grin. "Let's go inside. We can suffer together."

She looked absolutely charmed as she took my arm, walking the plank with me.

There were *so many* people in the auditorium. At least two hundred, I thought, and all the girls were milling around and chatting animatedly to each other while the boys stood back and looked uncomfortable. I hoped none of them would notice how much older I was than them.

Actually, no one noticed us at all. In my head, I had this vision of the entire auditorium falling silent and all swinging their heads en masse to *stare* at me. A few people glanced at us as we came in— mostly curious about my black eye—but otherwise, they were all busy with their own conversations.

"There she is." Bree had her eyes fixed over on the far wall. When I looked, Courtney was leaning against it looking quite pretty herself, but there was no one with her. "That's weird," Bree said. "If there's free food, Andrej's normally right in there. I wonder where he is?"

Before I could comment, two girls came rushing up to us. "Oh my god, Bree!" one of them said in what amounted to basically a single syllable. "You came!" They all hugged, and before Bree could introduce me, the other girl commented, "Hey, isn't that the same dress you wore last year?"

I inhaled sharply, but Bree just managed a really convincing laugh. "Hell, yes, it's the same dress!" she said, smoothing the fabric down as if she was really excited about it. "I fucking love this dress, and there was never any way I was going to wear it just *once*. Like, I was going through all the shops looking at all the stuff out there and I was like, all I want to do is wear this one, you know? So, whatever, there's no law against wearing the same dress again, so I *will* wear it, even if it's a bit tight!"

The girl laughed. "You're fucking crazy, Bree," she said, and then hugged her again. Both of them then looked up at me. I swallowed.

"Oh!" Bree said. "Oh, right." She introduced us, and as she did, I was *sure* the girls could tell something was up with me. They clearly couldn't, though, because they just greeted me a bit shyly and then went to go and grab themselves soft drinks from the refreshment table.

Bree fidgeted a little as they left, glancing over towards the far wall. "Um," she said to me, "I know this is really hard for you, but is it too awful if I just go over for a second to see if Courtney's okay? I'll be really quick."

I looked out towards the sea of students who were all largely ignoring me. "It's fine," I told her. "Go."

She gave me a grateful smile and made her way through the crowd over to the far wall. Courtney looked up when Bree spoke to her, and there was something about her expression. She looked embarrassed, I think, or ashamed. Bree pretended she didn't notice, and I watched her chat animatedly to Courtney as if no one had even come between them. Courtney began to visibly relax.

My heart *swelled* for Bree. There was no reason for her to have done that. She could have just paraded me around while Courtney was over there alone, and it would have been a glorious fuck you to her friend for choosing the flaky brother over her. She didn't, though. She went over there with a big smile and an olive branch extended.

Bree saw me watching them, and gestured at me to come over. I zigzagged through the students to where the girls were, my stomach clenching as I approached them. Courtney knew me from *before*, and I wasn't sure how she was going to react to me like this. *Maybe Bree's told her,* I thought. Or maybe she wouldn't recognise me.

I had completely forgotten she'd seen the painting, though, and when she looked up at me, she double-took and her jaw *dropped*. "*Whoa,*" was her assessment. Bree looked pretty pleased about it.

I winced. "Hello, Courtney."

"Hello, *Prince Charming,*" she said immediately, giggling. "You look *different.*" She stopped giggling, though, and her smile faded as she looked at the state of my cheek and eye. "Andrej did that." I nodded slowly, wondering who had told her. She swallowed and looked a bit distant for a moment. "I guess it's kind of better he didn't show up tonight, then."

"Don't worry, we'll keep you company instead!" Bree said quickly, and hugged her. "Would you guys like drinks? I'll go and get us drinks! They have chocolate over there, too. *Heaps* of it, and all these little salmon-cream-cheese things. They look *amazing.* I'll be right back," she said, and then zoomed off to get them.

We both watched her, amused. After a few seconds, though, Courtney looked back at me. "So, like, you're a guy now, or…?"

I grimaced and made a so-so motion with my hand. "Yeah…" I said at length, not really wanting to go into it. "Let's just go with that for now."

She squinted at me, looking interested in what I'd just said. I think she wanted to know more. She left it, though. "Hah, okay," she said simply and then asked a couple more questions about how Bree was doing in general, and then that was that. She didn't laugh at me. She didn't ridicule me, or look disgusted, or enlist her entire friendship group to harass me. She did look a bit curiously at my bulge and I was worried she was going to ask about it, but she didn't. It was all fine; the fact I looked like this was just an interesting quirk to her.

Bree returned with what could only be described as a whole armful of food, and took great joy in laying it all out on the bench beside us so we could select what we wanted.

While the girls started talking about teachers I didn't know, and gossiping about who'd brought who to the formal and why that was *so scandalous, oh my god*, my mind wandered.

Starting this weekend, I'd have to pack up my apartment, I thought as I took a bite of a 'salmon-cream-cheese thing'. Realistically, I probably didn't have that much stuff, and if Rob was rattling around Sarah's house looking for things to do, maybe I could enlist him to help load up my car. *My car*, I thought, thinking of the huge repayments on it. I was going to have to sell that, too. There was a lot of stuff I could sell, actually. I wanted all new things. Things that Mum didn't 'help' me choose.

There was *so much* to do, and, surprisingly, the more I thought about it, the more I found I was looking forward to it.

Later in the evening when we'd been joined by a couple more of Bree's friends, Bree leant over to me and whispered, "You're okay, right? Like, with everything? You're not too stressed out? If you are we can just go home."

I looked around me and shook my head. "No one can tell," I said. "Or if they can, they don't care. It's fine."

"Told you," Bree said smugly, giving me a quick cuddle. I kissed her head and then released her back to talk to her friends, watching her. Despite all the awful shit with Andrej, she looked happy. I wanted it to stay that way, and that probably meant she'd need a lot of support. Luckily, I had the headspace to give it to her now. Because she'd helped me get here.

Fuck, where the hell would I have been without her, though? Answering myself, I decided I'd probably just have been shut in at home pretending everything was great, and definitely never telling *anyone* about *anything*. I was *so* glad I was here now, in my suit, and not shut up in a house *hating* myself.

I surveyed the crowd, looking at all the other neat suits and pretty dresses. Everyone seemed relaxed and happy, and not one single student was paying any attention to me. I was invisible, and there was no feeling in the world better than that.

It meant that I *fit in*.

Bree and her friends were locked in enthusiastic conversation about university, part-time jobs, exams... all the things I'd expect to hear from final year students. Everyone around me was. They were all excited. They were all about to leave school and go out into the world to do the things they'd always wanted to do and be the people they'd always imagined they'd be. And this time I was joining them. For once, I wasn't hunched in a corner, hoping no one would notice me. I was *joining* them.

Sydney College of the Arts, I thought, enunciating it in my head.

Master of Fine Arts. I was actually going to do it, I was going to be the artist I'd always wanted to be. I didn't have to waste away in an office anymore. I didn't have to slave away at a job I was just pretending to enjoy. Someone had hit the reset button in my life and I could play it all over, and this time, *this* time I was going to get it right.

It was just so completely exhilarating. I was *excited* about university. I was *excited* about my future, it wasn't just something that was happening to me. I had friends who supported me, a wonderful girlfriend who *adored* me, and an invitation to a top arts school in my pocket. Most importantly, I *wasn't* pretending anymore; I didn't have to. *This* was who I was, this. In a suit, with my fantastically flat chest and looking to all the world like any other guy in this hall.

This is how it was always supposed to be, I thought. This is how it should have always been.

And now, finally, it's the way things are always going to be.

THE END

***

ABOUT THE AUTHOR

A. E. Dooland was born in 1981 in Adelaide, Australia. She moved to Melbourne as a preteen and despite having spent some time living abroad, she keeps finding herself back in Australia.

She has a series of unrelated qualifications and a diverse resume that includes acting, teaching, debt collecting, bookkeeping and accounting. You can now find her working with charities, supporting and advocating for families in financial crisis as a financial counsellor.

Her aspirations include changing the world, winning the lottery, and getting out more.

You can get access to free short stories, news and updates on upcoming web serials including the sequel to *Under My Skin* at aedooland.com

ALSO BY THE AUTHOR

Under My Skin
Flesh and Blood (forthcoming)

A FINAL THANKS TO OTHER FINANCIAL BACKERS

Alexa Ongoco
Meagan Begay
Jude DiSanto
Ben Christen
Ross Smith
Chris "The Epyon Avenger" Bergeron
Ruth Karlsson
David Jones
Caroline Smith
Vaula Rinne
fmorgana
Georgey Collier
Cynlinda Parga
Dr. Helgo Eberwein
Elle H.
Steven Lau
Tiarne Romey
April Damiani
Derek Sylva
Ms. Annie Nohn
Heather O.
Annie Ayres
Rowena Lam
Amy Watson
Laura Simarro
Aleksandra Borowska
Katrina Goodwin
Marie Cuenca
Noelle Adams
Kristen Madrid
Jaegen Clasohm